PopCo.

'Exuberant . . . Thomas restores the novel to its primary purpose: a blueprint for a revolution. It is an outright amazement.'
Scotland on Sunday

'Stories unravel within stories, and there are elaborate riffs on code-breaking, mathematical theorems and the pure pleasure of the hunt through numbers.'
Sunday Times

'An anticorporate fable with enough code-breaking tips, puzzles and graphs, charts, postscripts and appendices to satisfy that other mathematician storyteller, Lewis Carroll.'
New York Times Book Review

SCARLETT

Pop Co.

THOMAS

CANONGATE

Edinburgh · London · New York · Melbourne

Published by Canongate Books in 2009

1

Copyright © Scarlett Thomas 2004

The moral right of the author has been asserted

First published in Great Britain in 2004 by Fourth Estate,
a division of HarperCollins*Publishers*

This edition published in 2009 by Canongate Books Ltd,
14 High Street, Edinburgh EH1 1TE

The End of Mr. Y is copyright © Scarlett Thomas 2006

www.meetatthegate.com

British Library Cataloguing-in-Publication Data
A catalogue record for this book is available on
request from the British Library

ISBN 978 1 84767 335 0

Typeset in Sabon by Palimpsest Book Production Ltd,
Grangemouth, Stirlingshire

Printed and bound in Great Britain by
Clays Ltd, St Ives plc

For Francesca Ashurst and Couze Venn

Part One

In the postexperimental interview, when subjects were asked why they had gone on, a typical reply was: 'I wouldn't have done it by myself. I was just doing what I was told.' Unable to defy the authority of the experimenter, they attribute all responsibility to him. It is the old story of 'just doing one's duty' . . .

From Obedience to Authority *by Stanley Milgram*

Chapter One

Paddington Station feels like it should be shut. Late at night, long after rush-hour, it has an echo and the occasional blast of cold, thin air that smells of diesel. This really is an ideal time to be in train stations, when hardly anyone else is travelling. It is almost half-past eleven at night and I am looking for my train, which is due to leave in about twenty minutes. The station feels like it is on beta-blockers. A pulse – yes – but slowed. A medicated slowness; a pleasant fug. This speed, if it were healthy, would belong to someone who trampolines every day, rather than to the owner of the more dangerous circulation you see clogging the station at five or six in the evening.

For the first time in weeks I am wearing proper shoes, and I can actually hear my footsteps as I walk, a D Major scale playing on concrete. If you ever plan to hang around train stations in the middle of the night, you should always make sure you can hear your own footsteps, and, if you are at all musical, you should try to work out which notes you make as you walk, as it stops you from being lonely, not that I ever get lonely. Tonight I am wearing a long coat and a hat and I almost wish I was smoking an exotic cigarette in a holder because added to the coat, hat and suitcase, it would close the parentheses of this look, which I recognise from films and spy thrillers, but can't actually name, although I know people who could.

I know people who would make all sorts of assumptions about the clothes I am wearing. They would assume I had chosen a 'look'. They'd see my shirt and jumper and want to say, 'School uniform look today, Alice?' but then they'd see my tartan skirt, tights and sensible shoes and eventually conclude that I'm in what has been called in the past my 'Bletchley Park' look. Having named my 'look', these people would assume that everything was a deliberate part of it, that all my clothes and everything I have with me, from my purse to my suitcase to my knickers, had been chosen for a reason; to identify me, to give me my own code or stamp. Even if I wore – as I have done in the past – a truly random selection of old or weird clothes, this would simply be labelled my 'Jumble Sale' or 'Homeless' look. I hate this so much. They know I hate it, which is one of the reasons they do it, some logic dictating that when you act annoyed at something people do, it becomes funnier the more they do it.

I work at a toy company called PopCo. Most people love working at PopCo. It's a young, cool company with no dress code, no rules and no set working hours, well, not for the Ideation and Design (ID) staff anyway. Our team, which used to be called Research and Design, but isn't any more, has its own little headquarters in a red-brick building in Battersea and people are just as likely to pull all-nighters making prototypes as they are to suddenly all decamp *en masse* to Prague for a week, trend-spotting and fact-finding. Ideas are everything, everywhere, everybody at PopCo. We live to attract ideas: we are always in season for them; we fan our tail feathers and dance to attract them; our doors are always open if they decide to finally come over, drunk, when we had given up hope of seeing them that night.

Almost everyone in PopCo Ideation and Design is very cool. They devote themselves to it in a way I find impossible. Perhaps it's because I am a division all on my own, a solitary brand-cluster. I am an island despite being connected to land, a new girl despite having been at the company almost two years, an outsider despite being firmly on the inside. Sometimes, despite being on the run from them and their cool, all that happens is that I find myself at the end or beginning of a circle/cycle when everyone else is in the middle of it. Next year they will be the ones wearing shirts with jumpers and skirts, and their hair in sensible plaits, you can be sure of it. Perhaps at that point I will look like a college kid from Tokyo, as they do now, or like a junked-up space-girl, as they may do the season after next. With the people at PopCo there is a dilemma. If you dress like them, you fit in. If you dress in an opposite way to them, or in things so ridiculous they could never consider wearing them, you are cool, daring and an individual – and therefore you fit in. My constant conundrum: how do you identify yourself as someone who doesn't fit in when everything you could possibly do demarcates you as someone who does? If we were all children, it would be easier to rebel. Then again, if we were children, maybe I would actually want to fit in.

After a reception tomorrow lunchtime, the PopCo Open World event (P.O.W./POW), which is taking place at the company's 'Thought Camp' in Devon, will properly begin. PopCo is the third-largest toy company in the world, the first and second being Mattel and Hasbro. It has Corporate Headquarters in Japan and the US, and a smaller version here in the UK. Each country has its own separate ID section, but all the really crazy idea-generation (ideation) goes on at four main Thought Camps around the world, one each in Sweden, Iceland, Spain and the UK. We have all heard of this place in Devon but not many people have been there before. Since we usually have our annual POW somewhere really cool, we have all been wondering why, this year, we are basically going to a PopCo complex in the middle of nowhere. They usually throw money at these events; this year they must be spending next to nothing. I have to say I'm intrigued, and I like the idea of Devon, but for the last few weeks in Battersea everyone has been saying things like, 'It's not going to be like Asmara, is it?' Asmara, a city in Eritrea, is where the last POW was held. Asmara was a pretty bizarre experience. We were in the middle of a tour of one of the PopCo factories when a big civil disturbance broke out and we had to be flown home.

The words 'toy company' usually make people think of fluffy things and wooden blocks; elves, perhaps, in an industrial-revolution version of Santa's Grotto, hammering and carving and running around with dolls, farmyard animals and jigsaw puzzles, placing them in sacks for delivery to clean children who sit in front of fires. In fact, these days, toys are more likely to involve fast food promotions, film tie-ins, interactivity, 'added-value', super-branding and, of course, focus groups observed through one-way mirrors. Wooden blocks, at least the ones made by most toy companies, are apparently now designed according to a mathematical formula that tells you how many of each letter to include in which ratios on how many blocks so that children need to own more than one set in order to make proper words. I don't know if this is true but I know the sort of equation that would make it possible. Apparently someone did once suggest we started applying these sorts of equations at PopCo but she was then sacked. I don't know if this is true either. Although it is less than a hundred years old, PopCo has more folklore than some small countries, as well as a bigger GDP. The other major toy companies are the same.

The folklore, like everything else, is part of the fun. Fun colonises everything when you work in a toy company. You may have heard of things like 'Geek Cool' and 'Ugly Beauty'. Nothing is automatically uncool any more, which is another way of saying you can sell anything, if you know how. It isn't immediately clear to some people how this cynical, grown-up world of cool has found its way into the toy market. But those of us who work in the industry know that all marketing is ultimately aimed at children and teenagers. They're the ones with the disposable income and the desire to fit in. They spread crazes like they were nits, and make their parents buy things they don't need. Think of all the current buzzwords going around. A lot of people realise that they 'come from' school playgrounds and that what your nine-year-old kid says to his mates this week will be what you and your grown-up colleagues will be saying at work next week. Although these things germinate in playgrounds, they often originate in marketing departments. Kids have an accelerated, intensified idea of 'cool'. They go through friends, phases, crazes like flowers blooming on speed-cam. You can hit them, successfully, with something like 20,000 products before they are fifteen, at which point their tastes start to plateau and they buy less.

Toy companies don't necessarily make just toys any more – our most successful division is videogames, and our most financed research is in robotics – we simply make the things that kids want. We are in the business of the new and shiny, the biggest and the best, the glittery and magical, the fast and addictive. The toy industry has two big advantages over other industries. Our products are the easiest to sell, and our customers are the easiest to sell to. That doesn't mean that all products succeed, of course. But we can make things that explode or float or take you to fantasy lands, and, if we get it right, kids' eyes will grow big when they watch our advertisements.

That's not to say I am cynical. I am not. Neither do I hate my job. My job is to create new products in my three brands, of which one is for kids who want to be spies, one is for kids who want to be detectives and the third is for kids who want to become code-breakers. They are called KidSpy, KidTec and KidCracker respectively and are about to be rebranded under a new umbrella brand called 'Shhh!'. Focus groups and market research have shown that kids who buy one of my brands usually buy all three, and I am under pressure to square the triangle by coming up with a fourth 'killer' brand for a demographic of lonely, clever, devious, sometimes traumatised children, who can be boys or girls but who all basically like hiding, secrets and sneaking around catching/spying on criminals. This fourth brand (which will now become a sub-brand) will be the focus for relaunching the others. There will be an advertising campaign; possibly TV. It's very exciting. And having a really successful brand really makes you one of the gang at PopCo.

Nevertheless – and this is something that, for whatever reason, I feel quite strongly about – I don't want to be in this gang. Gangs make me feel uncomfortable. Being popular makes me feel uncomfortable. So this is what it's like being on the run from the fashion Gestapo; my own underground resistance movement: travelling one day before them, dressing in fabrics opposite to theirs, wearing clashing colours when they don't, and not when they do. However, I am not travelling one day before them to be different, but because I just don't very much like being squashed, unable to breathe, underground or any kind of emotional/spatial equivalent. Although I am normal in almost every other way, I don't really like it when strangers touch me. It makes me want to cry. Thus the night train.

Because of my 'condition' (human condition, medical condition, whatever), I often get to destinations one day before whoever I am travelling 'with' and, although travelling like this is something I do in response to a problem, I often forget the problem and just find the experience interesting, like riding a waltzer by yourself or making a cake to eat on your own.

My suitcase is on the ground. I suddenly feel nervous about it just sitting there. This is not a black and white film; it could get stolen, or dirty. I pick it up and look at the Departures Board. My train is going from Platform 9. I wonder if I am going to enjoy this journey. I did think about driving down but my 1960 Morris Minor (inherited from my grandfather) probably wouldn't do well on such a long journey. Without anthropomorphising the car too much (although this is a hazard when you work in a toy company – you find you can put eyes on anything and it will come to life), it seems to get miserable on long journeys now. It's a shame, because I love the feeling of travelling in my own bubble, sharing the sleepy motorway only with big lorries and their fuzzy orange space-ship lights. Still, the night train is also an adventure and I'm only going to be away for a couple of days. I am planning to travel back after the whole thing finishes on Monday night and I know I will be too tired to drive. Also, it might be nice to have a Martini or something afterwards, and I wouldn't want to drive 250 miles home after that. Maybe not Martini. I started drinking Martini because no one else did but now everyone seems to like it. Another conundrum.

I start walking to Platform 9. There are a few other people in the station: some on benches, some in hooded sweatshirts, some obviously drunk or vaguely dispossessed. On one cluster of benches, however, there is what must be a family: a man and woman and three children. They look tired and thin and are wearing clothes I don't recognise. Who are they? I am now lost in my own time-warp fantasy involving steam trains and romance, but they are a real time-warp, sitting on benches, sharing a loaf of bread. I am just about to stop staring and walk on when I notice that one of the children is reading a book with a red cover. Is this that moment that authors probably have all the time but I have never had? Is that small, thin, lost-looking child reading one of the books from the series I create? I walk closer to the bench, straining to look. When I get close enough to see, the book has gone and the child is holding a red lunch box. As I continue walking towards my plat-form, I think I can hear an owl hooting somewhere in the roof of the station.

Chapter Two

A steward checks me onto my train and shows me to my compartment. It has bunk beds, although the top one has been closed up against the wall. There is also a sink with a lid you have to lift up, and a little cotton towel. The bottom bunk bed is made up with crisp cotton sheets and a thin wool blanket.

The only bad thing about sleeping compartments in trains is what they do to my hair. I don't know if it's the air-conditioning, or the static, or the velveteen stuff with which the compartments are lined but something here makes my hair freak out like fluff stuck on flypaper. Perhaps I am vain, thinking like this. Perhaps frizzy hair makes you vain. I wait for the steward to check my ticket for the last time and then shut the door and apply a tiny bit of Vaseline (it's just like serum) to my hair, which I then tuck under a shower cap I have brought with me for this purpose. The shower cap is pink and cream, with a repeating pattern of kittens playing with balls of wool. I have lots of these shower caps. My hair doesn't respond well to getting wet, and it doesn't seem to enjoy becoming too dry either. It's like a fragile hanging garden that I constantly have to tend to prevent it from wilting or dying. I often wonder what I would have looked like in the Middle Ages, and what you would have done to control hair like mine before they invented products to do it for you. Would animals have lived in it? Maybe that would have been fun-ish.

I look at myself in the mirror over the sink and laugh silently at my odd reflection. Perhaps this could be the 'look' to finally shut them all up. What would they call this one? Lunatic Asylum? I pull faces at myself for a while, trying to make myself look as weird as possible, imagining situations I could ruin by turning up like this. I list family reunions and weddings among these, despite never having been to either. Could you have sex like this? What would someone say if you tried? Maybe there are shower-cap fetishists out there – there seem to be fetishes for everything else. Could this be my look for the whole POW event? If only I dared.

My old brown suitcase contains the following items: pyjamas; wash bag; plimsolls; hair products; spare shower caps; hair grips and bands; spare knickers; spare tights; clean shirt; spare cardigan; other assorted clothes, including my favourite corduroy skirt; nail clippers; guitar picks (although I have not brought a guitar I have to take picks everywhere); green tea; chamomile tea; a bar of 'emergency' chocolate; a flask of hot water; some muesli; three 1B pencils; a sketch-book; a notebook; my fountain pen; a pencil-sharpener; and spare ink cartridges for my pen. In a smaller army-style canvas bag I have two books, a few homeopathic remedies, my survival kit, my purse, a transistor radio, tobacco and cigarette papers, two or three miscellaneous items and various black and white hairs from my cat, Atari.

The survival kit is an experiment and contains items I think I might need in a survival situation, like plasters, water-purifying tablets, matches, candles, batteries, a small torch, a compass, a knife, several organic 'energy' bars, a large sheet of plastic and some Rescue Remedy. Rescue Remedy is great for almost everything – shocks, sick pets, wilting plants – and since it is suspended in brandy, it also works as an emergency antiseptic. Whenever I have had toothache, I have dropped some Rescue Remedy on the affected tooth and it has improved immediately.

The survival pack and my transistor radio are the two things I'd grab if, say, the enemy boarded the train now, and I had two minutes to escape. I would not take the shower caps. In a survival situation I don't think I would care about my hair at all. I read once that when packing you should ask yourself which items are necessities and which are comforts, and take only the necessities. Of course, hardly anything is really a necessity. If I was forced to choose only the absolute necessities from my bag I would take only my homeopathic Carbo Vegetabilis tablets, which I need due to my allergy to wasp and bee stings. Maybe also the plastic sheet, although I have already forgotten how you use it to collect water. I'd take my necklace, too, although I wouldn't have to remember that: it's been on the same chain around my neck for the last twenty years.

Everything else I have brought is really a luxury; even fantasies about the enemy. The enemies we have now are not the type to invade on foot or stop trains. Does anyone even know who the enemy is any more? Avoiding the real world as much as possible, I usually tend to think of 'the enemy' only in the context of my brands. This means I am constantly looking over my shoulder for shadowy, storyboard men with stubble: spies from the other side, or sterilised criminals on the lookout for animals or children to kidnap/use in crazy experiments. Perhaps this explains me also seeing my creations where they don't exist. That was certainly an odd experience I haven't had before.

My cat is called Atari not after the videogames manufacturer, as people have occasionally thought, but after a position in the game Go, which, like 'check' in chess, denotes a position in which one player can take another player's piece in one move. It's not as fatal as in chess, however, as Go has many pieces (stones), some of which you probably would not mind sacrificing as part of your strategy. My cat is black and white, as are the stones in Go. Go is about balance, yin and yang, sacrifice and victory; and many of its positions or sayings (there are thousands) can be applied, in metaphor form, to various situations in life, including military strategy. Atari is so named because his black and white hairs seem to be in competition, and are always falling out, as if they are constantly losing Atari situations with themselves.

Everyone at PopCo plays Go; it's virtually a prerequisite for working there. Each toy company has its signature game, in the same way that a sports team may have a song, or a mascot. At Hasbro, apparently, this game is Risk, which, along with Scrabble, is one of their bestselling boardgame brands. Risk feels like a less abstracted form of Go, and you can use many of the same strategies within it. It is about world domination but, of course, you are always at the whim of the dice. It is a long-term strategist's kind of game. The game they all play at Mattel is chess. Like us, they are very fixated on strategy. But while we are very philosophical about it all (you can't win without also losing and so on), they take the military stuff very seriously. There is no chance in chess. It's a very bang-bang game, where victory can sometimes happen in very few moves. In 1995 Mattel tried to take over Hasbro. It was an ugly situation.

Every year at PopCo we have a big Go tournament, which everyone gets very excited about. I didn't make it past the first round last year, having made one simple error in the first few moves of my only game. Since 1992, PopCo has offered a million-dollar prize for anyone who can write a computer program that can beat a professional Go player. No one has claimed it. While fairly ordinary chess programs are now beating world masters, no one has ever come up with a computerised form of Go that anyone other than a beginner or a child can't beat. However, the rules of Go are very simple. You have a 19x19 board, like a big chess-board, and two players – one playing white, one playing black – take it in turns to place their stones on it. You place the stones on the intersections (not in the squares) with the aim of capturing territory, and the other player's stones. You capture pieces and territory literally by surrounding them, although if you're not careful you can become surrounded while you are attempting this. Go is 3000 years old and has more potential formations than there are atoms in the universe.

The night train feels heavier than ordinary trains, in the same way that being asleep feels heavier than being awake. As it starts moving out of the station I get out one of my books and lie down on the little bed to read. I am soon distracted by the lights outside, though, and I put down my book and open the little blind over the window to see better. The window is one of those frosted things that you can't really see out of (or into, I suppose, which must be the point), and which can't be opened. But something about the way you can't quite see where the little orange and white lights are coming from outside makes them more interesting. I am hypnotised. This train does not shoot towards Reading like day trains do. Instead, it just ambles along as if there were something wrong with it. Soon it becomes possible to hear drilling, and to notice something that both looks and sounds like arc-welding. This feels like being in a post-apocalyptic Japanese videogame, travelling through a city ravaged by anarchy and war with a big sword and, possibly, some magic spells. I can't read with all this going on, so I get under the covers and lie there listening and watching until I eventually fall asleep.

Just before four in the morning, there is a soft tap at my door. Through my sleep I can hear an unfamiliar voice saying something like *Hello? Wake up call.* It feels like I only dropped off five minutes ago and opening my eyes is very difficult indeed.

The door opens slowly. 'Your water,' whispers a woman, giving me a small tray. 'We'll be at Newton Abbot in about fifteen minutes,' she adds.

With the door open I can sense the stillness in the corridor, and almost smell the sleep coming from all the cabins along it. I realise that everyone employed here must do everything softly, slowly, quietly. Do the people who work here whisper when they are off duty, in the same way I can't stop thinking about the kind of things 9- 12-year-olds would enjoy playing with, even when I am not at work? With various unformed thoughts emerging, I pull myself into a sitting position and take the tray from her, whispering a quiet, sleepy thanks as my shower cap rustles around my ears.

She closes the door – softly – and I am alone again. The tray has a small teapot on it and when I look inside they have indeed just given me the boiling water I requested last night, along with the Great Western Railway biscuits they seem to give you with everything. I take the small bag of green tea from my suitcase and drop a pinch of it in the water, watching it immediately swell. I blow and sip for a minute or two, needing the caffeine. I close my eyes for thirty seconds and then open them again.

My sense of time feels distorted and I suddenly don't know how long I now have to get ready before the train stops at Newton Abbot. Twelve minutes? Eleven? I tend to panic about getting off trains at the right time. Once, I was almost the last person to get off a busy train somewhere near Cambridge. After I had alighted, and as I turned to walk down the platform towards the exit, I became aware of someone shouting something. I looked back and saw a man still inside the train struggling to open the door. He had the window open and was tugging at the outside handle. 'I can't get this damn door open,' he said loudly. I turned to go and help him but at that moment the train started to move away. He suddenly became panicked and started beating the outside of the door with his fists. 'Hey!' he shouted. 'I'm getting off here!' It was too late for anyone to do anything, and the train pulled away with him saying something like 'Help me . . .' Perhaps missing your station isn't that big a tragedy in the scheme of things; maybe it just depends how inconvenient it would be to travel to the next station and then come back. In my case, if I miss Newton Abbot I will have to stay with the train until Plymouth, and then wait two or so hours for a connection back in this direction. Train connections become more difficult in the middle of the night.

While picking at my bag of muesli and taking sips from my tea, I quickly change out of my pyjamas and put on the clothes I was wearing only a few hours ago, although I can't face the shoes now and so wear my plimsolls instead. This means I have to fit my shoes into my small suitcase, which is already overloaded with stuff. It takes me a good 90 seconds to do this, which is a tenth of the total time I have to get ready and off this train. Slightly flustered, I soon emerge into the corridor where I wait for what feels like two hours before the train eventually slows, shudders and stops. Time is playing tricks on me, as it usually does.

I am the only person getting off the train at Newton Abbot. The first thing I notice is how clean and cold the air is here. Once the train pulls out of the station the silence is almost overwhelming, until a solitary early bird starts singing in one of the trees across the road. I have never been here before and I don't know what to expect. All I discovered when I booked my train ticket was that although this is not the closest station to Hare Hall, it is the closest station at which the night train stops. I worked out that a cab journey from here to Hare Hall would cost something in the region of £20, compared with something closer to £50 if I stopped at Plymouth instead. It's all expenses; but expenses I may at some point have to justify. My night travels have just about slipped through the net so far but I wouldn't want to have to try to explain why I needed to spend £50 on a cab, before dawn, as part of a trip for which everyone else will have normal, lower expenses.

Sometimes, night travelling can become depressing. If you feel at all depressed travelling at night, the trick is to remind yourself what an adventure it is, and how much more of the world you see when you are outside, awake and moving at a time when most people are inside, asleep and still. What a thrill to arrive in a place you have never been, when the sun has not yet risen in the sky and no one else is there. If the bomb dropped, killed everyone else and somehow missed you – perhaps because you were in a unique kind of bunker – this is how it would feel to emerge afterwards; to see the world uninhabited, as if people had left in a hurry. The night works for me, it really does. I am not scared of the dark, nor of strange men. I used to be but it turns out that being frightened is all in the mind. Once you strip down the fears you have of, say, walking through a town in the dead of night, or finding yourself alone in a dark forest, you soon realise that the only fear you actually have is of being alone. I remind myself that I know what to do in the event of many terrifying things – usually because I have studied them for work – and that I am not afraid of being alone, and start walking out of the station.

There are two or three taxis sitting in the small station car park, on standby, with half-asleep drivers smoking roll-ups or listening to all-night FM radio. I will take one of these taxis once the sun has actually come up. I cannot turn up at Hare Hall at five in the morning; that would be too strange. Instead I am planning to explore this little/big town under cover of darkness, to see if it generates any interesting or useful ideas, and then find somewhere to have breakfast. This is another habit from work: you can justify doing the strangest things on the basis that they may 'generate ideas'. This is actually not just bland justification – these oddities and displacements often do turn out to generate more ideas than anything else. Routine kills creative thought; everyone knows that. This, incidentally, is one of PopCo's many mottoes, all of which come from our crazy/brilliant CEO Steve 'Mac' MacDonald.

My suitcase probably makes me look like a runaway, I think, as I come out of the station and turn right, towards a small parade of shops. As there's no one to see me and think anything, I suddenly wonder if I exist at all. I can no longer hear my footsteps now that I am wearing plimsolls and this adds to the sensation of not really existing, moving silently through a town I don't know, before dawn, in a place where no one is watching.

Recently I have realised that almost every technique outlined in the KidSpy, KidTec and KidCracker kits are things I use in real life all the time, even if they are entirely unnecessary. For example, if I want to look at a person or some people walking down the street, I use reflections in shop windows. When walking, I take illogical routes in case someone is tracking me or noting my routines. I try not to leave footprints anywhere. This started as role-play. The ability to 'become' a misfit 9- to 12-year-old at will is a necessary part of my job, and the fact that after having that thought I then think, *Cool, a secret identity – it's like going into a phone box and coming out as someone entirely new with secret powers!* just shows how closely connected to the 9- to 12-year-old psyche I now am.

The KidCracker kit was easier to put together than the other two but somehow less fun. For the KidSpy and KidTec kits I was actually learning new things. Since codes and code-breaking have always been part of my life, that one didn't turn out to be so challenging. It was just a case of writing down all the stuff I've known for ever. Despite this, it has slightly outsold the other two kits. The people in Marketing – with whom I have to liaise about absolutely everything these days – say that spying is too 'cold war' and detective work seems 'lame' and 'old-fogey' to kids living in our terrorist/space-age matrix-world. It's never easy to know what to say to them. Because the KidCracker kit sold slightly more than the other two kits (despite being 'lame' etc., the other kits sold pretty well themselves), I am being pressurised to come up with something with more of a 'code-breaking feel'. So I am planning to make the next kit a survival-in-the-wilderness thing. KidScout, perhaps, although that sounds too much like the Scout movement and definitely uncool. I am having problems with the name, although this is something I am usually OK at. Of course, I cannot now explain how survival is like code-breaking, although I managed to do it in a meeting in such a way that my boss and the people from Marketing were convinced. I think I stressed the interactive elements (my brands are all heavily interactive, of course, as they all involve learning skills). The other proposal I put in was for a magic kit: KidCadabra, but this was rejected. They agreed that it would sell in the current toy climate but concluded that it might damage the overall PopCo brand to be seen selling 'black' magic items to children.

There is every chance that even my survival kit won't go ahead at all. It is fairly common for prototypes to be developed and then to fail in focus groups, or because someone spots something that might undermine the PopCo brand or lead to any sort of litigation. You have to be so careful with kids' products. Regarding this kit, I already have notes from a meeting reminding me to 'stress the back-garden elements of survival practice', i.e. don't tell 9- to 12-year-olds to actually go out into the wilderness and try to survive. Although it is hard, I am also having to take account of all the depressing statistics about children not really being interested in 'more traditional' toys any more. Younger and younger children would now rather opt for CDs, gadgets and videogames. Sometimes it feels like those of us stuck in the 'more traditional' parts of the toy industry are nowadays required to do little more than create decorative characters for hamburger containers, breakfast cereal, cartoons and films. There was a suggestion at one point that my brands could be 'updated' by linking each one with a pre-existing character: a martial-arts detective from a Japanese cartoon; a kid spy from some big-budget summer holiday film. I am glad this never happened.

So I am walking down this unfamiliar street in this unfamiliar town and I am thinking about being a runaway and this immediately does feed into my survival kit ideas, although it's a strange thought, that one of 'my' (this is also strange, that they are now 'my') 9- to 12-year-olds might be so traumatised, weird, loner-ish that they would actually run away and attempt to use the survival kit in a real-time, live situation, rather than in their back garden. Anyway, I wonder what would happen if you had run away and you were here, in this town, with these familiar shops casting unfamiliar dark shadows, and your parents looking for you. But . . . maybe your parents aren't looking for you. Perhaps they have been kidnapped by a biotech company and there is a big man looking for you – the company needs you to complete the family group and thus complete the genetic code for their vile experiment. What would you do? Where would you go?

I've been thinking about kidnap a lot again recently. I read some book that was lying around the office, which started it all off. It was about understanding fear when marketing to children. You could manufacture a talking pillow, it suggested, into which a parent could record soothing words so that if the child woke up scared and alone, they could simply press a button on a pillow to feel reassured. I found this terrifying, and it has left me with something, some memory-link to my own childhood, perhaps, in which I was so scared of being kidnapped I slept in the same room as my grand-parents for months. I didn't even have parents at that point, let alone their recorded, 'soothing' voices.

In the day this street is probably full of people, good and bad. You'd never notice the bad people in the day. They would dissolve in all the other bodies, smells, thoughts, intentions, decisions, cars, buses, mobile phones, footwear, magazines, job resignations, fast food, that affair with your boss that everyone warned you about. No. What would a child see here in the day? Toy shops, I think, as I approach one. This feels like work now. I look in the window and see a product that I knew about when it was an idea, in development, in design. My only almost-friend at PopCo, Dan, designed the packaging. I am not sure how I feel about packaging. He isn't either. He's into colour theory.

Perhaps a child would only see the bad people, even if they were partially dissolved in the fluid containing everyone else. They say that only children can see magical creatures, that by the time you are an adult, you have lost the ability. It's the same with the dark side. Perhaps it is because children are so close to death, if death comes before life in some grand cycle. Children; magic. Elderly people; insanity. Maybe it's all about proximity to death. And children can see bad things and bad people, too. They can see death in people's eyes. Children run from death in their fantasies, running towards what? Adulthood? To be the killer rather than the killed, the hunter rather than the prey, in the middle of the cycle where you feel safer from what exists at both ends.

Brand names, brand names, brand names. (A typical child is exposed to 8000 brands every day. I could clock up about half that in a couple of hours here, easy.) A small bookshop. A traditional department store, which makes me think of Christmas. But where could you hide around here? Not in an alley or a shop doorway. I am thinking (and have been thinking, for weeks now, actually) about A-frame shelters and ways of stuffing your clothes with dried grass to keep yourself warm and how to collect and filter water. I realise I need grass under my feet now, and keep walking.

After wandering for a while I come to a recreation ground with two old-looking cricket nets. There are recent chalk-marks on the worn green astro-turf. I think about my grandfather, for a second or two, and how he taught me to bowl leg-spin in our small garden in Cambridge. I imagine that the kids who play here have parents not that much older than me: shell suits, logos, designer glasses, office jobs. Yet somehow I still feel like a child, with a grandfather who played cricket in whatever he happened to be wearing at the time, smoking a pipe as he did so. The piece of netting hanging in-between the two practice wickets has a big hole in it, and flaps around in the light wind. I think about mosquito nets and children running away from home in a hot country and how my kit would work in different climates. Is it easier to survive when it's hot?

Perhaps, although there is dehydration to worry about. In the cold you can literally freeze to death. I will have to make battling against both of these things seem fun in my product.

I hate the word 'product'. I am having ideas, but they are not very good. Did I come here to have ideas? Yes. I did. I really did. I didn't come here because I didn't have anything else to do, alone in a strange town in the middle of the night. Sighing, I sit down on the driest bit of grass I can find and open my bag. I pour a cup of boiling water from my flask and place it on the ground, before adding a small pinch of green tea. I then take out a packet of blue cigarette papers and drop a slightly smaller pinch of brown tobacco into it, adding a filter tip before rolling it up, placing it in my mouth and lighting it. *Don't look at yourself from the outside. Don't see what other people see. You are sitting on a cricket field in a small town having a cup of tea in the middle of the night. It is completely normal.* But I am an anomaly. A night-time apothecary living on leaves. Green leaves to drink; brown leaves to smoke. I watch the sun come up like this, milky orange ice-lollies, and then I walk back to the station to take a cab to Hare Hall, via some forgettable breakfast place. I won't ever tell anyone I did this, tonight. To myself, I will explain it as work.

Chapter Three

The moor is a surprise. This is wilderness, real wilderness, in which you could genuinely get lost and die of exposure. There are several hills with broken-looking stone structures at the top of them. Forts? Ancient settlements? I will find out. Then mist, lots of mist and a drizzle that makes me think of see-through umbrellas and shower caps. One cattle grid, a 'Please Take Moor Care' sign, then some big, shaggy-looking cows and another cattle grid. It is not quite nine o'clock in the morning but I have already completely lost my bearings. The cab driver hasn't really said anything since Newton Abbot. It is vaguely freaking me out.

'The moor is actually quite big,' I say, lamely.

The cab driver snorts. We haven't seen any other cars, shops or road markings for about half an hour now. I am not even sure this is a real road.

'Just don't get lost in it,' he says eventually, and then laughs.

Hare Hall is a jagged shape in the mist, emerging incomplete, like something in a Magic Eye picture, perhaps a fantasy-style image of a castle with turrets. I imagine unicorns and fairies also living here. And I'm thinking about hares as well: the Hare and the Tortoise, which is a story I have always liked, and also some spooky, nightmare-inducing puzzle book I had as a child, which included clues for finding a magic, golden hare. That was around the time of the kidnap problem I had. I remember being scared to look at the book in case I somehow established the location of the golden hare and was kidnapped because of my knowledge, or that I accidentally found the hare and was kidnapped because of that. The golden hare book was a huge craze at the time and someone got it for me because I was interested in code-breaking.

The cab driver has to speak into an intercom in order for a rather large gate to be opened, although I am not sure how he knows to do this, as the intercom is tiny. Then we are on a long, curling driveway with, intriguingly, a small roundabout at the end. What kind of house needs its own roundabout? But this is a vast mansion, it turns out, made of what must be thousands and thousands of grey stone slabs. In the middle of the roundabout is a large statue of what from a distance looks like a gigantic garden gnome but actually turns out to be the PopCo company logo: a pale blue toy boat with yellow sails, set on a red circular background. The wheels of the cab resist the gravel and the car takes a second longer than it should to come to a halt.

I pay the driver. 'Can I have a receipt, please?' I say. I always say this. Today it makes me feel comfortable in a strange way; more like me. I may not know where I am, or where I have been recently, but I am on expenses. I have a job. It is, to some people, important. The cab driver writes out a receipt and drives off. I am alone.

So I am here, four hours early for lunch, the first event of the conference. I wonder if the mist will still be here when everyone else arrives, and whether anyone else will mistake our logo for a gnome. I am standing on gravel in my skirt, plimsolls, jumper and shirt, with my hair now in two plaits and my brown suitcase by my feet, wondering where to go next. Then a man appears. He walks towards me and – oh, shit. It's Steve 'Mac' MacDonald, our CEO. He is here, on the gravel, looking confused. Jesus Christ. I had hoped to 'check in', or whatever you have to do here, without anyone noticing, and then go for a walk in the grounds. In a worst-case scenario I would have been discovered doing something unusual, like turning up four hours early for lunch, by my immediate boss, Carmen the second. (The previous boss was called Carmen as well. It's a long story.) This is much, much worse than that.

'Hello,' he says.

Do I call him Steve, Mac, or Mr MacDonald? 'Hello,' I say back.

'Battersea?' he says.

'Yes.'

He almost smiles. 'You're a bit early.' He looks like a prime minister on a photo-op at an American president's ranch. He is wearing new-looking jeans and a thick sweater with green wellies. He is holding a dog leash. He is worth billions.

I mumble something about how I was doing some research locally and then stayed overnight with a friend. My brain is running to catch up with itself. 'And then my friend had to go to work this morning and she only had one key so . . .'

It's Saturday, error, error, but he doesn't seem to notice. I suppose my friend could have a Saturday job but when was the last time I knew someone who worked on a Saturday morning? Probably when I was about eighteen, and my friend Rachel worked in some fast-food place. 'Good,' is all he says, rather disconcertingly. Then he stares at me, as if he expects that I am going to do the thing I would have done next if he hadn't turned up. I don't know what that is.

'Well,' I say. And I want to escape from the CEO of this global corporation for which I work but I don't know where to go, and he knows I don't know where to go, so I just stand there dismissing everything my brain wants to do as either lame, stupid or totally ridiculous. In the end I do something lame anyway. I quote one of Steve 'Mac' MacDonald's mottoes back at him. 'Routine kills creative thought after all,' I say, not really knowing why, while all the cells in my body, including the ones making this weird smile I have on my face, are on a protest, telling my brain, *eject, eject*. This is an impasse. He's not moving. I'm not moving. A million years go by.

Eventually, a small black Labrador puppy runs over. 'Ah, there she is,' he says, starting to bend down to greet her. But instead of returning to him and his dangling leash, she runs over to me and wags her tail excitedly, her whole back half going off like a metronome. I love dogs. I bend down to stroke her, which really seems to get her going. She jumps up at me excitedly and when I look down I find I have two muddy paw-prints on my skirt.

'Oh, I'm so sorry,' Steve MacDonald says, walking over and clipping the leash on the dog. She jumps up at him a lot while he is doing this, and I realise that he is already slightly muddy. 'Oh dear. We're both muddy now. Oh dear.' Then he smiles. 'Now what are we going to do with you?' For a moment I think he's talking about the puppy but then I realise he's talking to me.

'I suppose I just need to find out where to go,' I say. 'Is there someone . . . ?'

'No, no, not this early. I'll show you where to go. I'm Mac, by the way.'

As if I didn't know. Oh well, at least I know what to call him now. Dan will possibly go pale and stammer when I tell him I have been this close to our leader. I suddenly realise that I am compiling anecdotes in my head before anything of note has actually happened. I hate anecdotes.

We walk in silence around the house, or at least this wing of it, to a small stable-style door, which Mac opens, and through which the puppy, now unleashed, runs. Somewhere inside a woman says something like 'Steve, there's not much milk left.' This feels more of a family kind of situation than a corporate one now, and I feel uncomfortable, as if I have turned up at the CEO's house, at a weekend, uninvited. Mac closes the door and turns to me.

'Right,' he says. 'Now.'

'Sorry to put you to this trouble,' I say. 'I would have come later if I'd known.'

'It's OK,' he says. 'And – sorry – you are?'

'Alice. Alice Butler.'

'Ah,' he says. 'Yes. The code-breaker.'

How does he know this? Has he memorised details of every one of the few thousand creatives in the whole company? Probably. It's probably in one of those management books about cheese or something. *Memorise your employees' names*. Or maybe not. This is weird. *The code-breaker*. Could he possibly know about my grandfather?

That's even more doubtful. What's going on? Help me.

The word *Yes* comes out of my robot mouth, and I am so polite it's killing me. I don't want to speak to anyone at the moment, let alone Steve MacDonald. Right now I just want a cigarette. Or maybe it's tea I want. Or sleep. I really, really want to put down this suitcase. I decide that when this is all over I am going to have a cigarette and a cup of tea and my emergency chocolate (even though I don't really like chocolate) and I am going to dance around my room, wherever that ends up being, laughing and pulling faces and taking deep breaths, celebrating the fact that this isn't happening any more.

'So if you could change one thing at PopCo, what would it be?' Mac says, as we walk back towards the PopCo roundabout and turn left down a gravel path.

I'm too tired for this. If I could change one thing at PopCo I'd fire all the marketing people, for a start (although we now, apparently 'are all responsible for marketing'). Or what about actually launching all those products that have been pulled due to some focus group research involving kids who are too young or too old or just too stupid for that particular product? And the coffee machine in the second-floor 'chill-out zone' at Battersea uses boiling water, rather than the hot-but-not-boiling water required to make good coffee. There is no car park. I hate our logo. I hate what is happening to the toy industry. I hate having to dumb down ('make accessible', in their language) my brands to appeal to more mainstream kids when my brands are obviously for the geeky ones. I would like to call a moratorium on staff conferences, under whatever name, and be paid about five times as much as I am.

We are still walking down the gravel path and I am really getting a sense of how big this place is. We have come to a stop at a little gravel crossroads with tennis courts to my right and the side of the main house to my left. The gravel path continues in front of me towards another little roundabout, with stables on the right and another gravel path to the left. I don't know why we have stopped. Maybe it's because Mac is still waiting for me to answer his question.

'Be honest,' he says. 'Don't try to impress me.'

'All right then,' I say bluntly, catching his eye briefly before looking back at the stables. 'I wish we could use less packaging, and I wish all the marketing promotions didn't involve bits of throwaway plastic.' His face tells me that this isn't quite what he'd expected, despite PopCo apparently having all these 'ecological' targets now. 'And I'd like it if we could take more risks,' I add. Does he like this one? Yes, he does. He's a CEO. They love talk about risks and danger, especially now that it seems impossible to do anything without the board's approval; without safety nets and parachutes. 'I wish that we could be, well, a little bit more autonomous . . .'

'You don't like it that everything is done by committee,' interrupts Mac, and I nod. 'Hmm. Interesting.' His eyes meet mine. 'I think you may find this conference – sorry – *event*, very interesting indeed. Although in defence of the committees, creatives do sometimes forget how much it costs to launch a product these days. Perhaps we'd *all* like to take more risks.' His eyes twinkle for a second and then die, like a pair of shooting stars. Have I just been approved of or told off? I'm not sure. He pulls a key out of his pocket and his manner seems to change from contemplation to business-as-usual. 'OK. If you could wait here, I'll be back in just a moment.'

This place, or at least its outside, smells like the perfect teenage girl's bedroom. The air is clean and flowery, with birds rising and falling in it as if in some sort of celebration. Suddenly, I imagine that I can also smell something like a school canteen, somewhere in the distance, this smell now cutting through everything else like a rusty axe. For a moment I also imagine I can hear children playing.

When Mac comes back he is carrying a clipboard.

'You're in the Old Barn,' he says. 'Not the grandeur of the main house, I'm afraid, but it's quiet, at least.'

'OK,' I say, because I can't think of anything else. 'Thanks.'

As we continue down the gravel path, past the stables and towards the second roundabout, the school-canteen smell becomes stronger, as does the sound of children playing. I frown, trying to pick out distinct sounds. There are definitely children here. This is playground noise: I would recognise it anywhere.

'Kid Lab,' Mac says.

'Sorry?'

'Kid Lab. That's what you can hear. We've got about fifty children on site at the moment. Focus groups, observation, research. Ideal location for it, isn't it? You'll probably get to meet some of the kids very soon. What you can hear might be some of them working with the Games Team, who, as you may know, are now based here on Dartmoor all the time.'

I didn't know that. I thought the gamers were all in Berkshire.

'Videogames?' I say, uncertainly.

Mac laughs. 'No, no. Real-time, live-action team games. Football, hockey, cricket, paintball. Only we're inventing a new game, of course. We have a Sports Hall, and a games pitch right here on site, just around that corner.' He points off to the right.

I wonder what he means by 'we'. *We're inventing a new game*. Is this just 'we' as in PopCo, or does Mac actually get involved in this himself? I have heard that this is his country retreat, paid for by the company. Does he hang around here at weekends, tinkering with these outdoorsy, wholesome projects? Is he a team-game type of guy? I bet he plays cricket, actually. I imagine him as a fast bowler who gets his wickets with well-timed slower balls.

'This is an amazing place,' I say. It is, too, even if I am trying to be polite.

'You haven't seen half of it yet. Used to be a boarding school, although you guessed that, right?'

No, but then I'm too tired. I say nothing.

Alone again, now Mac has gone. I am in what appears to be a dormitory in a converted barn. There are four beds in the room, each one screened off with these unstable-looking blue things on legs. I pick the bed on the far side of the room, next to the window, and put my case on it slightly tentatively. The idea of sleeping in the same place as other people does not appeal to me and I am irrationally hoping that no one else comes to share this room. The floorboards under my feet are dark and polished. Each bed has a cabinet next to it, as if this were a hospital, although each one is different. Mine has a small lamp on the top of it, three drawers and an open compartment at the top. It is made from dark wood like the floor. I sit on the bed and the blue screen adds to the hospital effect, leaving me with the feeling that I am about to be examined. I badly want to sleep now but I am not sure enough of my surroundings to allow any form of unconsciousness.

The water in my flask isn't completely hot any more but I use it to make some chamomile tea anyway. Then I roll up a cigarette which I smoke out of the window while drinking the tea. The emergency chocolate doesn't seem necessary any more; neither does running around celebrating. It's hard to know exactly what to do next. I don't want to leave this room in case I meet Mac again. What would I say to him? We've surely already had the only conversation we could ever have. Now I imagine him driving off in an SUV to get milk for his wife, vaguely laughing at this geeky girl he just met, a tiny atom in a tiny molecule of whatever metaphor you may like to use for this corporation. (A virus? A lump of green goo they sell in toyshops? A hive of industrious insects?) My brain keeps running this jerky film of Mac: planning his after-lunch speech, thinking dismissive thoughts about his underlings, thinking about playing cricket with members of the PopCo board, and then, suddenly, my mind becomes intriguingly blank of any ideas about anything else at all. No toys. No useful thoughts. Nothing. My inner 9- to 12-year-old child has gone off in a sulk. This is all too grown up for it. I yawn. And, although I have tried to avoid it, my internal scene shrinks to a repeated whisper, and a hazy fade-out takes me into sleep, propped up on my bed, still vaguely waiting for the enemy.

Chapter Four

Although I have many anxious dreams about sleeping through lunch (after arriving here, so conspicuously, four hours early, that would surely be the last straw), I am awake, washed and changed by half-past twelve. One of the miscellaneous objects I have with me is a small inflatable bag with suction pads attached to it. This was a prototype for a product that was never made, which was due to be called *Hide It!* or something else with an exclamation mark. (We've gone a bit exclamation mark crazy recently, I think because of some ironic, or even post-ironic, Japanese connection.) The idea with this product is that you put things in it, squeeze out all the air, then use the suction pads to stick it somewhere secret, where the enemy won't see it. It failed product testing because if you put too much stuff in it the suction pads don't work. It's a shame because initial focus groups loved it. The bags were originally going to be included with my KidTec, KidSpy and KidCracker kits, each one decorated accordingly with different types of camouflage, but the one I still have is just a see-through prototype. I put my credit card and a couple of other important things in it and stick it to the underside of the wooden cabinet. If it turns out that I really am staying in a dormitory with other people I may have to take other measures, but this will do for now.

I have no idea where lunch is. Maybe in the main building, the one Mac described as having some kind of 'grandeur'. I decide to go there to find out. As soon as I leave the barn I run into a bunch of people arriving with bags and cases. The mist has gone and it's not quiet any more. You wouldn't be able to hear the soft, breathless sound of the Kid Lab games now, what with all the extra sounds of people talking, coughing, arriving in taxis. I don't know any of the people who are walking towards me.

As well as involving the whole of the Battersea ID team, many of whom I only know to say 'hello' to, the POW event aims to bring together unique teams from other parts of the UK (like the videogame creatives, I suppose, although I don't really know) and the English-speaking ID teams from Iceland and Spain. I learnt this last week from an 'All Departments' e-mail forwarded to me at home. The group walking towards the barn are, at a guess, from Iceland. One girl in the group has pink hair, tied up in pigtails. She's wearing an obscure indie band T-shirt and a studded choker. Her rucksack has badges stuck on it, and various candy-coloured objects dangling from it: key rings, ribbons, a small soft-looking monkey toy. Just as she is about to make eye-contact, I spy Dan walking behind them, gesturing at me. A couple more hand gestures later, we are fleeing in the opposite direction.

'Where's your bag?' I say to Dan, once we are halfway up the hill behind the barn.

'In my room,' he says. 'I came to find you. You were on a list.'

'Why are we running away?'

'Escape is the only option,' he says.

Among a few other things, Dan and I share a love of military strategy and commando films. For me, it started with all the war stories my grandfather told me when I was growing up. For Dan, I'm not sure. At work, when we've had enough, we say things like,

'Escape is the only option', or 'Eject', and so on. We're not having sex, despite what people sometimes think. We once spent a whole night watching free porn just after Dan got cable TV but when I tried to get into bed with him afterwards he told me he was *gay-ish*. I don't know what *gay-ish* is. We're just friends, anyway.

'What's up here?' I ask him.

'According to my map? An old hill fort.'

'You have a map?'

'Oh yes. And a compass. Just in case.'

I wish I had my survival kit. 'Won't we miss lunch?'

'No. We'll just see this and then we'll go back down.'

At the top of the hill there is indeed a group of stones, some whole, some broken, arranged in a shape that could be a circle but is maybe actually a square. You'd have to go higher than this to see exactly what shape it was originally supposed to be, although there isn't anywhere higher than this in sight, that being the point, I suppose, of a hill fort.

'You can see everything from up here,' Dan says, although he doesn't really have to. Hare Hall now looks like a structure made from PopBrix (our version of Lego, although you're not really allowed to say that). I can see the large, grey structure that is the main house, and the little annexe that is joined to it. Closer to us is the top of the barn in which I am staying, grey slate on grey brick. There are other large PopBrix structures scattered around: various old barns; and a flat-topped, whiteish structure that must be the Sports Hall Mac mentioned. Being up here is actually useful, in terms of working out the layout of this place and what might be close by. Although in terms of what is close by, there doesn't really seem to be anything at all. There are no neighbouring structures or other houses that I can see. There is a stream off to the right and a thin, reddish-brown track to the left. As we watch, two taxis come down the track: more people coming to the POW event, presumably. Dan seems to get bored with looking down at Hare Hall, and soon starts to examine one of the stones instead. Then he lays both his palms flat against it and closes his eyes. I notice that he has a slightly pained expression.

'What are you doing?'

'I'm trying to connect,' he says seriously.

'Oh, for God's sake,' I say, laughing.

'Shhh. I'm concentrating. Becoming one with the rock. I see . . . a battle. Many warriors coming up the hill . . . We must hold them off! Hand me my arrows! Hide yourself!'

'Stop it. Tell me what you know – seriously.'

Dan breaks out of his trance. 'Hill forts are characteristic of the middle and later Iron Age,' he says. '500BC to AD50, roughly. They are supposed to be the fortified settlements of the Celtic people. At least twelve hill forts survive on Dartmoor. This isn't one of the twelve most people know about. This hill fort actually belongs to PopCo.'

'You've got a book, haven't you?'

'Oh yes.'

'Can I borrow it?'

'Indeed. But only if you tell me where you've been for the last two weeks.'

'Ideation, baby,' I say. 'Survival.'

'What?'

'I'll explain later. What time is it, incidentally?'

'Don't know.'

'Shit. I thought you had a watch.'

'Nope.'

We scramble into lunch with about thirty seconds to spare. It isn't even where we thought it would be. When we got to the Great Hall in the main building we were shooed away by a stern-looking woman who crisply informed us that lunch was being held in the 'cafeteria'. It didn't seem like a good idea to ask her exactly where that was, so, remembering the Kid Lab noises I heard earlier, and, crucially, the smell of food cooking, I led Dan in the direction Mac had pointed then. After walking past the full-sized Sports Hall, a cottage, and a smallish modern-looking structure, we eventually found this place. Presumably constructed from the remains of a large agricultural building, it is now a vast, modern rectangle, all white inside with exposed chrome pipes and fittings. It should feel like a school canteen – that must have been the idea – but it is way too glossy for that. The tables are laid out in a regular fashion, but are themselves irregular orange plastic designer shapes with Go boards etched into them. In one corner there is a DJ booth. One wall is taken up with a large plasma screen, currently showing kids playing with some PopCo products in slow motion. On the other side is a raised area with two more plastic tables, probably for Mac and his ilk. At the far end of this is – oh, my God – a flip-chart. In this business you can never entirely escape the flip-chart.

Dan and I are now standing in a queue, holding trays.

'What is this all about?' he says, looking around. 'Is this some kind of school-dinner thing?'

'Mmm. I think so. It's concept-driven, anyway.'

'Yes.'

Many of the expressions Dan and I use originally started off being things that other people said that we made fun of. Ending sentences with the word 'baby' was something that Carmen-the-first's assistant, Katerina, used to do. She was Russian and in the middle of an extreme love-affair with Western capitalism. When she came back from shopping (AKA 'research'), you wouldn't have to ask her what she'd bought because she would come into the office holding up paper carrier bags and saying 'Levi's, baby', with this proud smile on her face, like she was a feral dog returning with a bloody chicken. 'Concept-driven', 'High concept', and 'Concept-led' are forms of criticism that emanate from Richard Ford, Carmen the second's boss. His role in the company is to come into Battersea every so often and trash all our ideas. 'It's got an intriguing feel,' he will say. 'But ultimately it's too concept-driven.' Nobody has ever worked out what he means by this, or why it's a bad thing. Surely kids' toys are always concept-driven? Although I occasionally see Dan outside of work, we haven't got together that often since the cable TV incident. As a result, our friendship is strictly work-bound, full of references to work and office in-jokes. We are probably the closest thing to 'best friends' inside the office but outside we are still little more than strangers.

I am now at the front of the queue.

'Vegetarian or meat?' a woman asks, abruptly.

Dan pokes me. 'Go for veggie,' he hisses. 'Veggie. Veggie.'

'Ow! Sorry. Vegetarian,' I say.

The woman sighs, and then passes me a cling-filmed plate of sandwiches and salad. 'Next,' she says, and then gives Dan the same thing. It turns out that the non-veggies are being given an evil-looking stew.

'How did you know that?' I ask Dan. 'About being a veggie?'

'Ex-girlfriend. Boarding-school stories.'

This is the thing about Dan being 'gay-ish'. He only ever seems to have ex-girlfriends, never boyfriends. It's intriguing.

Because we were almost the last in, we are virtually at the end of the queue. The only other stragglers are the two people behind us, neither of whom I have ever seen before. As we are ushered over to the last free table by a woman wearing a blue boiler suit and headset, I try to work out where they might be from. The girl has long fawn-coloured hair, and is wearing a brown shift-dress and earrings made out of dark brown feathers. The guy is dressed all in black cotton, or possibly hemp: combats and a short-sleeved shirt. Are they Berkshire people? He has three biros in his top pocket, one green, one red and one blue, and is wearing black-rimmed glasses. Our eyes meet for a second before we sit down. For a moment I misread his expression and think he is about to say something to me, so I open up my face and half-smile. Then he looks away and says something to the fawn-haired girl instead. The connection, if there ever was one, is broken.

We are barely in our seats before the music starts.

'Oh Jesus. Please no,' Dan says.

It's this weird bouncy music I have never heard before. Or is it slightly familiar? I don't think so. 'What is this?' I ask Dan.

'You don't know? Oh yes, your TV thing. Lucky you.'

My 'TV thing' is that I never had a TV growing up and, although I have one now, I only really use it to watch videos or play videogames. I assume that what is playing is some sort of TV theme tune, in that case. I look over to the DJ booth and the source of the music becomes clear. I nudge Dan, but he's already watching.

'Christ,' he says. 'It's Georges. I might have known.'

Georges Celéri is the Creative Director of PopCo. He is like the company whirlwind, or perhaps our poltergeist. He's the PopCo prankster, the guy who *really* loves toys rather than business; the guy behind the ecology stuff. We know him as the sender of our weekly corporate e-mails, which often come with huge JPEG attachments or inappropriate jokes. He is also the director most likely to turn up on site just to 'see what you guys are up to', and then take the whole team out to dinner and a strip club. He is either French and grew up in Japan, or Japanese and grew up in France. I can't remember. He looks vaguely Japanese, is between thirty and forty, and has a good haircut. Like Mac, he has an accent stranded somewhere in the Atlantic.

'It's school dinner time!' Georges says into the microphone. I notice that Mac is standing next to him, holding a glass of wine, laughing. 'So, everyone . . . I'd just like to welcome you to the PopCo Open World Event. Don't drink too much over lunch, because there's a lot in store for you all this afternoon. Oh yes – the CEO's presentation, and after that, the games! Please meet at the sports field at four o'clock, dressed appropriately for running around. The theme of this conference – sorry – *event* is becoming more like children. Forget that this is work. We are PopCo! This is fun!'

Mac takes the microphone from Georges. 'Yes, welcome. Enjoy lunch,' is all he says before the two of them join the other directors, PAs and senior non-creative staff on the raised tables. Some people clap. A minion wearing a headset takes over the DJing, and, after the weird bouncy music finishes, a recent pop album comes on, at a lower volume. I notice that a couple of bottles of wine have been placed on our table; one red, one white. Dan has already filled both our glasses with red and I immediately gulp most of mine down.

'I needed that,' I say. I hate this already. The guy wearing black glowers slightly at us, presumably since we have hijacked the red wine. He fills his own and his companion's glass with white, wrinkling his nose slightly as he does so.

Over the rest of lunch, and while Dan eats my sandwich crusts, I explain to him about my recent 'ideation adventure': that for the last two weeks I have been at home, barefoot, reading about survival for my new kit. I don't go into too many details, it having been a calming, somehow private exercise. I also don't tell him I met Mac this afternoon. He'd probably get all excited about it and I am just not in the mood for that.

Ideation is an odd process. There are, of course, lots of ways of generating ideas. Ordinary people, stuck for ideas about normal things, like what colour to paint the sitting room, or what flowers to have at a wedding, may well decide to simply sit around and wait for inspiration, or use commonly available stimuli like magazines and shop displays in order to jog that inspiration into life.

When you are in the ideas industry, however, there are a vast number of techniques for ideation that you will just know. You will use these techniques not just at work, but in normal-life situations as well. You will know what sorts of results to expect from brainstorming, matrices, mind-mapping and so on, and if you want stimulating material you are more likely to rely on a trend-spotter or a fact-seeking expedition to somewhere bizarre, because it's just what you do. Last year at Battersea a couple of women ran these singles seminars after work in which, using flipcharts, matrices and mind-mapping, they came up with ideas as to how to find the perfect man. It was all a bit yucky. Dan and I called them the *Shagiators*, which was funny at the time.

There are several ways of becoming good at ideation. The first way is to be born with the gift. If you have been born with this gift, you are the type of person who will always be the one to say 'What if . . .' in any kind of situation. You will be the person who suggests the most outrageous idea to solve a problem, and you will find that, rather unpredictably, these sorts of ideas often work for you. You may believe you are lucky or even blessed with magical powers, but in fact you are just a natural ideator. The second way of becoming good at ideation is to spend a lot of time reading books written by creative or business gurus, or attending seminars and workshops either devoted to just ideation, or, more usually, to ideation and team-building. There are many books of this nature lying around the homes and offices of PopCo employees, recent hits including *Unleashing the Ideavirus*, *Creating Ever-Cool, a Marketer's Guide to a Kid's Heart* and *Funky Business*. Many industries use ideation techniques nowadays, often calling in a facilitator to help their employees bond, solve business problems or come up with a design for a new product. This is the realm of the flip-chart, the marker pen, lateral thinking puzzles and, of course, the Balloon Game.

If you have never played the Balloon Game you have played it twelve times less than I have. The basic idea is that a group of people – your team – are in a hot-air balloon which has become unstable and will crash if some people are not thrown out of it. The Balloon Game thus involves a debate about who should stay and who should go. This enforced suicide/murder ritual is supposed to help your team 'bond'. It is less disturbing if all the people in the game take on the personae of celebrities or politicians or something, so that begging for your life exists at one remove, but the whole experience is still rather disturbing. It's a particularly strange choice to use for team-building, as several people in the group will certainly have to (metaphorically) die in order that the team can prosper. I have heard of the Balloon Game being used in situations where companies are just about to lay people off. Apparently some companies deliberately use it to convince people that lay-offs are justified. Also – and this may actually be an urban legend – there was recently a fad in the City for Human Resources managers to watch through one-way mirrors and decide who to lay off as a result of the Balloon Game.

This isn't the most disturbing use of one-way mirrors I have ever heard of, though. PopCo was responsible for that. It involved six-year-old girls in a focus group testing a new cosmetics range for children. As far as I know, no one else apart from me was offended by the idea of various executives and marketers watching in extreme close-up while these little girls used the mirror to try out the lipsticks and eye shadows which, incidentally, never went on the market in this country but do pretty well in the US. Perhaps other people were offended but didn't say anything. Let's face it, I didn't actually say anything. I wouldn't have known what to say.

Corporations in the toy, clothes, fast-food and music industries are known for applying the most cutting-edge techniques for having/obtaining ideas. Many corporations have things called 'idea labs' or 'think-tanks'. McDonald's has something near Chicago called the Core Innovation Centre where they experiment with different ways of arranging queues, serving food, cooking it and so on. People at Levi's use a lot of trend-spotters and spend plenty of time in what they call 'infodumps', which are like brainstorming sessions. In these industries, if you can find a good idea and it works, it could well mean billion-dollar profits, happy shareholders, global brand-recognition and success. Because of this, there are many companies that just sell ideas.

At PopCo, however, we're not buying them. There has been a recent move towards keeping ideation in-house and, to some extent, intuitive. We are supposed to remain cutting edge without using any outside idea agencies. This is all part of Georges's long, rambling creative philosophy. Thus my two-week period of paid leave. I have been researching, alone, and now all this at-work stuff feels like it's killing me. I forgot how much you have to concentrate simply to be at work, interacting with other people. And I didn't bring a tracksuit, either. That 'All Departments' e-mail must have passed me by.

Chapter Five

It turns out that almost no one has brought any kind of sports clothing at all, sports clothing not being even slightly in fashion at the moment, and all the people in charge of this event obviously having forgotten to send the e-mail informing us that we would be needing it. One of the girls from Iceland claims to have two tracksuits, but despite her offering to lend one of them to someone, that still leaves roughly a hundred and ninety-eight of us without. I don't know what they would do in other industries, but as we all walk over to the Great Hall for Mac's speech, there is a buzz in the air that 'they' (the PopCo directors? the minions?) are ordering two hundred tracksuits to be delivered in time for four o'clock this afternoon.

The Great Hall is at the back of the main house: a vast, high-ceilinged space, the original structure of which seems, to my untrained eyes, faintly medieval. I glance at Dan as we walk in together, my initial look saying something like, *Wow, this is amazing,* and then mutating into something more like, *Don't start trying to 'connect' with the walls or I'll pretend I am not with you.* I'm not sure how much of this I could possibly have communicated with my eyes and Dan simply smiles at me. He doesn't touch the walls, though.

There are several rows of wooden chairs in the centre of the hall, with further seating available in one gallery at the top – 'The Gods!' Dan hisses as soon as he sees it and drags me up there – and two areas at the sides that go up, in a step-style fashion to several large stained-glass windows. At the front of the hall is a small stage, constructed from pale wood. It looks a bit like something a busy professional couple might create in their garden on a dry Saturday afternoon, inspired by DIY shop promotions and home-makeover shows. I am somehow able to make this connection without ever having watched a home-makeover show. It's funny; in the same way that Dan tries to connect with inanimate objects (albeit jokingly – at least I think it's a joke, it's relatively new behaviour), I seem genuinely able to pluck the details of mainstream pop culture from the air. It must be from the air. Bad TV shows do, after all, travel through it all the time; particles hitching a ride on passing waves of light. It's a sobering thought, actually, that as you walk around – doing your shopping or popping out to feed the ducks in the park – all this invisible stuff is churning in the air around you. TV broadcasts, radio waves, mobile phone signals, global positioning systems, fragments of advertisements. You probably have bits of advertisements trapped in your navel, in fact, along with all that pink fluff, and maybe also that radio play you'll never listen to. Perhaps this accounts for how I know many of the characters in the two most popular UK evening soap operas, and all the other stuff too. You can't escape these things – I can't anyway – no matter how hard you try.

This isn't why I am at PopCo. Before I got this job I didn't really pay much attention to the media, brands or toys. Roughly three years ago, someone at PopCo (Mac? Georges?) decided the company should headhunt a 'new type of creative'. At the time I was compiling crosswords for a broadsheet Sunday newspaper. After several years working my way up in the crossword world, I had my own code-name, and a particular style that the regulars could identify. I used to get letters, sometimes, from the occasional 'fan', although the job was in no way glamorous. I never went to the newspaper offices, only ever spoke to my editor on the phone and was paid very little. I spent most of my life in my pyjamas or, if I had to go out, old jeans. If I did go out, it was usually to hang around with my friend Rachel at London Zoo, where she works. Sometimes, when money was very tight, or I was feeling very lonely, I would think about applying for an actual job at the zoo. Other times, I would think about writing a book. Mostly, though, it was the crosswords and my grandfather's big project. These things occupied all my attention.

Most people who compile crosswords are retired vicars from Surrey or elderly military people. I was unique in my age and gender and thus appeared once in a small 'My Job' column in one of the business supplements. Rachel had already done it and had recommended me to the journalist. Shortly after the piece appeared, I got a letter from PopCo. They wanted ideas people, they said; ideas people with 'unconventional' ways of generating their ideas. Would I come in for an informal chat? I didn't know what they had me pencilled-in as, back then. Someone who would write the puzzles for their videogames? Perhaps I entertained vague notions of creating board games or puzzles. Perhaps that *is* in fact what they wanted me to do. They weren't very specific. During the two informal chats we had, they talked to me more about ways of generating ideas than my puzzle-creating skills and it was all very confusing. I remember it being a rainy kind of summer. My grandfather was in hospital and my car had conked out. I was going everywhere by bus, reading books about the war. I missed the stop for the Battersea offices both times I went there.

PopCo eventually offered me a job with a fairly large salary and a chance to actually go to a building and work with other people. At the time I needed both these things. The brief was fairly relaxed. 'Design something,' they said. 'Put in some proposals. No pressure.' Of course, my first ideas were fairly lame – hilarious in retrospect – but there really was no pressure. I was encouraged to blend into the 'team', to watch what they did and how they did it and learn by my own mistakes. In the end, I concluded that I should work with what I knew already; that advice writers are always given. Secret codes were what I knew already, so I put in the proposal for the KidCracker kit. I didn't just 'put in the proposal' of course. At Battersea, people are always coming up with new ways to present their ideas to the rest of the team. I made little teasers; in code. The idea was an immediate hit.

My grandfather, who taught me everything I know about cross-words, cryptography and cryptanalysis, died while I was working on this first kit. It was expected but I still couldn't bear it. Among other things, he left me with an unfinished project and a locket engraved with a strange code I was supposed to try to work out. I don't like thinking about those days very much at all, and when I see my grandfather in my mind, sitting awkwardly on our old brown carpet screwing up his eyes to see the letter on a Scrabble piece, or pushing a rook forward on our chessboard, I still want to cry.

*   *   *

Mac is standing on the decking-style stage going through sales figures for last year, via another plasma screen. Every so often people cheer or clap; sometimes little groups, presumably responsible for whatever brand is on screen at the time. My brands won't be a part of Mac's presentation, none of them having been launched last year, so I am able to relax. I try to pick out people I know in the audience. I see Carmen somewhere near the front, and, of course, Chi-Chi. Chi-Chi is a kind of evil genius, and is responsible for PopCo's main mirror-brand, K. Mirror-branding, when you first come across it, can seem perplexingly anti-brand – like, why have a huge international brand like PopCo unless you stick the logo on everything? Surely the logo is what makes the toys sell? Well, most of the time, except when you're selling to what has recently been termed the the *No Logo* demographic. The *No Logo* kids, also referred to in some marketing study as 'Edges', have money too and want to spend it on small, independent brands.

Completely web-based, K has several brands within it, the most popular being an orphaned space kid called Star Girl and a post-apocalyptic rabbit called Ursula. The whole thing has a Japanese-cutesy-cartoon feel but without the little-kid factor or the theme-park worlds. It's Hello Kitty injected straight into an ironic, wannabe alienated, sixth-form audience. Each character is a brand in its own right and kids from all over the world can buy T-shirts, purses, badges, hoodies, skateboards, bags, toothbrushes, bandanas, hairgrips, drawing pins and so on from each character's range. The Star Girl character is the most popular. Her motto is 'No one loves you in space'. The idea of K is that when people visit the website they feel that they have found something non-corporate, small, cool and exclusive. K claims to be based in a small lock-up in Tokyo, and even goes so far as to display its first screen in Japanese, with a little 'English' button. Somehow, this makes the kids feel they've really found something authentic. Dan worked on all the original graphics for the site but he doesn't work with Chi-Chi any more. They had a few problems working together.

Mac is going through the motions now, concluding this part of his presentation. Images flash up on the screen from the younger kids' brands: Doctor Dan, Lucy, The Bumblebuzz Babies, Sailor Sam and his Amazing Clam, Moo-Moo and Li-Li, the Drondles, the Smoogs, the Curly Cake Bake Factory, Grumpy Mr Duck, Laser-Eraser, Floppington Village, the Bubblegum Tree, Farmyard Friends, and the big hit of last Christmas, the Glitter Fairy Magic Glitter Wings and Secret Wish Wand Set. Most of the other little kids' brands are TV or film tie-ins or fast-food promotions. The term tie-in implies that the TV show came before the toys, although this isn't usually the case. Usually, these days, they are created together. It's quite surreal.

For some reason I start thinking about miso soup, and now, suddenly, I've got a real craving for it. This is what a lack of adrenaline does to you. Throughout Mac's final inspirational speech I consider how I could get some miso soup today. It took half an hour to get here from the nearest town. Would it even have a shop selling miso soup? Could I get back there? Unlikely. This is turning into a real craving. Oh, God. I can almost taste it in my mouth, salty, cloudy miso-heaven, with those little green bits floating on the top and the sea-vegetables on the bottom. And I realise that this is a complete flashback situation, reminding me of school assemblies during which I would think, exclusively, about food and yawn a lot. So I am feeling a bit off the planet when Dan nudges me.

'What the fuck?' he's saying.

'What?' I hiss back.

'Look.'

Mac appears to be about to start reading from a sheet of white paper.

'. . . in no particular order,' he is saying, sounding like he is carrying on from something he was saying before. He starts reading out names of staff. I don't recognise many of them. But, this being a big corporation, and Mac being our sort of God, the fact that he is mentioning individuals by name at all is rather thrilling.

'What's this for?' I ask Dan.

'It's . . . all he said was that he was going to read a list of names of people who he wants to stay behind afterwards or something.'

This really is like school. 'Probably to get sacked,' I say. A long time ago, my father worked at a factory making buttons. When the firm was on the verge of going bust they would read out a list, virtually every week, of people being laid off. He was on the list somewhere around week four.

'Maybe they want volunteers to give out the tracksuits,' Dan says.

We laugh quietly. Then Dan's name is called, and we abruptly stop. It's rather unsettling hearing such a familiar name being read out in a hall like this. It must be the context. Even if Mac was only calling a register, it would still feel somehow wrong. And – *oh, no* – then my name too. My stomach feels a bit electric-shockish as the last couple of names are read out. I vaguely note that my name was almost last, which is unusual – my surname being Butler usually means I am somewhere near the top of any register or list.

'We've got to what . . . ?' I say to Dan. 'Stay behind?'

He shrugs. 'Yeah, I think so.'

We are definitely going to be sacked. My head feels hot, and one of my toes starts to itch uncontrollably. I never really got into trouble at school and have never been in trouble before at work. What have I done? I feel sick. Is this something to do with meeting Mac earlier? What did I say wrong?

Someone comes in – is it Georges's assistant? It looks a bit like her – and whispers a couple of things to Mac. He looks down at his piece of paper and then back up to her and nods a few times. They laugh, briefly. Then Mac does that thing he did earlier, and rapidly switches his face back to business-as-usual. He walks back over to his microphone stand.

'OK, slight change of plan,' he says. 'Those people on the list are to come back here *after dinner* this evening, please. We are running slightly over time, so if everyone could leave via the main door, and take a tracksuit each from the boxes which have been placed there . . . Thanks.'

Georges's assistant, I think it definitely is her, now comes to the microphone, as Mac gathers up notes and prepares to leave. 'Thank you, Steve,' she says, waving one arm at him like a magician's assistant. Everyone claps. 'Right, yes, please do help yourselves to tracksuits from the boxes. I trust that you all have trainers but if anyone is in dire need, there are a few pairs which have been put in the changing rooms in the Sports Hall. Please get changed and make your way over to the Sports Hall for, let's say . . .' she looks at her watch. 'Ten past four. OK. Thank you.'

There are no clocks in this room. Dan nudges someone on the way out and asks them the time. It's apparently almost four o'clock.

'Ten bloody minutes,' the person groans before becoming lost, like everyone else, in the many-armed monster that is all the PopCo creative staff grabbing slithery plastic-wrapped packages from the cardboard boxes outside.

My arm doesn't feel entirely comfortable, stretched above my head like this.

'And over. Feel the stretch,' says one of the Games Team, a girl wearing a faded pink sweatshirt. She's leading the warm-up. 'And the other side. That's great.'

The last time I did any proper sport was when I played cricket with my grandfather, two or even three years ago. Since then I've had one disastrous game of tennis with Dan (he was way too good for me and I barely got to hit the ball, and when I did hit it I invariably got it wrong, leading with my elbow like you do in cricket) and two goes on a skiing arcade game we had for a while at work. So this feels odd, standing out here in this grassy field, stretching and bending and so on. We are in a group of about ten or so, and there are other similar groups dotted all over the sports field. I don't know anyone in this group apart from Dan. In the next group along I can see the dark guy from lunch and his companion, concentrating on what their Games Team person is saying. The next group beyond that seems to be full of people laughing and I feel a momentary longing to be part of that group rather than this one.

'OK,' says the girl in the pink sweatshirt, once we've finished warming up. 'These are called "Paddles".' She is waving around two things that look a bit like mini lacrosse sticks. My grandmother was a lacrosse champion before the war, and she once told me all about the game but I have never actually played it. 'You have two each,' the girl continues. 'Like this.'

She holds one stick in each hand. They are made from red plastic, rather than wood and string, and remind me of those soft-ball rackets you get in beach activity sets, but with a slight scoop in the centre, as if someone had used one to try to hit a tiny meteorite that hadn't quite burnt all the way through.

'Is this PopCo's new game?' someone asks.

The girl smiles secretively. 'Maybe,' she says. 'This is the first real product test, so who knows?' She looks back at the Paddles in her hands. 'So you have a Paddle in each hand, and a ball, like this.' She places a ball into the Paddle in her right hand. She immediately starts moving the Paddle around in this circular motion, and I realise that this is to stop the ball falling out. I actually remember my grandmother telling me about doing this in lacrosse. What was it called? *Cradling*. That was it. Cradling the ball. I always like the idea of that. It sounded comforting.

'This is called "Vibing",' the girl says. 'You do this to keep the ball in the Paddle. While you have the ball in your possession, you must move it between the Paddles like so.' She vibes the ball for a second or two and then flips it, underarm, to the other Paddle, in a sort of spooning motion. Sweeping up the ball with the other Paddle, she then vibes it for two seconds before flipping it back again, this time in a more overarm movement, this action seeming more like casting a fishing line than spooning. When the ball reaches the other Paddle she almost instantly tosses it back, this time using a different move, more overarm than before. Then a deeper underarm movement to bring it back. Suddenly she's doing it really quickly and the movements seem fluid and graceful. The ball moves from head height down to her knees and then way up in the air, her arms looking like they are conducting the most crazy piece of experimental music ever. Then she starts running with the ball, never keeping it in either Paddle for more than a couple of seconds but instead keeping it way up in the air, or just in front of her, each time passing the ball with one Paddle and catching it with the other.

'This is insane,' Dan says to me.

'I quite like it,' I say.

The girl comes back, slightly out of breath.

'OK, so that is the way you keep possession of the ball,' she says. 'There are goals at either end of the field, and of course the aim is to take the ball to the goal and score. There are similarities with football and hockey. You can play the game with either five or eleven a side and the team with most goals at the end of ninety minutes wins the game. But I'm getting slightly ahead of myself here . . .'

'How do you foul?' someone asks.

'Right, I'll come to that. Good question. I'll just run through a few of the rules first and then tell you about the fouls. The main thing is that you can't catch the ball in the Paddle you have just thrown it from. Throw with the right, catch with the left – or vice versa. You can't hold the ball in one Paddle for more than three seconds, so you have to keep it moving. You can only move when the ball is moving, too, which is slightly confusing.'

'Is it like netball?' someone asks.

'Yes,' the girl says. 'Or maybe closer to basketball. You have to vibe the ball when you stop, but you can't stop for longer then three seconds. You can't just stand there flipping it to yourself, basically. You have to be on the move when the ball is moving, which is most of the time. You might want to stop to look and see where your team mates are, or to pass the ball to one of them, so you have three seconds to do that. Anyway, when you pass the ball to your team mates, or even when you are flipping it to yourself, the other team will try to intercept the ball. They can use virtually any means to do this: they can hit your Paddle with theirs to get the ball out – if you are vibing at the time – or they can try to intercept it as you are flipping it either to your other Paddle or to someone else on your team. There is no body-contact between players, so if you shove against someone or trip them up, that's a foul. You must not hit another player with your Paddle, although that's sometimes difficult, and you mustn't break the general rules.' She has been talking quite fast, and now, having finished, she slowly sighs. 'I'm Rebecca, by the way, if you want to ask anything. Now . . . If everyone could just take two Paddles from the box here . . .'

It's not actually that easy to learn how to do this. The right-handed movements feel surprisingly natural, but trying to catch, and then keep, the ball in the left-handed Paddle is almost impossible for those of us, like me, who are right-handed. The lefties, like Dan, have the problem the other way around. I manage to vibe the ball OK in the right Paddle but then, having just about caught it in the left one, I only seem able to hold onto it in a vaguely egg-and-spoon way for about two seconds before it simply falls out onto the grass. Dan seems to have given up on his weaker hand and instead stands there flipping the ball up and down, and occasionally vibing it, with his left Paddle. It looks quite good but is, of course, wrong.

Rebecca comes up to me.

'Good,' she says, uncertainly. 'That's it, keep it going with the right hand. Now, flip!'

I toss the ball over to my left-hand side and catch it in the paddle, where it just sits there. I am too scared/uncoordinated to try to vibe it with this hand so I just hold it there for a second or so, my arm quivering with limpness, before trying to flip it back. It doesn't take flight very easily and immediately falls on the grass again. I go to pick the ball up with my hand but Rebecca shows me how to scoop it up with the Paddle. 'Like this,' she says, bending over and hoovering it up with one of her Paddles. 'Go at it quite quickly, though. Too slow and you'll just push it along the grass and it won't go in.' I practise this for a few minutes and then she drifts on to someone else.

'This is like trying to wank with the wrong hand,' Dan says, attempting to vibe the ball in his right-hand Paddle.

'Oh, yuck,' I manage, before we are called back together as a group.

There is going to be a small tournament, it transpires, even though we are all fairly rubbish at this. A rumour has started that Mac and Georges are both going to play, which is mildly frightening, and some people are also moaning that we are going to go way over time again and miss some activity that was supposed to happen before dinner. It turns out that two half-size pitches have been marked out on the sports field, so four teams can play at once.

Our team is comprised of the people with whom we warmed up and learnt skills just now, with Rebecca as our captain. We are sitting on the grass in the watery, pink grapefruit sunshine, watching the first teams play, feeling slightly nervous that we are up next.

'Does anyone know what they're supposed to be doing in this game?' a girl in new-looking trainers asks.

'No,' says another girl. She has black hair, blue eyes and turquoise eye shadow. 'I'm more worried about this fucking meeting with Mac. Were any of you on the list?'

I glance at Dan. 'We were,' he says to her. No one else says anything.

The others start talking about positions in this game while the three of us huddle and concoct conspiracy theories as to why we may have been chosen. It turns out that the girl with black hair is called Esther, and that although we've never seen her before, her base is at Battersea.

'Although I am out on research quite a lot, though,' she says, blushing slightly. 'Or over at the computer centre.'

'What do you do at the computer centre?' Dan asks her.

'Oh, just stuff,' she says. 'So anyway, what's this game called? Do we know? Was I just not listening or did they forget to tell us?'

'Yeah, that would make sense,' Dan says. 'That would be very PopCo.'

'Maybe they haven't given it a name yet,' I say.

'It's very similar to lacrosse,' Esther says.

'I thought that too,' I say.

'Do you play?'

'No, but my grandmother did. You?'

'Yeah.' Esther fumbles in her bag and pulls out two hair-bands, one of which she uses to tie half her hair into a bunch on the left side of her head. 'I was captain of the senior team at school, if you can believe that.'

Dan frowns. 'So you can do all the fiddly bits, then?'

'No.' She laughs. 'Well, only with my left hand.'

'Oh – I'm left-handed too,' Dan says.

'I'd rather do it with two hands, like lacrosse,' Esther says, sticking the other hair-band in her mouth and miming two hands cradling a lacrosse stick. It looks like she's grinding a really slippery pepper mill. Now she gathers the rest of her hair into another bunch and ties that. 'Fuck it. I'm just going to die running up and down here. I hate games where you can't legitimately keep still. I almost died playing netball once.' We laugh. 'No – seriously. I was rushed to hospital and everything. I kind of like hospitals, though . . . the atmosphere or something. Oh shit, I'm rambling. Sorry.'

'How do you almost die playing netball?' Dan asks.

'Yeah, good question. I don't know. I was really stoned; maybe that was it. It was in sixth form,' she adds, as if that explains everything. She looks at me. 'I bet you played Goal Shooter in netball.'

'Huh?' I say. 'Why?'

'You seem clever, but quiet. Sort of cunning. And you're tall. I bet you have a good aim, too.'

'I bet you played Wing Attack, then,' I say back to her.

'Because . . . ?'

'Wing Attack is even more cunning, because you have to attack without shooting. You're forbidden from entering the semi-circle, too, which is interesting . . .'

'What is this?' Dan says. 'The Tao of fucking netball?'

'Did you, though?' Esther asks me. 'Did you play Goal Shooter?'

'Yeah, I did most of the time. And you?'

'Yep. Wing Attack.'

'OK, you're both freaking me out now,' Dan says.

'Don't worry, there are only seven positions in netball,' I say to him.

'Please, no probabilities,' he begs.

I could have explained it, though. There are seven positions in netball, one of which, after the way she described it, Esther wouldn't have played, i.e. Goal Shooter. So that leaves six possibilities. I eliminated Goal Keeper because she's not tall enough, and Centre because she doesn't seem like a 'Centre' sort of person. That leaves only four choices. I guessed that she would have played attack, which leaves only two possible positions. A fifty-fifty chance of being correct, then – the same chance you'd have, incidentally, of finding two people with the same birthday in a room of twenty-three people. Was it that example that originally put Dan off probability? I can't remember, although it is the sort of thing he would argue about. Maybe it was the Monty Hall Problem that he got annoyed about: most people do.

The Monty Hall Problem, popularised by maths columnist Marilyn vos Savant, is this. You are a contestant in a game show and you have reached the final stage, at which point you are shown three identical doors. Behind one of these doors is a car. Each of the other two doors has a goat behind it. The game-show host asks you to pick one door. If you pick the door with the car behind it, you will win the car. If you pick a goat, you win nothing. So, you randomly pick one door out of the three. The host then makes a big show of opening one of the doors you didn't pick, and reveals a goat. The audience cheer. The host, of course, knows which door has the car behind it. Now he asks you if you want to change your choice. There is a car behind one of the doors, and a goat behind the other. You know that. You don't know whether you picked the car or the goat. The question is, would it be in your favour to change your mind now and swap to the other door?

Most people, given this choice, will stick with the door they had chosen originally. Most people will say that there is a fifty-fifty chance of the car being behind either of the doors, so really it makes no difference whether you swap or stick to your choice. But this is wrong. You actually have a greater chance of winning the car if you swap doors. The maths for this is pretty simple. When you first made your choice, you had a 1/3 chance of being correct, or a 2/3 chance of being wrong. The chance that you would pick the wrong door was greater than the chance you would pick the right door. The host has now eliminated one of the goats. Considering that there was a 2/3 chance that you picked a goat in the first place, you should now swap. If you do so, you will double your chance of winning the car from 1/3 to 2/3. If you swap, the only circumstance under which you would not win the car is if you had picked the car with your first choice. But, as there was only a 1/3 chance that you would have done that, it makes sense to swap.

But most people don't believe this.

Chapter Six

If you lie on the grass and close your eyes, this could almost be a Sunday afternoon cricket match. There are small, tentative bird sounds and the smell of freshly cut grass. On top of this, the wind-blunted voices of competitors: 'Now!' 'Run!' 'No!' 'Mine!'. Only – you don't have a bloody whistle in cricket. It seems to be going off all the time, presumably because of the three-second rule. This feels, or at least sounds, like netball: unpleasantly so. I keep almost-dozing and then being woken up by the whistle. In the end I stop trying to doze and sit up instead, wishing I had my tobacco with me, or a flask of something interesting.

Esther seems to be loading up a small pipe with skunk weed.

'We're on in a minute,' Dan says.

'Does anyone know what positions we're playing?' I say.

'Forward,' Esther mumbles. 'All forward.'

She lights the pipe and puffs on it urgently, holding in the smoke.

Without saying anything she passes it to Dan, who looks at it suspiciously before passing it straight to me. Dan's not big on substances. He did it all when he was 'younger', or so he tells me, and says that now all that kind of thing just gives him panic attacks. I, on the other hand, spent much of my youth in hibernation, wrapped up in a nest of grandparents and homemade stew and crossword puzzles and the wireless. Since then I have found many reasons to embrace some recreational drugs, adopting the same attitude towards them as I do towards other exotic things that never appeared on my grandparents' wonky old radar (Thai curries, seafood, tofu, miso soup, garlic, croutons, unsalted butter, Parmesan cheese and so on): if it sounds/looks nice, and has less additives than children's orange squash, it's worth trying at least once. (Although my grandfather's motto, *Everything in moderation*, applies very much here.)

Esther's pipe is a small green enamel thing on a chain.

'It's for crack,' she explains. 'But I only use it for weed.'

'Where in God's name do you buy crack pipes?' Dan says.

'Camden Market,' says Esther.

I take the lighter from her and light the mass of oily green leaves and buds in the pipe. Then I inhale the heavy smoke, trying not to cough. This is nice, actually: the weed tastes sweet and flowery, perhaps like thick honey. I pass back the pipe, nod a sort of acknowledgement and lie back on the grass for a few seconds, watching the clouds. When I sit up again, the sports field is pleasantly hazy. 'Thanks,' I say to Esther. 'I needed that.' She finishes the pipe and then makes another one. I don't want any more; just a taste is usually enough for me.

Her eyes are like tiny ink dots when Rebecca comes over.

'We're on,' she says.

'Us three are playing forward,' Esther says to her, firmly.

'Yeah, sure, OK,' says Rebecca, looking slightly scared.

'Hide your bloody eyes,' I say to Esther, as we walk over to the pitch.

'Why?' she says.

I laugh. 'You look totally insane. Like you may have explosives strapped under your tracksuit or something.'

'Good,' she says seriously. 'Let's kill the opposition.'

'Jesus Christ,' Dan says. 'No. Oh no. Don't look.'

But we do look. And it seems that Mac is playing for the other team. And – what's this? – Georges is jogging over in a silver (seriously) tracksuit, presumably to join our team. He winks at me before taking his position in the centre of the pitch. Oh God, why does he have to wink at me? Dan's looking at me in a worried way. Am I swaying or something? I make a question-mark face at him and then he just grins. I look over at Esther and she really seems like some feral street child: small and wiry; jumping up and down making faces at the opposition. The three of us are indeed the forwards for our team, which I know is going to be disastrous. Dan is playing in some kind of striker/shooter position and Esther and I are on the wings: me on the left and her on the right (she thinks this will work out best with me being right-handed and her being left-handed). I would have felt more comfortable as the shooter/striker but it wouldn't make any sense having the two lefties on both wings, apparently. Am I actually on the left or the right, I suddenly wonder, helicoptering my brain above the field and imagining an aerial view. I suppose it depends which way you look at the pitch. This is too confusing. I can do on and off sides. I can do slips and mid-wicket and cover and point and silly mid-off and square leg. I just thought I'd left wings behind ages ago.

The way this game begins is as follows: Mac and Georges play-fence with their Paddles for a few minutes before being told by the umpire, a member of the Games Team, to take their places in the small centre circle. At this point Mac steals the ball and runs away with it, before Georges somehow gets it back and hides it in his tracksuit bottoms. They are laughing so much that the game is in danger of never starting. Eventually they stop messing around, and the umpire blows the whistle to begin the game. The umpire throws the ball high up into the air and Mac catches it in his Paddle. He starts running in our direction before someone points out to him that he should be going the other way. Despite all this activity, there doesn't seem to be much reason for us to move at all. But yet – Esther has broken rank and has sprinted down the field where she is now tackling Mac, beating his Paddle from behind until the ball falls out. She scoops it up in one seamless movement and starts running back up the field with it, doing a not completely terrible job of passing the ball between her Paddles. It actually looks pretty impressive. Even Mac stands there looking pleased-ish.

'Alice!' she calls.

Oh God. The ball is flying through the air towards me. It's a perfectly timed pass, you have to give her that. All I have to do is run forward a few paces and . . . Shit. I caught it. OK, so now I am running forward and it's been like two seconds but I can't face trying to pass the ball to my left Paddle, so I flip it, underarm, back to Esther instead. Something happens in her dark, stoned eyes and before I know it she is doing the same thing: running with it in her left Paddle for a second or two and then passing it back to me. In this way, we make it down the field towards Dan, with a couple of defenders from the other team chasing, but not catching us. They were never marking us: perhaps they didn't think the balance of the game would change so quickly. This is actually a very efficient way to do this.

'Dan,' I call, once we are near him.

He shakes his head but I toss the ball as near to his left Paddle as I can. Somehow, like the bit of a dream just before you wake up, he catches it and slams it into the goal. The three of us run around wildly for a few seconds as the ball is retrieved from the netting and thrown back up towards the circle. Esther soon stops celebrating and goes all killer-eyes again. I accidentally catch Mac's eye as we walk back up the field to resume our positions. He mimes clapping. Is it sarcastic or not?

Then he is back in the centre circle facing Georges. What's this called? Teeing off? Bullying off? This game needs a bit more terminology as it's hard to know what to call everything. Anyway, Georges fails to get the ball again but this time Mac passes it straight to their captain, a red-faced guy from the Games Team. He runs the length of the pitch, passing the ball expertly between his Paddles, and then passes it to their shooter who immediately drops it. One of our team then makes a good effort at sweeping in and picking up the ball but then keeps it in her Paddle for longer than three seconds, and the whistle blows. Mac and Georges are talking to one another near the circle but most of the other players on the field are now closing in on the Forward from the other team who is playing the free shot. It doesn't make any difference. The player who takes the free shot is the red-faced guy, and the ball pings into the back of the net before anyone's really sure where it has gone. The whistle blows and it all starts again.

This time, Georges does get the ball but forgets to let go of it, or vibe it, or pass it to his other Paddle so the whistle goes and the ball is given to Mac for a free shot. Mac tries to pass the ball between his Paddles, like the red-faced guy did, but it all goes a bit wrong and Rebecca easily gets the ball from him as he fumbles it. She passes it to Esther, who passes it to me and we try to repeat our performance from before. The other team are onto us, though, and one player is getting a bit close to me, marking me slightly too aggressively for my liking (I think I said before that I don't like being touched by strangers). It is the guy from lunch, slight and fast and smelling of mint. I try to back off but he follows me. The next time Esther passes the ball in my direction, he intercepts it and starts trying to run down the field with it. Esther quickly attaches herself to his team mate – the fawn-haired girl – and Rebecca is marking Mac. Even Georges is doing some kind of tribal dance in front of the red-faced guy. The guy with the ball is therefore left without any passing options. He tries to pass it to himself but I slither in and manage to get the ball as it crosses awkwardly between his two Paddles. Esther is now being heavily marked by the fawn-haired girl so I attempt a long-ish pass down to Dan. Amazingly, he catches it and slams it in the net again. 2–1.

I almost slept with Georges once, which is why I try not to catch his eye as we come off the field. We have won, the final score being 3–1. Esther really does look like she might die now. Someone has very thoughtfully brought out orange and lemon quarters so Dan and I sit sucking on those while Esther lies on the ground and coughs a lot.

No one ever knew about me and Georges. He'd come over to take the team out one night and we did genuinely hit it off. I liked him. He had an air of rebellion and boyishness about him, but also a deep, deep power. We talked, first about toys, and then, later, about other things: an experimental musician we both liked; a writer. The conversation was not at all like one of those consumerist questionnaires that new acquaintances sometimes give you (*What's your favourite film? Band? Club? Album? Designer label?*). Instead we talked about how this musician – who I thought no one else had ever even heard of – somehow made you want to get into bed on your own with citrus fruits, and rub them all over your body;

and how the writer used crazy, semi-conscious metaphors that made you want to eat the actual book. It was one of those intense nights in Soho; close and hot, about to rain at any moment. When we left the club (a strip club, of course) the thunder started and we ran giggling into a company car. How far did it go? His hands on my breasts, on my thighs, my skirt pulled up in the back of the car and his hands creeping to the edge of my knickers and then . . . I stopped him. You don't sleep with the boss, do you? You just can't. But I did want him; I really did, even if I still don't know why. How is it possible to feel that attracted to a man more than ten years older than you, who regularly takes women – that he employs – to strip clubs without thinking they might be embarrassed, who has so many shares in this company it's just obscene, who probably has a wife back in New York? He even had manicured nails. But being with him felt like . . . Not like being in a film, which wouldn't have appealed to me as much. No, it felt a bit like being in a comic or a graphic novel, comfortably enclosed within squares on a page, with rainy, inked-in evil all around but one safe place, a secret, dark place that only exists at night: a hideout, or a whole identity. Secrets only work at night, really, don't they? Maybe that's why I couldn't do it. Perhaps I knew I wouldn't be able to face the morning. To his credit, Georges has never held it against me or even mentioned it again. He probably forgot it ever happened. He winked at me before but he probably winks at everyone.

'Alice?' It's Dan.

'Huh?'

'We're back on in a minute.'

'Jesus Christ.'

Afterwards we are given forms to fill out, like we're kids in a focus group. *Overall feeling about the game? Playability? Feelings about terms used?* And so on. Then, finally: *Suggestions for a name for this game? (Winner will receive PopCo shares and a crate of champagne.)* We got to the final of the tournament but lost 2–1 to the team who had laughed all the way through the warm-up, and which included both Chi-Chi and Carmen.

After we are all showered and changed back into normal clothes it's time for Georges's speech in the main hall. One exchanged look confirms that Esther and I won't be going. We have lost track of

Dan but he probably wouldn't want to skive off something like this anyway. Me, I just can't sit and watch that man for an hour or more, imagining his hands on my legs and so on, and Esther is just too fucked to be able to keep still in a big hall. She has that look of a cat that needs to be let out to piss, probably in the neighbours' garden.

'I think I overdid it,' she says, as we slip off towards the forest behind the car park. 'Too much running around.'

I quite like Esther, I think. I wonder why I haven't seen her around that much at Battersea. If I had seen her, I don't think it would have been possible to ignore her. She's like phosphorous or something, fizzing all the time. Perhaps we would have become friends, if I'd seen her at Battersea. She's not like the other people I work with, anyway. Now that we're changed, she's wearing a short green tartan pleated skirt, a T-shirt with a skull on it, an old cardigan and red scruffy trainers. She definitely wouldn't hit the right frequency with the in-crowd at work. I am wearing a knee-length corduroy skirt with my plimsolls and a thick jumper. *Preppy look today Alice?* But no one who cares is here.

'What did you say you did at Battersea?' I ask Esther.

'Just hang around and stuff.'

'I mean, are you a designer or what?'

We are in the forest now. It's dark and a bit damp-smelling. I am glad of my jumper: today is one of those days where you have to be either running around or actually standing in the sun to be at all warm. We start following a path through the trees and there are noises: lonely birds, damp insects; a brief fluttering and a constant hum. There is a fairly wide path on which we are walking, with reddish, dry earth beneath our feet. As I walk I become aware that my footsteps feel soft, and I entertain the idea that this path is the top of something hollow. It can't be, though, really. Perhaps it's something to do with the density of this earth. It makes me think a bit of pottery, especially old earthenware containers.

'I bet people have died in here,' Esther says, wrinkling her nose. I don't think she's going to tell me what she does at Battersea. And I don't think I should push it. I don't quite understand how it can be a secret, though, but whatever.

'This used to be a boarding school,' I say. 'So I bet all sorts of scary stuff has happened in here.' I think about my conversation with Mac again, and the Kid Lab noises. 'I wonder where all the kids went,' I say, suddenly.

'What, from the boarding school?'

'No. Sorry – two trains of thought. No, there were kids before, at the Sports Field. I just wondered where they all went.'

'You seem to know a lot about this place,' Esther says.

'Oh, I got here a bit early.'

I'm not going to tell her about Mac, or my night-journey. So now we are both keeping secrets.

There's a gazebo deep in the forest: old, with chipped paint on the outside and rusty hinges. We fall on it excitedly and start trying to open the door. It takes a few tries but eventually it does open, with a broken-sounding creak, and we enter it like naughty schoolkids who've found a secret grotto. There are crispy old leaves inside, and a platform for sitting on. The window frames are greenish with mould and all you can see through the smeared glass is the idea of trees. We sit on the platform and Esther starts rolling a joint.

'Fuck it,' she says.

'What?'

'Nothing.' She sighs. 'Why aren't you at Georges's speech, then?'

'Because I'm here?' I try.

'No, come on. Really, why?'

'*Really* why?' I sigh. 'Oh – can I tell you some other time?'

Esther shrugs. I half expect her to start questioning me – I have accidentally given her a question-mark after all – but she doesn't. She just kicks around some of the leaves under our feet.

'I wonder how it's going,' she says. 'Georges and his *speech*.'

'Huh?'

'Why do they think they're better than us?' she asks, suddenly.

'Who?'

'Mac. Georges. The *Directors*. Why? They're something here, yeah. But in, say, my local supermarket they'd be nothing. If you didn't know who they were, you could bump them with your trolley and not have to sweat about it for two months and send all your friends e-mails saying you can't believe who you saw in the supermarket and what you did to them . . . They'd just be a nobody, and so would you, and none of it would matter.'

'Well, they sort of are nobodies. We all are, really.'

'Not all of us. Not . . .' She kicks around some more with her scuffed trainers. 'Pop stars. Film stars. If the lead singer from say . . .' She thinks for a while and then names the most successful rock band in the country. 'If he walked in here now you wouldn't treat him like nobody. You couldn't.'

I would actually be more interested in the lead guitarist but I don't want to confuse the issue. In fact, it's odd that she's mentioned this band, as I often have odd dreams about the lead guitarist: not wanting to fuck him or anything, more wanting to be him. I even want his hairstyle. But I won't say any of this. 'So . . . ?'

'Are you going to any festivals\this year?'

'No. I don't like crowds.'

'You don't like crowds?' She sounds pleased.

'No.'

'Being in them, or from above?'

'Huh?' I frown. 'From above?'

'Being in a mass . . . You can only really see how horrible a crowd is when you see it from above, like when they televise festivals. When you're in the crowd, you'd be, what? A dot, a nothing, a statistic. Whose statistic? Some PR firm? An advertising agency?' She puts on an advertising-style voice. '*Wouldn't it be amazing if we were all connected to the same mobile phone network? Wouldn't it be just great if we could all text message each other pictures of ourselves watching the same band in the same crowd, at the same time?* I don't want to be in the fucking crowd. I'm not an insect. I don't want to be the same as the person I am standing next to. I don't want to be in the fucking audience anyway . . . I want . . .' She trails off, looking vaguely through the window at the almost-forest outside.

I actually know what she means, though, which is rare. Usually when someone starts talking passionately I end up tuning out, even if I don't mean to. I find it hard to connect. But then I've never liked crowds myself, and I'm not that big on advertising, either. I also don't like doing things that thousands of other people do.

'I want . . .' she repeats.

'You want to be in the band,' I suggest.

She looks at me strangely. 'Yeah. Maybe, but . . .'

'What?'

'Being in the band means that those insects give you meaning. Being in a band means that you'd be the reason for the crowd, you'd be responsible for an emerging demographic: fans of your band. *What can we sell them? Flame-grilled burgers or burgers with gherkins? Oh? This demographic is mainly vegetarian? OK, well let's have a brainstorm about the packaging for that fruit drink – I'm thinking a self-referential, knowing, playful Utopia pastiche, kind of hippy in style – and maybe something for those flapjacks.* Meanwhile, back at Team PopCo: *Oh my God, the cool rock stars are all wearing sweatbands this year! We have to design the Star Girl and Ursula sweatbands this week. Get them on the website now and I'll get on to Manufacturing . . .*'

'Does the band know this, though?' I interrupt.

'Of course they do. I haven't even started on the record companies yet. Big rock bands try to be anti-establishment,' Esther says. 'Some of them, anyway. And then we just sell anti-establishment stuff to their fans. We watch what they wear on stage and sell it off our websites. Their record companies don't care as long as there's a market – they just send out briefs for artwork that say "anti-establishment" on them. These cunts don't care if you're anti-them, as long as you make them some money. So you're a star in this system? You're famous? Great. You're making someone else loads of money. Let's all go and have hamburgers to celebrate! It's like a bunch of vampires sucking one corpse dry. Who wants to be a vampire or a corpse? No one. But everyone is. Everyone apart from Georges and Mac and people like them and all the fucking shareholders in the world.'

I think I have just heard the reason why Esther has skipped Georges's speech.

'Look, I know you don't want to say what exactly you do,' I say. 'But you must work with Chi-Chi on K. I mean . . .' People burn out all the time working on K. I've seen it happen. They get a kind of intense pop culture overload and it's very unpleasant; worse than the measles. It almost happened to Dan, then he and Chi-Chi fell out and he was spared.

Esther laughs and it comes out almost like a squeal. 'Shit, I'm totally ranting, aren't I? Look, you'll have to remember to just tell me to shut up when I start going on . . . Fuck. I can't end up like a malfunctioning version of one of Chi-Chi's evil automatons.' She gets up and starts staggering around the small gazebo like a robot, with her arms held out in front of her. 'I – will – be – cool – I – will – use – my – evil – thoughts – in – a – positive – way – rebellion – is – cool . . .'

'So you *don't* work on K?'

'I'm not actually allowed to tell anyone what I do,' she says. 'And I wasn't even supposed to say that, so you'd better stop asking me.'

'OK,' I say, too quickly. 'I heard nothing.'

Esther looks slightly alarmed. 'It's not that big a deal,' she says. 'But thanks. I fucking hate Georges, though, don't you?'

Chapter Seven

'I heard nothing.'

It's my dad, not very long before he disappeared. We're living in the centre of the city, about a month before the lay-offs started at the button factory. My grandfather has come over, but instead of sitting down to drink milky tea and play chess with me, he's arguing with my father.

'Please, Bill,' he says.

'Look, I told you. I *heard nothing*. It's zipped, all right.'

He mimes pulling a zipper over his mouth. When I do this with my friends it's a sign of absolute secrecy and trust, and we do it with big solemn eyes. But my father's eyes are blank and cold, and his fingers look wrong making the movement. They're too big and grown-up. His middle finger is stained yellow from smoking, and his hands shake. They always shake; more so when my grandfather is here.

'Yes, but Bill?' my grandfather says.

'What?' my father replies. I can't remember – this memory is as brown and dusty as our old sofa – but I think my dad is coating two slices of bread with lard while the frying pan heats up. 'What?' he says again.

'If they find out that I know anything I . . .'

'What?'

'Just – *please* – don't say anything else, all right? Think of Alice, if nothing else.'

'I am thinking of Alice,' my father almost hisses. 'Why do you think this is important to me? These things . . . This . . .' He seems to search for a word he cannot find. '*It* . . . It always seems to be just a game with you. A bit of fun, an intellectual challenge, like doing the sodding crossword. And this time, when it could actually be useful to us, when it's not just messing around but something real . . . You chuck it all away. You just chuck it away like it's rubbish, and . . .'

'No. You're the one treating this like a game.'

'Oh, come on. You talk about danger this and danger that . . . It's just fantasy.'

'No.' My grandfather sighs. 'But anyway, it is up to me, not you.'

'You've got a house, yeah? You've got a sodding house and a sodding garden and you don't have to worry about making ends meet in the real world. Look at what we've got. And then ask yourself why this matters to me.'

'It's just a stupid dream, though. It probably doesn't exist. It's bad enough that we are arguing over it. We are certainly not risking our lives over something that might not exist. I absolutely forbid it.'

'You forbid it?' My father can't seem to believe that my grandfather is speaking to him this way.

'Yes. I forbid you to do anything else that will put us in danger.'

'If you just told me, then I could . . . *I'd* take the chance . . . It wouldn't involve you.'

'No. Now – please – that really is the end of this.'

And I'm sitting there with a book, pretending not to listen, playing with my necklace, wondering if the secret it contains relates to the secret my dad isn't allowed to tell. *Think of Alice.* And I want to know it, this secret, so badly that I get a stomach ache that lasts for a week. I have examined this necklace but I can't make sense of it at all. It is a silver locket with a strange combination of numbers and letters engraved inside it: $2.14488156Ex48$, and a little swirling pattern.

Think of Alice. Think of Beatrice.

Beatrice was my mother. By the time things started to go wrong between my grandfather (her father) and my father, she had been dead for almost two years. She was the one who gave me my name, my books, my identity. She stamped it on me when I was a baby, a mark I refused to wash off. One night, during that winter when we hardly had money for the meter and he argued with my grandfather constantly, my father took my necklace. He copied out the numbers and letters, and the little swirling pattern, and then put it back around my neck when he thought I was asleep. You have to wonder about parents sometimes. You're not asleep when they are pretending to be Father Christmas, and you're certainly not asleep when they are stealing secret objects from you so they can copy them. How is it that they don't realise this?

Esther and I are now staking out the entrance to the Great Hall.

'Watch them come out, then *merge*,' she commands.

'Yes, sir,' I say, messing around.

Apart from the fact that she hates Georges and I did, well, what I did, with him, Esther and I have more in common than I would have thought. She must play Go, of course, everyone does. I wonder what sort of player she is; how she forms ladders and how far ahead she thinks. I wonder if she knows the moment she's made a losing move, as I do, even if the end of the game is still hundreds of moves away. She looks crazy, with her head poking out of this bush, but there's no one here to see. They must all still be inside. Yes – I can hear some clapping and a whoop or two of joy (Georges makes people whoop with joy and I have to say that if he hadn't turned me on so much I'd probably hate him too just because of that).

'Soldier: move out,' Esther says a few minutes later, as the first people begin to emerge through the door. The idea is that we will join the crowd and act like we were in there all along.

I can't help smiling at the cod military terminology she uses. It's obviously not just me and Dan, then. Does everyone end up doing this? Where do we get it from? Probably a combination of videogames, grandparents, Sunday matinees and news reports. Is this our language now – even though most of us have only ever used it in simulations? I'm not sure. Perhaps everything is a simulation, now. Anyway, this war-terminology stuff reminds me of a focus group for a board game that I observed when I first joined the company. (Observing a focus group was one of those induction activities, along with 'Use the Computer Safely!' and 'Manufacturing Techniques!') The game was so obviously based on Hasbro's Risk that it never went anywhere but the people playing it in the focus group didn't seem to care.

'Peasant revolt!' said one of the women players, as she attacked a country occupied by more armies than she could ever defeat. I remember her being the kamikaze queen of the game, lucky with the dice.

'Die, peasant scum,' said the man she was attacking, in a deep, put-on war lord voice. 'I will be ruler of the world!' He kept missing the ashtray and flicking cigarette ash all over the table.

'Terrorists!' said another woman when the other three players attacked her, one after the other. 'I have the biggest continent, I will rule the world. Those who oppose me are terrorists . . .' She was thin and ghostly with a pale, academic face. There was another man, too, although I don't remember him very well.

They banged their fists on the table as their global meltdown escalated. *Terrorism must be stamped out! Suppress the masses!* Of course, they were friends and all very drunk, playing the game after a dinner we'd laid on for them (with lots and lots of very nice wine that I was able to sample afterwards). At the time I was intrigued by their ability to iron the complexities of war into this thin sheet of banter; their playful neutralisation of horror. Now I wonder, do we all do that without even thinking about it? And do we all call our enemies 'terrorists', now?

We may as well be scuttling across the path under fake bushes and dustbins, we're that obvious. 'Look more natural,' I hiss, but Esther is in a semi-crouch position, looking furtively to the left and the right and – I do believe – holding her hand in the shape of a gun, as if she were about to pull it from a holster low on her hip. The last people pass and walk off towards the barns.

'All clear,' Esther says to me.

'Esther!' I whisper, but she's already made it over to the door. Of course, we've now completely mistimed this and she runs straight into Georges.

'Hello, Esther,' he says. 'Games before dinner?'

Her hand's still in the shape of a gun; two fingers pointing down.

'Nice speech,' she says.

He looks almost small in his black suit, his hair shining, looking newly cut. I am waiting for him to look over and see me but he doesn't. 'Thanks,' he says in an odd way. Then he's gone.

'Cunt,' says Esther when I join her by the door.

There's no one in the room in the barn when I get back but the smell of perfume tells me that someone has been here recently. I actually wish someone was here so I could ask them the time. It must be almost seven, and I probably should be walking over to the cafeteria for dinner but I just don't know. I left Esther about fifteen minutes ago and then went looking for Dan. He wasn't in the Great Hall, or up the hill, or around by the Sports Hall. I am not familiar enough with this place to know where to look for him. He was probably in his room, although I don't know where that is.

My *Hide It!* pack is still safe under the cabinet. It feels lumpy in my fingers as I pull it off and dump the contents on the bed. Somewhere in here is a small watch face that doesn't have a strap any more. Ah, yes: five to seven. The watch is five minutes fast, so I've got roughly ten minutes to get to dinner. Do I need to change? No. I'm not changing more than twice in one day, even if I do have to see Mac. I try thinking about seeing Esther again, as a sort of experiment. I don't feel sick. That's a good sign. Sometimes when you make a new friend it can feel a bit muddled and stupid afterwards; worse, even, than bad sex.

New friendships can also be like a children's birthday party; a big table laden with cakes, sweets, crisps and multi-pack chocolate bars wrapped in foil. It's as if there's just too much sugar there, all at once, piled on the table. You stuff yourself but it's too much and you just can't think about sweets again for a long time. Or sometimes new friendships – the ones destined to be focus-grouped but never launched – can be like playing an out-of-tune string instrument; when you find yourself carefully fingering the chords for your favourite song but hearing the sound coming out all wrong. Your input is the same as always but the thing responds erroneously, playing you back an unfamiliar non-tune which gives you a headache. Your favourite (and only) amusing story is batted back with a 'what happened next, then?', or a discordant, polite nod. So far, this isn't like either of those situations. Well, it isn't for me, anyway. But perhaps it is one of them for her. Making friends never gets any easier. Even if everything's right: you're having fun at the party and the music sounds OK, you might find you are a discordant sugar-overload for the other person. This happens all the time.

I yawn and wonder how quickly I can get to bed after seeing Mac. Will there be more activities? I heard someone saying something about after-dinner games before. Maybe I will wake up: I do like games. Maybe we are going to be fired, though, and we'll just have to leave after seeing Mac. *Time to get up off this bed, Alice. Don't fall asleep.* I'll count to five. I'll count to five and then I'll get up. Then I realise that something about my belongings, laid out on the bed, is not right. Nothing's missing – on the contrary, there are too many things here. There's something from my *Hide It!* pack that I didn't put there: a folded-up piece of paper. I feel prickly as I consider that someone else has been here and found my things. Then I open the piece of paper. It's a PopCo *With Compliments* slip, with the following letters written on it.

XYCGKNCJYCJZSDSPPAGHDFTCRIVXU

To an unaccustomed eye, perhaps this would seem like a barcode or maybe even a really crazy reference code from some official letter. It is, of course, a code, but neither of those sorts. This is a cipher that someone wants me to break.

I'm almost the last in line at the cafeteria. Dan waited for me by the entrance, so it's me and him again, standing just in front of the two people from lunch – the dark-haired guy and the girl with the feather earrings – as if coming to the cafeteria is such a small subroutine in the videogame version of our lives that it has been programmed to happen in only one way.

'Ah, it's the vegetarians,' the woman says from behind her hatch. She glances beyond me and Dan to the couple behind us. 'Many vegetarians,' she says, laughing to herself. 'Here you go.' Four plates appear, each with a pile of red sludge.

This time we've got it wrong, not that we had any choice. The meat-eaters are getting Steak au Poivre.

'Oh well,' Dan says, shrugging. 'There's a load of cheese boards on the tables.'

'I think I might actually become a vegetarian anyway,' I say, randomly. Even though I love Steak au Poivre, my stomach can't handle anything very complicated at the moment. The red sludge may actually turn out to be something hot and comforting, perhaps with lentils, which would suit me right now.

The coded note crackles in my pocket as I walk across to the dining area. Esther's there, waving. 'Saved you both seats,' she says. This is the only free table left anyway. In fact, it's the only table in the room that isn't full and won't become full, which gives me a thrilling sense of unpopularity, of being an un-clique. Glancing across the room, I can see Carmen and Chi-Chi sitting with some of the K people. They're all wearing T-shirts featuring nonsensical English expressions from Japan. '*Cream Pain*'. '*Oops! Hair*'. '*Bullying Peter*'. '*Moon Hazard: Space*'. Stuff like that. As far as I understand it, there used to be a little website devoted to this stuff and then PopCo bought it. They haven't amalgamated it with K or anything; they're just keeping it going as it is, but with the extra marketing push only PopCo can give. The K crowd always seem to be laughing (when they're not going bonkers, of course). I never understand why. Surely life isn't that hilarious?

The guy and the girl from the queue sit down at the other end of the table and grab the bottle of red wine before we get the chance. This time, though, as soon as they've tipped more than half of it into their glasses, a new bottle appears from somewhere.

'Cool,' Dan says, grabbing it. 'Wine, ladies?'

'Yeah,' I say. 'Thanks.'

'No. Don't drink,' says Esther. She has a plate of red stuff too.

'Ah, the vegetarian trick backfired on you, too,' Dan says.

'What?' she says back, confused. She thinks for a second. 'Oh, I see. No, I am an actual vegetarian. Well, a vegan, actually.'

I'm watching Dan. He didn't send the note. It's not there in his face. Oh, fuck it, I'm not going to panic about this. I don't even know what it says yet. It won't take me long to work out, though. It looked quite Vigenère-ish to me. Ten-minute job, maybe a bit more, although there isn't much text to go on. With anything Vigenère-ish, it helps to have as much enciphered text as possible, as you can see patterns in it more easily. The Vigenère method of cryptography was thought to be unbreakable for over 300 years but once you know how to unravel it, it is surprisingly easy, and very fulfilling to break.

It wasn't a Caesar shift cipher, that's for sure: you can tell one of those just by looking at it. A Caesar shift cipher is one of the most simple of all substitution ciphers, and involves one of two identical alphabets being simply 'shifted' one way or the other. If 'a', for example, is enciphered as Z then that's a shift of minus-one. Every letter will be enciphered as the one just behind it in the alphabet. In this system, with a shift of minus-one, if you found a C in the ciphertext, you'd know it was actually a 'd' and so on. One of the most famous contemporary uses of a Caesar shift cipher is, according to SF geeks, in the naming of the fictional computer HAL from *2001, A Space Odyssey*. Taking into account a Caesar shift of minus-one, *HAL* of course reads *IBM*. I used to have a little Caesar-shift wheel, where you could set the letter A to any other letter in the alphabet and the rest would just follow from there. But I did so many of those things when I was a kid that I eventually didn't need the wheel, and somehow became familiar with twenty-six different ways of, for example, spelling the word 'and'. *BOE, CPF, DQG* and so on. It must have been when I was nine or ten, and my grandfather communicated with me almost exclusively in this way until I learnt more sophisticated methods of cryptanalysis, at which point he began using more complicated ciphers to leave me notes that said things like: 'Gone to the shop for milk', or 'Back later'.

Another thing about Caesar shift ciphers, like almost all ciphers, is that they have their own little conventions that you can look out for. The text in my pocket starts with the letters XYC, if I remember correctly. Caesar shift ciphertexts don't usually start with two consecutive letters for the simple reason that not many sets of two consecutive letters in the English alphabet actually form the beginnings of sensible, common words. You've got A and B, which are pretty rare together at the beginning of words; S and T, which are the main two to watch out for – but I've already done it in my head and it's not S and T (the third letter would be X if it were); H and I, N and O, O and P, and of course D and E, which, rather worryingly, do start the word *death*. But, if this were a Caesar shift cipher and the first two letters were D and E, then the third would be I. Unless someone's writing to me about a deity this isn't very likely. The thing to watch out for, though, is that the Caesar shift could merely be the first layer of code and that when you look at the beginning of a message you may actually be looking at the end. Sometimes people will write something out backwards and then apply a simple Caesar code to it. But this doesn't feel like that.

The five most common words that begin coded communications are: *Meet*, *The*, *Take*, *Enemy* and *Go*. The ten most common words in the English language are *the*, *of*, *to*, *and*, *is*, *a*, *an*, *it*, *you* and *that*. The most common letter found in standard English language texts is always E, followed by T and then A, O, N, R, I and S (in various orders depending on which frequency analysis you read). The most common digraph in English is 'th'. More than half of all English words end with E, T, D or S. The most common letters beginning words in English are T, O, A, W, B, C, D, S and F.

I wonder what the bloody message does say, and prickle slightly. I wish I had time to just crack it now. It could turn out to be nothing at all, which would make me feel so much better. Maybe it is from Dan but contains such a small message, or joke or whatever, that there's no reason for it to be hidden in his face. Perhaps he has even forgotten that he put it there. He's never written to me in code before, though. Why would he start now? *Don't worry, Alice. You just decided not to worry.* OK. I drink all my wine and accept Dan's top-up. That feels a bit better. 'Thanks,' I say.

Dan's putting a small red hardback notebook into his pocket.

'What's that?' I say, more paranoid than usual.

He flashes me a weird grin. 'This? This is the future, baby.'

'Seriously. What is it, *baby*?'

He shrugs and passes it to me. Inside, on the first few pages, there are dreamy landscapes rendered in the same sorts of candy colours you see on Japanese toy websites: lemon, candyfloss pink, baby blue, strawberry, mint green and white. There are watercolours, pen and ink drawings and dark pencil sketches: thick dusty lines. I flick further through the book. There are various drawings of some sort of dome structure and some more or less illegible notes. Then more pen and ink drawings, in simple black and white, of people; characters, from the look of it, each one drawn from various angles, and in different poses. There's a thin, scrawny girl carrying a rucksack, and an ethereal presence that seems female and in some way magical. Then – and I can see where this is going now – a kid with a big sword and a small pet lizard in the palm of his hand.

'You're doing the graphics for a videogame?' I say.

'Let's see,' Esther says, holding out a small hand.

'They're really rough,' Dan says. And although he clearly doesn't want to, he passes the book to her. He looks at me. 'Not exactly,' he says, answering my question. 'It's more . . . I don't know. Research or something.'

'What for?'

'Hmm.'

'*Hmm?*'

'These are ace,' says Esther. I don't think I've heard anyone use the word 'ace' for over a decade. 'Really lush.' Ditto.

'Anyway, what's *hmm?*' I say to Dan.

He seems to be eating the red stuff rather tentatively. I've eaten most of mine. It's OK, actually, and comforting, just as I had thought. There's a nice-looking wedge of Stilton on the cheese board and I try to spread some on a hunk of ciabatta bread. It's crumbly and ripe and bits keep falling off my plate and rolling under the table.

'Nice hand–eye coordination, Butler,' Dan says.

'Yes, well,' I say. 'My life-meter has taken a battering today, what with all the sport and then strange military manoeuvres with Esther.'

'Don't blame me,' she says, still looking through the book, but smiling.

'I see,' Dan says. '*Life-meter.* We're using videogame metaphors now.'

'Yes. We are. So . . . ?'

'All right. I'm designing a videogame. There.'

'But you said . . .'

'It's not for work. It's a side project.'

I drop my voice to a hiss. 'For another company?'

'No. It's . . . hard to explain.'

'What is? Come on, why is it hard to explain?'

'My game. It can't exist. It's purely design.' Dan exhales as though he's just told his parents he made the next-door-neighbour pregnant or something. 'So . . .'

'Aren't all games purely design?' Esther says. 'None of them exactly *exist*. It's just binary code, isn't it?'

Someone on the K table drops something and there's a sharp crashing sound and then cheers and clapping. I thought they were supposed to be cool? You'd think they'd have sent out a trend-spotter to find a more interesting way of responding to a crash in a pub/restaurant/cafeteria. Am I jealous of them? I don't think so. Us three, here in the corner of the room, with no bright lights or spot-lights or anything: we're a huddle. We could be huddling under an old canopy and the effect would be the same – unless it was a really bright or stupid canopy and then everyone would laugh at us.

Dan is smiling at Esther. 'Yes,' he says. 'Exactly! It doesn't exist.'

'So you've basically done some artwork for a non-existent game?' she says, but with a cute smile like the thin rucksack girl-sprite from Dan's notebook. I notice that Esther has not changed her clothes since this afternoon but has changed her make-up. Now she has two very small spots of pink glitter at the top of each of her cheekbones, and two tiny blue smudges in the outer corners of each of her eyes. Apart from that there is no other colour on her face. I realise I am staring at her and glance down towards the end of the table instead. The guy in black seems to be staring at us/me but quickly looks away. He resumes a deep-looking conversation with his companion.

'You go to a dome,' Dan's saying. 'And the game is inside it . . .'

'But . . .'

'Hang on.' He pulls a cheese board towards him. 'Are you sure you want to hear this? You might think it's a bit lame.'

'Go on,' I say. 'I like domes.'

'Yeah,' says Esther. 'I loved your drawings.'

'The idea of the game . . . It's like a thought experiment. Look,' he pulls out the notebook and starts flicking through it. 'Here's the dome. OK, so you go to the dome and walk in.' He flips to another page. 'Everything changes. The climate is different, the vegetation, the light source . . . It's like being on another planet, or maybe a simulation of another planet. Perhaps there are different moons and so on, which you can see at the top of the dome . . . I haven't done much work on the sky yet. There are just a couple of images so far. Anyway, you walk into the dome and you're wearing a special suit which is so skin-tight you could actually forget you're wearing it. It could even be painted on. Hmm. Don't know about that.' He coughs. 'Anyway, you wear clothes over this material, whatever it is. The clothes are probably classic role-playing stuff: leather armour, leather boots and so on, certainly to start off with. The dome is huge, by the way, like half the size of Dartmoor or something, and you start wandering around waiting for someone – or something – to attack you or help you. You don't have any money at this stage, or any good weapons, so the best thing to do is find a friendly encampment and offer to do work for them in return for shelter. Alternatively, you could lay traps for another player, or ambush them and take their money and weapons. So far, this is like any other RPG . . .'

'Except that you're literally walking through a real-time environment,' Esther says. Dan nods enthusiastically. She frowns. 'How do you fight and stuff?'

'Ah. Good question. Well, the suit you wear is programmed in a particular way. This is where it starts to get a bit complicated. Your suit contains information about your . . .' he flashes me a look, '*life-meter* and all your other stats. As you progress through the game your life-meter grows, so it can contain more life and you become stronger. Also, you have a certain amount of magical ability, and this, also, can grow if you put the effort in and learn a lot of spells and so on. When you battle, the suit registers any injury you receive . . .'

'Like paintballing,' Esther says.

'Sort of. Except that if you take a blow to the leg, for example, you really can't move your leg for a while – say until you have it healed, or rest, or take a potion. The suit stops you.'

'God, I love words like "potion",' I say. I haven't played any sort of videogame for a long time. I played a lot when my grandfather was in hospital and I'd come home and literally not be able to do anything else. I would spend every Wednesday night haphazardly setting the crossword he was supposed to be doing (they didn't know until much later that it was me, although the people who actually did the crossword regularly had spotted the switch immediately), sweaty and pissed-off, and then for the rest of the week I would just let myself melt into the games the way I assume people melt into drug hazes or peaceful sleep. I don't sleep peacefully myself; I never have. Anyway, it's funny that from what are essentially memories of a bad time, good images occasionally do resurface – like the idea of potions – reminding me, I suppose, of what was comforting about the games in the first place.

Dan's still describing his game. 'There is a central hub, a bit like a computer server or something, which bounces all the information backwards and forwards. All the people in the game are attached to it, like being on a network, and it updates your skills, life, magic energy, resources, relationships – *everything* – in real time. Maybe you find a healer to fix your leg. Well, the machine sends a signal to your body suit and your leg suddenly works and some healing energy is taken away from the person who has helped you. Oh – and you know how in games you have to sleep to replenish your energy? Well, in my game you really do have to go to sleep for that to work. The suit takes information from your brain and when you get into that deep state of relaxation – something to do with beta hertz, I think – it triggers a signal back to the central hub and your stats are reset to the maximum.'

'So it's basically a way to properly "live" a videogame?' I say.

'Yeah, I suppose so,' Dan says.

Esther visibly shivers. 'And the hub is like God.'

At the end of the table, the guy and the girl laugh. I glance over at them but they're not looking at us.

'I read this article in a science magazine,' Esther says. 'It really fucked with my mind. It was like . . . There actually are theories that our world is a videogame or simulation constructed by higher beings or – and I couldn't get my head around this bit – by the human race in the future. Like we evolve to the point of being able to create artificial intelligence, so we do, and then we learn how to create worlds, so we do . . . We learn how to become Gods. We create a little self-sufficient world and then move on. Then the beings in the world we've just created, well they start progressing towards their *own* artificial intelligence projects and the whole thing starts again. Kind of fucks with your ideas about God. It would be . . . It's basically your game. It would work in the same way.'

'It wouldn't, though,' Dan says, shaking his head. 'It can't. That's why the game is only a thought experiment. Where would the energy come from really? How would you generate all that power to run something like that? Who would build the hub? It's insane. It's why we don't have magic, for one thing. Look at the laws of thermodynamics if you want to know how the world works, not crazy theories about artificial intelligence. Start with entropy; that'll tell you all you need to know.'

Esther looks unconvinced.

'Maybe we are actually a thought experiment then,' I suggest. And although it's meant to be a joke, it comes out a bit wrong and sounds more sinister than I intended it to. It's too late to add a smile. No one says anything for a few seconds and it all feels a bit ghost story-ish

'Anyway, sorry, folks,' Dan says, eventually. 'Didn't mean to do the whole meaning of life thing over dinner. I didn't even mean to show anyone the notebook. Fuck it. It's just a game, anyway.'

'So why the weird non-existent project anyway?' I say to Dan. I decide not to mention that I was thinking about life being like a videogame less than an hour ago, when we were in the queue. Normally I would: it's an interesting coincidence. But I feel Esther may start talking about glitches in the Matrix and so on if I do, so I'll tell Dan later if I remember.

'Don't know, really.' He shrugs, thinking about my question. 'I was thinking about AIs anyway after that memo from Georges but the main thing is that I really wanted to design something that wasn't just pictures. When I did, and when I started thinking about it and playing with ideas, I realised that this thing without pictures, it can't exist. All we can ever really create is pictures. So I drew pictures of a world that can't exist.' He laughs. 'I was pretty fucking bored at work when you were away, essentially.'

What was the memo from Georges? I didn't get that. Hmm. Pictures. I think about houses and chimneys and railway lines and boats and step-ladders and chairs and I wonder how much of it really is just pictures, in the end. The Bumblebuzz Babies; Moo Moo and Li Li and all the other toys that we – people sitting in this room – design, they're just pictures in the same way that videogames are. The plastic shape does the same job as the binary code; it stimulates the imagination, desire, pleasure . . . Whatever. We know that: it's OK. They always say that nowadays we just sell an image, an idea, anyway. The product doesn't matter. Manufacturing doesn't matter. Manufacture something and then add meaning later with marketing and tie-ins and promotions. Or maybe this is just a PopCo thing; PopCo-overload. Maybe it's working here that makes you think that all the world is just a cardboard box waiting for a plastic insert and some pictures on the front. I mean, my products aren't like that: they actually have substance, they really do. And, apart from the products on the K website, I don't know anything we produce for kids older than ten that doesn't have intrinsic value. And, as someone comes around clearing the tables, I still can't stop thinking about pictures, pictures that don't exist, and in an instant my memories plughole away from me, whirling towards a phone call I wish I could make, and memories of a book with pictures that didn't make any sense at all, not even to my grandfather.

Chapter Eight

Mac leaves the cafeteria on his own, carrying a slim folder.

'Shit,' says Esther. 'The big showdown.'

'What?' Dan says.

'Mac. We've got to go and see him, haven't we?'

It's not that I'd forgotten about seeing Mac, or that I haven't been wondering about what sort of trouble we're in and whether or not we will in fact be sacked, not at all. It's just that today's been so full of other things to think about that I simply haven't found time to properly worry about this. As we get up from the table I push two fingers into my skirt pocket to check that the PopCo *With Compliments* slip is still there. It is. The pockets on this skirt are not at all deep and I really don't want to lose this piece of paper. I so desperately want to know what it says, perhaps even more then I want to know what Mac is going to tell us. Perhaps with a less complex code I could have just slipped into the toilet during dinner and cracked it. This, unfortunately, is likely to need more than just vague frequency analysis and crossword-solving skills.

As we leave the cafeteria we are issued with torches from a big box by the door. Outside, it is now dark, and I can hear an owl hooting somewhere on the hill behind the PopCo complex. There are small lights fixed on the outsides of several of the barns, but the hazy glow they cast is not bright enough to really see by. All they seem to do is tell you that a building is there, or vaguely illuminate a door. I wonder if we have left too early: no one else is out here on the path. Something like a bird flutters in the dark, a fast vibration of black wings in the still air and then it's gone. Esther squeals.

'Fucking shit, what was that?'

'A bat,' I say. We had bats in the village where I lived with my grandparents. 'It won't hurt you.'

'You can get rabies from bats,' Dan says.

'Only if you're really unlucky,' I say.

'Don't they fly in your hair and stuff?' Esther says.

'No. They have sonar. They can *hear* your hair from ten miles away.'

With only the light from our torches, we make our way over to the Great Hall. Somehow, we are not the first to arrive; there are maybe ten people sitting on the seats near the stage. Mac isn't here yet. We all sit in an almost reverential, or perhaps just nervous, silence as more people enter the hall, and this feels like a church gathering, or maybe a meeting of a secret society or cult. For the second time in twenty-four hours I feel like I should be wearing an odd hat. I'm watching the door, looking for people I recognise. There's a PA from our office, and this eccentric guy from the next floor up who is still wearing the tracksuit from earlier. Most of the people, however, I don't know. There's a Chinese-looking girl who is dressed like a Goth, walking with an attractive, tall guy. The girl with pink pigtails comes in, walking arm in arm with another cute Scandinavian boy-girl. Then there's a tough-looking black guy in a pale-blue T-shirt, his various ethereal tattoos giving the impression that he works as a bouncer or a hit-man at night while studying art or philosophy in the day. He's with a group containing a guy in a retro grey suit who looks like a social worker on heroin, a guy with long, strange-coloured hair and thick-rimmed glasses, and a tall blonde girl with lots of make-up. Then – and they seem to be the last two people to come in – the guy in black and the fawn-haired girl from our dinner table. The guy makes brief eye-contact with me, raises his thick eyebrows slightly and then sits down and starts cleaning his glasses. Moments later, Mac walks onto the stage, accompanied by Georges and a woman from the PopCo Board called Rachel Johnson. She's in Human Resources, or whatever they call it now. The three of them sit down on chairs in a slightly too-casual formation. I wonder how they knew when to make their entrance. It's so PopCo to have everything timed correctly. They probably pay someone to stand in the shadows and count us all in or something.

'Thanks for coming,' Mac says, his voice echoing in the large hall. 'And sorry for all the mystery. I've heard a few rumours about why you all think you've been asked to come here. The most common is a fear that you are going to be sacked . . .' We all laugh nervously. 'Then there are the variations: you are in trouble, you are being relocated, your brands are being discontinued, and so on. It's interesting how rumours start, and how many people are touched by them. You will be learning about networks and rumours in due course.'

What? My brain says. I don't understand. Networks and rumours? OK.

Mac continues. 'I suppose I should get quickly to the point, after all this accidental mystery.' He glances at Georges and Rachel. 'Well. Over the last six months or so one particular consumer has consistently been an issue for those of us on the PopCo Board. This is a consumer who is difficult to understand, difficult to pin down and incredibly complicated in terms of taste and desire. This consumer is one for whom we haven't catered very effectively at any time in our history. To be blunt: we are just not selling products to this person, however hard we try. Who is this mysterious creature? Yes. The teenage girl. No surprises there. As you know, the Star Girl and Ursula videogame sales have been disappointing, and we had to withdraw the planned *Ophelia Dust* titles at the last minute. Teenage girls don't want videogames. They don't want trading cards. They don't want gadgets to zap their friends with. Too bad, really, because they are the most independently wealthy of all the under-eighteen demographics. They are likely to earn their own money earlier than boys, and they are also more likely to actively enjoy spending it. Where a teenage boy will tend to pre-order the latest mainstream videogame release in the most convenient way possible, the girl will browse in shops, looking for items that will give her positive peer recognition, enhance her looks or popularity. This much we know. But – even knowing this – do we have any products out there that will appeal to this girl? We do not. And that's where you guys come in.' He nods at us and then gestures to Georges, who now starts speaking.

'We suck at selling to girls,' he says, shaking his head. 'The good news is that Mattel and Hasbro and all the others haven't cracked it either. Should we celebrate? No. We all suck. And that's not good enough for us. Name me a craze,' he says, pointing randomly at the PA from Battersea.

'Oh. Um, Pokémon,' she says.

Georges points at someone else. 'Another one.'

'Power Rangers.'

'Good. You.' He points at Dan.

'From the toy industry?' Dan says.

'No. Anything you like,' Georges says.

'OK, um, skateboarding, then.'

People mention some other crazes. Most of them are built around specific brands although some, like skateboarding, are sports or leisure pursuits that inspired many tag-along, parasitic brands. As soon as someone says Hello Kitty, Georges holds up his hands.

'Well,' he says. 'If I was a teenage girl, I would only just have woken up. Thank God *someone* out there is speaking to me. Sanrio seems to be the only global company that knows anything about creating a craze among teenage girls. But is Sanrio actually about toys, or is it just merch?' *Merch* is short for merchandise, and has become a fashionable term lately. I think it originally came from the live music circuit, where it refers to all the T-shirts and CDs and badges sold off little tables during gigs. 'Let's face it,' Georges continues. 'You can't really play with Hello Kitty products. The whole thing is actually more of a fashion phenomenon than a toy craze. You can wear the stuff, you can collect it, but it doesn't *do* anything. There is no game play; no actual fun. So although it looks like a toy craze, it isn't really. But I am not going to bore you with the scientific details now.' He grins, and I imagine him off duty, in the back of a company car . . . *Stop it, Alice.* 'You still don't know why you're here, but perhaps you are beginning to hazard a guess. And you'd be right. You are our new crack team, our advanced squadron unit, our . . . OK, I'm running out of metaphors . . .' He laughs.

'Our *élite*,' Mac says, standing up, smiling. 'Here's the deal. You have all been selected from the PopCo Europe ID teams particularly for this project. Your brief is to design a new product, with specific potential to become a craze, for teenage girls. In order to help you do this, we have designed a programme of seminars, talks and ideation classes – as well as some other treats. You will encounter new methods of ideation as well as learning about how teenage girls operate and the networks they create. You will have access to cutting-edge research that hasn't been published yet. You won't be going back to your offices for a while, however. The deal is this: you stay here on Dartmoor. We feed you, look after you, stimulate you – *pay you* a bit more than your usual salaries – and you simply think. You think and plan and discuss and collaborate and wander in the grounds until – *zing* – you have the killer idea. We want to make something here that is more viral than SARS. Nothing of any use has been coming out of big cities for some time now. The good ideas are all coming from more remote ideas labs, and we just can't ignore that any longer. Perhaps there is too much stimulating material in places like London and New York, or perhaps these are now just places for old things: old ideas, old buildings, old products. Culture there, it's not rotting – it's actually dead. There are no nutrients left in the soil. We took them all already. So, breathe the clean air here and enjoy the countryside. I'll be around for at least the first week. Georges will put in less regular appearances. There will be lots of other people to help you.'

Shit. I feel like I have won a competition but I don't quite understand what the prize is. Is it a holiday? A prison sentence? This is . . . Well, certainly unprecedented. Why have I been chosen? I don't understand. I work on the 9 to 12 market, which is very different from teenagers – and I'm not even cool. You definitely have to be cool to work on teenage products. What's going on?

'Does anyone want to leave?' Mac says, seriously. More nervous giggles; but no one moves. Rachel is opening a file of documents on her lap. They look like they might spill onto the floor but she gathers them together at the last moment and blushes slightly.

'Good,' Mac says. 'Now. Some of you might be wondering why there are no people here from the K brand. Well, what can I say? We are looking for a different approach, right now. K is great but at the end of the day it is also just *merch* – I think that's the term Georges used. That's fine, and they do it very well, but it's not what we want here. You have been selected very carefully for this and we think you all have exactly the right skills for this brief. I ask only a few things from you – apart from a killer product of course!

First of all, I would like to keep this project a secret for the time being. Please don't tell your colleagues about this or discuss it amongst yourselves while they are still here. We know how easily rumours can start, after all. Back at your offices, you will all have auto-responders activated on your PopCo e-mail accounts, which will tell people you have gone away for a while. There won't be access to e-mail here, I'm afraid.'

Esther swears under her breath. '*Shit*.'

'Mac,' someone says, vaguely putting their hand up. 'What about meetings and deadlines and so on? I've got a full diary next week.'

I've been wondering the same thing. What about my KidScout pack (which I was actually thinking of renaming *KidTracker*)? I'm supposed to present roughs in just over a week.

'Your various team leaders will have been briefed, and everything will be postponed while you complete the assignment here. We're putting all your deadlines back and rescheduling everything for this. It's an important project. As far as everyone else in the company is concerned, you are all in the New York office, working with a team there on something relatively boring.' He clears his throat and looks at us all again. 'Yes, I'll admit that this is odd. Why haven't we planned this to take place in, say, two weeks, once you've all had a chance to at least tidy your desks, make it look like you've gone away to do something normal, organise the cat-sitter and so on? Well . . .' He glances at me and gives me a half-smile. '*Routine kills creative thought*. We all know that. So, we give you two weeks to prepare for this assignment. In the meantime, you anticipate it, think about it, develop ideas about how it's going to be and then you come here and . . . *Nothing*. All your energy would have been spent already. We wanted to give you a jolt; make you think differently. OK – it might not work. Hell, it might be a complete mess. But we decided that this would be the most creative way. And it's also the quickest, of course, time being a factor here as well. Your old routines are suspended as of now. Of course, there's nothing stopping you going back to London – or wherever – if you really need to. While you are here you are free to come and go as you like. But there will be a small team who will be available to organise any loose ends back at home if you would like them to, leaving you completely free to explore this problem in the most original ways you can. Seminars and activities start on Monday morning, so you should probably make use of the team if you need anything organised before then.'

Someone else is waving their hand about.

Mac smiles. 'Yes?'

'This might be a stupid question but why can't we tell other people in the company what we're doing? Why do we have to pretend to be in New York? Not that I mind . . . it's just . . .'

'No, no,' Mac says. 'Fair question. It's all about morale. Firstly, there are people out there who would feel, frankly, disappointed not to have been chosen for this. We have selected you all in a very particular way, and not everyone would actually understand how or why we did it that way. Someone who has worked on teenage girls' products for the whole time they have been at PopCo would feel, shall we say, aggrieved that he or she hasn't been chosen for this. Perhaps he or she would feel it was a mistake, and would send me e-mails about it. Then again, there might be other people who would feel that this is a competition. They may want to enter, again by e-mailing me with their ideas. I could do without all those e-mails! Some other people may simply feel like there's a party going on, to which they weren't invited. And I don't want to upset those people. It's not a new business theory but it works. *Don't make people feel that they're not special.*'

Rachel gets up, nods to Mac and starts handing out documents. 'OK,' Mac says. 'Now, the packs that Rachel is handing around contain paperwork that needs to be completed now. There are NDAs, new contracts, details of new salaries, terms and conditions and so on. Please sign them and hand them back to her. Anyone who doesn't want to be involved in this project should probably say so now . . . ?' No one says anything. 'Great.' He sits down on the chair and starts saying something to Georges.

Non Disclosure Agreements? Why? This is becoming a Fort Knox of ideas. I thought all our ideas, thoughts, everything were PopCo's property anyway. We all have NDA-type clauses written in to our normal contracts. Perhaps they feel they need extra reinforcements for their wall around any ideas we might generate here. I take my pack and start looking through it, still wondering why I'm here. I am not the kind of person you choose for special projects, I'm really not. I do my best to just get on with my life without being noticed, especially after all the odd things that happened when I was a kid.

Now it looks like I'm part of a secret again and I'm not sure how I feel about it.

After everything is signed and handed back, Mac starts wrapping things up.

'Please be as creative as you can, people,' he says. 'The old ideas can go out of the window because they just don't work. We want a fresh approach to this problem. There will be no research, as such, just pure design and ideation. And, remember – if you think an idea is just too crazy, you may well be on the right track. Thanks.' He looks down and then up again. 'You're free to go. Don't forget the PopCo disco over at the Sports Hall. Oh – Esther, could you stay back, please – and you, Hiro.' Esther doesn't give us the funny look we expect but instead just says something like *I'll see you later*, as we get up to leave. Both Mac and Georges seem to know Esther by her first name. I can't help wondering exactly what her job is.

As soon as Dan and I are outside we are both like balloons popping.

'What the fuck?' Dan says.

'We've been chosen,' I say, kind of ironically but with a sprinkle of genuine excitement. And then we look at each other in a thrilling-secret way, our eyes reminding us that we just signed forms to promise we wouldn't talk about this in public.

'Disco?' says Dan.

'I suppose so.' I feel dazed. 'But I do want to go to bed early-ish.'

'So what exactly *was* all that about, then?' he asks me in a low voice, as we walk down the path with our torches. 'Mac's *Weird Idea*.' He is referring to a book from work called *Weird Ideas that Work: 11½ Ways to Promote, Manage and Sustain Innovation*. The 'Weird Ideas' in the book include things like 'Hire Slow Learners (of the Organizational Code)', 'Find Some Happy People and Get Them to Fight' and 'Think of Some Ridiculous or Impractical Things to Do, Then Plan to Do Them'. Innovation seems to mean that corporations are pretty much up for anything now, however crazy. Innovation is everybody's best friend this century: share-holders love it, young bum-fluff managers adore it and even normal staff members quite like dressing up as rabbits for the day, pretending to be blind or being hired despite having no experience at all. The

vacuum cleaner company Dyson apparently only hires new graduates. The Sony Playstation was, legend has it, invented by people
entirely new to the world of videogames. I have a suspicion that
my own employment at PopCo came about as a result of a Weird
Idea. *Hire someone who has a strange skill but no experience in
the toy industry at all.*

I shrug. 'Don't ask me. I am genuinely baffled.'

'Does this mean that we're special, now?' Dan asks.

'I'm not sure. Perhaps.'

Chapter Nine

After spending the minimum time possible at the disco (half an
hour), I make some excuses and retire to the dorm, hoping that no
one else will return for a while. I tell myself that I am not scared,
walking the gravel track up behind the main building. I tell myself
that the night is beautiful, with its bats and silence and tiny waxing
moon, and that the snuffling in the hedge outside the barn is probably a badger.

The old wooden stairs creak as I walk up them. Again, I make
sure that I am not scared by concentrating on their music. It's all
minor chords here: no distinct notes at all. Perhaps minor chords
played on wooden stairs aren't the most soothing thing in the world
because I jump like I've been injected with adrenaline when I open
the door to the dorm and find a scruffy young guy standing by one
of the other beds, holding something white in his hand.

'Shit!' I say, automatically.

He jumps too. 'Fuck!'

'Sorry,' I say. 'You gave me a shock.'

'Yeah, you gave me one too,' he says back.

'What are you? . . . I mean . . .' I say. I want to directly ask him
what he's doing here but the words don't seem to come out. Surely
he isn't going to be sleeping here? I'd assumed that the dorms were
single sex.

'Yeah, sorry,' he says. 'I came to deliver this, but I don't know
which bed is whose.' The thing in his now shaking hands is an

envelope which he holds up to show me. It has my name on it handwritten in blue ink.

'That's me,' I say, pointing at the name on the front.

'Oh – great,' he says, and, after hurriedly giving me the envelope, he leaves.

'Thanks,' I say. But he has gone.

I immediately open the envelope. The message is typed. *Dear Alice Butler, Please move to Study/Bedroom number 23 in the Main Building as soon as possible. There has been a mistake in the allocation of rooms. Sorry for any inconvenience. If you need any assistance with any matters at all, including those of a personal nature, please get in touch with Helen Forrest on extension 934.* The letter isn't signed by anyone. I don't understand the extension number. There are no phones here that I've seen so far, let alone ones on a PopCo network. Maybe there's one in my new room, wherever that actually is.

My tobacco pouch is on the bed, where I left it. I reach for it and roll myself a small cigarette which I smoke out of the window, watching a large moth bump against the outside wall-light. Well, it looks like I'm on the move again. Once I have finished my cigarette, and my brain feels more low-frequency and normal, I start re-packing my things.

In the dark, the Main Building feels like a place you'd get to after trekking through a bandit-ridden forest on an RPG. Approaching it from behind (rather than through the main entrance, or the Great Hall entrance), it seems like a drawing from Dan's notebook, hazy with orange wall-lights and moth-shadows. There should definitely be flute and fiddle music here, I think, and the drunken clink of goblets held by goblins and elves. It is, however, silent. After walking through a stone arch, I can see a large rectangle of well-tended grass directly in front of me, to the left and the right of which are two residential wings, each containing what seem to be several little rooms. A few are illuminated, although I can see no people. Just as I am prepared to get completely lost, I see a small sign which says Study/Bedrooms 26–51, and has an arrow pointing around to my left. I turn my head to the right and find a similar sign pointing to rooms 1–25. This is where I need to be.

I walk on stone through a covered passage, with the grass on my left, as I count off the rooms on my right. Would people once have had sword-fights on this grass? It's easy to imagine, although I can't visualise corpses or blood, just people facing one another at dawn. Anyway, up one flight of stone stairs, through a small corridor with soft carpet and art on the walls, and then back on myself down another slim corridor and I am there. *Room 23*. There is an envelope on the door with my name on it. It contains the key, with which I unlock the door and go inside. Oh my God. This is more like it. The room has a polished, slightly uneven oak floor, a sloping, oak-beamed ceiling, and is furnished almost entirely with antiques: an old writing bureau with a little key (which immediately makes me think, *Great, I can lock away my things,* until I remember how easy it is to pick those things), a four-poster double bed, a little oak bookcase with a glass door on the front, and a comfortable-looking armchair. The room also has an en-suite bathroom containing a heavy-looking white enamel bathtub and a small sink and toilet. I feel a bit grubby so I immediately wash my hands and then dry them on a small white cotton towel. There is a little wooden mirrored cabinet above the sink, which I open. I expect it to be empty but find it instead full of expensive cosmetic and bath products, many in mauve glass bottles: seaweed and arnica bath soak; rosemary shampoo; seaweed shampoo, orange flower water, and quite a few other things. There are also delicate bars of French soap, two natural sponges, a new wooden hairbrush, nail-clippers, and a huge packet of condoms. For some reason this last find makes me blush and I leave the bathroom.

Back in the bedroom, I notice that the bookshelves actually contain books. There are many ideation and marketing titles (of course), a large dictionary, a bible and rather a lot of fiction that looks like it would appeal to teenage girls. So I am here because of Mac's Weird Idea. But why wasn't I here in this room in the first place? And why am I even part of Mac's crazy project? I still have no idea at all. But seeing this room answers Dan's question, anyway. Yes: for whatever reason, being singled out for this means we are special.

What I want to do right now is take a long bath, and then roll around luxuriating on the four-poster bed. What I actually do is take the dictionary out of the bookcase and walk over to the writing bureau. I unlock it with the little brass-coloured key and find – of course – that it is packed with expensive stationary. After packing away the complimentary stuff in one of the drawers, I take my notebook and pen out of my bag, place them on the desk, and sit down. The notebook is the type I always use – narrow-ruled in faded-looking pale blue – and the pen is my favourite of the many small fountain pens I own. I can't really write with anything else. There is a little lamp which I switch on. I quickly write half of a lame-ish To Do list (*1. Organise cat-sitter*), ready to stick over the top of what I am doing if anyone comes along. Then I take out the PopCo *With Compliments* slip from my pocket and lay it on the desk.

XYCGKNCJYCJZSDSPPAGHDFTCRIVXU

Time to make sense of this. Ignoring persistent thoughts like *Who sent me this?* And also the fact that I want to sleep so badly my eyes are watering, I start trying to pick out patterns. It takes me about ten minutes to pretty much confirm my original, intuitive theory that this isn't a simple mono-alphabetic substitution. So I am going to go down the Vigenère route and see what happens.

Patterns. You'd see more patterns in a longer piece of text, that's for sure. Still, I can see a couple of interesting factors here, and I start making some initial notes in my notebook.

Mono-alphabetic ciphers have been in existence, in various forms, for hundreds, if not thousands, of years. In these ciphers, each letter from the plaintext alphabet is replaced with another letter from a corresponding cipher alphabet. 'A' might be written as P, and 'b' might be written as S, for example. Each letter in the alphabet will have a corresponding letter which will always stand for it in the cipher. It is called 'mono'-alphabetic because there is only one cipher alphabet. I remember having this explained to me when I was a child and suggesting that it would be 'easy-peasy' to crack any of these sorts of ciphers. The Caesar shift, yes: that is easy-peasy. All you do is work out how many places the alphabet has been 'shifted' and you've done it. But if the cipher alphabet is sufficiently randomised then it does get a bit trickier. In fact, if you think of the cipher alphabet as a key, then the Caesar shift cipher has twenty-five possible keys (as there are basically only twenty-five ways of shifting the alphabet without actually rearranging it). However, if the cipher alphabet (a basic English twenty-six-letter alphabet) can be rearranged in any way, there would, as my grandfather once pointed out to me, be 403,291,461,126,605,635,584,000,000 potential keys to find, this figure being the factorial value of twenty-six (rather cutely written down by mathematicians as 26! and proving that they also have a thing for exclamation marks, just like the toy industry).

This was the first time I discovered factorials. If you ever need to know, factorials are calculated the following way: $3! = 3 \times 2 \times 1$ and $5! = 5 \times 4 \times 3 \times 2 \times 1$ and $13! = 13 \times 12 \times 11 \times 10 \times 9 \times 8 \times 7 \times 6 \times 5 \times 4 \times 3 \times 2 \times 1$, and so on. It's quite neat, actually. 100!, where all the numbers from 1 to 100 are multiplied together, gives a result bigger than the amount of atoms in the known universe. Anyway, as my grandfather explained, no one could check all those keys. It's true: even a contemporary computer would take – yes – longer than the history of the known universe to perform a calculation like that (perhaps while figuring out all the possible configurations of Go pieces.)

Even after my grandfather explained factorials to me, I was ready to take up the challenge. 'Go on, then,' I said. 'Create a random thingy alphabet, write a cipher in it and bet you I'll crack it.' He did, and I did, because the way you solve mono-alphabetic ciphers is never by trying to guess the key.

Say someone sends you a note written with a mono-alphabetic substitution cipher, and it says something like: QEPN BVQE C ASFN AXNYN GCZ C TSYU GXQ AXQBTXA ZXN PQBUH YNCH PSVXNYZ BEASU AXN HCK ZXN YNCUUK XCH AQ. You start in the following way. Is there a letter on its own? Yes. There's a C, twice. Well, there are only two single-letter words in common usage in English: 'I' and 'a'. So it's going to be one of those. Then you look for the most common letters. In this cipher they are: N, which appears 9 times; X, which also appears 9 times; C, which appears 7 times; A, which appears 7 times; Q, which appears 5 times; Y, which appears 5 times; and U, which also appears 5 times, including its appearance in a repeated-letter digraph in the third from last word. A digraph is a combination of two letters. A trigraph is a combination of three letters. Digraphs can be useful when you are cracking mono-alphabetic ciphers, and only certain letters are commonly found in repeating pairs, the most common being 'ss', 'ee', 'tt', 'ff', 'll', 'mm' and 'oo'.

Think about what you already know about the English language. You know that E and T are the most common letters in all 'normal' texts. The most common letters in the ciphertext are N and X. Is one of these going to be E or T? The most common word in English is 'the'. Are there any three-letter words in the text that look like they might be 'the'? In order to crack a mono-alphabetic cipher without guessing the key, you have to be a word-detective. You have to look for the patterns. You have to start trying to put in letters you think you know and see if anything emerges. If you do this, you will be able to unscramble the message.

Alternatively, you could always use frequency analysis, which is particularly good when you have a ciphertext that is not conveniently broken into words. Frequency analysis involves noting down the frequencies of *all* letters in the ciphertext so you have a list of the first most popular letter, the second and so on right down to the least popular letter. Then you get a frequency table (there are lots out there and people even post them on the Internet now) of the frequencies of letters in common English usage. You take the most popular letter from your ciphertext and replace it with the most popular letter in English (according to your frequency table). Then you take the second most popular letter and replace that with the second most popular letter and so on. It is surprising how often this works with only very minor adjustments. This method will certainly usually give you enough to see what the message is yourself. If the pattern-recognition method is like a Sherlock Holmes style of detection, then this frequency method is more like a twenty-first-century forensic skill.

This is the key you will get if you decipher the message:

A	B	C	D	E	F	G	H	I	J	K	L	M	N	O	P	Q	R	S	T	U	V	W	X	Y	Z
c	i	p	h	n	r	t	x	s	o	m	u	f	e	q	v	w	z	y	a	b	d	g	j	k	l

The first incarnation of my KidCracker pack came with an Alberti code-wheel, a Jefferson's Wheel, a battery-operated mini-Enigma machine and a laminated Vigenère square. Alberti was a fifteenth-century architect, and is known as the true grandfather of contemporary Western cryptology. His code-wheel formed the basis for all forms of poly-alphabetic ciphers that came later, including Enigma. I worked with two young engineers from the Mechanical Design team at PopCo

London to recreate these devices, which we did after researching many primary texts and objects at the British Library and various museums. As a result of this, my Age 9 to 12 code-breaking kit ended up containing miniature working models of some of the greatest cryptological devices ever invented. Originals of this kit now sell to collectors for almost a hundred times their initial selling price because of this, and have the same kind of appeal to adult cryptology enthusiasts as the famous Fischer Price Super 8 camera has for grown-up cinematographers. It probably also helps that my kit ended up being banned in various countries and had to be re-launched without the many interesting extras that were causing all the fuss. I thought I would be in all sorts of trouble for creating a toy that ended up being banned – and maybe I would have been if it hadn't worked to our advantage. As it was, a couple of newspapers ran short pieces on it and the publicity just about undid the damage the ban had caused. I was, however, given a talking-to by Carmen the first, during which I was given tips on legal research and much anecdotal evidence of product launches gone wrong as a result of fuckwitted creatives (the launch of the *Nova* car in Spain being the most obvious example; *Nova* meaning, of course, 'it doesn't go' in Spanish).

By the time the kit had been 'adjusted', all it contained was the Vigenère square. The Americans had made the most fuss over the original kit, saying that it contravened some law to do with preventing sophisticated encryption devices entering or leaving the country. (In fact, this is also why you can't get full versions of some Internet browsers outside of the States, because it is illegal to export the encryption software that goes with them.) I thought it was amusing that my Vigenère square was still allowed through, however. Would a 9- to 12-year-old ever be able to actually use it to start a revolution or overthrow a government? Possibly. But the chapter on Vigenère is probably the one that all the kids actually skipped, because it really is far too complicated.

Vigenère ciphers, unlike mono-alphabetic ciphers, do usually require you to crack the key, although the 'key' for a Vigenère cipher is usually a simple word, rather than a whole, randomised alphabet. The cipher itself, however, is much more complicated and impossible to break down in the way you would approach a mono-alphabetic cipher.

Mono-alphabetic ciphers involve only one cipher alphabet. They are easy to crack because, once you know what 'e' and 't' have been replaced with, the rest is just like completing an easy game of hangman. Poly-alphabetic ciphers, however, use several alphabets, at the same time. It's hard to describe what a breakthrough it was when Alberti suggested as a possibility the use of several alphabets in one encipherment. Mono-alphabetic ciphers are *always* crackable because of frequency analysis (even if the Sherlock Holmes method fails). But what if you could scramble the frequencies of letters by making different ciphertext letters stand for different plaintext letters throughout the message? This is what Alberti wondered. And he came up with a method that is, well, it's genius really. You draw up a square made of twenty-six different versions of the alphabet, each one shifting by one letter each time (see table). Then you choose a short keyword, say RAIN. You write the keyword over and over again on the top of the plaintext to be enciphered like this:

R A I N R
h e l l o

R A I N R A I N R A I N R A I N R A I
t h e h a r d e s t o f t h e m a l l

You then use the letter of the keyword to determine which 'line' of the Vigenère square you will use to encipher the letter below it. The 'h' in 'hello' enciphered using line R will be Y. 'E' enciphered using line A will be E (anything on line A will always be enciphered as itself, which is why many keywords don't have an A in them). 'L' enciphered on line I will be T. The next 'l', however, will be enciphered on line N, making it Y. So the first word, 'hello', will now read: YETYF, which does not look like a mono-alphabetic version of 'hello' at all. There's no clue to the 'll' digraph any more, and 'Y' stands for two different letters.

The longer message from above is encrypted like this:
KHMURRLRJTWSKHMZRLT
You are never going to crack this with frequency analysis or guesswork. To crack this, you need to know that RAIN was used as the key. This is the only way into a Vigenère cipher. Sometimes

Vigenère square

	A	B	C	D	E	F	G	H	I	J	K	L	M	N	O	P	Q	R	S	T	U	V	W	X	Y	Z
A	A	B	C	D	E	F	G	H	I	J	K	L	M	N	O	P	Q	R	S	T	U	V	W	X	Y	Z
B	B	C	D	E	F	G	H	I	J	K	L	M	N	O	P	Q	R	S	T	U	V	W	X	Y	Z	A
C	C	D	E	F	G	H	I	J	K	L	M	N	O	P	Q	R	S	T	U	V	W	X	Y	Z	A	B
D	D	E	F	G	H	I	J	K	L	M	N	O	P	Q	R	S	T	U	V	W	X	Y	Z	A	B	C
E	E	F	G	H	I	J	K	L	M	N	O	P	Q	R	S	T	U	V	W	X	Y	Z	A	B	C	D
F	F	G	H	I	J	K	L	M	N	O	P	Q	R	S	T	U	V	W	X	Y	Z	A	B	C	D	E
G	G	H	I	J	K	L	M	N	O	P	Q	R	S	T	U	V	W	X	Y	Z	A	B	C	D	E	F
H	H	I	J	K	L	M	N	O	P	Q	R	S	T	U	V	W	X	Y	Z	A	B	C	D	E	F	G
I	I	J	K	L	M	N	O	P	Q	R	S	T	U	V	W	X	Y	Z	A	B	C	D	E	F	G	H
J	J	K	L	M	N	O	P	Q	R	S	T	U	V	W	X	Y	Z	A	B	C	D	E	F	G	H	I
K	K	L	M	N	O	P	Q	R	S	T	U	V	W	X	Y	Z	A	B	C	D	E	F	G	H	I	J
L	L	M	N	O	P	Q	R	S	T	U	V	W	X	Y	Z	A	B	C	D	E	F	G	H	I	J	K
M	M	N	O	P	Q	R	S	T	U	V	W	X	Y	Z	A	B	C	D	E	F	G	H	I	J	K	L
N	N	O	P	Q	R	S	T	U	V	W	X	Y	Z	A	B	C	D	E	F	G	H	I	J	K	L	M
O	O	P	Q	R	S	T	U	V	W	X	Y	Z	A	B	C	D	E	F	G	H	I	J	K	L	M	N
P	P	Q	R	S	T	U	V	W	X	Y	Z	A	B	C	D	E	F	G	H	I	J	K	L	M	N	O
Q	Q	R	S	T	U	V	W	X	Y	Z	A	B	C	D	E	F	G	H	I	J	K	L	M	N	O	P
R	R	S	T	U	V	W	X	Y	Z	A	B	C	D	E	F	G	H	I	J	K	L	M	N	O	P	Q
S	S	T	U	V	W	X	Y	Z	A	B	C	D	E	F	G	H	I	J	K	L	M	N	O	P	Q	R
T	T	U	V	W	X	Y	Z	A	B	C	D	E	F	G	H	I	J	K	L	M	N	O	P	Q	R	S
U	U	V	W	X	Y	Z	A	B	C	D	E	F	G	H	I	J	K	L	M	N	O	P	Q	R	S	T
V	V	W	X	Y	Z	A	B	C	D	E	F	G	H	I	J	K	L	M	N	O	P	Q	R	S	T	U
W	W	X	Y	Z	A	B	C	D	E	F	G	H	I	J	K	L	M	N	O	P	Q	R	S	T	U	V
X	X	Y	Z	A	B	C	D	E	F	G	H	I	J	K	L	M	N	O	P	Q	R	S	T	U	V	W
Y	Y	Z	A	B	C	D	E	F	G	H	I	J	K	L	M	N	O	P	Q	R	S	T	U	V	W	X
Z	Z	A	B	C	D	E	F	G	H	I	J	K	L	M	N	O	P	Q	R	S	T	U	V	W	X	Y

keys can be arrived at by simple guesswork, of course. After the World Trade Centre attacks, one firm lost almost all its staff. The remaining few decided to try to keep the company going but were hindered by the fact that all the company passwords had been lost because everyone who knew them was now dead. The remaining employees then sat down and went through every aspect of their dead colleagues' lives, noting down locations of holidays, pet names and so on until they actually cracked all the passwords. I was told this story by someone at work who'd been particularly touched by the company spirit shown by these people. I just thought it was one of the creepiest things I'd ever heard.

However, considering it is unlikely that you know the key word for a message someone does not want you to read, you have to proceed in a logical fashion and look for patterns in the message that will give you a clue to what the keyword might have been. Most messages would be vastly more complicated than any example. However, in our example, we can start to find patterns.

KHMURRLRJTWSKHMZRLT

The same trigraph, it seems, has been repeated in the message, implying one of two things. Either this is simply a random result of the encipherment, in which case it can't help us, or perhaps it means that the same plaintext word has appeared under the same letters of the keyword and has been enciphered in the same way twice – in which case it will help us immeasurably.

It took a good 300 years after Alberti's initial ideas for someone to work out how to crack Vigenère ciphers in this way. Charles Babbage, the crazy and brilliant inventor of the Difference Engine (the first computing machine), turned his attention to it after a bizarre argument with someone who thought he had invented poly-alphabetic ciphers for the first time.

'I have invented a new, unbreakable code!'
'Well, actually, it's not that new. It's been around for . . .'
'I tell you, my code is unbreakable!'
'That's as may be – but you did not invent it.'
'Are you challenging me?'
'Well, yes, all right then, you imbecile.'
'Let's see you crack it, then!'

So Babbage, who could not resist a challenge from someone so obviously brain-dead, even if the challenge was absurd, eventually supplied us with our method. Babbage was a bit like this. As well as inventing the Difference Engine, he also invented the speedometer, the cowcatcher (a device fitted to trains to clear cattle from the tracks) and the basis of the modern postal system, where a letter can be sent anywhere in the country for the same price. He noted that if you could find patterns in a cipher like the one above, say the two instances of the trigraph KHM, you should then proceed the following way. Assuming you had a much longer piece of ciphertext, you would find as many instances as possible of repeated clusters of letters. Then you would count the letters from the beginning of each cluster to the beginning of the next. In our example above you would find twelve letters between the first K and the next one. What this tells you is that the keyword (the one that is written repeatedly above the plaintext during encipherment) must have a number of letters that is a factor of twelve i.e. 12, 6, 4, 3, 2 or 1, these being the numbers that divide into twelve. This makes sense, as we are assuming that the same letters repeat after twelve characters, in both the keyword and the plaintext message, resulting in the repeated cluster in the ciphertext. A two-letter key would have repeated six times before starting again; a twelve-letter key only once. With a longer piece of text it would be possible, usually, to narrow down the factors until the length of the word was obvious.

What happens next is rather complicated. If you had discovered that your keyword was four letters long, you would go through and label each letter in the ciphertext with a 1, 2, 3 or 4, depending on whether it would have been enciphered using the first, second, third or fourth letter of the keyword. Then you would perform frequency analysis on each set of letters; so for the letters marked with a 1, you would come up with a distinct frequency table which you could then compare with a list of normal frequencies. You would proceed the same way for each set of letters until you had each letter of the keyword, at which point you would decipher your message.

But this is not how I do it.

What I do is as follows. First of all I proceed the same way as Babbage would have done, trying to guess the length of the keyword by counting and factorising the letters between repeated clusters. But then I would be trying to find a short cut, being quite a fan of short cuts and not so much a fan of doing things the 'right' way, or going the long way around in general. So what I always do next is look for every repeated trigraph in the text and then go through trying each one as 'the'. I would be lucky with the sample above, as the first word is, of course, 'the'. I would work the letters KHM back using the Vigenère square (if K equalled 't', then the line of encipherment would have been R; if H equalled 'h', the line of encipherment would have been A and so on) and rather quickly come up with the following to work from: I would have a keyword that has a number of letters that is a factor of twelve and which possibly begins with the letters RAI. Intuition immediately tells me this could be the word RAIN. In fact, when I check in my dictionary I find other words that would fit as well: RAID, RAIL, and RAISIN, each being a word beginning with RAI and having a number of letters that is a factor of twelve. So what I do next is simply try them all. And of course, when I put the letters of the word RAIN repeating above the ciphertext, it unscrambles nicely.

I look down at my notebook, in which I have written the following:

XYCGKNCJYCJZSDSPPAGHDFTCRIVXU ?????????? CJ and CJ??
Repetition too soon.

The message is simply too short to have any useful patterns. Not that many short phrases actually contain convenient repetitions of the word 'the' or 'and' anyway. I yawn. Why has someone sent me this? Do they want me to read it or not? I sit there, listening to the noises outside in the dark, thinking how stupid this whole thing is. Why send a message with no key? I mean, it's not as if I intercepted this – it was sent to me!

I am staring at the piece of paper so intently that it starts to blur beneath my eyes. The letters of the code merge and smudge together with the PopCo logo in the top left-hand corner and the *With Compliments* lettering in the middle. And then I suddenly wonder: is the key in fact here, with the message? Vigenère used the concept of a 'priming key': could there be one here too?

With my heart playing fast percussion, and my brain suddenly alert, I write the ciphertext out on my pad again, cleanly, and write the letters POPCO repeating on top of it. My makeshift Vigenère square, which I have drawn on a piece of paper, gives me the following result:

```
P O P C O P  O P  C O P  O P  C O P  O P  C O P  O P  C O P  O P C
X Y C G K N C J  Y C J  Z S  D S  P P  A G H D F  T C R I  V X U
i  k n e w y o u w o u l d b e a b l e t o r e a d t h i s
```

I knew you would be able to read this. What kind of message is that? And who has sent it to me? I don't like this very much, and the late-at-night factor doesn't really help. I can't relax now, so I pace the room smoking roll-ups until it is calm-ocean blue outside and only then do I get into bed.

Part Two

Bertrand Russell once shared a dream with G. H. Hardy. Russell dreamt he was on 'the top floor of the University Library, about A.D. 2100', said Hardy. 'A library assistant was going around the shelves carrying an enormous bucket, taking down book after book, glancing at them, restoring them to the shelves or dumping them into the bucket. At last he came to the three large volumes which Russell could recognise as the last surviving copy of Principia Mathematica. *He took down one of the volumes, turned over a few pages, seemed puzzled for a moment by the curious symbolism, closed the volume, balanced it in his hand and hesitated . . .'*

From The Man Who Loved Only Numbers *by Paul Hoffman*

Chapter Ten

It's hard trying to cook dinner for yourself when you are nine.

For one thing, it's actually impossible for me to reach the grill unless I stand on a chair. I wasn't allowed to do this before my father left; am I allowed to do it now? No. If I slip and fall now there'll be no one to look after me or go to the phone box to ring for an ambulance. I have to be more careful now, like the way I'm being careful not to cry. Anyway, things you use the grill for, like sausages, are too complicated and I can't afford sausages any more. Today, for the third day in a row, I am making porridge with water from the tap and the big box of oats in the cupboard. I haven't told anyone what has happened. I haven't told my best friend Yvonne, who isn't talking to me anyway, and I haven't told a teacher or a grown-up friend. I can look after myself.

Ten days ago I came home from school to find that my father had simply gone. There was a note: *Sorry. Had to go. Ring your grandparents and they will look after you.* Why haven't I rung them? I don't know. Perhaps it's something to do with being so angry with my father that I can't bear to follow his stupid instructions. Anyone knows that you don't leave a nine-year-old child on her own. And maybe it's something else, too: a vague sense that, if I can just hang on and weather this storm of unreality, the big waves of loneliness, fear and uncertainty will pass and things will just steady themselves back to normal. Dad will return from wherever he has gone, kiss me on the top of the head and apologise. However angry with him I am, my rationale is that I have to give him that chance. Phoning my grandparents would be tantamount to telling tales on him; I mean, if they knew he had left me here alone they would go ballistic. They've been complaining lately about me being what they call a 'latchkey kid', something to do with the fact that until my father stopped working, I used to let myself in when I came home from school. I have a feeling they will view this much, much more seriously than that.

I am using sailing words a lot and thinking of things in terms of the sea because there are sailing books all over the house. In fact, they must be due back at the library soon. Dad will probably get a fine as well as everything else. I don't think he cares, though. Maybe I'll take them back for him. But I'm not sure I can carry them all. And they're interesting, too. I have been reading one of them; a true story called *Survive the Savage Sea*, about a family stranded in a dinghy in the Pacific for two months. This book makes me feel better. If I have an orange while I am reading, I split it into small sections and give them to myself in rations, as if this was the last food I had in the world, and I pretend I am on an adventure with my family, far out at sea. I imagine a big family, with laughter and exciting stories and the ability to survive even a shipwreck.

I wish I had a pet. Not a dog or a cat or anything – that would be asking too much. A gerbil, guinea pig or fish would be ideal. I would give it a really nice name and feed it and look after it all the time. I would teach it to do special tricks, and tell it all my secrets. Dad always says the 'novelty' of a pet would wear off but I know it wouldn't. He said once that I won't know how I'll feel in the future and that your future self is always going to be a surprising stranger with thoughts and feelings you don't recognise. He didn't say things like that before Mum died but now he says them all the time, with a misty, philosophical look in his eyes. *You don't know who you'll become, Alice.* I only wanted a bloody gerbil. This is why I haven't risked asking for a dog or a cat.

Has he gone sailing somewhere? Are the books connected to his disappearance or merely a red herring? Dad gets a lot of strange, sudden ideas and goes to the library to research them – but they very rarely lead to any direct action. Has this been an exception? Ideally he will just come back or – and this is what I think about late at night – I will work out where he has gone, find him and bring him back. If he comes back then my grandfather and grand-mother won't need to know that this ever happened. This is the plan at the moment.

You have to be careful with porridge because it is dangerous when it is boiling. If you spilled it on yourself you could get scarred for life – maybe even on your face if you were really unlucky. So after I have let the water and oats boil in the pan for one minute precisely (which I count in my head: *one elephant, two elephants* and so on because my digital watch doesn't have a timer) I simply switch off the gas and leave the pan to cool before I touch it. This is one of my emergency survival procedures. I am making a list of what these are. So far I also have: *Do not stand on chairs; Do not use the grill; Do not plug things in or unplug them unless the switch is definitely turned off.* One of Dad's friends recently told us a story of being 'thrown across the room' by an electric shock. I don't like the idea of that happening to me here on my own. Every time I remember something I have been told not to do in the past, I am adding it to the list. That's the system. Sometimes you have to trust grown-ups, perhaps more so when they are not there to actually supervise you. It is only in the middle of the night that my resolve fails and I want to ring my grandfather but the phone box is two streets away and I am not allowed out after dark.

I am concerned about where I am going to get money for the gas and electricity meters. My food money has also almost run out. The food money came from my piggy bank in my bedroom. There was six pounds in there only ten days ago but it's surprising to note how quickly it goes. It probably didn't help that I had fish and chips for the first three nights, and spent one whole pound at the sweet shop a few days ago. Again, though, it's hard to budget when there are no grown-ups around telling you what you are and are not allowed to buy. This, perhaps, is why children are not usually allowed to be in charge of money.

The Hoover is out-of-bounds so I don't use it. I am also not allowed to use bleach. I have never actually done much cleaning: I used to help Mum before she died but after that Nana Bailey came to 'tide us over'. Nana Bailey never lets me help with anything. 'Get out from under my feet, Alice,' is what she always says whenever I go anywhere near her. Dad's pretty good at cleaning but was always 'too tired' when he came home from work. This is why Nana Bailey was helping us but she stopped when Dad lost his job. I was quite pleased about this but I didn't say anything. Anyway, at least I don't have to worry about her coming around now – I really do have enough to worry about. Still, I haven't done a very good job of the washing up over the last ten days. My first big mistake was to leave it to build up for about four days before tackling it properly. Then I couldn't get any hot water to come out of the tap. I still don't know how hot water works. I think it's something to do with the red switch next to the boiler but I was always told not to touch that. It isn't easy washing things in cold water, though, although I expect this is what you would do on a boat.

My bed is my boat. I have moved it away from the wall and put things from the bathroom (two rubber ducks and a fish-shaped sponge) around it as if they were bobbing in the sea. I have stuck the broom in the end of the bed, wedged between the mattress and the frame, and attached a sheet to it so it looks like a picture of a sail in my book. Notches in the side of the boat tell me how many days I have been here, alone at sea. There are ten so far. I have several books in my 'boat': obviously *Survive the Savage Sea*, a dictionary to help me with the complicated words (I have a reading age of sixteen but it is an adult book), a book of maths puzzles my grandfather got me last Christmas and two other sailing books I found lying around the house. I know three knots, now: the bow line, the reef knot and the clove hitch and I think – although I am not sure – that I have my sail rigged correctly. I think that tomorrow I will stay in my boat and not bother about school. Yvonne still isn't speaking to me and I want to finish my book. Our maths topic is long division (which I can do already) and our English topic is 'the seasons' (which is boring) so it's not as if I am going to miss anything.

*

PopCo Towers, as we have christened it, is again shrouded in mist on Monday morning. Sunday turned out to be a bit of a blur. After staying up thinking about the coded message until about five, I slept until almost midday. This nocturnal thing is becoming a bit of a habit, actually, which I am going to have to watch out for. Could it be natural? It's hard to say. Being at home for the last couple of weeks researching my KidScout/KidTracker kit was relaxing mainly because I made the most of the night. I found myself still up at three in the morning usually, reading by my desk lamp. For two nights I actually camped in my small garden and made notes on 'Creatures You Can Observe When Camping'. Because of the 'back garden feel' that was requested at the last product meeting, I have made sure that the animals in this section of the book are mainly common, suburban or domestic in nature. While in my own garden I saw one cat (Atari), one hedgehog, two frogs, a toad, several slugs and snails and a dead mouse. I heard one owl hooting, the rustling of one fox/burglar and next door's rabbit moving around its hutch.

By the time I was up and about yesterday it was too late to do anything useful, so I ended up getting a quick lunch on my own in the cafeteria and then walking around the gardens thinking about my survival research and trying to identify flowers and shrubs. I didn't catch up with Dan until the evening and then we simply sat around playing cards until bedtime. I tried not to think of the message I received, although it has left me with an uncomfortable sense of anticipation. Will the person contact me again? It seems probable. *I knew you would be able to read this* does sound like a set-up for further correspondence. In my rational mind, I know that anyone who had my KidCracker kit would be able to send a message like that. And sending it to me would be logical: of course I would understand it – I invented the kit. Yet a paranoid part of me is saying, *What if?* What if it has started now, all these years later? Could someone know about the necklace? This is the kind of thing everyone was worried about back then. But no. I am being stupid.

There were events going on all day yesterday but I didn't go to any of them. And as for Mac's 'Goodbye Speech', well, it's not goodbye, really, is it? Dan called me a 'terrible skiver' when I caught up with him and it's true – I *do* skive off all the time. I don't know why but sometimes I just get a complete mental block on organised activities. I never have a problem with any actual work but for some reason being in a specified place at a specified time and doing what I've been told to do sometimes trips the wrong set of switches in my brain. Sadly, the seminars planned for the following few weeks at PopCo Towers are all completely compulsory so it's probably a good job I gave myself Sunday off. I have also ticked off the one item on my To Do list. I phoned Helen Forrest and organised for someone to go and collect Atari and take him to Rachel's house. I have been imagining him travelling in a corporate cat box on a red cushion in a PopCo limousine. I think he would quite enjoy that.

Dan and Esther both have study bedrooms in the West Wing.

Mine is in the East. Other things I have discovered about being housed in the Main Building: there are small kitchens at the end of every hallway; each wing has its own 'Common Room/Library' and there is another, almost secret dining area down near the Great Hall in which, it turns out, there are actual chefs available to cook for us. Dan and I had dinner there last night, and are planning to have breakfast and lunch there today. Apparently, the chefs will make you up a packed lunch if you want to picnic in the grounds, or go walking on the moors. And we haven't told them we are vegetarians – although I think I am definitely going to become one.

In the end I don't see Dan in the dining room at breakfast time. I am bleary-eyed and confused, and manage only one slice of toast before I decide to take a cup of tea outside with me. As I walk out of the dining room I note a general sleepiness, but also a slight buzz in the air.

Esther is already outside smoking.

'Bloody early,' she mumbles.

'Yeah,' I say, lighting a roll-up.

'Good idea,' she says, gesturing at the fact that I have brought a cup of tea out with me. 'I might get another cup before this all starts.' She yawns. 'Fucking hell.'

'So how's it going?' I ask her. I haven't actually seen Esther properly since Mac's talk on Saturday night. I don't even know what he wanted to talk to her about. Can I ask her directly? Probably not, although I am curious as hell.

'All right,' she says groggily. 'Not sure about all this, though.'

I smile. 'What, our secret assignment?'

'Yeah. I don't know. It's sort of exciting to be chosen but . . .'

'Weird.'

'Yeah. *Weird*. I totally can't work out why we were all picked. I don't know anyone here apart from you and Dan, and I only met you on Saturday. Who are all these people?'

'I don't know either,' I say. 'Maybe they're robots.'

'Maybe.'

Two men go into a restaurant and order the same dish from the menu. After tasting his food, one of the men goes outside and immediately shoots himself. Why?

I don't believe this.

'Jesus Christ,' says Esther. I am in a 'team' with her and Dan. We have been in this room for only about two minutes so far and we have been asked to split into teams to solve this lateral thinking puzzle. I think it's a hello/bonding exercise. There's been no sign of Mac yet today, just the guy leading this seminar.

'I know the answer anyway,' I say. 'So I'd better sit this one out.'

'Why – or *how* – do you know the answer to such a stupid question?' Esther asks.

'My grandfather was an expert on lateral-thinking puzzles,' I explain. 'I think I know them all. By the way, I'll give you a million pounds if you can get the answer to this one.'

Esther is looking at the whiteboard in a confused way. The puzzle is written on it in electric blue board-marker. She frowns and then draws a neat square in her notebook. Then she adds perspective lines and makes the square into a cube. She starts shading one of the sides of the cube; a perfect shadow. How odd. I doodle in exactly the same way as this, although I sometimes add spirals drawn inside rectangles.

'What do you think?' she says to Dan.

'Fuck knows,' he replies. 'Are the clues in the question? They must be.'

'A million pounds,' Esther says absent-mindedly.

'Why the sullen expression, Butler?' Dan asks me.

'This is the stupidest lateral-thinking puzzle in the world,' I say. 'It doesn't make any sense at all. He could at least have asked us to do the one about the black and white stones, or something. At least that one's satisfying.' *He* is the guy leading this seminar. His name is Warren and he is an expert in team-building and problem-solving. He's from a small, exclusive London ideation facility called Lattice.

We are in a south-facing room in the small block adjacent to the main building. At least, I assume it's south-facing – sunlight is already streaming in. I remember when I was a kid I became briefly obsessed with compass readings and charts. But now all I know about points on the compass is that south is the direction in which middle-class, young, professional people want their gardens to face. There are about twenty-five or so people in the room: basically everyone who was at Mac's 'secret' meeting on Saturday night. Warren is sitting at the front looking over some notes while everyone tries to work out this strange puzzle. I glare at the itineraries we have been given: lateral thinking until lunchtime today, then something called 'How to Think'. Early this evening we have a meditation class, and then team-building all day tomorrow. All the team-building I have ever done has been the urban, flip-chart sort. I remember some article I read once about trainee managers walking over hot coals and sailing unsteady rafts across a raging river, taking it in turns to be blindfolded. I hope we don't have to do that kind of thing here.

'What's the "black and white stones" puzzle?' Dan asks me.

'It's long-ish,' I say.

'Go on,' he says, putting down his pen. 'I can't get my head around this one. Maybe if I have an example I'll know what I'm supposed to be doing.'

I glance at Esther. She looks interested, too. 'All right. Well the problem is this. A merchant has fallen on hard times and has borrowed some money from a very rich, but very evil man. The merchant pays the first instalment of the loan but the next day the rich man's servant comes and informs him that he also needs to pay rather a lot of interest. The interest is so high that it's impossible for the man to pay. He tells the servant to inform his creditor that he cannot pay such a huge sum and offers some of his livestock in lieu of this interest. The servant returns again with a different proposition. The merchant has a very beautiful daughter, who is also very clever and is coveted by all the men in the kingdom. If he will give his daughter to the rich evil man for him to use as his slave . . .'

'Sex slave?' says Esther.

I smile. 'Yeah, possibly. Anyway, if he will give his daughter to the rich, evil man then his debt will be written off. If not, he will lose everything and his whole family will starve. It's a horrible choice to make but eventually the daughter herself makes it. She appears in front of her father carrying her suitcase, ready to offer herself to the rich man. Her mother and father cry as she leaves in one of the rich man's carriages: they fear they will never see her again. Now, the rich man is not just evil but also sadistic and cunning. One month later he calls the beautiful girl's family to his castle, saying he has a proposition for them. When they get there, they find various people from the town assembled in the large castle courtyard, waiting to see what spectacle is going to occur. The courtyard is covered with small black and white stones – legend has it that this exotic, elegant gravel is the rich man's pride and joy. It reminds him of his favourite pastime, chess, and he has the stones shipped in regularly at great expense. It's a shame he wasn't into Go, actually, as these things are basically like thousands of Go stones all over the ground.

'Anyway, once a big enough audience is assembled, he comes forward to address the crowd. In as humiliating a way as possible, he relates the tale of how this hapless merchant owed him money but offered him his daughter instead. At this the father becomes very angry. He didn't simply "offer" his daughter – he was tricked! His wife calms him down. She fears the worst if he makes the rich man angry. Executions have taken place in this courtyard before now and she doesn't want her daughter, or her husband, to be the next victim. Eventually the rich man comes to the point of his long speech, speaking directly to the girl's father. "I have here a bag," he explains, "into which I will place one black and one white stone from the ground. If your daughter can pick the white stone from the bag, she is free to go home with you today and you will owe me nothing. If, however, she picks the black stone then she is mine for ever and you will never see her again. Do you accept this proposition?" The man has no choice. He accepts it.

'The girl is brought out to the courtyard by a servant. She is not crying but instead seems calm and brave. The challenge is explained to her and she nods. A 50–50 chance of being free is more than she thought she would be able to hope for, and she prays that she will be able to pick the right stone. Then the rich man bends down to pick the stones from the ground. He does this in such a way that the audience can't see what he is doing but it is absolutely clear to the girl that he has picked up two black stones and placed them in the bag. This is so unfair! She can't be condemned by trickery to spend the rest of her life in his service, available to indulge his every sadistic whim . . .'

'Are you embellishing this a little bit, Butler?' Dan asks, laughing.

'No, no,' I say, also laughing. 'This is exactly as I heard it when I was ten or so.'

Esther looks worried. 'What does she do?'

'Well,' I say. 'That's where the lateral-thinking puzzle comes into it. There is something she can do. What is it?'

'Is it kicking the man in the balls and running away?' Dan asks.
'No. It's nothing like that. It's a lateral-thinking puzzle, which means that it has a neat answer that, if you haven't thought of it yourself, feels like . . . a bit like the punchline to a joke or something and it seems so obvious you think you should have thought of it yourself.'

'She can't just tell on him?' Esther says.

'No. She can't call the man a liar or a trickster without the fear of being executed. She has to trick him back. How can she do it?'

Chapter Eleven

Warren has been on the loose for some time. Now he's suddenly at our table, peering down at our notebooks. Esther's is almost a cubist tableau by now and mine is blank. Dan has drawn a front-on view of an Italian restaurant with a man lying dead in front of it, a gun in his hand.

'Good,' Warren says, pointing at Dan's work. 'A visual mind, eh?'

'I am a designer,' says Dan.

'So, how are you getting on?' he asks us.

'Slowly,' says Esther.

'I think it's something to do with an albatross, although I can't think why,' I say, innocently.

'You've heard it before?' Warren says, sounding a bit alarmed.

'No, definitely not. I just think it's something to do with an albatross. It's just a hunch.'

Warren walks away with slightly narrowed eyes.

'So, there are two black stones in the bag,' Esther says. 'Hmm. Did you work it out when you heard it?'

'What me?' I say. 'No. God, no. I'm terrible at lateral thinking. I only know all of the answers because of my grandfather. He wasn't that great at solving them either, actually. But years ago he used to do the puzzle column for a weekend newspaper and he always used to have a lateral-thinking puzzle in there. Like, "A man pushed his car. He stopped when he reached a hotel at which point he knew he was bankrupt. Why? He was playing Monopoly."' It's really years since I've thought about the Mind Mangle. While doing the crossword for one newspaper, my grandfather was the Mind Mangle for another. And at the time, I thought this was really quite ordinary. Then I became a teenager and it all seemed a bit strange.

'I give up,' Dan says eventually.

'Yeah, go on,' Esther says. 'But I know I will kick myself . . .'

'All right,' I say. 'This is what the girl does. When the rich, sadistic man holds the bag out to her, she picks a stone out of it, just like she is supposed to. Then she pretends to fumble and drops the stone. "I beg your pardon sir," she says – or something like that – to the rich man. "I seem to have dropped the stone." The rich man is angry. "We will have to start again," he says. "Pardon me, sir," the girl says. "But perhaps there is another way. If you look in the bag to see which stone is left, it will be clear which one I dropped. If the stone in the bag is white, then I must have dropped the black one and will remain here for ever. If, however, the stone in the bag is black, then I picked the white one and should go free." The crowd murmurs its approval. Of course, the stone in the bag is black, there having been two black stones in there to begin with, and the rich man is forced to let the girl go free. Her trick was ultimately better than his trick.'

'That is very cool,' Esther says. 'I like that.'

Dan looks like he's going to start a *What if*-type conversation but at that moment Warren asks everyone to stop working on his puzzle. My eyes are already itching with that heavy, trapped classroom feeling. I wish I was outside. I wonder if we are going to be able to go for a break soon but when I look at the clock on the wall it says it's only 10:30. I yawn as everyone stops talking and looks at Warren.

'Anyone got any ideas?' he says.

Everyone is silent. I look around the room. The dark-haired guy and the fawn-haired girl are sitting together without any other 'team' members. Elsewhere in the room, people seem to have paired up or got into groups of three with people they knew already. The PA I recognise from Battersea is sitting with a designer I don't really know at all but who I *think* is called Lara. The PA's name, possibly, is Imogen, but I really can't remember.

'You two,' Warren says, pointing at two people I have never seen before this weekend. 'What are your names?'

'Richard. Well, I'm Richard and she's Grace,' says one of them. He has got spiked, blond hair and she is the Chinese Goth I noticed at Saturday night's meeting.

'Good,' says Warren. 'Grace, did you solve the riddle?'

'No,' she says. 'Sorry. We had a go, but . . .'

Warren chuckles. 'Pretty impossible, isn't it? Now, more importantly, what did you learn about your team-member?'

'He's a twat?' Grace offers. We all laugh, including Richard.

Warren looks concerned. 'Do you two know each other already?' he asks.

'Yeah,' says Grace. 'Of course. He's my boss. So I probably shouldn't call him a twat, and . . .'

Warren interrupts. 'Who else is in a team with people they already know?'

We all put our hands up.

'OK.' He frowns. 'Right.'

'I think it's all gone tits up,' Esther comments in a whisper loud enough for most people in the room to hear. I feel someone's stare tickling the back of my neck and look behind me to my right. I am just in time to see the dark-haired guy look away from us disapprovingly. What is up with him?

'Did anyone get the answer to this puzzle?' Warren asks, tiredly.

'Was it something to do with the meal they ate?' Lara asks. 'Was it poisoned?'

I wonder how the actual answer is going to go down with the people in this room. Poor Warren. I see what he was doing now: giving us something impossible to work out and hoping that we would 'bond' while doing so. I imagine him planning this class on the train from London, visualising us all laughing together over the stupidity of the lateral-thinking puzzle, having just made friends with the person on our right. He wasn't to know that most of us already are friends with the person on our right. Mind you, you would think that Mac would have briefed him.

'One of the men is an executioner,' offers Richard. 'Like a Mafia hit-man or something. He has taken the other man out to talk "business" but this guy knows for certain that he is going to be killed. Once he has tasted his food, nausea rushes over him. He decides that he would rather die by his own hand, and excuses himself from the table. Then he blows his brains out in the road outside.'

That's actually very good, compared to the real answer. I think I prefer it.

'Very imaginative, Richard,' is what Warren says, in a slightly patronising way.

'I do imagine for a living,' Richard says back.

This isn't going very well. You know the way you can just tell what a group is thinking, when you are a part of that group? I know that everyone now thinks Warren is a bit of a wanker. He has now reached a critical mass whereby he has changed from being someone 'in charge' to being someone we don't particularly respect. If Warren was plotted on a graph, he would currently be flat-lining somewhere near zero.

'All right,' he says. 'Here is the answer. I'll just read it out to you quickly and then we'll have a break before moving on. The answer was never the main part of this – what I wanted to do was introduce lateral thinking in a "fun" way while you all got to know each other. But, since you already know each other we will get straight into the learning section after our break.'

'Warren?' says Lara's companion, Imogen.

'What?'

'We don't *all* know each other, most of us just know the person we're sitting next to. You could, like, jumble us up or something.'

Warren sighs and tells us the answer to the lateral-thinking puzzle.

Esther's already skinning up by the time me and Dan get outside.

'Drugs already,' Dan says, disapprovingly.

'That's not a fucking puzzle,' Esther says. 'That's a soap opera. I need drugs after that.'

'I told you,' I say, rolling a cigarette.

'So it's like . . . The dish they ordered was albatross. The man knew as soon as he tasted it that whatever he was eating was something he'd never tasted before. From this he surmises that when he had "albatross" on some desert island all those years ago he must have been eating his son, who had died just after they reached the island.'

'Yep,' I say.

'That's fucked up! You could never work that out from the infor- mation you're given. Plus, surely the guy would check that they hadn't just given him the wrong meal or something before shooting himself? Jesus. Or what if the people on the island gave him, I don't know, swordfish or something and said it was albatross? It doesn't follow that he ate his own son. God. I am so over this Warren guy. I'm over this whole thing. Fucking hell. We – or at least you – already know how to have ideas and do product proposals and stuff. Why do we need all this extra tuition?'

'It would be all right if he knew what he was doing,' Dan says. 'Maybe it'll improve this afternoon. I was quite looking forward to learning how to have good ideas and stuff . . .'

'What do you do? Normally, I mean,' Esther asks Dan.

'Not telling,' he says.

She smiles, as if she's in a joke she doesn't quite understand. 'Huh?'

'Well, you haven't told us what you do.'

I try making a face at him but he's not looking.

'Oh, haven't I?' Esther says casually. 'I'm in the computer admin team. I thought I said.'

'Oh,' Dan seems slightly wrong-footed by this. 'Oh. Well, I'm a designer. But not like Alice. I don't design products on my own. I get assigned to people who need artwork, on the whole.'

'You get *assigned*?'

'Well, sort of. Like, sometimes the people who do the mechanical stuff have a particular mechanism that needs a product shell. That's probably when I get to be the most inventive. I'll get a brief saying something like: "This is a doll that crawls", with technical diagrams and so on, and I will then design the way the doll looks, or at least the roughs. Occasionally I get to design the whole thing once the mechanics are done, but that's rare. Usually if it's a new brand another team will have decided on the name, the personality and so on and I'll just be briefed to present, say, fifteen different eye-colours and a collection of skin-tone swatches. Most of the time, though, I'll work with someone like Alice, and do the artwork on her proposals and finalise images and colours and so on for the actual product. I'm basically just an art guy.'

'You're not *just an art guy*,' I say, slightly defensively.

'Yeah, I am. I don't really mind, though.'

'So of the three of us you're the only one who has ever proposed an actual product?' Esther says to me. 'That's weird, isn't it, considering the project we're working on?'

'Yeah,' I say. 'Especially since I've never done anything for the teenage market. And the two other people here that I recognise – one's a personal assistant and the other is just a junior designer. It is odd.'

'They wanted a new approach, though, didn't they?' says Dan.

'Maybe they've already tried everyone else,' Esther says.

We finish smoking and go back into the classroom.

I don't believe it. It's the fucking Balloon Game.

'So, the criteria for this exercise is that you're in a group of about four people, with *no one you already know*,' Warren says. There are twenty-six of us in this room. How many different ways are there of dividing us into sets of four or five? How do you take into account the parameters of the existing associations between us? Wasn't there some classic maths problem along these lines? The Travelling Salesman problem, or maybe something to do with students in college dorms? I can't remember and I am way too tired to try to work out what the maths might be. I just have a suspicion that it's one of those almost-impossible things. In any case, I just stay where I am until three people I don't really know drift towards me and sit down.

My group eventually contains, apart from me, Richard, Lara and the guy with the dark hair from the cafeteria. His name, it turns out, is Ben. He very briefly smiles at me, as if we sort of know each other, and then says nothing. Richard, who works in robotics, and Lara, who is, as I'd thought, a junior designer, both present entertaining cases for why they should stay in the balloon. When it is my turn to plead to stay in the balloon, I don't bother. I offer myself as a willing sacrifice. This is not what is supposed to happen in the Balloon Game.

Ben looks at me in an odd way and then says, 'Yeah, chuck me out too.' His voice is deep, like he's stuck at the bottom of a very dark well.

This is pretty much the end of the Balloon Game.

*

There are now thirteen notches on the side of my boat. I haven't been to school since about notch seven. I haven't had a bath, or washed my hair. I am allowed in the bath on my own but I am not allowed to run it. Apparently you can get the water too hot and scald yourself when you get in. However unlikely this sounds, I have to follow the rules.

On the fourteenth day, and before I have had a chance to add my notch, my grandparents turn up. They have, apparently, received a postcard from my father apologising for disappearing 'like that', and asking after me. They have obviously been panicking. What did my father mean when he wrote, 'Thanks for looking after Alice'? Could I be dead? When they find me alive my grandmother actually cries and my grandfather beams as if he has just won the Pools.

'You're coming to live with us, now, Alice,' my grandmother says, gently.

'And not before time,' says my grandfather.

I tell myself that I have been picked up by a fishing trawler.

Going to live with my grandparents actually turns out to be better than staying at home on my own with all my self-imposed rules and restrictions. The trip there is like books where a summer holiday begins and children are ferried off to somewhere far more exciting than home, to have adventures involving wilderness, mud, hastily constructed camps and small deserted islands. As we travel up the dual carriageway in the Morris Minor my grandparents whisper hasty plans while I look out at the grass verges and think about the wildlife they might contain. I have only stayed overnight with my grandparents on a handful of occasions, and not for ages. They have recently moved from their big red-brick house in the centre of Cambridge to a cottage in one of the villages nearby. Will I be able to ride horses there? It's hard to tell.

I am given my own bedroom, which is not at all similar to my old bedroom. It is painted pale pink with a sloping, low ceiling and has really old furniture including a big brown chest of drawers that is entirely empty when I open it. Is it all for me? More intriguing: I have been standing in the room for about five minutes, wondering whether to unpack my things, when my grandfather walks in and presents me with a hand-made wooden sign that says *Alice's Room*. He must have made this ages ago, not in the space between hearing I'd been left on my own and rushing into the city to pick me up (I estimate this space as being something not exceeding five minutes). So I always had a room here and my grandfather even made a sign for it. No one told me that.

'We always hoped you would come and stay,' my grandfather says in a happy/sad way, and I sense grown-up politics that I don't understand. Is there a connection between the arguments my father and grandfather have been having and the fact that I have never been here? Almost certainly; although I don't know why. It's not as if I was involved in their disagreement.

'Do you still wear the necklace?' he asks me, after I have taken the door sign from him and put it on the bed.

'Yes, of course,' I say, pulling it out on its thin silver chain to show him. *Of course* I still wear it: he told me never to take it off.

'Good,' he says. Then: 'We're going to have fun, you know.'

'I know,' I say. And then, once he has left the room, I cry, thinking of my abandoned ship, and all the bowls of porridge I made.

Chapter Twelve

There is a five-columned matrix on the desk in front of me. This is what is says:

Product Category	Special Powers	Theme	Kid Word	Random Word
Ball	*Lights up*	Pirates	*Cool*	Round
Board Game	*Explodes*	Witches/ghosts	*Clever*	Lawn
Wheels (bikes, skateboards etc.)	*Floats*	Wilderness	*Scary*	Mountain
Doll	*Big*	Saving the world	*Silly*	Elves
Videogame	*Small*	Animals/fish/ environment	*Mysterious*	Complex
Building kit	*Invisible*	Outer Space/ UFOs	*Gross*	Serpent
Activity set	*Fast*	Martial arts	*Special*	Extinct
Plush/soft	*'Real'*	Acquiring/ collecting	*Cute*	Bubble
Robot	*Shows emotion*	Mastery	*Grown-up*	Armour

Everyone else has roughly the same thing in front of them, as this matrix is what we have been making all afternoon, with a facilitator called Ned. Most of the columns have been created by us all just shouting ideas out as they have come to us, but now we have been left on our own to finish compiling the random word columns individually. Ned is young, together and certainly *not* a fuckwit like poor Warren, who was almost crying by the end of the morning session. With Ned, we are 'recapping' the process of compiling matrices, most of us having done it before, and adding this new thing: the random words column, which is pretty new to most of us.

The notion of randomness is a big part of any kind of lateral/creative thinking. It's all connected to that idea that you can't really trust your brain, that any ideas you have on your own may well turn out to be simply bad ideas or just ones that aren't at all original. Just as routine kills creative thought, so too apparently does, well, thought itself. Our brains are just not wired up to be original on their own. But with this thing called 'Random Juxtaposition' (an idea of Edward de Bono's, of course), well, you can have many good ideas.

My random words aren't entirely random, however. When you use a dictionary to search for random words, you end up with things like *fritillary* and *droshky*, which don't really work in this context. So what I've been doing instead is picking a random *page* of the dictionary and then finding a product-matrix type word on that page. It may be cheating but now my notebook has ideas crawling over it like cockroaches. It's uncanny.

What you do with a matrix is as follows: you write the columns out, as I have done, and then you take one thing from each column until you have made an entirely new thing. For example, you could have a small ball that is connected with mastery and is perceived as special. So this could be a brand where each ball is unique, perhaps with its own signature pattern or design (like Cabbage Patch Dolls, which each came with a unique 'Adoption Certificate'). Using mastery, you would be able to learn tricks with the ball, and perhaps take part in regional or 'street' competitions. If we add a word from the random column we could take, for example, 'complex' and make this product complicated and challenging to learn. This would fit in with children's desire to be special, to learn special (secret?) skills and 'be the best'. This product would also have collecting/trading appeal because of the uniqueness of each ball. Perhaps kids could be encouraged to buy the whole set of a particular theme (sea, space, monsters, etc.). You wouldn't know which type of ball you were getting when you bought it and then you might want to swap. To further encourage kids to buy more than one ball, there would also be multi-ball tricks that could be learnt.

Or what about a 'Snake Board': a skateboard that is 'real', connected with animals and the words 'silly' and 'serpent'? This would be a product for 9- to 12-year-old boys and would be sold in the form of a 'create-your-own' kit. The 'real' factor would be the wood and wheels and so on, which the kid can put together in various ways. Each Snake Board kit can take on the shape and character of different types of snake. There'd be the Python, the Adder and so on. The 'silly' factor could be achieved by having things like 'wobbly wheels', 'crazy eyes' and 'killer tongues' as features that could be added to the board. Perhaps the boards could also shoot 'venom' when you stamp on a foot pedal?

What about a building set that shows emotion, is connected to the environment and the word 'cute'? This would be something like Meccano (a product that makes all toy creatives, engineers and architects go a bit misty-eyed due to the fact that everyone learned to build things with it and it isn't made any more). However, when you build things with it, it becomes 'happy' or 'sad', depending on certain factors. A wall without windows would be 'sad', perhaps? Or the building material would become sad about things that are bad for the environment? I'm not sure this is feasible – it's a bit too AI – and sounds altogether too educational. Still, a building set with 'cute' features would work – definitely for girls. I add the random word 'elves' and spend the next fifteen minutes working out a product with which girls could build miniature elf dwellings, shops, and, in theory, whole towns, which they would then put in their gardens. Like bird tables – but for magical creatures! At the point when I catch myself thinking, *How would you know if the magical creatures had visited or not?* I give this up and start doodling instead.

My brain actually, physically hurts. I can't switch off, though. My doodle – several cubes and a large spiral – makes me suddenly think of a way you could make Go three-dimensional. And now I have a mysterious board game that is big, clever and complex. This matrix has embedded itself in my brain. How would you play three-dimensional Go? You would still place stones on the intersections but to surround a stone you would need to control not just the four intersections around it on the plane but the six that you would find in the three-dimensional equivalent. My doodle breaks down and I am not even sure that six points would connect each intersection. My head really is fucked now.

To my right, Dan is writing away furiously like he is in the most important exam he has ever sat. Esther, on my left, is looking dreamily out of the window.

'So,' says Ned. 'How many product ideas have each of you managed to create?' He looks around the room at people and they start calling out figures, which he writes down on the whiteboard. Grace has got four, Richard has got seven. I learn a few more names as he goes around the room. The big tattooed bloke is called Frank, Ben's fawn-haired companion is Chloë and the girl with pink pigtails is called Mitzi. I am able to match the name Hiro (which Mac called out on Saturday night) with a skinny Japanese guy with short black hair. They all have six ideas each.

'Seventeen,' says Dan when Ned's glance falls on him. Bloody hell. I offer my four ideas, and Esther slightly apologetically offers two.

'So, in this classroom, in the space of one afternoon, we have created exactly two hundred and one ideas. Pretty good going, don't you think?' Ned smiles. 'Of course, the important thing about matrices is the creative use of columns and parameters. I'm seeing you again on Wednesday, so perhaps between now and then you could think about what other parameters we could use. And I'd like you to develop one of your ideas into a full proposal, please.'

There is a lot of scraping-chair noise as we all get up to leave.

My new home is much quieter than my old flat. Trucks don't go past all the time, and people don't shout at each other underneath the windows. I don't have to go to school as it is almost the summer holidays and there's no point enrolling somewhere for just two weeks before everything breaks up. So I am free. My grandmother is working in her study all the time and my grandfather is researching a new series of his Mind Mangle columns at the University Library. So I spend my days exploring the village. I am alone most of the time, which is OK. At least I am not shipwrecked any more.

I have started working on my necklace. When I say 'working on it', I mean that I am working on deciphering the strange letters that are engraved in it. 2.14488156Ex48. What does that mean? And what about the little swirly shape? I haven't got very far but I think that this necklace holds the secret of why my father went away, and why my grandfather has been acting strangely recently. He was always such a cuddly, sweet-shop kind of person before. Now he looks like there is a ghost following him around all the time that no one else can see. In order to work on the necklace I have to be very secretive. In the middle of the night I have to do stealth-walking to get downstairs to see if I can look up the symbols in any of the books (or, indeed, find evidence of what the whole thing is about). Stealth-walking is a special skill I made up. To do it, you have to wear thick socks, and you have to place your weight down on your feet very slowly and carefully so as not to make a sound. You have to imagine each foot almost melting into the floor; *heel, ball* and *toes* slowly, like that. When walking down the stairs, you have to keep to the outside edges, because the middle bits creak.

One night I got caught! I was in the sitting room, about to open a book, when I heard a bed-spring noise from upstairs and then the sound of a door opening. I considered hiding but knew that wouldn't work. What if whoever it was checked my room before coming downstairs? They would know I was hiding and would then also know I was up to something. No. Something else. I could feel different parts of my brain clicking around like the dials on a safe, struggling for the right combination. By the time my grandmother came into the room I was already walking around with a glassy stare, almost bumping into things.

'Oh, Alice,' she said, leading me gently back up the stairs.

'Have a good sleep-walk?' my grandfather asked me over break-fast.

I feigned ignorance.

By the time the real summer holidays start, my grandfather is spending more time at home. He has cheered up, too. He shows me card tricks and leg-spin bowling and substitution ciphers. Now that it is summer, the village even has its very own gang of kids, which I am supposed to want to join. This gang consists of two quite stuck-up rugby-playing brothers, James and Vaughan; a girl called Rachel who has her own pony; and a girl with pierced ears called Tracey. Tracey seems like some sort of outcast, though. Apparently, they all go to private boarding-schools and she doesn't. As I haven't started my new school yet, I am an unknown quantity. I am suspicious of them all and, much though I would dearly love to ride Rachel's pony, I initially choose to hang around with Tracey instead. I teach her the substitution cipher and send her secret messages which she can unfortunately never decipher – even though she is a whole year older than me. I have a plan whereby, using stealth, we will take territory from the others; particularly some strategic points on the playing field by the stream where they hang around playing kissing games. Tracey doesn't want to. She wants to teach me about make-up and pop music. I begin to suspect that she would probably enjoy kissing games. I quickly defect and join Rachel instead. During the course of the summer Tracey joins the boys (we think she may have held hands with James) and we wage war against them, relentlessly, until term starts again. I am sometimes allowed to ride Rachel's sister's horse, Pippin, if she is away. Riding is scary but fun and you have to watch out not to get beheaded by low branches.

My grandfather plays cricket for the village team. The other players say he will carry on playing until he literally just dies at the crease, which I don't like the sound of very much, although it makes them all laugh. On Sundays they sometimes travel in their rusty old van to away fixtures in various nearby villages, and I am allowed to go too, supposedly to help with the teas. I hate helping with the teas, though. Tracey's nan is in charge and she always smells like sour fruit. There are always wasps, and they always get in the jam, which makes me feel funny. Anyway, I would much rather be playing cricket than fiddling around with jam, and I do have my own bat and pads now (which I got for my birthday in July). But however long I stand there hopefully, knocking a ball around on my own, they never ask me to play. Even when they are a man down I am not allowed on the team. It's not fair. They say I am too young but Colin Clarke plays if they are really short, and he's ten as well. I think it's because I am a girl.

One day I hear my grandfather talking to the captain about me.

'Come on, Mike,' he's saying. 'Give her a game.'

Mike's frowning. 'Where would she get changed?'

'She doesn't need to get changed. I never use the changing rooms.'

He's right. Like most of the team, he turns up for matches in his old cricket jumper and trousers, and goes home like that too. Only Bob the accountant ever uses the changing rooms and that's because he also plays squash.

'Yeah, but we'd have to provide facilities anyway. There's a law.'

'So we'll *make* her a changing room. I'll bring a tent! There. Solved.'

'What'll we say to the bowlers on the other team? They'll feel like they have to go easy on her and it'll be unfair. They won't want to bowl to a, you know, a *kid*.'

'They bowl all right to Colin, though.'

Mike shrugs. 'Well, he's playing for the Under-11s now. He can handle himself all right.'

'So can Alice. She's a decent little spin bowler, you know. Come on Mike, stick her in at number eleven just once. It would make her summer.'

But my grandfather is wrong. My summer has already been made by overhearing this conversation. He thinks I am good enough to play! My chance to join the team never actually comes though, due to my grandfather mysteriously deciding to resign from it.

'We'll play cricket our own way,' he says. 'In the garden.'

*

Mac is there for the meditation class. He speaks to a few people (but not me), and then settles down at the back to join in. I can't believe that it was only two days ago that meeting him seemed like such a big deal. Now he's around all the time, and my 'secret' – that I had that conversation with him when I first arrived here – has lost power as quickly as an engine with no fuel. We are gathered on the sunken lawn in front of the main building, under a very old, gnarly tree. Our meditation tutor is a softly-spoken woman with long brown hair tied in two long bunches. I have never meditated before but, now that I am having a go, I find that it is somehow like drugs, this feeling of shrinking back into yourself. It's not as hard as I would have thought. All you do is shut your eyes and concentrate on something, and you almost don't realise you have been doing it until you stop, open your eyes and the world suddenly seems sharper, yet more distant. I thought meditating involved clearing your head of all thoughts but the woman says it's OK to keep your thoughts in a back cupboard in your mind while you bring one thing to the foreground and focus on that. She says meditation is like tidying up before you sit down, as opposed to sitting down in a mess. She also says it's good for when you get that brain-overload feeling, which I definitely do have. When it's all over I feel lighter, and also very tired. I walk slowly back to my room and, without fully intending to, I immediately fall asleep on the bed.

An hour later, or possibly two. I have probably missed dinner. What time is it? I feel disorientated, sleepy. Am I still myself? I think so. I force myself out of bed, splash water on my face in the bathroom and then use some of it to smooth down my hair, as I sense the beginnings of frizz. But this is more habit than anything. Do I care if my hair is frizzy? Not particularly. I walk slowly back to bed and get in. The sheets are still warm, and the pillow still has the small indentation from where my head was resting a few minutes ago. It's not that I'm sleepy any more, actually, far from it. I simply feel bread-warm and comfortable in here, with my legs drawn up, as if someone has been singing me magic, calming lullabies. At the moment I feel like the kind of person to whom no one would ever send notes in code. I feel like someone with no work to do. To complete the effect, I reach over to the bedside table and pick up my bottle of valerian. A few drops and then a bit more semi-meditation, concentrating on a crack in the ceiling. I am overdosing on relaxation. This is great. More valerian; now I could do with some chamomile. I really could do with some chamomile tea, some miso soup (that craving never completely went away) and possibly some dope. Where is Esther? Will the chefs have heard of miso soup? Can I answer these questions? I drop off again while wondering if I can even be bothered to masturbate.

Eight o'clock. I really have missed dinner now. The valerian has slightly rag-dolled my body but not so much that I can't get up and smoke a cigarette. I pull on my skirt, a shirt and a cardigan and my plimsolls. I have attached my door key to a piece of ribbon and I slip this around my neck. Hair in a ponytail? No. Two thick plaits. Great. *Time to leave the room, Alice.* Can't go back to bed again. Can I? No. I vaguely recall that I was planning to do some work this evening but I need soup, tea, anything. I am hungry and I need to walk around. When the air hits my face outside, it is like an unexpected kiss.

Over in the West Wing, Dan is buried in a book about lateral thinking.

'Hi,' I say to him.

He looks at me with gleaming eyes. 'This is so . . . oh, God. What happened to you?'

'Huh?'

'You look wasted.'

'No, no. I'm fine. Meditation-overload. It'll be all right.'

'Oh. We were looking for you at dinner.'

So I did miss it. 'I had to go to bed really urgently. Any sign of Esther?'

'In the kitchen, possibly? It's at the end of the hall.'

'Thanks,' I say. 'What time will you be up until?'

'One-ish.'

'Cup of tea later, then?'

'Yeah, cool. Will you require my notes for the purpose of copying?'

'What? Oh, yeah, maybe.'

'You're such a skiver, Butler.'

It's not that, really. I just know I will be able to do this work quickly, when the deadline is looming in a more threatening way than it is now. But I say nothing and walk down the corridor towards the kitchen. I can smell toast, and steam. The door is closed but I push it open anyway, for some reason expecting Esther to be sitting in there on her own, making toast. Instead, I find Ben, Chloë and Hiro talking in an intense kind of way. It's one of those situations where, as soon as I walk in, they all stop talking and look at me, all with raised eyebrows. Oh God.

'Sorry,' I say automatically. 'Looking for someone.'

Actually, they don't all have raised eyebrows, nor are they all looking at me. Ben keeps his gaze down on the table, his brown eyes lost behind his glasses. Does he not notice that I am here? Is he not going to give me one of his unreadable expressions? No, not now, obviously. Strange. It was only this afternoon that we were talking about jumping out of an imaginary balloon together, which gave me a nice, fizzy feeling, I must admit. As quickly as I can, I close the door behind me and start walking back down the corridor. I briefly knock at Esther's door, but there is no reply. I walk slowly down the steps to the stone passage below. The air is fresh and damp with the smell of grass. What is my mission now? Shall I abandon the hunt for Esther? She is a difficult person to find, so much so that I have been wondering if she can shape-shift, or even whether she turns into a bat after dark and simply roosts somewhere. Perhaps I will go and find out if the dining room is still open, or see if there is anything to cook in the East Wing kitchen. Maybe I will even do some work, now, since that's what everyone else seems to be doing.

As I turn out of the West Wing I become aware of footsteps breaking into the quiet behind me; fast footsteps, as if someone's running to catch up with me. Instinctively, I look behind me but there's no one there. I hesitate for a moment but the footsteps have gone. Perhaps they were some echo from the past, or simply belonged to someone going the other way. I wander through the arch and then across the grass to the big oak door leading back into the main building.

There are indeed chefs still in the dining room. Could they even be 24-hour chefs? Anything's possible when PopCo is in charge. I slightly apologetically ask if it would be possible for me to have something to eat, and then present them with a list of my unusual requests.

'Miso soup,' repeats one of the chefs. 'Chamomile tea. *Pain au chocolat*. Scrambled eggs on wholemeal toast.' He grins. 'I think we can manage that. Got the munchies, have we?'

'Er, sort of. I missed dinner,' I say.

'No problem. You know we are here all night?'

PopCo really do think of everything.

'Do I have to eat it here?' I ask. 'Or . . .'

'You want take-away? Yep. We can do take-away.' He shouts the order through to someone else and I go to one of the small tables to sit and wait. I wish I had something to read.

Back in my room, I pick a 'young adult' title from the bookshelves and then pull the foil off the plates and start to eat. The miso soup has come in a big flask and my craving is satisfied after two cups of it. The scrambled eggs have grated parmesan and basil leaves sprinkled on the top. I eat them all, with the wholemeal toast, reading the beginnings of this novel, which is about a lonely girl and her horse. The girl is lonely because her family has moved to a remote house on a moor in Scotland and she has no friends. Every day she has to get up at five to groom her horse and then walk two miles to the bus stop to be taken to school. When she is there she is too sleepy to make friends with anyone and gets behind with her work. At the weekends she pretty much just gets into dangerous scrapes with her horse. The first time she tries to ride him over unfamiliar moorland they get lost in a storm; the next time they get stuck in a bog. On their third time out, she meets a wild boy riding his own horse. They look at each other and then, without speaking, ride faster and faster into the wind, challenging each other, competing in an uncertain event. He doesn't stop to tell her his name but simply disappears over a hill, shouting something like, 'Tomorrow . . .'. But tomorrow he isn't there. She then starts looking for him, trying to find him again so she can at least ask his name.

The tea is finished and I am smoking. This is actually quite a gripping book. Will she find the boy? Who is he? I could finish reading this right now but that feels greedy, somehow, and faintly absurd. What time is it? Nine, ten? Maybe I'll have another go at finding Esther. Or maybe I should just stay here and read after all, with cigarettes and more valerian. There is also, of course, the possibility that I could do some work, now I am reaching my peak time for alertness and enthusiasm, not that I feel particularly alert, or enthusiastic. A blast of wind hits the window and there is a curious whistling noise outside. Is there a storm coming in? Maybe I will go for a wander now rather than later. Even if I don't find Esther I can have a cup of tea with Dan. Then there'll be loads of time to come back and actually get on with something. I brush my teeth and put some lip-balm on my lips before I leave, pulling my cardigan around me against the wind. As I cross into the stone walkway on the West Wing I again imagine I can hear footsteps, just like before. I am so distracted by the sound that I almost walk straight into Ben, who appears to be walking in the opposite direction to me, towards the East Wing. It has started to rain.

'So this is where you are,' he says, his deep-well voice soft and uncertain.

What my eyes do now must require the activity of about a billion neurones. *You were looking for me?* they say. And, then, subtly, *Come with me, then, through this arch. I dare you.* His eyes say something almost question-markish back, but he does; he walks with me through the arch. We walk, slowly, in the rain, around the outside of the main building towards the steps leading down to the sunken lawn. We must seem like old drunks; Ben is so close to me that we are swaying and bumping together as we walk. At some point I put my finger to my lips and make a *Shhh* noise but I don't have to. Neither of us is going to say anything. In this almost-gone light Ben looks like a solemn ghost; his wet black hair and rain-spattered glasses giving the impression that when alive this ghost was a South European intellectual, perhaps sometime between the wars. My heart is a tap-dancing speed-freak, despite my evening of downers, and my legs suddenly feel crazy, like they could be a tail. For a second I am a mermaid. Could I have been thrown out of the storm to tempt him? Did he come out of the storm for me? Again, I think back to the moment we shared earlier on during the Balloon Game. For once in my life, I am pleased I played the Balloon Game.

Did I intend to lead him to the gazebo? Perhaps. But neither of us can wait that long. As soon as we are in the forest and well out of sight of the main house, we take a sharp left, look around to finally check we are alone, and then, as intensely and as hard as we can, we kiss. We kiss as if neither of us had names, addresses, To Do lists, phone numbers, friends, enemies or anything else in our lives at all. Ben's arms are surprisingly strong as he presses me against a tree. 'Don't speak,' I whisper, and he doesn't speak, not once, as he pulls up my skirt, takes a condom out of his pocket, and then begins to unbutton his trousers.

Back in my room I take off my wet clothes and put on the white PopCo dressing gown. Delicious, delicious. I will not wash tonight. I sit on my bed and it all seems quiet, perhaps too quiet. There is less rain now, and no sounds from anyone along the corridor. Should I have stayed with Ben? Should we have talked after-wards; swapped details of our childhoods and our jobs and our ex-partners and our unsavoury habits? No. This is right. This is how I wanted it. And, of course, I won't talk about this, or tell anyone what happened, especially not a woman. *You didn't speak at all? You did it against a* tree? *Well, he'll think you're easy, won't he? You've got to make them run, Alice. You can't let them have you so easily.* Of course, he didn't 'have me'; we had each other. But you try explaining that to a woman who thinks that all men are out for one thing and won't respect you if you 'give' it to them. I wonder what Esther would say? Probably not that, at least. But I still won't tell her.

It must be past eleven now. I get up off the bed and sit down at my desk. *Teenage girls.* I write this on a piece of paper and then look at the words suspiciously. Are we supposed to be diving straight into this problem or practising lateral thinking and matrices first? What would happen if someone came up with the definitive teenage girls' product tonight? Would we all simply go home tomorrow?

I've only been sitting there for three or four minutes when there's a soft knock at the door. For a moment I think, *Ben*, but when I open it it's Dan, carrying two mugs of tea and smiling almost naughtily.

'This is like some boarding-school story,' he says, walking into the room. Then: 'Oh – you're not dressed.'

'Just had a bath,' I lie, taking a mug of tea from him. 'Where did you get these?'

'Made them in the kitchen.'

'Great. Thanks. So . . . Do I need to get dressed or can you handle me in a dressing gown?'

He grins. 'I'll control myself, Butler.'

'Good.' I start rolling a cigarette. 'So how's stuff?'

'Really cool. I am *so* into all these lateral-thinking ideas. And the matrices . . . I haven't really thought about things this way before. I am definitely going to crack this teenage girl problem. I mean, how hard can it be?' His eyes are sparkling orbs of enthusiasm.

'God. You've gone a bit . . .'

'What?' He sounds slightly defensive.

'Well, it's a change from all that "The world is only pictures" stuff from the other night. You've turned into, I don't know, *Super PopCo Man* or something. Don't get too sucked in. Remember: they *are* an evil cult and they *will* brainwash you.' I don't actually mean this. It's just, like so many other things, something we say because it sounds funny. Dan doesn't laugh, though. He just looks thoughtful.

'It's all because, well, I've never been asked to actually pitch a new product before. I don't know. I know you probably think it's a bit sad or something, that I'm so excited about this. But I just . . . No one's ever valued my ideas before. It's always been, "Oh, Dan, that's a lovely blue," or "Oh, Dan – can you help me with this story-board?" I'm sort of enjoying there being no "Oh, Dan" about this. It's a chance to work on my own and actually do something important.'

'Until we get to the teambuilding class tomorrow, when, I guess, we're going to be told how to work effectively as a team.'

'Maybe.' He sighs. 'Oh, you know what I mean, anyway.'

I smile. 'Yeah, I do.'

Dan sips his tea. 'So, there's a man lying dead in a field beside an unopened package. There is no one and nothing else in sight. What has happened?'

'His parachute didn't open. Please don't tell me that you have actually learnt how to solve those things, because that would be too scary.'

He grins. 'No. I like them though. I also really like what de Bono says about using chance to help generate ideas, or solutions to problems.'

'What, all that open-the-dictionary-to-a-random-page stuff?'

God, Alice, can you sound any more dismissive?

'Yeah. I've never thought of things that way before. Do I sound lame?'

'No! Not at all. Sorry. It's me. I think I'm a bit tired.'

Yes, because you've been outside in the rain fucking for the last hour.

'You can shoot me if I defect,' Dan says.

'I will be the first to shoot you if you defect,' I assure him.

But later it occurs to me that we are at war with no one, no one at all.

Chapter Thirteen

There is a boat in the middle of the Great Hall.

'What the fuck?' says Esther.

'Cool,' says Dan. 'Sailing.'

I experience some brief butterfly-wing memory of having seen a picture of something like this a long time ago, and then I am distracted by Mac's voice from the small stage.

'Hello,' he says. 'Welcome to *SailTogether*.'

'Do you think that's one word, or two?' I ask Dan.

'It's one,' he says, indicating the logo painted on the side of the boat. 'Look.'

We are standing in clusters around the hall, like pictures of a virus. I haven't made any sort of eye-contact with Ben yet, although he is in the next cluster along, standing with Chloë and Hiro. Everyone is looking at the boat. How did it get here? Why is it here? It's peculiar, seeing a boat out of water, like this. And something is missing from it but I can't work out what.

'What's wrong with that boat?' I say to Dan. 'It looks, I don't know . . .'

'There's no keel,' he says. 'And they've flattened the bottom. It must be just for demonstration or something.'

'Demonstrating what?'

'Probably how to sail.'

'This is Gavin Samson,' Mac says in a loud voice, gesturing towards the tall, thin, suntanned man standing on the stage with him. 'Gavin has worked with PopCo on many different occasions. When he first joined the company, in 1980, he worked as an artist for the General Mechanics division, completing technical drawings for various mechanised toys. He then moved on to work more closely within the "Bath Time" brand, eventually creating successful sub-brands like the Tiny Trawler and the Saturday Sailboat.'

The Tiny Trawler isn't made any more but it was one of PopCo's big successes in the 80s. When I was a kid I knew people who had Tiny Trawlers. They were little wooden fishing boats that came complete with their own miniature string-operated outboard motors. You could play with them in the bath or, if you had the remote control model, the local fish pond, river or lake. The Saturday Sailor was a small toy sailing yacht which came with little masts, sails, rigging and rope. Again, you could actually sail the boat, but not anywhere out of reach as you had to be able to get to it to set the sails (and retrieve it when it shot off in the wind). However, the product did OK-ish with sailing families and was often bought as a novelty gift for the grown-ups, or as an educational aid for their kids to play with in the bath or the paddling pool.

Mac continues. 'Gavin's particular successes at PopCo also include the original drawings for Sailor Sam and his Amazing Clam, who, I am sure Gavin won't mind me saying, started life as simply a doodle on an abandoned technical drawing. Those who know their PopCo lore will also recognise Gavin as one of the co-designers on the 1984 PopCo logo redesign project. The design consultants were so taken with some of his boat and ship diagrams that he was brought in to help modify them into the graphic we now use. Gavin left the mechanics division some years ago to complete his solo voyage around the world, which, some of you may remember, PopCo sponsored.' Mac pauses at this point and we all clap Gavin's achievement. 'Now it seems that we are collaborating again. Gavin's new company has designed a range of products intended for the trainee sailor or for those who want to learn to become a team through sailing. We are trialling it here over the next two weeks and I am sure you will give Gavin all your support in making this work for him and for PopCo. And for those of you surprised to see a boat inside this hall – shame on you! Read your lateral-thinking notes again. And be prepared, because there are a lot more surprises in store for you with Gavin. So I will hand you over. Ahoy!'

'He is so embarrassing,' mutters Esther.

Mac leaves via the stage door and we are left standing there looking at Gavin.

'Hello,' he says. 'Well, I don't think I'll be able to live up to that introduction.'

He has an honest face and scruffy blond hair. We laugh politely.

'Before I begin, any questions?'

Dan puts his hand up. 'What was it like sailing around the world?'

Gavin smiles. 'It was, well, hard to describe, actually. Tell you what, I couldn't walk on dry land for almost a week afterwards.

My balance wouldn't adjust. Anyway, the whole experience was very intense. There are these amazing moments when you just feel like you are part of the sky, and then the sun starts to set and you suddenly really understand that you live on a planet. Some nights the sun would seem to set for hours, and the whole sky would be red. Then there were the storms. One time I didn't think I was going to make it. I couldn't get the sails down quickly enough and I lost my jib in the sea. And then there was the loneliness, which could get very intense. You just don't speak to anyone for weeks at a time. But then that's all part of it; the solitude. You come out of the experience a different person, that's for sure. And no one recognises you because of the suntan and the beard.' He looks around himself awkwardly. 'I think I might get off this stage now. I feel like I'm at a book event, although there are far too many of you for that to be true.'

He hops down and walks over to the boat. He pulls a chair over and sits down. Those of us who aren't sitting down now do so as well. 'There, that's cosier,' he says, although he looks odd sitting down, like he's the kind of person who should be constantly moving around, doing things to sails.

'Did you write a book?' asks Mitzi.

'Yes. But don't make me tell you about it. Then this really will feel like a book signing. And there's nothing more depressing than a book signing.' Gavin gets up again and starts walking around the boat, touching things. 'OK. Now, Mac has told you that the purpose of this is teambuilding. That's true. You are going to learn to sail, in small teams. But I am hoping that some of you have sailed before, because those who have are going to function as team-leaders. Mac did indicate that some of you had included sailing as a hobby on your CVs. So who here is an experienced sailor?'

Five or six people put up their hands, including Dan and Chloë.

'Great,' says Gavin. 'Marvellous. You can never be sure with PopCo admin.'

Weird. I'd have said that PopCo admin always get everything spot on; mysteriously so.

Gavin calls the experienced people over to the boat next to him. 'Great. Now, could each of you tell us a bit about yourself? You could include where you learnt to sail, your strong points and your weaknesses and anything else you want to add.'

The first person to speak is Chloë. She pushes her long hair behind her ears before starting. I don't think I have actually heard her speak before. She has a soft accent that I can't place but sounds vaguely Celtic.

'Hello. My name is Chloë, for those of you who don't already know. I'm based at the videogames division in Berkshire, working with the RPG team, where I work on concept design and storyline development. Um, I learnt to sail with my parents, from being really very small. There isn't really anything more to say. I've sailed small yachts on my own. I've got a couple of RYA certificates and that's about it.'

'Thanks, Chloë,' says Gavin.

The next person up is the guy I thought looked like a bouncer/philosophy student before, Frank.

'Yeah, um, hi. I work with Kieran's team in the Virtual Worlds Development division in Berkshire. I grew up in a children's home by a river and they taught us all to sail there. After I left there, I crewed boats for a while before I came to work for PopCo.'

Next up is Xavier, a designer from Spain, who has his own yacht. Then Imogen, the PA, who sails every summer with her boyfriend. Then it's Dan's turn. I never knew he sailed, so this is new for me too.

'My grandfather was a fisherman in Dartmouth before the war,' he says. 'My father learnt to sail from him and I learned from them both. There's not much more to say. After I graduated from art college I did a brief stint working for a racing yacht design firm before I applied for the PopCo job. I haven't sailed for a while but I remember everything about it. It's not really something you forget; like driving a car.'

'Dartmouth, eh?' Gavin says. 'Well, we'll be going there soon, and you can visit some of your old haunts. Right. Now, so I can just get acquainted with what these people know, do the rest of you want to take a break for half an hour or so? See you back here at, say, 10:45?'

I notice that not one of the experienced sailors has followed instructions and talked about their strengths and weaknesses. No one does that voluntarily: you have to really interrogate people to get that kind of information out of them.

* * *

Esther and I fall into step and walk outside into the sunshine.

'I'm scared of drowning and stuff,' she says.

'Yeah, me too.'

We lie down on the grass and start smoking. Ben and Hiro seem to be coming in our direction and Esther waves at them to come and sit with us. 'That guy was looking for you yesterday, by the way,' she says to me. 'Did he find you?'

'Yeah, thanks,' I say.

Hiro flops down next to me. 'Hi,' he says. 'How's it going?'

'We were saying that we are scared of drowning,' I say.

'Nah, there's no water around here. This is all going to be theory, I reckon.'

Ben has sat down too. He is cleaning his glasses on the edge of his shirt.

'What do you do? At PopCo, I mean?' I ask Hiro.

'Computer admin,' he says quickly.

'Oh, Esther does that too,' I say. 'Don't you, Esther?'

She gives me a funny look. 'Yeah,' she says.

Esther and Hiro are fizzing now; something's going on. They're sitting still but yet they seem as if they are dancing around each other like spinning quantum particles. And suddenly they're not looking at each other. Why? What did Mac want to see them both about on Saturday night? Maybe the computer admin staff needed some sort of special dispensation to come here. But I am fairly sure Esther doesn't work in computer admin. Otherwise, surely she would have told me the other day in the gazebo, instead of saying that she couldn't tell me what she did.

'I can't even bloody swim apart from the doggy paddle,' Esther says, breaking the unnatural silence. 'And a stupid head-in-the-air kind of breast-stroke.' She mimes what she means and we all laugh.

'I think we'll have life-jackets,' says Ben.

'I love the phrase "breast-stroke",' says Hiro.

I lie on the grass, smoking my cigarette, listening to Esther, Hiro and, to a lesser extent, Ben, finish the sailing conversation and start chatting about clubs that play guitar music and where you can get dope around here. I have caught Ben's eye only once and we have exchanged a half-smile. Now, mixed in with birdsong and the chatter of my colleagues, I can faintly pick out the noise of children playing: the Kid Lab sounds I first heard last week. Where do the kids go? I haven't even seen one child in the time I have been here so far.

The Great Hall is cool and echoey despite the escalating heat outside. Once inside, we are quickly divided into our sailing 'teams', according to what seems to be some strange mathematical function in Gavin's head. Some people have been split apart from friends and jumbled up but Esther and I are both assigned Dan as our team leader, while Hiro and Ben are put with Chloë. Our team also includes Grace from robotics, while Chloë's team has Richard, her boss.

After an introductory lesson on 'Parts of the Boat', each team is assigned a half-hour slot to play around on the training yacht with Gavin and their particular skipper. Our slot isn't until half-past four, so, after lunch, Dan, Esther, Grace and I get the chefs to make us big flasks of tea and we climb up to the hill fort to clear our heads. It's already a hot day and I have my cardigan tied around my waist.

'So how come you specialise in AI?' Dan asks Grace, once we are settled among the old stones with our tea. 'Did you have experience before you joined PopCo?'

'Yeah, I worked on an Internet project after university.'

'What was it?' I ask.

Grace pushes some black, crimped hair out of her eye. 'It was this chat-room programme,' she says. 'Designed to mimic real conversation. We programmed in responses to typical statements, and "taught" the programme how to respond to various types of conversation. If the human chat partner ended a statement with an exclamation mark, for example, the bot would say, "Really?" It didn't work that well, although research is still going on in that area.' She sounds a bit jaded by it all.

'Weren't you that into it?' Esther asks.

'It was all right.' Grace frowns. 'I did always want to work in mechanical robotics, though. It's what I specialised in at university. There are so many exciting things going on in robotics. I mean, it's such a young area. No one even knows how to get a bot to walk on two legs yet.'

'Really?' Dan says, sounding surprised.

'Yeah. Well, have you ever seen a fully functional two-legged robot?'

'I'm sure I have,' Dan says. 'Don't they have them on all those

Science Channel programmes about Japanese inventions? I'm sure I've seen two-legged robots.'

'Yeah, but have you ever seen the way they move? You can't get them to navigate any sort of three-dimensional terrain; they just fall over. Getting a robot to navigate its way across a flat surface takes more programming than you'd imagine. It would take millions of neural processes for your brain to get your body to climb over one of these rocks. Trying to replicate those processes in a robot is pretty impossible. It makes you wonder about GM food . . .'

'GM food?' Dan says. 'What's that got to do with it?'

'We have had various forms of robotics much longer than we have had gene technology,' Grace explains. 'And we can't even make something walk on two legs. When you work in something like robotics – and I have heard biologists say this too – you start thinking all sorts of things about nature, and about whether living creatures were designed or not. It's easy for normal people to forget just how complex creatures and plants are. When you think about all the billions of things a biological organism can do at the same time as walking on two legs, such as think, sweat, talk, menstruate and so on, you realise that its design is something so far beyond our understanding. We couldn't make anything that complicated, or a hundredth as complicated, or a thousandth as complicated . . . How anyone thinks they can splice genes in and out of different species and actually improve on nature is just absurd, you know? It's like breaking something you can't fix. It's a one-way function, if you know what that is . . . ?'

I am nodding. 'Yeah,' I say.

'What is it?' asks Dan.

'In maths, it is a function that only goes one way,' I explain. 'It is sometimes called a "trap door function" as well. The idea is that, like falling into a trap door, it is something that is easy to do but hard to get out of. You can feed a number into a one-way function and get a result, but, for whatever reason, you can't easily take the result, feed that into anything and get the number you started with. So the function works one way.'

He looks blank. I am not explaining it very well.

'It's like, if I take the function $x+5$, and say the result equals y, I can always find x again by taking 5 away from y. But many one-way functions are so complicated, or lead to numbers so big, that you simply can't unravel them. It's the mathematical equivalent of mixing paint. If I have a tin of blue paint and a tin of yellow paint and I mix them, I will get two tins of green paint. Once I have that green paint, there's no way of getting the tin of blue paint back again. You can't un-mix paint.'

'That's it exactly,' Grace says. 'With GM technology, you could mess around mixing up genetic equivalents of the blue paint and yellow paint not even realising that you'd never be able to get those paints back again. We already see super weeds, resistant to any kind of herbicide or predator – they already exist. You can't undo the spread of mutation once it's there. It's terrifying. Don't even get me started on nanotechnology . . .'

'I heard that some of the bio-tech companies have made plants with no seeds,' Esther says. 'So that the growers have to go back to the company each time for more. I imagine that if that spread it would be the end of the world. If all plants stopped producing seeds . . .'

'Well, at least that can't happen,' Grace says. 'Think about it. If there are no seeds, the attribute can't spread. Barrenness seems to be the one thing nature forbids. It can't spread because there are no seeds.'

'Oh yeah,' says Esther. She looks embarrassed. 'I still don't like the idea of eating all that stuff, though. I don't like the idea of having vegetables with locust genes in them or whatever, especially since I'm a vegan.'

'Me neither,' says Grace.

For a few minutes we lie on the grass in silence, all our eyes looking up at the sky. I think about how I am looking at the same sky I looked at when I was a kid, but everything underneath it has changed. And when you are a child you know things will change, because everyone says that things do, and they do, too, but slowly enough for you not to notice. Political regimes change, things blow up and people die and suddenly the world is completely different. But the sky stays the same, and the moon waxes and wanes the same each month. But if people could change those things they would. Imagine if you could advertise using the moon. It could be – what? – a giant hamburger, or some company's logo. Usually when I think things like this I get a tingle and then think about something else. For some reason today I vow that if this happens in my lifetime I will seriously think about killing myself. What sort of person would sell the moon if they could? For a million pounds, would I sell the moon if I could?

'No one ever cracked that Go problem, did they?' Dan says lazily.

'No,' Grace says. 'That would be such a breakthrough. It's not just PopCo offering prizes for the person who works out how to get a machine to play Go properly. I think Microsoft has a huge prize, too. Half of us in Robotics and AI are working on something in our spare time but it's pretty impossible. Are any of you any good at Go?'

'Alice is,' Dan says.

I shake my head. 'I'm not *that* good.'

Esther's rolling a joint. 'You know that guy I was talking to before? Hiro? Well it turns out that he's the reigning PopCo champion. Cool, huh?'

'You should play him,' Dan says to me.

'I'm really not that good,' I say again. 'I bet Grace is good.'

'Are you?' Esther says.

'Not really. I'd never played before I came to work here,' Grace says. 'But I play almost every day now. It really is the ultimate AI geek game, it turns out. Don't know how I never played it before.' She grins.

'Why can't computers play Go?' Dan asks. 'I've never really understood that.'

'Pattern recognition,' Esther says, frowning. 'Or something like that.'

'Yeah,' says Grace. 'Machines can't recognise subtle patterns the way humans can. It's one of the main things that separates people from machines, actually: machines process data a lot faster than normal humans, but humans can recognise faces and voices in a way that no one can get computers to match – or even come close to. You could pick out your best friend in a crowd but a computer would only see light and shade. With Go, a lot of it is about seeing patterns. The Go masters think a lot about the shapes they create on a board, and strive for beauty as well as victory. Computers can't do that. Another problem is that computers can't understand that sometimes you may have to sacrifice some territory to make gains later on. You know all that vaguely Zen stuff about not being able to lose without winning and vice versa? That's what you can't teach computers.'

Dan frowns. 'Can't they be taught to do something like a risk assessment, to work out the consequences of every possible move? Then, if it seemed that the computer would be successful from making what seems to be a "losing" move, it would simply see it as a winning move and play it anyway?'

'Well, that's how chess programs work,' Grace explains. 'They call it the "brute force" method. A chess programme simply runs a set of *what if*s to see whether particular moves would be successful. But there are too many possible moves in Go. A chess-board only has 64 places you can move but a Go board has 361. The computing power required to work out all the possible combinations of moves would be pretty staggering. But it's like the whole thing with recognising faces. A good human player can look at a Go board and instinctively know whether territory can be captured or not. It seems to be almost impossible to teach a computer to do the same thing. People are just better at seeing patterns.'

361. The square of 19. Still looking at the sky, I find myself thinking about prime numbers. It used to be a habit – almost an obsession – of mine, to immediately wonder if a number is prime or not. I even just did it with 361, even though I know it's a square. Perhaps it's because I have a prime number birthday: the 19th of July 1973. 19 is prime, as is 7, as is 1973. These numbers have no whole number divisors apart from one and themselves. There aren't many prime years in which to have been born, actually. In the twentieth century you've basically got 1901, 1907, 1913, 1931, 1933, 1949, 1951, 1973, 1979, 1987, 1993, 1997 and 1999. When I realised I had a prime number birthday, I then wanted everything about my life to be prime. The primes are, after all, the most mysterious and beautiful numbers in the universe. You can't ever break them apart, but every other number breaks down into its prime factors eventually. They are the building blocks of everything.

So I am sitting here on sun-warmed earth, leaning against grey rock and I close my eyes. Behind them, all I can see, suddenly, are building blocks abstracted in the dark. The rock behind me, the rocks under the ground, the blocks in all the structures on the PopCo Estate below me. You can build something and you can smash it up and bury it, but the blocks always stay the same. Prime numbers, genes, atoms. The blocks have to stay the same, don't they?

Chapter Fourteen

My grandfather is making marmalade while my grandmother works in her study.

'What does she do up there all day?' I ask, keeping away from the big pan like I have been told to do.

'She does maths,' he says simply.

'What sort of maths?'

'Complicated maths.'

'What sort of complicated maths exactly?'

'She's trying to prove the Riemann Hypothesis.'

'The *what?*'

He laughs. 'Quite. And she says *I* set myself impossible tasks.'

I don't know what he means by this.

At the end of the afternoon I am allowed to help slip pieces of muslin over the jars and secure them with elastic bands. Then we write on the labels, *Orange, 1983* and put them in the larder. Soon after that, my grandmother comes down from her study and yawns, which is my grandfather's cue to pour her a whisky over ice.

'What's the Riemann Hypothesis?' I ask her immediately.

She laughs. 'It's the work of the Devil.'

'Is it important?' I ask next.

'Yes, to some people,' she says, with an amused expression.

It's always hard to know what to talk about with my grandmother. It's not that she is frightening but she really is incredibly busy, all the time. My grandfather will chat with me about anything: how weather works, Ian Botham, electrical circuits, the right way to sand wood, how to mix paint and so on; but my grandmother has always been frustratingly enigmatic. Occasionally I have shyly asked her questions like, 'What are we having for supper?' or 'Do you think it's going to rain?' and she has just absent-mindedly said something back like, 'Oh, um, ask your grandfather,' and then disappeared upstairs to her study. Once, to avoid this response, I asked her what her favourite colour was. She just looked at me with a really puzzled expression and then simply said she didn't know. I think she likes me, but definitely not as much as my grandfather does. Anyway, I have asked her about the Riemann Hypothesis because this is obviously the thing she is most interested in and perhaps she will like me more if I understand the thing she is most interested in. But answers are not forthcoming, so I change tack.

'What's the most important maths anyone has ever done?' I ask.

My grandfather comes and sits opposite me on his favourite chair. 'Now there's a question,' he says. 'There's a question indeed.' He glances over at my grandmother, and then back at me. 'The most important maths. Hmm.'

'Euclid?' says my grandmother, more to him than me.

'Hmm. It has to be Bletchley Park, really, doesn't it?'

She looks sad for a second. 'Well . . .'

He looks at me. 'Have you ever heard of Bletchley Park?'

I shake my head, imagining ducks in a pond.

'This was classified information until very recently . . .'

'Is it to do with the war?' I ask, instantly thrilled.

'Oh, yes.'

My grandmother sips her drink while my grandfather starts telling me all about how, during the Second World War, the most intelligent mathematicians, linguists, crossword addicts, music theorists and chess players were rounded up and sent to this secret mansion between Oxford and Cambridge to crack German codes. He tells me in such detail about this mansion, with its outside units called 'huts' and its ballroom and its gardens that it almost seems as if he was there himself. My grandmother is quiet as he speaks but occasionally she nods and raises her eyebrows, as if confirming what he is saying. He tells me all about something called the Enigma machine, which turned messages into (supposedly) unbreakable code, and how the German operators often made mistakes in its use so that it was easier for the British cryptanalysts to break their messages.

'The German keys changed at midnight,' he says. 'Intercepted messages would start pouring in and then the race would be on to find that day's key . . .'

'What do you mean, the key?' I ask.

'The setting for the Enigma machine,' he says. 'Once you know what the setting is, you can unscramble the message. There was a certain amount of information that the cryptanalysts would use to their advantage, like how the same setting couldn't be used more than twice, that the new setting couldn't use consecutive wheels and so on . . . Enigma would never encipher a letter as itself, so that also helped to narrow things down . . . But people really did think Enigma was unbreakable. Sometimes, British Intelligence forces even had to stage events – the movement of a particular fleet, perhaps – so that they would know what the German messages for that day would say. Of course, once you know roughly what a message says, it is easier to unravel the cipher version of it. The cryptanalysts would also look for encrypted messages that looked like they might be weather reports. After all, everyone knows what the weather has been. But with Enigma, a key is only valid for twenty-four hours and then it changes. The Allied Forces needed to find a way to crack the code, not just get individual keys.'

'So how did they do it?' I ask.

He chuckles. 'Bombes.'

'Bombs?'

He spells it out. 'Bombes. They were early computers, originally conceived by a Polish scientist but refined by Alan Turing, who was the most well-known cryptanalyst at Bletchley. In fact, Turing's machines formed the basis for all computing today.'

I have never seen a computer, although I have heard that James has something called a ZX Spectrum on which he plays games to do with space. Before I became shipwrecked and moved, there was a craze at my school for hand-held games, which are like little computers. I had a go on my friend's Frogger game once, but my frog died immediately and then she took the game back.

'Turing,' says my grandmother wistfully. 'He really was a genius. How could they have let that happen to him?'

'What happened to him?' I ask.

'He killed himself. With a poisoned apple.'

'Like Snow White?'

'Just like Snow White.'

I shudder. I've only recently become aware of people killing themselves and the very concept gives me nightmares. I cannot imagine any reason that someone would actually want to die and I don't think I'll understand it as a grown-up, either.

'Turing was a great man,' my grandfather says. 'As well as his bombes, he invented "mind machines", imaginary computers that showed what would happen with certain maths problems.'

'But they did actually have computers in the war?' I say. I thought they had only just invented computers a few years ago. Everyone talks about them as if they are new.

'Yes, sort of,' says my grandfather. 'Anyway, it was because Turing was such a mathematical genius that he was able to construct all these ways of cracking the Enigma ciphers. Of course, there were lots of other people there too, working in the same sorts of ways, but they say that without his input the Allied war effort would have been put back several years. Interestingly, Turing also wanted to prove the Riemann Hypothesis. Anyway, there you go. The most important maths. It won the war for us, or so people say.'

'Why did they have musicians and crossword people at Bletchley Park?' I ask, not yet finished with this conversation.

'Because people like that are good at seeing patterns. A lot of cryptanalysis is about having half of something – or less – and being able to guess the rest. Obviously, crossword people would be good at that, and linguists. Meanwhile, the mathematics experts were able to finish patterns using their knowledge of the patterns of numbers, and probability and so on. Those who know a lot about music theory understand music mathematically, and music has patterns based on maths. Musicians understand intuitively which notes fit where in a melody. A lot of code-breaking demanded those sorts of skills as well. And music is, after all, completely based around numbers . . .'

'Is it?' My eyes must be wide. I thought music was the furthest thing from maths in the world. I thought music was all about letters: A, B, C and so on, all the way up to G, which is where the notes run out and you have to start again.

'Oh yes. Have you ever heard of Pythagoras and his urn?'

'No.'

'Have you heard of Pythagoras at all?'

'No.'

'Well, Pythagoras was a famous mathematician in Ancient Greece. He invented something called Pythagoras's Theorem, which will be very important when you do geometry and trigonometry in a couple of years . . .'

'Can you explain it now?'

'No, we'll get so far from our starting-point we'll never find our way back.' My grandfather smiles. 'I can show you tomorrow if you're still interested. Anyway, Pythagoras filled his urn with water and banged it with a stick – or something like that. The urn made a pleasing sound. A *musical note*, is how we would describe what he got. Pythagoras experimented with water in the urn until he came upon the following observation. If, after playing his first note, he tipped exactly half of the water out of the urn and hit it with his stick, the note he got was very pleasing next to the first one. If he tipped half the water out again, so he was left with a quarter of the amount he started with, and banged it with his stick, this note was also pleasing when played next to the first two. If he tipped out two-thirds of the original amount, leaving him with a third, this was a pleasing note too. If, however, he left some other quantity of water in the urn, an amount that wasn't a precise fraction of the original amount, he got *dissonance*, which means that the note sounded wrong. And that's the basis of music theory.'

'Did he use lots of urns?' I ask.

'What do you mean?'

'Well, rather than keep filling and emptying the same urn . . .'

'Yes. I've never really thought about that but yes, he must have done.' My grandfather looks pleased, like I have just solved one of the riddles he always gives me, but it's so obvious. In my mind, when I imagine this man Pythagoras, I don't see him all flustered, trying to mark off points on one urn, with his robes all twisted and his face all red. I imagine him calm and serene, with a row of urns lined up like keys in a glockenspiel, all measured out perfectly, playing beautiful music. But something else about this doesn't make sense to me.

'Why does a third work?' I ask.

My grandfather makes his concentrating face. 'Sorry?'

'You said he kept halving the amount of water. One, a half, a quarter and so on . . . Why a third?'

'Oh, Alice,' he says. 'You do ask good questions.' He laughs and glances over at my grandmother, who is also smiling. 'The pattern is 1, $\frac{1}{2}$, $\frac{1}{3}$, $\frac{1}{4}$, $\frac{1}{5}$, $\frac{1}{6}$ and so on. It doesn't reduce by half every time, but by whole number denominators of one . . .'

'Whole number . . . *What*?'

'In a fraction, the bit on the underneath is called a denominator,' my grandmother explains. 'That's the bit that goes down by one every time.' And this is amazing, because it's the first time she has ever explained anything to me – and she has made an effort to explain it in child-language as well. At this moment, I feel closer to her than I ever have before and I resolve to really try to understand what she does, so we can talk about it all the time.

Also: I bet I could solve the Riemann Hypothesis, whatever that is. I bet I could solve anything if I tried hard enough. I am definitely going to be famous for solving a mystery or a puzzle that has stumped grown-ups for ever. This is my plan. Sometimes, when my grandfather is out and my grandmother is working, I make up recipes in the kitchen. I am absolutely certain that one day I will stumble on the special combination of ingredients that will make me rich and famous. Magic biscuits that make you fly; invisible blancmange; mould that has healing properties. I imagine having the Riemann Hypothesis explained to me and the answer arriving in my brain a split-second later, like it was running for a train.

I look at my grandmother, wisps of her grey hair escaping from her long plait, and my grandfather, with his blue shirt-sleeves still rolled up, and they suddenly exchange a comfortable, happy smile. The house still smells heavy and sweet with freshly made marmalade and the sun is now setting outside. I know that in about five minutes my grandfather will get up and switch on the electric light and my grandmother will play one of her records, probably something by Bach. But just now, as they exchange their smile and sip their drinks, I imagine us suspended here in this moment of happiness for ever and I have no shipwrecked feelings at all.

The next day my grandfather receives a package.

'Aha,' he says. 'This is it.'

'What is it?' I ask him, intrigued. His face is lit up like Christmas. 'Is it a present?'

'What? No. Not a present. But very exciting. Look.'

He shows me pages of what seems to be a copy of an old-looking manuscript. There are handwritten words that I can't read, and strange pictures of plants and people and animals. Something about it makes me feel strange. I don't quite know why. Perhaps it's because I don't recognise anything on the pages. It looks like you should be able to recognise things: the words, the illustrations and so on; but it's like a book you'd find in a dream; almost real but not quite.

'What is it?' I ask.

'This is the Voynich Manuscript,' my grandfather says proudly.

'And what do you do with it?'

'You try to read it.'

'Is it in code, then?'

'Oh yes. Or at least, that's what people think. This . . .' He fans the pages carefully. 'This is one of the oldest unbroken codes in history. And I am going to break it.'

'Can I help?' I immediately ask, unable to stop myself.

'Yes,' he says. 'You certainly can help.'

What? I am actually being allowed to help with an important, secret, grown-up project? Bloody hell. Slightly dazed, I go upstairs and immediately sharpen all my pencils.

Once school starts, I fall into the following routine. I get up at seven-thirty, which leaves me just enough time to get dressed and have breakfast before I have to run for the village bus. Tracey waits at the same bus stop as me for her special school bus (which I will also take next year when I move up to the comprehensive) but we never speak. Sometimes on the bus I reply to letters from Rachel, who is back at her boarding school. More often, though, I take a fragment of the Voynich Manuscript that I have traced the night before, and study that. After school, I walk to the bus stop in town, breathing the bonfirey, marshmallowy smells of autumn. I love this time of year, when people start to rehearse for Christmas plays and pantomimes, and the air feels like it's full of magic spells. This is the time of year when arriving home after school feels cosy, like going back to bed.

When my bus arrives back in the village it is usually almost dark and I walk across the green and through Hang Man's Lane, down the alley leading to our garden and then in through the back door. My grandfather cooks stew most evenings, with root vegetables and prunes, and while it bubbles away on the stove, we sit down and he fills me in on the work he has done so far that day. I am not old enough to have homework yet, so we spend most of the evening working on the manuscript, except for when my grandmother comes downstairs, and we are expected to put our work away and fetch drinks for her. We also stop for dinner, and sometimes I watch my grandparents play chess or Risk together afterwards. Occasionally I am allowed to play too, but I never win. The only night our routine is different is on a Tuesday, when my grandfather compiles the crossword for the local newspaper. On a Wednesday morning he cycles into town to deliver it to the newspaper offices. (He has decided that using the car all the time is too 'lazy'.) He always buys toffee on his way back, and so on a Wednesday evening we eat toffee while we work, and I have to clean my teeth for twice as long on a Wednesday night.

One Wednesday afternoon, I am waiting at the bus stop thinking about toffee when these two men come up to me. I wouldn't notice, except that, as they approach, I can hear one say to the other, 'No, that's definitely the Butler kid. Look at her hair.' I consider running for it but that always looks suspicious so I stand my ground.

'Hello,' one of them says to me.

I say nothing back. Is this danger? Or are these people just friends of my grandfather? I remember that in our Stranger Danger sessions at school, we were told not to believe a grown-up if they say something like, 'I'm a friend of your dad and he asked me to drive you home.' So I am ready for this. I don't have many self-defence moves but I will knee one of them in the balls if I have to.

The other one takes a step towards me and I instinctively move back.

'Don't scare her,' says the other one. Then to me: 'Don't mind him. He's got no manners. My name is Mike and my friend is called John. We've been trying to get in touch with your grandfather.'

Still, I don't say anything.

'We had his number a couple of years ago but we lost it. And we don't know where he lives any more. We wondered if you could point us in the right direction? We're old mates of his from the Fountain. We've got a proposition for him. So . . . ?'

Now I know they are lying. My grandparents have only had a telephone in the house for about a year at the most. And it was my father who always drank in the Fountain, not my grandfather. Knowing this makes me frightened; my small heart an elastic-band ball, bouncing in my chest. These are definitely bad men. Do I run now?

'I'm not allowed to talk to strangers,' I say.

'We're not strangers. We're friends of your . . .'

The one called John interrupts. 'Oh leave it, Mike. They're taught to ignore all this stuff now. You can't ask kids the bloody time these days. Let's just leave it. This little bitch isn't going to tell us anything.'

Tears spring into my eyes. No one has ever spoken to me like this before. My bus, welcoming, warm and full of nice grown-ups pulls up but something tells me not to get on it. If these men know my bus route, they'll have a much greater chance of working out where I live, and I really, really never want to see these men again. So, although every part of me wants to get on the bus, I glance at it dismissively and then look at my watch, as if I am thinking, *Hmm, this isn't my bus. Wonder what time my bus will be along?* The bus soon moves off and I am left alone with the two men again. I wait until the split-second when it seems right and then, seeing no alternative, I run for it. I run through the shopping arcade and out into the main part of town, not looking to see if they are running after me. In a few minutes I make it to the police station, and, after telling them that some strange men asked me to go with them to look at some puppies, they drive me home.

When the police have gone, I tell my grandparents everything.

'Excellent,' my grandfather says. 'You did the right thing.'

My grandmother isn't so pleased. 'You should have got on the bus, Alice.'

'But then they would have known . . .'

'There are other ways of finding out where someone lives. You shouldn't put yourself in danger.'

I can't help it. I know I have been brave, but now I start to cry.

'And lying to the police . . .'

'That was quite right, Alice,' my grandfather says, emphatically. He looks at my grandmother. 'We *don't* want other people knowing about this. Especially not the police. Imagine going to court and having to be completely public about all of this? It would cause mayhem. And it served those two right. If they get picked up for this then . . . Well, it'll teach them to swear at a child.'

'Maybe the police *should* know. What are these people going to do next? Kidnap Alice? Try to take the necklace? I don't know why she even has the bloody necklace anyway, Peter. It's like you've made her into your walking, living proof. You've branded her. It's like Hardy's postcard: utterly ridiculous. It's not safe. And it's not fair, either.'

I have never heard my grandparents argue before. I wish they would stop. This is all too confusing. What on earth is Hardy's postcard? What's wrong with me having the necklace? Although it's the most exciting thing I own, I suddenly don't want it any more. My grandmother gets up and pours herself a drink, which she almost never does, and fetches me a glass of water.

My grandfather is pacing the room now.

'This is nothing like Hardy's postcard. He didn't have proof. I do.'

'Well, why don't you just publish it, then?'

'Beth, we have talked about this. You understood.'

'That was before strange men started abusing my granddaughter in the street.'

'Look, can you stop making this more dramatic than it actually is? Yes, I admit that those men aren't particularly nice but they would never, ever hurt a child. They want my address so that they can come and try to persuade me to tell them what I know. They, like every other bugger out there, think that one day someone is simply going to give them a treasure map and they'll be able to just go off around the world and claim something that doesn't belong to them. Well, I'm not having it. Even if they did come here, I could deal with them. What happened tonight was very frightening for Alice, I know, but it's not as sinister as it seemed. Alice did the right thing, and I am very proud of her. Now, I am going to go out for a while to make sure this does not happen again. Give Alice some strong, sweet tea, please.'

The door slams and I am left alone with my grandmother. Although she is obviously cross, she makes me a cup of tea with several sugars in it, and strokes my hair for a while as I drink it. Then she distractedly makes herself another drink and looks at the clock on the mantelpiece. She sits down and sighs.

'What is going on?' I ask, simply.

She laughs nervously. 'Where would I start?'

I put on my best grown-up voice and say: 'At the beginning.'

Chapter Fifteen

At half-past four we walk down the hill to the Great Hall and clamber into the boat. I had expected it to feel solid but it is actually on some kind of spring system and wobbles when you walk on it. We learn what things to hold on to to avoid going overboard and Gavin explains that if we were on water we would have to wear lifejackets. On rough water, he says, we would be tied to the boat with a line. Gavin controls the 'wind' with these big fans and we have a go at putting sails up and taking them down again. We learn not to get in the way of the big boom when it gybes from one side to the other (being hit by it is, apparently, the number-one cause of going overboard) and not to get the sails tangled when putting them up. Gavin keeps explaining that this thing or that thing is much better on water, and easier to understand, which is odd considering that he has invented this indoor training boat. It's quite thrilling when the boat heels over in the 'wind', though, and I feel quite excited imagining doing that in the water. In fact, the more I think about it, the more keen I am to actually get in some water: it's turned into a very hot day.

There is a swimming-pool next to the Sports Hall complex, apparently, so after our sailing session is over I leave the others and walk back to my room and dig out some navy blue knickers that look like shorts and my bikini top, which I put on under my clothes. I grab a towel from the bathroom and start walking slowly across the grounds, thinking about cold water on my body. As I walk, I hear the Kid Lab noises again but they fade as I get nearer to the Sports Hall. When I get there, the sounds have completely gone. There are no children anywhere.

The small swimming-pool is entirely deserted, the water as flat as a mirror. It is not full of leaves and dead things as I had feared but is surprisingly clean and fresh-looking. Next to it are some gazebo-style changing rooms, which, it turns out, have cardboard boxes full of little plastic packages containing PopCo swimsuits and towels. The swimsuits are white, with PopCo written across the chest. I decide to stick to my own clothes. After stripping down, I drop my towel by the edge of the pool and dive straight in. That's better. Ice, ice, and then, gradually, body temperature. I swim a couple of lengths and feel almost normal again. My hair is getting wet, which is a bad thing, but I may just keep it plaited for the foreseeable future and then it won't matter what happens to it. Two plaits, and a slick of Vaseline; that'll do it. I don't think it's actually that normal to put Vaseline on your hair but I refuse to pay for all that brightly packaged funky-hair shit they sell in chemists. It's all just grease, whatever they call it. It's bad enough that I buy anti-frizz shampoo and conditioner.

I am sitting on the edge of the pool, dangling my feet in the water, when I realise someone is walking this way. *Ben*, I think, for a second. But it's not. It's Georges. What's he doing here?

'Alice,' he says, coming over to where I am sitting.

'Georges,' I say back.

He's wearing knee-length shorts and a thin linen shirt with some expensive-looking sports sandals. He slips these off and sits down next to me, dangling his feet in the water next to mine.

'God, it's a bit cold,' he says.

'You just have to get used to it,' I say. 'How are you?'

'Me? Busy, stressed, you know how it is.'

I laugh. 'I'm a creative. I never get stressed.'

He laughs too. 'So . . .'

'What?'

'How are you finding all this? The project?'

'I'm not sure,' I say honestly. 'Ask me again in a week.'

'I hear that some of the lateral thinking hasn't been up to much.'

'It's all right,' I say. Then I frown. 'Are we focus-grouping or something?'

'What? Oh, no. Sorry. I did actually come looking for you, because . . .'

'Because . . . ?' I turn to look at him, trying to erase what's in my eyes before he sees it. There's always been something about Georges; there always will be. I notice how skinny his brown legs look in his shorts and I can see him, suddenly, as he must have been as a child. But this man is the corporate face of all the creatives at PopCo. He is our boss. He is almost as remote as the moon. When he turns to kiss me, I allow myself to want him for five seconds, which I count in my head, as his lips meet mine, his hand resting lightly on my arm. But then I pull away and stand up.

'In a parallel universe,' I say, before I walk away. And then, perhaps not loud enough for him to hear me: 'In dreams.'

My room feels cool and almost dusty after the heat outside. Somehow I manage to get inside and flop onto the bed before I realise that two envelopes have been pushed under the door. For a few more seconds I lie there with the pleasant chill of the duvet on my back, frozen in time, *incommunicado*. Then I get off the bed and pick them up.

One envelope has my name on the front. The other is blank. I open the one with my name first. It's from Georges. *On my way to find you to give you this*, it says. *If I don't find you (or if I screw it up) here it is anyway.* There is a business card, blank except for Georges's name and his mobile phone number. I hold the thin card in my hand as the highlights of another life play in my head. I don't know how this life ends, or even how it would begin.

The next envelope is exactly what I feared it would be. Another thin *With Compliments* slip, this time with the following letters on it: PFTACJVPRDNN? I sit down at my desk and start working it out, using only the POPCO lines of a Vigenère square, which I quickly draw up on a piece of paper. It's cool in this room but yet I suddenly feel desperately hot. As I work on each letter of the text, I find myself hoping that the completed message will tell me something about who the sender is and what he or she wants. But this message turns out to be even weirder than the last one. It finally comes out as: areyouhappy? *Are you happy?* What? What does this mean? Why has someone sent this to me? It has definitely been sent by an amateur, I know that now. The use of the question mark has given them away. No one uses punctuation in cryptography; there really is no point. Rather than consider the contents of the note, I turn my attention to other factors: mode of sending, ink, handwriting and so on. The PopCo *With Compliments* slip is an innocuous enough piece of paper to use, I suppose. Everyone has piles of those things at work. *But we're not at work.* Did someone bring compliments slips with them to Devon? Did he or she bring them specifically to use for this purpose? I haven't seen any compliments slips since I have been here but then I didn't know that there were swimming costumes provided for us, or chefs. I examine the *With Compliments* slip again. Something about it is different from the ones we usually have, not that I even see those very often. Of course. The address. The address on these slips is the address here, not the UK headquarters in London. Does this mean anything?

Whoever sent this must have delivered it by hand today. Quite obviously that means that it is someone who works here, someone on the project, or Mac or Georges. Georges was at PopCo Towers both times I have received one of these notes, but why would he bother to send me one message in code and another in plain text? And giving me his phone number is far more incriminating than sending a note simply asking whether I am happy. I don't think it is likely to be him.

I roll a cigarette and, after lighting it, I use my lighter to burn the partial Vigenère square and the decipherment I have just completed. I know what it says and don't need evidence of it lying around. I am not sure yet that I want my correspondent to know that I am easily deciphering these messages. In fact, I am not sure I want this correspondent to know that I care. More importantly, though, I particularly don't want someone to find the deciphered message. This would compromise not only the message itself but also the key. However insignificant or absurd a message seems, you must never compromise the key.

You have to do things now, if you are going to do them at all. You really don't know what is going to happen in five minutes' time. If I don't burn this stuff now, I may never get the chance again. Anything could happen. I could go back to the swimming-pool, bang my head and wake up three months later in hospital. 'We cleared out your room, Alice. What were those weird bits of paper? Why were you decoding messages?' Since I don't know who is contacting me, I don't know whether or not I want to be connected with them. Putting things off is one of the great comforts of our lives. *I'll be home at the end of the day. My husband will come back. There will be food in the supermarket. If I run out I will just get some more.* But you never know. People threw food away before the siege of Leningrad because they didn't know what the next day would bring, and a few months later they were boiling up hand-bags for soup. You never know if you will wake up one day to find your mother dead or your father gone or that war has broken out. You just don't know.

Am I happy? I really don't know.

I look down at the surface of the desk, at Georges's card and the *With Compliments* slip. Then I burn them both, too.

*

'If you want me to start at the beginning,' my grandmother says, 'this may take some time. We have to go back to the start of the Second World War, or even a bit before.'

'The war?' I say.

She nods and sips her drink. 'You may have noticed that I seemed sad when we were discussing Bletchley Park recently. I was surprised that you didn't ask whether or not your grandfather was there during the war . . .'

'Was he?' I ask, thrilled at the thought of this.

'No. I was.'

'*You* were?'

'I was one of very few women cryptanalysts. I worked with Turing on the Naval Enigma. It was hard work but very exciting. Your grandfather and I were already lovers by the time war started, and we planned to marry. However, war puts so many plans on hold and there weren't many weddings in those years, I can tell you. We had both studied at Cambridge. I was one of the first women to actually be allowed to take a proper degree, and I, like your grandfather, read mathematics there. Alan Turing was a Fellow at Cambridge when I was an undergraduate in the thirties. I remember that he was very passionate about the anti-war movement at first, before things became more muddled after about 1934 or so. Hitler was doing all kinds of things, whipping and murdering people in the streets of Vienna and so on, and we were hearing stories all the time but no one knew what to believe. Hardly anyone wanted a war. But then it was suddenly inevitable.

'In the last two or three years before the actual declaration of war, I had graduated and started working towards a fellowship thesis but your grandfather was in a lot of trouble. He was a stubborn man even then, and was always on the wrong side of those in authority. He was passionately against war of any kind, and, one night not long before his graduation, he wrote a series of pacifist messages in chalk on some of the walls around the university. He was forced to own up eventually, and although it was chalk and washed off perfectly, they wouldn't give him his degree. They said they would do so only if he made a formal apology, but he refused. It had been a political statement, not a silly prank, he said, and then he simply left the university, vowing never to return. He stayed in Cambridge, however, and still socialised with a big group of us from the university but he always refused to apologise for what he did. It was a funny time. Turing had gone to Princeton, hoping to meet a mathematician called Gödel, but had met another Cambridge man, G. H. Hardy, instead.'

'Is this the Hardy who sent the postcard?' I ask.

'Gosh, you've got a good memory. Yes, it is the same man.'

'So what was his postcard?'

My grandmother laughs. 'This is slightly off the subject but at least it will explain your grandfather's comment earlier. Hardy was an eccentric mathematician, not unlike your grandfather in some ways. He was obsessed with cricket and proving the Riemann Hypothesis. And God. He was obsessed with a strange war he was determined to fight with God. He was always trying to trick God. He would turn up at cricket matches with a pile of work to do, pretending that he hoped it would rain so he could get some work done. He was actually double-bluffing God. He thought that God would see that he hoped for rain and give him sunshine instead – which was what he actually wanted all along. Hardy's postcard was well known. He sent it to a friend just before he was about to get on a ship to sail on some very rough seas. The postcard said he had found a proof for the Riemann Hypothesis. By this time, the Riemann Hypothesis was one of the most famous unsolved problems in mathematics. Hardy knew God wouldn't let him drown after he had sent this postcard. He would have become famous overnight if he had drowned, for ever known as the man who had solved the Riemann Hypothesis and then died. He just knew that God wasn't about to make him immortal like that, thus his "insurance policy". One very funny thing, actually, was when Paul Erdös met Hardy. Erdös is a completely eccentric mathematician as well. His name for God is the SF – the Supreme Fascist. You can imagine how the two of them got on! Anyway, that should explain Hardy's postcard.'

'I see,' I say, although I'm not sure how this fits into the argument before.

My grandmother makes another, smaller drink for herself and puts on the kettle again, possibly for more tea for me. It has started to rain outside, tiny hooves on the window, and I hope my grandfather is all right. My grandmother does make me more hot sweet tea, and switches on the gas fire before sitting back down on the sofa.

'Where were we? Oh yes. Turing had been working on the Riemann Hypothesis for some time, and meeting Hardy had made him wonder if in fact he should be working on disproving, rather than proving it. He returned to Cambridge in a strange mood, filled with even crazier-than-usual ideas about mind machines and real machines that he would build. He particularly wanted to create a machine to work on the Riemann Hypothesis, and I assisted him for a time at Cambridge. I remember my head was full of thoughts about my heroine, Ada Lovelace – Lord Byron's daughter, another woman mathematician – and I was a little bit in love with Turing although that was silly because he was, at least at Cambridge, openly gay.'

'Gay?' I say, shocked. At school, someone is 'gay' if they do something stupid. I know it really means men loving men, or women loving women, but I just find the idea confusing.

'Yes, Turing was gay. He was persecuted because of it and that is why he killed himself.' She looks at me sharply. 'Never judge anyone like that, Alice, ever. You don't know what it will do to them.'

'I won't,' I say, seriously.

'Good. Now, when war was finally declared, several of us from the mathematics department were advised to go and offer our services at this place called Bletchley Park. There were rumours about it being somewhere intellectuals could spend the war solving puzzles, which sounded right up your grandfather's street. He hadn't been told to go, having been ostracised from the university, but he came along anyway. Unfortunately, he was one of the few who were turned away. He didn't have enough discipline, they said, and couldn't be trusted with official secrets. I was accepted, which was a shock to us both. We said farewell and promised to write to each other. For years – even after the war ended and we were married – I was forbidden by law to tell your grandfather what went on at BP. He was always so good about it but it had hurt him deeply, being turned away like that. I don't think he was ever jealous of me being there with several of our friends, though, and I loved him all the more for that.

'After he was turned away from BP, he hung around for a year or so doing nothing much of note. By then he wasn't quite the pacifist he had been. Reports of what Hitler was doing were now coming through thick and fast and, mingled with the wartime propaganda, well, you couldn't have not been against him. Your grandfather tried to join up to go and fight on several occasions but was always declared mentally unfit. One day he came up to take me for tea on my day of leave. I had heard of people coming through the French Resistance to England and then being sent off to train with a secret organisation based somewhere in London. Members of this organisation were being parachute-dropped behind enemy lines all over the world where their brief was simply to blow things up, cause mayhem, indulge in sabotage – anything that would help stop the Germans. Some members of this organisation were to be sent in to help the Maquis – French freedom fighters who were organising themselves to try to overthrow the occupying army. France was of course occupied by the Germans at this time . . .'

'Yes, I know,' I say. 'I've read *lots* of war books.'

'Oh, good. Well, your grandfather went to London and made the necessary contacts. He was interviewed in an apartment somewhere near Baker Street. This organisation – SOE, it was called – was the one that attracted all the rebels during the war. The strong ones were trained up to be dropped behind enemy lines – into France, or elsewhere – but others stayed behind working on things like local customs, dialects and particularly disguises, which involved researching French dentistry, German sewing methods, the best ways to conceal cyanide pills and so on . . .'

'What?' I say. '*Dentistry*? Why?'

'Well, everyone dropped into France was to pretend to be German or French. The Germans were on the lookout for any inconsistencies at all. Everybody who was dropped into France had their dental work redone. You couldn't turn up in France with English fillings – that would be the end of you. You had to be completely fluent in French as well, of course, which your grandfather was, then. Anyway, your grandfather's stunt at Cambridge actually impressed the people at Special Operations Executive. It was the fact that he had stuck to his guns and not caved in. They needed strong-willed people like that who would not crack under interrogation. During the psychological test, a doctor showed him ink-blot pictures and told him to say what he thought they looked like. Your grandfather went mad. He hated all that psychological mumbo-jumbo, and so he basically told this chap to stop wasting his time with pictures of nothing and get out there and fight Hitler like a real man. He couldn't help himself. These outbursts were the kind of thing that meant he so often failed these sorts of tests and hadn't made it into the Army or Navy. But this was again exactly the sort of thing SOE wanted. He was accepted, and then sent to their remote training camp in Scotland, where, for thirteen weeks, he learnt how to parachute, how to kill people with his bare hands, how to pick locks, make bombs and the best way to blow up bridges. He was even observed to make sure he wouldn't sleep-talk in English! He was in his element. By the time the training was over, he was desperate to go to France, but there was a lot of waiting around in SOE. He spent a lot of the war simply waiting.'

My grandmother looks at the clock. It is almost half-past eight.

'Without going into too many more details, your grandfather had a rather peculiar time in SOE. You could ask him about it when you are a bit older. But, although I have been rambling a little, I wanted to set the scene for you properly. Your grandfather is a brave man, fiercely proud and stubborn, and he never fully forgave BP for not letting him in. Of course, he ended up having a more interesting war than any of us, but he knew – we *all* knew – that, barring Turing and a few others, your grandfather was the best crypt-analyst in the country. After the war, I settled into the work I have been doing ever since, trying to formulate a proof for the Riemann Hypothesis and teaching mathematics. But your grandfather retained a certain anti-establishment attitude, a sort of *I'll show them all* spirit. After Turing died, he became more certain that he was going to show "them". The officials at BP – the cream of the British crypt-analysts at the time – had put Turing under severe pressure. Later, of course, he was pushed over the edge by an unfair arrest to do with his homosexuality. All of this made your grandfather all the more determined to resist authority. To him, codes and ciphers were like rules – there to be broken. He wanted to show people that he, Peter Butler, could break the unbreakable, which was why he started work on the Stevenson/Heath Manuscript almost immediately.

'The Stevenson/Heath Manuscript had first come to your grand-father's attention in around 1934 or 1935 but he hadn't paid it quite as much attention at the time. The manuscript, basically a pamphlet containing an intriguing background story and then a series of strange numbers and letters, was essentially an enciphered treasure map, and, not being that interested in treasure, your grandfather glanced over the article about it in *The Cryptogram* noting only the important or absurd details, which I remember he told a group of us over dinner one night. I remember we were all quite taken with the whole idea of it, that, although the enciphered "map" had been available to the public for almost a hundred years, no one had yet claimed the treasure.'

'Did *The Cryptogram* exist all those years ago?' I ask. There is a pile of magazines with this title on the bookshelves and I know my grandfather gets them every few months or so from the American Cryptogram Association.

'Oh yes. Your grandfather was one of the very first members. It was another reason that he was so annoyed about the BP affair – most members of the ACA did work on cryptanalysis during the war in some capacity or other. Anyway, the Stevenson/Heath Manuscript was to cryptanalysts and treasure-hunters what the Riemann Hypothesis is to mathematicians. Anyone who could break it would receive not only the wealth the treasure would bring, but the immortality of being the person who actually cracked it. Your grandfather has always been obsessed with the Dumas novel, *The Count of Monte Cristo*. Do you know the story? It is about an honest sailor called Edmond Dantés who is betrayed by his friends and sent to an island prison where he is locked on his own, in a stone cell, for thirteen years. One day, another inmate, a priest, accidentally digs his way into Dantés's cell while trying to dig a tunnel out. They become friends, and the priest teaches Dantés to read and write and together they spend several years digging a tunnel out of the prison. The priest knows of some buried treasure and, just before he dies, he gives Dantés a map. He tells him to finish the tunnel and find the treasure. But although he warns Dantés to use the treasure for good, Dantés swears to use it for revenge. Once free, and rich beyond his wildest dreams, he concocts the most complex plans for this revenge and eventually brings down all those who betrayed him. But in doing so, he also loses everything he held dear, including the woman he loves. The moral of the story is that revenge doesn't make you happy in the end, but your grandfather never read it like that. He started fantasising that he would solve the puzzle of the Stevenson/Heath Manuscript, find the treasure, become famous and rich and then do something crazy like buy Cambridge University and turn it into a school for underprivileged children, or a rescue-centre for animals. It was completely absurd, the whole thing, and we argued about it. Eventually he admitted that yes, he did understand that revenge was wrong and no, he wasn't that interested in the treasure. But he still worked on that manuscript every day for about thirty-five years.'

'Then what happened?'

'He solved it.'

Chapter Sixteen

Francis Stevenson was at first taken to be a basket of eggs when he was found on the doorstep of the Younge family in a village near Tavistock, in about 1605. It was Mary Younge, the wife of the yeoman Thomas Younge, who found him. She thought he was eggs because he was in a tiny wicker basket covered with a piece of cloth. She thought he was eggs because Fanny Price had said she would leave some there. History doesn't explain why this would be: the Younge family had many of their own chickens, enough to supply the whole village with eggs. Perhaps it was because Fanny had claimed to have a very particular kind of egg she wanted her neighbour to try. Perhaps it was some sort of debt. But the basket didn't contain eggs, anyway. It contained a baby.

Mary had a fairly good idea where the baby had come from. She had recently befriended a poor young woman called Elizabeth Stevenson whom she had met at the village market. Elizabeth, heavily pregnant and desperate, was there waiting while her husband and sons tried to find work in the area, having been turned away from the Tavistock stannary. Enclosure had recently taken away their small plot of land and their cottage in a Cornish village and the family were on the move, their few possessions piled into a tiny, haphazard wagon. They had already been stopped by highwaymen three times, the last of whom had taken such pity on them that he had actually given them a few pence and spared them and their few remaining possessions. Mary had bought this poor woman some bread, and in return, heard her life story, which was just sadness itself. Mary's own family had been small farmers but had retained their land. She knew that she was lucky. She had married well – to her childhood sweetheart – and she and her husband had land, animals and money. Her male children would soon attend school. In fact, she had hopes that the eldest, Thomas the younger, might make it as far as grammar school and then, perhaps, university. Her life, she knew, could have been a lot worse.

The Younge family opened their doors to Elizabeth Stevenson, her husband Robert and their children. Thomas found work for Robert on the farm, and the children worked as much as they could in the house and the fields. There was talk of opportunities in the town of Taunton, in the next county of Somerset, which had many new jobs in textiles and wool. Robert had also considered a life at sea but was too old, and didn't know what his family would do while he was away. In the end, Mary never knew what happened to the Stevensons. One morning, she got up and simply found them gone. There had been a small argument the evening before – one of the Stevenson children had stolen some cheese – and this had obviously made them feel unwelcome. Mary cursed herself for even mentioning it. Why had she done such a thing? But perhaps it was time for the family to be on their way anyway. Winter was approaching and there was less work for them anyway.

She knew without a doubt that the baby that appeared on the doorstep a week later was Elizabeth's. And she understood why she had left this child; of course she did. This tiny, blue-eyed boy's future would have been wholly uncertain with his parents. The few certainties of their lives weren't at all pleasant to contemplate. They didn't have a home, or work. They might not have enough food, or adequate shelter, for many years to come. At any stage, Robert might be accused of vagrancy and put in the stocks or flogged. On their way to Taunton, or wherever they were going, they would certainly be robbed again. A baby's chances of survival in a big town, with unsanitary conditions, was very slim – if it even arrived there safely at all. A mother has to do what's best for her child. Mary, with her four strong children, knew she would have done the same for them in the same circumstances. By leaving her newborn at the farm, Elizabeth had done the only thing she could do for her son. She had given him a small chance in life. Fresh air, food, shelter; if the Younges were kind to him and didn't just dump him somewhere, he would have a good chance. After a short discussion, the Younges indeed decided that, as they could easily feed one more mouth, it was their Christian duty to look after the boy until such time as he could make his own way in the world. And they thought maybe his parents would come back for him one day, although they never did.

Another male child was a useful addition to a farming family, of course, and Francis grew to be a strong, useful worker. At six he was already capable of much of the work of a fully-grown man. He sowed seeds, milked cows, picked fruit, mucked out horses, tended to chickens and pigs, churned butter and helped Mary and her daughter Molly make cheese. Molly, the same age as Francis, was the youngest of the family and by the time she and Francis were nine or so, the older boys from the family were attending grammar school. The family was still doing well. The surplus from the farm was going to market twice a week or, increasingly often, it was instead being taken by carriage to distant markets where a better price could be obtained. This angered local people. The Younges had always been well-liked, and known as a good family. But now their popularity seemed to wane. Thomas the elder didn't see anything wrong with making good money from sending his best cheeses, hides and preserves to markets in London and Bristol, but the villagers didn't agree. It was the job of yeoman farmers to provide cheap food for local people, they maintained. There were two good arguments for this. The first was simple. Villagers had to buy food from somewhere. If the local farmer wasn't selling it to them, how would they get it? Would they have to give up their own trades and all become farmers? If they did, who would make shoes, weave cloth, provide medicines, play the fool? Everyone had their role, and the role of the yeoman and the farmer was to sell food to local people.

There was also a wider economic argument. The villagers pointed out that Thomas and Mary didn't buy shoes and cloth in London; they bought these items locally, in the village market. But how could they expect the local weavers and cobblers to work with no food?

If the villagers were forced to buy more expensive food at market – rather absurdly brought in from farmers miles away, for much higher prices – they would have to increase the prices of their own services in order to survive. Making money from distant trade would always be a false economy, they said. The Younges might make a profit today, but tomorrow it would all even out again as prices went up to reflect what was going on. All prices would go up eventually, and for what? Far better to simply trade locally. But Thomas Younge had made agreements and was not about to go back on them now. These arguments simmered for several years.

Francis always knew his family background, but the villagers didn't. As far as they were concerned, he was simply a member of the Younge family. He got on well with most people as a child. He was strong and friendly and, some said, rather handsome. People even said he looked like his 'father', Thomas the elder. One of the village girls, a physician's daughter named Sarah Marchant, soon developed strong feelings for him. But she was always frustrated, since Francis was always to be found with his sister, Molly. However many excuses Sarah made to go over to his family's farm, she'd always find them together, working or, in summer, messing around in hay barns or riding horses over the rough land, into some faraway, probably forbidden forest. Sarah never liked horses, and couldn't ride. Sometimes she would hang around with Francis and Molly for a whole morning, helping with their work and sharing a lunch of apples, bread and ale, only to see them disappear on their horses all afternoon, leaving her behind on her own. She would occasionally stir trouble when she arrived home, bored and lonely: 'Father, why does Molly Younge dress in that odd fashion?' or, 'Father, the Younge children really are rather wild. I fear they may turn to robbery before very long.' Most of this fell on deaf ears, until Sarah stumbled upon the best piece of gossip she could ever wish for.

Francis knew that his position in the Younge family was unstable. Although he felt great fondness for the Younges, and they for him, it was clear that he wouldn't be taking over the family land after Thomas the elder died. This would fall to either Paul or Thomas the younger. So what would he do? He would have to learn a trade. For that, he would have to take an apprenticeship somewhere, but he didn't want to leave his comfortable, warm house. Every night he dreamed of this grey, rainy urban future, without his adopted parents and without Molly, and he wept. He also wept for the mother he would never know and the education he would never receive. The Younges were kind people, but their kindness did not stretch to an education for a foundling child. Francis knew he was going to have to make his own way in the world, but where and what? And when?

As he approached his twelfth birthday various things happened. Firstly, he and Molly learned to read and write. John, the most wayward and rebellious of the Younge family, had stopped attending school. Now he was at the farm during the day, he worked alongside the others, which made the work disappear more quickly, leaving the children more time to get up to mischief. Francis and Molly were able to show John how to navigate the woods on a horse, and where the local highwaymen kept their hideouts; and in return he was able to tell them how to conjugate verbs in Latin, and how to write down these verbs. A year later, John left for Plymouth to go to sea on a merchant vessel bound for Africa. But Molly and Francis had learned a lot from him. They started writing messages to each other in a strange combination of Latin and curious words and symbols that they had made up. Most people in the village couldn't read, but even those who could would never be able to decipher this hocus-pocus text. The strange letters they sent did, of course, contain details of their love affair; not just notes about meeting places and times, but poems and declarations, sometimes five pages long. For the next couple of years they also both kept personal journals. The two of them were obsessed with writing – the only thing they cared about more was each other.

Molly was already pregnant on the day Sarah saw them kissing in the orchard, but nobody knew that. Of course, Sarah had seen all she needed to see, and had run home, feeling sick, to immediately tell her father. What she thought she had seen was incest: brazen incest, in the open air. As Francis and Molly lay half-clothed beneath the trees, they had no way of knowing that they had been seen and that this would be their last time together. You never really know what is going to happen in the next five minutes of your life. Sarah's father would perhaps have told his daughter not to be so silly – he was one of the few people who knew of Francis's genealogy, having tended to him as a young child – had he not been as aggrieved by the Younges' trade practices as the rest of the village. So, despite what he knew, and despite the fact that he had been a family friend, he went to complain to the Younges about what Sarah had seen. By now, Sarah had also made up a story about Francis trying to proposition her. Was there no end to his evil? Lying with his own sister and then trying to lie with the physician's daughter: it was too much. There were stiff penalties for this kind of thing in 1618 and Francis Stevenson had no other option than to run for it as soon as he heard what was going on. He had no desire to be lynched by the villagers. Mary was sad to see him go, but not as distraught as poor Molly. The two women helped him make his getaway as Thomas Younge and the physician sat in the parlour discussing what Sarah had seen. It was clear that Francis would soon be apprehended and accused. Mary grabbed a few clothes for him and some bread, cheese and cider, while Molly just cried. Perhaps she already knew she was pregnant with his child. Stuffing his things into a knapsack along with a small purse filled with coins, Mary told Francis to take one of the horses and put as much distance between himself and the parish as possible. He obeyed.

As he went, he called to Molly, 'Sister, I will be back for you!'

She responded: 'I will wait, brother.'

It hadn't been incest, but perhaps it may as well have been.

Plymouth was as grey as a dead man's face when Francis arrived. Wet with night-time mist, it smelled rotten. Fish, sweat, blood and grime mingled in the filthy streets. Everything was encrusted with salt. When Francis licked his lips, he tasted salt. Salt even seemed to be in his eyes, making them sting. The docks were noisy, dangerous, foul. But at least he was safe, away from the village, far from the possibility of lynching. But something was making him feel uneasy. There was no colour here, and no open spaces. It felt almost as if he was being crowded into the sea.

There was one inn near the docks that Francis could afford, in theory, for a week, while he tried to get a place working on a ship. You could make good money going to sea, if you were prepared to take some risks and work hard. In a few years you could make your way up to mate, or even captain, if you did not drown or die in some other unpleasant way. The possibility of death didn't frighten Francis now, however. He was grieving for his lost love and didn't particularly care what happened to him. He missed his home and his adopted family but knew that part of his life was over. The long-term plan, inasmuch as he had one, was of course to go back for Molly as a rich man, possibly in disguise. But how to get to this position of riches? Much later, a wise man would say that going to sea is like going to prison with the added possibility of drowning. But Francis thought the sea would bring him his freedom. He sensed it in the fetid air around him. This was to be his life.

After two nights at the inn, Francis had learned something of what he could expect at sea, and of the fates of recent adventurers connected with this port. All Plymouth was still abuzz with stories about Sir Walter Ralegh, who had so recently been captured here and then beheaded in London on a charge of treason and piracy. Francis became rather fascinated by the story of Ralegh, the soldier who had become a sailor and then a favoured courtier, before turning sailor once more. Francis Stevenson was not old enough to remember anything of Elizabeth's reign but Ralegh had apparently been quite a favourite of hers. The new king, James, on the other hand, didn't feel the same way and, on a vague charge of treason, had imprisoned Ralegh in the Tower of London for thirteen years. In his time in the Tower, Ralegh wrote his *History of the World*, which Francis certainly later read. King James eventually set Ralegh free on the condition that he would immediately go treasure-hunting on his behalf. There were still men from this ill-fated voyage hanging around Plymouth, talking of the supposed gold mine on the great Orinoco river that was never found. Instead, of course, Ralegh and his men took the Spanish settlement of St Thomas, killing and plundering for what turned out to be only two bars of gold. Baffled and humiliated, Ralegh returned to Plymouth, only to be taken to London to be swiftly beheaded, his last words apparently being: 'This is a sharp medicine, but it will cure all diseases'. King James was suddenly trying to impress the Spanish, it turned out, although no one seemed to have told Ralegh that. Francis Stevenson lapped up all these stories about Ralegh, beginning what would become a lifelong fascination with narratives of adventure, piracy and life on the high seas. Of course, Stevenson was to come to live this life of adventure himself. But before this life could really start, he still had to find his first job.

After a couple of days, he happened to meet someone who knew someone who knew a captain who was urgently looking for crew on a merchant ship due to sail the next day. After a bit of smooth talking, he secured his position as almost the lowliest member of this crew. Despite what he must have told the captain, Francis knew nothing at all about sailing. But he did know how to work hard, and he was good at watching and learning. It becomes easier to learn when your life rests on your knowledge and, of course, once on board the ship, Francis soon found that tying the right knots in the right places could mean the difference between going overboard and staying on the ship in a storm, or during a battle. Of course, he hadn't known in detail about the battles there were likely to be at sea; how hard-fought every single passage was. It wasn't until the voyage was under way that the other crew-members started to tell him about the time John Ford lost an eye to a pirate, or the time Stephen Falconer fell overboard in a storm but was pulled back up by a halyard to which he had become attached. This was a dangerous business indeed, from which only the most brutal seemed to profit, and only the luckiest survived. Occasionally, Francis heard the men complaining. When John Ford lost his eye he wasn't compensated by the merchants at all. If he had been on a pirate ship, they said, he would have been given 100 pieces of eight – as specified by a document called the Articles of the ship – which could be used on various distant islands to buy rum, women and a life of general fun and debauchery.

Francis Stevenson's first voyage was a fairly simple passage across the Mediterranean. For the first three days he was terribly sick, probably due to the deep, churning water. Then he started to pay attention. As the only crew member who could read and write (apart from the captain and the officers) he was occasionally called on to help with navigation, and learnt as much as he could about stars, sextants and charts. Most of the time, though, he was wet and cold, hanging off ropes, halyards and rigging, adjusting various sails on the ship. Being below decks was somehow worse, however, with crowded conditions leading to rashes, boils, coughs, breathing problems, dysentery and the dreaded itch. For several weeks Francis was either too hot or too cold; always hungry and often sick. There was hardly any fresh water on board the ship, and what there was soon became riddled with bacteria and disease. He learnt a particular method for dealing with the cramped, dangerous conditions. This method was simply to clear his mind of everything, to not think of open spaces or Molly or his former life. Instead, Francis fancied he was a small part of a bigger whole, his job being to keep very still. He never panicked, although many people did. He concentrated only on his breathing, keeping it slow and steady, and survived many rough nights of the crowded voyage that way, almost meditating. Two crew members died on that first trip.

Back at Plymouth, Francis wrote letters to Molly – letters he would never send. He spent his small wage in less than a week, even though he was careful with the money. He stayed at his former inn and waited for the next opportunity to arise. He now had experience, and the beginnings of a good reputation. After a few days he desperately wished to be back at sea, unpleasant though the experience was sure to be. He took the next position offered to him, as a crew member on another merchant vessel, this time bound for the West Indies. He did become ill on this voyage but was helped immeasurably by an excellent physician on board the ship who carried mugwort, which he said cured almost everything, and a tincture of crushed bone and red wine for everything else – especially dysentery. Francis learned from the physician as well: how to cauterise severe wounds or amputations with boiling tar and pitch, using rum to deaden as much of the pain as possible; and the practice of giving small pieces of lemon or lime as a protector against scurvy.

This routine, going to sea and coming back, always learning, continued for the next couple of years until 1621, when Francis was offered a position on board the *Fortune*, a 55-ton ship containing thirty-five pilgrims emigrating to the new colony across the Atlantic which had been created by the people who had left on the *Mayflower* earlier in the year. The trip was fairly clandestine – emigration was still illegal – and funded by a shady group called the Merchant Adventurers, but would at least be interesting. Francis would get to see the New World, and would be able to read books on the voyage as the pilgrims were taking virtually a whole library with them. He had been caught up in the excitement of the *Mayflower* leaving like everybody else, and had heard about these paradises overseas. Recently, the Virginia Company had sent something like a travelling circus around the whole of Devonshire, trying to drum up interest in their colonies. You could invest, they said, and reap vast rewards. Or you could become a settler and sail away to a paradise where all you would have to do was pick some tobacco occasionally and package it up to be sent back to England. Francis didn't like the idea of settling; he enjoyed his life at sea too much. In 1619 he had been on board the 200-ton ship from Plymouth that had managed to obtain and trade £2000 worth of furs in only six weeks. For the first time in his life as a mariner, he had actually made a decent sum of money – £20 – which he invested in the Somers Islands Company, an offshoot of the Virginia Company. Investing, yes. Settling, no.

It is hard to know exactly what Francis Stevenson would have read on his 1621 voyage across the Atlantic, although for various reasons many people have tried to work it out. Stevenson would certainly have been well acquainted with the Bible by this stage of his life, and would have seen various miracle or morality plays in his locality as a young man. In one of the many secret letters exchanged between him and Molly in about 1617, there were several references to a play they had attended in the local market square, thought to be called *The Hog Hath Lost His Pearl*. In this performance, the most engaging character had been the Devil, with the best lines and the only jokes. The idea had been to keep the 'yokels' interested in the religious and moral elements of the performance by including some bawdy, naughty bits, but it had led, certainly in Francis's case, to some intriguing ideas about good and evil which would not fully surface until later. It is thought that as well as religious texts, Stevenson read Chaucer's *The Canterbury Tales*, Sir Philip Sidney's *Arcadia*, Spenser's *The Faerie Queene* and, a bit later, the works of Ben Johnson. Although the first folio of Shakespeare's plays was not published until 1623, it is thought probable that Stevenson also read these later. When Tavistock Abbey was dissolved back in 1539, all the books had been burnt, sold for small sums or given away. Tavistock would have had a flood of books at this stage and although no one knows what their availability would have been seventy or eighty years later, it may also in part account for Francis Stevenson being so well-read as a young man.

By 1621, Francis had become a member of the congregation of St Andrew's in Plymouth. It was common for seamen to pray there before a voyage and afterwards, too, thanking God for carrying them home safely. Many people forgot to give thanks afterwards, however, heading straight for inns where ale and women could be found, only remembering God before the next voyage. But Francis always went straight from the ship to the large church. He got to know the vicar, Henry Wallis. Wallis, along with many of the most important merchants and political figures in Plymouth, was a Puritan. Having been on the wrong end of the Spanish Inquisition for thirty years, Plymouth people were not impressed by any sort of Catholicism, and embraced this new, disapproved-of Christianity wholeheartedly. Francis Stevenson passed by the church occasionally when a lecture was being given from someone with Puritan sympathies. He understood its central ideas, although whether he genuinely supported Puritanism at any stage remains unclear. Still, while he loaded people and their belongings on to the *Fortune*, he understood why the women looked so deliberately plain in their white bonnets, and why the men had no ribbons or fripperies on their costumes. They must have looked quite elegant, despite the simplicity, and these God-fearing people even influenced fashion, eventually. It was only after the Puritans that simple, well-cut outfits in dark colours came to be worn by courtiers and nobles.

The *Fortune* sailed from Plymouth on August 9th, 1621. Francis watched as the walled town, his adopted home, gradually faded from view, the St Andrew's church tower being the last thing to disappear. The passage was rough, although Francis was a good seaman by now. He had been promoted within the hierarchy of the crew, now occupying the position of second mate. But what he really wanted, of course, was a position as captain. But this would come. On the journey, he became friendly with a young woman called Dorothie Pope, an ironic name for a Puritan, who was travelling to the New World with her parents. Francis risked severe punishment if caught being indiscreet with this woman on the ship, so the two of them decided to wait until they had docked at their destination. When they arrived, however, the mood was fairly grim. The original settlers had expected the merchant adventurers to send supplies with the new pilgrims but there were none. The merchants were apparently annoyed at the lack of goods being sent back to pay for their investment. In the end, Francis and Dorothie never got their moment together, although it is thought that she asked him to stay there with her and he refused. It was a life at sea or nothing at all. And there was Molly, of course, for whom Francis had promised to go back.

Loaded with beaver pelts and other furs worth about £500, the *Fortune* set sail again on December 13th 1621, an unlucky day to begin any sort of undertaking. Later, someone said that a rabbit had crossed the Captain's path on his way to the ship, an omen of such terrible proportion that he would have been better advised to camp for the night and set off the next day. But yet the ship sailed. It should have been an enjoyable passage, as there was certainly more space now, but Francis spent the first month wet and cold, bailing out the ship during the several storms almost certainly brought on by the rabbit. Waves of over thirty feet high washed over the boat, probing under her hull, or occasionally catching her broadside, threatening to tip her over. During these storms, Francis may have prayed. He certainly would have got used to the strange bucking rhythm of the ship as it rode up to the top of gigantic waves, hung peacefully for a moment and then fell, slapping the sea with such ferocity that he would have believed it must surely break up. For days at a time, all he heard was the rumble of sea and thunder and rain, and the cries of men for help.

As soon as the ship found itself in calmer waters and everyone was drinking rum to celebrate, a French privateer ship attacked. Privateering was still a very lucrative enterprise in 1621, although by now everybody knew it was just piracy with an official seal. All Francis would remember of the attack – the first he had ever faced – was the noise of gunfire, and shouting, French and English voices dissolving like salt in water. It sounded distant, even though it was going on right in front of him. Gunfire, smoke and the horrible metal-and-egg smell of gunpowder and sulphur. Men losing control; throwing themselves in the water, their clothes smeared with blood and other bodily fluids. It seemed like a hundred years before the ship and her paltry cargo was taken.

Ropes, tight and burning on his wrists. Hardly room to breathe. No room to turn around. Francis spent the next month as a prisoner on board the privateer ship, on his way to a prison in France. Every day that he found himself still alive felt like winning top prize in a raffle. With no physician, no clean water and no fresh air, it is a wonder that the men taken from the *Fortune* survived at all. Francis knew of the practices of pirates and privateers, of course.

Not knowing that his destination was a French jail, he wondered whether he might be thrown overboard, marooned or sold as a slave to a galley ship. A ball and chain around his ankles; the whip. The idea was too much to bear. He made a pact with God at that moment. As images rose and fell in his mind like the waves outside, images of men with their liberty taken away, forced into labour for another's profit, whipped, bleeding and trapped, he promised God that he would never make another man his slave and would personally wage war on those who practised this – the Spanish and the Portuguese in particular. Francis would never make another man fear what he now feared. He vowed to God that he would have revenge on his captors, too. He would seek out the French and make them pay. Francis remembered a story he heard about Sir Walter Ralegh. He had apparently freed some island people who had been tied up and tortured by the Spanish – for his own ends, of course, as he needed the people to help him defeat their common enemy. But he had freed people who were not free, from the people who would use them – against their will – for their own profit. And Francis would do the same, he now decided. He would give people their liberty when he could. Life or death – but no imprisonment or slavery, he decided. This would be his new way of life.

After a short time imprisoned in France, Francis Stevenson and the rest of his crew were freed, and sent to London. Francis had never seen London before but his weak, diseased body couldn't cope with the excitement of it now. His shares had made some money while he had been at sea, so he cashed them in and obtained some medical help and a carriage to Plymouth. Once there, recuperating in his usual inn, he set down some of his political thoughts in the form of a pamphlet which, like the letters he used to write to Molly, he never actually showed anyone. However, this pamphlet, entitled 'Liberty For All Men', was a profound document that would eventually be picked up by a group aligned to the Parliamentarians some years later during the Civil War.

The physician Stevenson paid to tend him during this period was thought of locally as a 'witch doctor'. Known as John Christian, and having been converted to Christianity, this unfortunate 'Indian' had been captured somewhere in Virginia some years ago and traded for some trinkets. As the 'property' of the captain of the ship to whom he had been traded, this man was brought, bound in chains, to Plymouth, to be sold eventually into servitude in London. At the time, it was not very common, but not unheard of, for 'Indian' or African people to be traded in this way and brought to England as exotic servants. John told Francis his story, from the horror of his entrapment and passage to England to his dull, repetitive and humiliating period in service to a wealthy noble family in London, virtually a slave until a mysterious woman had met him one night and given him money and helped him to escape. John, previously a peaceful sort of man, had armed himself and set off on the road to Plymouth, tackling all the highwaymen who set upon him, intending to retrace his steps back to America. However, over two years later, he was somehow still in Plymouth, selling his services as a physician, still trying to get the money for his passage back. Francis asked why he hadn't got a position as a ship's surgeon, or even a deck-hand on a ship bound for Virginia. 'I will not work for the people who sold me,' he said. 'And they will not employ me anyhow.' John always had to be on his guard in Plymouth, ready for those who would call him a heathen or a beast. However, sailors in Plymouth did a lot of trade with 'Indians' like John, and, although not particularly friendly towards him, at least did not treat him like a monster. He and Francis became good friends.

Francis knew what it was like to be unable to go home. By now, thoughts of returning to his childhood village had all but vanished. Molly must be married now and would have forgotten him. Perhaps if he was really rich . . . It was too much to hope for that she would even recognise him now.

Around this time, it came to Francis's attention that a certain John Delbridge, a wealthy merchant from Bideford in the north of Devonshire, was trying to find a captain to sail a ship to Bermuda, where Delbridge was hoping to set up a colony. He was part of the Somers Islands Company in which Francis had invested. Somehow, this investment history and a meeting with Delbridge were impressive enough that Francis was offered the position as captain of the first of these Bermuda-bound ships. He would sail a 180-ton ship to Virginia, where he would offload some settlers, pick up a cargo of tobacco and trade with the natives there. At this point his ship would leave Virginia and sail for Bermuda, carrying more settlers and several people from the Virginia colony who had agreed to relocate. Then he would sail back to Plymouth. Delbridge was glad that Francis had agreed to this commission. Although he had not captained a ship before, he was now a respected seaman. More than this, he was the only person who would agree to sail to Bermuda. For some reason, many mariners would not go there. It was a fearful place, they said.

Francis called for his physician the following night.

'Are there others like you?' he asked John. 'Others who require passage home?'

When the ship *Ophelia* left Plymouth, its crew of forty men included John as ship's surgeon and several recently escaped servants who acted as gunners, cooks and boatswains. Francis was strict with his crew. As well as the usual rules to do with not smuggling women on board dressed as men and not gambling and so on, Francis had a new rule on board his ship. The 'Indian' crew members were to be treated like other men, he said, and anyone found treating them as anything less would be marooned immediately. And so, with its crew of escapees on their way home, and captained by a runaway, the *Ophelia* moved silently through the deep blue waters of the Atlantic, making a speedy passage to Virginia, arriving only fifty-one days later. The reception in Virginia was not quite what Francis would have hoped for, however. The new settlers were delivered without too much difficulty, but the leader of the existing settlement decided to cause trouble. As soon as the Indian crew members were off the ship, he took them prisoner. Francis was livid with rage. Had he brought these men all this way for them to be captured immediately and sent back as servants – or worse? Had he brought them to their historic homeland so they could serve the men who had arrived little more than five minutes ago? After consulting with his remaining crew, he decided to launch an attack on the settlement to release John Christian and the others.

With the ship loaded with tobacco and furs and ready to go, Francis and his crew waited patiently for darkness to fall. They attacked just as the settlers thought the ship was about to leave. With considerable gun power, and armed with their sharp swords, he and his men cut through any resistance they found until John and the other captives were freed. Unfortunately, in so doing Francis had killed the head of the settlement. He knew the punishment for that. *Death*. That was what would await him on his return to Plymouth. In the darkness of the night, with gunpowder fumes and the cries of women and children ringing in their ears, he and his men – including John and the other released captives – re-boarded their ship and sailed away into the night, not at all sure about what to do next. The ship held over £1000 worth of tobacco and £500 of furs, but its captain would soon be a wanted man. There was only one thing they could do. They turned pirate.

Francis asked the men to vote. Anyone who didn't vote for piracy could be marooned somewhere habitable, he offered, but he couldn't have any dissenters on board his ship. The vote was unanimous. The ship was renamed the *Rebecca* and the new Articles of Agreement drawn up. The Articles of the *Rebecca* have never been found but would have included the usual stipulations and rules found on Articles of pirate ships of this period. There would have been the usual 'no prey, no pay' principle, of course, although the *Rebecca* did start her pirating adventures already in possession of valuable goods. The Articles would have outlined exactly how this and any further plunder or profits would be divided, how the men would be compensated for injury and what practices would and would not be acceptable on board the ship. After the men had agreed on the Articles, they voted for their captain. Of course, they chose Francis Stevenson. Then they set off towards the West Indies.

The tobacco was sold easily in Jamaica, and the men of the *Rebecca* were suddenly rich. Then the real piracy started. There were enough targets nearby: Spanish ships, Portuguese ships, French ships. Francis had an intriguing policy regarding the taking of other ships' treasures. Once he had captured the ship, he would apologise to the crew and then, after asking them to avert their eyes, he would kill the captain. Having disabled all the ship's guns, and confiscated all hand weapons, he would simply bid the crew a good day before sailing away. It was this practice that gave Stevenson the nickname 'The Gentleman Pirate', although how much of a gentleman he really was remains uncertain. Stevenson would have been as violent as all pirates in this period, his business after all being to kill for treasure. The only thing that could be said in his defence was that he stood by the pact he had made with God, and took no man prisoner. He killed them instead. Still, as his intentions had been humanitarian from the start, it is also thought unlikely that he engaged in cruelty, rape and torture, as many pirates did.

He had no need to take towns. He was a pirate who existed purely at sea, plundering ships and selling the resulting treasure in the islands of the Caribbean.

This continued for several months before things started to go wrong. Various crew members had decided to settle in Jamaica or other islands with which the *Rebecca* traded, meaning that new crew members had to be found. John Christian and some of the other Indians settled on a Caribbean island, urging Francis to stay with them. But he could not abandon his ship. 'We will keep a place set at our table for you,' John assured him. 'You will come and join us one day, perhaps.' And perhaps that is what Francis meant to do, eventually. He never had the chance. Within a month he had been marooned on a remote island by the new crew. Not wanting him as captain any more, with his strange ways, and wanting to properly plunder towns and engage in more serious forms of violence, they simply voted for someone else and then marooned him.

Francis had been clever, though. Before John and the others had left the *Rebecca*, he had buried one particular haul of treasure, probably on one of the Pacific islands near what is now Tahiti. Francis was the only person in the world who knew where this treasure was. Although it is not clear how he achieved this, he did record that he had made 'devilish' use of blindfolds and trickery, at that point not trusting his crew at all. Francis made a map of the location of the treasure, which he wrote using one of his secret codes from years ago, concealed it about his person, and the *Rebecca* set off again. No one knows why exactly Frances buried this treasure at this moment. Perhaps he knew that he wouldn't be able to carry on pirating for ever and meant to go back for it. No one knows what he planned. Marooned on an island probably near Hispaniola, he set about trying to build a boat. It is unclear exactly how long he managed to live off the land, although some of his history and day-to-day life was recorded in a journal before the paper he had and the one pencil he used to write with ran out. Francis did one other thing while on the island. He wrote out a version of the treasure map, encoded of course, and addressed it to Molly Younge. Then he sealed it in the one bottle he had – the bottle which had contained the small amount of water he had been allowed to take with him when he was marooned – and threw it into the sea.

Chapter Seventeen

Wednesday morning. I am bored with all my clothes. Maybe not bored, exactly, that's probably the wrong word. Perhaps the problem is simply that everything I have here now feels slightly grubby. What did the PopCo coordinators think we would do about clean underwear and so on? They must have thought of something; they seem to think of everything else. There is probably a whole room full of clean designer knickers and pants somewhere in this vast building; it wouldn't surprise me at all. Or a laundry service. That's it. There must be a laundry service. Why didn't I think of that before? I will ask someone later.

There is a small group of girls here – one of them works in dolls, I think – who all wear their hair in a similar way. I have been studying it. They pin sections of it back with small silver grips, these grips forming a halo of attractive, slightly odd, flat sections in their hair. Why do I have the urge to do something similar to my own hair today? I would never, ever act on this urge. So why is the thought even beginning to form? Have I been impregnated with some vile, emerging trend? Abort, abort. This trend is unwanted. While I am thinking, considering the enemy thought trying to lodge itself in my brain, I slip on my corduroy skirt and a T-shirt and plait my hair again. I do like my plaits: they make my hair look like two pieces of rope. And nobody else does this with their hair – not here, anyway.

Skirts over jeans, that's another thing. A few months ago, someone came into work wearing a tiny A-line denim skirt over these faded, flared jeans. It looked peculiar at the time. Then, a few weeks later, maybe ten people in the office were wearing similar outfits regularly. Of course they all 'individualised' these outfits. One girl favoured thin flowery skirts that bounced just over her bottom as she walked, skirts so short that jeans underneath were pretty much compulsory. Another tried the look with a knee-length pencil skirt over extreme-flare jeans with flowers embroidered on the legs. Now, if you wear plain, un-skirted jeans into the office you seem almost naked. How does that work? And how is it that while there are still people starving in the world anyone has time to think about all this? In some form or other I suppose this has always happened, though. Look at Elizabeth I's amazing dresses, worn while peasants starved in the countryside. Perhaps it's no wonder that when the pilgrims ejected from this country a few years later they did so in the plainest clothes possible.

I remember one of Chi-Chi's many scary, cocaine-induced speeches explaining how we, at our small red brick building in Battersea, are actually at the centre of the world. 'We're a young team,' she said. 'We're artists and designers and visionaries. We create the very foundations of youth culture every day. We make toys, sure, but we also make catch-phrases and attitudes and lifestyles. This is what we do for a living. Then we go out drinking with people from Levi's and Diesel and MTV. Everyone knows everyone. Watch *Top of the Pops* next week and you'll see kids in bands wearing clothes, or combinations of clothes, that originally started life on someone in this office, designed or marketed by one of their friends. What we do is important. We, and our friends, are the centre of this fucking town.' Chi-Chi scares me, she really does. I have never been drinking with any of those people. I have never worn anything that would appeal to someone in a girl group or a boy band. I am nowhere near the centre of anything.

The first seminar of the day consists of us all reporting back on the product plans we have made using our matrices. I quickly present my plan for an alien frog bandit character, and then drift off while everyone else presents their ideas. All I keep thinking is, *Am I happy?* I really don't know.

At lunchtime, Dan and I take some sandwiches and a flask of tea up to the hill fort. I almost want to confide in him about the coded messages and Georges and everything else, but he gets in first.

'What were you like as a teenager, Butler?' he asks.

'Huh?' I say. 'What? As a teenager? Why?'

'Well, I just . . . Come on, what were you like?'

'Is this audience research?' I ask, suspiciously.

'Well, yeah, sort of. I've got no idea what teenage girls think about anything, or what life is like for a teenage girl. I just want some insights before I seriously start work on my draft product plan.'

'Aren't we going to be doing this all afternoon?' I ask. This afternoon we have a speaker coming to talk to us about emerging trends in youth culture. He's a researcher from a major new study called *Branded: Loyalty, Recognition and Awareness of Consumer Brands in 13-17 Year Olds*. We are having this research presented to us before it is made public in book form, and PopCo is 'very excited' by this, according to the memo we all received yesterday.

'I want some real stuff,' Dan says. 'First-hand. You are a girl, so . . .'

'I wasn't normal, though, as a teenager. Not at all.'

Dan laughs. 'Why doesn't that surprise me?'

There is a haze over the moor today. It is still hot, but with almost zero visibility. Looking down, I can't see much more than a thin film shimmering over everything like fairy dust. The enemy could attack on a day like this and you wouldn't know they were coming until they had arrived.

'What sort of things did you do when you were, I don't know, say, fourteen?' Dan asks me.

'Fourteen? God. Um, got up, went to school, came home, did my homework, went to bed.'

'Butler!'

'What?'

'Well, what about when you weren't doing those things?'

'I read a lot. I helped my grandfather with his various projects. I learnt how to compile crosswords . . .'

He shakes his head. 'So basically you really were the most boring teenager in the world.'

He's joking but I suddenly feel angry.

'So at age fourteen your spare time would have been filled with what? Saving the world? Talking to aliens? Being a spy?'

He doesn't seem to know if I am joking or not. 'I don't know. When I was fourteen I think I just watched loads of cool stuff on TV.'

'Oh right. TV.' Now I really am cross. I can't help it.

'What? What's wrong with TV?'

'TV fools you that you've had a life you haven't had. Don't you know that? At least I had a life, even if it was, as you say, boring.'

'God, settle down, Alice.'

'No. I hate it. All that retro stuff that's around at the moment.

Remember when we all watched that thing on TV in the seventies and it was so ironic? I don't even know what any of it's called because we didn't have a TV. It all just seems to be this stupid nostalgia for something that never existed in the first place. Just shapes on a screen. You were the one talking about everything just being pictures the other day. You must know what I mean.'

'I do. But I don't agree.' He sips his tea calmly.

'What? You think all that stuff has some sort of point?'

'Yes, I do. I think that there is no difference between a narrative on TV and a narrative in a book. They are both told in pictures, really, it's just that the little pictures on the page – the letters – spell out words, and the pictures on the screen are visual references. But you can't tell me that sitting down and reading something is intrinsically better than watching the same story acted on a screen. That's just snobbery.'

'No it isn't. When did you last see a fifteen-hour-long TV drama that had no adverts and wasn't written so a child could understand it?'

'What? I don't . . .'

'Or a TV drama you could cast yourself? Choose your own locations? Edit your own script? That's what happens when you read a book. You have to actually connect with it. You don't just sit there passively . . .'

'You are such a snob, Butler!'

'I'm not. Anyway, for the record, I never said that books were *always* better than anything on a screen. All I know is that on the whole I prefer books, but I have to say that I'd rather watch a classic film than read a trashy novel. And I love some videogames, of course. But that's just my choice. I don't care what anyone else does . . .'

'Snob.'

'Dan!'

He smiles. 'What?

'I hope you know you are really winding me up now.'

'All right, all right. Sorry. You are a terrible snob, though.'

'*Dan.*'

'Oh all right.' He throws a sandwich crust for some invisible bird. 'I can't even remember how this started anyway.'

'You said I was a boring teenager.'

'Oh, yeah. Sorry.'

'Then I said you can't have been that much more interesting.'

'I wasn't. I just wanked all the time.'

'Yuck!'

'And dreamed about being a fighter pilot or an astronaut.' Dan pours some more tea from the flask into both our cups while I start rolling a cigarette. 'So, what did you dream about? What were your teenage fantasies?'

'The interview continues,' I say, sighing. 'Fantasies? Do you mean sexual ones?'

'You know very well that I don't.'

'All right. Well, most teenage girls fantasise about men, or boys, or whatever you call the opposite sex at that age. Boyfriends, true love, marriage, babies . . . Or friendship. That's a big part of everything.'

'So that's the kind of thing you were interested in, then?'

'No. God.'

'Well, what did you think about?'

'Um . . .'

'This is like getting blood out of a stone.'

'Sorry. I did tell you I wasn't normal. Um, well, I worried about things a lot. My dad ran away when I was a kid, as you know, so I wondered about him. You know, where he was, whether he'd ever come back and so on. I read a lot of books as well, adult books. It gives you rather an odd perspective on life when you are a child reading adult books . . . Um, I thought about maths problems, and chess, and all these weird revenge fantasies. I started working on a plot to take over the world but it got too complicated . . . A lot of the time I was just trying to stay afloat in an incredibly complicated world, where you could be popular one minute and bullied the next, where coming into school wearing glasses for the first time would see you relegated from normal kid to "Four Eyes". I didn't get glasses until I was almost fifteen. One time, they broke and my grandfather mended them with gaffer tape. I didn't really have any friends at the time but if I had, well, I doubt they would have been speaking to me that day.'

'I had my glasses mended with sticking plaster once,' Dan says. 'My girlfriend dumped me because I looked so stupid. I must have been about twelve.' He looks sad for a second. 'Have you got contacts now? Instead of glasses?'

'Yeah. I think I might go back to glasses, though. Contacts hurt my eyes.'

'Oh, I know where you can get the coolest glasses . . .' he starts saying. I don't want cool glasses, though. Inside, I suddenly feel odd for a second or two, like I might cry. *Cool glasses.* Why? I just want some cheap glasses that I can mend with gaffer tape when they break and I don't want any part of that to be a style statement. Why doesn't that seem to be possible, now? And what's wrong with me? I should want to be stylish, I know, but I just can't.

More NDAs before the talk this afternoon.

'We don't want the press to see the results before we draft the press release,' an assistant explains when I hand mine back. 'Thanks.'

The speaker is David Furlong, head of the *Branded* research team. Furlong introduces himself, makes a few jokes about the research process (some responses that fell in the river, an e-mail that accidentally went viral) and then tells us that, as instructed by Mac, he will mainly focus on what this study has to say about teenage girls today. After telling us something about the sample group size and other statistical details, he starts his presentation.

'Furbies, Beanie Babies and your own brand, Finbar's Friends.' Pause. 'What do these brands have in common? Well, we found that they inspired love, loyalty and recognition in a very large percentage of the girls in our sample. *Love.* That's a strong word, but it was the word most often used by these girls. Here are some other comments. "I just adore my Beanie Babies." "If my house was on fire and I could rescue one thing, it would be my Finbar." "I am physically incapable of seeing a new Finbar's Friend and leaving the shop without buying it." "I have a collection the same size as my friend Marie, and that makes us, I don't know, even better friends."'

I have ended up sitting next to Esther.

'I think I am going to be sick,' she says under her breath.

'Jesus,' I hiss back, and we exchange a smile.

David Furlong presses a button on a hand-held console and some images come up on the plasma screen at the front of the room. They are pages from websites, a second or two for each. Furlong speaks over them.

'Here we can see fan-sites created by girls around their collections.

Most of them are Japanese girls' sites and most of them, you will no doubt be pleased to hear, are sites devoted to Finbar's Friends. Outside of the entertainment industry and websites connected with the cult of Ana – the pro-anorexia sites – these are the most high-visibility sites created by teenage girls.' He presses another button and a different image appears. It's a plain-looking bedroom. 'This is wrong, isn't it? If I told you that this was a teenage girl's bedroom, you wouldn't believe me.' He's right: there's nothing in it. 'We asked these girls – using a variety of research methods – which things were most important to them. On the basis of their responses, we can add to the room. Most important was clothes, of course, and then music.' He presses a button and the room now has a stereo and a haphazard pile of CDs. The bed, chair and floor are strewn with clothes and fashion-brand carrier bags. 'Items connected with music or celebrities came next.' Now there are suddenly posters and gossip or style magazines in the room. 'Next were cosmetics.' A hairdryer, make-up, hair products and bottles of various cleansing fluids now appear. This room is a bit messy now. 'Then mobile phones.' In the picture, a small top-of-the-range mobile appears next to the hairdryer, connected to a charger. 'Next, however, very high on the list, were soft toy products.' A few people in the room sort of clap when the picture changes again to include teddy bears, Beanie Babies, Finbar's Friends and other branded plush toys. 'Teenage girls placed their collections of soft toys far higher on their priority list than games consoles, dolls, books, computer equipment, televisions and other accessories. So, what does this tell us?'

He puts down the little console he's been using to change the images and walks across the room.

'Well, firstly, girls in this age group value motherhood a great deal and aspire to it in a lot of cases. We found many fantasies connected to caring and responsibility. Many girls carry a soft toy around with them on a daily basis. They put them in their school lockers, use them as key rings or attach them to rucksacks. We observed an emerging trend for girls to have rucksacks or small handbags which in themselves look like soft toys. This trend looks set to continue. Traditionally, Japanese culture favours the "cute". Here in Europe, the use of soft toys was often combined with acces-sories and clothing derived from the aesthetic we would recognise as belonging to punk, or sub-cultural movements now known as post-punk and ska. In other cultures, notably in Japan and some Scandinavian cities, the soft toy would be juxtaposed with technology – mobile phones and MP3 players mainly – creating something of a mother-cyborg, a girl trying to embrace her natural urges as well as her urge to consume the latest products. Girls, then, will combine teenage rebellion and consumerism with a genuine – or in some cases ironic – nod to motherhood and caring. *Soft, cute, lovable, huggable, dinky, sweet, tiny, adorable, baby, fragile*. These are all positive words for this age group. On various levels we also found that these were words that girls would like to use about themselves. Are they just caring for their cute, miniature toys or do they identify with them as well? As I am sure you are aware, one of the only toy crazes ever to affect teenage girls was the Tamagochi craze of the 1990s. This addressed the teenage girl's need to care for something, although there were problems with this craze, as it didn't last. In friendship patterns, too, we observed a need to care, far more than a need to be cared for. "I want to be there for my friends when they need me" was a typical sentiment expressed by the girls in our sample.'

Esther glances at me. 'I am so bored I am going to kill myself,' she whispers. Dan is busy taking frenzied notes. I look behind me and see Ben and Chloë, who both have expressions of extreme concentration, although Chloë is frowning.

'An interesting fact about these girls is that they are non-competitive, as a rule,' Furlong says. 'This may seem counterintuitive. Teenage girls are known for being bitchy, for bullying others and for going to all lengths to get a decent boyfriend. What our study shows, however, is that in terms of priorities, girls from all cultures placed friendship above all else. For them, friendship was about sharing items of clothing and make-up, telling secrets, trust and so on. For boys, friendship did not have the same priority level, and was based far more on competition and 'fun', thus the importance of videogames and sport for boys, these being the two most popular ways to combine competition and fun.

'The word "sharing" was very important for girls. Hardly any placed any importance on the word "winning". This is perhaps why toys based around competing or swapping have never taken off with girls in the same way. Girls do not want to be seen to be trying to be better than their friends. Thus the comment earlier from the subject who wanted to own *as many* Finbar toys as her friend and *no more*. Younger girls will swap and even squabble over items. Older girls, however, are more interested in lending, sharing and giving. These are the ways they gain acceptance in their peer groups. These are also the ways that products proliferate in this consumer group. Something that can be lent, given or shared – or is connected to lending, giving or sharing – will do well with these girls. Note how much marketing to this group emphasises sharing a drink or a portion of fries or a day at the beach. Of course, girls do compete – to be the thinnest or the most popular – but, crucially, they will never admit that they are engaged in competition. Girls will try to refine their identities to further their more general aims: to have important social relationships and find a "perfect man". It is around these desires that product-gaps can certainly be found.'

Furlong bounces on his toes for a couple of seconds and crosses the room again. The image from before is still on the screen and he points to the mobile phone.

'Communication is also of vast importance to this group. Hotmail is a brand which has particular significance for them. MSN Messenger is something used by 79 per cent of girls who are connected to the Internet. Hotmail and its sub-brands, like MSN, have achieved the same global recognition as Coca Cola in *less than five years*. This is a very visible brand. We asked the girls what they liked about e-mail and instant messaging. "It's easy." "I can stay in touch with my friends when we're not at school." "No one can overhear an e-mail." "My parents don't know what I am doing and that's cool." These are just some of the responses. Mobile phones are very important to this age group. Closeness and telling secrets are such an important part of these girls' experience that the family landline phone – often placed somewhere where the rest of the family can overhear – is just not good enough. Boys, traditionally lovers of gadgets, didn't have the same recognition around phone and e-mail technology. Too tied to their game consoles as usual!

'Over 50 per cent of the teenage girls in our study owned a mobile phone. SMS text messaging is the most popular way for these girls to keep in touch, however, with e-mail in second place. Communicating using text in this way reinforces the need girls have to exchange messages perceived as 'secret'. It is interesting to note the ways in which all teenagers use some form of code in their communications.

This goes beyond what you may recognise as 'text speak' and into the heart of language itself and the way it is used. Words like 'evil' have positive and negative connotations for these teenagers. English-speaking kids have their own grammar, as well, inspired by American TV shows, videogames and pop music. "I'm so, like, over him," is the way one teenage girl in our study articulated her dislike of the Harry Potter brand. Many teenagers in the study showed a profound level of brand and consumer awareness. They are aware of fads, phases and product cycles. "Move on", "So last year", "Get over it", and "Bargain basement" were phrases with a high level of recognition and their own analogous uses within the language of these teens.

'What I was asked to do here today was to present you with an overview of the results from our study that would be applicable to the market for toys and interactive entertainment products for teenage girls. As you know, not many brands from these categories currently have much success with teenage girls. The few that have achieved recognition with this group involve activities to do with exercise, karaoke, and updated versions of fashion crafts. These girls love making their own T-shirts, for example, or weaving friendship bracelets. As you know, the small company Lucky Dog has had a great success with its Friendship Loom, which girls can use to create friendship bracelets in a fraction of the time it would take to make them by hand. In fact, at the rate these things are selling, lots of little Asian children will probably be out of a job by the end of the year.'

He laughs in the way people do when they have just made a slightly risqué joke. No one else in the room joins in, though. I'm trying to digest what he has said, and wondering whether it was as offensive as it sounded, when a chair scrapes at the back of the room. I look around. It's Ben.

'You disgust me,' he says to Furlong, before leaving.

A few minutes later, the rest of us are sent on a break. Dan, Esther, Hiro, Chloë and I all head for the West Wing kitchen, looking for Ben. It's another hot afternoon and the still, thick air doesn't clear my head at all as we walk around the main hall to the residential wings.

Ben's there, drinking black coffee. Hiro gives Ben an odd look that I can't read and then puts on the kettle.

'*Vive la revolution*,' Chloë says to Ben in a rather intense way.

He glares back at her. 'Come on. I couldn't bear any more of that. That guy could be straight out of ZoTech.'

Now she visibly softens. 'You know that's not what I mean.'

'What's ZoTech?' Esther asks. 'Are they like the evil baddies in a game or something?'

'Yeah, pretty much,' Chloë says.

'What's the game?' asks Dan.

'It's called *The Sphere*,' says Ben. 'It's what we would be working on if we weren't here.'

'Are you having trouble, you know, switching it all off?' I ask Chloë. 'For all this teenage girl stuff, I mean.'

She frowns and sips the coffee Hiro puts in front of her. 'Yeah, totally. I mean, you get so . . . *crazy* with it. Up until this weekend we were just living in Terra all the time – that's the game-world. Now . . . I don't know. Planet Earth and all the fucked-up ideas people have about it. I don't like it here as much.'

'Terra,' says Dan. 'Earth.'

'Yeah, it's a bit obvious,' Chloë says. 'But it fits with the concept of the game.'

'It's an RPG?' says Dan.

'Yeah,' says Ben.

RPG. *Role Playing Game*. I think about the worlds in which I lost myself when my grandfather was so ill. I think of brightly coloured landscapes, somewhere beyond the past and the future, in which death was only temporary and in which your virtual friends fought by your side, everyone with different skills. A young kid with a big sword (like Dan's drawings from the other day, but more), a female healer, a female mage, with dark powers. I ache, as I think of it. There's something so comforting about being a hero in a fantasy world, with a big bag of chocolate raisins and lots of tea, still on the sofa at three in the morning.

I hadn't played any videogames at all when I discovered RPGs. I remember a Saturday, rainy and sad; I was standing in the local Woolworth's, trying to choose something to go with the new console which I had bought, literally, to console myself. I remember thinking this, weirdly. Console. *Console*. As the words sing-songed in my head, and as the rain pounded the dirty south London street outside, I rejected game-concept after game-concept until there was only one game left I could buy. Ideas that would have been three or four years in the making, which had extensive marketing plans and favourable focus group results; I rejected them all in a second. *Too American. Too childish. Not childish enough.* I thought of Japanese otaku kids in their bedrooms, hiding from the world, and since this was closest to the experience I wanted to emulate, I picked the game that looked most like it would appeal to this kind of alienated, agoraphobic, sociophobic Japanese kid. I picked the game with the most sweet-shop colours – rubber-duck yellow, mint green, baby pinks and blues – and spiky-haired heroes and pictures of strange other-world animals on the back. Soon, I was so busy customising weapons and armour and learning to ride around on these strange yellow birds that I couldn't worry any more. My world was now two-dimensional, fifteen inches squared, and I never wanted to switch it off.

The others are still talking about Ben and Chloë's game.

'So what's ZoTech's evil mission?' Dan asks. 'Presumably they have one.'

'Yeah,' Chloë says. 'It's like . . .'

'It's the usual stuff about taking over the world,' Ben interrupts. 'ZoTech are this corrupt corporation who control Terra. They've developed these dangerous chemical weapons because they want to colonise space, but the weapons programme has unbalanced Terra. ZoTech don't care about this very much. The natural resources on Terra are pretty much spent anyway, especially since ZoTech started mining for the Lost Elements and using them in their weapons technology . . .'

'What are the Lost Elements?' Hiro asks.

'Fire, water, air, electricity, ice, earth, dreams, spirit and magic,' Chloë says, in her gentle voice. 'The story goes that humans living on Terra abused powers they were given at the dawn of time and as a result these powers have been taken away or hidden. Magic was the first to go, then spirit. It's set in the future, obviously, and by this time all the natural elements are gone, too: ice, fire and air and so on. The game is called *The Sphere* because Terra has basically become just that: a central sphere and various interconnected bubbles in which people live and work. The Spheres are powered by dreams. Although the ability to dream was lost by humans a long time ago, one ancient mutant tribe still has the power. No one in Terra particularly cares that this tribe, the Maki, was captured by ZoTech long ago, and that its members are now bred like farm animals and forced into perpetual sleep, drugged in such a way that their dreams become even more powerful. This dream power is harnessed, and used as fuel for the spheres. When the lights flicker in the spheres, you know that one of the Maki has died, or woken up. If a Maki wakes up, he or she usually dies from the shock anyway, and the lights flicker even more.'

'How does the game start?' Dan asks.

'One of the Maki has escaped,' Chloë says. 'He has been dreaming of this beautiful girl all his life, and at first, his mission is to escape from the Maki Dream Lab and find her. Of course, it turns out that the destiny of the escaped Maki and the girl from his dreams are intertwined. When he finds her, and she hears what has happened to him, they join forces to fight against ZoTech, using his special dream powers, and her magical healing powers. They meet more comrades along the way but I won't say any more in case I spoil it . . .'

'Is it pretty linear?' asks Dan. 'Or do you get to do your own stuff in the game-world?

Chloë sips her coffee. 'It's not as nonlinear as we would have liked,' she says. 'It's all been a bit of a nightmare, to be honest. Marketing people don't like "nonlinear". It's a bit too challenging for them. They don't want cult. They want mainstream. It's the same old story.' She sighs.

'But what about the online games?' Dan says. 'You know, EverQuest and Ultima and all that . . . ? They're nonlinear, aren't they? I was talking to that guy Kieran yesterday about all the virtual-world research his team are doing. Apparently they have a completely free reign to develop virtual products for these virtual worlds. I mean, PopCo must know that nonlinear environments are where it's all happening, surely?'

'Not in the console market, apparently,' Chloë says.

'Someone actually has a job here inventing virtual toys?' I say, disbelievingly.

The door squeaks open and Grace sticks her head around the door. 'The second half's started,' she says. 'I was told to come and find you.'

'Shit. I wasn't going to go back,' Hiro says.

'No, come on, we'd better go,' says Chloë.

Although I've been avoiding catching his eye, I now look at Ben. He briefly shifts his inky eyes to the left and then back to meet mine. He raises his thick eyebrows and I nod. Message received. We let everyone else filter out of the kitchen and then we follow them at a distance, going only as far as the archway before we double back and go to my room.

He kisses me as soon as the door is closed, and we fall onto the bed, his wiry, strong arms pushing me down, and his hands removing only the most critical items of my clothing: knickers, T-shirt, bra. He leaves most of his clothes on, just pulling down his trousers at first, only pausing for a moment to put on a condom. This soon becomes blurry, unreal sex, perhaps the kind of sex videogame characters would see in their dreams. I am on my back on the bed, then, suddenly, on my front with my skirt up around my waist. Oh, God. I like this but is it too much, too soon? I can't move anyway, so I let myself enjoy the sensation until it becomes overwhelming. Then I push Ben onto his back and climb on top of him, noticing the big scar breaking up the pattern of hair on his chest. I run my finger down it but he grabs my wrist and moves it away. Then I am on my back again and his thrusts are suddenly more violent. Blurry sex, with fingers and scratching and more hair-pulling and then it's over, for both of us.

Ben gets off the bed and runs some tap water into a glass. There's silence for a minute or so while he drinks it.

'Sorry,' he says, eventually, looking at the floor.

I am rolling a cigarette with shaking hands. 'What for?'

'If I was too . . . If it was too . . .'

I smile. 'No. That was pretty great.'

Now he suddenly smiles too, a sweet lopsided grin in his usually serious face.

'Really?'

'Yeah.'

'Am I allowed to talk now, then?'

'Huh?'

'You told me not to talk that time before.'

'I don't like talking during sex,' I say.

'Yeah.' He frowns now, the serious face back.

'This is afterwards, though. We can talk now.'

'Is this, you know, all this . . . Is it just fucking?' he asks me. 'Just so I know.'

'I don't know, yet,' I say. 'Are you and Chloë . . . ?'

'What?' He shakes his head. 'Oh. No. Just colleagues.'

'Oh. Good. I mean . . . I still don't know, but . . . maybe we should just wait and see or something.'

He nods, almost too quickly. 'Cool.'

'I'm sure there's some public health campaign warning young people about this sort of thing, though . . .'

'Good.' Ben takes a puff of my cigarette. 'I hope we catch lice and the plague and gigantism from each other.'

I smile again. 'Yeah.'

We fall asleep on the bed until well after dinner.

Chapter Eighteen

When I wake up for the second time, Ben has gone. I removed my contact lenses some time ago and the room is now a night-time haze of fuzzy furniture-shapes and dulled edges. I walk the short distance to the bathroom and start running a bath, the steam making everything even less clear. If Ben was still here he would be a shape too, a lump in the bed. He'd also be a collection of smells, small noises and mysterious connections. If he was staring at me I would know, even if I was facing the other way. I read this ESP book about six months ago while briefly considering proposing something called the KidKenesis pack. The whole idea was doomed from the start. Kids developing their ESP and holding séances is not considered very wholesome entertainment in today's market.

In the bath, I finish the rest of the book about the girl and her horse, holding it up close to my face so I can read without my lenses. She finds the boy in the end, of course, and learns his secret. It turns out that he is an orphan with no money, living in a barn with only his horse for company. At the end of the book the girl is planning to ask her parents if he can move in with them. It all becomes a bit overdramatic, a bit Cathy and Heathcliffe, although

I would certainly read Book 2 of the series if it was here. What did the book tell me about teenage girls, though? Not very much. The girl in the book never bought anything; she was just interested in her horse. What would you sell to a girl like that? I expect that girls like that grow out of their horses and their Heathcliffes by about age fifteen and then the brand-awareness kicks in. Even then, what could you sell to a girl like that, apart from mobile phones, CDs, make-up, clothes and cheap alcohol? It's certainly a conundrum.

My hair has achieved the consistency of straw mixed with glue over the last couple of days. I rinse it in the bath, having previously noted the absence of a shower attachment in here. I need a container to pour clean water over my head. I look around for one. Then, suddenly, the idea seems rather wasteful. Perhaps it something to do with the moors, and not being in a city. In the city water is like magic. You turn on the tap and out it comes. From nowhere! It's a miracle. But out here, where the cold water is supplied from a spring (and doesn't taste like bleach) it seems as if the water still belongs to the earth, or, at least, belonged to it much more recently. Out here, the earth might be watching to see what you do with its precious, clean water. I know what's making me think of this, actually. It's all that stuff about the Lost Elements. If I waste water rinsing my hair, will it be taken away from me? Also a conundrum.

I rinse my hair in the bath water again in the end and wrap myself in a fluffy towel before replacing my contact lenses. The room snaps back into focus, suddenly including distinct colours and actual corners. I need some food. Perhaps some company? It is only once I am dressed and ready to leave the room that I notice the white envelope that has been pushed under the door. Irritated by the timing of my unknown correspondent, I chuck it on the desk until later, forgetting to worry about it being discovered or intercepted.

Noodles with hoi-sin sauce and little grilled shitake mushrooms and spring onions on the top. Iced coffee. Is there anything these chefs won't make? Someone's left a style magazine in the dining room, so I flick through that as I eat. The magazine turns out to be not much more than a catalogue for products you could buy to support your slightly non-mainstream lifestyle. I'm sure magazines used to contain more than just advertisements and features about products. Perhaps it's just because I work in this kind of industry and am constantly in contact with marketing people that I see an interview with a controversial rap star as a 'feature about a product'. An infomercial, perhaps. Anyway, this guy has just done a deal with one of the soft drinks companies and now they're asking him to clean up his act. The magazine interviewer asks him if he thinks he's selling out. How is being in a magazine like this not exactly the same thing? All this stuff just bewilders me. I find myself looking at some 'anti-ad' ad for jeans, considering the model's black/grey nail polish, wondering if it would look good on my toenails, and then remind myself that I don't want to be cool and I don't want to look like everyone else. I push my plate away, knowing that someone else will clear it up, and for a second I think about my favourite supper from when I was a child: homemade soup with bread and cheese, followed by tinned fruit.

Back in the East Wing, there's noise coming from the kitchen area, so I go in to see what's going on. The East Wing kitchen is bigger than the one in the West Wing, and is joined, by an archway, to a large drawing room. It's a chilly night tonight and someone has lit the large open fire and stocked it up with dry wood. There are lots of people in here – almost everyone on the project – milling between both rooms, making toast and jam and coffee, or helping themselves to wine. Lots of people seem to be gathered around the table in the drawing room, where Hiro is playing Go with someone I can't quite see. I look in the fridge and find it full of cold beer. I almost wish it wasn't there, and that I could experience the sensation of wanting something and not being able to have it. Then again, maybe having it is nicer after all. As the cold, bitter liquid slips down my throat, I can't imagine drinking anything else.

'Alice Butler – the skiving cow!' Esther says as I turn around, smiling at me from the kitchen table. 'Do you want some of this?' She offers me a half-smoked joint.

'Go on, then,' I say, taking it and sitting down next to her. 'So what did I miss?'

'Fuck all. Loads of statistics about how many brands kids are aware of by the age of seventeen, how their brand loyalty works at that age and stuff. Turns out that all the cradle-to-the-grave marketing bollocks really is bollocks . . .'

'The what?'

'That theory that you can make £100,000 out of someone in a lifetime of consuming if you can get them interested in your brand at an early age. Turns out that kids today just don't have any brand loyalty at all. They know what's cool, but that changes regularly. Even the big names are losing out to new brands that come along and claim to be cooler. Ha!'

'Why "ha!"?'

'Well, it's just a bit sinister otherwise, isn't it?'

'Yeah. Although the other way sounds possibly a bit too Chi-Chi.'

'Hmm. Oh, actually, you did miss something this afternoon,' Esther says. 'Mac was there, and . . .'

She pauses to relight the joint I've just passed back to her and Ben comes to sit with us. We exchange a shy smile.

'What's up?' he says.

'Ah – the other fucking skiver,' Esther says, blowing smoke out. 'I'm just telling your partner in crime about what you missed this afternoon.'

'It started off being "fuck all",' I say to Ben. 'But she's just remembered the important bit, I think.'

'Yeah,' she continues. 'Mac was there, all smug and smiling. So Furlong's presenting all this crap about marketing to teenagers. All the stuff we basically know but the marketing people don't seem to accept: don't make brands look too mainstream; don't make them look like something your parents would buy; emphasise anti-authority messages and stuff about not fitting in; don't advertise on TV – make the kids think they've found the brand themselves and so on . . .'

'I told you,' I say. 'This just sounds like K to me.'

'Yeah, well, K works, doesn't it?'

'So . . .'

'So halfway into all this, some of the videogames people and that weird virtual-worlds guy start asking Mac questions about why PopCo doesn't do any of this, and asking how we're supposed to compete in the teenage market with our marketing teams stuffed full of dinosaurs that think of demographics in terms of 'age' or 'gender', not in terms of skateboarders, ska-girls, Rage Against the Machine fans and so on, and then a couple of people mention that they've been telling the marketing people this stuff for ever anyway and just get ignored, and we're all creatives, so what's the point of telling us because we can't do anything about any of this . . .'

'Breathe, Esther,' Ben says.

She inhales. 'Oh, yeah. Thanks. Anyway, Mac says that as a result of this research, we're going to have these new mirror-brands. One for videogames, which Chloë seemed well chuffed about, one for the robotics people, one for the plush-toy lot and one for the teenage-girl product – if anyone ever thinks of one. Within the mirror-brands, we're going to create marketing plans ourselves, like, make the marketing plan as part of the product . . . Or the product as part of the marketing plan? . . . I can't remember which way round it was. Maybe the product *is* the marketing plan. Oh, and he said a lot of this would become clearer tomorrow and that he expected the "missing persons", i.e. you two, to be present at the seminar because it will be very important.'

'Jesus,' Ben says.

'Everyone's well chuffed because they think all this is going to mean more freedom to design crazy stuff without being told we're not allowed to,' Esther says. 'But I have a funny feeling it's just going to mean lying to teenagers a lot.'

'That's a very nasty anti-corporate attitude you've got there, Esther,' says Ben, with a half-smile.

'Yeah, well. Call me old-fashioned, but . . .'

'Who's old-fashioned?' asks Dan, coming over.

'Esther,' I say. Then, jokingly: 'Can you believe she doesn't want to lie to children?'

'Who lies to children?' Dan says.

'We do,' she says. 'All the adverts and . . .'

'Oh, don't be silly,' Dan says. 'Kids can see through all that stuff. They're more sophisticated than we were. That's why we have to hit them with more sophisticated messages. They're able to sort through the information they are given and find the relevant bits. Don't worry about it.'

'I think she's joking anyway,' says Ben. 'Aren't you, Esther?'

'What? Yeah, whatever.'

'Hey,' Dan says. 'Did you know that Grace is doing pretty well against Hiro in there?' He gestures to the drawing room. 'Thought you might want to see.'

We all walk through to the other room, where the heat from the fire immediately covers us like a soft woollen blanket. The game must almost be over, from the look of the board. Not much space is left at all; the whole 19×19 area has already been colonised by black and white formations of stones. Every final Go board is different, of course, and the patterns unique. Yet, although they are unique, each pattern made by stones on a Go board looks like an ancient symbol from a forgotten language, or a collection of pixels from a bigger picture. Great Go players can look at the final patterns on a board and tell you pretty much everything that has happened in the game – much in the way that forensic detectives can tell you exactly how, where and when a crime took place from looking at little more than a speck of dust. A glance at this board tells me that it has been a very close game indeed, although I couldn't say who has won. The players know, of course. They won't have to count the intersections, they will just know.

Ben has been talking to a guy I recognise from seminars but can't name. He is pretty scruffy, wearing old jeans and a black T-shirt. His hair is shoulder-length and a bright ginger-pink colour which I'm not sure is entirely unnatural. He is wearing glasses with thin silver rims and has a strange symbol tattooed on his right arm. At first, when I look at it, it seems to take the form of an uncompleted figure 8, lying on its side, a bit like the symbol for infinity but with unclosed tail lines at both ends and a small line underneath it. Then I recognise it. It's $\aleph_1$, AKA aleph-one, the symbol for Georg Cantor's second level of transfinity. I am still contemplating this when Ben turns and smiles at me.

'Alice,' he says. 'Meet Kieran.'

'Hi,' I say. 'You're . . . ?'

'Kieran does the virtual-world stuff,' Ben says. He looks at Kieran and raises an eyebrow. 'Alice doesn't believe you exist.'

'Someone said you were designing virtual products to be sold in virtual worlds,' I say suspiciously.

'Yeah, that's right,' he says, swigging from a bottle of beer.

'Seriously?'

'Seriously. Although I get other people to do the actual design. I'm more of a grand-designer.' He laughs a technician's laugh. 'I work out what sort of products would work, create tests and commission artwork. We've released a couple of beta versions inside a controlled virtual environment, with avatars that will support additional customisation, and, yeah, it's going pretty well.'

'What's an avatar?' I ask.

'It's like your on-screen character,' Kieran explains. 'You know, the little picture of the person that moves around on the screen. It's actually a term borrowed from the Hindu religion that usually means the incarnation of a deity . . .'

'What products can you make for a picture of a person?' I ask uncertainly.

'Ha.' Kieran laughs, again. 'Well, how long's a piece of string?'

I have noticed that this is the generic computer-person's response to everything. That, or something involving the acronym WYSIWYG: what you see is what you get, pronounced *wizzywig*. This last always intrigues me as it doesn't seem to apply to anything at all in life, which seems to run on completely invisible forces, power, religion, desire, electricity and so on.

'Go on,' I say. 'Humour me.'

'Well, the trainer and clothing companies are in this research big time, which should tell you something,' he explains. 'The big corps have whole teams on it, 24/7. The idea is that in a few years' time you'll log on to your online multi-player game, EverQuest, or whatever, and be able to buy little branded sneakers and T-shirts for your character. Have you ever been on EverQuest?'

I shake my head. 'No.'

'Ah. Well. EverQuest takes place in a world called Norrath. The whole thing is, shall we say, *huge*. Norrath's GDP per capita is higher than China's and India's, its GNP is somewhere between that of Russia and Bulgaria and its currency is more valuable in US dollars than the yen and the Italian lira . . .'

'What, really? And this is a virtual world?'

'Oh yes. It's owned by Sony. Someone said that if you were a citizen of Bulgaria, the most economically sound decision you could make would be to give up your job to play EverQuest all day. You'd make more money in the long run.' He swigs from his bottle of beer.

I frown. 'How do you make money playing a game?'

'People sell their avatars in online auctions. Or they trade the Norrath currency – Platinum Pieces – with pounds or dollars on auction sites. A typical person can make about $3.50 an hour working on EverQuest by farming the bots and selling them on. You'd be amazed what rich kids and addicted executives will pay for a customised character, or Platinum Pieces, so they don't have to go through the difficult parts of the game themselves. They have money in the real world, with which they can purchase power in the virtual world. Imagine what people like that would pay for a pair of Nikes for their avatar, or a Porsche for him or her to drive around in. The characters are usually supposed to walk everywhere, of course, that's always been a convention of fantasy gaming, but, well, what if your character could buy a car? How cool would that be?'

'Maybe horses would work,' I say, uncertainly. Ben has returned from the kitchen with more beer. He passes me a bottle. 'Is this stuff real, though?' I say to Kieran. 'Is this actually true?'

'True, yes. Real? Of course not. None of it's real. That's the point.'

'Do you know about all this?' I say to Ben. 'Selling virtual branded products in virtual worlds and so on . . . ?'

'Yeah, of course. Kieran's based in Berkshire with us. He tried to convince us to get the characters in *The Sphere* to wear virtual K clothing.'

'It would have rocked,' Kieran says to Ben. 'You know it would. And there's still time . . .'

'Not up to me anyway, is it? But I don't think it would work at all. Gamers don't want brands like K shoved down their throats. We don't want them to think we're opportunistic scum, after all.'

'Way too cynical. Way too cynical,' Kieran says, shaking his head. 'I can already see Zuni in a tight little Ursula vest-top with her tits almost spilling out. Oh, *baby*.'

'Zuni's meant to be about twelve,' says Ben.

'Oh, baby, baby,' says Kieran, before grinning wildly and drifting off towards the kitchen.

Somehow, Grace and Hiro's game is still going on.

'That guy's kind of odd,' I say to Ben.

'Kieran? Yeah. They all are in his team. They all live in those online worlds almost all the time. Don't know how he's managed to stay offline for so long here.'

'Maybe he's got a secret computer,' I suggest.

Esther comes over to stand with us, drinking a cup of black coffee.

'You know that Kieran and his lot are inadvertently creating the most vacuous profession ever, of course,' Ben says.

'Which is?' I say, putting my empty beer bottle down on a table.

'Virtual retail assistants to sell the products in the virtual world. Not automated ones, but actual people who will log on and hang around all day at the store peddling branded goods.'

'Why not automated?'

'Cheaper to have real people.'

There's a big groan from the people closest to the game. Someone must have made a bad move. I can't quite see from here. Hiro has his head in his hands, though, so I am assuming the bad move was his.

'Were you talking to that Kieran guy?' Esther says to me.

'Yeah. He's a bit odd, isn't he?'

'He was a bit full-on with Mac this afternoon. What was he saying?'

'Just talking about all this virtual product research.'

'That stuff's scary,' Esther says. 'Imagine, you're in your online game world, walking around looking for something to kill, or information, or healing magic or something actually relevant, and then some twat comes along trying to sell you a pair of imaginary trainers.' She frowns. 'Kind of like life, I suppose. Hmm.'

'Kieran never actually said which PopCo products were going virtual, if that's the expression,' I say. 'Apart from the K stuff, obviously.'

'I know they're trying to do mini-games,' Ben says. 'One of our team is working with one of their team on it.'

'Mini-games?' I say, confused.

'Like games within the game?' Esther says.

Ben nods. 'That's right. One idea was to develop mini virtual hand-held consoles you could buy for your avatar, which is a bit of a mindfuck, if you think about it. The idea they went with, though, was for a card trading game. You can buy, sell or trade these virtual cards inside the game or outside it, and then when you meet someone in the game you can challenge them to a battle using cards.'

Esther suddenly bites her lip. 'Do you think that in a hundred years' time we'll all be living in these games, working in virtual industries buying and selling imaginary products, while some invisible underclass of people actually collects the rubbish and makes our food and does all the work in the real world?'

Her question hangs in the air for a second or two. I am tempted to say that we already are almost living in this world, when a squeal of victory from the Go table implies that Grace has won.

*

When my grandfather returns, I am still full of questions, but it seems that none of them will be answered tonight. I put myself to bed while he and my grandmother talk in hisses downstairs. This must be the latest I have ever stayed up. At three o'clock in the morning I am still not asleep. My grandfather knows the location of some hidden treasure. How can I sleep with that knowledge? I switch on my lamp and look at my necklace, with its odd number–letter combination, 2.14488156Ex48, and the strange symbol – almost like a figure 8 but not quite – and I wish I knew what it meant. I am also, of course, kept awake by the realisation that this whole business – the treasure map, the necklace and so on – was the reason for my father's disappearance.

The next day I am too tired to go to school. My grandfather lets me sleep in until about ten o'clock and then makes me a big bowl of porridge for breakfast. I have so many things I want to ask him that my brain jams and I sit silently at the kitchen table, not knowing where to begin. In the end, I ask something rather strange.

'Can I see it?' I say, looking into my bowl at the bits of melting sugar making swirly patterns on the surface of my porridge.

'See what?' my grandfather says.

'The Stevenson/Heath manuscript.'

'Why would you want to see that?' he says, as if I have asked to look at something as boring as the inside of an umbrella, or the back of a teaspoon.

I can feel my face burn with a weird sort of anger. 'It's the reason for everything!' I say, more forcefully than I intended. 'Surely I've got a right to see it? I wear this necklace . . . I don't even have a father any more because of this. I just want . . . I just want to *understand*, that's all.' This is the first time I have ever been angry with my grandfather, and this fact, combined with everything else, makes me start to cry. And now I am a cry-baby too, which makes me angry with myself. This anger is exploding inside me like a parcel-bomb. While it wrecks my insides, my grandfather just looks at me as if he doesn't know what to say or do. I am sure we have reached some kind of stalemate, with me crying into my porridge and him drinking his tea as if nothing is going on, when he suddenly gets up and puts his cup in the sink.

'Hang on then while I find it,' he says.

Telling me the back-story of how this manuscript came to be in existence takes the best part of the morning. The story is all about a pirate called Francis Stevenson who threw a coded treasure map into the sea over 300 years ago. The map was intended for his lost love, a woman called Molly Younge. The instructions on his accompanying letter told her to find his friend, an ex-servant called John Christian, and that John would have the key to unlock the code. Francis trusted that his friend John would not betray Molly, or she him, and left instructions that they should share the treasure. Of course, what he sent off in the bottle was actually a riddle that would baffle people centuries later.

The message never got to Molly. In fact, it wasn't seen by human eyes for at least a hundred years. Tide and current took the bottle and its intricate instructions to an uninhabited bay somewhere near Cape Cod. From there, it was washed behind a cluster of rocks and simply rested there until it was covered in debris from a rock-fall. The area was first excavated in the late eighteenth century and it was then that the bottle was discovered. One of the excavators thought it looked interesting and put it in his pocket to take home to show his wife. She suggested showing the contents – a strange scroll of paper covered in numbers, and a short note mentioning something about a key and a man named John Christian – to a scientist they knew. This scientist was Robert Heath. Heath and his friend worked on the manuscript together for several years. Heath was able to examine portions of the text that had faded over the years and establish what the tiny numbers were, thanks to some lemon juice, charcoal powder and his new magnification device. The two men knew that what they had was a treasure map. And they were determined to find the treasure.

They both died some years later, having made no progress at all with the cryptanalysis of their document. On the death of Robert Heath, the original manuscript, along with his notes and corrections, were placed in a museum near to Heath's home. There they stayed for almost another hundred years, until someone working at the museum realised that this exciting collection of papers could be used to stimulate interest in the local area – perhaps attract more visitors to the museum. Pamphlets were printed containing a copy of the original manuscript and Heath's notes, and sold at the museum for a dime apiece. Before long, other towns were doing the same thing with their own mysteries and treasures. Treasure hunting was becoming a popular activity, particularly in places where there had been pirate and merchant traffic in the past.

Everyone knew about Captain Kidd's treasure, for example. The writer Edgar Allan Poe had become very interested in it, and in cryptanalysis in general. As well as taking a keen interest in a coded document called the Beale Papers (which some say he even authored as an elaborate hoax, perhaps as a result of his interest in the Stevenson/Heath manuscript, as the two are similar), Poe evidently spent a long time in the area near the museum, trying to solve the riddle of Francis Stevenson's treasure. At some point, he wrote a foreword to a reprint of the pamphlet, but these copies were almost all lost in a fire at the museum, which also destroyed the original bottle containing Francis Stevenson's last message to the world.

While my grandfather tells me this story, and while rain beats relentlessly on the windows, I gaze at the small pamphlet in my hands. Inside the thin, blood-red covers, are Francis Stevenson's original words, now set in some twentieth-century typeface, and then the columns and columns of numbers which hold the secret of the treasure. It's hard to believe that something that sounds so much like a story could ever be real.

'This is the American Cryptogram Association version of the pamphlet, of course,' my grandfather says, nodding at it. 'Real treasure-hunters might do better to try to find one of the ten or so copies of the original Edgar Allan Poe pamphlet that survived that fire.'

'Why?' I say. 'Are they better?'

'No, no.' My grandfather chuckles. 'They are rare, collectible items. Each one is worth something like three-quarters of a million dollars. They are treasure in themselves.'

'Gosh,' I say, making the sort of impressed whistling sound that people use at school sometimes if someone has a particularly good sandwich in their packed lunch, or scores a decent goal playing football at lunchtime.

'You know that the Voynich Manuscript was originally found by a rare-books dealer, of course. These people are the source of many of these mysteries, and some of them become rich on it, although not, of course, poor Voynich, who could never sell his book and was never able to read it.'

'Poor Voynich,' I repeat.

My grandfather gets up to put the kettle on, talking as he bustles around the kitchen. 'When I first came across the story of the Stevenson/Heath manuscript, I was sure it would turn out to be a hoax, possibly a Poe hoax. Everybody who was interested in crypt-analysis knew the story "The Gold Bug", by Poe, which was agreed to be the first time an actual cipher and its explanation had been included in a fictional work.' My grandfather smiles, reaching for the tea caddy. 'Of course, if you want to find actual codes and ciphers hidden in texts, they are all over the place. In Shakespeare, according to the Baconians; in the Bible and so on. Anyway, as I said, I was pretty sure that this one would turn out to be a hoax. I had glanced at some material connected with it before the war, but then of course, my and everyone else's attentions were else-where.' He pours water into the teapot, which he then places in front of me on the kitchen table. He places two mugs along with it, and the milk and the chipped little sugar bowl. Then he sits down opposite me again and starts messing around with his pipe.

'Just after the war I had reason to visit an aunt of mine in Torquay. While I was there, I got thinking about the Stevenson/Heath manuscript again. The Torquay library has an archive of historical documents, and I thought I would pop in and have a look at the parish records for St Andrew's church in Plymouth in the early 1600s, to see what I could find. Of course, I wasn't trying to find details of Francis Stevenson's birth or anything quite so obvious – especially as he hadn't been born there. One of the things that had struck me as fictional in the story I'd heard, actually, was that Stevenson was supposed to have been an orphan, with no family ties. Anyway, I looked in the St Andrew's register for things like John Christian's baptism, or records of Stevenson's church atten-dance. I found nothing. Then, out of the blue, I found parish records for the area of Tavistock in which Stevenson had been adopted.

And then I found it. 1605, October. A baptism of a boy called Francis Stevenson. Thomas Younge was listed as his godfather, and Mary Younge as the godmother. The baptism was witnessed by a doctor, Christopher Marchant.'

'So you knew it was all real?'

'Well, not quite. I knew then that Francis Stevenson was real, at least. Poe wouldn't have had access to parish registers for Tavistock. Neither would any plausible American hoaxer of the correct time period – or, at least, it would have taken an awful lot of effort for them to get the information. I had always been surprised that the story was so English, if it was supposed to be an American hoax, anyway. Too many of the details are correct. It just felt like an English story. And it would have been just too much of a coincidence for a Francis Stevenson to appear in the correct parish register if the whole story had been made up. Of course, just because Stevenson was real didn't make the treasure or the code real. Someone who had known about the pirate Francis Stevenson could easily have added the story about the treasure. That happens all the time. Anyway, I put together a lot of the Francis Stevenson story from my own research, and other historians and treasure-hunters filled in the rest. Molly's childhood journal survived, for example, and some records from ships Francis Stevenson was on. His log and journal from his *Fortune* voyage are in a museum in Plymouth. It all started to add up.'

'When did you know for sure it was real?' I ask. My tummy feels tingly with all this excitement. If I can get my grandfather to tell me where the treasure is, like he must have told my father, I will be able to find him and bring him back. Or – more exciting – my father may return any day now with treasure, and we can live in a palace and I will be a princess! However unhappy you are, as a child, stories about pirates and treasure cannot fail to cheer you up, especially *real* pirates and *real* treasure. My porridge tears now feel as far away as Australia.

'I never knew,' my grandfather says. 'You can never know if something like this is real, or at what point the hoax, if there is one, begins. Francis Stevenson himself could have been the perpetrator of the hoax, for all we know. But the main thing was that the story added up. Here we had a boy who had definitely gone to sea on the right ships, who could read and write and was interested in coded messages. It was enough for me to start work on it.'

'What do all these numbers mean, then?' I ask, flicking through the little red pamphlet again.

'That's the code. Not a cipher, mind. A code.'

A cipher is where symbols stand for letters, and these letters make words in a language. A code is where symbols stand for whole words or ideas. I remember this, which is good and means I don't have to ask about it.

'In this kind of code, which wasn't at all popular in Stevenson's time, incidentally, each number usually stands for a word. The key is usually a book or manuscript available to both the sender and the receiver of the code. The number 01 in the ciphertext would relate to the first word of the key – or in some versions, the last word of the key. The number 211, then, would usually mean the two hundred and eleventh word of the text. It's actually one of the best methods of encryption around, as long as the key is kept secret. Particularly today, when there are millions of books out there. You and I could agree to use a little-known science-fiction novel as our key and no one could ever find out that's what we were using unless they watched us all the time and noted the books we were reading. It's one of those situations where all the keys could simply never be checked.'

'Why don't people use that to send codes all the time?' I ask, sipping my tea.

'Well, it's all right under normal circumstances between just two people,' he says, lighting his pipe. 'But if we were at war, for example, and I was on a ship, it wouldn't be very good at all. The enemy could raid the ship and discover a well-thumbed novel next to the communications equipment. They wouldn't even have to capture and distribute the book; they would just radio the title back to their HQ and the cryptanalysts would easily be able to get hold of copies of it. Changing the key would mean supplying all communications personnel with a copy of the new novel. You could find out what that was just by watching the bestseller lists in the enemy country! Or by having spies in bookshops or book distributors.'

Smoke curls upwards from my grandfather's pipe, the comforting smell of his cherry tobacco filling the room.

'But Francis Stevenson used this method?'

'Yes. The numbers he wrote down related to a text that he told

John Christian he would use in this situation. A perfect key for his purposes.'

'So all you had to do was work out what book he had used?'

'You make it sound very simple! But yes, once I'd put together the story of his life, I turned my attention to those texts he may have used to encode his message. It wasn't as simple as just trying different books, however. I worked in reverse as well, considering the length of the coded message, its possible or likely structure, words that may have begun or ended the message or portions of it. I studied sentence-structure and grammar use from the early seventeenth century. I discounted books that wouldn't have included words he would need to use, like *gold* or *treasure*. I felt more like a detective than a cryptanalyst, to tell you the truth. Would Stevenson have been here? Would he have read such-and-such a book? What would the seventeenth-century version of the text have looked like? Would the numbers run backwards or forwards? Would he take into account the folio page or not? All these questions were part of my life for years.'

I look down at the worn wood of our kitchen table, looking for patterns in the grain. I do this a lot when I am thinking. I look at patterns in wood, or on curtains, or even in cracks on the ceiling.

'Were the numbers themselves a clue?' I ask.

My grandfather smiles at me. 'Very good,' he says. 'So, you tell me.'

I blink hard, trying to reset my big eyes. 'What?'

'What have you noticed about the numbers?'

I'm still looking at the table. An old burn looks like a little bird, I suddenly realise. Or possibly a rabbit.

'The numbers are all three digits or fewer,' I say, frowning. 'Um . . .'

'What's the highest number there?'

I open the pamphlet again. 'Two hundred and something,' I say, flicking through it. 'None of the numbers start with a three.'

'Excellent. If you look at something like the Beale Papers, the numbers get quite large. In the first one of the three, the numbers go up past 2000. Was a larger text used in that case? Or a less common range of words? Of course, we now know that the first of the Beale Papers was encoded using the American Declaration of Independence as a key. Anyway, it is indeed a very good point to start asking questions.'

'So what was the book Stevenson used?' I ask, sipping from my mug of tea.

'Oh, Alice.' My grandfather looks at his hands and sighs. 'I can't tell you that.'

'Why not? I won't tell anyone.'

He sighs again. 'I can never tell anyone, I am afraid. I can tell you that it doesn't exist any more, and that I had to virtually put it together myself, backwards . . .'

'But you told Dad!'

'No I didn't. He thought he'd worked it out for himself.'

'Had he?'

'No. But he wouldn't be told he was wrong. And I couldn't tell him why he was wrong without revealing the right solution.'

So my father isn't coming back with treasure. Great.

'Did he get the answer from my necklace?' I ask, touching it under the collar of my T-shirt.

'No.'

'But it is the answer, isn't it?'

'No.' He pauses, relighting his pipe. 'It's a key to the answer.'

My grandfather infuriates me when he speaks like this. I want answers, not riddles.

'Why won't you tell anyone? Are you going to get the treasure in secret?'

'No. I am not going to get the treasure in secret. I'm not going to get the treasure at all.'

'You're not going to get the treasure! Why not?'

'There is more to life than money and possessions, Alice.'

'But . . .'

'They say pirate treasure is always cursed, you know. I don't necessarily believe in supernatural curses, but people who go treasure-hunting rarely find happiness. Your friends and relations become quite interested in you when they realise you are going to look for treasure. You can be sure they will want more than just love and friendship when you return. If you do return with treasure, you'll find you suddenly have a lot more friends and maybe even relatives, too; people you didn't even think you knew. So many people will want what you have got. Of course, that's if you even make it back. So you go to some remote place and dig up a big chest full of antique gold, jewels and money. How do you transport it? Where do you take it? What do you do with it? There are plenty of people in the world who, if they knew what you were doing, would quite easily relieve you of something like that, and probably kill you too. Or maybe you would have to use some sort of violence to stop them. And all for what? To come home and have a private swimming-pool and some fur coats? We have all we need here – why would we risk our lives for more?'

He has got a point. Treasure-hunting sounds quite terrifying.

'Couldn't you send someone else to get it?' I ask.

'Like who? And what would you pay them? If they dig it up, why wouldn't they just keep it? There'd be no incentive for them to bring it back and give it to you, would there?'

'Gosh. I suppose not.'

I hear the pad, pad, pad noise of my grandmother coming down the stairs.

'Have you told her about the bird sanctuary yet?' she says to my grandfather when she enters the room.

'What bird sanctuary?' I ask.

'Ah,' he says.

'What?'

'Well, there is another reason why I won't reveal the whereabouts of the treasure.'

'A *bird sanctuary*?'

'Yes. The treasure – if it exists – is situated in an area that is now part of a bird sanctuary. This is where I am afraid I seriously fell out with your father. He believed that digging up the natural, protected habitat of some almost-extinct birds was a small price to pay for the treasure we would find. I disagreed. When I told him this was my reason for not going to get the treasure – or one of them, at least – he simply treated it as a clue, listing all the bird sanctuaries in relevant parts of the Pacific and Atlantic, trying to guess which one it was. I am afraid I got very angry with him.'

'He never had money, Peter,' my grandmother says. 'You can understand his attitude.'

'He had enough. He was able to work. He didn't want the treasure so he could survive. He wanted it so he could be rich. I'm sorry Alice. In many ways your father is a good man, but in this he was mistaken. People have to respect the natural environment.

Otherwise, what will you have left? A society made of greedy, unhappy people, and a lot of extinct animals.'

'So no one knows that you've solved the puzzle?' I say, filing the information about my father away for more careful perusal later.

'No,' my grandfather says.

'He did it for the intellectual challenge in the end,' my grand-mother explains. 'He wanted to be known as the person who solved the most difficult hidden-treasure question in recent history. But now there's no way he can be known for it – because once people know he has a treasure map he doesn't intend to use, he – we – will be inundated with people who do want to use it.'

'Like those men at the bus stop?'

'Exactly.'

'And they knew because my father told them?'

'Yes.'

My grandparents start bustling around the kitchen, making lunch, while I sit there at the table feeling tired and quite small. I am angry with my father; the anger feels bigger than me. He was the reason for those men who approached me yesterday. How could he have been so stupid? And how could he go off on some stupid, dangerous, ill-fated treasure-hunt? How could he go without me? How could he do that? My thoughts blur into confusion over a lunch I can only pick at. I am not sure I understand about the bird sanctuary. I think I do but, given the choice, I would have the treasure. I'm sure the birds wouldn't mind really. But then I love the fact that my grandfather is so solid and predictable. He would never run away and leave me on a whim. He wouldn't think it was right. And my grandmother. Does she know where the treasure is? She must do. *I wish I wish I wish* I knew. After lunch I go for a lie-down and I take the pamphlet to read in private, in bed. I will find out where Francis Stevenson buried his treasure, just to prove to my grandfather that I can. My necklace is a key. That's what my grandfather said. My necklace is a key and I have the code right here. I will do it. With these thoughts I fall asleep, the open pamphlet on the floor by my bed.

Chapter Nineteen

The white envelope is still on my desk where I left it. I have brought a bottle of beer with me from the East Wing kitchen and I open this and take a few sips before considering the envelope. It isn't frightening me so much any more, the fact that someone is contacting me in code. Nothing bad seems to have happened as a result of it, not yet, anyway.

It only takes five minutes or so to decipher this one; it is written using the same key as the others. *Need help to send longer message,* it says. *Very important.* What? Need help to send longer message? Well, OK. Sure, I can tell you how to do that, but *who are you?* You haven't told me how to get in touch with you! I realise that I am speaking these thoughts aloud and stop, quickly drinking some beer instead. Really, though. This is stupid. I burn the note and consider my reply. As I have no idea who I am dealing with, I can't think how I would respond to this. Is my correspondent observant or not? Is he or she capable of following clues? I really don't know what to do. Could I just do nothing? Unlikely. I do want to know who this is and what they have to say. I really, really hope this isn't just some teaser for a new product.

When I first joined the company, e-mail viruses and 'viral' style e-mails were a new-ish thing, at least for people who had only just started using computers all the time. At the launch of one product, a young guy from the marketing department decided to create and send out a viral e-mail telling people about this new product, which had been hyped in-house as that year's most likely Christmas must-have toy. The e-mail went around the world in about fifteen hours, and then started going around again. Before too long, people were sick of getting this e-mail, and then started asking questions about where it came from. When people realised that this was a corporate marketing device, they went mad. The toy had to be withdrawn, and the marketing guy was sacked. The team who had created the concept for the toy were very pissed off. All that work for nothing. Which just goes to show. You can give people information a couple of times, but do it too often and they just won't want the information, or anything relating to it, ever again.

It's almost eleven o' clock. I switch on my radio, and wait while the soft voice of the woman presenter bleeds into some experimental organ music. As she finishes speaking, I realise that this is a special programme about a woman composer who eventually killed herself. Her music is spare, strange and magical. I lie back on the bed and suddenly there is nothing in the world except for an F sharp and me, then an A, majestic but alone. I am suddenly not there; somehow observing from a point of invisibility, perhaps as a cloud or a wisp of nothingness. I can see a forest with a cottage, all made up of one note, the A, and then an unexpected friend coming to visit, a B flat, carrying a gift – something made of hay, or grass. Am I asleep? I must be because there's no answer when I ask myself this question, nothing at all.

When I wake up, it is about six o'clock in the morning and the radio is still on. My instinct is to switch it off, take off my clothes and snuggle back into bed for an hour or so of 'proper' sleep before I need to get up for breakfast. However, once I have gone to the loo, looked blankly at my odd reflection in the mirror, fiddled with the radio and started to undress, I realise I am actually no longer tired, and go to the kitchen to make tea instead.

From the kitchen window I can see that dawn is just nibbling at the sky as if it's a biscuit it doesn't really want. There is still dew on the grass outside, and I remember someone telling me that dew is a magical substance, if you gather it in moonlight. Back in my room, with my tea, I think again about how to respond to the message. It's frustrating; I know what to tell but not how to tell it. Sending a long message is, of course, easy. You use a book as the key, and then make the code out of numbers relating to the placing of words in the text. But how do I tell this person that? Even if I just write a message with that as the content, using the PopCo code (which would take ages), I wouldn't know where to deliver it.

There are other ways of sending a long message, of course. One of my favourites, even though it is really for kids, is one I described in my KidTec kit. You have to glue one large envelope inside another one, and then you conceal your message in the 'hidden' envelope. When the receiver gets the package, they know to cut it open to find the hidden message inside. Could that work here? Fuck it. Not knowing what else to do, I write *KidTec page 14* on a Post-it note, and stick this to the outside of my door. (I know it's page 14, because there were problems laying out the envelope image when the book was at flat-plan stage and I have virtually a whole folder of e-mails on my work computer with the subject header: *Page 14 Problems*).

Back inside the room, I pace for a bit before opening the door again and removing the Post-it note. It's too obvious. Anyone could walk past, read it, check what's on page 14 of the KidTec book and know I am up to something involving double envelopes. They wouldn't even have to be the enemy to be intrigued by that. Not, of course, that I even know who the enemy is. I screw up the Post-it note and throw it away. Then I take it out of the bin and burn it. The smoke alarm in the centre of the ceiling flashes a single red pulse. Perhaps I should stop setting fire to things in here?

At breakfast, Kieran and another guy are giving everyone packs of cards. Each pack is made out of thick, pulpy, recycled-looking orange paper and fastened with string and the sort of button you get on duffel coats. Mine contains five cards. The cards themselves look like an odd combination of Tarot and kids' trading cards. The symbols on them are both familiar and unfamiliar to me. I have one with a man's head on it, this head comprised entirely of leaves and vegetation. The legend on the card says 'Green Man'. Around the edge of the card are numbers corresponding to the north, south, east and west edges, which are themselves implied by a semi-transparent compass graphic behind the Green Man's head. On this one, north has a value of 31, east has a value of 15, south has a value of 1, and west has a value of 25. I have four other cards. One is a picture of a crossbow, which has values of 4 on all its edges. Another is a winged dragon, with the values 5, 6, 12, and 4 for N, S, E and W. The other two are almost identical, and carry images of wood sprites. One seems stronger than the other, having a value of 10 on its west edge, and 3 on all the others. The second one has a west value of 7, and 3 on the others.

'Enjoy!' calls Kieran, as everyone starts examining and comparing their cards. I am on a table with Ben, Chloë, Dan, Esther, Grace and Richard. Richard, Dan and I are eating poached eggs with muffins. The others are all eating cereal or toast.

'Don't show anyone your cards,' Ben says to me.

'Why not?'

'You have an advantage in the game if other people don't know what you've got. And you should definitely hide that.'

'What?' I look down at the cards on the table. The Green Man is my favourite, so I have put him on the top of my pile.

'That,' Ben says, again, gesturing at the Green Man. 'It's a powerful card. You don't want people to know you have it.'

'Oh. OK.' I shuffle the Green Man into the small pile of cards. 'How do you know all this?'

'Oh, Kieran's been going on about it for days. It's his *big idea*.'

'What, for teenage girls?'

'God no, he couldn't give a shit about that. No, this is his online card trading game. He thought he could try it out with a bunch of people offline, to see if there were any bugs or anything.'

'I see. So . . . he's not into the teenage girl thing at all?'

Ben pours some more cereal into his bowl and adds milk from a blue jug on the table.

'Don't think so,' he says.

'So what's he doing here? I mean, why doesn't he just go back to work?'

'He's having too much fun here. Pagan symbols, witchcraft legends – you get more of that stuff on Dartmoor than you do in Reading. In fact, we've been invited to go along on this weird nature ramble with that lot on Saturday, if you're up for it.'

We've been invited. God, that sounds so coupley.

'We?' I say.

'Well, me,' Ben says. 'But I asked if you could come.'

'And how is it going to be "weird" exactly?'

'Not sure. At best, it may involve tree-hugging. At worst, we might be required to help summon something.'

'Yeah, count me in, then,' I say, laughing. 'It sounds unmissable.'

'What's unmissable?' says Dan.

'Kieran's crazy nature ramble,' Ben says. 'You should come, too.'

'There might be more hill forts,' I say.

'Cool.'

While we are talking, the question of how to respond to my odd correspondent keeps turning in my head like cement revolving on the back of a lorry. And then, suddenly . . .

'Where are you going?' asks Dan, as I jump up from the table.

'Back in a tick,' I say.

'You'll be late,' he warns.

'No, no. I really will only be a minute,' I say. I don't want to be late for the seminar but this is important – or at least, it feels important, which is the main thing. As I am going, I see Ben give me a raised-eyebrow look. I shake my head almost imperceptibly and try to send him the telepathic message *See you later*.

It is dusty in my room; the early sun picking out millions of dark particles dancing in the air or lying lazily on the desk. Which book? Which book? I select the teen novel about the girl and her horse in the end, not wanting to waste any more time. I scan the first page, looking for the word 'use'. It's not there. I scan page two. Yes. It's there, in the second paragraph. A neighbour is telling the lead character, 'Take care when you use the stony path after dark, strange things lurk there.' The page is 2, and the word number is 197. I write 2, 197 on a sheet of writing paper, then the numbers 2, 243, which lead to the word 'this'. There. *Use this*. As long as the right person cracks the code (which isn't hard), it will tell them all they want to know. If anyone else picks up the book and cracks the code, they won't know what 'use this' means. Satisfied that this is the best way of responding, I tuck the sheet into the book and leave my room, already five minutes late for the seminar.

The only thing now is . . . Where to deposit the book? I have it tucked under my arm as I walk briskly down the steps towards the main part of the building, and I am thinking so hard about what to do with it that I don't notice Hiro walking in the other direction and almost bump into him.

'Sorry,' I say, smiling.

He looks embarrassed. 'Do you have something for me?' he says.

'Huh?'

He grimaces. 'This is well embarrassing. All I'm supposed to say is, "Do you have something for me?" I don't know. It might be like a message, or a secret, or something. I really don't know any more than that.'

'Who asked you to . . .'

'Can't say. I'm just the messenger. Really.'

'Oh. Well, perhaps they mean this?' I hand over the book and he accepts it without even glancing at it.

'Cheers,' he says, walking away. I watch him go, half expecting him to fade into invisibility, cackle loudly, or spontaneously combust. He does none of these things, of course; he simply walks away like he's on his way to the most normal place ever. I stop watching him and keep walking in the direction I was going.

So Hiro is involved in whatever this is? Where was he going when I bumped into him? To find me? To break into my room to see if I had left a response there? Again, I find myself hoping that this is not just some silly game, endorsed by the PopCo Board. Or perhaps I do hope it's a silly game. The idea of it being something else isn't actually that appealing, now I think about it. As I walk over to the seminar room I realise that I am tired, and wish that I'd gone back to bed again this morning after all. Not one particle in my body wants to go to this seminar but there will be big trouble if I don't. Sighing heavily, I approach the room and quietly open the door, pretending to be invisible as I slip into the seat Esther has saved for me.

'Glad you could join us, Alice,' says Mac, from the front of the room. This really is just like being at school.

There is a man at the front of the room with Mac. I am assuming his name is Mark Blackman, as this is what is written on the board behind him. He is older than the other speakers have been, with slicked-back grey hair and black-framed spectacles. He is dressed rather eccentrically in a tweed jacket, yellow cravat and jeans.

'Hello,' he says, now, getting up to speak. 'As Mr MacDonald has already done such a good job of introducing me I shall not waste time re-introducing myself. The only extra thing I can tell you is that I have an Erdös number of 3. Does anyone know who Paul Erdös was?' He pronounces the name correctly: *air-dish*.

I put my hand up. 'A Hungarian mathematician,' I say when he nods at me.

'Thank you. And my Erdös number means?'

'That you have written a paper with someone who has written a paper with someone who wrote a paper with Paul Erdös,' I say.

'Very good. Are you mathematically inclined, yourself?'

I can hear Dan groan in the seat behind me.

'My grandmother was,' I say. 'She had an Erdös number of 2.'

'Wow!' He looks impressed. 'Does anyone else know what we're talking about?'

I look around the room. Kieran has his hand up, as do Grace,

Richard and the blonde girl I've seen hanging around with Kieran who either works in videogames or in Kieran's strange team.

'OK, thanks,' Blackman says. 'You can put your hands down now. All right. What we are talking about here is networks. If you want to take over the world with some undoubtedly pointless plastic moulded product, as Mr MacDonald assures me you do, then you need to understand network theory. You need to understand why your toy, or even your disease, or your idea – it's the same principle – can be relatively unknown one day and then, overnight, be the thing everyone has. Or not. OK. Forget Erdös for a moment. Who has heard of Kevin Bacon, the movie actor?' Most people put up their hands. 'Good. You, boy, with the long, odd-coloured hair.'

Kieran looks up. 'Me?' he says, grinning.

'Tell us about the game Six Degrees of Kevin Bacon.'

He starts talking in a lazy voice. 'Six Degrees of Kevin Bacon, or "The Kevin Bacon Game" appeared in 1997, I think. Originally invented by a group of fraternity brothers, it posited the theory that Kevin Bacon was the centre of the movie universe, as it was possible to connect any other actor in the history of films to him in, on average, less than four steps. The way it works is this: if you have acted in a film with Kevin Bacon, you have a Bacon number of one. If you have acted in a film with someone who acted in a film with Bacon, your Bacon number is two and so on. The idea was supposed to prove Stanley Milgram's thesis about "Six Degrees of Separation" – that everyone in the world can connect to anyone else in six steps or less. However, in a closed network like movie actors, the number was found to be much less than that . . .'

Blackman is almost laughing. He looks at Mac. 'Looks like you could have saved my fee and paid this young man instead.'

Mac smiles. 'Kieran has an alarming mind,' he says. 'Anyway, please go on. This is fascinating.'

'As I'm sure you could all guess, an Erdös number is the same as a Kevin Bacon number, but it relates to degrees of separation in a network of mathematicians rather than movie stars. Scientists have found that these networks, whatever – or whoever – they are comprised of, will display the same structure and properties. We call this the "Small World Phenomenon". This is interesting when we come to consider how disease, or products, or ideas, can infect these kinds of networks.

'A small-world network is itself defined as a group which displays a level of interconnectedness whereby each "node" on the network can be reached from any other node in six steps or less. Your company, PopCo, will, no doubt, display properties of a small-world network. Perhaps the whole of the toy industry would. Other small-world networks have been found to exist in the US power-grid system and the neurological system of the microscopic worm *C. elegans*. They have also been found to exist in the World Wide Web, the metabolic network of *E. coli* and in the network of boards of directors in US Fortune 1000 companies. Kevin Bacon and, particularly, Erdös numbers occur when the group is aware of its own interconnectedness. Erdös, incidentally, for those of you who don't know, was a very famous mathematician who created a model for random graphs – which, coincidentally, happen to form the basis for much of the initial mathematical work in this area of study.

'Small-world networks have to display a particular combination of "clusters" – say, groups of friends in the same town, or the people in your actual office – and "random links" – you and your most remote friend, or you and the person from accounts with whom you smoke, probably in the rain, outside the office building. These random links provide "short cuts" through the network. Mr MacDonald is an important node in the PopCo network, as so many people connect to him. He is like a big airport, in that sense, linking many smaller places. So, out in the real world, you might not know anyone who lives in Australia, but I do. If you know me, then you are connected to my Australian friends by only two degrees. What is surprising about scientists' findings is that only a few random links seem to have the effect of connecting the network in such a way that it will suddenly display small-world properties. Not only does this happen, seemingly 'naturally', in many different types of network, the 'critical point' where this type of connected-ness occurs is also familiar: it is the same, mathematically, as the moment a polymer solidifies or water freezes. It looks like a phase transition. It is a natural value.'

Mark Blackman pauses dramatically and then turns to the whiteboard. For the next ten minutes or so, he attempts to draw examples of what he means. I am thinking of cobwebs while he does this, I don't know why. Just as I am at the point of drifting away, I click myself back in and look at the board. This is an exciting idea, I realise, that some property that you find in nature – the point where one thing becomes another, where water becomes ice or steam – is replicated in this odd network theory. I don't understand the physics of it but I know that there is a mathematical reason for these things. How can that apply to people too?

Other people are completely lost.

'What is a phase transition again?' asks Esther, rocking back in her chair.

'It is the transformation of a thermodynamic system from one phase to another.' Blackman scratches his head. 'You don't really need to understand it to understand network theory; it's just very interesting to note that a network changes from being unconnected to being connected in the same mathematical way that, say, water turns into ice.'

Esther frowns. 'I still don't get it.'

Kieran speaks up. 'You've heard of "critical mass", surely? Or a "critical point"?'

'Yeah,' she says.

'When something reaches its critical point, it changes from one thing into another, or, you know, *explodes*. What Mark is saying is that it's the same with how we all connect. Say you move to a new town, yeah, and you don't know anyone? For a few weeks you don't know anyone, then maybe you start a college course. On the first day, you talk to one person but this person isn't very well connected. You now know one person, and you aren't connected to many more. Slowly, you make some more friends until, say, you come across some really popular person who seems to know everyone. Because this person knows everyone, she invites you to a party. You meet more people. You start going out with some guy you met at this party. His dad, say, is the mayor of the town. Suddenly you have connected with two important hubs in the network and you find you are only a couple of steps away from anyone in the town. The moment you tip from being a no one into being really connected – that's the phase transition.'

'OK,' says Esther. 'I get it.'

Kieran slumps back in his chair, a little as if he was a coin-operated information machine that has just been deactivated and is waiting for someone to insert more coins. Blackman puts down his chalk and addresses us all again.

'What this young man has just explained,' he says, pointing at Kieran, 'is how "short cuts" appear in the network. These short cuts are what turn ordinary networks into small-world phenomena. However, although we all have access to these "short cuts", it seems that the problem is how we find them. However well-connected we are in theory, it is very hard for us to evaluate our links beyond the local level. I may know that I know you, but I do not know everyone you know. I certainly don't know anything about who your friend Simon (whom I have never met) knows. Yet I am connected to his friends by only three steps. The problem isn't the connectivity but our ability to navigate it. Stanley Milgram found this with his small-world study, where he asked randomly selected people in the US Midwest to try to get letters to a stockbroker in Boston, on the east coast. The letters could not be posted. Instead, those taking part were asked to hand them to people they knew who might have social ties that might take the message closer to the target. Although Milgram did prove that the letter would get to the target eventually, he didn't show people using their contacts very well.

'So, if we apply this to your desire to spread a plastic product among the world's children – a commendable aim, I am sure – then you may have to navigate the network on behalf of the children. Build something into your product that means it spreads itself. Disease works like this. You may never come into contact with the person on the fourteenth floor of your office block, but you may spread your germs to them none the less. This is called "unconscious" or "automatic" transmission, and I believe this is what marketing departments want built into products they are responsible for selling. Of course they do! Automatic transmission does their job for them. Lazy bastards!

'Consider Hotmail. Every time you send a message using Hotmail, it comes with an advertisement for Hotmail itself. The message is the ad. The product spreads itself. Or, perhaps more pertinently, consider MSN Messenger, used, I believe, by teenagers everywhere – certainly by my son, who doesn't allow me access to my own computer in the evenings. In order to talk to other people on MSN, you have to have the MSN technology yourself. This piece of software promotes itself!

'All this mathematical network theory relates also to disease epidemics, the "madness of crowds" and the breakdown and recovery of network systems. Why did so many people go crazy buying tulips in Holland in the seventeenth century, even selling their houses to do so? Why did seemingly rational people get carried along by the 1990s dot-com hysteria? It seems that we, in our networks, are wired up in such a way that we are both resistant *and* vulnerable to 'infection' from diseases and ideas; system failure and so on. However, one very important rule holds true: you are more likely to get a disease or buy a particular book if *everyone else has it too*. This is called a power law, or is sometimes referred to as the Matthew Principle. What is the Matthew Principle? It is, of course: "for whomsoever hath, to him shall be given", otherwise known as "the rich get richer while the poor get poorer". The more people that have a product, the more people will buy it. Now. Kieran, I think it was?'

Kieran seems to wake with a jolt. 'Huh?'

'Who was Stanley Milgram's mentor?'

'Um . . .'

'Ha! Thank God you don't know everything. Milgram's mentor was Solomon Asche, who demonstrated that people would give the wrong answer to a simple question if enough other people in the room had given that answer first. He conducted a very fascinating series of experiments, whereby, for example, the subject would enter a room in which he or she believed the other people also to be subjects in an experiment to do with reasoning or some such. The other people in the room were, however, actors. The people in the room would be shown a series of shapes, like this . . .' He approaches the whiteboard, rubs out his diagrams from before and draws a circle, a square and a triangle, in a horizontal line, starting from the far left-hand side of the board, as if they were letters in a word. Circle, square, triangle, from left to right. Then, on the far right-hand side of the board, he draws a vertical line, like an 'I' or a 'l'.

'Now,' he says. 'Asche asked the people in the room to say whether they thought the square was closer to the triangle, or closer to the line. Obviously, it is closer to the triangle. However, he found that when he asked the actors first – who were primed to give the wrong answer, and say instead that it was closer to the line – the subject would often give the wrong answer too. Such is the madness of crowds. We may not like to think we follow the crowd but, to differing extents, we all do. We do odd things – eating meat, praying to an invisible, non-existent bearded man – because everyone else does. Crazes in your own industry often involve children wanting the toy that everyone else has got, particularly at Christmas, as I should well know having bought my son Transformers, Mutant Turtles, Power Rangers and goodness knows what else before he grew out of them.

'Once you have got your odious plastic object to the stage that everyone wants it, the craze is set. But to get it there in the first place, you have to build in a way for the product to navigate networks and proliferate itself as widely as possible. How is your product going to be spread not just between friendship groups but beyond them? It only took one infected rat on a ship to spread the bubonic plague to a whole new country, remember, because once the plague was there, among a network of local rats, it could look after itself. Perhaps television is the way that an idea for a toy can spread to "remote" nodes on the network. Or perhaps you will do as other toy companies have done – or so I read in my weekend newspaper – and give the toy away to the most popular child in every school. Once you have infected the most connected hubs, the other nodes will soon follow! In this way, *you* would be the connecting point between various networks. But remember, of course, that any toy or product which involves communicating, swapping, giving, comparing and so on, has built-in automatic transmission. Think of your vile plastic objects as dandelion clocks strewn by the wind. The dandelion seeds wouldn't fly in the wind had they not been designed that way. Any questions?'

Kieran puts his hand up immediately. 'Who designed the dandelions?' he asks. 'You can't mean God, because you already said . . .'

'The creators,' Blackman says dreamily. 'The original mathematicians.'

'Cool! So . . .'

Mac stands up. 'I think we have taken enough of Mr Blackman's time now. What a fascinating discussion. Thank you.' He looks at his watch. 'OK, now I think you are expected for your sailing classes soon. Can you please refer to the times on the noticeboard for each group please. Mark, I'll see you out.'

* * *

The daytime is all right, and if I have to be alone in the light, I can cope. At night, however, I have to be with people. To find myself alone at night is just too hideous a proposition. What would I do if it actually happened, and I did find myself alone in the dark? I think I would probably scream until I passed out, or until someone came. I understand that, in many ways, this is an irrational fear. By definition I cannot be hurt if I am alone, because being alone means that no one is there. Yet in my most panic-stricken moments I would even wish the enemy there in the dark with me. *The enemy.* The enemy is a two-headed man, or sometimes two heads on the body of an insect or a spider. I could not ever describe this to anyone. I could not describe the way that, since the incident at the bus stop, those men have become super-real in my mind. Only I understand the way that one whisker has become four, blue eyes have become red and a sneer has become a grimace with fangs; fangs dripping with blood and gristly bits of small schoolchildren. But I'd still rather they came than that I was left alone in the dark. Perhaps it's because I would rather just get on with dying than wait for the inevitable, alone and unseeing. It is because of this that I have been sleeping in my grandparents' room.

Interesting things have happened as a result of my fear (which my grandparents say is actually a 'phobia': like fear, but more impor- tant). Because the nights are so potentially horrific, so mind-curdlingly, heart-stoppingly terrifying, everything outside of this set of 'things of which I am afraid' (we have been doing sets in maths) seems just brilliant. For example, the daytime is brilliant. If, during the day, I ever feel sad about my father being lost, or I feel bored at school, or upset because of a fight at playtime or anything like that, I simply have to remind myself that it is not night and it is not dark and I am not alone. Other people seem moderately happy, or just the same kind of happy/sad, all the time. If the way they felt was a graph, it would be a single flat line, with maybe a blip for Christmas and another for their birthday, perhaps. But the graph of my moods has mountains and valleys galore. Dawn, for example, can make me soar on its own. A whole nine, or maybe ten, hours until it starts to get dark again! Hooray! In the summer it will be brilliant, because there will be a good deal less darkness than there is now. In some ways, fear is a good thing. It makes you appreciate life more: the bits it hasn't spat all over seem all the more delicious for it.

For these reasons, I do not think I need to go to the doctor about my fear, and I have explained this to my grandparents. Of course, I never want to go to the doctor about anything. The doctor's surgery is a potentially dangerous place from which I would not want to have to escape (if he got out his pliers, or revealed himself to be an alien with a bacterial weapon – *bang!* – I'm melting!). Also, I have heard that if a doctor thinks you are being mistreated, he can send you to live in a children's home. I have never been mistreated but my family is unlucky in some ways, and we seem different, and sometimes that's all it takes. If I got sent to a children's home they would undoubtedly lock me in dark rooms and I would be forced to either run away (which would itself inevitably mean ending up in the dark on my own, probably in a forest) or kill myself. I don't like the idea of killing myself but I would do it if I had to. I wish I had an emergency cyanide pill, like my grandfather did during the war.

It is almost two months since I met the men at the bus stop. Christmas is coming, and I have opened ten windows on my Advent calendar. My grandparents are still letting me stay in their room with them at night, and Rachel is coming home soon. Things don't feel so bad. Some days I don't think any bad thoughts at all, which is very nice, especially compared to some of the days I have had, where bad thoughts are snakes in a pit and you just fall into it with no ladder.

I am thinking about sets a lot. A set is something from maths that means a collection of things that share a property. You could have the set of even numbers, or a set of all numbers less than 100. You can make a set of anything and it seems neat and tidy, like putting thoughts in a drawer in your mind. Some sets are potentially confusing, though. For example, you could have something called 'the set of all sets'. Would this set contain itself or not? It would have to; but how could it? This situation, where something seems to be right and wrong, or true and false, at the same time, is called a paradox. I love paradoxes! When I grow up I am going to have a cat and call it Paradox. A paradox is what happens when you go back into the past and kill one of your distant relatives. If you kill them, of course, you prevent yourself from being born. But if you did not exist, you couldn't go back and kill them. I read a science book that said that this is why time travel to the past is never possible. It said that any system that supports paradoxes is inherently flawed. Like sets, maybe?

My grandfather told me some more paradoxes. He uses them a lot in his magazine column. My favourite one is about time travel (lots of paradoxes are either about sets or time travel, it turns out). A scientist, Henry Humphrey, develops a method of travelling to the future. While there, he goes to a library and reads some science books that are way more advanced than those in his own time. One book in particular grabs his attention, and then he realises it has his name on it! He must have written this book in his own time. Extraordinary. When he gets back to his normal life, he starts his groundbreaking work, replicating the material from the book he saw in the future (well, it had his name on it – why not?). He publishes it to breathtaking acclaim, and only then realises that he has created, or been a victim of, two huge paradoxes. Who wrote this book? Where did it come from?

Henry Humphrey suddenly doesn't know if he has committed a gross act of inter-temporal plagiarism. Did he originally write the text of this book or not? In the story, he first encounters the book in the future. *Then* he writes it. Does this imply that the book existed in the future 'before' it did in the past? Or simply that Henry writes it after he returns from his trip to the future? Does it imply that it was actually written by someone else? It's hard to tell. Even if the book 'was' written by someone else in the future, it will have Henry's name on it when he sees it, as he is of course about to go back to the past and write it earlier. So who wrote the book? Can we ever know?

The real paradox, however, is in the existence of the book in the first place. To recap: Henry goes to the future, sees some information in a book, comes back and uses this information to create his own book which becomes the book he finds in the future, from which he gets the ideas, etc. etc. This is a very neat loop except for one thing. The information in the book comes from nowhere. It is never originally written! The scientist gets the information from the future. But who put it there? He did! So where did he get it? The future! This loop continues indefinitely.

'I've solved it,' I say to my grandfather one crisp day towards the middle of December. 'It's simple. Someone else writes the book . . .'

'When?'

'In the future.' My grandfather frowns but I continue anyway. 'So the book is there, with another author . . .'

'Can we give him – or her – a name?'

'Yes. It is by a woman called Tabitha Paradox.'

'All right.' My grandfather stirs the soup on the stove.

'OK, so Tabitha writes this book. When Henry comes to the future, this is the book he finds.'

'But it has his name on it.'

'Yes, I know! That's what I'm trying to explain. The moment he sees the book, time shifts and her name changes to his, as it is this moment that alters history. He doesn't notice this, of course, as it happens in less than a split second. Perhaps all he feels is a crackle in the air, or a sudden rush of cold wind.' I have been reading a lot of science-fiction books lately, and I think I have a feel for the sorts of things that would signify a ripple in time.

'But he still goes back to his own time and writes the book?'

'Yes.'

'But then the paradox is still there. Tabitha can't write her book because it will already exist. It will have been written before she was born. Her ideas won't be groundbreaking, because they will already be there – in this book by Henry Humphrey . . .'

'That *she* wrote!' I say. 'How could he write it without her?'

'Well, there's the paradox,' my grandfather says. 'Who did write it? If it was Henry, then he got the information from nowhere. But it can't have been Tabitha, because by the time she is born, the book will already exist, with Henry's name on it.'

While we have been talking, my grandmother has emerged from her study. Now my grandfather gets up to pour her drink, and to start making his pipe (he only smokes one after dinner now and it is the highlight of his day, so much so that he spends a good deal of time before dinner making and tinkering with it).

'What have you two been mumbling about?' my grandmother says.

'Paradoxes,' my grandfather says, straightening out his yellow pipe-cleaner.

'What sort of paradoxes?' she asks, sitting down with her drink.

'Time travel paradoxes,' I say.

She laughs. 'Oh dear. No wonder you both look confused.'

I tell her our paradox, and she laughs some more. The soup is simmering on the stove and I can smell sweet carrots, parsnips and herbs, as the windows steam up. I feel safe like this, even though darkness is falling. The steam on the windows is a protective film and I am not alone because my grandparents are here.

'So you have a made-up story that doesn't make sense,' she says. 'Is that actually a paradox, or just an implausible story?' She is addressing my grandfather with a shiny look in her eyes and an almost naughty smile.

'If you could travel to the future, and back, it could happen,' he says. 'That's the point of the story.'

'Perhaps it means that time travel will never be possible,' I say.

'It's rather likely that travel to the past will never be possible, certainly,' my grandmother says.

'How do you know?' I say, widening my eyes. In our family my grandmother is always, always correct. My grandfather is brilliant, with his crazy ideas and lateral solutions to his puzzles, but she is a flawless logician. If she says there will never be time travel to the past, there never will be.

'Yes, how do you know?' my grandfather says.

'I know because I have never met anyone from the future,' she says. 'If there was ever going to be a way of coming back, people would be coming back. It is logical. History would be full of strange twists and turns caused by future people turning up and messing around with things. Betting shops would be full of people from the future. Things would disappear all the time. But none of these things happen. So, people can assume that time travel to the past will never be invented or discovered.'

'Maybe it just hasn't been discovered yet, in the future,' I say.

'Think it through logically, Alice,' she says. 'It doesn't matter when in the future time travel to the past is invented. If it is *ever* invented, people could come back to this time, now.'

'Maybe you can't see time travellers,' my grandfather suggests. 'And they can't change anything. If that was the case, then people could be travelling to the past all the time and no one would know.'

'Well, yes, that would solve your paradox problem, wouldn't it?'

'Why do you keep saying "time travel to the past"?' I ask my grandmother. 'What about time travel to the future?'

'Well, time travel to the future is theoretically possible, using Einstein's theories. All you need to do is get in a space-ship and travel somewhere very, very fast. When you come back, more time will have elapsed on Earth than in your speeding space-craft.'

This shuts me up. I never knew this. While I think about whizzing off to the future, a place where women wear silver mini-skirts and have hard cones for breasts, my grandmother gets up and puts a Bach record on the turntable.

Later, while we eat our soup, I keep asking my grandmother questions about time travel and the potential paradoxes it could create. It seems that all these paradoxes specifically concern travel to the past: changing something that has already happened. There are no paradoxes in going to the future, just as long as you don't try to come back.

'Einstein's universe is a one-way system, that's for sure,' she says, and my grandfather laughs a lot.

'What we really need is a bypass,' he says, still laughing.

They have just built a small one-way system in our village centre, which everyone is always joking about for some reason. There is also a plan to build a bypass, whatever that is. Cue more jokes. I didn't know roads could be so funny.

'A bypass,' she repeats. 'Ha ha ha . . .'

'What about wormholes?' my grandfather says suddenly.

'What's a wormhole?' I ask.

'It's a potential short-cut through time,' my grandmother says to me. To my grandfather she says, 'Don't be so silly, Peter. It's quite clear that wormholes can't exist, or if they did, no one could actually travel through one.'

'Hmm,' is all he says. I know what that *Hmm* means. It means *Maybe not mathematically; but then you can't explain ghosts mathematically, or telepathy.* He has been interested in such things only since we began working on the Voynich Manuscript, but it is almost an obsession now: that there might be 'things' out there that we don't have the tools to understand. Is the Voynich Manuscript then one of the tools, or one of the things?

It strikes me then that he and my grandmother are engaged in completely opposite occupations. He in the realm of the 'what if', and she in the realm of the 'not very likely'. In order to progress, my grandfather has to sometimes formulate hypotheses that are counter-intuitive, or seem ridiculous. What if aliens created the Voynich Manuscript? What if it isn't supposed to be read? What if it came from the future, written in a language we don't yet know (another reason for all the time-travel conversations)? Then again, my grandmother works with imaginary numbers all day, and something called the zeta function. Maybe I am wrong. Maybe what they do is exactly the same; creeping up on impossible problems with a few made-up stories and invisible theories and trying to convince them to come out of the bushes. My grandmother's leaps into the unknown are just slightly harder to understand, sometimes.

My grandmother has been explaining to my grandfather about wormholes, and now they are talking about some other part of time travel, and she is saying something about the mathematician Gödel, whom she met once, a long time ago. She finishes what she is saying and glances at me.

'If you really want to investigate paradoxes, Alice,' she says. 'You should look at what Gödel did with them.'

My grandfather gives her an odd look.

'What did he do?' I ask.

'Well, I can't explain the whole thing right now, but do you know of the Liar Paradox?'

'"All Cretans are liars"?' I say. 'That one?' The Liar Paradox is one of the oldest puzzles in the world. Epimenides, a Cretan, makes the statement, 'All Cretans are liars.' If he is telling the truth, then he is lying. But, if he is lying, he is telling the truth, which means he is lying. This kind of thing makes my brain fuzzy, in a nice way. It's like the set of all sets, anyway.

'Yes,' my grandmother says. 'Well, Gödel proved that the whole of mathematics could be seen as a paradox, just like "All Cretans are liars". Because it is self-referential and provides its own rules, there has always been a fear that mathematics may include inconsistencies at a profoundly basic level. That's what he showed – in a much more complicated way, of course. I'll lend you a book, if you promise to be careful with it. It has number codes in it, too. Gödel invented a code that you will find interesting, I think.'

Number codes and paradoxes at the same time! How exciting. And this reminds me that I should get back to work on the Stevenson/Heath Manuscript before too long. I just have to stop being afraid of it, that's all.

* * *

Our sailing time isn't until three o'clock, so after lunch I go back to my room to see if there's been any response from the mysterious person to whom Hiro delivered my message. There is nothing. It's funny how you get used to things, sometimes. The idea of someone letting themselves into my room and leaving something for me or taking something away just doesn't bother me as much as perhaps it should. My credit cards and other important objects are safely stashed where no one – this time – will find them. My necklace is always around my neck. If I was at home it would be different, perhaps. But this room isn't mine. It's just my temporary space.

There's nothing here, however. No change at all since I left this morning. I put down my bag and take out the slim, soft pack of cards Kieran gave me at breakfast. I still don't know what you would do with them. I do like this Green Man image, though. It reminds me of something, an old book. The Voynich Manuscript – of course. And all the hundreds, possibly thousands, of books I read while trying to find any link at all to what it might mean. We never got the answer, of course. As far as I know, people are still trying to decipher the strange text and images. Perhaps I will go back to it one day, but without my grandfather, there seems to be little point. Even if I solved the riddle, there'd be no one to tell. If I could tell the whole world, there would still be no one to tell.

So many of my interests – and a lot of my general knowledge – come directly from studying the Voynich Manuscript. When I was a kid, I learnt about plants and herbs and art movements to help with my grandfather's research. He'd ask me for things like a list of common and Latin names for every blue flower, say, or for the first time two colours were used together in ancient art. When I got older, the knowledge became more sophisticated, and related more to my own work on the manuscript. My grandfather and I both needed as much distraction as possible after my grandmother died. We moved to London because we couldn't cope with the space left in our old house after she had 'gone' (departed, passed over, passed away, never *died*). We simply left the space behind.

In London I became obsessed with herbalism and then with homeopathy. Partly, it was because the Voynich Manuscript looked for all the world like a medical textbook, with pictures of plants and so on, and I was convinced that this route would help us understand the kind of material it might contain. My grandfather had taught me that if you want to decipher a document, you have to be an expert in what you think that document might contain, otherwise you will have no idea how to fill in blanks as they come up. He told me that when my grandmother was at Bletchley Park, she had to learn all sorts of things about German engineering practices and methods of ship design, for example. But my interest also came from a genuine desire to heal. I didn't want my grandfather to die – and I certainly didn't trust the doctors who had failed first my mother and then my grandmother. I became convinced I could keep him alive myself, if only I learnt the correct art.

Homeopathy is definitely an art, as well as a science. The names of the remedies have always thrilled me. *Arsenicum, Lachesis, Pulsatilla, Tarantula, Sulphur, Natrum Muriaticum* . . . There are thousands, all in Latin. When you buy a homeopathic remedy, you can get it in various forms – liquid, soft tablets, pills. I always buy remedies in their most common form, as little round, white, lactose pills that you dissolve on your tongue. Each of these pills contains only a wispy, whispery remnant – like an afterthought or a forgotten dream – of the original substance, which would have been diluted and shaken, sometimes thousands of times, to release the energy (and stop it being poisonous, as all homeopathic substances are poisons). I wasn't convinced at first that there was anything in this strange medical system, so different from anything I had ever known before. Then I saw the remedies work. Since I discovered homeopathy, I haven't been to the doctor once. I couldn't save my grandfather, though. In the end, he refused any kind of medication at all.

The Green Man stares at me, his eyes almost lost in the curled leaves of his beard and hair. I read once that you can still see Green Men hidden high up in churches, evidence of our pagan past, created by the pagans who had to build the churches. I smile at the Green Man but he just carries on staring at me. I put him away and get out my notebook.

Mark Blackman's talk has actually made me a bit more enthused about this project. I jot down some extra notes and thoughts at the end of what I wrote while he was talking, then glance back over the whole lot. Model student that I suddenly am, I find myself neatly drawing up a matrix of attributes I feel a teenage girls' product could have, and then I add one column with only two words in it: 'Automatic Transmission'. The product must be able to spread itself.

I write another note to myself: *If possible, the product itself should be the means of transmission.*

There is a knock at the door, which makes me jump. There I was, telling myself that I am OK about all the weird stuff going on here; now someone knocks at the door and I almost fall off my chair. Could this be Hiro, or Hiro's friend, with this 'longer message'? I open the door and instead find Ben, smiling.

'Good. You're here,' he says.

'Hi,' I say back. 'How was sailing?'

'All right.' He grins, and walks into the room. 'When's yours?'

'Three. I was just getting some work done and then I was going to have a nap.'

'Do you want some company?'

'Yeah, that would be nice. I do have to get some sleep, though. I fell asleep with my clothes on last night and then woke up at six with my radio blasting in my ear.'

'Yuck.'

'Yeah.'

I get onto the bed and sit there with my legs crossed. Ben sits on the armchair.

'So what's this work you're doing?' he asks me.

'The teenage girl thing.'

'God, you're keen.'

'Keen? Hardly. I've only just started.'

'This whole thing . . .' Ben looks distracted, his dark eyes flicking around the room.

'What?'

'It's pretty sinister, don't you think?'

'What is?' I ask. He really does look freaked out. 'Ben?'

He crosses his legs, then re-crosses them the other way. 'All that stuff about networks and phase transitions and viruses. I don't know. It just spun me out a bit.' He looks at his hands. 'Is it right?'

'Yeah, I think so,' I say. Then it occurs to me that he doesn't mean 'right' as in 'correct'. He is asking if our project here is morally right. 'We're just doing our jobs,' I say. 'We don't make up the rules, or assign the projects. If people don't want whatever we make, they won't buy it. It is their choice.'

'Yeah, but we're learning to create addictions. To tell lies. To make products that act like viruses . . .'

I frown. 'Yeah. I know.'

'If you know, then why are you doing it?'

'Um . . .' I want to say that I am doing it because we are supposed to: because that's why we're here. But that doesn't ring true at all. I'm not like that – I've never liked doing what I am told. But the real reason is somehow worse. 'I like the challenge,' I say eventually. 'I like the idea of solving a really hard problem, or getting the solution to a puzzle. I know it's a bit lame . . .'

'God. I bet you like crosswords, too.' He frowns.

'I used to compile crosswords. That was my job before they asked me to come and work at PopCo.' I look down at the floor. The rug on the floorboards has an interesting tiling pattern, regular geometric shapes.

'You were headhunted, weren't you?'

'How do you know that?'

'Something someone said. So PopCo decided that your puzzle-solving skills would be just what they needed. Interesting . . .'

'You've gone all weird,' I say. He has. He's acting like I am a mystery he is trying to solve.

'What? Oh, sorry.' He shakes his head. 'It wasn't just the seminar. I'm feeling a bit . . .'

'What? What happened?'

'Oh, I was looking for something on the way back from sailing and I ended up over in that strange Kid Lab bit of the estate. Have you been over there?'

'Not really. No. Not further than the canteen building.'

'God.' He lights a cigarette. 'It fucking freaked me out. There's this guy over there called Oscar. He's in charge of the Kid Lab activities. He saw me bumbling around and offered me a tour. I had no idea what they did over there.'

'I'm guessing that they have scary one-way mirrors . . .'

'Yeah. Fucking hell. And they have this whole room laid out like, I don't know, like some kind of paedophilic reception room or something. That's what it made me think of. It made me think, *This is the kind of place little kids would sit around waiting to be fucked by old men.* It was horrible. It was all clean and glossy, with all these boxes of toys and carefully selected old junk that kids traditionally play with – like socks, washing-up liquid bottles and things like that. There were little play mats on the floor, and beanbags, and a fridge full of fizzy drinks and fruit. Oscar said that they bus in kids from nearby towns in term-time to take part in trials. In the holidays, like now, they give poor, inner-city kids a "free holiday" in return for the kids' participation in focus groups. They get the room ready, depending on what test they are doing, so the children might have just PopCo toys or a collection of found objects, or both. Say a little kid would rather play with an old sock than with Sailor Sam or something – or the Bubblegum Tree or whatever else we produce – then the researchers want to know why. And then they try to work out what PopCo could make that's based on the principle of playing with an old sock. Oscar was telling me about something called the Sock It to Me kit . . .'

'Yeah,' I say. 'That's in development. I didn't know that's where the idea had come from, though.'

'What is it, exactly?'

'It's a kit that enables you to, I don't know, funk up your socks or something. As far as I know, there are two kits in development. One, mainly for girls, is a kind of embroidery set – with loads of iron-on-ability – that lets you add eyes to your socks, and patterns and so on. I think the tagline is *Friends You Can Wear*. The other one is called Monster Foot, and it's mainly for boys. It's essentially a puppet-making kit, with stick-on googly eyes, crazy tongues made out of felt and so on. I think they were trying to work out which one would sell better.'

'How do you know all this?'

'It's all very intense at Battersea,' I explain. 'Everyone knows what everyone else is doing. Plus, I go outside and smoke, just like Mark Blackman said, and because of that I know a girl who was working on that project. Bloody hell, though. I didn't know they got ideas like that. It is a bit creepy.' Except I do know. I know what focus groups are like and this is no different. You just tune it out, though. You have to, otherwise you can't get on with your job. And everything looks odd, if you look at it for long enough, even the word 'and'.

Ben puts his cigarette out in a PopCo ashtray. 'What I don't understand is that if kids like playing with old socks, why we can't just leave them to it. Why do companies like PopCo have to jump in there and ruin everything? Is it just greed? I don't know.'

'Maybe one of the shareholders needs even more money,' I suggest, and then we both laugh.

After this, we get into bed and sleep for about an hour until I wake up sweating, still half-stuck in my dream that I am late for the sailing class. In my dream, when I get there I find that the boat has simply sunk into the floor.

Chapter Twenty

Saturday morning. We are leaving on our strange nature ramble in about half an hour. I have a sore throat, so I am chucking Aconitum down my throat like there's no tomorrow (in homeopathic terms, this means I have actually taken two doses). I hate colds. I will do almost anything to avert a cold, including taking high doses of vitamin C, Echinacea and spoonfuls of honey virtually every hour if I think I have one coming on. I do have my reasons for this. When I was a kid, my dad and I lived in a damp council flat and since then I have always had a weak chest. Plus, it was colds (or, actually, varying degrees of the 'flu) that finally killed both my grandparents. Whenever I get a cold, it cuts through to my chest with the sharpness of a sickle and I go around wheezing like an old woman for weeks. I have told myself that the next bad chest will be the sign that I have to stop smoking. I am not looking forward to that day, not at all.

Aconitum is the Latin prefix for the Monkshood family of flowers and is poisonous, of course, in crude doses. In fact, Aconites are some of the most used poisons in history. *Aconitum angelicum* is the wild version, but *Aconitum napellus*, the domestic variety that you can still see in gardens today (and the variety used in homeopathic prescribing), was originally introduced in order that everyone could have his or her own supply of poison. Sixteenth-century herbals commonly warned that its charming, shy, blue flowers are not to be trusted. If you eat Monkshood, it kills you. The poisoning comes on suddenly, and always makes the victim panicky and terrified of their approaching death. If you find that you have an illness which has come on suddenly, and you think you might die (and even feel that you could predict the time of your own death), then you might need homeopathic Aconitum as a remedy. This is the thing about homeopathy: *similia similibus curentur*. Like cures like. Suddenness is therefore a particular keynote of Aconite, and many homeopaths suggest taking it at the first sign of a cold; when you go, in an instant, from feeling sunny and relaxed and normal to having razor blades in your throat and an inflated balloon in your head. I have quite a high-strength bottle of Aconite with me – 1M – so I think I have a good chance of staving off this thing.

What do I need for a day on the moor? My mind briefly fills with thoughts of jam jars with wire handles, magnifying glasses and sandwiches wrapped in greaseproof paper. But no, I am an adult. I will take my survival kit, a bottle of mineral water and perhaps a packed lunch from the chefs, depending on whether anyone else is doing the same thing. We have been told to take a compass and a notebook. I have a compass in my survival kit, and I take my notebook with me everywhere. Are these adult things to take? I'm not sure.

Thinking about my survival kit is like an electric shock of normal life, reminding me of a world outside PopCo Towers. I suddenly wonder if Atari is OK with Rachel, and if he enjoyed his corporate-sponsored ride over to her place. I realise that if I wasn't here, on this odd project, I would be preparing the roughs for my survival kit presentation, originally due on Monday. Who knows when that will happen, now. And how long will it take me to finish? I am out of survival kit mode now and well into this other thing, whatever it turns out to be. Have I gone through a door that only opens one way? Will I be able to go back? I hate leaving things unfinished, and always have these fears about not being able to go back to them. I'm not sure I can even remember anything about survival. God.

Before I leave the room I check again that no notes or letters have been delivered but there is nothing. I am meeting Ben, Kieran and the others by the sports hall in about twenty minutes so I had probably better go. I am planning to go the long way round, since I am not in the mood for playing Kieran's card game (now christened *Jack*), and people tend to challenge you to games whenever they see you walking around. I simply feel too odd and sore-throaty to concentrate on anything today.

So I am skulking around like some kind of weirdo, keeping to a route I think others will avoid: through the sunken garden, around the edge of the car park and along the side of the wood. I have found these Echinacea pastilles in my bag but I have been trying to resist sucking them because of the menthol they contain. Early twentieth-century homeopaths like James Tyler Kent thought that menthol (or camphor) and coffee work as antidotes to homeopathic remedies. I have never been sure what to think about this but I don't want to take any chances with the Aconitum.

I am thinking about Kent, and wondering whether to take another dose of Aconitum. It's important not to repeat a remedy too soon, especially if it is working. Is my Aconitum working? I'm not sure. Quite lost in these thoughts, I almost don't notice Georges walking briskly towards me. When I do see him, my stomach flips over like an extreme fairground ride. I never did anything about his note, or his business card. Oh yes, I did. I remember now. I burnt them. I burnt his mobile phone number, which I can never get again by any other means other than from him. What is wrong with me? When he speaks to me, perhaps I can ask him to give it to me again, just in case? But he doesn't stop. He gives me a slightly strange look, and then a sad-ish smile, puts his head down and keeps going. Oh well. I suppose there's only so much running a person can do before they just get tired and stop. Alan Turing may have found that some programs simply never terminate but this one obviously has. Does love terminate? Fucking hell. What am I thinking? I must be ill.

My stomach flips again but doesn't end up the right way around. I whisper it to the forest. *I love him. I do fucking love him. I am in love with Georges Celéri.* Then I feel like crying. OK. Calm down, Alice. That was a bit loud, for a whisper. Yes, yes, big revelation; and I think that maybe I am in love with him but I will never, ever do anything about it. I am a scruffy creative with a barely affordable mortgage. He is a millionaire. Yeah, if this was a romance story we'd be a perfect match. But it's the real world and I am not for sale. It was OK talking to Georges about books and music; and when I looked into his eyes I felt something amazing, like we were the two missing pieces of an ancient puzzle. Yes, I admit it. I did feel those things. But they don't mean I could ever fit into his world. What would I do? Move to New York and learn how to use cutlery properly? Spend my days having my nails done and buying art? It's just not viable. Or he could move in with me and slum it for a while before eventually we have a conversation that begins, 'Darling, I . . .' and he persuades me to go for the first option after all. 'All my friends are in New York,' he'd say. And he'd point out that I have no friends in London, which is almost true, and it would all just go horribly wrong. My whole life would seem like a pathetic little novella to him, or a short poem about loss. *Join me in my multi-volume, leather-bound saga, darling.* No! Maybe he does just want to fuck me and nothing more. But if that's the case, I'd rather not find out.

No one would understand this. Everyone else finds Georges deeply annoying. Is it only me who sees his charisma? Or is everyone else simply daunted by it? I really don't understand why I am in love with him and it definitely has to stop. Ben is exactly right for me at the moment. Maybe it is just sex – but it is pretty intense sex, which seems to be what I need. And we are not asking each other for anything. There are no promises that we'll end up breaking. Ben probably lives in one room in some inner-city house-share in Reading, with mouldy coffee cups and science-fiction novels in little piles by his bed, probably a mattress on the floor. All his possessions would probably sell at auction for less than Georges would spend on a meal. Why am I thinking like this? It's almost embarrassing to find myself thinking like this. Surely the point of love is not simply to find two guys and then go to bed with the poorest one? I don't know if Ben is even poor, anyway. But he does have a hollow look, and he wears second-hand jackets.

And I bet Georges has a massive family. I bet he has all kinds of wonderful warm relations in France and Japan and New York. I can just see myself on some big, shiny ship with an expensive scarf and possibly a lapdog, on my way to meet Mama and Papa and various cousins and aunts. And me, an orphan with nobody. I can contribute nothing to this fantasy world. Do people like me have children because it's the only way of having a family again? But I don't want that. I just don't know what I do want. Perhaps Ben is the solution to my puzzle after all. Or perhaps there is no solution: not all puzzles have solutions, after all. Turing again.

I am early for my rendezvous, and no one is anywhere near the sports hall when I arrive. Not wanting to be the lame one who has arrived first, I keep going in the direction of the Kid Lab buildings, walking purposefully, as if I haven't yet reached my destination. I wonder if this guy Oscar will be around, but when I get there, there is no one at all. The door is open, however, so I go in, finding myself in a square-shaped entrance foyer with bright coat-pegs all around its walls. There is also a coatstand painted to look like a frog, and a few chairs around a coffee table in the shape of a lady-bird. The lights are off, and perhaps that's why everything looks wrong, but I immediately register the same sort of sensation that Ben was talking about. This gets worse as I walk through an archway (with 'cute' spiders painted around it), and into a large play area. My skin tingles. Is this where they watch the kids? It must be. There are play mats everywhere, and boxes of different kinds of toys. I am a giant in this world, with doll-tables and doll-chairs and imaginary objects everywhere. I almost trip over a wooden building block and instinct makes me pick it up. I have this thing about reversing entropy. If something is disordered, I have to tidy it up, if something is out of place, I have to put it away. If I see that something has fallen off a shelf in the supermarket, I always have to pick it up and put it back; always. I can't stand things being, well, not exactly out of place, but on the way to *disorder*. The block has a big red 'A' on two of its faces, pictures of acorns on two more, and apples on the other two. *A is for Alice*, I think, and smile before putting it back in one of the toy boxes. It's a false smile, however. Why bother with a false smile when no one is here? Maybe there is someone here, though, watching me. I wouldn't know. All I can see when I look at the mirrored walls is myself. Oh God. It must be the darkness that is unsettling me. Darkness and childhood don't go well together. Time to leave. Ben's right about this place. Something about it is frightening.

What would I think if I was a kid and I had arrived here to test some product, or to be observed playing? How different would that be from what has happened to me anyway; coming here and being told I have to come up with a unique product plan? I expect I would be far more excited if I was a kid, of course. And perhaps I would feel important, too. It would have been explained to me, probably, that some exciting adults from the toy industry would be observing me, and maybe asking some questions about toys. I bet I would have loved that, as a kid.

*   *   *

'Alicia!' says Kieran when I arrive back at the sports hall. Why has he added two unnecessary syllables to my name? Still, he gives me a joint, for which I am grateful. Will it help my throat? Would Kent approve? Who cares? As well as Kieran, the group of people contains Grace; Niila and Mitzi from the plush-toys team in Iceland; the blonde girl, who is introduced to me as Violet; the black tattooed guy called Frank; and a guy I haven't spoken to before called James (the one I thought looked like a social worker on heroin). Kieran starts giving out photocopied sheets to everyone.

'Where's Ben?' I say to him when he gives me mine.

'No idea,' he says.

I look at my sheet. It is a map of Dartmoor with no place names. Instead of place names, it has names of animals. In the north is something called Great Bustard. Slightly to the west of this is Sea Eagle. In the south-east, there is a cluster of names: Polecat, Night Jar and Turtle Dove. Woodcock, Raven and Lapwing appear in other places on the map. On the bottom left-hand corner of the map there is a legend in ornate script: *Map of Dartmoor Illustrative of its Zoology*, it says. Next to this there is a compass rose and a date: 1839. This reminds me of a treasure map. Still no Ben. I don't know anyone here apart from Grace and Kieran. I wander over to Grace.

'What's this all about?' I ask her.

'Psychic orienteering,' she says, smiling.

'Huh?'

'Yeah, mad, isn't it? It's just another one of Kieran's crazy ideas.' She laughs and pushes some of her long black fringe out of her eyes. 'With just this map and a compass, we have to find our way to . . . Hey, Kieran? Where is it we're heading?'

Kieran stops talking to James and looks around.

'Yeah, good point babe. I probably should tell everyone what we're doing,' he says. 'Right. We will today be attempting to get from our current position, roughly three miles east of Honey Buzzard – I have marked it on the map – to Corn Rabbit, via Goshawk, Moor Buzzard and Buzzard.'

Niila puts his thin arm in the air.

'How will we know when we are there?' he asks.

'We will see corn rabbits, of course,' Kieran says.

'This map's from 1839, yeah?' says Violet. 'Everything's going to be fucking extinct by now, surely? And what the fuck is a corn rabbit anyway?'

She's leaning against the sports hall wall like a sullen teenager, scowling. There's something about the way she looks that I quite like. She reminds me of someone I used to know as a kid, a girl called Tracey who lived in my village. Violet's blonde hair is scraped up in a tight, high pony-tail and she is wearing a lot of make-up: dark eyes and almost white lips against a pale, matt face. Her clothes don't say 'cutting-edge fashion' like Chi-Chi and her crowd's, or even 'anti-cutting-edge fashion' like mine and Esther's. Violet's clothes are the kind of High Street fashion that real teenagers wear, not the ones Chi-Chi invokes, who always tend to be pop stars or international skateboard champions. Her pink T-shirt doesn't quite reach the hipster waistband of her blue jeans, and her navel is pierced. James and Frank are laughing at what Violet has said. I get the impression that these four – James, Frank, Violet and Kieran – hang around together a lot.

'What's the thing that looks like a cat's arse-hole?' Frank asks, pointing at his photocopied map. Is that something you could, you know, fall into?'

'I think that's a quarry,' says Grace, peering closely at her sheet.

'All right,' Kieran says. 'I'm handing you over to James, now, since this is really his experiment after all.'

I am wondering how I can escape from this. It's not that it doesn't sound interesting but I don't feel part of it at all. Kieran has his gang and, judging from the vibes I can pick up, Grace is here because she is connected to Kieran somehow now as well. Are they an item? It certainly feels like it. Niila and Mitzi form a little unit of their own. They make me think of slender fairies: creatures you'd be more likely to find on a slightly supernatural day out on the moor rather than part of the exploration party. And then there's me: awkward, alone and feeling more and more ill. James is fiddling with a piece of paper. Shall I make my escape?

'What would you rather be: a Short-eared Owl or a Thick-kneed Plover?' It's Ben's voice, and his breath on my ear.

'Hello,' I say. 'I thought you weren't coming.'

'Slept in,' he says, smiling. Ben's smiles are always faintly surprising, as if something so flippant could only very rarely occur on such a serious, bushy-eyebrowed face. 'So?'

'Um, a Short-eared Owl.'

'Hmm. Me too. I'm not sure I like the idea of thick knees. And I don't even know what a plover is. What exactly is this?' He waves the map around, and the small breeze catches it, almost blowing it out of his hand.

'It's our map.'

'There are no actual places on it.'

'I know. Apparently this is "James's Experiment".'

'Ah,' Ben says, as if this all makes sense now.

'Who is James?' I ask. 'What does he do?'

'James is a psychologist. What he does isn't entirely clear. In my division there's a little think-tank, all about game theory and education and so on and he runs that. But it only meets once a week. I think he was brought in to work on a couple of educational titles but as far as I can tell, he spends all his time over at the virtual-worlds research centre with Kieran and that lot. The set-up at Reading is a bit weird. It was all designed around the themes of hot-desking and the paperless office. No one has a desk, basically, and it's hard to know what anyone is doing, or who is connected to whom.'

'And that girl?' My eye keeps being drawn to Violet. Everything she does – now, for example, she is applying more of her pale lipstick – is utterly compelling. Why would this be?

Ben laughs. 'What, Violet? Have you never come across her before?'

'I've seen her in seminars. I just assumed she was something to do with plush toys or dolls.'

'Violet has a Ph.D. in pure mathematics,' he says.

'Bloody hell.'

'It's not that clear what she does, either,' he says. 'But that little team . . . They're like PopCo's élite. Mac and Georges pop in to see them all the time. They'll find that they haven't produced anything for a couple of weeks and turn up to find them having a séance. You'd think they would get into some sort of trouble, but no, they really can do no wrong. Incidentally, who do you think Violet is going out with?'

'Um, Frank?' I suggest. He's big and tattooed and, I don't know, their aesthetics seem to match.

'Yeah. Frank. *And* James.'

'Both of them?'

'Yep.'

'And they know?'

'Yep.

'Fucking hell.'

Ben smiles. 'And now Kieran's after Grace, of course . . .'

I look over at them. They are deep in conversation. 'Yeah, I noticed that something was going on,' I say.

'Richard can say goodbye to her.'

'What do you mean? Were they . . . ?'

Ben shakes his head. 'No, no. But she'll be joining Kieran's team after this, I bet you anything. She is exactly his type. An engineering graduate Goth who knows all about robotics. And she is likely to become the PopCo Go champion soon, too.'

'A trophy girlfriend indeed.'

'Oh yes.'

'Can people just move divisions like that then?'

'Only if it's to Kieran's team. He can choose anyone he wants – anything he wants – and he gets it. He could request Prince William on his team and he'd probably get him.'

Over by the wall, James clears his throat. I can't help picturing him and Frank and Violet at it together. I imagine Georges turning up at their offices to see them all, this 'élite team'. Does he think about fucking her too? I would. My bloody throat hurts. I fish around for a pastille. It won't help in the long run but it will take away the pain for five minutes or so. The Aconitum really isn't working. I probably need another remedy but I'm too fucked to think about which one. And I don't have any of my books here, either.

'If you look at your maps,' James says. 'You'll see only a few landmarks. The River Meavy, for example, on the banks of which we will, hopefully, find Corn Rabbit later today. The thing that Frank and Grace deduced between them was either a depiction of a cat's arse-hole or a quarry is actually a tor or hill fort.'

'Where's Dan?' Ben hisses at me.

I shrug. 'Don't know.'

'Did he say he was coming?'

'No.'

James continues. 'We will be getting our information mainly from ancestral memories of the people and animals who have lived on the moor, which we will obtain through a process of meditation. Together with this map and a compass, of course. Anyway, this should, hopefully, be an interesting way of getting around and you may find all kinds of memory traces of beautiful extinct creatures, or other things from the moor. When you think you have reached Goshawk, our first destination, ask the Goshawk to show itself to you. You may then see a vision. If you don't, then perhaps you are in the wrong place. If you do see a vision, make a sketch of what you have seen. I'm sure some of us will need reminding about what a Goshawk actually is.'

A few people laugh.

'The trouble with this lot,' Ben hisses to me, 'is you never know when they're being serious. This could be completely real, or it could be an elaborate hoax. For all we know, Kieran could have a real map and a GPS unit in his pocket. The actual experiment could be something to do with how we respond to this.'

'Why isn't Chloë here?' I ask.

'Oh, she hates this kind of thing. It's too bourgeois for her.'

Bourgeois. That's a word I haven't heard for a long time. I wouldn't have put it with Chloë, but then I don't really know anything about her.

'What is the purpose of this experiment?' Mitzi asks James.

'That's complicated,' James says, with a smile. 'On one level it's part of my own research into the ways people interact with the zero-point field. On another level it's part of some ongoing research to do with mapping the virtual world. OK. Shall we get going?'

Mitzi doesn't look completely satisfied with her answer but doesn't seem to care too much. We all start walking down the forest path towards the back of the PopCo complex. I pull out my compass, and tree-shadows fall on it like a zombie's fingers.

'20 degrees north,' I say to Ben in a hoarse voice.

'Are you all right?' he asks me.

'Yeah. Well, no. Bit of a sore throat.'

'Yuck.'

'Yeah. Well, I just hope it doesn't turn into anything.'

'Don't give it to me.'

'I thought you wanted to catch my diseases,' I say.

*   *   *

Somewhere near Goshawk (or a long way in the direction of what we all think might be Goshawk), I somehow end up walking next to Violet.

'So who's the grandmother, then?' she says to me.

'Sorry?'

'The one with the Erdős number of two.'

'Elizabeth Butler,' I say. 'Why?'

'I know some of her work. I thought I might. I'm Violet, by the way.'

'Alice,' I say back. 'Don't come too close. I've got some kind of sore-throat thing developing.'

She walks close to me anyway and I can smell rose, and vanilla. She smells powdery, like there's no moisture in her at all and she could just crumble into dust at any moment.

'You do those spy kits and that code-breaking stuff, don't you?' she says to me.

'Yeah.'

'I research puzzles in virtual worlds, among other things. We're like the real and pretend versions of each other.' She laughs. 'The offline and online versions.'

'Yeah,' I say, unconvinced. We walk on in silence for a minute or so. I don't know what to say next. Since we left PopCo Towers, the landscape has changed abruptly. I say *abruptly* because the change really was abrupt. We came out of the forest, and found a road. The PopCo side of the road was fairly normal: trees, bushes, grass in kids'-colouring-book green. The other side of the road marked the beginning of a wilder kind of countryside. The grass was like a thick yellowing carpet; no hedges or trees. This new grass is springy when you walk on it, and has wild flowers growing in clumps everywhere. The flowers are gorsy or prickly in places and are species that I couldn't name. I could confidently say I have never been anywhere like this before. I have never really seen proper moorland before this (it was too misty when I arrived here last week) but yet, if you had shown me a picture of this, I could have told you it was a moor. I don't know why.

We have just passed a boggy area, which I suggested we didn't try to cross. I don't know anything about bogs and marshes but I have read *The Hound of the Baskervilles*. We scramble down another big dip to find ourselves close to an old stone wall. There are

Dartmoor ponies everywhere, and sheep. Some flowers are growing up the wall: wild pink daisies, and some blue flower that could even be Monkshood. The wall seems to be the remains of some kind of battlement. On the other side of it there is a mossy-looking hill with the remains of a stone structure at the top.

'You know, I haven't been able to look at flowers the same way since I learnt about the Fibonacci sequence,' Violet says, stroking the pink daisies with her thin white hand as we walk along the wall. 'I don't know which is better: simple beauty with no explanation, or knowing exactly how and why seed pods are organised.'

'I can barely remember what the Fibonacci sequence is,' I say, stopping to look at the map again, and check the compass.

'Didn't you do maths?'

'No. English.'

'Oh.' She looks disappointed. 'I thought you were a fellow maths chick.'

'No. Not really. Not beyond the odd bit of recreational maths.' I frown, self-deprecatingly. 'Is the Fibonacci sequence the one that goes 1, 1, 2, 3, 5, 8, 13 and so on?' How did I find this in my cluttered mind? I do recognise it as another Voynich memory, though. How much stuff did I learn because of that blessed manuscript? Not enough, obviously, because I never did find out what it contained.

She beams. 'Yeah. That's right.'

'And each new number is the sum of the two before?'

'Yep. And the rate of growth?'

I smile. 'You've really lost me now.'

'It's phi, the golden number. Or as near as dammit. 1.618 . . . and however many decimal places you want to go to.'

The golden number, phi. Of course. I remember now.

'Flowers have Fibonacci numbers of petals,' I say. 'Is that it?'

'Yes, that's pretty much it. And Fibonacci numbers of seeds, and seed-heads. The golden number controls a lot of nature's patterns.'

She strokes the petals some more before we set off again.

'You can create your own universes, if you know the code,' she says. 'Or you can try, anyway. Do you like videogames?'

'Yes,' I say, nodding.

'Are you online?'

'In what sense?'

'Part of a virtual world?'

'Oh. No, not yet.'

Yet. I don't know why I have said this. Dan and I talked about virtual worlds a while ago, when he started researching Dungeons and Dragons artwork. I was scared of addiction, and still am. I know I would love it inside a world like that so much that I would never come out. Dan said he was scared that they wouldn't measure up to his idea of what a world like that should be. I almost smile at this recollection. Now I've heard about the world he would create, I know why.

'Wait until ours is ready, then try that,' she says.

'Yours? I didn't know you were making a virtual world. Someone said that you research products to be sold inside them. I didn't realise you were building them too . . . Wow.'

'Yes. Outside of pornography and eBay, virtual worlds are one of the few online businesses that are making money. We have to be doing it. It's very cool. Like being a God. Some of the programming is pretty boring but the boys do that. I am in charge of the patterns. I've been looking at the basic Fibonacci stuff again because of that. I want to write a programme to make the natural landscapes in the virtual world create themselves, just like ours do. You have to build in rules for that, just like whoever created us must have done. The Fibonacci sequence is great. It entirely explains why things like flowers grow outwards, in a circular fashion. You don't see square flowers, do you? Or naturally occurring straight lines? Isn't it amazing that there is a mathematical rule for things like that, that nature seems to understand that circles and spirals are the most efficient way to organise things?'

The grass is longer now as we walk past the hill and the structure and off towards another one. We soon come to a tiny stream, and people start splashing themselves with water. All this walking does make you hot, although I am not hot. I feel shivery all over. While they mess around in the stream, Violet and I stand next to what looks like the remains of a very old train track. I didn't know they had trains on the moor. It's all grassed over now; grass claims everything that humans abandon. Violet is applying more lipstick.

'What's the actual difference between a world and a virtual world?' I ask her suddenly, frowning.

'Good question. But don't ever say that to Kieran. He will start talking and not stop for several hours. He thinks we really are gods. He says that the reason there were so many Greek and Indian gods was because they created us just like we are creating Efila – that's our virtual world – and you need a team to do it. He says the idea of God as an individual is total bollocks. Anyway, the difference between a world and a virtual world is obvious, if you think about it.'

Everyone has set off again, so we do too. 'Go on,' I say.

'A virtual world must have one dimension less than the "real" one in which it is created. We are three-dimensional creatures, yet we can't create anything very complex in three dimensions; not something that imitates life, anyway.'

'I see what you mean,' I say. 'Who was I talking to about this recently? Um . . . Oh yeah. It was Grace. She was explaining how difficult robotics is because of that.'

'Exactly. If you look at, say, a rabbit's leg, it's so bloody complicated that you could never recreate it. We can't make prosthetic hands that are a convincing reproduction of the real thing. We can't even begin to understand the human foot. But if you look at the latest generation of videogames and online worlds, we are very good at making two-dimensional worlds that, in some ways, work better than this one.'

'Better?' I think about the fragmented, geometric landscape of the last videogame I played and compare it with where I am now. This landscape is alive and exciting. The other one was a collection of dots.

'Not better in every way. But in a two-dimensional world there is no pain. There is immortality. There is fairness. It's a nice place to spend some time.'

My brain hurts. Did a 4-dimensional being create us? Can you have 'life' in two dimensions? I remember my grandmother explaining to me that the most complicated part of the Riemann Hypothesis is that all the maths is four-dimensional. That's what you get when you run imaginary numbers through the zeta function: points you can only plot on a four-dimensional graph. For a second I imagine some 'being' in Violet's two-dimensional world trying to figure out the secrets of its own universe. Would it try to do three-dimensional maths, even though it would never be able to see a three-dimensional object? Would it come up with theories about there being other dimensions 'out there', like we do? Would it consider an afterlife? Would it ever become aware of a lost book, accidentally (or, more likely, mischievously, as nothing is really an accident) dropped into its world: a blueprint for something, perhaps some world that never got made, and spend its life trying to work out the language and the pictures . . . ?

I don't feel very well.

While I have been thinking, Kieran has ambled over. I realise that he has all sorts of things strapped to him. A utility belt holds a pair of binoculars, a pair of pliers and a small flask. He has a compass hanging around his neck. Slung over his shoulder is a bag that looks a lot like a knapsack. He looks like a Hollywood version of a Victorian gentleman explorer.

'What are you ladies talking about?' he asks. 'Hairstyles? Babies?'

'Fuck off,' says Violet, smiling.

Kieran looks at me. 'So, tell me about your mate, whatshisname.'

'Who?'

He feigns concentration. 'Dan? Yeah, that's right. So what's he like, then?'

'He's a nice guy,' I say. 'Why?'

'He approached me looking for a job in my team when we leave here. Don't know if I'll have anything for him. Good artist, though. Some odd ideas, however.'

Good artist. Odd ideas. Dan must have shown him the artwork he created for his non-existent world. Perhaps he realised that a non-existent world could easily become a virtual world. Who knows? We walk along through a small area of forest, trying not to trip over roots coming out of the ground. I'm thinking about zombie-fingers again, and I'd prefer to be out in the open.

'So what are you into, Alice? Who are you, really?'

'Huh?' The way Kieran talks isn't good for my head at the moment. 'Sorry?'

'What do you do when you're not, well, doing PopCo?'

'Ah, you want to know my hobbies,' I say. Violet smiles at me and walks off to join Ben and Frank, who seem to be having an intense discussion. 'I like crosswords,' I offer.

'What's in your DVD collection?'

'DVD collection?'

'You can tell a lot about someone from their DVD collection. It used to be books, of course. And maybe videos. You'd go round someone's house and decide whether to have sex with them on the basis of what they had on their shelves, wouldn't you? Not that I'm deciding whether or not to have sex with you, you understand. Although if you weren't already taken . . .'

'I don't have a DVD collection anyway,' I say quickly.

'Videos?'

'Nope.'

'CDs?'

'Yeah, I've got a few CDs. But not on shelves. Nobody would look at them and decide to have sex with me. Or not.'

'Dan said you'd be like this.'

'What's Dan got to do with it?'

'He said you were hard to get to know.'

I frown. 'I'm not "hard to get to know".'

'But you won't tell me anything about yourself!'

'I won't tell you what I own,' I say. 'Which is different.'

'Shall I tell you what's in my DVD collection instead, then?'

'If you like. It won't make me want to have sex with you, though.'

We exchange a grin. Kieran happily rambles for the next ten minutes or so about American remakes of Japanese independent films, B-movies, anime and old westerns until he seems satisfied that I know what he is all about. He doesn't tell me where he grew up, how many brothers and sisters he has, what he is scared of, whether he likes his toast done well or not, whether his hair colour is actually natural, what he would do to improve the world, whether he believes in God (although I already know the answer to that one, I think), who he would vote for, what his perfect political party would stand for, what items he would take with him if he was to be stranded on a deserted island or anything at all about this cyber-paganism in which he is supposed to be so interested.

Is this how it works now? Do we just let film-makers create identities for us that we can buy for £12.99? Is that what identity costs? Or is it how you put the units together that counts? Does a zombie film plus an experimental Parisian inner-city heist film make you a different person than two Hollywood romantic comedies do? Would either of these people get on with the person who has every series of their favourite SF TV show on DVD, arranged in such a way that their edges make one picture on the shelf? You can string this stuff into lines of cultural DNA that can be seen without any kind of microscope, until anyone looking at your shelves can use this

244

information to establish 'who you are' and whether or not they want to have sex with you. Can't people just desire you because of your breasts any more? Maybe they do, sometimes. But if your cultural DNA can't link up with theirs then they'll fuck you and leave before you wake up, just like everyone said they would. Or you'll do the same to them, because they like alt country music two years after it was fashionable, or they own *Titanic* on DVD.

*

The numbers of the Stevenson/Heath manuscript form a strange wallpaper in my bedroom. You can look at them until you get dizzy but they don't mean anything without the document that will turn them into words. I have asked my grandfather to tell me what it is so many times but he never will. He doesn't like it when I bring the subject up anyway, not any more.

My job in the evenings and at weekends is as follows. I have to count all the words on each page of the Voynich Manuscript and note down the results in a column for my grandfather to look at. Winter turns into spring, and snowdrops and then daffodils come up, and there I am, night after night, transcribing first the numbers of words, and then the numbers of letters, on every page of this huge manuscript. Sometimes I have to use a magnifying glass, and I think about being a detective. Mostly, though, this is boring work and sometimes I wish I could just read a book with real words instead.

On April 1st, my grandfather announces that he has completed his decipherment of the Voynich text. Then he laughs and says *April Fool!* Many years later this will become a tradition of ours, to claim, every April Fool's Day, that we have solved this riddle. Something else happens on this date as well. On April 1st, 1984, my grandfather's first book, a collection of his Mind Mangle columns, is published. He has received a sum of money for this that he will not disclose. 'Not quite enough for a swimming pool,' is what he keeps saying. On April 2nd, we have a new burglar-alarm system installed. My grandmother is against it.

'We can't live inside a fortress,' she says. 'It's unhealthy.'

But it happens anyway. Thanks to my father, people in Cambridge know that we have a treasure map in here. My grandfather has become increasingly convinced, since the incident at the bus stop, that someone will break in to get it. Personally, I say good luck to them. I live here, and I haven't had any luck finding it. And I have the biggest clue of all: my necklace, with its strange numbers that don't mean anything to me. I think that perhaps I, with my necklace, *am* the treasure map – or at least the proof that my grandfather knows what it is, which must amount to the same thing. So I am the treasure map and even I don't know where it is. I do not point any of this out, however. There are other reasons for the alarm, it turns out.

On April 3rd, my grandfather comes home with a big box.

'Here you go, Beth,' he says to my grandmother. Her eyes shine as she unpacks a BBC microcomputer. The Riemann Hypothesis, which I now know to be something to do with a line of zeros plotted on a four-dimensional graph (the question being, *Does the line go on forever, or eventually stop or change?*) is now put to one side for a whole week while she sits in her room making a tap-tap-tap noise, occasionally asking me in to test programmes she has written in BASIC that, on the basis on a Y/N input, reveal more information as you go along.

```
Is your name Alice?  Y/N
Y
Do you want to read Part Four of 'Alan Turing
and the Computer'?
Y
```

This particular instalment of the story takes me back in time to learn about someone called Georg Cantor. He invented set theory! And he also found out that there isn't just one level of infinity but various levels of something called transfinity. I love the names for the levels of transfinity. Aleph-null is the first one; ordinary infinity that everyone understands. Aleph-one is the next level, and is obtained when you take 2 to the power of aleph-null. It's confusing but I still like it and I *almost* understand Cantor's famous diagonal proof.

My grandmother loves the computer. She, of course, actually discussed Turing's ideas with him as he was having them. She has read Ada Lovelace's thoughts on programming Babbage's Analytical Engine. She knows the mechanics of this thing, and nothing about it scares her. I am fascinated by it for various reasons, but partly because she has it connected to a new black and white portable TV. A TV in the house! But it will never, ever be used to pick up broadcasts. It isn't even referred to as a TV. We all call it the 'screen'.

After I read what my grandmother has written about Georg Cantor, I start talking about aleph-null all the time. When my grandfather asks now many biscuits I want, for example, I say 'Aleph-null, please.' He twinkles whenever I do this, so I do it more. One day, I am sitting reading on the old armchair in the sitting room. I am flicking through the Mind Mangle collection, although I have read most of the pieces before (and only understood about half of them). I look at my name in the acknowledgements for the aleph-nullth time and only this time do I notice that, on the following page, there is a symbol: $\aleph_0$. I realise that this is the symbol from my necklace! My grandfather is out, so I tear into my grandmother's study.

'What is this?' I demand, out-of-breath from running up the stairs.

'It's aleph-null, silly,' she says. 'Your favourite expression.'

'Aleph-null? But . . .'

She suddenly smiles. 'Oh, of *course*. You would never have seen the symbol, would you? I can't type Hebrew letters on my keyboard so I just wrote the words out phonetically. Gosh, how funny.'

This isn't funny at all. I've been trying to work out what that symbol was for ages.

'So it's a clue, then?' I say. 'To the treasure.'

'No,' she says firmly. 'Not at all. Your grandfather puts that symbol on everything. Have you not noticed before?'

Of course I haven't. But now it's been pointed out to me, I do start to notice the way he adds it to his letterhead, or to envelopes before he posts them. He even has a little stamp so he can print it on everything. How could I not have noticed this before? Oh well. Now it's just me and this other thing: 2.14488156Ex48. What on earth does it mean? I know better than to ask my grandmother anything else about the necklace, though. Neither of them like talking about it. I don't know why.

Soon, my grandmother starts writing programmes for her computer in assembly code, complex little things of no more than 22k, which she uses to back-up and password-protect some of her most secret and important work. She keeps all this work on tapes, which only run with her programme and her password. Then she starts building cellular automata. I have been a bit worried that my grandmother can never share any of her work with my grandfather and I, because it is simply too complicated for us to understand. Now, however, she calls us in all the time to see what she has done. Cellular automata are ace! My grandmother has been in touch with another mathematician called John Horton Conway, and he has told her about his 'game', which is called Life.

The game isn't really a game. A grid, rather like a chess-board, is created on the computer. Each square on the board is known as a cell and there can be infinite numbers of them, although in reality you can only see a certain amount on screen. A black cell is known as 'living' and a white cell is known as 'dead'. In Conway's version, there are four rules: A black cell with zero or one black, or living, neighbours dies from isolation. A black cell with four or more living neighbours dies from overcrowding. A dead, or white, cell with exactly three living neighbours becomes alive. All other cells remain unchanged. You start the programme and it really does seem to take on a life of its own, like a very basic cartoon, as all the rules are implemented simultaneously and little kaleidoscopic patterns move around the screen. You can do it by hand if you want to see what happens, by placing black markers on a white grid, but it is slower that way, and you don't get such a good impression of the expanding /contracting patterns as new generations of cells are 'born' or 'die'. It is fun to make up your own shapes to begin the 'game' and see what happens as a result of them. Even very clever people can't necessarily work out what the outcome of every starting position in this game could be. That's why my grandmother finds it so interesting.

I am occasionally allowed to sit with my grandmother and feed in the numbers which set the programme off, and we watch while the black blobs expand, expand and die, turn into little flashing lines or just die after a single generation. With this odd background of pixels on a black and white screen, we sometimes talk about other things. I have learnt some more about the Riemann Hypothesis at last, and I know how to use four-dimensional co-ordinates (although I don't know what the resulting graph would look like). My grandmother has explained that after all these years of working with four dimensions, she can actually see them in her head, even if it is supposedly impossible. I have read a science-fiction book that says the fourth dimension is time. My grandmother corrects this.

'Time has only one dimension,' she says. 'In the physical world we can experience three dimensions of space, and one of time.' A fourth dimension of space would be very different, she explains, with outside and insides of things becoming infinitely complicated, and cubes becoming simply the edge of something else.

As the game of Life trickles away in the background, we talk about mathematical proof, and my mother and father, and even what my grandmother was like as a young woman. One day I ask about my necklace again.

'What did you mean,' I ask, 'when you said I'd been turned into a living proof? Is this actually the answer, written on here?' I pull out my necklace and open the small silver locket. I point at the numbers inside. 'I know now that the aleph-null symbol is a red-herring, but this – this other bit – is that his proof?'

'You should ask your grandfather,' she says, like she used to when I asked her about the weather.

'I can't ask him,' I say, sadly. 'He won't talk about it any more.'

The screen on the desk has been full of activity – large geometric patterns in every part of the screen – for the last five minutes. Now, inexplicably, the patterns start to die off, eventually ending as three small lines of three blobs each which flash horizontal and then vertical *ad infinitum*. I think it's OK to say *ad infinitum* about these patterns as everyone knows they are final positions in this game; they won't change any more, now.

'It's a code,' she says, after a long pause. 'A code he thinks you will be able to work out.'

'But I can't . . .'

'Not now. When you grow up. When he is dead, you will inherit all his papers, you know that, don't you?'

I didn't but I nod dumbly anyway.

'He thinks that, if you want to, you can work out the code then and make your own choice about what to do about it. It's hard for him. He doesn't want anyone to recover the treasure, but at the same time he very much wants to be known as the person who solved the Stevenson/Heath puzzle. Perhaps one day there won't be a bird sanctuary on the site any more, or perhaps, rather than digging up the treasure yourself, you would want to give the solution to an archaeology department of a university and let them organise a proper dig . . .'

'Why doesn't he do that?'

'He hates universities.'

'Oh, yes.' We both smile.

'Perhaps war will break out again, or perhaps one day you won't have all you need like we do now. It's there and you do have the key. What you do with it will be your choice.'

'Unless there is no treasure,' I say, experimentally. I have been considering what my grandfather said about the Stevenson/Heath manuscript being a hoax. Even if Stevenson did exist (which, according to my grandfather's evidence, he certainly did), it could still be a hoax.

My grandmother nods. 'Unless there is no treasure,' she repeats. 'Although, if there wasn't any treasure, it doesn't really matter. Your grandfather solved the puzzle, and that's what he would like known.'

'And the answer is really here, in my necklace?' I say.

'Yes.'

'Do you know what it is?'

'No.'

We now know, thanks to many hours of boredom and toast, the number of words and letters on every page of the Voynich Manuscript. But now my grandfather wants me to come up with the prime factors of all these numbers. Until he started talking about prime factorisation, I didn't know how complicated prime numbers were. Every number, it turns out, is either prime or can be expressed as the product of prime numbers, which is why primes are sometimes known as the building blocks of the universe. The number 2 is prime, as are 3, 5, 7, 11, 13, 17 and 19 and so on, all the way to infinity (or aleph-null). If a number is prime, then it cannot be divided by any whole numbers apart from 1 and itself. The number 4 is not prime as it is comprised of 2×2. The number 361 is 19×19, or 19^2. The number 105 is made of the primes $3 \times 5 \times 7$. The number 5625 is made up of $3^2 \times 5^4$, or $3 \times 3 \times 5 \times 5 \times 5 \times 5$.

Apparently, once we know this data for all the pages of the Voynich Manuscript, my grandfather will assess it. He has had all kinds of hypotheses in his head all along. Will the numbers, or the prime factors, once we have them, form a pattern? Will there be square numbers of words on every page (there aren't), or a Fibonacci number of letters (he doesn't know yet)? Will all the numbers connected with the book turn out to be prime? These sorts of baffling questions are the reason for him wanting me to do all this work, and, while I am excited about being trusted with such an important task, even I realise that it is going to take ages. Counting the words and the letters on each page took for ever. This is going to take longer than for ever and a day.

My old calculator is going a bit wrong so on Saturday we go into town and I am allowed to choose a shiny new scientific calculator all of my own, with loads of buttons. I also, of course, want a ZX Spectrum, and games, and all the pens and pencils in the shop but my new calculator is so shiny and big that I soon forget all of this. I expect it will have a button that will enable me to complete these prime factorisations in an instant, but when I ask my grandfather that evening, he just laughs.

'Ah,' he says when he stops.

'What's "Λh"?' I say.

'Well. Yes. That's the thing about prime factorisation. No one's ever found a short cut. No one knows very much about how primes behave, that's the problem. Problems to do with primes have puzzled the greatest mathematicians. Now your grandmother . . .'

'What about me?' she says, coming down the stairs.

'I was just about to tell Alice that your work might one day help to predict primes and lead to quicker ways to do prime factorisation.'

'Mmm. Yes,' she says, uncertainly. 'Maybe one day.'

'But in the meantime, Alice, I'm afraid it's going to be a bit of a long old job for you.'

'Have you got that poor girl doing your prime factorisation for you?' my grandmother asks, as my grandfather gets up to pour her drink. 'Shame on you.'

But they both laugh, as if prime factorisation is just another bypass.

This is a challenge all right. Still, maybe I will learn the secret short cut as I go through these numbers. It's complicated enough for me to quite enjoy it, although I don't know how long all this is going to take. You need a list of the primes, to start with, which

I have obtained from my grandmother's study and copied out on to fresh sheets of paper. I have written out the first hundred from 2 to 541, which I hope will be enough, although my grandmother has more than ten thousand primes up there, like they're pets she collects. The hundredth prime squared, however, is 292,681, which is far bigger than any of my numbers, so I think I will be all right.

To do prime factorisation, you have to remember the following rule. Every number that exists is either prime or can be expressed as a product of prime numbers (or 'prime factors'). A number that can broken down to prime factors is called 'composite'. 7 is prime, because it is only divisible by 1 and itself. But 9 is not prime. 9 is composite because it has a prime factor of 3. The number 21 has two prime factors: 3 and 7. Prime factorisation, then, means taking a number and trying to work out which primes divide into it. This is a trial-and-error process. And it really does take ages.

There's something I don't understand about this, though. I am a child and, although I am quite good at prime factorisation, I wouldn't trust me to do it, if I was my grandfather. I have a suspicion that he checks all my results as they come in, but if he's doing all that, why not do the prime factorisation himself? It's confusing. I suppose it is much easier to check a result than generate it in the first place but I still think it's a little odd. I don't think he checked my results of the numbers of words and letters in the manuscript, either. Perhaps all my calculations are wrong.

Sometimes I see prime factors in my sleep.

*

Eventually, Kieran drifts off and I find I am walking on my own. Well, I am not exactly on my own, since I am walking in a group, but no one is walking alongside me, chatting. My throat is full of broken glass. This is all so beautiful; the landscape swelling around me. But I just want to go to sleep. In fact, when we get to what we think is Goshawk and sit on the slightly damp grass to start to meditate, I take the opportunity for a little nap, leaning against a big old tree, and have to be woken up by Ben afterwards. When we set off again my legs are full of molasses and feel too heavy to take even a single step.

Somehow, using this bizarre method of meditation and compass reading (neither of which I am doing myself but I can independently verify that most other people here are), we do eventually end up on the banks of the River Meavy, just after two o'clock. There is a sign confirming that it is the correct river, and everyone cheers. And, as we follow the river down, preparing to try to 'see' the original corn rabbit, we come upon a pub which we all fall into, breathless and hungry. I eat a bowl of soup and drink a Bloody Mary but this cold is too far gone now. I will not be saved. After we have eaten, I can't take it any more. There is an open fire in the pub, and it makes the whole place feel hot and syrupy. There are horrible things like stuffed stag's heads and hunting photographs on the walls. These bleed into nothingness as I close my eyes, put my head down on the table, saying goodbye to it all.

'I'll take her back,' I hear Ben saying. 'She isn't feeling too good.' Then gentle arms, cool air outside and a car engine. Finally, the sound of gravel confirms that we are back.

*

At the same time as I work on these prime factorisations, I read the book my grandmother lent me, the one about Kurt Gödel. Apparently my grandfather was obsessed with Gödel's work a long time ago. You can see why. With the same kind of dour anarchism to which my grandfather is prone, Gödel set out to show that you can never completely prove a mathematical theorem is true, not exactly because mathematics isn't consistent but because it will never be completely flawless.

In 1900, a German mathematician called David Hilbert gave a famous lecture in which he set out the twenty-three mathematical problems he felt would be key challenges for the new century. The first problem was the Continuum Hypothesis; the theory that there is nothing between the infinities aleph-null and aleph-one; no value to be found between Cantor's concepts of the countable and uncountable (or the 'continuum'). The Riemann Hypothesis was number 8 on Hilbert's list. But Hilbert also called for the very principles and foundations of mathematics – its axioms – to be sorted out once and for all. This was problem number 2. People were already starting to worry about whether or not the closed system of mathematics was actually consistent, and whether the axioms were correct.

If it wasn't consistent then all the proofs of all the theorems to date would amount to nothing (if anyone even knew what nothing was). What if, say, the Riemann Hypothesis was true and false at the same time? If $1 + 1 = 2$ and $1 + 1 = 3$ at the same time? That sort of thing would never do.

Axioms are the very foundations of mathematics. Axioms are things that you can't necessarily prove but form the basis for all mathematical proofs. Proofs, in mathematics, are logical evidence that something will always be the same way. Euclid formulated a proof that there are an infinite number of primes, for example, and Cantor narrowed this infinity down to aleph-null, or $\aleph_0$. A proof is never the same as experimental evidence though. A proof of Pythagoras's theorem (and I know what this is now, because it's in this book – it says that the square of the hypotenuse of a right-angled triangle is always equal to the sum of the squares of the other two sides) is not based on someone looking at lots of right-angled triangles, measuring the lengths of the sides and saying, 'Yup, everything seems to be in order here.' A proof, elegant and simple, will explain why this will be so for eternity, for all right-angled triangles. There are many proofs of Pythagoras's theorem.

Axioms, the things on which proofs are based, like $1 + 1 = 2$, are sometimes referred to as 'self-evident'; others have been proved. *You can always join two points with a straight line. All right angles are equal to one another. All composite whole numbers are the product of smaller primes.* These are axioms. Axioms are a bit like starting points on a journey. You can start at one point and, using a set of directions, walk to another place. However, you need to know where your starting point is before you can obtain or use the directions. If you got a set of directions that were correct, but you had started in the wrong place, you would end up somewhere very unexpected. If you formulate a proof using axioms that are incorrect, you will end up in the wrong place.

By the time of Hilbert's lecture, set theory had thrown up a lot of problems in mathematics. You need sets in consistent mathematics. They tell you what things are and what things are not; which ideas share the same properties or rules (as well as what sorts of different infinities you might get). Axioms are based on them. You can say, 'A set of triangles is a set of all three-sided, two-dimensional shapes with three angles adding up to 180 degrees,' and, as long as you were talking about triangles on the plane, not triangles on a sphere, you'd be OK. But in 1903, Bertrand Russell came up with various paradoxes to illustrate the problem that a set (or class) cannot contain itself. Imagine the Barber of Seville. He shaves every man who does not shave himself. So does the barber shave himself? If he does, he doesn't and if he doesn't, he does. It's just like the liar paradox! Despite his clear love of paradoxes, Russell went on to try to sort out these sorts of problems by writing the *Principia Mathematica* with his teacher Alfred North Whitehead, which was published in 1910. In three vast volumes, this work set down the basic axioms and rules for mathematics. Everything was OK in mathematics after this, or as OK as it ever was, with no pesky paradoxes spoiling everything, until Kurt Gödel came along and messed everything up again in 1930, when he proved two theorems which would together become known as Gödel's Incompleteness Theorem. In these theories, he explained how you could find fundamental paradoxes within the system of mathematics. He did this using code.

As I understand it (and I am, after all, a child, so this is the simple version), Gödel worked out a clever way of assigning number codes to statements. The way he did this was by assigning numbers to all parts of mathematical (or other) statements, and then using these numbers to create a unique, large number. It turns out that this is just like making a secret code! Gödel's code was a little more complicated, but say you assigned the following values to mathematical symbols:

Symbol	Code Number
x	1
÷	2
+	3
-	4
=	5
1	6
2	7
3	8

All the symbols now have a number that you can work with. The statement $1 + 1 = 2$ would, in this system, be represented by the sequence, 6, 3, 6, 5, 7. Now comes the clever bit. To turn this into a unique large number, you have to use primes. You take the series of prime numbers – remember, the series of prime numbers starts 2, 3, 5, 7, 11, 13, 17, 19 . . . – and then you raise the first prime to the power of your first number, the second prime to the power of your second number and so on. Then you multiply them all together. In this case you would get the result of $2^6 \times 3^3 \times 5^6 \times 7^5 \times 11^7$, which is 8,843,063,840,920,000,000. That's a huge number! It won't even fit on my calculator properly.

Every composite number is a unique product of its particular prime factors. 3×7 *only* makes 21. It never makes any other number. It's the same with this large number we have created. It can *only* be the product of that particular arrangement of primes. As it can only be the product of that particular arrangement of primes, then all you have to do to get your original statement would be to prime factorise the number. But really! It takes me over an hour to prime factorise three-digit numbers, sometimes. Who would sit down and crack that one apart, just to find out that $1 + 1 = 2$? But it turns out that this system of encoding is not intended for practical use. It is just there to demonstrate what *could* happen. Gödel's theorem says that any statement at all could be encoded this way. It doesn't matter whether or not you can easily do the resulting calculations; it's the point that counts. Gödel proved that, with his system, it was possible to have a situation whereby the number 128,936 (for example) was the code for the statement: 'Statement number 128,936 cannot be proved.' Not altogether likely, perhaps, but possible all the same.

Before Gödel, people believed that if you did find something wrong with the foundations of mathematics, a break or a gap, you would just patch it up with a new axiom or two, or maybe a new proof of something. What Gödel proved was that it doesn't matter how much you do this; using his coded statements you can always create (or have the possibility of creating) self-referential, para-doxical statements. It's not exactly '1 + 1 = 3'. It's more: 'If 1 + 1 = 2, then $1 + 1 \neq 2$'.

This is the liar paradox all over again. And the fact that, using just maths, you could create this type of paradox, where something is true and false at the same time, meant that mathematics was inherently, well, not so much inconsistent, but inconclusive. This kind of thing can give you a headache if you think about it too much. Anyway, poor Hilbert was going to have to deal with the fact that mathematics could not be tidied away neatly. Imagine. You set a problem for people to solve, hoping that the answer is going to be reassuring, and it turns out to be anything but. And poor Gödel. Convinced he had a heart condition, he became paranoid and thought that all his food was poisoned. The only person he trusted to feed him was his wife, Adele. When she went into hospital, he literally starved to death.

My grandfather is keen to know how I am getting on with this book; I don't know why. All I want to know is what happened next. Did mathematics collapse? And if not, why not? Was Gödel wrong?

My grandmother smiles when I ask her this one evening in her study.

'If it collapsed, then how could I still be doing it?'

'But . . .'

'Gödel did not destroy mathematics. He inspired it. Everyone was inspired by Gödel, particularly Turing. Cantor proved that you could always add infinities to infinity. Gödel proved that you can always add new axioms to mathematics – and never be sure that it's possible to prove something that is true. Turing proved that there are some computer programmes that may simply never terminate. It's very exciting, when you think about it.'

'Never terminate?' I say.

'That's right.' She smiles. 'Say you give a computer a really hard problem to solve. It could take a million years to come up with an answer but it *will* come up with an answer – at least, you think it will. But how would you know? You won't be around in a million years to check, so how can you know, in advance, if something is computable or not? Turing tried to prove that there would be a way of finding out but, in the end, he had to conclude that the problem was undecidable. Sometimes, you just can't know if a problem has a solution or not.' She turns to the computer and fires up one of her homemade programmes. 'I think you might be ready for the next part of the story,' she says.

Part Three

A bit beyond perception's reach
I sometimes believe I see
that life is two locked boxes, each
containing the other's key.

Piet Hein

Chapter Twenty-one

A dream: I am lost in a forest, with no one there apart from me. I can hear strange whispers which I try to follow but I know there isn't any point. Soon, I come to a cottage, with wild roses growing outside, and walls green with ivy. I think, *I am in a dream and can therefore enter this cottage: this is the kind of thing it's OK to do in dreams.* Inside, I find that the cottage walls are covered with letters and symbols. The aleph-null symbol is there, repeated like wallpaper over the hallway. The numbers from my necklace are there too: 2.14488156Ex48. The rest of the hallway is randomly decorated with images and ideas from the last week: the Green Man, the PopCo code, a diagram from Mark Blackman's seminar.

I enter the living room to find it arranged like a library. There are DVDs, videos and books lining each wall. I remember some conversation where I claimed not to have these collections myself, or be interested in anyone else's. However, I am impressed by this one. All the films are favourites of mine, or my grandparents. There are maths films, war films, code-breaking films, films that make you cry because the world has changed and people don't help each other any more. I look at the books on one shelf and realise I am looking at my grandfather's collection. Books about Gödel, books about astrology and flowers and alphabets. There is a biography of someone who put together an ancient language from mere fragments, and my grandfather's most well-thumbed code book, *Secret and Urgent: The Story of Codes and Ciphers* by Fletcher Pratt. This book, published in 1939, contains my grandfather's favourite frequency table of occurrences of letters in English.

Another set of shelves also contains books; and I realise that these are all mine. Mary Shelley, Edgar Allan Poe, H. G. Wells, Jules Verne, Samuel Beckett, Raymond Chandler, William Gibson, Umberto

Eco, Marge Piercy, Margaret Atwood. The kits I have created for PopCo are here too, but changed. Instead of colourful boxes carrying the PopCo logo, the material now appears in grown-up books, with my name, Alice Butler, on the spine. For a second I feel like an author, how I have always wanted to feel. Then everything feels odd. I realise that this cottage is the inside of my brain, and I think that it's probably dangerous to go wandering around inside your own brain, even if it is disguised as a cottage, and you are, objectively, inside a dream.

On the floor, there is a single wooden block, with the letter A on two of its faces. The other four faces are blank. It's not that messy in here, apart from the block on the floor, but I am thinking, I have to tidy this up! I have to make it make sense! I have to get out of here. I concentrate as hard as I can, almost meditating, and everything in this room starts to melt into code. I wonder where it's going – the cottage and its contents – and then I realise that it's filling the blank faces of the wooden cube. I don't know how this is happening but, some time later, I blink and find that the process is over, the cottage has gone and I am in the forest alone again. When I touch my necklace, as I always do after some dramatic or dangerous event has occurred, I find it has changed shape. I frantically pull the chain out and see that instead of carrying a locket with a number inside it, it now carries a little wooden block, with all the information from the cottage inscribed on its six faces. Even though I know the necklace number by heart and haven't really lost anything, I shout *No!* so loudly that my voice echoes in the whole forest, and birds fly out of the trees like dust beaten from an old sofa.

When I wake up, it is the middle of the night. I have slept for hours. With a thick head and a gravelly throat, I think about getting up but somehow can't, so I just lie there on my bed in Room 23 feeling sorry for myself instead. I wonder whether anyone will come in the morning or whether, as usual nowadays, I will have to be ill on my own without anyone's help or comfort. Even Atari doesn't usually care that much when I am ill. In the language of Paul Erdös, cats arc bosses, not slaves. *Don't be pathetic, Alice.* There's no point, anyway. Being pathetic only has a point if there's somebody watching. Aching all over, I get up and run myself a glass of tap water. I take a book from the shelves and get back into bed. It's cold in here, or maybe that's just the fever. I probably should take something for this.

What have I got with me? Some Arsenicum, some Lycopodium, some Nux Vomica and some Gelsemium. Hmm. Not a very big choice considering that there are tens of thousands of homeopathic remedies. But I feel cold, and I still feel like tidying up all the time. Do I feel nervous about the future? No. Do I think I might die from this? Yes, irrationally, I do. I think every cold I get will kill me. Fastidiousness implies both Arsenicum and Nux, as does coldness. However, I don't feel particularly angry or snappy (Nux), and the fear of death is certainly Arsenicum. I don't feel as restless as Arsenicum usually does but, still, I take an Arsenicum 200 and, without even looking at the book I have selected, I go back to sleep.

*

By the time the summer holidays start, I have finished as much of the prime factorisation as I can do without going mad. I ask for a two-week break. My grandfather says I have done enough, anyway, and takes me off the whole project for the time being. My grandmother approves of his releasing me from this huge task to enjoy a 'normal summer' like 'other children'. I feel exhilarated at being able to abandon the rest of this task but, as the holidays get under way, I get an aching sense of having left something unfinished. I hate this feeling. It's like being away from school on the day of a test: you miss the test but also the nice feeling of the test being over.

On my birthday, my grandparents present me with several gift-wrapped boxes: a new fountain pen to use when I go back to school (I am changing up to the comprehensive this year, which I am excited/nervous about), an RSPB bird-watching book, a set of my own cricket stumps, a David Gower mug, a radio cassette player and a small silver digital watch. This is the best present haul I have ever had! Perhaps it's because I am a prime number of years old. My grandfather explained to me last year about my prime number birthday but of course I was ten then: 2 x 5. Now everything about me is prime! Once I have finished opening my presents, my grandmother starts to explain about the large tea-chest my grandfather is dragging into the sitting room.

'It's from your mother,' she explains. 'Books. Diaries. I don't know if you are too young . . . But she did say that she wanted you to have them when you turned eleven. So here you are.'

My grandfather finishes dragging it into the middle of the room and then stands there looking at it, puffing slightly. I don't know what must be happening to my face. My mother? Bloody hell.

'Well . . .' He says. And I think this is going to be a 'Well . . .' that means I am going to have to examine this box now, with them both watching me. Instead, my grandparents exchange a slightly concerned look, and leave the room.

Oh God. I'm sitting there staring at the box, not sure what to do. I didn't know my mother had left me anything of hers. Why did no one tell me sooner? When I still lived with my father I would have given anything to touch even a hair of hers. If I could have found anything at all – a single earring, a thin bangle, a small torn-off corner of an old shopping list – I would have guarded it more carefully than I guard anything in my whole life, even my necklace. But there was never anything. As if my mother was a habit my father had given up, every tiny trace of her was removed less than a week after her death. When I returned to the flat (I had been staying in my grandparents' old house in town) everything to do with her was gone. *Everything*. There were no bras, no books, no chewed old biros, no brown bread, no postcards of ballerinas, no tins of mints, no pot plants, no cassette player, no tapes, no note-books, no apple cores, no lipstick, no violin, no nothing. And he thought I wouldn't notice.

Now this. A whole box of things that she has touched; books she has actually read. Diaries? Imagine that. With my eyes wide, I approach the box. It is open at the top. Bloody hell! There aren't just books in here. There is a teddy bear, old and battered, his head poking out from a pile of novels. There is also a cassette which I later discover contains a series of violin recitals taped from the radio. I spend the rest of my birthday morning slowly and care-fully taking my treasure upstairs in small, easy-to-carry piles. Then I take the empty box up and re-fill it with the piles of books. The teddy is now on my pillow. I play the tape in my new stereo. I still haven't opened any of the books.

I don't know anything about my mother at all. When she died, there was no one to ask. Everyone was just too upset to deal with questions from me so I just learned not to ask them. Perhaps everyone thought I was too young to understand. This is why I am surprised when, suddenly, today, my grandparents offer to tell me anything I want to know about her.

'Really, Alice,' my grandmother says gently over lunch. 'Anything at all.'

'Did she like maths?' is all I can think of to ask.

They both laugh. 'Oh, no,' says my grandmother. 'Not even through her music. She didn't have any interest in it whatsoever.'

My grandfather looks a bit sad, so I don't ask anything else. After lunch, he settles down with the Voynich Manuscript calculations, and my grandmother puts on a silk scarf and goes over to Tracey's nan's house to make the birthday tea for my party.

I spend the afternoon on my bed, flicking through novels and music books. There is a diary that I haven't plucked up the courage to examine yet. When I eventually do, at about four o'clock, I don't actually read it. I simply sit there touching the writing, wishing things had been different, not allowing myself to cry.

There is hardly any time to get ready for my party. I'm not sure I even want a party now but the village hall is booked and invitations have gone out and the tea is probably already made and on its way to the hall; flowery china plates covered in cling-film, and jugs of orange squash. My tummy hurts just thinking about it. I begged and begged to have this sort of party because all my friends have them but I don't really like any of the people I have invited. Will anyone from school actually come? I have seventeen returned slips from the invitations – all with little ladybird patterns on them which I liked when I chose them from Woolworth's but on reflection seem a bit babyish – but I sent out twenty-five. And this was before we broke up for the holidays, so maybe everyone has forgotten. My grandparents agreed to the hall but not to a professional disco, so my grandfather will be in charge of the music, using my cassette player and some borrowed tapes (mainly Rachel's). Will this be a disaster? Boys are coming, too. Will *this* be a disaster? How many disasters can one party have? I wish this was someone else's party, not mine.

I end up wearing my blue dress and red sneakers. I am not sure they go together but I don't really care. I brush my hair and braid it carefully into two plaits, the way I have been doing since I was about six. Then I rub a flannel over my face and go downstairs. My grandfather is still there with the Voynich Manuscript.

'Time to go,' I say.

The village hall is like a witch's house; small, grey and pointy with climbing plants all over it. You enter it through a vast, wooden, creaking door that can be held open with a huge brass hook (which is good, because this door is so heavy, and on such a tight spring, that children could easily be crushed to death by it trying to close). This door leads to a tiny foyer, cobwebby and dark, with five rusty coat-hooks and a broom. Then another door, thin wooden slats, leads to the hall itself. This hall is a repository for memories of bingo, bridge tournaments, chess club (which my grandfather created but which is no longer going), Brownies, Scouts, Guides, Boys' Brigade, Girls' Brigade, the Woodcraft Folk (also defunct), the Wallflower Theatre Society, the Women's Institute and the Amateur Operatic Club. A local rock band also practise here on a Thursday evening. Even our house, which is half a mile from the hall, vibrates on a Thursday evening. The band has a girl singer who always dresses in black. She smokes long, thin cigarettes, too. When I first saw her, I wanted to be her so much that my stomach ached for two weeks. She was carrying an electric guitar.

In the afternoon, the sun coming through the windows of the village hall is like something coming from heaven, and you imagine angels playing in the dust-storms inside. Directly in front of the doors, about twenty paces beyond them, is the stage, made of dark, shiny wood. You can't climb on to the stage from the hall if you are a child; it's too high. Instead, if you want to go on the stage, you have to negotiate the maze of little back rooms – kitchen, back-stage, dressing rooms, broom cupboard and store – to get to the actual stage door, beyond which there are seven shiny wooden steps which lead up to it. I used to come to Brownies here, which is how I know all of this.

Everyone at my party wants to get on to the stage. I am the queen of all hostesses in my blue dress, because only I know the ancient secrets of the stage. While the grown-ups stand around the fold-out tables talking, and my grandmother regards the geometry of the birthday tea with evident satisfaction (right-angled jam sandwiches, cheese footballs as neatly spherical as Riemann's zeros, jellies in the shape of ellipses) we all take off our shoes and creep through the haunted passageways until we get to the seven magical steps and then we spend about half an hour skidding up and down the shiny stage in our stockinged feet. My grandfather fires up my new cassette player and selects a tape from Rachel's collection. The first five or six songs are recent pop hits that everyone knows from the weekly chart countdown on the radio. My guests and I create a game where we stand on the very edge of the stage, waiting for the climax of the song, at which we all jump off simultaneously. This seems to have been inspired by something called *The Kids from Fame*, although I don't know what this is. After we have jumped off the stage we immediately race around the back again, almost forgetting about the ghosts, ready to jump off at the next climactic bit of the song. Even the boys do this! Could I be having the best party ever?

Rachel, back from boarding-school for the summer, is easily the most sophisticated person here. As an outsider, and the only person who doesn't attend my school (which, like the Brownies, I have actually left but this hasn't sunk in yet), unspoken children's rules suggest that she shouldn't fit in: that no one should talk to her or want to be seen standing next to her. However, Rachel has developed a special kind of presence since she's been at her boarding-school. She walks in a floaty way, and sometimes wears mascara. She's like a pretty ghost-child from a film. When the first of two slow songs come on, she has the pick of the boys to slow dance with. And, because she and Robert, the most eligible boy in the class (Rachel also has impeccable taste), are slow dancing, everyone else does too. I am not sure how I feel about the idea of being in such close proximity to a boy but, somehow, my slow-dance partner happens to be the only boy in the class that I like. He's called Alex and is good at maths. He is Russian, too!

'Do you have no parents?' he asks me, as we sway on the spot, his accent as round and soft as a doughnut.

My head is on his shoulder. 'No,' I whisper back. 'I don't have any parents.'

'Me too,' he says. 'I have no parents as well.'

Later, Alex kisses me on the cheek. Rachel, of course, kisses Robert on the lips.

I sleep with my mother's teddy bear that night, and I feel happy.

*　　*　　*

It's about ten o'clock on Sunday when I am awoken by someone banging on my door. It is Ben, carrying a tray.

'Breakfast,' he says, following me into the room.

I fall back into bed and he places the tray on the small table and starts bustling around like some sort of home-help, opening the curtains, opening the window and, finally, leaning behind me to fluff up my pillows. Then he places the tray on my lap. I am only half-awake and I stare at him with sleepy eyes, not knowing why he is doing this, but grateful all the same. In fact, I am so grateful that I can feel tears welling up in my eyes. *Don't cry, Alice. Never cry.*

'Thank you,' I say.

'Just call me Nurse Ben,' he says, grinning. 'And sorry I was in a shit mood yesterday. Of course I still want all your diseases.'

Was he in a shit mood yesterday? I was too ill to really notice.

I look down at the tray. There is a pot of boiling water, a selection of teabags, a mug, two slim jugs of milk, a bowl, two mini boxes of cereal, a plate with two slices of wholemeal toast, a tiny dish containing two pats of butter, a small jar of Marmite and a selection of jams.

'I didn't know if you were a meat-eater or a vegetarian or a vegan or what,' Ben says. 'There's milk and soya milk there. The soya milk is in the pale blue jug. I didn't know whether to bring butter or not so I did. I thought you had butter with your roll yesterday but I wasn't sure.'

'I'm a vegetarian,' I say, sleepily pouring water from the teapot over one of the tea-bags: Green Tea with Lemon. 'Recently converted by the unmentionable stew last Saturday.'

He smiles. 'That stuff looked foul. What did it taste like?'

'Oh, I didn't eat it. It was the fact that I was spared by claiming to be a vegetarian that actually made me one. That was the day when me and Dan drank the red wine and you looked at me disapprovingly.'

'That was supposed to be "I want to go to bed with you", not "I disapprove of you".'

'Really?'

'Mmm.'

'Oh.' I smile, then look awkwardly down at my two jugs of milk. I wonder what soya milk is like. 'Apparently there are lots of vegans here,' I say conversationally, my mind still trying to wake itself up, not wanting to deal with the horror of how I must look and smell after lying in bed feeling like death for almost twenty-four hours.

This seems to make him flinch, slightly. 'Who said that?'

'The chefs.'

'I'm a vegan.'

'Oh.' I start buttering my toast. 'So what does that actually mean?'

'I don't eat any animal products at all.'

'What, no cheese or milk or butter?'

'That's right.'

I consider saying something like, *So what can you eat, then?* Or, *Doesn't that get really boring?* Or, *I could never give up cheese.* However I suspect that these sorts of things must sound a bit clichéd if you're a vegan. Logic suggests that Ben must eat all sorts of things or he would waste away and die of either starvation or boredom, so I say nothing and carry on buttering my toast, vaguely wondering what could be wrong with butter. Then I find myself thinking about Gödel starving himself to death, imagining an old man in a grey dressing gown looking at the contents of a larder and being able to touch nothing in it. From Gödel I move on to Virginia Woolf, and I think of her method of suicide, damp and silent. What did she eat before she walked into the water? Did she care? My thoughts are a mess. I could think about the suicides or untimely deaths of geniuses all day but this probably wouldn't be a good idea. But my thoughts won't switch off so easily and I find myself thinking of poor Ramanujan, the Indian mathematician who worked at Cambridge with G. H. Hardy. He was so unhappy, so far from home, so sick of trying to live as a vegetarian in the twenties at Cambridge that he tried to throw himself under a train. He was saved from this death and then tuberculosis got him. People are still deciphering the amazing formulae in his notebooks. Then I think about Georg Cantor, burnt out at forty, and persecuted to the point of madness by people opposed to his ideas about transfinity.

Morbid thoughts. I always think morbid thoughts when I am ill. At least my throat doesn't hurt today. But my limbs all ache and my head feels heavy. Could the Arsenicum have caught this in time? Gödel could have done with some Arsenicum, I realise. Ben is in the bathroom with the door closed. I can hear water running, and the clink of glass. A few moments later he comes back into the room with some water and three small glass phials.

'What's this?' I say.

'Bach Flower remedies. If you laugh or call me a hippy or a ponce, I will leave,' he warns. 'My mother gave me flower remedies when I was growing up and that's how I know how they work. I'm not into any crazy middle-class alternative medicine . . . I just know these work, that's all.'

'It's OK. I know about flower remedies,' I say, smiling.

Of course I do. One of my grandfather's early theses about the Voynich Manuscript was that it was a blueprint for flower remedies and it was my job to look them all up for him in the local library. I was never quite as fascinated with them as I became with homeopathy, however. Homeopathy seemed to be more of a challenge somehow and both mathematical and poetic at the same time. Only in homeopathy do you get specific remedies for people who believe they are made of glass, have a delusion that they are selling green vegetables, or have an aptitude for, or a horror of, mathematics. Using homeopathy to solve the problem of illness is similar to using functions in maths. If you know how to, you can input data and generate a useful result. In homeopathy, you note down all of someone's symptoms, pick the important ones (especially any key mental symptoms), and then look them all up in a big repertory, which is like a dictionary of symptoms and the remedies that cure them. Each symptom in the repertory is expressed in a 'rubric'. Under each rubric is a list of all remedies that cure the symptom it describes. You have to try to find the common remedy (or remedies) that appear under all the rubrics you have selected. Then you cross-reference with a *materia medica* – a list of all the remedies and what they do, like a backwards version of the repertory – and select the one that best 'fits' with the patient.

Examples of rubrics from the 'Mind' section of my repertory include: *Anxiety, mental exertion, from,* and, *Amusement, averse to,* or *Fear, evil, of,* and *Noise, inclined to make a.* This backwards way of putting things, and the nineteenth-century language (which you find in all repertories) makes the process of selecting a remedy similar to the process of cracking a code. Selecting the correct rubric in the first place requires a poetic sort of imagination. *Delusion, Prince, is a* (patient thinks he is a prince) does not literally mean that the person thinks they are a prince. You have to break the idea down and understand the kind of person who would think that he was a prince. Would this be a very ambitious person? Someone who has 'delusions of grandeur', perhaps? Perhaps someone who has great things expected of them by their family? Someone who has the delusion *Glass, she is made of*, does not literally believe herself to be made of glass but rather feels fragile and brittle, as if she might break. This might be someone who constantly thinks bad things are going to happen to her, or someone coming off drugs, perhaps, feeling she might break down. In homeopathy, the mental symptoms are so important that even if the person you are treating simply has a sore knee, you have to try to understand their mental state before you prescribe anything for them. After my grandfather died, I began experiencing horrible migraines. I lived for about a month on Ignatia, the classic remedy for bereavement and disappointment. I didn't feel much better about losing my grandfather but the headaches did go.

Ben is mixing two drops from each bottle into the glass of water.
'So what am I getting, then?' I ask.
'Rescue Remedy, Wild Rose and Crab Apple,' he says.
I think of my bottle of Rescue Remedy in my bag, that I forgot I even had. 'Because . . . ?'
'Because, um, well . . . I put Rescue Remedy in everything. Wild Rose is for resignation and apathy. Crab Apple is for detoxification, and it's really good for colds and flu. It's also useful for people who feel the need to clean up a lot.'
'How do you know all this?' I say, surprised. 'I mean . . .'
'Well, I think everyone here feels a bit of resignation and apathy,' he explains. 'It should probably be put in the water.'
'But what about the cleaning-up thing?' I say. 'How would you know . . . ?'
'Before you passed out at the pub yesterday you stacked up your bowl and plate neatly and pushed them to one side.'
'That was because I wanted to put my head on the table.'
'Oh. So you're not . . .'
'Oh, yes. No. I mean, I am prone to fits of cleaning and tidying when I'm ill. I just didn't know how you would know that. I . . . We don't really know that much about each other, do we?'

Ben smiles in a slightly sad way. 'No.' He looks as if he might say something interesting and then gets up off the bed. 'I'm going to run you a bath,' he says.

'You don't have to,' I say. But he is already in the bathroom.

Why is he looking after me like this? Do I deserve it? Probably not. It will probably end, that's it. He'll do this for a few hours (if I am lucky) and then get bored. I will make sure I don't get too used to it. Who is Ben, now? I think about how I wrote him off as a guy with battered science-fiction novels by his mattress bed just yesterday. How does 'Nurse Ben' fit into this? Have I classified him in the same way Kieran tried to classify me, as nothing more than a collection of cultural objects? Should I ask him lots of questions about politics now? I yawn. I am too tired. When my bath is run I slip into it as if it were a new form of sleep, and then I read a novel about dreams while Ben sits by my bed reading something about philosophy. Every so often he stops to ask how I am, and I assure him I am OK. He does not leave until dinner time, though, and then he comes back with another tray.

Chapter Twenty-two

It's hard to get to sleep on Sunday night. Perhaps I have slept too much during the day. My mind won't switch off, anyway, and I have persistent thoughts. For example: I still haven't had any response from my unknown correspondent. Being ill like this makes me feel less capable of dealing with this kind of thing. As I try to get comfortable in bed, I imagine running, and promptly cough a lot. I couldn't run in this state. I can barely make it to the bathroom without feeling terrible. I feel vulnerable when I know I can't run away. I would so much rather die running than, say, in my sleep, or standing still, powerless. I would like to be the kind of person who resists until the end. In this state, resistance is impossible.

I miss my grandparents. I miss my cat. In a parallel universe I am at home, asleep, having anxious dreams about presenting roughs for my survival kit tomorrow. Which is more real? That or this? Where was the choice I made that sent me spinning into this version of my life rather than the one before? Will I get a secret message tomorrow? Will Ben come? Will I be able to get back to the ideation seminars or will I still be too ill? At about three or four I finally drop off, too hot and on edge to sleep properly at all.

Ben comes with another tray at about half-past eight and then dashes off to the first seminar of the morning. With sleepy words, I ask him to tell 'them' I am ill. I don't know who he will tell, or what they will say. I will be well enough to go back tomorrow; I'm sure I will. But for today I am stuck in bed with my cough and my morbid thoughts and a few books and a box of tissues. My bed is my world, for now.

There's a knock at the door at eleven. *Ben*, I think but – shit – it's Georges, standing at the door in an expensive-looking grey suit and a black polo neck. My room suddenly feels grubby and small, like it is a train carriage he is going to get into and not even notice. I feel like a drug-addict or vagrant he will not even see.

'Hello,' he says.

I can feel myself blush. Stupid, stupid.

'Sorry,' I say, coughing. 'I'm a bit . . .'

'You aren't well, I hear.'

I clamber back into bed, wanting to conceal as much of myself as possible. 'Yeah. Look, I . . .'

'Sorry to hear it,' he says crisply, interrupting me.

What had I been going to say? Something in a soft voice about 'losing' his mobile phone number, perhaps. Maybe it's a good job he cut me off. Everyone knows that no one ever loses a phone number they want to keep. If someone ever tells you they have lost your number it means that they didn't care about it enough to keep it somewhere safe or, if there is sex involved, it means that they thought they had a better offer but it went wrong somehow. Wanting your number again makes you a second choice, usually, and if someone couldn't be bothered to keep it then they really don't deserve you. Georges will know all this. What he won't know, and what I can never tell him, is that I burnt his number because of a minor personality disorder involving a combination of fear and the desire to burn things. I want(ed) him, but I know I don't/can't want him. What the fuck is happening to my brain? Jesus, I feel ill.

'I'm going back to London,' Georges says. 'Then on to New York. I thought you might want to come.'

'Sorry?' I do a weird double-take. 'But I'm . . . I can't . . .' I start having a coughing fit instead and reach for my water. 'Georges . . .' It's the soft voice again.

He doesn't belong in this room. In his suit, he looks like the executive he is. He is a teacher visiting a student, a parent visiting a child, a doctor visiting a patient. He frowns.

'Georges, I can't . . .' I start to say.

'Oh, God, Alice. Please don't make this dramatic. We know that, well, *that* is over. I know you're seeing Ben now, which is great. Congratulations! You are a perfect match. I'm just offering you a lift back to London, as your boss, which I still am. You are ill and, it would seem, can no longer take part in this process. I have a company car organised for this afternoon. It can drop you home after it drops me at the airport.'

'I'd rather stay,' I say quickly, embarrassed. 'I've . . . had an idea. I want to work on it here.'

'An idea?'

'Yes. A product for teenage girls. I think . . . I think it might come to something.' I am clutching at nothing here. I have had a vague idea, yes, sometime last night between worrying about my unknown correspondent and missing my cat. But why do I want to stay here really? Is it that I like this room? I enjoy being looked after by Ben? I am scared of being alone? I really want to know who has been contacting me and what they want to say? Maybe I just like feeling special, tucked away here on Dartmoor. Maybe I am enjoying the fresh air. I don't know. But I don't want to go home and I definitely don't want to get into another company car with Georges, especially not looking/feeling like this. Pathetic, perhaps, but there you are. Maybe I do regret burning his number. Perhaps not. At the moment I'm really not in any position to judge.

'And this is going to be impressive, this idea?' he says.

'Possibly.'

He walks over to the bedside table and picks up one of the bottles of Flower Remedies that Ben left behind. He makes a face as he scans it and then puts it down. Ben's philosophy book is there too, and I notice that he has kept his place with a scrap of paper, rather than turning down the page. I realise that Ben has left a little space here, with his book and his flower remedies, and that means he is definitely coming back. He is going to come back, with his serious face and his dark eyebrows, and he is going to look after me.

'Take some antibiotics, for God's sake,' Georges says. 'I'll organise for a doctor to come. If you're not better in a few days you will have to abandon this project. OK?'

He's looking at this room the way I looked at Ben's room in my mind. Do I hate him for that? Do I hate him for being frivolous rather than serious, powerful rather than alienated, practical rather then mysterious? What is it about him? I really, really don't understand. Georges is the kind of man who goes away and does not come back. You can see it in his eyes. What you can also see in his eyes, however, is the existence of an exception. There is a woman in this world for whom Georges will always return, for whom he will do anything. Perhaps I realise that being this woman would be like being the first Riemann zero found to lie off the line. If you were this woman, Georges would search for you for years. You'd be the result of an amazing challenge, complete with a probability-value less than the chance of winning the lottery while being repeatedly struck by lightning at the same time. Perhaps that's where the attraction is. Imagine actually being that for someone. It would be the most incredible experience. I stare at Georges in a deliberately blank way, hoping he'll fill the blank with something interesting or warm.

'OK?' he repeats.

'Fine,' I say back.

'Good.'

'Georges . . . ?'

He is on his way to the door. 'Yes, Alice?'

'I'm afraid I lost the number you gave me, and . . .'

'It's probably for the best,' he says. 'Let's just keep this to worker and boss, shall we?'

Slave and boss, I think, as he leaves the room. Erdös again. Of course, I have passed up the chance to be the boss while he is the slave. Or maybe it never was that. With tears in my eyes, I settle down into bed, feeling like there are razor blades in my soul. Tears = humiliation. Razor blades = betrayal (where I am the betrayer and I don't even know why). When Ben comes at lunchtime, I pretend to be asleep.

*

There are four houses at my new school. Each one has a name and a colour associated with it. The names are of places, I don't know why. I have never been to any of these places and I don't think they are even close by. Gloucester is yellow, Windsor is red, York is green and Buckingham is blue. I am in Windsor House. Alex, not that I am trying to notice, is in York. Our forms are named in a special sort of code. I am in 1WP, which means I am in year one, in Windsor House and my form tutor is Mrs Pearson (this accounts for the P). I am fascinated with this way of naming classes and I think about it a lot. If Mrs Pearson died (she drives a rusty car so decrepit that there must be a fairly good chance of this), would they have to find us another tutor with the initial 'P'? Or would the name of our class change?

My school uniform is a navy blue A-line skirt that comes down to just below my knees, a white blouse, an electric blue jumper and an electric blue and yellow striped tie. When you get to the third year, you are allowed to wear a navy jumper. I can't wait for this day to come! Most girls in my form look like me, awkward and a bit lost. But there are a few girls who seem to know things no one else does. They have short pleated skirts, rather than long A-line ones. They also have scented erasers (which they all seem to collect), fruit-flavoured lip gloss, which they also collect, pencil cases in the shape of animals or chocolate bars and baggy electric blue jumpers, rather than the Age 11–12 ones most of us are wearing that are too tight and a bit itchy. How do they know to do all this? Did they all know each other before school even started? I know for a fact that Emma, a girl from my primary school, didn't know any of the people she is hanging around with now, so it can't be that. Maybe you are born with it, this élite, expert sense of fashion, popularity and where to buy all the things that go with it.

In my first week, I do all the things my grandparents said I would do. I lose my fountain pen and, miraculously, find it again. I have trouble finding the classrooms I have neatly written into the slots on my timetable. I also learn things they didn't warn me about. I learn not to ask anyone for directions, finding that this is the surest way to get sent somewhere ridiculous. Honestly. This school is like the living embodiment of all the liar paradoxes you've ever heard. *There are two pupils of the Groveswood School, one who always lies and one who always tells the truth. They are both standing in front of you and you can only ask one of them one question. You have to find your maths classroom. What do you do?* The answer, of course, is that you ask either pupil where the other would tell you to go, and then do the opposite. In reality, however, there is no such thing as a Groveswood pupil who always tells the truth so you are better off finding the classroom yourself. No one ever gives you a map of the school, I have noticed. You are expected to learn by trial and error that room 401, an English room on the top floor of the school, is not next to room 400, which is actually a Portakabin in the Rural Studies department, which is itself a field.

The classroom in which we have maths on a Wednesday is on the third floor of the school, next to the language lab. I am in my second week at this school but have not actually had a maths lesson yet. The maths classes last week were given over to 'induction' during which we met our tutors, learnt to use the library and various other things. We have French on the third floor on a Tuesday, so I know where to go, thank God. There isn't very much else on this corridor, and the lights don't seem to work. As there is only one grimy window, this means it is rather dark up here. I wish I had someone to walk to class with but I haven't made any friends in my form yet. I have realised that the key to making friends is finding someone as much like you as possible and then talking to them about how much you both dislike everyone else. Then, if all goes well, one of you will go home with the other after school, for tea. For about half a day, I had my sights on a girl called Becki, but it turned out that she is too stupid. It's a shame; in every other respect she would have been perfect. She also does not have her ears pierced, and she wears a long skirt like mine. I heard that her parents are divorced, which in this school is almost as bad as having no parents at all. Becki also has a packed lunch, rather than school dinners, like me. But, like I said, she is stupid.

So I walk to maths on my own. I thought maths would be my favourite subject but everything is so different here.

'So,' Mr Morgan, the maths teacher, says. 'Welcome, small people of the first year.' (So far so good. No more or less mad than other teachers.) 'In my class we will have no talking, laughing, chewing, eating, drinking, passing notes, brushing hair, farting, copping off . . .' Everyone laughs nervously at this. 'Copping off' is what some teachers seem to call snogging. There's a craze for it here – but not in the first year! We are far too young for this. Morgan continues:

'The reason that it is possible to have copping off in classrooms at this school is because boys and girls are mixed together. If this was my school, boys and girls wouldn't even get within spitting distance of each other. Women – sorry about this, girls – but women ruin everything. If I had my way, you girls would get double domestic science in this period. We can do the sums while you bake the pies. What's wrong with that? Ha ha ha . . .' He starts laughing while we all look at him, confused.

I am sitting next to Emma. She puts her hand up.

'That's sexist, sir,' she says, bravely. Some of her gang murmur their approval of this.

'Nothing wrong with a bit of sexism,' Morgan says back. 'Before we start the lesson, I have to tell you about chess club. Wednesday lunchtime, in the library. And computer club. Thursday after school. Got that? Groovy. Right. Let's get on with the lesson then. Adding fractions.'

Emma and I exchange a look while he turns to the blackboard. She starts writing a note to me on a scrap of paper. *What an idiot!!!* it says. Just as she has passed it to me, Moron (I have already started calling him this in my head) turns around and sighs crossly.

'*Girls*. I knew you'd be trouble. Girls always are. Let's have the note, then.'

He looks at me and Emma.

'What note?' she says.

'I haven't got a note,' I say.

'Right. Both of you, outside.'

I have never been sent out of a class before in my life. I would definitely cry if I was on my own but I am not on my own. I am with Emma.

'Thanks for not telling on me,' she says.

'That's all right,' I say back awkwardly.

'Do you want to come around with us lot, at lunchtime?' she says.

'Us lot' is all the popular girls with pleated skirts and lip gloss. Bloody hell!

'Yes,' I say back, although I had been thinking of going to chess club. And then I can't think of anything to add to the 'yes' so I lean back against the wall in the dark hallway. I think of other things I could say, like, *Do you think there are ghosts here?* But you can't say things like that. Ghosts are far too babyish to talk about. Of course, at home, everyone reads books about ghosts and witches and gangs of plucky children. But that is home. School is the complete opposite of home, and anything you do in one can't really translate into the other.

This school has far more rules than my old school. These extra rules are not made by the headmistress or the teachers; they are made by the children themselves. Not just *Don't talk about ghosts or anything babyish*. If you're a girl, you can't talk to a boy. Ever. If you talk to a boy (and I know this because I made the mistake of trying to say hello to Alex last week) he will blush while his gang of friends laugh, jeer and make licking/snogging noises. Girls will then ask you directly, with a kind of sneer, why you were talking to a boy. Talking to a boy attracts too much attention and the last thing you want at school is attention. It is for this reason also that putting your hand up in class to answer a question, or being really good at PE or something is also frowned upon. No one likes a show-off.

If you do want to do something odd, it helps to have a gang. A gang makes this all right. Emma could only say what she said in maths class because the rest of her gang were there, backing her up. If you are in a gang, you can do anything, really, within reason. The only thing you have to be careful of is being thrown out of the gang for being 'weird' (say, wearing your hair differently from the other girls) or 'a slag' (talking to boys) or 'a gyppo' (wearing anything second-hand or mended) and so on. If you are in a gang and you do want to talk to a boy, you send someone else from your gang to do it. You never, ever, ask someone out yourself. If your friend's mission is successful, and you end up going out with a boy, you still don't get to speak to him. Not that this is likely to happen to me, of course. It's still very confusing, though.

A gang is not called a gang. If you are in a gang, you are 'going around with' the people involved. I can't believe that I have been asked to join Emma's gang. Is it just for lunchtime, or for ever? I have the wrong skirt. My ears aren't pierced. I don't have a TV at home (this would be seen as so weird and abhorrent by people at my school that it is already my biggest secret). I don't have any lip gloss. As if she can read my mind, Emma pulls a small pot of lip gloss out of her pocket.

'Do you want some?' she says.

Could this be a trick? On Monday, I saw one girl, Kali, offer another girl, Liz, one of the leftover sandwiches from her lunch box. 'Do you want it?' she said, sweetly. The moment that Liz reached over to take it, Kali pulled it away and she and her friends laughed, acting disgusted. 'What a greedy gyppo,' Kali said. And Liz has been known as 'greedy' or 'gyppo' ever since. She is fat, which doesn't help. You have to watch out for these tricks. I should be fairly safe with this interaction with Emma, since there is no audience, but I still have to be careful. Is using someone else's lip gloss 'gyppo' or 'gross'? And if I refuse, will I be 'stuck up' or 'posh'?

'Are you sure?' I say in the end.

'Yeah. It's grape flavour,' she says, smiling.

'Thanks,' I say, taking the little mauve pot from her. I put my finger into it and take a little bit, which I smear on my lips. I can see why that lot like lip gloss, now. It really tastes/smells of grapes! And my lips feel softer already. If I am going to be in their gang, I will have to get some lip gloss of my own. How would I do that? What shops sell lip gloss? I don't have any money of my own. Can I ask my grandparents for money for lip gloss? It's doubtful. I could never, ever explain to them why I need it, so it's likely that the response would be something like, 'Really, Alice. What a strange thing to want. You don't actually *need* things like that, you know.'

I am learning that the paradox of being a child is as follows. At school you are desperately embarrassed about everything you do at home. But at home, the odd rules and conventions of your school friends are just as weird and embarrassing. Is it possible that I still have seven years of this hell ahead of me? Still, at the moment I want to go around with Emma and her friends more than anything. I will find a way of obtaining lip gloss, and a pleated skirt.

My heart beats fast all through RE, which is the last lesson before lunch. Then it's time. I worry that Emma will have forgotten her offer but when the bell goes she walks over to my desk.

'Are you coming, then?' she says.

Some people eat their packed lunches in the hall with the school dinner people. But Emma and her friends have found a way to sneak into one of the Portakabins in Rural Studies. One of them, Michelle, has brought a small portable stereo in her bag, so we can play tapes in there and make up dance routines to go with songs.

This is really ace! There's one song in particular that they are working out a routine for but I don't know it. I manage to wing it today but tomorrow, if I am invited here again, I will have to know this song. Today, I learn about my new friends. Michelle is small and blonde, and goes ice skating after school. She has a real, actual coach! She wants to get to the Olympics but swears us to secrecy about this. If the other kids found out she would be seen as a terrible snob/show-off. Sarah and Tanya both like horses and go riding together at weekends. They both want to work at the local stables when they leave school. Lucy does ballet. Emma and I both don't really do anything like that outside of school. Lucy and Michelle are actually on diets, even though they are very thin. No one eats their packed lunch at lunchtime, which seems odd. Lucy and Michelle don't eat anything at all and the others just eat chocolate bars they got from the van on the way to the Portakabin.

The van is a burger van which parks in the school car park at lunchtimes and sells hot-dogs, burgers, ice-cream, fizzy drinks and chocolate. You can go to this van to buy sweets and drinks and that's OK, but if you buy actual food from it you are a gyppo. It's all so complicated.

I don't get to eat my lunch at all on Wednesday, so I throw it away before I get the bus home. I throw it away because I don't want to hurt my grandfather's feelings (he always makes my lunch) but once I have done it I feel guilt like a boulder in my stomach. Instead of talking to him about the Voynich Manuscript, I escape upstairs as soon as I get in, claiming to have lots of homework (another lie; another boulder). Then I lie on the bed with one of my mother's books, listening to the radio and waiting for that song to come on – the dance-routine song. When it eventually does, I tape it, and by the next day I have it memorised.

Chapter Twenty-three

My notebook is filling up . . . *The wooden block with the 'A' on it. Kieran asking who I am. Identity. DVD collections. My dream.* I am writing so fast my hand hurts. I have never had something pop out of a dream quite like this before, but it makes sense to me. A necklace bearing an identity, a proof; a locket with a lock of hair. Not just a necklace, necessarily. A bracelet, perhaps. Bracelets carry all sorts of things: hospital details, festival entrance ID, charms that your aunt gave you. But you can shrink this stuff, the mess of identity, in the same way my grandfather shrank all he thought I needed to know about the Stevenson/Heath Manuscript. You can shrink it and wear it and then everyone can know who you are (or the people you want to know can know, if they can read your code). Cultural DNA. A DVD collection can say things about you, sure, but you can't carry it around with you. Teenage girls, perhaps a bit young for the DVD-identity test, have all sorts of unwieldy ways of expressing who they are. You can wear some of it – black nail varnish, Hello Kitty hair clips, torn fishnet tights, cute tartan skirts – and give some people some idea of who you are. But this entire 'who I am' process could be made a lot simpler.

This is the basis for my idea.

You can wear your identity. Of course you can. But why not go further? If you like a certain pop star, don't put a poster on your wall, wear the code that says you like him or her! So, you're best friends with the most popular girl in the school? Don't just tell people – wear the code for it. Something, perhaps, that she gave you. Yes! You give these things away – thus the automatic transmission factor. You give someone a 'bead' (which I am seeing as like the thing in my dream, a tiny cube like a kids' wooden block, with six faces and a space inside) that means 'You're my friend', or 'best friend'.

Eventually you end up with a string of these things (like a string of DNA, or computer code). The 'beads' will be colour-coded, perhaps? Pink for friendship, say. Blue for things you like? Mint green for memories. Black for politics. I don't know. But you could instantly look at someone and know where their priorities lay in life. An environmental activist loner may choose to wear only one black bead, with pictures of animals on the outside and some earth inside. The popular but boring girl-next-door type would have various pink beads from her friends. Megan or Jackie or Sally would each have given her a bead, with little photos of their holiday together on the six faces, and a Friendship Stone inside it (Friendship Stone . . . ? Could be a good addition). Perhaps the inside of the beads is the private bit, where you can store something that relates to whatever is on the outside of the bead. A modifier, perhaps. Teenage girls could hide drugs in these things! That would give them cult appeal. Their boyfriend's pubic hair. A miniature version of their favourite poem.

The locket and the charm bracelet updated for a kick-ass, post-punk generation. The (think of a name, Alice) is a unique way of creating and broadcasting your own special identity. People say that all today's teenagers think about is themselves. *Who am I?* is the number-one question on teens' lips today (the number-two question, of course, being *Who are you?*). Teenage girls buy products that tell people things about who they are – clothes, make-up, CDs, DVDs. We can give them that sort of product, too.

I can see the kits already. This would have to be done right, probably using the mirror-brand concept. The kits would be heavily customisable, of course, and would have to have organic potential built in, i.e. the kids must be able to customise these things in ways we haven't even thought of. A kit would come with several different choices of string for your neck or arm. You could choose from a chain, a piece of ribbon, a leather string . . . Whatever. You could make or find your own. It doesn't matter at all. You would get a 'starter' kit of, say, ten pink blocks and various other colours (pink being most important, as these are the ones you give away and thus spread the concept of the product). Each block has six faces and an inside. The six faces either have little doors, or transparent slots, so you can insert little pictures, or whatever you want (locks of hair, magical symbols, initials, mathematical formulae . . .). Then of course there is the secret chamber inside the block where you can put anything you want . . . This would be the place to hide secrets. Teenagers could come up with their own language about what this means . . . ? We could include different coloured 'rocks' or 'stones' (like tiny Go stones) in the kits. Possibly set up a website with guidance on the 'mysterious meanings of the stones'? (Not sure about this bit.)

We could sell all kinds of miniaturisation technology, which is perhaps where the real profits would be. A miniature Kodak-style camera that prints out pictures exactly the right size for the blocks, for example. What about mini scrolls, on to which love letters and poems could be copied? Little sets of laminated letters, perhaps, so you could spell out a secret message and carry it around with you inside one of your blocks/beads.

People have always worn various forms of their identity around their neck. People don't wear crucifixes so much any more, but this was an obvious sign, telling you about the person's religion (and taste in religious jewellery). People who are allergic to penicillin have to wear a necklace saying so. This would be all that and more . . . Possibly launch in Japan, with a Japanese name? Or is Japan too over/ too K? This will be the Pokémon for teenage girls. It has 'trading' potential. You get to build up your necklace/bracelet in a unique way. It has broad, multi-cultural appeal.

Tie-in potential: every time a new product (outside PopCo – I'm thinking new fizzy drink, pop group, movie) is launched, a new 'bead' (limited edition?) can be given away with it. Other corporations will want to give away beads to go on our necklaces/bracelets because the concept will be so popular . . . (And we can make them.) Fans of the product can wear its bead (along with all their others, adding to their unique identity). You will easily be able to spot another fan of *The Matrix*, as he or she will be wearing the same bead you've got (will this have appeal to guys, too? Possibly not, but could be some potential . . .). People can wear the bead of their favourite band until they decide they don't like this band any more and then just throw the bead away. No! The bead can be recycled. You can whip out the pictures of whoever was number 1 last week, and replace them with pictures of whoever's in this week. Or, if you're a different sort of person, you will wear the same bead for years. This really can appeal to a lot of people.

The customisable element of this means that people can always express their identities, by making up beads as cult or as mainstream as they want. Badge-makers and T-shirt printing sets have become popular because people want to create customised messages about themselves. But this has much more potential than that. You will be able to download themes, perhaps, from the Internet? Just as you can currently download 'desktop themes' for your computer from fan sites, you'd be able to download themes for your beads/blocks (must think of good name). PopCo (well, mirrorbrand) would create the 'hardware'. People create their own 'software'. We sell them tools to help them create their own 'software'. And it's all about expressing yourself. PopCo are not telling someone who they are. We give them a blank canvas and say, 'You already know who you are. Here's how you can tell other people.' In this way, it should have wide appeal across different teenage girl demographics. If we can get this concept out there as something that *everyone has to have* (using viral marketing, network theory, etc.), no one will even notice us selling it. It won't be a fad that will come and then go. It will be the constant. Different 'beads' themselves may come and go but we won't make those, just kits and blanks and miniaturisation devices.

Imagine something that combines the appeal of tattoos, piercings, badges, slogan T-shirts, posters, certain styles of clothing, friendship bracelets . . . Yes, it's the new concept (insert name here).

So this is my idea. I read back over the notes I have just made. Then I go and throw up in the bathroom.

At about half-past four, the doctor comes. Already, I have that being-ill sensation of time moving very slowly. Half-past four feels like two weeks later than this morning when Ben brought me breakfast. I think it's been quite a hot day outside, although it always stays cool in here. The day outside my window has been almost silent, apart from a single bird singing occasionally. I wish I had my guitar here.

The doctor is a guy in his forties with expensive glasses, chinos and a linen shirt.

'What's the problem?' he says.

'Nothing,' I reply, coughing. 'Just a cold.'

I hate doctors. The last doctor I saw was the one who told me my grandfather was dead. In my life, I have been told by doctors that I am asthmatic twice (I am not) and offered anti-depressants three times, despite not being depressed. When I was about seventeen I was going through a very rough patch and they tried to give me Prozac. I didn't need pills, I just needed to get hold of my life. Even that isn't shocking compared to something I read not long ago about ten-year-olds being stuffed full of pills because they are, apparently, hyperactive. Not just a few, either, this report said that something like one in seven school children were on these drugs: Ritalin, or similar. Some schools were saying that children couldn't attend unless they agreed to take drugs for their 'behavioural problems'. The piece suggested that kids were bound to be hyperactive given their lifestyle: TV, videogames, junk food. If I watch TV for more than a couple of hours I feel sick. Imagine what kids must feel like. Living on sugar, salt and fat; over-stimulated by bang-bang visual culture. Are pills the answer? I don't think so, but what do I know?

The doctor wants to listen to my chest.

'You are very wheezy,' he tells me.

Well, I knew that. 'I'm taking something homeopathic for it,' I tell him.

He ignores this. 'Are you allergic to anything?' he asks me, reaching for his bag.

'No,' I say sullenly, thinking, *I'm allergic to doctors, to work, to contemporary life. At this moment I want to live in a bubble on another planet, if you must know.*

'Good. I can dispense all the items you need right now.' He reaches into his bag and starts pulling out white boxes with blank labels that he fills in with my name and instructions. He leans on the bedpost to write, like he's a man who doesn't have time to sit down. 'Here are some antibiotics. I don't think you've got an infection but better to be on the safe side. Are you asthmatic?'

This again. 'I shake my head. No. Definitely not.'

'Well, I'm going to give you an inhaler anyway, just in case. And some painkillers – nice strong ones, these, not usually available in the UK – and some decongestant and . . .'

I look at the labels on the boxes he is giving me.

'Isn't Vicodin what Hollywood stars keep getting addicted to?' I ask. 'And this stuff . . .' I look at the decongestant. 'Isn't that what people test positive for at the Olympics?'

He sighs. 'Are you planning to take part in the Olympics?'

'Well, no . . .'

'Then you don't have to worry about being drug-tested, do you? It has a little tiny bit of amphetamine in it, that's all. All decongestants have it. And if you don't want the Vicodin, don't take it. But I think you'll find it will make you feel better. It has a cough-suppressing action as well as being a painkiller, which is why I have prescribed it for you.' He smiles at me. 'Is there anything else you would like, while I am here?'

'Sorry?' I say. Outside, the bird sings again. I love birds.

'Well, is there anything else I can give you?'

This doesn't happen on the NHS. 'Like what?'

'Amphetamine? Your boss mentioned that you want to get back to work as soon as possible. If you want to take some, I've got some wonderful sleeping tablets you can have as well – the amphetamine can stop you sleeping, you see.' He's standing over me a bit like he is planning to operate. I look at his bag, placed on the end of my bed and I imagine it full of pills: pink pills, blue pills, a sweet shop of pills.

I frown at him. 'I thought you said there's amphetamine in the decongestant?'

'Well, yes, but not really enough to make a lab rat run around for longer than about five minutes.' He laughs, and reaches for his bag. 'So. You'll want some of this, and . . .' He's taking out another box.

'No, really,' I say.

'Take it. If you don't want it, you can always give it to one of your friends.'

'But . . .'

'And here are the sleeping pills.'

'Hang on . . .'

I now have a pharmacy on my bed.

'Actually,' I say, 'there is something I want.'

'Yes?'

'Nicotine gum. I really could do with some nicotine gum, if you have any.'

He frowns. 'Nicotine gum? No. Sorry.' He shakes his head and then adjusts his shirt. 'No one's ever asked for that before.' Now he's back in his bag. 'I've got some tranquilizers, which can have a similar effect to nicotine. Valium, perhaps?'

'Isn't Valium a bit out of date, now?' I say. I'm thinking about Mother's Little Helper and that sort of thing. That was the 60s. That was last century.

'No, no. Still does the same old job. Works in an hour or so. Makes you feel nice and relaxed. That's what people want. Not three weeks like these new drugs. Although if you were actually depressed I could find something a bit more up-to-date . . .'

'I'm not depressed,' I say quickly. I cough again, and look down at the white boxes on the bed. Christ. 'So what would happen if I took all this stuff at once?' I ask. He looks alarmed. 'Not the contents of all the boxes,' I say quickly. 'I just mean, well, won't these things all clash with each other?'

He smiles. 'No, of course not. What will happen if you take all these drugs properly, as per the instructions, is that you will feel a lot better. Any infection you have will go. You will have no pain. You will be able to go back to work. You will be able to sleep at the end of the day. This miracle is what medicine – proper medicine – can do. Now, sign here.'

He offers me a printed-out sheet, from which he has crossed off the few drugs in existence that he hasn't given me. My name and address are already printed at the top which makes me do a double-take until I realise that my details must simply have been pulled off the Human Resources database. The bill for this will, of course, go straight to them, or Georges's office, or some dark, remote part of PopCo. I am tired now, so I sign the form without asking any more questions. I just want to make him go.

Once he has gone, I look at all this medicine that I don't need or want. I wonder what would happen if I did take this lot all at once. Would I have a quiet death? A sleepy death? A pain-free death? A paranoid, angst-ridden death? I open the bottle of Vicodin and look at the clean white tablets inside. Maybe I could do with some serious pain-killing at the moment. I didn't want these but now I've got them maybe I will give them a try. Just one. Maybe it will take the cigarette craving away a little. Or was it the Valium that was supposed to do that?

There's a knock at the door which makes me jump. I haul myself out of this mountain of medication and open the door. Ben comes in, looking tired.

'Fucking hell,' he says when he sees all the drugs everywhere. 'Where did all this come from?'

'Doctor Death,' I say, getting back into bed. 'I don't know if he's the official PopCo doctor or what. Georges sent him.'

Ben doesn't pick up on the reference to Georges, for which I am grateful. Instead, once I have got back into bed, he sits on the edge of it and starts looking at all the packets.

'Shit. You've got Vicodin here. This is totally addictive. You haven't taken any of it, have you?'

I shake my head. 'No. I didn't want it. He just kept giving me more and more stuff. I don't know what to do with it all, to be honest. Maybe I'll just flush it all.'

'No. I'll take it to a chemist where they can dispose of it properly. Don't want to flush all this into the water system.' Ben frowns. 'Fucking hell. What a racket. I bet that he gets a commission from the drug companies every time he prescribes one of their products. It must be great being a private doctor, employed by corporations. You can give out as much of this shit as you want, knowing that a big accounts department is going to unquestioningly pay your bill, knowing that you're getting a nice kickback from the drug companies as well.' Ben picks up one of the boxes, which contains the inhaler. 'Are you asthmatic?' he asks me, looking concerned.

'No! I tried to tell him but . . .'

'They give inhalers away to every second person these days. It's not healthy to take this sort of medication if you don't need it. God.'

Ben seems to be getting more and more angry but after frowning for a few more seconds, he looks at me and laughs.

'Sorry. Too many paranoid-conspiracy books, perhaps. Blame my job, and all the bloody research I have to do.'

'No, I think you're right,' I say. 'It all makes logical sense.'

'Depressing, though.'

Now I smile. 'Well, if you're depressed I could offer you, oh, I don't know. Some Valium? Some speed?'

'Don't tempt me. It wasn't too long ago that I would have fallen on these boxes with joy. Especially the speed. Let's look at it?' He takes the box. 'Oh yes. Could get a few fun all-nighters worth of coding out of this. Mmm.'

I take the box away from him.

'What happened?' I say. 'Why did you . . . ?'

'What? Give it all up? Dunno. Got too old, I think.'

'How old are you?' I don't even know this about him, I suddenly realise.

'Thirty-one.' He sighs.

'That's still young,' I say.

'Yeah, but . . . OK. Maybe it wasn't just age that did it.'

'What did, then?'

'I don't know. A lot of things . . . How can I put it? A lot *changed* for me about a year or two ago. Got rid of the drugs, got healthy again, went vegan.' He stares past me at the wall, a lost expression in his eyes. 'I . . . Oh, I can't really tell you the whole story but . . . I read a few books while I was researching *The Sphere* that made me think differently about the way the world works. Investigative reports about the environment, animal rights, the effects of junk food, corporations. All the reading was because of the central idea in *The Sphere*, that there's this evil corporation which dupes the public into believing that what it is doing is good for them. We've modelled the Dream Prison on various ideas from battery farming, animal experimentation labs and sweatshops. So I had to read a lot of horrible material.' He snaps his eyes away from the wall and shakes his head, looking at me. 'It really wakes you up when you know what's going on. But it's hard to talk to people about it, because they think you're nuts, or you're making it all up. I mean, there's stuff going on out there that certainly sounds made-up.'

'People would rather believe in a thirty-second bit of marketing than the truth anyway,' I say. 'It's easier to listen to stuff you want to hear.' I know this because I, too, am like this. I fit into this category myself. I don't like the amount of packaging we use at PopCo but whenever they send an e-mail around saying that we are reducing it, or that we have met 80 per cent of our 'environment targets' I allow myself to feel a warm glow. But deep down I know it's all bullshit and we still use hard plastic wrapping on everything.

'That's true,' Ben says.

'But I don't think you're nuts,' I say. 'So this stuff actually made you vegan, then?'

'Yeah,' Ben says. 'There's something about the way we treat animals that just seems so, I don't know, *dystopian*: like contemporary life is like some far-fetched science-fiction novel.' He gives me a serious look that mutates into a grin. 'You know, I read about this series of experiments where they got animals to ask for food by pressing buttons. Birds had to balance on a lever. Other animals like pigs and cows used their snouts. The researchers found that cows liked to be stroked, so much so that they would press a button to make it happen. The pigs in particular were so advanced that they learnt every single thing they were taught. They were happily pressing buttons for food, for strokes, for toys. I looked at the pictures of these pigs sitting in front of these consoles and I thought, "Fucking hell, I can't eat an animal that can play videogames," and then I became a vegetarian. I hadn't felt right about eating meat since I got my dog, actually, and this book I read just confirmed it. Then, a bit later, I did the whole thing and went vegan. That's my vegetarianism in a nutshell, actually,' he laughs. '*Don't eat anything that can play videogames.*'

'Where does butter come into this?' I ask, also laughing. 'I mean, why go totally vegan . . . ?'

'Do you really want to know?' he says, frowning suddenly.

'Yeah. Why not?' I say back.

'Well, do you know how milk is produced?'

Do I know how milk is produced? I'm not sure. I scan my mind for images but all I can come up with is a scene from some of the marketing material for Farmyard Friends, where a ruddy-cheeked milkmaid is sitting on a milking stool next to Daisy or Buttercup in a green plastic field. That's not how you get milk now, is it? I can see a grainy image of cows in stalls in my mind but nothing else comes. This is stupid. I drink milk all the time. How can I not know how it is produced?

'Dairy cows have a pretty horrible time,' Ben says, cutting into my thoughts. 'Forced to be pregnant year after year, killed once their milk production dies off a bit — usually when they are only about two or three years old – and in this constant torment looking for their calves . . .'

I frown. 'Looking for their calves?'

Ben nods. 'Yeah. Well, the calves are taken away as soon as they're born. Then they're killed for veal, or just killed. It's . . . it's so sad the way that the cows keep calling for their calves and looking for them. I don't know. It got to me, anyway.'

We sit in silence for a few seconds while I digest this.

'Where is your dog?' I say, eventually.

'With my cousin. We live together. He's looking after her while I'm here.'

'Do you miss her?'

'God yes.'

'I have a cat,' I say. I think for a moment. Then I say to Ben, 'I don't know much about it, but conventional farms don't really have yards any more, do they? They're not like the "farmyard" toys we sell, are they? I mean, it's not just the dairy cows that have shit lives, is it?'

'No,' he says, shaking his head. 'No. Now farms are like prisons.'

Usually, when I think about the word 'farm' I see it in terms of toy cows and pigs and little pretend fences. Perhaps thinking about the world in terms of toys makes things easier to cope with (even the fences are cute!) Or maybe not. What about when you realise that the fences aren't pretend? I know one vegetarian (Rachel) and now one vegan. But it's not a 'normal' thing to be, is it?

And then I think another odd thought. Does marketing do this? Is it marketing that makes us think that something like being a vegetarian is as stupid as wearing shoulder pads and too much blusher? Is it just marketing that makes us feel good about tucking into a 99p slab of dead cow at lunchtime? That, and the fact that everyone else does it too, perhaps. Who said that recently? Mark Blackman, in the network seminar. *The more people that do something, the more likely you are to do it too.*

And I wonder. Was Ben right about cows liking to be stroked?

'I think you're brave,' I say to Ben, eventually.

'Me, brave? Why on earth would you think that?'

'Most people would think you're nuts being a vegan,' I say. 'But I don't know why. Now I think about it, everything seems a bit nuts.'

He gets onto the bed next to me. 'Yeah. Well.' Ben strokes my head slowly while we both look at the ceiling.

'Are you happy?' I ask him. *Are you happy?* I think of the coded message that asked me that. I still don't know the answer. What does my happiness matter anyway? Perhaps that's the most logical response. *Does it matter?*

'What, now?' Ben says.

'Yeah.'

'Yes. I'm happy now. Right at this tiny moment in time, I am very happy.'

'But everything's so fucked up.'

'Yes, but you just do what you can about that. You do what you can, and then you stop. Believe me, you can almost go mad otherwise.'

'Do what you can? Like being a vegan?'

'Yeah.' He sighs. 'And other stuff. I . . . I wish I could talk to you about everything.'

'Why can't you?'

He bites his lip. 'I just can't.'

I pause for a second. 'Does being a vegan help, then?'

'Yes. Well, I think so.'

'How? I mean, does it help more than say, just being a vegetarian?'

'I think so. I mean, you're not buying anything connected to the meat industry, which has to be good. Look it up sometime and you'll see what they do to geese and pigs and chickens. By being a vegan you're not giving profits to the scum in those industries. You're, I don't know, unplugging yourself from the Matrix a bit.' He shrugs.

I think about Mark Blackman again. 'But you're just one person. Everyone else is still buying animal products.'

'Yes, but I spend, what . . . ten thousand or so quid a year on food. At least. We all do, well those of us with salaries like ours do, anyway. None of that is going into the meat industry now. Like I said, you do what you can do and then stop. Those things are what I can do.'

'And the "other stuff".'

'Yes. And the other stuff.'

'Is it legal?'

'Huh? Oh yes. It's not that. I just really can't talk about it now.'

'Ben?'

'What?'

I look at all the stuff on my bed. 'Shall we just take a load of these drugs?'

'No. They'll make us feel worse.'

'Are you sure?'

'Yes.'

'I really wish I could have a cigarette.'

Chapter Twenty-four

At my old school, getting changed for PE took place in a comfortable warm room next to the school hall, in which we did self-expression (dancing around with bits of material) and dance (dancing around without bits of material). Otherwise we would go outside to play netball on the courts just beyond the classrooms. I don't remember it being at all traumatic.

PE is not like that here. At my last school, if you forgot your PE kit you just had to sit quietly and read a book while the other kids did PE. At my new school, if you forget your PE kit, you have to do PE in your underwear. This isn't a joke! The actual PE kit is almost as bad as underwear, anyway. For girls it's a very short blue pleated skirt, blue PE knickers and an aertex top in the colour of your school house. There is no comfortable heated changing room here. Instead, there is a concrete outbuilding split into Boys and Girls. The girls' half is a dank cave of dark metal hooks, thin wooden benches and – horror of horrors – communal showers. PE is the most evil and stupid thing ever invented. At eleven years old, with all the precise codes and conventions of being that age, the very last thing you want to do is be naked in front of your class-mates. The second last thing you want to do is be forced to walk around outside in the cold wearing a skirt so short and revealing that, if you tried to wear it in any other normal life situation, people would stare and whisper and probably have you arrested for inde-cency. Yet we have to do both these things, three times a week.

'I'm not wearing this outside,' Emma says, during our first proper PE lesson. This takes place on the Friday of our second week at school because of all the induction activities. 'Miss?' She starts waving her hand in the air, trying to get the attention of the PE teacher, Miss Hind. 'Miss?'

'What is it?' Miss Hind says.

'Do we have to go outside wearing this?'

'What's your name?' asks Miss Hind, sharply.

'Emma.'

'Well, yes, *Emma*, you do.'

'But it's disgusting, Miss.'

'I'm sorry, Emma? It's *what*?'

'Disgusting.'

'Yeah,' I say, backing her up.

'There's boys out there, Miss,' says Michelle.

I will later find out that what Michelle wears for ice-skating is much, much more revealing than our frumpy PE skirts. But I will also learn that she would rather die than have anyone see her in these outfits.

'Why don't boys have to wear skirts?' says Tanya. 'It's really sexist.'

'Why can't we just wear tracksuits?' I say.

'Professional sportswomen wear skirts like yours,' Miss Hind says.

'But we're not . . .' Tanya starts.

'Or, if they're athletes, they wear just knickers. Haven't you seen them on the telly?'

Our classmates are looking at us with a mixture of admiration and awe. It is so great going around with this lot. I have never had people look at me like this before. But so far we are the only girls who will stand up to the teachers so I suppose we do deserve some sort of recognition.

'In fact,' Miss Hind says. '*You* will be the ones wearing only knickers if you complain again. All of you. Do you understand?'

'We'll go on strike if she tries to do that,' Emma whispers to me. But we do stop complaining at this point. We know deep down that resistance is futile in these situations and that teachers always get their own way in the end.

'Right,' Miss Hind says. 'All jewellery in here please.'

She starts walking around with a tattered cardboard box. This bit takes ages. Various girls have only recently had their ears pierced, and can't take out their studs in case their holes close up. These girls are issued with bits of tape to stick over their studs. It looks very stupid. Although all my friends have had their ears pierced for ages, I'm not going to have mine done until the holidays (if my grandparents even let me). There's no way I am going to draw attention to myself by going around with tape stuck to my ears. Other people have valuable crucifixes that they don't want to put in the box, even though Miss Hind assures them that the box will be locked in the PE safe during the lesson. When she gets to me, I'm so busy talking to Emma that I hardly notice she's there.

'Necklace, please,' she says sternly.

Everyone looks at me. I can feel myself blush.

'What, me?' I say stupidly.

'Necklace, please. Hurry up.'

'But . . .'

'Necklace!'

'I'm not supposed to take it off, Miss.'

She is cross now. 'I have just about had enough of you girls. Put the necklace in the box, please.'

'I had a note from my parents . . .' I can't say grandparents. No one knows that I don't live with my parents like any normal child. No one in this room attended my birthday party, and even if they had they wouldn't know my domestic set-up because of the village hall. Alex is the only person to have ever noticed I don't have parents. '. . . at my last school. I just need a new one. I . . .'

'Have you ever seen someone's head ripped off because they have been wearing a necklace during sport? It's not very nice. Or watching someone's face turn blue as they choke to death, strangled by the crucifix they "have to wear because of Jesus"? I am not going to lose my job because one of you girls is too stupid to listen and follow rules correctly. No excuses. In the box.'

I am almost crying as I fiddle with the clasp on the necklace. I don't even know how the clasp works, as I have never taken it off before. In the end, Emma helps me, for which I am very, very grateful. I go to drop it in the box but Miss Hind grabs it as it is about to slide in.

'What is this thing, anyway?' she asks, opening the catch and looking inside the locket. As she does this, the small picture inside (of my mother) flutters onto the ground. I go to pick it up but she is quicker than me. Now she's holding the locket in one hand and the picture in the other hand. I thought she would look at the picture but it's too late. She's seen the code.

I feel like I will definitely cry in a minute. Why is she doing this?

'What on earth is this?'

As an adult, you could say something nonchalant, like, 'Oh, it's from a boyfriend. It's a coded message of love.' Or, 'Oh, my grandfather was interested in cryptography a long time ago. It simply says "I love you, Alice" in secret code.' But I am a child.

'It's a picture of my mother,' I say, playing dumb.

'Not that. These numbers and letters. 2.14488156Ex48,' she reads out, slowly. 'What do they mean?'

'I don't know,' I say.

'You don't know?' Miss Hind sneers at me. 'You wear this on your neck. You must know what it is.'

Everyone is staring at me. Even my new friends are looking at me like I am a weirdo or something.

'I don't know,' I manage to say, again, as tears start to form in my eyes. If only there was something I could say. But there isn't. I can't say it's a phone number or a birthday or anything like that. No one goes around with a jumble of numbers inside a locket. No one. I can't tell her the story of why I have it, in front of the whole class. Apart from it being weird and embarrassing, my grandfather told me never to tell anyone about the necklace. This is why I put the picture in it. But I never thought anyone would actually be able to examine it the way Miss Hind is doing now. The silence seems to go on for ever.

'Well?' she says.

Will I ever escape from this?

'It is probably a hallmark, surely?' someone suddenly says, in an odd accent. I look around and see that it is Roxy, this French girl no one ever speaks to. Being French is even weirder than having no parents in this school. Don't ask me why. 'Perhaps you have never seen one before?' she says to Miss Hind. 'If it's a Paris hallmark then you would only have seen it if you bought the most exclusive jewellery, which I find doubtful . . .'

All I know about Roxy so far is that she previously went to an English-speaking school in Paris and speaks English and French perfectly. She is a year older than the rest of us and gets picked up from school every day in a sleek black car driven by a good-looking man in blue jeans. I am thinking, *Yes, I'll say my dad bought it for me in Paris*, but Miss Hind has already lost interest in the necklace. In about one second it is in the box and she is on the other side of the room, pinning Roxy up against a rusty sanitary towel machine.

'You little . . .' she starts to say.

'Put her down, Miss.' This is Emma. 'Miss, you shouldn't do that.'

Roxy's pale face is still defiant. 'Hit me if you want,' she says to Miss Hind in her soft French accent. 'But if you do, my father will make sure you get the sack.'

This PE lesson is definitely not going well.

Miss Hind releases her hold on Roxy. 'You three,' she says, meaning me, Emma and Roxy. 'Get out of my bloody sight. Now!' Teachers don't usually say 'bloody'. Michelle, Lucy, Sarah and Tanya are regarding us with both sympathy and distrust.

'Where are we supposed to go?' says Emma.

'Headmistress's office. Now.'

We leave the changing rooms still wearing our PE kit. All I keep thinking, as we walk across the concrete playground into the main building, is that my necklace is in there, in that box. How will I ever get it back now? I can't go home without it and leave it here all weekend. I want to be wearing my proper school uniform, not my PE kit. But I am not going to cry.

'Thanks,' I say to Roxy.

'Bloody hell,' says Emma. 'We're in so much trouble.'

But it is thrilling, in a way.

'You know, there is no such thing as a Paris hallmark,' Roxy says.

We all laugh. We are in trouble, but we are free. The only problem with my laughter is that there is a terrible anxiety hidden inside it. I have to get my necklace back.

The headmistress is called Miss Peterson.

'Why are you three here?' she says, once we are inside her room. Her room is off the newly refurbished school foyer, which is next to the school hall. It is hot and stuffy and smells of glue and school dinners.

'We have no idea,' Roxy says, sweetly. 'There was a minor disagreement with Miss Hind and . . .'

'Miss Hind pinned Roxy against the wall,' Emma blurts out.

'We were really scared,' I add.

'All right,' Miss Peterson says. She sighs. 'I am fairly sure that you are exaggerating, as girls your age are prone to do. Members of my staff do not pin people against walls. Roxy?'

'Yes Miss,' she says. 'I think it was a misunderstanding.' The way she pronounces the word 'misunderstanding' makes it seem to go on for ever. She turns the 's' sounds into 'z', rolls the 'r' in a disconcerting way, and when she gets to the 'stand' bit of the word, she pronounces it 'stond'. She spoke more normally when she was just talking to me and Emma. I wonder if she just plays up her accent when confronting people like Miss Peterson. I would if I was her, and a bit braver than I am.

Miss Peterson sighs again. 'You have been here less than two weeks,' she says. 'The fact that I have seen you so early is a bad sign. A bad sign.' I hate it when teachers repeat things like this. It's as if they think they are performing Shakespeare, not talking to eleven-year-olds. 'I am going to keep an eye on you three,' she continues, pointing at us. 'Understood? If I see you in here again before the end of term it will be letters home. Now get out of my sight.'

We troop out into the glossy foyer. It has a weekend feeling to it already. The canteen at the far end of the hall has its silver shutters rolled down and there are no oniony cooking smells. A couple of men seem to be bringing equipment in from a van outside. It must be for the senior disco, which is happening tonight. The junior disco isn't for another two weeks but my friends are all planning to go. I don't know how I will be able to go. I wouldn't be allowed to go home on the bus afterwards but being picked up by my grandfather could be fraught with problems. Anyway, I can't worry about this. I have to get my necklace back.

'Why didn't you tell on Miss Hind?' Emma says to Roxy, as we walk out of the main doors into the car park.

Roxy rolls her eyes. 'You don't tell on teachers,' she says. 'If they find out you have told tales on them they will go out of their way to give you hell. Besides, headmistresses always back up the teacher. It is better to get revenge your own way.'

There is another hour left until the end of the PE lesson and therefore the end of school. We wander out of the building and around to the deserted changing rooms.

'Do you think we should get dressed, then?' Emma says.

Roxy is already changing into her school skirt.

'Yeah,' I say, shrugging. 'I don't see what else we are supposed to do.'

This lost hour into which we have tumbled is very difficult for us to understand. Everything is so planned and structured at school. You never find yourself floating free of structure and timetables and supervision. But we are, somehow, free and unsupervised. For the next two or three minutes we struggle into our school uniforms, scared that someone will turn up and we will get into more trouble. Then we look at each other blankly. We are not allowed in the library or the canteen (which is shut now anyway) or in any of the playgrounds while lessons are going on.

'Bloody hell,' says Emma. 'Shall we just go home?'

'I have to wait for my father to come,' Roxy says.

'I get the bus.' I say. 'And I have to get my necklace back.'

'Miss Hind is a right cow,' says Emma. 'What are we going to do, then?'

'We will break into the safe,' Roxy says.

'She'd know,' Emma says. 'Then we'd get letters home.'

'Yeah,' I say. 'She would know if we took it.'

'If we could even break into it in the first place,' Emma says.

I bet I could get into it but I don't say this. 'I'll have to wait for the end of the lesson and then ask her for it,' I say instead. The thought makes me shiver.

'We will stay here with you and wait for her,' Roxy says. 'No one should be with that bitch on their own. You don't know what she might do.'

Emma and I exchange a glance. No one our age uses the word 'bitch', especially not in this film-star accent. Roxy is someone we shouldn't be friends with. She's too odd. But yet we know we will be friends with her. Especially me. I am odd too, of course, although I do a better job of covering it up.

Waiting for Miss Hind turns out to be a complicated affair. We realise that if we are still here in the changing rooms, dressed, when the others come back, we will definitely be called lesbians. You simply can't watch other girls change and shower unless you are doing those things yourself. So we end up doing a strange tour of the very edge of the school boundaries until we end up at the top of the Rural Studies department where the goats are kept. Apparently, when you get to the third year you have to learn to milk the goats. Yuck! And you have to dissect things in biology. Emma and I have already talked about going on strike when this happens. Striking is a very fashionable thing to talk about at school at the moment, perhaps because of the miners. Emma brings it up all the time.

We manage to time it so that we get back to the changing rooms two minutes after school has ended. This has to be quick, because my bus is waiting in the car park already, and Roxy's father will be here soon as well. Miss Hind is there on her own, sorting through a box of hockey balls.

'Excuse me, Miss,' I say.

She turns around. 'Yes?'

'I came to collect my necklace.'

'I'm sure you did. I see there are three of you here. Is this neces-sary? Are you too much of a baby to come and see me on your own?'

I want to shout at her. I want to say that she is violent and unstable and has already pinned one of my classmates against a wall today. I would be mad to see her on my own. Instead, I just say, 'Can I have my necklace, please?'

She sighs and gets the cardboard box. 'I was going to confiscate this over the weekend but I can't be bothered really. Here you go.'

She throws it at me but I am too slow to catch it. It falls to the floor, almost in slow motion. My poor necklace! I let out a yelp as I bend down to pick it up.

'What do you say, then?' says Miss Hind while I am trying to rub stagnant water off the necklace. She says it in the kind of voice people use to prompt you to say thank you.

'What?' I say back.

'What do you say?' A bit more stern – but she actually wants me to thank her.

I look at her with hatred in my eyes, then I look back at my friends. 'Shall we go home, now?' I say to them. I am not thanking this woman. No way. I am not the bravest person in the world but I will not be intimidated by this. I don't care how hellish she makes my life at this school. If I have to, I will run away to Russia, perhaps with Alex. Without saying anything else, the three of us walk out of the changing rooms.

I spend most of the weekend in my room. School now seems to be one long complicated knot of things that I can't tell my grandpar-ents about. I certainly can't explain about the necklace, not that I have to now, since I actually got it back. But everything at school – all the painful inadequacy I feel – comes from the fact that I am not normal. I am not normal because I live in this village, with my grandparents, in a house with no TV. I imagine living where Emma does, on the estate just in front of the school building, with normal furniture and oven chips and parents and catalogue clothes. This would be heaven. I could invite Emma over for tea, then. I could dream about Alex coming around one day and not laughing at me. (He may have no parents but I bet he has a TV and normal books in his house.) So now I have actually wished my grandparents and everything I love away, all because of what people at school think. *If your friends threw themselves off a cliff, would you do it too?* Well, no. If they threw themselves off a cliff, I wouldn't have to worry about what they think any more, so that's a stupid question. I can't deal with this. My grandparents are both too caught up in their work to take me into town. I will not have a pleated skirt by Monday. I will not have lip-gloss. I have to do something about this. But what? Will my friends like me for another week without these things? I have a plan to ask my grandparents if I can have dinner money instead of a packed lunch, so I can buy chocolate at the van at lunchtime like my friends do. Perhaps I can save some of the change for lip-gloss? So next week I will have to feel guilty because of that, too. What am I turning into?

My mother's diary turns out to have been written in the 1960s, when she was a teenager. Her life then seems a million miles away from my life now, however. She went to the girls' grammar school and was obsessed with her violin. Every entry in her diary mentions how much practice she has done that day, as well as whether she has any spots! I wish I was at the grammar school. Why did no one tell me that everything was going to be like this? I thought my mother's diary would be the secret way into her mind but there isn't that much in it apart from the notes to do with her violin practice, or homework. I feel guilty about this as well (guilt is my new best friend), but I feel almost cheated by the diary. I have searched it for secret messages or code, but there is nothing. On the plus side, however, some of the novels in the box are very interesting. Some of them even have dirty bits! I have decided to get to know my mother by reading these books instead. Although I am not cold, I snuggle up in bed with these books all day on Sunday and try not to think about going back to school. I wish I could contract a terminal disease so I don't have to go to that place tomorrow. My stomach ache starts at about six o'clock on Sunday evening and I can't listen to anything my grandparents say at all.

*

Ben and I wake up at dinner time. He gets out of bed with messed-up hair and walks through to the bathroom. I can hear him peeing and then the taps running.

'What do you want for dinner?' he asks me when he comes back.

'You don't have to . . .' I say.

He smiles. 'Shut up. Just give me your order.'

'Oh. Well, just bring me whatever you're having.'

'Do you mind if I eat here too?'

'Of course not.' I yawn. 'Bloody hell. I didn't think it was possible to sleep as much as I have over the last couple of days.'

'You need rest,' Ben says, walking to the door. 'Oh. There's something here.' He bends down and picks up a white envelope. 'There's nothing written on the front. Do you want me to . . . .?'

'No,' I say quickly, holding out my hand. 'That's OK.'

He passes it to me. 'All right. Well, I'll see you in a bit.'

'Yeah.'

Is this the longer message from my unknown correspondent? I tear open the flap and pull out the contents of the envelope. It's definitely not the longer message. There is just one thing in here: a white business card with a mobile phone number on it. There is a message in blue ink on the back. *Alice*, it says. *Forgive my jealousy. If you ever change your mind . . . ??? Oh, well. Here's the number again anyway.* G.

My heart is beating fast. Shit. What if Ben had seen this? It's not just that this is a secret note from another man; this is evidence that I have had/will have some sort of romantic entanglement with one of the PopCo Board. This isn't just ludicrous, it's deeply, deeply lame and uncool. Of course, I don't care about being cool most of the time but this is the one issue on which I think cool has it right. Creatives are creatives and bosses are bosses. That's it. You can't mix the two groups. Also, though, I think about the way Georges stood here in his suit looking down at me. I think about Doctor Death and his Vicodin. Then I think about Ben. Suddenly, it's not just sex with him. With a strange sense of déjà vu, and without thinking any more about this, I get out of bed, find my lighter and burn the business card.

'What's that smell?' Ben says, when he comes back.

'What smell?' I say.

'Oh, nothing.' Ben puts down the two trays he is carrying.

'So what have we got?' I ask.

'We have got . . . Um . . . Sticky onion tarts; braised red cabbage with apple and red wine sauce; and potato, parsley and celeriac mash. There was beans and chips but I thought I'd get the posh stuff. For pudding we have lemon cake with mint leaves. One of the chefs said they call it *Let Them Eat Cake* cake. Some kind of Marie Antoinette thing. I think they're a bit bored down there. I brought you some green gunpowder tea as well. I've had a real thing about gunpowder tea lately.'

'I love green tea,' I say. Ben passes me my tray. 'This looks amazing. Is it all . . . .'

'What, vegan? Yep.'

'Cool.'

'Shall we have the radio on?'

'Yeah,' I say. 'It's just up there, on the windowsill.'

Ben gets up. 'What station?'

'Um . . . Well, it's not late enough for Radio 3 to be any good. I don't know. Maybe 4? You choose.'

Ben fiddles with the dial, switching reception from FM to SW. It crackles and hums a lot and then, suddenly, an intense bass noise kicks in, with ethereal flute sounds. The two melodies, high and low, twist around each other like alien tentacles.

'Cool,' Ben says. 'They're on.'

'Who's "they"? What's this?'

'Zion Radio.'

'Pirate?'

'Yeah, sort of. As much as anything is on short wave.'

'Zion as in *Neuromancer*?'

'Yeah. These two postgrad students in Poland run it. They play math rock, experimental jazz, classical, drum and bass and . . . oh, here you go.'

A woman's voice fades up over the track.

'She's speaking Polish,' I say.

'Wait,' says Ben.

She stops speaking and then starts again, this time in English. A new track starts softly in the background. It is one of Bach's fugues – something my grandmother used to play all the time. But there's something else coming in and out of it, another track; very faint drums. The woman keeps speaking, the English words softened by her accent. I recognise that she is reading something, and I quickly realise that it's Gibson, but I'm not sure which one. Then I hear the word *Wintermute* and smile.

'She's reading *Neuromancer*,' I say, bemused.

'Yeah. They do this most nights. They don't read a whole book, or even the same one, they just broadcast music and excerpts of whatever they choose to read that night. It's brilliant.'

'I love this,' I say. It's an odd experience, sitting down to eat while a Polish woman reads William Gibson on short-wave radio, but odd in a very, very good way. 'Oh yum,' I say, trying some of the mash. 'This is amazing.'

'Those chefs are pretty good.'

We are silent for a while, listening to the radio and savouring our food.

'Ben?' I say eventually.

'What?'

'Thanks for looking after me.'

He smiles back at me. 'Any time,' he says. He finishes his onion tart. 'Do you really like this?' he asks.

'What?'

He gestures at the radio. 'The Gibson stuff?'

'God yes. Especially done like this. I wrote my thesis on cyber-punk at university.'

'As part of what degree?'

'English.'

'I thought you'd done maths or something like that.'

I smile. 'You're not the only one. Violet thought so, too. I had a mathematical grandmother, which is how I know the few bits of maths I do.'

'Had?'

'She died. Just after I finished university.'

I tell him briefly about how I lived with my grandparents when I was a child and what a good job they did of bringing me up, even if I didn't always appreciate it. I tell him about my mother dying and my father disappearing. Even the short version takes almost an hour, during which time it gets dark outside, the bird finally stops singing and Ben smokes a cigarette out of the window while I enjoy the passive smoke. We drink gunpowder tea.

'So your father just went?'

'Yeah.'

'With no explanation?'

'No.' I don't tell Ben about the necklace and all that stuff. There are lots of reasons not to tell him but at the moment the main one seems to be that I want him to be intrigued and fascinated with me, not with my past. If that's not possible, then the programme can terminate. I will not put an artificially infinite loop into this relationship. The algorithm is already wonky but is at least looping at the correct point. I will not make him want me because of intrigue/money.

'That's horrible,' Ben says, about my father.

'Yeah.' I want to change the subject. 'What did you do at university?'

'Philosophy and Theology.'

I hadn't expected this. 'Wow.'

'Yeah. Doesn't make you very obviously employable. It was interesting, though.'

'So how did you end up in the videogames division of PopCo?'

'That's a pretty long story.'

Ben starts clearing the trays away. He pours more gunpowder tea for both of us and passes me my cup. I smell the smoky, green tea aroma. I hadn't had gunpowder tea for ages before tonight. It's amazing.

'Too long?'

'Probably. But the bare bones are that I needed money fast, for various reasons. I've always coded, ever since I got my first BBC Microcomputer in the 80s. I used to create Othello games for fun, and little text adventures. Obviously, as a kid, I got heavily into science fiction and fantasy. I was a right little geek. I started wondering about other worlds, and other forms of consciousness. I ran these crazy astronomy programmes on my computer and persuaded my parents to buy me a telescope. It's . . .' He laughs. 'It's a long story, like I said. I basically became obsessed with making contact with other worlds. Then, when I hit about fifteen, or so, I suddenly started thinking about things in a different way. What would it mean if there were other worlds? Could computers ever develop consciousness? How do you define life? When it came to choosing A levels, I decided to go for Religious Studies, Philosophy and Psychology. I left science behind. There was also this girl . . .'

'Isn't there always?' I say, feeling an unfamiliar discomfort. Jealousy? What was this girl like? Did he reject her or she him? Does he still dream about her?

'At university I became interested in thinkers like Deleuze, Baudrillard, Virilio. I think I may have done the same as you – left the scientific stuff behind and then picked it up again as part of an arts degree.'

'Yeah. That's exactly what I did.' For a moment it all comes back to me; how quickly it happened. One minute I was playing chess and doing maths all the time, the next I had been re-routed into more 'normal' girls' activities: reading, writing stories and worrying about my clothes. 'How did you do it?' I ask him. 'What sorts of things were you interested in?'

Ben sips his tea. 'Artificial intelligence, machines, control screens . . . I loved all that stuff. In Theology, I did a lot of work on Indian religions. Going back to my roots, kind of. I'm half Indian but I had pretty much repressed my Indian side for years, especially at school, where you just try not to be too different. People would think I was Greek, or maybe Italian. I didn't correct them. In my final year thesis I looked at Artificial Intelligence, Otherness and the Enslavement of Consciousness. It was something to do with reading the capitalist economy as an AI programme. I had stopped looking for aliens by that point. Anyway, I started an MA immediately after I graduated – I wasn't about to go and start working for the establishment I'd been criticising – but then my dad was made redundant and I had to leave the MA rather quickly, get my hair cut and get a job.'

'You had to leave?'

'Well, I didn't have to. My parents didn't ask me to or anything, but they had a huge mortgage and no income. I had to help them. So I started sending my CV out to, well, everywhere really. So many of the people on my degree had ended up in call-centres or doing media sales and these did seem to be the only jobs you could apply for with an arts degree and no real work experience. I even applied for work at fast-food chains, can you believe that? I had this vague idea that I would try to get the most pro-capitalist job ever and try to screw the system from the inside. But these places know better than to employ philosophy graduates. Anyway, I also sent my CV to a few videogames companies. Amazingly, one of them picked me up. My coding skills weren't that up-to-date by then but they liked my degree, combined with my background. They put me on storylines, continuity and tea-making with the RPG team. A year later the company was bought by PopCo and I paid half my parents' mortgage with the bonus. PopCo liked me and soon they paired me up with Chloë and told us to create and project-manage a game of our own. So we came up with The Sphere. And now here I am.'

I finished my tea a while ago so now I reach for my little bottle of Arsenicum. You need to take homeopathic remedies on a clean mouth, so it's good to wait five minutes or so after finishing tea or whatever before taking them. I tip a little pill into the lid and then chuck it onto my tongue. In the background, the Polish woman is still reading *Neuromancer*, this time with Miles Davis in the background.

'I'm glad we ended up here together,' I say.

'Me too.'

'If only I didn't feel so ill . . .'

'What's that you've just taken?'

'Arsenicum. It's homeopathic. I don't think it's the right remedy but it's the closest one I've got.'

'What happens if it's not the right remedy but close?'

'Um, it doesn't really work properly. But I haven't got anything else.'

Ben looks concerned. 'Where would you get the right remedy?'

'The Internet. Or, if it was a low potency, from a health-food shop. But I don't know what the right remedy is. I have to note down all my symptoms and then look them all up. I don't have any of my books here, so . . .'

'Is there no other way?'

'Well, yeah. They have online repertories. But there's no Internet here so I'm just going to have to make do.' I smile. 'It could be a lot worse. Mind you, I really could do with some nicotine gum as well. And . . .' I sigh. 'I really, really feel like some sweets. I don't know. It's hard with there being no shops here.'

'I could go to the shops for you.'

'No, really . . .'

Ben gets up and pushes his black glasses up his nose. 'Hang on,' he says. 'I think I have an idea. I may be able to get you on the Internet. Back in a bit.' Then he leaves the room.

If he is going to get me on the Internet (I can't think how) then I will need to have my symptoms ready to look up. How am I feeling? It is very odd, trying to repertorise your own symptoms and prescribe yourself a remedy, but I don't really have much choice. *So, how do you feel, Alice?* I feel like shit. *Can you be more specific?* I think about what I would do with a patient. I have never had any patients, of course, not real ones. I have prescribed for Atari, for Rachel and for Dan. This is how a lot of homeopathy occurs. Someone learns the art and then uses it casually with friends, colleagues and relations, like the neighbourhood witch. I imagine myself with a cape and a pentagram, and smile. This isn't helping. I take out my notebook and a pen and flick to a new page before writing my name and the date at the top of it. On the way to this clean, new page, I pass my idea: pages and pages of brainstorm-style notes and diagrams. Is this idea any good? Do I care? I'm not sure.

The key to this is writing down what you would notice about yourself if you were an impartial observer. My necklace idea at least proves my mind is active. Is my mind *unusually* active, though? I'm not sure. Maybe I should do the 'generals' before I do the mentals. I am cold and I have a desire for warm drinks (especially gunpowder tea and – still – miso soup). Miso soup is salty, as well. In fact, I am craving salt. I imagine plates of chips and crisps and soy sauce. I feel better keeping still in bed and movement makes me worse. But do I feel better from coughing, or talking? These are forms of movement as well. I cough experimentally. Nope. Don't feel any better from that. I make some notes. Is there anything else that makes me feel better or worse? I feel better when Ben is here. I add *Better from company* to my notes and then think some more. Following my strange dream on Saturday night, all I have dreamt of is birds, oddly enough. *Dreams of birds*, I write down. It is so hard to try to note your own mental symptoms. Come on, Alice. What thoughts are you having? What, if anything, has you obsessed?

Here's one thing. Earlier, when I was talking to Ben about milk, something happened in my mind. I can't exactly describe it but something changed. All I've been thinking since then is this: just because everyone does something, does that mean it is correct? Mark Blackman proved that people will do something just because everyone else does. And I've been wondering: since I have devoted a lot of my life to *not* doing what everyone else does, why is it that I accept so much that is obviously wrong? Why is it that even I assume that some things are OK simply because everyone accepts that they are? Of course, I always knew that bad things happen in the world. I am not an idiot. But my attitude has always been that you just have to try to get through life, for as long as possible, without deliberately making things worse but, also, aware of the fact that you can't make anything better. In the end, there's probably no four-dimensional being watching us to see if we make the right choices. There is no judgement. You live your life and hope that you won't be involved in any wars and then what? It's all over, and you become earth.

War. When Hitler was around, it was quite clear who the enemy was. But who, or what, do people fight now? I sense that people simply fight their own, individualistic wars against their noisy neighbours, or drug addiction, or the mobile phone receiver in their garden (but not the one in the next town, or the unjust war 1,000 miles away). Perhaps the world seems like too big a thing to try to save, especially when there are so many enemies out there. It's too late! Save yourself! Does that make more sense? I have always felt incapable of 'saving' anything: myself, the world, whatever. One person doesn't matter. One person can't matter, unless that person is a head of state. I think about my grandfather and all the small personal battles he fought. He was against greed, and acquisitiveness, and plundering the environment for whatever treasure you thought it might contain. If he received bad service in a shop, he would never confront the assistant. Instead, he would come home and write a long letter to the Managing Director of whatever company it was, complaining about their exploitation of their staff and how, since this company so obviously exploited its staff, and since this led to a bad service, he wouldn't be shopping there again. One time I suggested to him that perhaps the member of staff *was* to blame. Surely people should take some responsibility for their actions? If their company was that bad, surely the employee could just leave? 'We *all* have to fight the system,' he said to me. 'Otherwise no one will.'

Another strange memory: an essay I did at university. *Is* The Tempest *a racist text?* I remember drawing meaning out of the word 'text', using Barthes to argue that text lives in a dimension of its own, not stuck in its own time, and needs the reader to take things to it in order for it to make sense. As a text, *The Tempest* is racist if you read it as a story about Caliban, the indigenous inhabitant of the island, being colonised and enslaved by Prospero. But what about theatre companies who cast Caliban less as a 'monstrous' native and more as an ambiguous magical creature? Are those texts racist? Is it OK to enslave magical creatures? No one seems to mind Prospero's domination of Ariel, after all. At the time of this essay, we had a seminar in which someone argued that *The Tempest* could not be seen as a racist text because in Shakespeare's time people hadn't been educated to recognise racism or be against it. You couldn't blame Shakespeare and his audiences for their attitudes, this person argued, because they hadn't been educated to have different attitudes. Educated by whom? The Disney Corporation? I argued back that everyone is capable of logic, and everyone is capable of moral reasoning. Just because most people think something is OK does not mean you should think so too. Slavery would never have been abolished if everyone just sat back and said, 'Oh, everyone else says this is all right and after all it is jolly convenient . . .' I remember at the time wanting to mention Francis Stevenson, who was against slavery before it even became popular. But no one had heard of Francis Stevenson, or (officially) proved he existed, so I didn't say anything.

Yet, here I am and I am fighting against nothing, nothing at all. And suddenly I don't know if this is right, any more. And I don't know what has made me think about this; whether it is this cold, or Ben, or Georges, or Kid Lab or Mark Blackman or Kieran or Doctor Death . . . And I have no idea what to do about it, either, and I still don't know who the enemy is.

It doesn't go on the list, anyway.

By the time Ben comes back, I have the following list of symptoms:

    Cold > warmth
    < Touch
    < Movement
    Desires salt, sweets
    Desires company
    Fear of disease
    Dreams of birds

Ben has Esther with him. She is carrying a laptop case. They almost fall into the room.

'For God's sake,' Esther says.

Ben laughs. 'We're here now.'

'No one's supposed to know I have this thing. Hi, Alice.'

'Hi,' I say. 'What's going on?'

'Internet access,' Ben says. 'Brought to you, by us.'

Esther puts the laptop case down on the bed and sits next to me. 'How are you feeling?' she asks.

'A bit shit,' I say. 'Thanks for bringing this . . .' I gesture at the laptop. 'I didn't know . . .'

'Don't tell anyone I've got it,' she says. She leans over and unzips the case. The laptop inside is small, thin and silver. She opens it and fires it up. 'I'll jack you in,' she says, 'and then we'll go and get you some tea or something.'

'Thanks,' I say.

Esther presses a few buttons. I don't know what she is doing.

'There,' she says.

'Huh?' I say. 'It's not connected to anything.'

'It's in the walls,' she says.

'It's wireless technology,' Ben explains. 'This whole estate has wireless broadband. You can just open a laptop in any of the rooms and immediately connect to the Internet. It's pretty cool, actually. I wish I had my laptop here.'

'It's the future,' Esther says. 'And it's here.' She laughs. 'Well, have fun. Ben? Tea.'

They leave me alone with the laptop.

At home it takes ages to log on, and then twenty or so seconds for each page to load. On this thing, it's all instantaneous. The homeopathy site I like most is French, with an English section. It has electronic versions of all the most important text books, and entire *materia medica* that, if you bought them, would cost hundreds of pounds and run to several large volumes. I load up Kent's repertory and start looking up the symptoms. *Company, desire for* and *Fear, disease of impending* have many remedies listed under them, in varying degrees. Two remedies, however, Kali-Carbonicum and Phosphorus, appear in the most serious degree in both. *Fear, touch of* has only five remedies listed under it: Arnica, Coffea, Kali-Carbonicum, Lachesis and Tellurium.

*Dreams of bird*s. I look this up under *Sleep, Dreams* but find nothing. Sometimes this happens in the repertory. You don't find what you are looking for in the place where you expect it and you have to be a bit more inventive. I am sure I have seen references to birds in the repertory before. Often, when I think I have seen things in the repertory but can't remember where, they turn up in the *Mind, Delusions* section, since this is the part I browse most often. The delusions are like poetry. *Delusions, choir, on hearing music thinks he is in a cathedral. Delusions, existence, doubted his own.* I love the *Delusions* section. I bet I will find something about birds there. I click around from page to page until I find it. *Delusions, birds, sees.* Sees birds. Is that the same as dreaming of birds? It doesn't really matter. If birds are a theme you have to take them where you can find them in the repertory. I note down the remedies under this rubric: Belladonna, Kali-Carbonicum, Lac Caninum.

Cross-referencing with the Generalities sections for coldness, warmth and so on, and the section in Stomach for desires and aversions, I find Kali-Carbonicum in all the relevant rubrics, except *Desires salt.* Phosphorous is there, as is homoeopathic salt itself, Natrum Muriaticum. I have come up with Kali-Carb on all but one of my symptoms, however, including the most odd one (sees birds). This is what I need, I am sure of it.

I type the name of my favourite homoeopathic pharmacy into the browser and the page pops up instantly. I click through to the K page and select Kali-Carbonicum in both 200C and 1M potencies. I press 'add to cart'. Then, excited to be actually shopping (sort of), I select the P page and order the same potencies of Phosphorous, just in case the Kali-Carbonicum doesn't work. Then I order some organic hand cream to make myself feel better. I click through to the payment page and type in my credit card number (which I know off by heart, having an affinity for learning long numbers). Blah blah blah. Click, click, click. Oh. Delivery address. I hesitate for a moment, and then type in Room 23, East Wing, Hare Hall (although I almost typed PopCo Towers), Dartmoor, Devon. That's enough information, surely? Maybe not. I have the feeling we may have moved on from the days where you could draw a picture of the pub next door to where your friend lived and an arrow pointing to their flat with just the name of the town and the Royal Mail would get it there somehow.

Ben and Esther knock at the door while I am still wondering whether to press 'Confirm'. Ben is carrying a tray with a teapot and some cups on it.

'Do either of you know what the address here is?' I say.

Ben shakes his head. 'It's Hare Hall,' he says. 'That's all I know. He puts the tray down on the table.

Esther is checking the pockets of her hoody, and then her denim skirt. 'Um, I thought there was one in here,' she says. 'Oh yes. There you go.'

She passes me a PopCo *With Compliments* slip.

'It's all on there,' she says.

*

Roxy only stays at Groveswood Comprehensive for one more week. In that week she attaches herself to our group like we are a host and she is an unknown virus. She spends this time pouting, smoking (really!) and explaining how to shoplift. Then she is gone. We later hear that she has started at an all-girls private day school in town. I am jealous that she has escaped.

During that week, I use her presence as a cover for the fact that I still don't have any of this right. My grandparents are giving me £1.75 a day dinner money now, so I save this every day, pretending I am on a diet like Lucy and Michelle. I don't think Lucy and Michelle like me, though. One day I was a few minutes late into the Portakabin at lunchtime and noticed that the conversation died the moment I walked in. Later, I asked Emma what they had been saying. 'I stuck up for you,' she said mysteriously. 'But you know what they're like.' Do I know what they are like? I'm not sure. I know they pick on girls who smell, are fat, wear the wrong clothes, speak up too much in class, don't brush their teeth, don't shave their legs, eat food that is bigger or smellier than a chocolate bar, don't wear deodorant or don't have permed or styled hair. I have been pretending that my hair is permed which has gone down well. I am not fat and I don't smell. But I need to get a different skirt.

On Wednesday the maths sets are announced in Mr Morgan's class. Roxy sits there sighing and painting her nails with Tippex. Perhaps she already knows she is leaving. We haven't done a test to see what sets we should be in, like we have in some other subjects. Instead, Morgan (Moron) has decided to set us on the basis of the two pieces of homework we have done so far, and our general attitude in class.

Emma and I are put in set 2, along with about four other girls, none of whom we know. Our friends all go into set 4, except Roxy, who is way down in set 5. I am disappointed not to have made it into the top set. The boys who are in top set all go to chess club and computer club, unsurprisingly. They must be really clever. Also, perhaps it's a good thing that I didn't get into the top set. Imagine being the only girl in a class, with none of your friends. It would be horrible. One thing I have been learning this week is that the more time you spend with your friends, the less time they have to talk about you behind your back. You really do have to be on constant alert all the time at school. I have been on DEFCON 1 since the necklace incident which, while it could have been a lot worse, marked me out as odd.

Along with Emma and Sarah, I have been put into the top set for English. This setting was done on the basis of a test that included spelling, comprehension and a little essay on the subject 'My Favourite Book'. My new favourite book is *The Count of Monte Cristo,* which was in my mother's book box, so this is what I wrote about. In my essay, I repeated what my grandmother said about revenge. *This book shows that revenge is a bad thing.* But, like my grandfather, I am not so sure I really agree with that. I want Moron to get it, and Miss Hind, and Lucy, actually, and Michelle. The English teacher, Mrs Germain, wrote on this essay 'Very mature' and gave me an A–. I like Mrs Germain much more than all the other teachers.

The rest of this week is spent plotting the purchase of my skirt. I have actually managed to ask Emma how much her skirt cost. Not being sure whether it was 'gyppo' to ask something like this, it took me two days just to formulate the question. But I now know that they are £6.99. I also need thick black tights, which I have noticed Tanya and Emma wearing on colder days. I think I will have enough money for both these items by Saturday but that doesn't solve the issue of how to get into town to get them without my grandparents knowing. I know that some of the others go into town every Saturday. They invited me once but I said I lived too far away and I haven't been invited since.

'I wish I could come into town with you lot on Saturday,' I say to Emma on Thursday. 'It's really boring at home.'

'Well, why don't you come for tea on Friday and then stay the night?' she says. 'We can go in together on Saturday. It'll be brilliant.'

This is inspired of Emma, although I can't say I didn't have the idea myself first.

'Will it be all right with your mum?' I ask.

'Yeah, I'm sure it will. Look, give me your phone number and I'll get her to ring your mum to tell her it's OK.'

My heart beats as I tear a scrap of paper out of one of my folders. 'I'm staying with my grandparents at the moment,' I say, coolly. 'So she'll have to talk to one of them.' My life really is full of lies right now. At least I don't have to worry about being afraid of being alone in the dark any more. I have so many other things to worry about that this fear has been squeezed out of me like the last bit of toothpaste in an old tube.

Emma and I have a plan. We will get up early on Saturday and go into town before the other kids get there. We will purchase my skirt and tights from a shop she knows and then go and hang around with the other kids afterwards. I will have the embarrassment of carrying a plastic bag around all day but it will save the embarrassment of having to take the whole gang along to buy the skirt.

My preparation for this operation is so complex that I don't have time to do any homework on Thursday night. I resolve to catch up over the weekend. I examine my whole wardrobe for something suitable to wear into town on Saturday. There really is nothing. I don't know what they all wear out of school but it's reasonable to assume that I don't have it. Shall I take something anyway, or simply pretend to have forgotten? If I pretend to have forgotten, will Emma lend me something or not? If she doesn't I will have to come home, as I can't go into town in my school uniform. Will asking to borrow clothes make me a weirdo or a gyppo? I'm not sure. Still, it will probably be better to be called a weirdo or a gyppo by Emma for five minutes than to be called one by all the other kids in town all day. I decide to take nothing.

During Friday afternoon break, when I get a minute alone with Emma, I see an unexpected opportunity. Clapping my hand over my eyes, I feign sudden revelation.

'Oh bother,' I say.

'What?' she says.

'I haven't brought any clothes for tomorrow.'

She laughs. 'You're so absent-minded, Alice. It's all right. You can wear something of mine. I borrow clothes off my sister all the time.'

My heart sings.

The skirt shop is in a bit of town I haven't been to very much before, near Mill Road. The ground floor is full of army surplus stuff that older teenagers wear: combat trousers, army boots, green shirts. It is dark inside the shop, and the man behind the till smiles lasciviously at us as we walk inside.

'Hello, girls,' he says, through rotting teeth.

Emma and I exchange a look and then run upstairs, giggling. There's no one up here except for us. It smells slightly of rain, and school lockers.

'You could nick stuff here, and they'd never know,' Emma says in a whisper. We have been a little bit fascinated with shoplifting since Roxy told us all about it.

'I know,' I say.

'Have you ever . . . ?' she says.

'No. Have you?'

'No.'

There are racks and racks of school-uniform style clothes up here and other things I have seen people at school wearing: parka jackets, leather jackets, cheap fashionable shoes. I wonder if the clothes I am wearing now – a black skirt and a shell-pink jumper – come from here. I am so glad I am not wearing my own clothes.

'Can I help you?' says a girl's voice.

We turn around. The girl looks young, possibly a student. Her hair is dyed bright blue and she is wearing a female version of the clothes from downstairs: big DMs, tiny combat trousers and a baggy T-shirt with the words Amnesty International on the front. I want to be her! I am too scared to speak, so Emma asks for the skirt and tights, saying they are for me.

'You'll want a size bigger so she can roll it up, presumably,' the girl says, winking.

'Yeah,' says Emma.

I know this is how they make their skirts shorter as I have watched them getting changed after PE. This girl knows that too –

and she has even made a joke about it. I feel sick inside. I know that the rest of my group would call this girl a weirdo but I would give anything right now to be her age (about eighteen) and working in a shop like this, with blue hair and crazy clothes.

'Did you think she was pretty?' Emma says when we leave the shop.

'Did you?' I say. I have the impression that Emma thought, like me, that the girl was pretty but I want her to say it first. She hesitates.

'No. Do you think I'm a lezza? Come on.'

We walk into the centre of town to the market square, looking for Lucy and Michelle. Sarah and Tanya are at the stables, apparently, so it's just going to be us four. We are early, so Emma suggests that we look in Boots. Her lip gloss has almost run out, and she wants to get a new one. I wonder if I have enough money left to get some myself. I know that the rest of the gang always get cheeseburgers from the new McDonald's on a Saturday, regardless of diets and everything else. If I want to do this too, I definitely can't afford lip-gloss. It's a conundrum.

So we are in Boots, looking at flavoured lip-gloss, and there are no members of staff around at all.

'Are you thinking what I am thinking?' Emma says.

'What . . . ?'

'You know.'

I do know. So many of our conversations seem to operate according to the surreal, hardly there principles of not-saying-something-first, guesswork and basic telepathy. I know what she's talking about, and she knows that I know. But neither of us has mentioned it first. No one is a gyppo. No one is to blame.

'Yeah,' I say. 'But . . .' I gulp. 'What if . . . ?'

'No one's looking, though.'

'No.'

'Go on, then.'

'You first.'

We giggle. 'We'll do it together,' Emma says.

Objectively, I seem to be better at this than she is, and I notice her watching and copying me. I pick up two lip-glosses in my hand, one with my forefinger and thumb; one concealed in my palm. I say something loud to Emma about already having this one and then I put one of them back, using slightly too theatrical movements. I still have the other lip-gloss concealed in my hand. I quickly put this hand in my pocket. We leave the shop.

Outside, there is a stall giving out leaflets to do with animal experimentation, which I have heard people talking about at school, but never really understood before. I look at the people on the stall, briefly, and their posters of rabbits with electrodes in their brains, and dogs tortured and shut in cages. My stomach turns over. This can't really happen, can it? I want to cry. But I can't really think about this because I am a thief now and Emma and I have to get away from Boots. We are running, suddenly, and we don't stop until we get to the park.

'Did you really do it?' Emma says.

'Did you?'

'Yeah. Look.' She shows me the lip gloss she stole.

I smile, and get mine out too.

'Do you think they'll be following us?' she says.

I frown. 'I don't know.'

'We'd better not go into Boots again for a while, just in case.'

'No.'

We are brave. We are on the run. We have new lip gloss! We promise not to tell anyone else we have done this. Later, Emma asks me if I will be her best friend. It is logical – in our group, Lucy and Michelle are best friends, as are Sarah and Tanya. I had a feeling that Emma has brought me into the group and groomed me for this purpose and when she asks me now I get the feeling of finally having done things right.

We meet the others later and go to McDonald's, where, even though we are scared of being seen/caught, we cannot resist getting out our lip glosses. Of course, we do not say how we obtained them. I can tell that Lucy and Michelle approve of me a bit more today. I have lip gloss. I am wearing fashionable clothes. After lunch, we all eat chewing gum (to make our breath fresh) and then we go to the small shopping centre and sit on a bench watching a group of boys from our year who are sitting on another bench watching us. We giggle, and they occasionally call things out and hit each other.

At about three o'clock, just before I have to leave to get my bus, one of the boys comes over. His name is Michael and everyone knows he wants to go out with Lucy. He comes over to Emma and takes her off to one side, whispering something in her ear. She comes back, grinning.

'Do you like Aaron?' she asks me.

'Which one is Aaron?' I say.

'The one with blond hair.'

'Oh.' He is in my class for history, I think.

'Well? Do you like him?'

This is a potential minefield. If I say yes, and she sends the message back to the boys, there is every chance they will just jeer at us and shout out things like 'No chance', or just make gross noises meaning 'You're ugly/yucky'. This is the kind of thing that happens at school. However, things are different in town.

'Why?' I say, in the end.

'He's asked you out,' she says.

Bloody hell. A boy has asked me out. Is this a joke?

'Don't take all day,' one of the other boys shouts from their bench. I glance over and see Aaron punch him on his arm.

'Tell him yes,' I say quickly, to Emma.

She nods in the direction of the boys, and three of them cheer, while Aaron blushes. I avoid catching his eye. It's almost time for me to go and get my bus. It is arranged, via Emma and Michael, that my new boyfriend will walk me there. All the way to the bus stop, and with the others walking behind saying things like 'Oooh', and 'Kissy kissy', I ask Aaron things about whether he likes school, and other things that pop into my head. I have this idea that if you are going out with someone, you should get to know them. Aaron doesn't say very much but, when we reach the bus stop, he checks to see that his friends aren't looking and then kisses me on the cheek. He blushes, says, 'See you at school', and then runs away.

As soon as the bus has pulled off, and my friends are no longer in sight, my stomach clenches like something in a vice in wood-work. I am the only person on the top deck and it is too quiet up here. I close my eyes and see a mess of images: animals in cages, rows of cosmetics, children jeering, beef burgers. I see Aaron's face leaning in to kiss mine. He wanted to kiss my lips but I turned away. I have a bag of contraband school uniform, that I stole dinner money to get, and a lip-gloss in my pocket that I stole from a shop. I am a liar and a thief.

Walking home from the village bus stop, I look at Rachel's house and wish she was home. I will write her a letter tonight, I think. What have I become? Still, I am in too deep to go back now. I will not show my grandparents that I am upset. I will conceal the lip-gloss and new school clothes from them. I will only cry on my own, when no one is looking. I think of Aaron's kiss, and I wish it had been Alex. I wish I went to chess club.

There is a car in the driveway that I haven't seen before. Is it the police? With my heart beating wildly, I walk around to the back of the house and let myself in. I feel sick crossing the threshold to my own home, as if the Alice that should live here is dead because I killed her. That makes me an impostor. I don't want to be found out. I want to hide for a million years.

'Ah, the wanderer returns,' says my grandfather when I walk through the back door. He sounds happy, so maybe the visitor isn't the police. She doesn't look like the police, actually. She is sitting in the kitchen with my grandfather, drinking a glass of wine.

'Hello,' she says to me. 'You must be Alice.'

She is about my grandparents' age but more glamorous. She is wearing a black kaftan and a crimson silk scarf. Her lips are the same shade of red as her scarf and glisten like a cut beetroot.

'Hello,' I say shyly. Then I remember that I am an impostor and cannot say too much in case I am discovered. In fact – I must look like an impostor in Emma's clothes. Just as I have this thought, my grandfather glances at me again and does a double-take.

'Is it the wine or is there something different about you?' he asks me.

'I borrowed Emma's clothes,' I mumble as I walk through the kitchen and go upstairs to my room. From up here I can hear the sounds of laughter downstairs. I place the carrier bag (which hasn't been noted, thank God) on my bed and take out my lip-gloss. I apply some of it to my lips but it feels wrong so I wipe it off with the back of my hand. I slip it in my school pencil case instead and think about doing some homework. I half-heartedly take out a couple of books and my folders but my life feels like an open wound at the moment and I can't focus on homework. Instead, for the next hour or so I lie on my bed with the radio on, trying to convince myself that I like Aaron. Then there is a knock at my bedroom door. It's the police! No, in fact it is my grandmother.

'I think dinner is almost ready,' she says to me. 'Did you have a nice time with your friend?' I climb into my grandmother's head and imagine her ideas about the kinds of things two friends would do on a Saturday. I see two girls playing Ludo, helping with each other's homework, talking about life, families, dreams and ambitions. My grandmother would never understand what I have done today.

'Yes, thanks,' I say.

'Jasmine is here for dinner. Did you meet her? She's an old friend of ours. Very interesting woman.'

'Yes,' I say. 'I did meet her.'

'Alice?' says my grandmother. 'Are you all right?'

I immediately bristle. 'Yeah, of course. Why?'

'No reason. Well, see you downstairs in a minute, then.'

'OK.'

Jasmine reminds me of a very grown-up version of Roxy. She has been travelling, it transpires, which is why my grandparents haven't seen her for so long. She has been to India, Africa and even China! No one knows anything much about what goes on in China so for ages she tells my grandparents things she has seen there. After we have finished our main course, she lights a long, black cigarette and leans back in her chair like she has no problems in the world. Why can't I feel like this? Then my grandfather serves his famous home-made Black Forest gateau, and something about this scene is so comfortable and homely that I want to cry. I want to cry and tell them all that I never want to go to school again.

'So how's the world of cryptography, Peter?' Jasmine asks.

'You mean cryptanalysis, of course.' He laughs.

She laughs too. 'I was never too great with all that terminology. Code-breaking, then, that's an easier term. How's it going?'

'It's going well. I – well, Alice and I – are working on a fascinating project at the moment. I'll show you after dinner. It's called the Voynich Manuscript . . .' His voice fades out slightly. In my head, every synapse I have is singing, 'Alice and I, Alice and I . . .' My grandfather has described it as our project! I am so proud, I want to burst. When my grandfather's voice fades up again, he is about to talk about something else.

'Since you asked about cryptography, though,' he is saying to

Jasmine, with laughter still dancing in his eyes, 'I feel compelled to tell you the latest developments.'

'So this is what . . . ? Code making rather than breaking?' She smiles. '*Graphy* from *Graphein*. *To write*.'

'That's right. Have you heard about Public Key Cryptography or RSA?'

Jasmine laughs again. 'Peter, have I ever heard about something scientific before you or Beth have told me? Come on, just tell me. It sounds bloody complicated.'

My grandfather starts by way of a kind of introduction, explaining problems in cryptography, telling her that, historically, even supposedly unbreakable ciphers have always eventually succumbed to cryptanalysis. He talks about Charles Babbage breaking the Vigenère Cipher a hundred years ago and the operatives at Bletchley Park breaking Enigma. This leads the three of them to make various comments about the war, and my grandmother says something about Turing and BP while we finish our cake.

'So,' my grandfather says, getting up to put coffee on the stove. 'The challenge has been for the cryptographers to come up with something truly unbreakable. Since Enigma tumbled, the ball has been truly in their court. Now, Alice, tell Jasmine what the biggest problem with cryptography is.'

Me? I gulp. What is the biggest problem of cryptography? I force my mind into reverse and try to remember all the conversations we have had on this subject.

'The distribution of the key?' I say uncertainly.

'See, I told you she's a genius,' my grandfather says. 'Exactly. The distribution of the key. Most ciphers are enciphered and deciphered using the same key, often a jumble of letters or numbers or a word. I could decide to communicate with you using the Vigenère Cipher, or even a mono-alphabetic cipher. We would both know that the key was, say, the word "lapsang". No problem. I use the key word to encipher the message, and you use the same word to decipher it.'

'How do you encipher a message using the word "lapsang"?' Jasmine says.

My grandmother smiles. 'Don't ask him that. We'll be here all night.'

We all laugh. This is true.

Still, to help this make sense for Jasmine, he quickly explains how you could start a ciphertext alphabet with the word 'lapsang' (but without the second 'a', of course) and then follow it with all the other letters of the alphabet backwards. He writes it on a scrap of paper like this:

a b c d e f g h i j k l m n o p q r s t u v w x y z
l a p s n g z y x w v u t r q o m k j i h f e d c b

If both sender and receiver knew that the key word was *lapsang*, any message sent would be easy to unscramble (he doesn't explain that any message sent using this cipher would unscramble easily anyway due to frequency analysis, though).

'Now, say our key had fallen into enemy hands,' he says. 'We would need to change it. But how do I, the sender, get the new key to you, the receiver? What if, to avoid compromising the key, we decided to change it every day? We would still have to exchange it. I could phone you and say, "The key word is now 'Darjeeling'", but our telephone may well be bugged. In fact, if we knew our telephone not to be bugged, we could exchange secret information over the phone without any need for a cipher at all.'

'I see,' says Jasmine. 'So in order to send a secret message using a key, you first have to send an un-secret message telling the other person what key you are using.'

'Quite,' says my grandfather. 'And that is the weak point – the point at which the enemy can intercept the information.'

'What if, every day, you sent a message and then, in the same code, sent the new key word for the following day?'

My grandfather brings the coffee pot to the table and fetches the best cups from the dresser. 'People have used methods like that,' he explains. 'But you can see that in that situation, if one message was deciphered by the enemy they would be in the loop for all time. They would only have to crack one message to be able to crack all the others for ever.'

'Ah,' says Jasmine. 'So, how do you do it, then? I know you want to tell me . . .'

'Well, there are a couple of ways. The first way, known as the Diffie–Hellman–Merkle key-exchange system – named after the people who invented it – is based on one-way functions and modular arithmetic, which Beth knows more about than me.'

My grandmother smiles. 'Believe me, Jasmine, you don't want to know. It's basically a complex mathematical trick where two people think of a number, run it through a function – much more complicated than "think of a number, double it and add five" but similar – and then swap the results. The exciting thing about this method is that even if the two results are overheard, the enemy can't crack the code, because you need to know one of the original numbers to break the code – not the results. It's very complicated to explain but it is a very clever trick indeed. It didn't catch on because it turned out to be impractical. The sender has to communicate with the receiver beforehand every time they want to send an encrypted message. But mathematically, at least, this system is very exciting. Imagine being able to swap a key in public, rather than in secret, knowing that even if the enemy hears what you say, it doesn't matter. It's brilliant.'

My grandfather sips his coffee. 'What people really needed was an asymmetric key, rather than a symmetric one. In other words, a system where the thing you use to lock a message is different from the thing you use to unlock it. If you had a system like this, you could send the *lock* to someone who wanted to communicate with you, not the *key*. The best analogy is an actual padlock. Say I had a secret box to send to you. I could buy a padlock and key, then lock the box with the padlock and try to work out how to get the key to you without it being intercepted. Or, alternatively, I could tell you I had a secret box to send to you, at which point, *you* could purchase a padlock and key and just send me the padlock. It wouldn't matter who intercepted the padlock – they wouldn't be able to do anything with it. When I receive the padlock, I just snap it on the package and send it to you. Once it's locked, even I can't open it, because only you have the key.'

'That's so clever,' Jasmine says. 'I like that.'

'Couldn't someone pick the lock?' I say. 'If you intercept the padlock, you could then make the key, surely?'

'Well, this is the clever bit. The padlock and key is simply an analogy for – sorry – more maths. In fact, people came up with the concept of an asymmetric cipher several years before they worked out how to do it, mathematically. For a while, no one could think of a function that would have this effect. But, then, three chaps at MIT did it. What if I told you, Alice, that the key in this story was actually two very large prime numbers. What is the lock?'

I think for a moment. ' I don't know,' I say.

'Well, what do you get if you multiply two large prime numbers together?' he says.

'A very large composite number,' I say. 'With two very large prime factors . . . Oh! I see.'

Of course. If you choose two large enough primes, keep them a secret and multiply them together, someone who wanted to prime factorise the big number would have to start from 2, 3, 5, 7, like anybody else doing a prime factorisation. They wouldn't know where the prime factors would be found, and I know as well as anyone that prime factorisation has to be approached methodically. My grandmother proved to me once that with a big enough value of N (with N being the composite number that is a product of two large primes, p and q) it could take thousands of years to find the answer, even if you could try one prime a second. Of course this is a great method of encryption. You send the large composite number to the person who wants to send you a message, they use it to encrypt this message in such a way that you need the prime factors to decrypt the message and then, bingo! Only you can read it. You could tell everybody in the world what N is but only you would know p and q.

For the next half an hour or so, we all explain prime numbers and prime factorisation to Jasmine. I am able to join in with this like a grown-up, as I spent so long doing those prime factorisations for my grandfather. Eventually, she understands.

'But surely computers could do it in a second?' she says.

My grandmother shakes her head. 'With a big enough composite number, N,' she says. 'You could have ten billion computers in the world, all working simultaneously, each checking a thousand different prime numbers every second and they would still take a billion years to come up with the answer. Yet, just one of these computers could generate N from p and q in a second.'

'That's amazing,' Jasmine says.

'Martin Gardner, the chap who writes the Mathematical Games column for the *Scientific American* . . .' My grandfather begins.

'A bit like an American version of the Mind Mangle,' my grandmother explains.

My grandfather continues. 'Yes, well, back in '77 he set a challenge for people to crack a code with a public encryption key that ran to 129 digits. Remember, although encryption is based on the large composite number N, it is not just used on its own. There is some modular maths in there as well. However, the security of the cipher relies on N being impossible to factorise quickly. This, then, was the main challenge: to come up with the prime factors of this large number.'

'So how long did it take to crack it?' Jasmine asks.

'Oh, people are still working on it. Beth was asked to join a team trying to crack it actually. But she's too busy with proper maths.'

'I'm surprised you didn't give it to Alice to try,' my grandmother says, laughing. 'Since she did all that other prime factorisation for you. And there is a prize of $100, I believe.'

A prize of $100! I file this away to think about later. We all move into the living room and Jasmine starts talking about new developments in her own area, psychology. She talks about a man called Stanley Milgram, and his controversial book, *Obedience to Authority*, in which he describes a series of experiments designed to determine how far people would go if their actions were condoned by an authority figure. The study is about ten years old, now, but has apparently inspired all sorts of exciting research.

'In these experiments,' she explains, ' a subject would come along to take part in what he or she believed to be one of a series of memory tests. Milgram did the experiment in various ways, but essentially the subject was shown another person, the 'learner', who was hooked up to a device that would administer electric shocks. The subject would 'teach' the learner a series of word pairs, from a sheet. Then he or she would test the learner. The learner was always actually an actor, primed to start giving wrong answers fairly soon. When the learner gave a wrong answer, the subject was prompted to administer an electric shock, using a button. Of course, the shocks weren't real, but each time the button was pressed, the actor would say something like, "Ow!" or "I can't stand the pain." With each wrong answer, the subject was prompted to give the learner a more powerful electric shock. Milgram wanted to know at what point the subject would refuse to take part any more, and how the presence of the authority figure would influence his or her decisions. The authority figure had a set script. At the point the subject complained or questioned what he or she was doing, the authority figure would say, 'Please continue.' The next complaint would have him saying, 'The experiment requires that you continue.' The last level was: 'You have no other choice. You *must* go on.' There were various variations as well, in which the learner claimed to have a heart condition, for example.'

'It sounds extraordinarily cruel,' says my grandmother.

Jasmine smiles. 'Well, fortunately or unfortunately, depending on your perspective, the same experiment could not be conducted today. All the subjects were properly debriefed after the experiment, however, and asked what they felt they had learnt from the experience. One person, when he found out what he had really been doing, was so fascinated he asked for a job.'

'So what did Milgram discover?' my grandfather asks, poking at his pipe.

'He discovered, essentially, that a large number of people would indeed continue to administer what they believed to be painful, very painful or even dangerous electric shocks to the learner when told by an authority figure that it was OK to do so. The book makes for very sobering reading. Milgram starts off discussing the Nazis, and the idea that any brutal regime or army needs to have great levels of the kind of obedience to authority he explores. It is very, very interesting to look at human cruelty, and how often it has to be endorsed by an authority figure. Left to themselves, I suspect, most people are kind and sensible. But give someone an electric shock button and tell them it is all right to use it and many people become monsters.'

My grandfather starts talking about various things he believes fall under this category. People thinking it's OK for the police to beat up striking miners because the police are authority figures and the miners are not. People believing that it is OK to experiment on animals because the government endorse it and because the people who do it are important scientists in white lab coats. People believing that it is all right to have nuclear weapons pointing at other countries because some political scientists and logicians say it makes us safer. Then the three of them start talking about Nazi concentration camps, and the officers there who were 'just acting out their orders'.

But I am thinking about school. I am thinking about an incident last week, when our group came upon Liz eating lunch on her own. 'Got no friends, then?' Lucy said to her. 'She's too fat to fit in the dining hall,' said Sarah. And we all laughed. Even me. I believed it was wrong to laugh at Liz but I still did it, because Lucy and Sarah made it seem OK. I also did it because I don't want to be like Liz. By laughing at her, I was able to distance myself from her. I am the one who laughs, not the one who is laughed at. That, for the time being, is my identity.

Going around with the popular girls gives me a shell. I can't afford to lose this shell. There is too much about me that they can pick on: too much that wouldn't stand up to their examinations. I can't allow myself to be in Liz's position because it would be just so easy to pick on me, if they knew how. After all, the best way to avoid having an enemy is to join that enemy. For the first time ever, I understand what made people into collaborators in the war. Every time I read a story about someone who sold their friends to the Nazis I could not understand how they had done it. I would be brave, I always thought. If it was me, I wouldn't talk even if they tortured me to death. Yet I have become a betrayer over nothing more complicated than not wanting to be teased at school. What is wrong with me?

I am so lost in thought that I don't realise that all three adults in the room are looking at me, smiling.

'So?' says my grandmother.

'Sorry,' I say. 'I was miles away.'

'There's a pink elephant in this room,' Jasmine says to me.

Have I heard her right? What's going on? Maybe it's the start of a joke.

'OK,' I say, waiting for whatever comes next.

They laugh.

'I said this wouldn't work on Alice,' my grandfather says.

'Is there a pink elephant in the room?' Jasmine says to me now.

'No,' I say.

'Are you sure?' she says.

'Yes,' I say. 'Look around. There isn't a pink elephant here. How would it get in? Also, pink elephants don't exist, so I know that there can't be one here.'

'I say there is a pink elephant in the room.'

'OK,' I say, shrugging. I don't know where this is going.

'Can you prove that there isn't?' she says.

Bloody hell. I think for a minute, frustrated. This isn't maths.

This kind of thing won't submit to a proof, I can see that instantly. All you've got is the evidence of your senses, plus your inherent sanity, plus a faulty non-logic based on experience. I could prove Pythagoras's Theorem if someone gave me a piece of paper but I can't prove that there is no pink elephant in this room. I think about everything I have learnt at school over the past few weeks, and the strange games I now know how to play and I look Jasmine in the eye.

'No, I can't prove it,' I say. 'Therefore I conclude, like you, that there is indeed a pink elephant in this room.' There. I have a feeling that this is not how you are supposed to play this game but I sense I have won.

Jasmine smiles and shakes her head. 'Do you know, I have never had that response before. How bizarre.'

'That's Alice for you,' my grandmother says.

'I've tested hundreds of children, who all tear their hair out trying to convince me that there isn't a pink elephant in the room.'

'Why have you tested hundreds of children?' I say.

'It's an experiment about how people define reality, and how they feel reality is constructed,' she says. 'It's about the forms of reasoning people will use to convince me that there isn't a pink elephant in the room. Some children say, "Look, you can see there's no pink elephant." So then I say, "Well, if I was blind, how would you convince me?" They go through the senses one by one. After that, I say that the pink elephant is invisible, which is why they can't see it, and then ask them again to prove that it is not there. Most of them say that invisibility is cheating, or not real – but they find it difficult to prove. Or they say, "So how do you know it's pink if it's invisible?" and that takes us down a whole different avenue altogether.'

'What does Alice's response mean?' my grandfather asks.

'I don't know,' says Jasmine. 'Alice? Why did you agree that there is a pink elephant in the room when it's obvious that there isn't?'

I am tired now, and feeling contrary. 'Isn't there?' I say. 'I thought you said there was.'

Jasmine laughs. 'Yes, yes. We both know there isn't one here really.'

'Prove it, then,' I say.

And I'm thinking that the reason I agreed with her is because I am tired, and I stole and lied today, and I really don't care if there's a pink elephant in the room or not. If Jasmine wants to believe there is, well, then, that's fine. I'll even agree with her. What do truth and reality matter anyway? Right now, the only thing a pink elephant could do to actually change my life, if it were in this room, would be to sit on me and put me in hospital long enough so I never have to see my 'friends' again.

The grown-ups laugh, again.

'All right, clever clogs,' my grandfather says. 'Time for bed.'

Chapter Twenty-five

Shortly after breakfast on Tuesday morning there is a knock at the door. When I open it I find a woman I haven't seen before, and a man who looks like an engineer. The woman is carrying a clipboard and a pile of magazines, and the man is wheeling a large trolley with a TV and VCR on it.

'Are you Alice Butler?' the woman asks.

'Yes,' I say.

'Good. We have a TV for you here.'

I frown. 'I don't need . . .'

'And videos. Since the material being presented to the other delegates today is in video format, someone suggested that you needn't actually miss out because you are ill in bed. So we have brought the videos to you. This is John, our site technician. He's going to hook you up.' She smiles a big smile. 'OK?'

'OK,' I say. 'Thanks.'

She pulls a few A4 sheets from her clipboard and gives them to me. The heading is just a number: *14*. The sub-heading is: *Adult or Child?* She marks something off on the remaining sheet on her clipboard, and then gives me the pile of magazines too.

'Everyone is being issued with these. They are to help with your research.' She places the pile of magazines on the end of my bed, gives me another big smile and leaves. Why do people with clipboards always have big smiles? Maybe I should get one.

I feel the same today as I did yesterday, which I am finding frustrating. Being in bed ill is all right for a couple of days but then the whole thing starts to feel a bit old. I have tried to will myself better overnight but the cough is still there and my insides still feel so heavy that I can barely walk across the room without feeling incredibly tired. When I woke up this morning I did what I do every morning when I have the 'flu. I went through a series of experimental steps: breathe, cough, sit up. When I am ill, I always have this hope that one day I will wake up and find that I feel miraculously better, and that my cough (or whatever it is) will simply have gone, taken away in my sleep – perhaps by fairies or other magical creatures. But today there is no change. Still, while I was in the bath earlier someone came and changed my sheets and brought me back some clean laundry, which was nice. I could have changed the sheets myself, though. It makes me feel uncomfortable that someone is doing these things for me, that it is someone's job to do this for me.

John is fiddling around with a remote control, having set up all the other equipment.

'There you go,' he says, handing it to me. 'Video and TV controls both on there. If you want to ditch the corporate video and watch soap operas or satellite TV, press this blue button here.' He grins. 'Hope you feel better soon.' Then he leaves.

The magazines, glossy and perfumed, look precarious on the end of my bed, so I reach forward and move the pile so it is next to me. There are about seven or eight of them altogether, all this month's issues. I remember a couple of the titles from when I was a teenager but things have changed a lot since then. Some of the more successful women's lifestyle magazines now have baby-sister versions of themselves, their main brand name suffixed by the word 'Girl'. Then there are the newly invented magazines for a whole new demographic of girls who are under fourteen but also want to be told about pop stars and make-up and sex. Videos first, I think.

Ben has filled up my flask with boiling water, so I make myself some green tea before pressing Play on the remote control. Someone told me recently that the universal Play button, the > sign, has only been in existence since Sony invented it in the 60s or 70s, they weren't sure which. Now, of course, it's a universal icon. I think of more universal icons: the picture of the wastepaper bin on a computer desktop, the 'mute' button, the letters www, the Golden Arches, the letters 'txt', triangular ready-made sandwich containers and the @ sign. All these things found their home in my lifetime, along with the digital watch, the video recorder, the Walkman, the microwave, the laptop, the chilled ready-meal, the satellite dish, the CD, the mobile phone, the DVD, the Post-it note, the retail park, the blog and even the remote control. I think about everything that a teenager today would take for granted that was pretty much unheard of even fifteen years ago: text-messaging, e-mail, instant chat. There are kids who can't even remember a time when the Internet didn't exist in the way it does now, when you had to go to the library to look everything up or actually ask in record shops for the 12" you heard at that party. Shall I write some of this down in my notes? I can't be bothered, even though my notebook is next to me on the bed, along with the magazines and my lip balm. Maybe I'll jot some ideas down after the video has finished.

The programme is about to start, so I fluff up my pillows and lie back in bed, sipping my tea. An introduction informs me that this series of documentaries forms part of a study – the first of its kind, blah blah blah – of teenagers in Britain today. What are their attitudes on sex, life, money, school, work, porn? Are they children or adults? Should they be allowed to vote, leave school, have sex? The production company's logo flashes up, and a voiceover explains that this series of documentaries has been partly funded by one of the terrestrial TV channels, and sponsored by PopCo. Our logo flashes up briefly, and then the first programme starts. I expect that when this is broadcast on TV, our logo will not be there any more. This is the corporate, rather than the mass-market version of the recording.

The first documentary is about a group of ten fourteen-year-olds – five girls and five boys – living together, with no adults, in a suburban house for a week. There is no TV, music system or any videogames. As if they are protesting about not being supervised ('Will we get into trouble?' 'There's no one here, is there, so we might as well do what we want . . .'), the teenagers immediately trash the house. I can't help smiling as they cover the walls with painted slogans. Over the course of the week, the two most 'popular' girls (the ones who look most like TV presenters) flirt with the boys, play a few kissing games, and then decide they don't want to do that any more and gang up with the other girls against the boys. At one point, the boys hang one girl's Finbar toy from a light fitting, with a noose around its neck. 'Kill the bear,' they shout. She cries and then they stop. The girls give each other make-overs, talk about boys and make up dance routines in the garden while the boys create extravagant water bombs and laugh at them. They live on crisps and microwave meals. The kitchen disintegrates.

The next programme shows a similar experiment, but this time a different set of kids are put in a luxury apartment containing a huge home-cinema system, some decks, a big stereo system, a Jacuzzi and a mini-arcade. The kids do not trash this place. For one week, they – almost literally – sit in front of the TV watching music videos and advertisements, and discuss which items they would buy if they could, what it would be like to be famous, and who on the screen is 'cool' and who is not. These kids still make a mess of their kitchen but organise themselves in an almost eerie way. They decide to have a 'club night' on the Wednesday, and an 'Arcade challenge' on the Thursday. These are the only times they leave the TV, except to go to bed. Later in this experiment, two of the girls get into bed with two of the boys, and their parents, who are allowed to watch all the time on a hidden webcam, want to intervene but the production company persuades them not to.

I start to make a few notes. I am intrigued by the homogenisation of youth culture. They all watch the same things on TV, they all seem to have similar aspirations (basically, variations on 'Be famous') and most of the southern teenagers speak with exactly the same London accent. This isn't the 'Mockney' of my own youth but a black, south London, hip-hop voice. I can't say I don't like it but it is intriguing. Where does it come from? Is it a nice example of multiculturalism, that all these kids try to speak the same way, in a voice that to my grandparents would have sounded distinctly foreign, or is it a weak protest against the blandness of their culture – *we'll be different, but we'll all do it the same way*? There even seem to be regional versions of this voice. Oh well, at least people can't complain about Estuary English any more (which I have always been accused of speaking, despite never having been anywhere near the Thames Estuary in my life).

The only ones who speak differently are the public-school kids, but even their voices aren't the normal Received Pronunciation you'd usually associate with public school. If the other kids have taken Urban Black as their language, these ones have Beverly Hills Shopping Mall. In each programme, the token public-school girl was the thinnest, the most attractive and was wearing the 'coolest' (to my adult eyes) clothes. Yet it took both girls a while to fit into the 'group'. They seemed more style-magazine, somehow, with their designer ballet skirts, turned-up jeans, striped socks, leg-warmers, sweatbands, cute tees, personalised denim jackets and baseball boots. The instantly popular girls seemed to go for the safer option of hipster jeans, vest tops, studded belts, and trainers. All the girls (apart from one in each group – the unfashionista) wore sweatbands, which are this year's coolest accessory (I know this because of Chi-Chi et al.), and seemed to deliberately expose their bra-straps. Why wasn't fashion like this when I was a teenager? When I was that age the whole point was to try to find a bra that *didn't* show, an almost-impossibility. If you had gone around then, as kids do now, wearing a red bra under a sheer white vest-top, with the straps showing, people would have instantly condemned you as a freak/drug addict. How times change.

When I was fourteen, people still wore leggings. No jeans fitted properly. Good clothes were baggy and the size 'skinny' didn't exist. Nothing was hipster; nothing was flared (apart from the clothes of lame 70s kids in school sex-education videos). I probably looked like the non-fashion girls in these documentaries, with their frizzy hair, badly cut jeans and non-branded long-sleeved tops. These girls are making no effort to fit in. Is it because they can't or because they won't? I suspect the former, although the possible reasons for this must be almost infinite. I notice that what is objectively different about all the other girls is that they are simply covered with iden-tity markers. They are saying 'look at who I am', while the other girls are saying 'I am nothing'. It is intriguing to note that the point at which the less fashionable girls were allowed to enter the main group of girls was usually via a make-over, or by the girl borrowing some fashion item from her new 'friend'.

This is all starting to connect with my necklace/bracelet idea now. I note down what the main identity-tags seem to be, and make a few sketches from freeze-frames. Then I give up on the TV for a while (it's making me feel ill/iller) and flick through the magazines instead. The same things are here, too: cute bags, turned-up jeans, 'customised' laces, rings, sweatbands, plastic bracelets, string bracelets, chokers, strings of beads, hair slides, blue/pink/black nail polish, cute hair bands, cute socks, cute tees, cute smiles . . . When did teenage girls become so cute, anyway?

I am still reading and making notes when Ben turns up with lunch on a tray.

'Fucking hell,' he says when he sees the TV.

'Yeah,' I say. 'The mountain to Mohammed.'

'Nice of them.'

'I know. I even have magazines.'

He starts taking greaseproof paper off the plates on the tray.

'We all have them,' he says. 'Kieran's gone off to his room with his. He was last heard saying something like, "Oh, baby, baby."'

I laugh. 'Oh, yuck.'

Ben laughs too. 'He has an unhealthy obsession with teenage girls.'

'Yeah, him and the rest of society . . . Oh, thanks.' Ben has just passed me a plate of sandwiches with a side salad and chips. I peer into the sandwiches. 'What's in here?'

'Falafels with onion relish.'

'And why are there flowers in the salad? Can you eat them?'

'They are nasturtiums, apparently. Everyone was asking about them. The chefs say that yes, you can eat them. They're from some local organic farm.'

'Cool. I've never eaten a flower.'

'Me neither.' He smiles and picks up a magazine. 'What were you saying about Kieran and the rest of society?'

'Oh, just an observation about the sexualisation of teenage girls,' I say. 'It just hit me when I was reading through those magazines how much more, I don't know, *pornographic* kids have to be these days. Maybe I'm just getting old. Anyway, I'm not surprised at his reaction, really. Surely it's the logical conclusion to all this stuff.'

'Fucking hell,' Ben says, flicking through one of the magazines. 'Yeah, I think you might be right. Are they wearing less clothes than when I was a kid or have I just got old finally?'

'It's less clothes,' I say.

'I don't find it attractive, though,' Ben says. 'I just find it a bit freakish.'

'I'm not sure you're supposed to find it attractive. I think that teenage girls are supposed to find it attractive.' I peer over his shoulder watching a cascade of images of teenage girls, TV presenters and pop stars; advertisements bleeding into features. 'You know what I think?' I say. 'I think the overall message of these things is *I'm getting ready*. You know, *I'm getting ready to go out. I'm getting ready for sex*. I just, I don't know, I just find it disturbing that there's so much childishness in those magazines, and so much about sex at the same time. Not just the problem-page stuff, either. You are encouraged – in a playful, "childish" way – to pay so much attention to the detail of your "cute" socks and your "cute" bag and the cut of your kids'-TV-presenter jeans and your bubblegum-coloured nail varnish because, well, basically because you want boys to think about fucking you. They don't say that explicitly, though. They talk about fancying and snogging and crushes. What they don't say is, "Here's how to make boys your age want to fuck you."'

'And Kieran,' Ben says.

I smile. 'And, obviously, Kieran.' For a moment I think about history and I realise that there was a time when paper wasn't glossy like this, and didn't smell of mass-produced perfume. 'What's disturbing as well is this thing where people my age are supposed to want to look like these kids. Because they are thin and small and have good skin – essentially because they are still children – grown women look at them and think, "I want to look like that too", because that of course is the ideal. So then even they're buying these products, the cute socks and so on. Even I persist with the same hairstyle I had when I was six.' I pick up a plait in each hand and wiggle them around. 'I would never have got away with looking so childish twenty years ago.'

'We're a nation of paedophiles,' Ben says.

'We're a nation of paedophiles,' I repeat, raising my eyebrows.

'I like your plaits though,' he says. 'They are quite kinky.'

I smile. 'Thanks. I think.'

'Look at this.' Ben shows me the front cover of one of the magazines. There's a young American pop star on the front, her bare midriff taking up a lot of the cover space. She's wearing a white crop-top with a pink bra underneath, cut-off pink fishnet tights on her arms, black nail varnish and blow-job pink lip gloss. On her neck she has a studded red choker, which is connected, with a chain, to a smaller version of the same choker on her wrist. 'What's this saying? *I'm a porn star?*'

'I particularly like the bondage angle,' I say.

'*For girls who love to shop*,' says Ben.

'Huh?'

'The tagline.'

'Indeed.'

He flicks through the rest of the magazine while I eat my sandwiches.

'Where is the problem page, anyway?' he asks, eventually. 'I thought at least that would be interesting.'

'I don't think girls like that are supposed to have problems,' I say.

*

Sunday. I am going through the box of my mother's books again. I am a detective looking for clues, clues about life. I have worked out that my mother must have had all the answers. Here's my rationale. There are no answers. She is not here. The answers must be with her. Why did she die? Why did I never know her? Why hasn't she left me any clues at all? There must be millions of words in this box but so far I haven't found any that mean anything. Of these millions of words, she herself wrote only about a thousand. The odd diary entry ('Violin practice frustrating again') and the odd place in a book where she has marked her name, or the date. There must be something else here. This can't be it, can it?

Then, after lunch, I find something. It's an old, battered copy of *Woman on the Edge of Time* by Marge Piercy. My mother has written inside it – but not just her name. *Please return this book to Beatrice Bailey*, it says in her curly writing. OK, well, several of her books say this, or the same thing with her maiden name, my name: Butler. But there is more. She has written something in this book for me! *Dearest, darling Alice, I have just finished this book and I am wondering what to say to you. Perhaps you have forgotten me already. I wonder how old you are now? Will you even get this book? I have asked your grandfather to add it to the box of books I have left for you but sometimes people say they will do something and then they forget. This is a very important book to me.*

It explains . . . A lot of things. Please take care of it. Alice, please know how much I love you, and how much I will always love you. This love doesn't die. I will die, a bit sooner than I would have hoped, but I will never, ever disappear. I feel like I should say something profound now but, since the margins of this book are too small for all my reflections on the world I will say only this. CHANGE THE WORLD. It doesn't matter how big or small the change is but make sure it's for the better. I look around me and I see nuclear missiles, vivisection, cruelty, poverty and hunger. Will things be different when you grow up? I hope so. I will wait on the other side for your report. With all my love, Mummy.

I gulp, tears forming in my eyes. She is waiting somewhere for me! She loves me! And now I understand that this is how the dead speak to you. This is how they stay in touch. My mother has travelled in time for me. My identity swells. I am not just Alice Butler, orphan/shipwrecked child. I have a mother who loves me. Once I have stopped crying, I start reading the book. It is quite grown-up, but I am going to savour every word. I will understand it. I have to. And I don't know how I am going to change the world but, later, as I look out of the window into the infinite space outside, I vow to my mother that I will. Does she live in the clouds? In the stars? Inside a rainbow? She is there somewhere, though. I know that now.

Later on Sunday afternoon, I get the feeling that my grandmother might be sad since I haven't visited her in her study for a few weeks. I have had a lot of school things to think about, but is this any excuse, really? Why isn't it the summer holidays? I don't want to go back to school. Would my mother like, or even understand, the person I have to be at school? Would she see me as I see myself now, as a cowardly collaborator? I look out of the window but there is nothing. No answer attached to a shooting star. No message on an interstellar laser beam. *Change the world.* I wish I knew how. Even though I still have two days' worth of homework to complete, I wander down the landing to my grandmother's door and knock.

'Alice,' she says. 'Just the person. I need you to read out these numbers to me, so I can write them down . . .'

It feels like I have just returned home after a long journey.

A stomach ache prevents me going into school on Monday. I stay at home instead and read. In the afternoon my grandfather asks me if I am too ill to make a list of some rare red flowers for him. I have my dinner downstairs with my grandparents. On Tuesday, my stomach ache is worse. When my grandparents say that I should see the doctor I refuse, as usual. Thus, I am back at school on Thursday.

It is too late. Leaving your friends alone for an hour is really too long, let alone three whole school days. You can lose a best friend in five minutes. All it takes is a short conversation. 'Do you really like her?' 'Well . . .' 'I mean, she is a bit weird.' 'I know.' 'She's such a know-it-all.' 'I know.' 'I wish we were going around together.' 'Me too.' 'Well, why don't we . . . ?' 'How will I tell her?' 'Oh, she'll get the message.'

It's not that Emma has exactly dumped me, just that while I have been away she has been going around with this girl Becky, who is in maths with us. They both present me with the sad but inevitable news that Aaron is going out with someone else now. And, of course, it is round the whole first year that I am tight because I wouldn't kiss him (I did kiss him! Well, sort of.) Is being tight worse than being a slag? Aaron also told everybody that I talk too much. Even Alex looks at me oddly now, if he looks at me at all. I am wearing my new skirt (which I had to change into in the alley on the way to catch the bus) but it hasn't made very much difference. I have lip gloss but so does Becky. Anyway, lip gloss isn't quite as important any more, suddenly. The new craze, which I have missed entirely, is for stationery: glitter pens, coloured Tippex, stick-on stars, felt pens, highlighters. All of my group now spend every lesson decorating their work with different-coloured underlining, or coating their rulers and protractors with coloured Tippex. They all know a really good way of drawing heart shapes. I can't draw heart shapes at all. And why would I draw a heart shape anyway? It's not as if I have another set of initials to go with mine inside the heart.

'We'll help you find a new boyfriend,' says Becky, at lunchtime on Thursday.

'Yeah,' says Emma. 'Aaron's not worth it anyway.'

Meanwhile, my homework is piling up. The only lesson I am doing OK in is English. I keep seeing Emma and Becky in intense-looking conversation. I feel like a virgin queen, plotted against by everyone. Actually, I don't. I feel like a lonely eleven-year-old with an overflowing locker, a dirty PE kit and dinner money obtained under false pretences. I hate school. At home I can think about private things: books, my mother, the Voynich Manuscript, cricket. Here, they'd know if you even thought about subjects as embarrassing as these so it's best not to even try. Thinking is something you are not allowed to do anyway. At break on Thursday we see a girl sitting on her own on the bench outside the science block. She's called Sophie and she wears glasses.

'What are you doing, four-eyes?' Emma asks Sophie, in a sneery voice.

'Thinking,' says Sophie.

'Thinking?' says Lucy, while the others laugh. 'Who do you reckon you are, then? Mrs Einstein?'

'Leave her alone,' I say to them. And this is the beginning of the end for me.

On Friday I have to stay behind after Geography to explain why I haven't done my homework. My life is such a mess. Afterwards, I don't feel like going to lunch with the others. They have just about got over the incident with Sophie yesterday, but I just can't keep up with them, I realise that now. Someone has brought in a magazine with pop stars and gossip and song lyrics in it. I have never read this magazine. I've seen it for sale in the village shop but I would never, ever be able to summon up the courage to buy a copy. Surely the newsagent would refuse to sell it to me. I am not fashionable enough, or old enough, to understand it. He would know that. Someone said it even has swear words in it, worse than 'bloody'. Of course, I already know all these swear-words from the books I now read but no one knows about that. The newsagent would definitely tell my grandfather that I am buying grown-up magazines with swear words in them and I would die of embarrassment. I have realised some other things, too. I won't get Emma back from Becky, not ever. Even if I did get her back, it is my turn to invite her for tea. What could I ever do about that? Living in one of the villages is embarrassing enough, but how would I even approach the subject of having no TV, or any fashionable non-school clothes? How would I tell her that I am not simply 'staying with my grandparents for a while' but that I live with them all the time? No one lives with their grandparents. Also, I would have to admit that I lied. Being a liar is worse than being a slag, or fat, or even a gyppo. Lying is worse, even, than thinking.

Sometimes, if you want to tell your best friend a secret, and you want it to stay a secret, you do this thing where you swap secrets. On a sleepover, usually, you start whispering into the darkness about embarrassing things you have done, boys you have kissed, or people you don't really like. For each secret you offer, the other person has to offer one back of equal value. This way, you are both taking out a kind of insurance. If they tell your secret, you will tell theirs. I have done this once with Emma. I told her that I kissed Alex ('Who?') and she told me that she really fancies Michael, even though Lucy likes him. But there is no way on earth she will have enough secrets to match mine. Even if she had aleph-null secrets, I know I have aleph-one. And anyway, my secrets make me really weird.

Can I use the fact that I know two secret things about Emma (the Michael thing and the fact that she stole that lip gloss) to secure my exit from their group? Will Emma make sure they leave me alone if I threaten to blab? It's unlikely. Leaving the protection of the popular group takes power away from anything you might have to say about its members. There's a big difference between manœuvring from within the group and attempting manœuvres outside it. Inside, you can whisper to one other person and cause all sorts of trouble. But outside, all you are is a slag spreading rumours because you are jealous. Still, my position in the group in untenable. I cannot keep up with all the rules, conventions, things you have to buy. I will jump, before I am pushed. If I could leave this school, everything would be easier but how would I even explain why I want to?

So I am in the dinner hall, instead of the Portakabin. It turns out that all the boys eat in here, big plates of beef burgers, fish fingers, chips, beans. They don't have to worry about being seen eating this kind of food. Anyway, I am standing in the queue on my own (horrors), when all the popular boys from my year come in – Michael, Aaron and that lot. There are about twenty people behind me, and only two in front. The boys all bound up to me like oversized rabbits.

'Let us in, Butler,' says Michael, getting in the queue in front of me.

'Yeah, thanks, Butler,' says another one of them, called Mark.

Aaron gives me a slightly embarrassed look and then also slips in. I expect this is the last time any of them will talk to me in a friendly way but who cares? Actually, I do care, but I can't do anything about it. I just can't afford my special shell any more. I think about Roxy, and how she didn't care about this sort of thing at all. Could I Roxify myself? Would I dare?

'Why are you in school dinners, anyway?' Michael asks.

I blush and look at the floor.

'Don't you lot normally just stay in that Portakabin eating air at lunchtime?' Mark says.

'No,' I say, although I suppose it would have been better to giggle coquettishly and say yes. But it's not at all clear what I should say. You are not supposed to come in to contact with boys like this, on your own. That's why girls go around in pairs or groups all the time.

As if the boys can already sense something of the outcast about me, they soon stop speaking to me at all, and punch each other's arms all the way to the till. I am just in time to see Alex go off on his own, with his free lunch (he has special tickets). I could never, ever, sit with him, because he's a boy. So who shall I sit with? There's no one, so I sit on my own. I sit on my own and eat pie, chips and beans on my own and every single second of it is like a little death. But at least I am free.

This is the weekend that Rachel comes home for something called *Exeat*, which is Latin for *weekend at home* or something like that. We go riding together on Saturday morning, and I am faster, more daring than usual. In the afternoon we groom the ponies and talk about our schools. Rachel's school is different from mine but in its own way is still a maze of awkwardness and embarrassment. You have to get changed in front of the other girls every night. You have to have a 'crush' on an older girl and then she becomes your 'crush' and you her 'crushlet'. (Imagine what the girls at my school would say about that? It would be the most lezza thing they ever heard!) Rachel says it's not at all to do with love or sex or anything, your crush is just something you have to have because everyone else has one. She says that popularity is measured by things like how many letters you get from friends outside (rather than from parents) and how good you are at music and acting.

I tell her about all the problems I've been having.

'Bloody hell, Alice,' is what she says.

'I know,' I say.

'I'm so glad we don't have boys at my school.'

'Yeah. I know.'

'You could move schools, you know,' she says. 'You could come to my school. You could move into my dorm and we could be best friends. It would be brilliant!'

Indeed it would. But when we bring it up with my grandfather, he simply says no. He has always had a soft spot for Rachel, but however much she cajoles him and smiles sweetly at him and asks for another jar of his delicious marmalade for her mother, he still says no. Well, he says yes to the marmalade, of course, but no to changing schools.

'Even if we could afford it,' he explains to me later, 'I don't believe in private schools. You're better off where you are, mixing with ordinary kids.'

So I will have to get the money myself. I add up in my head what I could realistically expect to make from a bit of car-washing, factorising the RSA encryption code and working out what's on my necklace and claiming all the treasure. Probably about one million, one hundred and twenty pounds. Or would some of it be in dollars? Anyway, I make myself a list and resolve to get cracking as soon as Rachel has gone back to school.

*

By about four o'clock I have created several montages in support of my bead/necklace idea. Using images cut from the magazines, and inspired by freeze-frames from the videos, my montages each take the form of a one-scene storyboard. In each one I have created a black-and-white pencil sketch of a group of teenagers and then added 'colour', both literally and figuratively, in the form of the objects cut from the magazine. It's very similar in feel to the teenage girl's bedroom we saw in the seminar last week. But of course this is all about the teenager as an individual. What do teenage girls actually wear/keep with them? What does it all mean? I make a note that as well as using markers to say 'This is what I like,' the beads on the necklaces/bracelets could also say things like 'I'm available', 'I'm not available', 'I live in London', or whatever.

At about half-past four, Dan turns up. He's carrying a bag.

'Hard at work, then?' he says to me when he sees my montages. Instinctively, I push them out of sight. 'Kind of,' I say.

'How are you feeling?' he asks, sitting down in the armchair which is still by the bed where Ben moved it.

'So so,' I say. 'What's in the bag?'

'Navigation, baby,' he says. 'Compass, sea charts.' He passes the bag to me. 'You have been nominated as our navigator, so they're for you.'

'Oh.' I pull out the contents of the bag. There is a big chart, folded down; a pair of binoculars; a ruler with wheels embedded in it and a compass which is rather different from compasses I've seen before. It's a big plastic thing with a hole and no actual face or dial.

'What's this for?' I ask Dan, still examining it.

'It's a hand-bearing compass,' he says. 'You use it to take bearings.'

'How?'

'You point it at things and look through the little window.'

I try this, pointing at the wall. The reading is 13 degrees north-east.

'Oh.' I try the other wall. 'Where's the sextant, then?'

'Sextant?' He laughs. 'This isn't the Middle Ages. We've got GPS, so we won't exactly need a sextant.'

GPS. Global Positioning System. 'If we've got GPS, why do we need all this?'

'You still need to be able to plot bearings,' Dan says, sighing. 'And this is cool. You'll like it. It's all to do with triangles and maths. That's why we nominated you to do it.'

'So you haven't just given me the duff job because I'm ill, then?' I say.

'What? No! The navigator is always one of the coolest crew members. You get to sit down below with your ruler and your charts and only poke your head up when you want to take a bearing. Everyone else is getting wet as fuck but the navigator is always warm and comfortable in the cabin, drawing triangles and trying to establish where the boat actually is. The thing about the sea is that it is huge, and it all looks the same. It is also full of rocks, remains of shipwrecks and so on. It's a real skill learning how to find where you are in it.'

I think of Pythagoras for a moment and imagine that this will have something to do with measuring the hypotenuse of triangles, or something like that. I have to admit that it does sound better than fiddling with sails on the slippery foredeck, something that Gavin said wasn't much fun if you're at all scared of falling in the water/drowning.

'OK,' I say. 'It does sound interesting.'

'The only thing is, are you going to be well enough to sail on Saturday?'

'Saturday. Um, yeah, I would have thought so. Bloody hell, it's only Tuesday. If I'm not better by Saturday, I'll be dead. Yeah, of course I'll be OK.'

For the next hour or so, Dan explains how to take a bearing on the hand-bearing compass and then how to use this information to plot your rough position on the chart. Since we are, in theory, not going out of sight of land on Saturday, this involves looking for landmarks in real life that relate to things you can see clearly marked on the map. We are planning to sail into something called Start Bay. Notable landmarks, according to the chart, include the Dartmouth Day Beacon, the Start Bay lighthouse, the spire of a church in the nearby village of Stoke Fleming and the coastguards' cottages – where, apparently, Dan's grandfather grew up.

'How will I know if I've chosen the right landmark?' I ask.

'I'll help,' Dan says.

I peer down at the large chart. There are several 'wrecks' marked on it. These must be boats that have sunk, and now provide a similar hazard to rocks: dark masses underwater that you just don't see until it is too late.

'What do you do if you have just sailed to somewhere for the first time and you don't have anyone with local knowledge on the boat and you can't distinguish between one church spire and another?' I ask.

'Um, you guess and hope for the best. Or you use another landmark, one that's more easily recognisable. You can't miss the lighthouse, for example, or the Day Beacon.'

'Oh. OK.' This doesn't sound foolproof to me.

Apparently, what you do, once you have identified your landmark, is you point the hand-bearing compass at it and then look through the little window until you have established the bearing.

Say the bearing is 19 degrees north-west, you take your ruler with wheels, and line it up so that its edge cuts through the value 19 degrees north-west on the compass rose on the chart, then slide the ruler along so it cuts through the landmark and then draw a line. Now you know you are somewhere on this line.

'So now you simply take another reading from a landmark in another direction to find out where on the line you are!' I say, triumphantly.

'No, Butler. You take *two* more readings, which give you a triangle. You then know you are somewhere inside the triangle.'

He demonstrates with various made-up readings, eventually drawing a small triangle on the chart in pencil.

But this makes me uncomfortable. Surely the point of this is to plot a one-dimensional point, a certainty in the sea – not an uncertain, two-dimensional triangle. There's infinity in a triangle, lots of it. What if you ended up with a right-angled triangle measuring 1 unit by 1 unit on the sides A and B? The hypotenuse would go on for ever! The square root of 2 never terminates, everyone knows that. (Or at least, no one has ever seen it terminate.) But a square root that never terminates would surely be dangerous out at sea. Perhaps that's what resulted in the Bermuda Triangle. No wonder you could disappear in it and never be seen again. This is what happens when you tumble into infinity.

Anyway, I have got the point of this now. You make your triangle, make sure there are no rocks or wrecks in/near your triangle and then tell the captain what bearing to take to go in the direction you want to go to avoid rocks/land/shipwrecks/shallows. Next, Dan starts to explain to me how to read tide charts, and how to tell whether there will be enough clearance over certain rocks or not. My brain is now undergoing phase transition from absorption to rejection.

'Enough!' I say to Dan, clutching my head with my hands. 'Leave the stuff here and I'll just practise or something. Do you have a book I can refer to?'

He does. I am free.

'Shall I get us a cup of tea?' he says.

'Yeah. Green, please,' I say.

He goes off to the kitchen while I try to make the pile of navigation stuff look tidy on my bed. I suddenly realise that I didn't take account of my tidying urges when I worked out my remedy yesterday. Then again, I am always a bit like this so it probably doesn't matter.

After about five minutes, Dan comes back with two steaming mugs.

'Did you watch the videos, then?' he asks, nodding at the TV and VCR.

'Yeah,' I say. 'Well, I managed two of the documentaries. How many are there?'

'Four.' He laughs. 'Oh, did you see the bit where that Finbar toy gets hanged off the light? It caused a total episode earlier on.'

'An episode?'

'Yeah. Esther completely flipped out.'

I frown. 'Esther did? Why? What happened?'

'Well, when the boys on the documentary were all going, "Kill the bear, kill the bear . . . " Kieran and a couple of others joined in, just as a joke. Then those plush-toy people, the ones from Scandinavia . . .'

'What, Mitzi and Niila?'

'Yeah. Well, they told them to shut up. They designed the Finbar's Friends brand, so they were pretty upset about it. Anyway, we went outside for a break, and Mitzi's there, all upset, and Niila is comforting her, and so Esther walks up to them and she's like, "How dare you get sentimental over some piece of shit made in China using slave labour!" Then she starts laying into Mitzi about how all PopCo's plush toys are made in sweatshops in China or South-east Asia. So now Mitzi's really crying and your mate Ben has to come over and take Esther away. After that, Esther still wouldn't stop going on about the conditions in these Chinese factories. How people there are paid less than a dollar a day, how they regularly lose limbs in the factories, blah blah blah . . .'

I think that if I had lost a limb, I wouldn't suffix a description of it with the words 'blah blah blah'.

'Is that true, though?' I say. 'I thought our toys weren't made in sweatshops. I thought there was some policy . . .'

Dan shrugs. 'I expect it is true. I mean, it would make economic sense. But it's too simplistic to take Esther's approach, isn't it? We don't really know what it's like over there. It's better that people have work in places like China. What are we going to do? Take work away from them?'

'I'm not sure about that,' I say. 'I think I'm with Esther on this one, if it is true. It really isn't ethical . . .'

'Who says it's not ethical, though? You can probably live like a king on a dollar a day in places like that,' Dan says. 'I mean, you're not going to pay someone thirty grand a year to make toys in a factory in China, are you? It has to scale down.'

'A dollar a day isn't that much anywhere, though,' I say. 'And anyway, it can't be that good in these factories if people who work there lose limbs regularly. They must feel they have to work there or something. There can't be any other choice.'

'There is always choice,' he says. 'People can always choose not to work in them.'

And what? Lose their houses, lose their only source of income? It's always easy to say that someone else should walk out of their job until you have to think about doing it yourself. I think about Dan, with his mortgage and his gym membership and his car. What would it take for him to give that up? Add a young family and a pregnant wife and a rise in interest rates and you've suddenly got a situation where losing your job means you could lose it all. Imagine telling your pregnant wife that you are going to have to move out of your large south London terrace with the parquet flooring you laid together and find somewhere cheap to rent instead, somewhere with horrible carpets and a greasy landlord who comes around every six months to examine the place and can throw you out with only two months' notice.

But people don't think of Chinese factory workers in the same way they think of themselves. I remember a writer I like saying that we sometimes look at old gravestones and see records of babies that have died at six months old, or nine months old – sometimes several in one family – and we think that these losses are somehow less painful because they happened often, and to strangers, and at some distant point in history. We think that these remote people would have 'got used to it', and that their pain would be less than ours would be at losing a child. But in doing this, we dehumanise these people. Of course the pain is the same. By imagining Chinese factory workers like this, as strange people, perhaps living four or five to a room, eating mainly rice, living on the scraps thrown to them by the companies that exploit their labour, and by thinking that even this imaginary, exotic version of these people are happy with what they have got . . . Well, it's the same sort of dehumanisation, surely?

I suddenly remember something else. A saying. Where does it come from? I think that an ex-boyfriend's father used to say it, a long time ago. He said: 'Beware of cheap goods. If you buy cheap goods, you are stealing someone else's labour.'

I look at the teenage magazine Dan's flicking through now and suddenly think that probably 90 per cent of the clothes, purses and bags in there have been made or stitched in a sweatshop. Probably 95 per cent of the cosmetics have been tested on animals. How much blood, pain, slavery and torture exactly does go into creating all this stuff, which we are told is so frivolous, so much fun? People like us are paid vast amounts to come up with the concepts, and then the actual objects are made and tested . . . Where? Somewhere invisible. Somewhere that doesn't matter. Somewhere very, very distant. Of course, we all know that actual objects don't matter any more. What matters instead is the logo, the idea, the lifestyle, the brand. Companies are now required to spend millions of dollars establishing this brand, paying sports stars and actresses to endorse it, paying marketing gurus to tell them how to make it 'go viral' and so on. How can they compete otherwise? Perhaps there really is nothing left over to actually pay to make the product. Perhaps that's why the people who make it have to live in poverty, and why the materials are substandard and glue shows on even the coolest trainers. They pay only to make the label, nothing else.

I wonder what my grandparents would say if they were alive today and someone took them on a whistle-stop tour of 'cheap' Britain (a place that they never really chose to visit, even though it had started to exist in their lifetimes). Would they stock up on cheap meat, cheap clothes and cheap knick-knacks that no one needs (but can't resist because they're so *cheap*)? Would they see it as progress that you can now buy a hundred different types of hair-grip in the supermarket? Or would they in fact notice that, as so much has been loaded onto this side of the equation, a hell of a lot must have gone from the other side?

Dan drifts off eventually. I find I haven't got very much more to say to him. The last ten days or so have fucked with my head. I feel like I have been reformatted, and Dan, an obsolete registry file, has been overwritten with something else, maybe blank space, maybe question marks. I wanted to ask him about his rumoured move to Kieran's team but he didn't bring it up. What's wrong with me? Where are all my jokes about retreating and collaborating and being shot? It used to be that we would joke about the enemy, not really believing that the enemy existed. But maybe the enemy does exist after all. Maybe I have some idea of who the enemy is now. Maybe the enemy is me.

A few minutes after six and there's another knock on the door. It must be Ben. But it's not. It's Chloë.

'Hello,' she says shyly, in her soft Celtic voice. 'Can I . . . ?'

'Oh, yes. Of course,' I say, stepping back to let her in.

She walks into the room, everything about her soft and somehow feathery. She's wearing black linen trousers today, with a black polo-neck sweater; her hair twisted up behind her head in a large, translucent crocodile-clip. She's holding a white envelope which she gives me.

'You have a correspondent,' she says, something dancing in her eyes. 'It was outside.'

I take the envelope from her. It has the PopCo logo, the little sailboat, on the top right-hand corner, and my name typed in bold on the front. Am I being sent home? Sacked? Could this be the return message from the mysterious encipherer? I can't look at it now so I put it down on the desk and then sit on the bed. Chloë half-sits on the chair as if she wants to be ready to spring up again at any moment.

'How are you feeling?' she asks.

'OK,' I say, although I do not feel OK. I wonder why she is here. I've barely spoken to Chloë since I have been here. I have the feeling I would like her a lot if I got to know her but there is something about her that makes me feel uncomfortable, too. It's as if she wouldn't let you get away with something if she thought it was wrong. Not that she seems judgemental at all, just that she seems certain. Of what, I don't know.

'I was looking for Esther,' she says.

'Esther?' I think about the laptop, and her giggling with Ben. When was that? Yesterday? The day before? 'I haven't seen Esther for ages,' I say.

'Has she not been to visit you?'

I shake my head. 'Not today.'

'Oh.' Chloë looks disappointed. 'I can't find her anywhere.'

'She seems to be good at disappearing,' I say with a little smile. I don't share my hypotheses from last week that Esther can make herself invisible or turn into a bat. Sometimes I do say these kinds of things to people, as surreal almost-jokes but they tend to look at me blankly and just say something like, 'Er, right . . .' and then change the subject.

'She does indeed,' Chloë says. She pauses, and looks at her hands. 'Not that I've seen much of Ben lately, either.' She looks up at me and I am braced for a sad/possessive look which will complicate everything between Ben and I. But instead of this look, Chloë's face becomes one big, kind smile. 'He's happy with you, you know,' she says.

'Oh,' I say. 'Um . . .'

'I haven't seen him this happy for a long time.'

Oh God, now I see where this is going. There's a long pause, though. Am I supposed to say something now? I'm not sure I know what to say.

'This isn't just a conference fling for you, is it?' she asks.

'I don't know,' I say honestly. 'I don't think so.'

Her eyes flick to the floor, like she's embarrassed.

'He thinks you're pretty great, you know?'

I laugh, also embarrassed. I hate conversations like this. 'Um . . . That's, er . . . God. I think the same about him, I think.' I look around at my room and across my bed, in which I have been living for the past few days. For a second it blurs and seems like a boat, stranded at sea. Then it's a bed again. Old memories. 'I don't know why he would think that, though,' I say. 'I don't think I'm great. In fact, the way I feel now, I . . .' I'm about to go on about how ill and un-sexy I feel but I don't know Chloë very well so I take a few steps backwards in my head. 'I don't even know who I am half the time,' I say instead.

Do I sound like the lame teenager I almost certainly once was? *I'm just mad. I'm SO confused. My life is so complicated. Me, me, me. Look how muddled I am. Do you think I might be on drugs? My madness makes me sophisticated. Oh, I need more strong coffee and more French cigarettes.*

But Chloë just smiles and says, 'He's a good judge of character.' So now I am expecting the big 'Don't hurt him' speech but it doesn't come. Instead, Chloë gets up and fiddles with a strand of hair that has come loose from the clip.

'If Esther does turn up, will you tell her I'm looking for her?' she says, walking towards the door.

'Sure,' I say.

And then she is gone.

So what's in today's envelope, then? I pick it up off the desk and consider taking a short cut and just burning it before I have even read it. But I don't. I ease open the flap and pull out the contents. There's a letter, written on PopCo headed paper, and something else, another sheet of paper. I open this out. Fucking hell. It's a share certificate. What's going on?

Dear Alice Butler, the letter says. *Thank you for taking part in our Games Testing programme and for offering the suggestion of Paddle Z as the name for the game you played. Although we received many feedback cards and suggestions, we all felt that your idea most strongly encapsulated the feel of this product. We particularly liked the playful juxtaposition of the functional word Paddle with the symbol Z. We were very excited by the versatility of this conjunction. Does the 'Z' refer to some sort of 'Z' factor (much more impressive than an 'X' factor), or does it imply a cutting-edge plural: PaddleZ? The options are all there. Therefore, we are pleased to inform you that we have now officially selected it as the brand name. Please find enclosed 1000 PopCo shares. A crate of champagne will be delivered to your home address when you return from your current assignment. Thank you once again for your valuable input. With best wishes, blah blah blah . . .*

Bloody hell. I only wrote that because I couldn't think of anything else. 1,000 shares. What are they worth? Probably a lot less than you'd pay a professional brand designer to come up with a product name, but a lot more than I would earn in a month. Maybe I won't burn this piece of paper. What am I going to do with a crate of champagne? I could share a bottle with Rachel, perhaps while I tell her about my strange adventures here. Perhaps Ben will want to come round and share a bottle with me. I shiver unexpectedly, imagining Ben in my house, in my bed. Will this indeed be more than a conference fling? Will he want it to be more?

Where is he, anyway? Bizarrely, I find that I am really missing him.

*

My new strategy for surviving at school is a constantly evolving entity. At first, I take a jumble of things – images, ideas, people – and pack them for school every day as carefully as my grandfather packs my lunch box (I told him that school dinners weren't working out). I take ideas about imprisonment and freedom from *Woman on the Edge of Time*. I tell myself that no one's life is as bad as the heroine Connie's life. She is locked in a cruel mental institution despite not being mad. I am trapped in this school but at least I can lock the door when I go to the toilet. On the other hand, Connie has the ability to time travel to a better world. I do not have this ability. But sometimes, when things are really bad, I imagine that I too can summon this future up in my head and step into it as easily as stepping through a door. I take this image of another world around with me all the time, folded up in my head like an old map.

Other things I carry around with me, in my head: snapshots of Roxy, of Jasmine, of the blue-haired girl in the clothes shop. They wouldn't take any shit, I know that. (I am using words like 'shit' now a lot in my head. This is what happens when you are exposed to so much adult literature before you are even twelve.) Sometimes, if one of the boys says something to me, something designed to hurt my feelings or humiliate me (and there are myriad ways of doing this at school, believe me), I say something so horrible back that they leave me alone for a while. When Mark came up to me recently and asked why I don't have any friends, I looked at him with Roxy eyes, and imagined myself with blue hair and said, 'Get fucked, Mark.' No one says things like this at school, not in the first year. Another time, the other kids got hold of one of those anti-vivisection leaflets. 'Where's your cat, Butler?' they kept saying. I didn't know what they were talking about until they slapped this image down on my desk – a cat with wires coming out of its exposed brain – and said, 'We found your cat, Butler. Sorry to say it's not in a very good state.' They all laughed, probably imagining that I was about to cry, or wet myself or something. Instead, I looked coolly down at the image and then looked up at them in a confused, grown-up way and said, 'I don't have a cat, you morons.' I didn't let them see that they had upset me. I have learnt various rules. Cry in the toilets, not in public. Use the scary, dark toilets on the third floor for this purpose, as no one else uses them. Use swear words that they don't understand. Scare them before they can scare you. Never appear weaker than them.

Every day, I eat my lunch with the Rural Studies goats, and I do my homework there in the field, so I have more time to spend with my grandparents when I get home. I mark off days on a sheet of paper I carry around as well. I have worked out that my sentence here is something like 1,205 days. It's slightly depressing that I have only served about thirty of them but I haven't completely given up on Plan B yet either, although it's almost as hard to find people in the village who want their cars washed as it is to work out what my necklace actually means.

Gradually, though, the other kids do stop picking on me. I have made it quite simple. I am weird and I am mean and if they do try to pick on me I give it back to them worse. There's no way I can keep this up for longer than a couple of weeks but, as I thought, I don't have to. Hit the weakest targets first, that seems to be the main agenda of the popular kids. And I won't let myself be a weak target, so they move on to other people, eventually. My strategy has worked. I can't have a best friend, of course, or any sort of friend. It would be too dangerous, as there would be a definite risk of this person feeding information back to the popular kids. Divide and rule. But if you don't add yourself to anything you can't be divided. I don't disclose any of my secrets and I have my special reflector shield, too. They can't get me!

A few weeks into this experiment, I decide that I might join chess club and computer club after all. If you're popular you can never contemplate doing anything as geeky/weird as this. But I am not popular. I can do what I want. And what would they say to me anyway? 'Alice, you like playing chess!'? Here are some more rules I have learnt. You must never ignore them. You must never use sarcasm back at them. You shouldn't try to reason with them. You must never talk to them in a soft voice, or avoid eye contact. All these things are losing moves. If one of them says to you, 'You like playing chess,' you say back to them something like, 'Well, you like playing with yourself, but I'm not making a big deal of it.' You make it short, snappy and loud enough for the rest of the class to hear (but never the teacher). Remember that you have the advantage. You know in advance what embarrassing hobbies you are about to take up, so you can work out responses beforehand. The only danger in this method is that you will occasionally get challenged to actual physical fights, but that's OK in my case because all arranged fights take place in the field after school and I am already on my bus by then.

Sometimes, if you go too far, the other kids will say you are 'gross' or 'disgusting'. Then you simply say, 'Do you want me to tell everyone how disgusting you are? I've heard all sorts of things about you . . .' When you have spent some time inside the popular group, this will make them nervous. Sometimes this person will try to catch you on your own and say things like, 'What did you hear?' Then you know you have won. And you also know that they do have a disgusting secret. After all, who doesn't? At school we may all act like those neutered dolls you can buy, the ones with a smooth plastic space where their genitals should be, but under our clothes we all have holes through which we pee and shit.

So, one Wednesday, not long before Christmas, I go along to the orange-carpeted library in which chess club takes place. The boys look at me nervously and/or contemptuously as I take a seat at one of the desks to wait for Mr Morgan/Moron to come. But I have forgotten how awful Moron actually is. When he enters the room he performs a comedy double-take and then laughs at me.

'What do we have here?' he says. 'A damsel in distress?'

'I've come to join chess club,' I say.

All the boys in the room, including Alex, are looking at me.

'You've come to join chess club,' Moron repeats. 'Oh dear. Tell me, Miss Butler, what set you are in for maths.'

'Two,' I say.

'Now boys,' he says to the others in the room. 'Tell Miss Butler what set you are all in for maths?'

'One,' they chorus.

'I'm afraid this is a top set club only,' Moron says to me.

He starts to say something else but I am already out of the door, my face red, tears starting to form. I flee from the main buildings and up to the field. I intend to eat my lunch with the goats as usual, but I am not really hungry. I am too angry to be hungry. How dare he?

This is now war. I am an agent of the French Resistance, lurking in forests. I am an SOE saboteur, armed with a knife and some plastic explosives. I will blow up their bridges and murder them in their sleep. Well, once I have stopped crying, that is. Miss Hind is still giving me trouble. Well, she'll get it. Moron will get it in triplicate. Any kids who give me any more trouble will get it, too. Who am I? I am Edmond Dantés.

For the next two weeks I plot and plan and then I go to work. I can't believe I am actually doing this! I spend a lot of time on the third floor of the school, lurking in the dark toilet, so I already know the rhythms of this strange floor, full of cobwebs, echoes of *écouter et répéter,* and the chalky smell of Moron's classroom. I know that Moron only teaches up here, in his horrible poky little maths room, and nowhere else. This classroom is never used for anything other than his vile, élitist maths lessons. I fully expect that when Moron dies and turns into a ghost, this is where he will hang around. Oh God. I am terrified of being found out. I am terrified of being sent to Miss Peterson again, but I know logic will get me through this. So I superglue his windows shut on a Monday (while he is on lunch duty) and let off a stink bomb on the Tuesday (lunch duty again). Girls never touch stink bombs and I have no link with this classroom. Teachers' logic will suggest that a boy from Moron's class has done this in order to get off the lesson. No one will suspect me. And I am right. Apparently, when the crime is discovered, Moron storms out in a rage and his precious chess club are kept on detention for a week while he waits for one of them to own up. Knowing that I was the actual perpetrator of this gives me such a surge of adrenaline that I can hardly breathe for a week. I never, ever would have thought that I would actually do something like this. Up yours, Moron!

Rachel and her family are away over Christmas so I spend my time reading and concocting new schemes in my imagination. I could never carry out any of these ideas – they are too complex and the stakes too high if I was caught – but I find that I get almost as much pleasure from simply dreaming them up in my head and then watching myself carry them out in the dark space behind my eyes. I break into Miss Peterson's office and change all the popular kids' reports; I write *Miss Hind Sucks Dick* on the sports hall wall (it's those adult books again). I steal Lucy's school skirt from the changing rooms on a day when PE is before lunch so she has to go around for the rest of the day in her PE skirt. In my mind, I am unstoppable.

Sometimes I think about kissing Alex, and doing things with him that adults do in the books I read. I imagine looking up his number in the phone book, ringing him and arranging to go walking in the park on a Sunday evening. We will both wear scarves and he will kiss me in the snow. Then he will say, 'You know, I've never told anyone this before but I am a millionaire/spy/time traveller with my own lavish apartment. Would you like to come and see it?' And it will just so happen that I am in possession of a magic button that stops time for everyone in the world apart from me, and whoever I am with. (I wear this button around my neck.) So we go back to his place and I press the magic button and then we go to bed like adults for as long as we want, and . . .

I'm not sure if my new fantasy world is good or bad. Sometimes I write up very sanitised versions of my stories for English assignments and I always get an A or an A+. I think I might like to become a writer one day. I don't plan any more actual sabotage missions for the time being; it turns out that thinking about them is enough. But I do plan one major *coup*. Just one.

In the summer term, there are tests and exams and all kinds of scary things, so this is when teachers plan other things like Sports Day (hell) and Non-Uniform Day (double hell). There is also something called the Groveswood Chess Tournament. And anyone can enter. I read the notice on the board every day, just because it thrills me so much. *The Groveswood Chess Tournament*, it says. *Open to all pupils. Winner will play Mr Morgan. Sign up or come and watch. Will someone take Mr Morgan's cup away from him this year?* Oh, joyous day. It is not lost on me that most schools would not have a tournament in which any pupil can take part but a teacher always wins. Wouldn't it be brilliant if it could be different this year?

I make my grandfather play chess with me every night. Practice, practice, practice. Will I be good enough to win any games, or will I get beaten by one of the obviously-much-cleverer-than-me chess-club boys? It doesn't matter. Every moment I manage to stay in the competition will be a moment Moron will hate and that's good enough for me. As long as I don't have to play Alex. That would be too much, I think. I think if I had to play Alex I would throw the game almost immediately. I couldn't sit looking at him for all that time, not after the thoughts I have been having. But I don't play Alex. On the day of the tournament, a bright June Saturday, I sit in the ghostly sunbeams in the main hall and play Robin and Neal and Gavin and Stephen and I beat them all. My grandparents sit in the audience among chess-club parents and clap every time I win a game. I can't believe how well this is going! I suppose my grandparents are not surprised that I am beating all these boys; and it probably doesn't seem that odd to them when I make it to the final. But I know what an anomaly I am. I know I won't be able to breathe properly for a month after this.

All through the 'final' (the real final is against Moron, of course, but this is the final between two pupils) I am so nervous that I almost lose. My opponent, a kid called Wayne, is actually very good. He is playing a kind of Queen's Gambit game with which I am not familiar. It could go either way for a while. Then almost too late, I understand what he is doing. Luckily, I still have time to trap his king and, with my hands shaking so much I think I might drop the pieces, I win. I am going to play Moron!

I expect him to be impressed, and possibly humbled, by the fact that I am facing him at all. I imagine that he might say something like, 'Well, Miss Butler, I was wrong about you.' But he doesn't. Instead, as we shake hands before playing, he says quietly, 'Women always get to the top by nefarious means. Well, let's get this over with then. I reckon you'll be a five-minute job, maybe less.'

I am actually quite scared of playing Moron. I expect he is really rather good at chess and, after all, he has never let a pupil beat him before. However, once he has played his first few moves, I recognise his attack completely. It's a Rubinstein attack, exactly the one used by Kasparov in a game I studied in one of my grand-father's chess books. My grandfather even wrote a Mind Mangle column about it. So when Moron moves his queen to c2 and gives me a smug look, I am totally prepared. His big error is to completely ignore what I am doing and press on with a carbon copy of Kasparov's attack. Ten minutes later, I have won.

I had planned to say something nice and polite like, 'Well played, sir', and none of the horrible things from my fantasy world. But Moron doesn't give me the chance to say anything at all. With a hurt, confused and humiliated look on his face, he simply leaves the hall without saying anything. The boys, who have all been watching, look at me as though I am some kind of toxic end-of-level monster from one of their videogames. In my fantasy they all clap the over-throw of the vile despot Moron but in reality it's only the parents and my grandparents clapping. But that's enough for me.

Chapter Twenty-six

When Ben finally turns up, he's with Esther.

'We're on the run,' Esther says as she comes in. 'We're not here.'

What am I missing? It looks fun, whatever it is. The two of them are flushed and slightly breathless, like kids playing in snow.

'She means *she's* not here,' Ben says, coming over and sitting next to me. Esther perches on the end of the bed.

'Where have you been?' I ask.

'Totnes,' Ben says. 'It's this little hippy town not too far from here. Well, it didn't look far on the map. It took, what, forty minutes to drive there? Something like that.' He looks at his watch. 'Bloody hell, it is late. I'd better sort dinner out soon.'

'Who drove?' I say, confused. 'I thought we were all trapped here.'

'Esther's got a car,' Ben says. 'She was planning to escape so I hitched a ride with her as far as Totnes. Then she decided not to escape and gave me a ride back.'

'Totnes is so cool,' Esther says to me. 'It has a castle, and about seven different health-food shops. I think we went to all of them.'

'Why did you want to go to Totnes?' I ask Ben.

'To get you some stuff,' he says, slightly shyly. 'Here.'

He gives me a carrier bag. I look inside and immediately find a paper chemist's bag with a pack of nicotine gum. I expect Ben took all those drugs from Doctor Death to the chemists to dispose of as well. I hope so.

'Thank God,' I say, grinning and unwrapping the gum. I put some in my mouth and instantly feel a lot better. 'Wow, what's all this other stuff?' The rest of the bag is full of sweets, exotic-looking packs of miso soup, fruit, organic chocolates, lavender shampoo and conditioner, and aloe vera gel.

'Just a few things I thought you'd like,' Ben says.

'I chose the shampoo and stuff,' Esther says. 'And the aloe vera gel is for when the itching starts.'

'Itching?'

'Have you ever given up smoking before?'

I shake my head. 'No . . . Why?'

'Give it a couple more days and you'll start itching like fuck. Trust me. When you do, you just need to get Ben to rub this stuff into your skin before bed and it'll be a lot better.'

'Thanks, Esther,' I say. I have some half-memory of something on the radio about Dylan Thomas getting some sort of itching if he didn't drink. What did he call it? Rats in your vest, or something like that. Is it the same thing? I don't think I am going to stop smoking for that long anyway, but still.

I fish around in the bag looking for some sweets to open now. It's an odd experience having a bag full of sweets and chocolates and not recognising any of the packaging or brand names. It's not unpleasant, though. It feels a bit like being on holiday. There are three little hard tubes of CJ's Dynamic Peppermints; two round wooden boxes of Booja Booja chocolates (one box of banana flambé and one box of 'around midnight' espresso); a slab of Cayenne chocolate, which, according to the label, is dark chocolate with pepper in it; another slab of chocolate with nuts and peel pressed into it; three macadamia and fruit bars, a thin paper bag of liquorice; a box of organic cola bottles; a box of organic pineapple sweets and a box of something called VegeBears that look like Jelly Babies.

'Why are they "Vege" bears?' I ask Ben, opening the box and offering them around.

'They're vegetarian,' he says, taking one.

'Oh,' I say, remembering something from my student days. 'No gelatine, right?'

'Yeah.' Ben smiles. 'No ground-up pig trotters and cow brain.'

'Mmm, pig trotters,' says Esther, reaching into the box for some sweets.

'Shut up, Esther,' Ben says. He looks at me. 'She's been doing this all the way back from Totnes.'

'I can't help it if I crave meat,' she says.

'I thought you were a vegan too,' I say to her.

'I am,' she says. 'I just crave meat all the time. The more evil the better. I horrify myself, I really do. I think it comes from spending my entire childhood at McFuck's. I think they make that stuff addictive, I'm convinced of it. I just can't wait to die sometimes, because I have this theory that when you die you get to heaven and then you can have anything you want because it's not real any more . . . I'll be there and I'll be like, "Hi, Supreme Being.

Yeah, I'm ready to order now. I'll have a quarter-pounder with cheese and chips, please, with extra gherkins, and a portion of fries, a portion of onion rings, and a strawberry shake . . . "'

'Don't they do meal deals in heaven?' I ask, laughing.

'I dunno,' Esther says. 'But you never get a shake with a meal deal anyway, just watered-down cola or whatever . . .'

Ben is making a face. 'Shakes at those places are essentially the secretions of imprisoned animals mixed with pus, blood, chicken fat, artificial flavouring and sugar,' he says. 'But I suppose if it's what you really want . . .'

'It's not real in heaven,' Esther says. 'Anyway, as well as all that I would also have an iced latte . . .'

'More pus, more blood,' says Ben.

'Shut up, Ben!' she says. 'Where was I? Yeah, an iced latte, a full Devon cream tea – shut up, Ben – a family pack of B&H, a huge pile of cocaine, an E, or maybe two, and I dunno, chuck in some heroin as well, maybe.'

'I told you,' Ben says to me. 'She's nuts.'

'I am not nuts. It makes sense!'

I'm laughing. 'What does? I'm lost.'

'That all the stuff you don't have in life you are allowed to have in heaven. Obviously up there it's the cruelty-free, no-pain version of everything. So if you spend your life eating McFuck's and ready meals, you have to spend an eternity eating lentils. But if you spend your life eating lentils, you get to spend an eternity eating fast food. The same with smoking. The same with drugs. An eternity's better than a lifetime, isn't it? So you may as well do the right thing now, so you get all the good stuff after you die.'

Ben's shaking his head. 'Only you would imagine heaven as an eternal fast-food restaurant full of drug dealers.' But he's smiling, and I know he likes Esther.

'Hang on,' I say to Esther. 'You smoke, so you wouldn't get your B&H in heaven.'

'No,' she corrects me. 'I only smoke dope now. I used to smoke, like, thirty cigarettes a day. Then I just gave up. That's how I know about the itch . . . Anyway, the whole experience was just too painful and I realised that I *had* to smoke something. I thought of smoking cigars or a pipe but I didn't want to have to learn how to do it. I always liked a spliff so I thought I'd just smoke a couple of joints a day. That turned into, well, I guess about ten joints a day but at least I'm not smoking fags any more.'

'Isn't there tobacco in your joints, though?' Ben asks, laughing.

'Yeah, but I reckon the Supreme Being doesn't know about that.'

'Doesn't the Supreme Being know everything?' I ask.

'Not necessarily,' Esther says. 'Look at Newcomb's Paradox.'

Ben is laughing so much I think he might cry soon.

'Esther, you are so nuts,' he manages. 'What the fuck is Newcomb's Paradox?

'Newcomb's Paradox?' she says. 'Oh, well, it's all about these two boxes. You are told the following information: Box A contains £1000 and Box B contains either a million pounds or nothing.' She takes another VegeBear and bites its head off before looking at Ben, who has stopped laughing. 'Have you settled down now, Ben? Good. So, the Supreme Being can see into the future and, depending on the decision he/she/it decides you will make, will either fill Box B with a million pounds or leave it empty. If the Supreme Being predicts that you will take the contents of both boxes, he/she/it will leave Box B empty. If, however, the prediction is that you will take the contents of *only* Box B, the Supreme Being will load it with a million pounds.'

'So there are four possible outcomes,' I say, trying to catch up. 'You can leave with £1,000, £1,001,000, £1,000,000 or nothing.'

'Yes, that's the mathematical way of looking at it,' she says.

'How can you leave with the million pounds and the thousand pounds?' Ben asks me.

'Shut up both of you,' Esther says. 'Just let me tell it. All right, so the Supreme Being makes the prediction a week before you are offered the choice of boxes. This prediction is almost 100 per cent accurate. The Supreme Being knows what you are going to do and loads the boxes accordingly. Remember, Box A will always have a thousand pounds in it, and Box B has either a million pounds or nothing depending on the prediction. If the supreme being thinks you will pick only Box B, it will contain the million quid. But if the prediction is that you will take both boxes, it will contain nothing. Your goal is to maximise your winnings from this game – you have to leave with as much as possible. The supreme being can't change the contents of the boxes once they have been loaded. So what do you do?' She smiles, and eats another sweet.

'Take Box B,' Ben and I say together.

'That's what I said!' Esther says. 'But if you think about it logically, you should actually change your mind at the last minute and take both boxes. The supreme being will have loaded Box B – a week ago, remember – with a million pounds, based on the choice it predicted you will make. Obviously you're going to pick just Box B, as this is your only way of winning a million pounds. So, considering that your aim is to maximise your prize, having chosen Box B, with the million quid, you may as well take Box A as well. It *always* contains a thousand pounds, so you may as well take it.'

'Hang on, though,' Ben says. 'If that's the logical thing to do, surely the Supreme Being will have predicted it. If it's been predicted that this is what you will do, then there won't be the million pounds in Box B at all . . .'

'Which still makes it sensible to choose both boxes, in order to make sure you leave with a thousand pounds rather than nothing,' I say, uncertainly.

'Which means that, in actual fact, it is after all much better to just choose Box B, because that's your only way of winning a million pounds,' Ben says.

'Which takes you back full circle,' Esther says. 'You choose Box B, which is the only sensible option. But, having done that, don't you just take box A as well at the last minute?'

'No,' Ben says. 'You only take Box B.'

'But the Supreme Being can't change the contents of the boxes after they have been loaded,' I say. 'So you can change your mind and it can't go back in time and take the money away. I see why this is a paradox now. Will the Supreme Being predict that you will change your mind since, according to the rules of the game, that is the most sensible thing to do? If this is the prediction, then you should take both boxes, since it's your only way of winning anything. Or will the Supreme Being think one more step ahead which is that, actually, you will choose Box B after all, since it's the only way to get a million pounds?'

'Exactly!' Esther says. 'It's a cool puzzle. Grace told me it. She said there were good mathematical arguments for both positions but that no one has ever proved which one is actually correct.'

I chew on my gum, wondering if this is a question that simply has no answer.

'I still say go for Box B,' Ben says. 'You decide you are not going to cheat, and the Supreme Being knows that you are a moral person who will not cheat, and you get your million pounds, simple. After all, it's only when you try to cheat the Supreme Being that the whole thing starts to go wrong. So you take Box B, and you don't try to take Box A as well, because if you do take it, you can guarantee that the Supreme Being will have predicted it.'

'Yeah,' I say. 'That is an interesting way of looking at it. Does the Supreme Being have a moral dimension, or is it pure logic?' And I suddenly wonder if that is what greed actually is, a game played with logic only and no morals.

'Must be just logic, mustn't it?' Esther says. 'Otherwise Ben's right and that is the solution. There'd be no paradox.' She eats another sweet. 'My Supreme Being isn't like that, anyway.'

'Your Supreme Being?' I say.

'Yeah. I reckon we all invent our own Supreme Beings. It's the point of life. You invent your own religion complete with an after-life, a Supreme Being if you want one and anything else you want, and then you pretty much get whatever you expect after you die. People who don't believe in anything or who don't bother to come up with their own belief system really don't go anywhere after they die. People who believe in some complex system of reincarnation and cycles of life get that. People who belong to organised religions get whatever that offers, although it usually isn't very good . . .'

'But that's a paradox in itself,' Ben says. 'Your own invented religion is essentially that everyone in the whole world gets to choose their own religion, etc. etc. So if you are right, and everyone does get to choose their own "meaning of life", then you have made this up as part of your own meaning of life theory. So someone else could say, 'Oh, I believe something else', and that might negate yours . . .'

'It's a positive feedback loop,' I say. 'Although I do like the idea of it.'

'You and your bloody theology,' Esther says to Ben. 'And your bloody maths,' she says to me. 'My head hurts.'

'One thing I don't understand, though,' Ben says. 'You weren't sure of the gender of your Supreme Being. Surely you'd have all that worked out . . . ?'

'When?' she says, confused.

'Just now in that Box A or Box B thing.'

'Oh, that. No, that was Newcomb's Supreme Being, not mine,' she says. 'My Supreme Being wouldn't fuck around with boxes.'

'She'd be too busy flipping your hamburgers, I suppose,' Ben says. 'So didn't Newcomb know what gender his Supreme Being was?'

'Probably,' Esther says. 'But I forgot. I think in Newcomb's Paradox, the Supreme Being can be whatever you want. That's why I left it open. Why has Alice gone all quiet?'

'Huh?' I say. 'Oh, I was thinking about the SF. The Supreme Fascist. It's what Paul Erdös called God. It's his version of the Supreme Being, I suppose. He said that life is a game that you can never win, because every time you do something bad the SF gets one point, but every time you do something good, neither of you score. The game of life is to keep the SF's score as low as possible but however you play, it's a game you can never win.'

'Sounds about right,' Ben says.

'Actually, now I think about it, Erdös had a whole Supreme Being/afterlife system worked out just like yours,' I say, looking at Esther. 'He believed that the SF keeps a book – with a transfinite number of pages – in which perfect proofs for every mathematical problem in existence are recorded. Whenever someone came up with a really elegant proof, Erdös would say, "It's straight from the Book." He believed that when you die, you get to see the Book.'

'That's cool,' Esther says.

'I heard this theory once,' Ben says, 'that you can't go to heaven until we invent it. The argument is that the point of our life on Earth is to construct some kind of viable afterlife for ourselves – not just in our imaginations, but to actually construct it. Perhaps it will be some way of releasing our consciousness at the point of death, possibly into a computer simulation or something like that. Anyway, until then, we are all reincarnated, and new people are born and the population is exploding . . . Once we learn how to release our consciousness from our bodies, we will stop being reincarnated, and move on to the next level of evolution, where we exist as pure energy.'

'Like the advanced beings you see in science-fiction films?' Esther says.

'Exactly.' Ben laughs, and reaches for a sweet. 'It's a slightly warped form of techno-Buddhism,' he says. 'I can't remember who thought of it. What do you think, Alice?'

'It's almost convincing,' I say. 'But if the point of evolution is to reduce ourselves by a dimension, is our ultimate goal to not exist at all? I don't know. I've always had this hope that when you die you go to a big library which has not just Erdös's Book, but a trans-finite number of books explaining everything you would ever want to know about life. I imagine that as well as being able to read all these books, you get to watch any events on Earth, from any period of history, from any perspective you want. You could spend fifty or so years living Hitler's life, if you wanted to understand him, or a hundred years sitting inside a tree in a park in France watching people go by, or a few lifetimes inside ordinary people's heads. In my afterlife, everything has been scaled up to another level. Knowledge is infinite facts – answers to as many questions as there are in the world – and entertainment isn't fiction any more but real lives . . .'

'Come on, Ben,' Esther says. 'Now tell her that her afterlife is the Reality TV channel on cable . . .'

'No,' he says. 'I think her afterlife sounds cool. What's the point of life on Earth, though, in this version? Why do we live at all?'

'For two reasons,' I say. 'Firstly, to understand what life is and to learn as many skills as possible for interpreting it. Life is where we get to have a good guess at solving the puzzle before we die and get to see the answer, and also where we learn what questions to ask. Secondly, the point is to live a good life and be nice to people.'

'Why bother, though?' Esther says. 'If you're going off to your cushy afterlife afterwards?'

'Oh, because in your afterlife, there are lots of other dead people. At first, you sort of choose who you want to hang around with in the afterlife. But of course, if I got to the afterlife and looked up some old friend from school, the first thing I would do is go back and look at her life to see what she was really like. If it turned out that she had simply pretended to like me for all that time, I would ditch her in the afterlife. So if you go through life betraying people and lying to people, you could end up on your own up there.'

'You see,' Esther says. 'Everyone has their own afterlife worked out, just like I said.'

'Hang on,' I say. 'Ben hasn't.'

'What?' he says, getting up and stretching. 'Oh. Um, I think I'll join your religion if that's all right,' he says to me. 'I'll go to the big library in the sky with you.'

'Oh, yuck,' says Esther. 'You two make me sick.'

'I like the way we've bypassed planning for our retirement or anything like that and gone straight for the afterlife experience,' I say. 'Pretty good going after a week.' Ben's face falls. Oh shit. It was just a joke . . . Backtrack, Alice. 'Anyway,' I say. 'I would *love* to have you in my exclusive religion. You can even be the co-founder.'

'Yeah, well, unless I get a better offer,' he says back.

Esther sticks around while Ben goes to get dinner for all of us.

'Chloë was looking for you earlier,' I say. 'It seemed important-ish.'

'Maybe I should have escaped,' she says dreamily.

'What were you escaping from? Not Chloë?'

She gestures around her. 'No. Just . . . this. Everything. PopCo. I don't suppose you know that I'm Mac's niece, do you?'

'You? You are Mac's niece? Not really, though?'

'Yep. Not by blood or anything – yuck, imagine that. No. My mother's sister was his secretary years ago when he was MD of a carpet firm. They fell in love and he married her. She wasn't exactly the right class or anything but Mac's parents thought she was charming. Well, they would. Aunt Sarah is that type. She did elocution lessons and ballet and always had proper hairstyles and manicured nails. She knew that the way she could become rich and pampered was to marry an MD. So she did. But my mother was pretty much the opposite. She was an art-school hippy with a drug habit and the beginnings of a drink problem. She would turn up at Mac and Sarah's country house for 'spontaneous' weekends with them, dragging along whatever dropkick she was seeing that week. When she became pregnant with me, they disapproved – she wasn't married or anything and this was 1974 – so they fell out of contact for a long time.

'So, fast forward quite a while, and there I am, and I'm, like, twenty-one and I've just finished my degree and I don't have a job or anywhere to live. My mum's still drinking, and we're both living in Teignmouth – not far from here, in fact – but I badly want to move to London and get a place to live. I was sort of a loser, to be honest, but I had a good bunch of friends from university, and we wanted to set up our own company, creating videogames. My mum was like, 'Why don't you call Uncle Steve? He's CEO of PopCo now. He'll give you a job in videogames.' And I was like, 'Who wants to work for that corporate shit bag?' But, hypocrite that I am, I phoned him and asked for a loan of some money to go towards this company we wanted to set up. Anyway, he said no to the money but did offer me a job. He said I could work up in London at the Battersea office and that he had a really special role in mind for me.'

'So obviously, you took it?' I say.

'Yeah. What could I do? At first I had plans to use the money I was earning towards art projects but you know how it is. Friends drifted away, I got caught up in my job. I live online now, mainly.'

I think of Kieran and his virtual worlds. 'Online?' I repeat.

'Yeah. You know, you can get caught up in newsgroups and bulletin boards and Ultima and EverQuest. I've got some good friends online. And a few enemies . . .'

'Esther?' I say, suddenly. 'What is your job?'

'My job. Ah.' She gulps. 'You'll hate me if I tell you. Or I almost hope you will . . .'

'I don't understand.'

She takes a deep breath. 'I make websites.'

'What? You work on the PopCo site?'

'No, no. I make websites. I come up with a persona, like, oh . . . On one site I'm a girl from London called April, and I make April's homepage. The idea is that I keep a diary, like a blog, as April, and lists of likes and dislikes and whatever, and every so often – not often enough so it would be obvious but enough to have an impact – I become "obsessed" with a PopCo product, usually some K thing, or Finbar's Friends. So one day I'm April, writing in my blog about this new Finbar toy that's just been released that I just *have* to have. The next day I might be Tabitha, battling with anorexia, pictured wearing K products, looking sexily underweight. I might be a couple of friends who have set up the "unofficial" Finbar fan club. I tend to do that one over the weekend. I'm also supposed to mention PopCo products on Ultima and EverQuest and various chat rooms. It's called guerrilla marketing. That's my job. That's why I had to see Mac afterwards last Saturday. He was sorting out for me to have a laptop so I could maintain the sites from here.'

'And Hiro, too,' I say slowly.

She looks down at the floor. 'Yeah. Hiro, too.'

'He does the same thing? As teenage boys?'

'He doesn't have personas as such. It's not so important for boys to see personas online. Hiro does all the videogame fan sites. Well, not all of them. I expect PopCo have twenty or so of us doing these jobs. We don't know about each other. Well, we're not supposed to, but I've known Hiro for a while.'

'How did you meet?' I ask.

'What? Oh, a chance meeting online.' I can tell she's lying but I don't know why.

'At least I see now why it's a secret,' I say.

'Yeah. No one wants anyone to know about these jobs, even staff. I suppose it seems dishonest.'

'It is dishonest,' I say. I shrug, but then don't say anything else.

'It's all dishonest, though, Alice,' she says. 'All of it.'

She's right. The way the products are designed, focus-grouped, manufactured and sold. It's all dishonest, all of it.

*

For the next three years my grandmother continues failing to prove the Riemann Hypothesis (but writes some interesting papers about subjects connected with it); my grandfather continues failing to solve the Voynich Manuscript (but publishes two more Mind Mangle collections); and I continue to fail to crack the necklace code.

For GCSE English we have to do a project on a book of our own choice. I pick *Woman on the Edge of Time*, the moving and disturbing book I last read when I was almost twelve, and didn't properly understand. I pick out themes of oppression and resistance and write an essay well beyond the requirements of the syllabus. For this, and all my other GCSEs, I get A grades. After the chess-tournament incident, Moron went on sick leave for a long time. A new teacher came, a woman called Miss Rider, and I moved up to top set in time for the exams. It's a good job I did – people in sets 2 and 3 were only put in for the Intermediate paper, where the highest possible grade you could achieve was a C.

Rachel gets the same results as me and we confer about where we should do our A levels. I am, of course, not keen to go back to Groveswood for what will surely be another few hundred days of torture. Rachel has become bored with being locked up in the middle of nowhere with what she calls 'a bunch of anorexic rich kids'. It's all changed at her school in the last few years. Fitting in there is as complicated as fitting in at Groveswood, but you never get to go home. Everything has to be right: the way you shower, your deodorant, the tapes you listen to in your Walkman at night, the records you bring into school, the boys you know, the letters you receive. While Rachel was in the 5th year, I would sometimes send her letters as a boy called Rupert, which apparently helped somehow. She started smoking at school because there was nothing else to do. I am learning to smoke now, too. We have promised each other that we will give up when we are twenty (ages away) but we both love the advertisements: the purple piece of silk slashed through in so many different ways. Cigarette companies soon won't be allowed to advertise directly and this one company is already cleverly making their advertising into code. When Rachel and I go into town together, the summer we are both sixteen, we look at these big, glossy billboards and, without having to talk about it, we understand that these pictures represent our futures. This is what our village is not. This is London and glamour and sex and being grown up. This is art films and kisses and having your own car.

We are both accepted to do our A levels at the local sixth-form college. Over the summer we spend hours in a coffee shop off the market square in town, scaring/thrilling ourselves with stories of how the people at this college are all in bands, or have dyed hair, or take drugs, or are weird, loser-ish dropouts. We are both scared of these things but we both also want to be them. We each want an identity more complex than, simply, 'Virgin good-girl from village who brushes her hair properly every night'.

We sit in this cafe, drinking espresso even though neither of us like it, and smoking cigarettes from our purple and white packets. We say things to each other like, 'I really *need* a cigarette', until the point when it's not a lie any more. We dare each other to go into the dark, smoky record shop and mingle with thin boys in black. We wish and hope and pray that one day two young guys will ask to share our table in the cafe: two guys with long black coats and DMs and badges and record collections and their own flats. This never happens.

We save money from our babysitting jobs and buy ripped 501s and black polo-neck jumpers. We go on diets. We rent films from the local video shop, films about fucked-up ballet dancers and holiday romances and kids from small towns where parties are illegal. We rent French art films in which girls no older than us swish around smoking and having intense-looking sex. We plan our own 'first times'. We buy postcards of naked black men holding white babies, stylised pictures of beaten-up pink ballet shoes, and that big poster of the tennis player showing her bum. We cut out Sunday supplement versions of the cigarette advertisements we like and stick those above our desks with Blu-Tak. We decide that chart music is for 'plebs' (Rachel's word) and we contrive to get into what is called indie music. In order to do this, we get big floppy music newspapers and we buy whatever these papers say is 'in'. We sit around in the evenings listening to music and carefully fraying our jeans. We sew on patches – the American flag on one leg and a VW patch on another; or paisley patches and yin and yang signs. We talk about stealing real VW signs to wear in other ways – this is a craze we have read about. We also read about how it is 'trendy' now to wear branded sports trainers with our 501s, so we start doing this. We think about going to America. We dissect song lyrics looking for hidden meanings. We obsess, briefly, over Marilyn Monroe. We wear loads of black eyeliner and pink frosted lipstick. We are going to hit our college with force.

One day, about a week before term starts, we are in town as usual, pretending to be older than we are, on drugs, in the middle of interesting crises and so on – our usual fantasies of adult life. We are on a mission to buy new lipsticks: they have to be exactly the right shade of pale pink. We *have* to have them. Really, we live for this sort of thing. We occasionally see people I used to know from Groveswood in town. For example, Emma is now a junior assistant in Miss Selfridge, and Lucy works in the bank. We think they are really stupid, and we laugh at their hair and clothes and jobs. We would never fall into the establishment rat-race rut of working in something as pathetic as a bank or a mainstream clothes shop. They spend all day doing what they are told, with their backcombed pony-tails and their red lipstick and blusher, and we talk about how ridiculous they look. Only someone who had sold their soul to Thatcher/Hitler/Reagan would seriously want to look like a cheap doll in red (of all things) lipstick and black skirts and tights. And they all wear high heels. Every mission that Rachel and I go on is about not being this. Our lipstick, our jeans, our hair – these things, so carefully put together, say that we don't like what everyone else likes. Or, at least, we don't like what the plebs in this town like. In London, or Paris, maybe somewhere like that, maybe we'd fit in.

So we are on this mission for our pink lipstick. Outside Boots, the animal-liberation stand is there as usual. We approach it, smoking cigarettes.

'I want to join that,' Rachel says to me. It's not a surprise. She loves animals and always has. She wants to be a vet. She's wanted to be a vet since she was about ten.

'I do, too,' I say. 'But I'm scared.'

We giggle. 'I am too,' Rachel says. 'But I don't know why.'

'I think they might tell us off for smoking,' I say.

'Yeah. And wearing make-up,' Rachel says.

'Do you think it's true, what they say they do to the animals?'

'I don't know,' says Rachel. 'It must be a bit exaggerated.'

'Yeah. It would be too horrible otherwise.'

'No one would let them get away with it.'

'No. Exactly.'

'But I do agree with them, though.'

'Yeah, me too.'

So, having added that to our identities, we swish into Boots in our jeans and we buy our lipsticks. We laugh at the tragic pictures of models on the make-up displays, and we giggle at laxatives and Durex. We don't think any more about the animal-rights stand, and the people outside in the rain. We don't make any particular connection between our lives and theirs. We don't consider not coming to Boots any more. After all, no one else stocks our favourite lipstick! But mostly, we expect that while we are being young and doing this, someone else will care, and someone else will sign the petitions and we can simply tell all our friends (the ones we are bound to make) that we support animal liberation. We don't really think that the stands, or the people in the rain, will ever just go away.

*   *   *

College is everything we thought it would be. There are rocka-billies and psychobillies and girls who dress like punks and boys who dress like 50s American movie stars. These people, however, look at us as though we are children. We need to raise our game but we don't know how. We look OK. We like the right music – although there's no easy way of getting this across. We sit in our favourite cafe and dream of the day when we will have been coming here for enough years so that we can send funny postcards from abroad and they will be displayed on the wall. We plot ways of being invited to the other kids' parties and invent ways of getting into the pubs where they all go. We think about how to obtain some cannabis and where/when we could learn to smoke it like they all do. We long for the day when one of the skinny boys in black will speak to us.

More than anything, we wish there were more things for us to buy, and easier ways of finding out what we should buy. We trawl charity shops and fancy-dress shops but we still don't quite know the secret of being as trendy as the other people at college. We could be saying so much more with our style. Rachel, who started doing Biology, Chemistry and Physics, swaps so she is doing Biology, English and French. This won't get her into university to study to become a vet, but all the interesting people are in the arts groups, not the sciences. I am doing Sociology, English and French. A lot of the most interesting people are in my group for sociology. On the day the Gulf War starts, we have a discussion about the end of the world. Then we organise a sit-in protest.

'We thought you two were just really aloof,' a girl called Harriet says to me and Rachel during the sit-in. We are all telling secrets and making friends and flirting. Harriet is a couple of years older than us and has only recently come back to college after some-thing thrilling like a nervous breakdown or a period of drug-rehabilitation.

'We thought you just didn't like us,' Rachel says, honestly.

And then we can't stop talking.

We have just become friends with Harriet! After the sit-in, she invites us to our first party. We ring up our parents/grandparents and tell them that the sit-in is going to go on all night, and because of our political beliefs, we really feel we have to stay on. When my grandfather says he is proud of me for standing up for what I believe in, I feel a little bit sick. But then I reason that all the people at the party are all the people from the sit-in so it's almost like an extension of the same thing. It's not a complete lie.

When Rachel tells her parents, they say, 'Just stay with Alice, she's sensible.'

The party is in a squat in a huge mansion off Mill Road. This is simply the most amazing place we have ever been to. They have it all connected up so there is a second-hand or stolen telephone in each room, all networked so that, say, the girl who lives upstairs can call the sitting room downstairs and ask for a spliff to be brought up to her. All the people who live here ride bicycles, many of them stolen. They are living the same kind of anti-establishment life we have seen in films and magazines!

This turns out not to be a dancing/eating sort of party. Instead, everyone sits around in the big, dusty living room or in the dirty, cramped kitchen, passing round spliffs and talking about politics or music or protest marches they have been on. Rachel and I don't have to go home until the morning and so we definitely won't. We drink cider and vodka and smoke our first spliffs. Our eye make-up smudges and our breath goes sour. Our stomachs rumble. We haven't eaten since lunchtime. A student called Toby starts talking to me, while his friend, a musician called Gary, talks to Rachel. We both lose our virginity that night, on opposite sides of the same room, each while we think the other is asleep. Voodoo Ray is playing on an old, half-broken stereo when it's my turn.

Over the next few months, the various accessories and props from our discarded identities pile up in corners of our bedrooms like we are both holding never-ending jumble sales. Broken Walkmans, watches that aren't cool any more ('cool' is the new word for anything good), copies of French existentialist novels that we bought one Saturday from the bookshop to go with our French cigarettes, dinky notebooks half-filled with poetry and lists of what we thought was 'in' or 'out' at the time, Zippo lighters (branded matches from interesting clubs are better, we decide), silk scarves, berets, menthol cigarette papers, perfumes, deodorants, lipsticks, black nail varnish, indie albums (we like house now) and posters for demonstrations from when we used to hang around at the squat. Even my tarnished old necklace is under there somewhere, and my now battered copy of *Woman on the Edge of Time*.

How much life can the two of us fit in to the smallest space? We squeeze our few experiences like oranges, telling our new friends how wasted we always are, and how much sex we are always having. I say I was fucked up by my dad abandoning me, and Rachel turns her boarding-school into a reform school for the purpose of anecdotes and discussions. We claim to have seen cutting-edge TV programmes that last aired when we were both ten, and despite Rachel being at boarding-school and me not having a TV. We even lie to each other. 'Yeah, I tried a bit of coke once,' Rachel says. 'Someone brought some into school.' 'Yeah, me too. Same,' I say. As if anyone would ever have brought coke to school. Suddenly, trying things for the first time (coke, acid, speed) can't even be that because doing something for the first time is too uncool. We don't even admit to ourselves that we are the inexperienced sixteen-year-olds we are. We hitch rides home after the last bus has gone. We read 'feminist' novels about prostitutes being raped and we think they are profound. We even find them titillating, which we have no problem admitting to each other. We still think we might die if Saddam launches a nuclear missile at us. We fall in with another group, at another squat, and Toby becomes Mike and Gary becomes Dave. Dave already has a girlfriend with a kid on the way but Rachel doesn't care. She is younger, prettier, poutier. And anyway, we are grown-ups now, doing grown-up things, like in the books we read. There will be casualties, of course there will. But that's not our problem.

But summer changes everything, as summer always does. Did I think I would ever get away with this? Did I think I would ever manage to be cool and liked and myself, all at once? How stupid of me. It's over – bang, bang, bang, bang – all of a sudden, just like that. Bang! My first-year exam results are pitiful and Rachel fails altogether. Bang! Rachel is pregnant and can't tell her parents. Bang! Her mother is diagnosed with breast cancer. Bang! My grandmother goes into hospital, having suffered the first of the many strokes she will have. My life is like a firework display that has just finished; with cold, greasy hot-dog wrappers and charred remains of fun lying everywhere. I have hardly spoken to my grandparents for months. Now I find I simply have to be at home. I have to be the right sort of granddaughter for my grandfather. I want to work with him again like when I was a kid, before these pretty, meaningless lights exploded around me. But even this is tarnished. Of course, I still have to sneak around with Rachel, trying to organise an abortion, trying to convince doctors that she really cannot tell her parents.

By the time it is all over, my bedroom is tidy again, my necklace is back on, and my hair dye is growing out. Life doesn't seem quite so frivolous any more. Rachel starts her A levels again, back to her science subjects, and I pull my socks up for my second year. When I leave for university the following year, I take a recipe for root-vegetable stew, my gaffer-tape glasses and lots of books connected to the Voynich Manuscript. I send my grandparents long letters every week, written in fountain pen, on nice paper. I look at the other first years, smoking their first joints, agonising over their first sexual experiences and trying to come up with a 'logo' for every society they invent and I know that I have already had enough of all this.

*

My remedies arrive on Thursday morning, in a little brown padded envelope. This cheers me up a bit. I love getting remedies through the post. Little brown bottles with tiny white tablets inside, each labelled with the Latin name and potency of the remedy inside. I take a Kali-C, one of the 200s, and then get back into bed. I haven't slept well at all, and the remedy knocks me out, too. I pretty much sleep through breakfast.

Eleven o'clock. I sit up in bed, switch on the TV and then immediately switch it back off again. I go to the bathroom and wash my face. I walk back into the bedroom and look at my storyboards from yesterday. What a load of shit. For the first time in ages, I think back to my own teenage years. I think about how we all built ourselves up like AIs or online avatars, as if identity was something you could put together only if you bought the right bits first. However, when I was a teenager you at least got to do the thinking yourself. You at least had to be inventive about where you got the bits and how you put them together. Teenage girls haven't changed that much, but now there is so much more for them to buy. Now there are people only too willing to stick a bunch of them in a focus group and say, 'Now, girls. Tell us what exactly you want a lipstick to *do*.' I suddenly think back to the question of the moon. If I was a scientist and I had worked out how to brand the moon, how to shine logos on it so that everyone in the world could see them (100 per cent coverage, well, except blind people), would I sell my idea? Would I sell the moon for a million or more? No. I absolutely would not.

I think about all the marketing books I have read, and all the little tricks that we learn in our industry and I suddenly realise that Esther is right. It is all dishonest. We are twenty-first-century con artists. Marketing, after all, is what you do to sell people things they don't need. If people needed, say, a T-shirt with a logo on it, no one would have to market the idea to them. Marketing, advertising . . . What started off being, 'Hey, we make this! Do you want it?' turned into, 'If you buy this, you might get laid more,' and then mutated into, 'If you don't buy this, you'll be uncool, no one will like you, everyone will laugh at you and you may as well kill yourself now. I'm telling you this because I am your friend and you have to trust me.' Marketing is what gives value to things that do not have any actual intrinsic value. We put eyes on a bit of plastic, but it is marketing that actually brings the piece of plastic to life. It is marketing that means we can sell a 10p bit of cloth for £12.99. We spy on kids and find out that they like playing with socks, so we sell them socks. I don't want to do this any more. I really, really don't want to do this any more.

I burn the storyboards in the bath.

'You're looking a bit better,' Ben says when he comes later, with dinner.

'Thanks,' I say, smiling a watery smile.

'We're going on an excursion tomorrow,' he says, just as we finish eating.

I put my tray down on the table. 'An excursion? Where?'

'Totnes. You should come if you feel better. We can have lunch. We're all getting things for sailing . . . Deck shoes, funny hats. All that stuff.'

I smile another smile, even more diluted than the first one.

'What's wrong?' Ben asks.

I can't help it. I start to cry.

'Alice?'

'I miss my grandfather,' I say. 'And my grandmother.'

I talk incoherently while he fetches me tissues. I doubt that what I am saying is making any sense. I'm talking about how I don't think they'd be proud of me doing this and I don't know who I am or where my life is going and how this is the third time I have let them down. I think this might have something to do with not smoking, or the remedy, or even a touch of PMT. But it's what I really feel, and it's coming out because I don't have my barriers in place properly.

'It's all right,' he says, stroking my arm. 'It's all right.'

When I stop crying, we lie down on the bed together, both staring at the ceiling.

'I'm leaving PopCo,' I say, eventually.

Ben pauses for a minute, then props himself up on an elbow and frowns.

'Why?'

'I just don't believe in it any more,' I say, seriously.

He starts laughing. 'Alice . . . bloody hell. No one believes in it. You don't have to leave.'

'No. I do have to leave.'

'But . . .'

I won't listen to any arguments. My mind is made up.

Ben disappears shortly afterwards to take the trays back and I am on my own again. He is gone for longer than I expect, and soon I fall asleep, dreaming of the moon.

Chapter Twenty-seven

We are going to Totnes in Esther's car. That's the plan. Other people are getting taxis. Some people are going to Newton Abbot instead, or Plymouth, or Exeter. I like the sound of Totnes.

Standing in my clothes in the bathroom feels very odd, a bit like those mornings when you find yourself robotically getting into the car at 3 a.m., washed and dressed, having set your alarm wrong, or having simply been woken by a brain that will not rest. I've been lying in bed in my pyjamas for days. That's why this now feels so odd. I do feel a lot better, though, today. For some reason, things feel different. Not just emotionally, but literally, too. It took me ages to get out of bed once I had noticed how soft my sheets actually are. Then, while I was getting dressed, I had to stop and consider every fabric I touched. The worn-out cotton of my knickers, the soft downy feeling of my vest, the thin, tissue-paper feel of my cotton top and the warm woollen texture of my blue cardigan. My skirt moves in ways I hadn't ever noticed. When it brushes against my knees, the sensation is like being licked by a cat. And thinking of cats: Atari, I will see you soon.

The plan, the plan. Do I have a plan? Well, yes. For something that arrived in such an unexpected way, spontaneous and emotional, my future feels rather well planned, actually. I will spend tomorrow sailing with the others and then on Sunday I will go home. I will say that I am sick and Georges advised me to take myself off the project. Then I will write a letter of resignation. My old editor is still a good friend, so I will see if I can't get my old crossword slot back – or maybe even some sort of Child of Mind Mangle column, although that sounds a bit like a horror film. I will clean the house and brush my cat and not be too tired to have Rachel round for dinner. I will help at the zoo again. I will cash in my PopCo shares and go travelling – there's somewhere I have wanted to go for a while. I will unlock the dusty old chest in my bedroom and get out the Voynich Manuscript. I can report back to my grandfather when we meet in my own personal heaven. Will I have much to report to my mother? Maybe not. I wonder if my father is up there somewhere, or whether he is still here on Earth. It probably doesn't matter, and I probably don't care. You're supposed to pine and ache for missing fathers but I didn't spend much time on all that. He left me when I was nine years old for some vague idea of treasure. I was over him by the time I was ten. If I did see him again, maybe I would ask him why but I doubt that his answer would make too much difference to me.

Even my hair feels different today, like child's hair, soft and delicate. *Come on, Alice, Ben will be here in a minute.* I put in my contact lenses and even the sensation of things snapping into place feels new, as if I don't have that sensation every single day. *New eyes,* I think. Perhaps today I really do have new eyes. I splash Orange Flower Water on my face and then apply a touch of tinted moisturiser, some lip balm and a tiny bit of rose-scented mascara. The hand cream that came with my remedies is smooth and cool and I rub some of it into my hands just for the feel and the smell of it. I am looking forward to some fresh air; to seeing something beyond PopCo Towers.

There's a knock at the door a couple of minutes later. When I open it, Ben's standing there with a small white package, sealed with Sellotape. It's about the size of a book.

'Here,' he says. 'This was by your door. It's for you.'

'Thanks,' I say, taking it quickly. My correspondent at last? It must be. I slip it in my canvas bag, where it sits awkwardly on the pack of nicotine gum, my tobacco (which I crave more than I can describe), my purse, my remedies, a little notebook, a pencil, a pen and my survival kit. This last gives me a pang. I won't ever present those roughs in a meeting, now. I won't ever be able to teach thousands of kids how to go out and survive in the wilderness. Then again, I could write a proper book about survival if I wanted. In fact, if I was going to write a book it could be about anything at all. Perhaps I will make the survival research into a free website for kids.

'Are you sure you're OK to come out today?' Ben asks me.

'What? Oh, yes. Of course I am. I just won't do too much walking around, probably.'

He smiles. 'I'm so glad you're feeling better.'

I smile back. 'Me too. Of course, you know what this means?'

'What?'

'Prepare to be jumped on later. That's all I'm saying.'

'Jumped on? Sounds nice.'

'Will be.' I grin at him as he pushes me against the door and kisses me hard. Even this sensation is more intense than usual. What will sex be like in this state? I almost want to ditch the excursion and stay here all day with Ben finding out. Then again, I've actually spent enough time in bed this week. Later, though. If I anticipate it all day, maybe it will be even better.

He's suddenly holding on to me like I am about to get on a train and go to war or something.

'Ben?' I say, pulling back to look at him. 'What is it?'

'Nothing. I'm going to . . . Nothing. I'll just . . . miss you. That's all.' He frowns. 'And I wanted . . .'

'What?'

He looks away from me. '*This*. I wanted this to go on for longer.'

'This . . . ?'

'For God's sake, Alice. Me and you.'

'Well, why can't it?' I say.

'Do you want that? Even after you leave this all behind?'

'The first weekend you get out of here, I will expect you at my place. How about that? I'll even cook.'

His eyes are sparkling now. 'How about this?' he says. 'Next weekend I'm going to fuck this place off, get on a train and come to see you regardless. That sound OK?'

'That sounds lovely,' I say.

'Good.'

Esther's driving is bizarre. It's like she is on a constant safari. She doesn't drive at more than about thirty-five miles an hour, which is a good thing because she doesn't ever seem to look at the road.

'Bunny rabbit,' she says, as we drive across the moors. 'Oh, look – fluffy cow! Spooky forest. Witch's house . . .'

Soon I'm doing it too. 'Little steam train line,' I say, as if we're ticking off items on a list. 'Oh – more cows. These ones don't look very happy, though . . .'

As soon as we get near Totnes, Ben says, 'Esther, earthlings!'

'Shut up, Ben,' she says.

As we enter the town, I briefly see the castle, round and grey, before we turn off to drive into a half-empty car park. I have an urge to see what it looks like from the air. Maybe I will find a post-card while I am here.

Esther is explaining the layout of Totnes.

'It's basically one long road on a hill,' she says. 'Top of town has more interesting shops, but the best health shop is at the bottom. Um . . .'

'Is there a museum?' I ask. This is a curious habit I have. If ever I visit a new place, I have to go to the museum.

'Yeah,' Esther says. 'Top of town. Well, about three-quarters of the way up the hill.'

We park and get out of the car.

'So . . .' Ben says. 'I'm going down the hill to that amazing health-food shop and then I'm on a mission to find some vegan deck shoes. Alice?'

'I'm not sure I want to walk all the way down a big hill and then back up again,' I say. 'I'm going to wander around up here a bit and maybe go to the musuem. Shall we split up and meet later for lunch?'

'Yeah,' he says. 'Shall I text you when I've finished?'

'I don't have a mobile,' I say.

'How can you not have a mobile?' Esther says.

I shrug. 'I don't like them.'

'What are you doing, Esther?' Ben says.

'I'm meeting Chloë at the bottom of town,' she says with a slight frown. 'We're having lunch.'

'Shall I just meet you somewhere up here?' I say to Ben.

'Yeah, OK,' he says. 'Shall we say . . . outside the museum at one?'

'Great,' I say.

I walk up towards the main street, passing two pubs and a fish and chip shop. After crossing a road, I feel like I have crossed over into another dimension. This is a place from books. The street is tiny, with old-looking buildings crowded on either side of it. I pass a shop selling Indian clothing and wind chimes, a health-food shop, an organic cotton shop (with an amazing soft-looking brown blanket in the window), an Oxfam, a Fairtrade clothes shop and a second-hand music and book shop. I stop by the music and book shop and go inside. I need to ask directions to the museum, and I just can't resist shops like this. With a sharp pang, I remember how my grandfather would always stop in places like this, looking for old herbals or occult books, always hoping to see a replication of a picture or a fragment from the Voynich Manuscript. The shop itself is large and airy, although almost everything in it is brown and dusty. Old cassette tapes, drums, tambourines, records, comics, books, dream-catchers, maracas. An Asian-looking woman is in an intense conversation with a dark-haired girl who is playing a haunting tune on a red acoustic guitar. The woman laughs and then the girl does too. I wander around looking at old books, remembering the time I picked up a three-volume Synthetic Repertory in a shop like this. They only wanted a fiver for it but I made them accept £20. They were connected to a charity and I couldn't rip them off too much. The set was worth over a hundred pounds.

After asking directions to the museum (around the corner and down the hill), I leave. The package in my bag is knocking around. *Open me. Open me.* But I can't open it until I am sitting down somewhere relatively private. Perhaps a quiet coffee shop? I walk on. A normal-looking hiking shop and photographic shop are huddled in amongst an ethical shoe shop, a small organic supermarket and a big, swollen coffee-shop, whose frontage takes up the whole of the large corner. I don't fancy this place but there is a sign pointing down a tiny side street. An arrow and one word: Café.

I almost miss the door. It's tiny. Inside, there is a wooden floor and a few tables, some pretty plants and a piano in the far right-hand corner. It's almost empty so I pick a table at the back and sit down. What am I going to order? I have been eating vegan food for the last few days and I do feel a compulsion to continue the experiment. Will it get boring? Will I waste away? Only time will tell. I order a black coffee and some wholemeal toast with marmalade and no butter. Then I get the package out of my bag.

It's a white padded envelope, wrapped with clear Sellotape. My name is written in inky blue capitals. Whoever sent this has cleverly or accidentally Sellotaped over my name. When I remove the Sellotape, the blue writing disappears, ripped off in a second. At least I know this hasn't been tampered with since it was sealed. Once I have eased open the flap, I reach in my hand and pull out the contents. It's a small book that I would recognise anywhere. I drop it on the table, my hand shaking. It's a 1979 Women's Press edition of *Woman on the Edge of Time*. The same copy I have at home, the one my mother left me all those years ago. Of course it's not my copy: there's no writing inside. But there is a sheet of paper, neatly folded in two.

Someone comes to the table, looking for somewhere to put down my coffee and toast. I move my bag, and the book, and mumble some sort of thanks. My hands are still shaking. Can I risk a cigarette? Maybe half of one. Maybe in a minute.

'Can I smoke in here?' I ask the guy just as he wanders off.

'Yeah, sure. I'll bring you an ashtray.'

I'm not hungry any more, but I eat the toast quickly anyway, not wanting to waste it. The coffee is strong and rough in my mouth and I take three more shaky sips before I wipe my hands on a paper napkin and reach for the book. A small, handmade ashtray appears on the table. I roll a thin cigarette, light up and cough experimentally. It feels OK – well, except for my head being almost blown off by the sudden rush of chemicals and nicotine. The room blurs and comes back into focus again. The book. I open it and take out the sheet of paper.

Here, at least, I find what I expect. A list of numbers:

263, 18; 343, 9; 363, 97; 363, 98; 325, 27; 106, 120; 300, 52; 20, 7; 71, 40; 92, 18; 151, 60; 258, 6; 71, 40; 58, 38; 104, 5; 34, 143; 342, 18; 342, 19; 342, 20.

I take out my notepad and pencil and turn to page 263 of the book. Word 18 is *don't*. Don't what? I am just turning to page 343 when the little door clatters and a bunch of PopCo people come in: Grace, Kieran, Frank, James and Violet. Shit. I quickly stick the book and the sheet of paper back in my bag before they see me. Then I make a little doodle in my notebook, as if this is what I was doing all along.

'Well, this is a nice little place,' Kieran's saying, in his loud drawl. 'Oh, look. There's what's-her-name.'

'Alice,' says Violet.

Sitting in a café on your own is always great until a group of people you know walks in. Now they've said my name, I have to look up.

'Hi,' I say.

'How's it hanging?' Kieran says. 'Are you digging this medieval town thing as much as we are?'

'Yeah, it's nice,' I say.

'We'd join you, except . . .'

'No, no. I'm just going anyway,' I say.

I gulp down the rest of my coffee and put out the cigarette. I pay at the counter and leave quickly. Where can I go to decode this message in private? I join the main street again and turn left down the hill. I walk through a tiny covered parade of shops in medieval-looking houses on one side of the street, while a busy market hisses and hums on the other side of the road. I see Boots in the distance, with no animal liberation stands outside it, nothing at all. I walk past a boring-looking bookshop with shiny, corporate bestsellers in the window, and a world music shop. There must be somewhere I can go to do this. Then I come to the small museum. *Of course.*

Feeling rather paranoid, I check I haven't been followed and then duck inside. The burble of market traders, cars, children and swishing carrier bags stops as if someone has thrown a switch. I am in a cool, silent room with a polished wooden floor and a desk on the far side. I walk over, past racks of T-shirts with pictures of the castle and the museum on them, local history books and historically inspired toys: finger puppets, cut-out dolls, the sort of things PopCo stopped making in the 80s.

'Hello,' I say to the elderly woman behind the desk. 'One adult, please.'

'Are you a resident of Totnes?'

'No,' I say, looking down at a pile of leaflets advertising some of the exhibits. I glance at the picture on the front of one of them, showing that this museum used to be a merchant's house. Inside, there is information about current exhibits. There's a Victorian apothecary display, a historical costume display and – what's this? – the Charles Babbage Room? This is too weird. Why would they have a Charles Babbage room here? He worked in London, I know that. It was from London that he waged his relentless campaign to ban organ grinders and street musicians. I shake my head the way you do when you are trying to shake dreams and illusions away, and look again. *Charles Babbage Room*, it still says.

'That's £1.60,' the woman says.

I get out the change. 'I'm interested in the Charles Babbage Room,' I say.

'Oh yes,' she says. 'It's the room at the top of the house. History of computing. Very popular. It's those stairs there that you want.'

The wooden stairs creak as I walk up them. Are there any other people in the whole museum? It doesn't sound like it. I pass one floor, then another, going, I think, forwards in time the higher I climb. There are nooks and crannies and I can see rooms with sloping floors, a sign to the apothecary display and various snatches of period costumes. When I reach the top floor, I am actually awed and almost frightened by the silence and stillness here. There's a sign. *Charles Babbage Room*. I go in. And there, in the corner of the room, is Babbage himself, sitting at the desk.

'Oh my God,' I yelp, springing back.

If he looks up at me I will die on the spot. I will die. I look back. Nothing happens. I look again. It's a life-size model, posed at the desk like a waxwork. Who would do that? This is one of the scariest things I have ever seen. He's so . . . real. I'm sure his plastic eyes follow me as I walk around the room, looking at pictures of models of the Difference Engine and plans for the Analytical Engine (the real ones are in museums in London). I discover that Babbage was born here and has had a road on a local industrial estate named after him. I look at displays about the history of computing; a frieze about Babbage's life. In a glass display case, there are little ZX Spectrums and a BBC Microcomputer that look almost as old as the Difference Engine.

On the far wall there is a portrait of Ada Lovelace. I go and look at it. *Ada Lovelace, daughter of Lord Byron*, a caption says. A printed sheet tells me things I already know: her mother didn't want her daughter tainted by poetry the way her father had been, so had her schooled in mathematics and science instead. In 1843, Ada married the Earl of Lovelace. When she translated an Italian summary of Babbage's plans for the new Analytical Engine, Babbage suggested she add her own notes. These notes turned out to be three times the length of the original article. Ada and Charles continued to correspond. Ada wrote an article that was published in 1843. In it, she predicted that the Analytical Machine could be used to compose complex music, to produce graphics, and for both artistic and scientific endeavours. Her predictions turned out to be correct. She was my grandmother's heroine.

No one is coming, Alice. Relax. Can I do the decode here? Is anyone else going to come and look at Babbage? I suppose I will hear the creaking steps if anyone does come. I work out that I will have at least a minute-and-a-half's warning of anyone coming up here, and slip down on the floor under the picture of Ada Lovelace, my legs crossed on the hard wooden floorboards, my bag by my side, ready to abort this mission if need be.

Don't. That's the first word. OK. I flick to page 343 of the book. The 9th word is either 'go' or 'to', depending on whether my correspondent has counted a hyphenated construction (self-educated) as one word or two. *Don't to.* Well, that doesn't make sense. *Don't go* . . . Bloody hell. Who has sent me this? The next two numbers are similar: 363, 97 and 363, 98. Two words together. I flip to page 363 and count words. Word 97 is 'fight' and word 98 is 'back'. *Fight back.*

I sit there counting words for the next ten or so minutes until I have the following: *Don't go fight back struggle against corporate enemy meet in your room to night at eight it's a war.* Bloody hell. Refusing for a moment to actually digest the meaning of this, I suddenly think of Francis Stevenson, and the mystery text he used to code his treasure map. I remember my grandfather explaining that you always have to think about what sort of books would contain the right words to create a particular kind of message. I look at the language of this one. Fight, enemy, corporate, war, struggle. You wouldn't find any of those words in the horse book I sent. I smile at the broken-up nature of the word 'tonight', written as two words in the message. You wouldn't think so, but sometimes it's hard to find a simple word like *tonight* in even a long text. *Woman on the Edge of Time* is written in the past tense, which means that you would only find a present-tense word like 'tonight' in a piece of speech.

But maybe none of this matters right now. I read the message again, inserting my own punctuation. *Don't go. Fight back. Struggle against corporate enemy. Meet in your room tonight at eight. It's a war.* Who is this from? What is going on? And then it hits me. I didn't think the enemy existed. Then I realised it was me. Then I decided to desert. Now – is this possible? – I am about to find out that there is another side. I suppose there has to be, if there is an enemy. My mind is running the tape of the last couple of weeks again, like a password-descrambler checking every letter in every space to see what fits. I can almost hear the click, click, click as faces, coincidences, events fall into place. And, suddenly, I think I can make a pretty good guess about who will be coming to my room tonight. It's like playing Cluedo, really.

There's a sound, like marbles falling onto concrete, and the patch of sunlight in the room suddenly disappears as if it was a rug that someone had simply pulled away and rolled up. It's funny how dark it is in here now that the sunlight has gone. I shiver. It's cold, suddenly, too. Babbage's eyes still seem to follow me as I get up and go to the window. Hailstones as big as gobstoppers are falling from the sky. I stand in the chilly, dark silence in here and watch as people outside duck into shops and doorways or open their just-in-case umbrellas. One man runs down the suddenly deserted pavement with a supermarket carrier bag over his head. A smell of wet leaves comes through the window.

Change the world. Has my mother been time travelling again? Has she violated some cosmic law to send me this book with this new message? Do I believe in coincidence? Do I believe in synchronicity? *Stop it, Alice.* Hail beats against the window and outside, people are still huddled in doorways, looking at the sky. I remember thinking I had encountered a huge coincidence once, when looking up a word in a dictionary. Usually, it takes me ages to find the right page but once, just once, I picked up the dictionary and opened it to the correct page immediately. *Amazing*, I thought. Then I worked out that, since I have been using dictionaries all my life, the probability is that this would have to happen at some point. There's what, a thousand pages in a dictionary? When you open it, there's therefore a 1/1000 chance you will open it on the page that contains the word you are looking for. These odds are greatly reduced by the fact that people don't open dictionaries randomly: they aim to open it as close to the word they want as possible. If you are searching for a word beginning with 'C', you don't open the dictionary at the end, you open it fairly close to the beginning, where you guess the 'C' section might be. It is likely then that you will hit the correct page more than once in a lifetime, especially if you use a dictionary a lot (although it could, of course, happen the first time you ever use one).

Probability – remember – also proves that, if you get twenty-three people in the same room, you will have a 50 per cent chance of finding that two of them share the same birthday. Probability is a funny thing, something that humans don't intuitively understand. We declare as coincidence events which aren't actually that unlikely, mathematically. It's like the story of Marilyn vos Savant and the Monty Hall Problem. *Of course* you have a greater chance of winning the car if you swap doors. There was a two in three chance you made the wrong choice in the first place, so you should definitely swap. But, when Marilyn vos Savant said this, even Erdös was convinced she must be wrong. But she wasn't. She got hate mail from male mathematicians saying she was wrong, but she wasn't.

So, you've picked one of three doors. You've been shown a goat. Do you change doors? You've chosen a life that seemed to make sense. But there are two other options. One is, perhaps, a goat. One is a mystery. Do you open the mystery door? Do you abandon the game and (metaphorically) embrace the goat? What's wrong with goats anyway? I'd actually rather have a goat than a car. I already have a car, but I do not own a lawnmower.

Or perhaps there are two boxes, A and B. Box A contains £1000. Box B is either empty or contains a million pounds . . .

I pick up my bag from the floor.

'What would you have made of Newcomb's Paradox?' I whisper to Charles Babbage. 'What would you have chosen?'

I smile, then turn and walk towards the door.

'*Choose Box B*,' says a deep male voice.

Babbage? I turn around but the dummy is still and lifeless. My heart is a fish trying to escape from a hook as I run, clattering, all the way downstairs.

'Goodness me,' says the woman at the desk as I fly past her.

'Sorry,' I call back. 'I'm late . . .'

Out in the street, the hailstones have stopped falling and people are wandering about again, their shoes and trainers and boots scuffing up dirty bits of sleet, little puddles forming between cobblestones. I look at the town clock and see that it is half-past twelve. I cross the road and walk back up to the funny little parade of shops on what I now see is called the Butterwalk. One is a health-food shop and I duck into it and buy a huge bottle of Echinacea tincture on PopCo expenses. It's quite crowded inside and I end up standing in the queue for ages next to a noticeboard covered with business cards. *Personal Journeys, Yoga for Health, Reiki, The Individual and the Spirit, Reflexology, Colour-therapy, Psychic Healing, Chanting Workshop, Jungian Therapy, Psychodynamic Counselling, Hypnotherapy, Hypnobirthing, Womb Chanting, Qigong, Crystal Healing* . . . Each card has a mobile phone number on it and for a second I am reminded of prostitutes' cards in London call boxes. Eventually I get to the front of the queue and pay for my Echinacea.

I go next door, into a funny little department store. It smells of leather, a smell which follows me through into a small womenswear department, all floaty scarves, incense and 'handmade' Indian tops. Then I walk into the footwear department and up the stairs. At the front of the first floor (and this is the reason I came in here at all, because I saw it in the window) is a large rocking horse, with tradi-tional toys displayed all around it. I touch its mane, thinking about how much I wanted a rocking horse when I was about five. I'm not convinced about the rest of this shop but up here it's nice. There are wooden toys, building blocks, sharing toys, caring toys. There are wooden train sets and farmyard animals and fairy costumes. There are no big brand names, no guns, no electronics, just simple, well-made toys. I touch the silky outsides of juggling balls. I look at glass marbles, pick-up-sticks and rainy-day cricket sets. I see something that partly inspired the bead/necklace idea I will never develop, something you see in a lot of department stores: little pick-and-mix beads and strings so you can spell out your name on a necklace or a bracelet. I smile. Yes: this is nice.

I walk around to another display. Oh no. Something I recognise. A cardboard stand with smudgy, child's-finger-painting-style images of two children. One is a yellow smudge with brown plaits and a red hat. The other is a pale green smudge with yellow-smudge hair sticking out at all angles. *Milly and Bo*, a sign says. But I already know Milly and Bo. On the shelves by the cardboard stand are various Milly and Bo products: a fire-fighter's uniform for Milly. A nurse's outfit for Bo. A Milly and Bo doll's house which has solar panels, a composter and encourages equal gender roles. Although there is no sign anywhere and no familiar sailboat logo, Milly and Bo is a brand made by PopCo.

I feel sick. But why? What's wrong with the fact that PopCo makes and sells nice politically correct toys? What's wrong with this little department store selling this range alongside small, non-corporate brands? Well . . . What's wrong is that PopCo haven't got their logo here anywhere. This is yet more mirror-branding. This means that parents can buy these products without ever realising that they are lining the pockets of the third richest toy corporation in the world. What's wrong is that everyone in the industry knows that PopCo ripped this idea off from a small co-operative toy company based in Scotland called Daisy, who couldn't match PopCo's distribution or afford to sue. What's wrong is that PopCo really don't care what they make as long at it sells. I rip open the plastic package containing one of the male nurse uniforms and check the label. *Made in China*, it says. Did someone lose a limb so that middle-class children could experiment with gender roles? How nice that in this country we are on to messing around with gender roles while in so many foreign-owned factories it's still impossible to form a union and get fair pay, whether you are a man, woman or child.

Children who make footballs in factories, or stitch trainers and sweatbands and purses for us . . . they won't ever play with toys like these. They will make them but never play with them. I reach into the packet I have just opened and feel for a seam. Once I have located it, I rip it all the way down. Then I leave the packet open. There. That's one unit PopCo won't be making a profit on.

I leave the shop and cross over the road again and head for the museum to meet Ben. I feel this stupid glow inside – something I have only felt once before in my life, after I played a prank on a maths teacher who humiliated me. I have cost PopCo one unit of stock. I have not hurt any animals today. It's not much but it's more than I was doing before.

Later, when we drive back to Dartmoor, the sky is a dusky blue, with an almost full moon punched in it like a hole.

'Bats,' Esther says, as soon as we leave town. 'Look.' But I am still looking at the sky.

It was a Sunday evening, almost a year ago, when I began finally to let my grandfather go. I was driving back from Cambridge to London, having just broken up with this guy called Paul who I'd been seeing for a few weeks. The relationship was never going to work out. For one thing, it kept taking me back to Cambridge, a place I didn't want to be: a place buttered with memories like the crumpets I used to eat in my grandparents' garden. For another thing, I had this problem, this inability to feel anything at all. I had even argued with Rachel over it.

Paul was an artist/art director who had come into the Battersea offices to get some props for an ad he was doing for one of our products (I forget which one). A couple of after-work drinks had turned into sex at my house, after which he told me that he wasn't planning to come back to London for a while, and asked me to spend the next weekend with him in Cambridge. Although my mind was still foggy with loss, and generally over-stimulated from work, it was a fun-ish weekend. He had three flatmates who all looked alike and were the sort of people who were 'up for anything'. I'd taken a prototype of a board game and we all played it together, shouting like we'd known each other for ages. At the time I was much better in company than alone, although the rainbow of my possible moods/emotions/feelings had merged into a dirty brown mess in my mind and I just couldn't bring myself to feel anything for Paul. On the third weekend he said he was falling in love with me. On the fourth, I drove there to tell him I wouldn't be coming back. I couldn't tell him why. I just sat there spewing clichés and thinking, *Actually, this stuff makes sense.* It really is me and not you. I really don't know why.

I never drive back from Cambridge on the motorway (which comes out in north London eventually) but always on the back roads, with hedges and scenery and occasionally wild animals. It was mid-July and the days were still long. I'd eventually said my final goodbye to Paul at around ten o'clock and then hit the road, quite fast, still not really caring about anything very much. As I was driving up a steep hill, with fields on either side, I suddenly became aware of a strip, like a ribbon, of pale blue light on the horizon. At first I didn't know what it was. Then I realised that this was the last part of sky that hadn't yet been taken by the already impressive sunset: a baby blue sliver of day, which I could only just glimpse through the trees. At one point, when there were no trees, I saw it span the whole horizon; the day dying before my eyes, with blood everywhere. Then a hedge obscured it and the whole, tantalising scene was just gone.

Higher ground. I had to get to higher ground. Instead of taking my usual turn-off, a downhill section like driving into the centre of a very deep bowl, I turned off randomly, pushing the car upwards, further, trying to find a place to look down on the dying sky. I had to see it; all of it. For some reason nothing else mattered and I raced against the clock to get up the hill before night-time reached critical mass and the sunset was gone. Finally I found the perfect viewing spot: an abandoned, darkened shell of an old burnt-out petrol station. Switching off my car headlights made all the difference. The sunset now spanned the entire horizon in front of me: miles and miles of sky. Behind me, it was already night-time. But I was like a furtive god up there, surveying the last long sliver of the day, still with its afternoon-blue set beneath not just oranges and reds but grey, black, purple: all these swatches of sky bruising and smearing together. You couldn't draw this. You couldn't capture any of this in a photograph. I had never even seen anything like this in my life. This was the sky ripped in two with its insides spilling out. Black silhouettes of trees and houses looked like burnt-out ruins set against the bright mess in the sky. I realised that I was actually sitting in a real burnt-out ruin, randomly, on my own, with no family left in the whole world. I started to cry.

And it all made sense. The world was beautiful, even if people you loved died. In fact, if this sky was a kind of death, then maybe it wasn't so bad. Was heaven in there somewhere, behind all those colours? This sky made me believe, for the first time, in heaven. It made me believe in heaven and ghosts and the afterlife in a way I had never imagined I could or would. This wasn't an intellectual belief, with empirical proof or rational argument. This was a feeling of miracles and love and a vast, infinite future. This was a sky from fiction, and I believed in it, then. I believed in it all. If this was nature, then maybe nature was all right. Maybe death was as natural as this sky. And suddenly I didn't need that brown veil any more. All I felt was hope; and the loss I felt about my grandfather's death seemed to bleed away with the remains of the sky until I was sitting there in complete darkness with my face wet, unable to move.

Chapter Twenty-eight

It's 7:58 and my mind is running at 100 per cent processing power, my heart pumping blood around my body at what feels like three times the normal speed. Ben has gone. I've tidied up. I've had a cigarette. I've smoothed down my skirt and looked at myself in the mirror. What did I see in the mirror? A twenty-nine-year-old woman with schoolgirl plaits, shiny lips and understated eye make-up. What else did I see? A lonely child? A confused adult? Who am I today? What is this war in which I am being enlisted? Do I even want to join up? *Choose Box B.* Even the ghost of Charles Babbage seems to know more about my life than I do.

War thoughts again. I think back to the business cards from that health shop earlier on. I think about the miniature wars that individuals fight all the time. They fight against cellulite, or negative emotions, or addictions, or stress. I think about how we can now hire all different sorts of mercenaries to help us fight against ourselves . . . Therapists, manicurists, hairdressers, personal trainers, life coaches. But what's it all for? What do all these little wars achieve? Although it is part of my life too, and I want to be thin and pretty and not laughed at in the street and not so stressed and mad that I start screaming on the tube, it suddenly seems a little bit ridiculous. All the time we do these things we are trying to enlist ourselves into a bigger war. We are trying to join up, constantly, with the enemy. It's the enemy voice in your ear that tells you your kitchen is too untidy, or your bathroom does not sparkle; that your hair isn't shiny enough, your legs not thin enough, your address book not bulging enough, your clothes not cool enough. My grandparents did not collaborate. So how did I slip so easily over to the other side? Perhaps it was because no one told me that anyone was even at war.

Hitler tried to impose his shiny, blonde, neat, sparkling world on us all and we resisted. So how is it that when McDonald's and Disney and The Gap and L'Oréal and all the others try to do the same thing we all just say, 'OK'? Hitler needed marketing, that's all. His propaganda was, of course, brilliant for its time, everyone knows that. What a great idea, to make people feel that they belong to something, that their identity makes them special. If Hitler had been able to enlist a twenty-first-century marketing department, would he have been able to sell Nazism to everyone? Why not? You can just see a beautiful, thin woman with her long blonde hair moving softly in the breeze, and the tagline 'Because I'm worth it'. I am worth it. *Me*. I am worth the lives of others.

There's a knock at the door. I gulp. As I open it, I expect to find a group of people standing there (including Ben). But there's only one person at my door. It's Chloë.

'Hello,' I say.

'You got my note?'

'Yes,' I say. And then: 'I was expecting you.'

She comes in and sits down. 'You knew it was me?'

I smile. 'You're the one who seems to tell everyone off when they step out of line.'

She laughs. 'Yeah, it's been a bit weird having a group of us together all at once here, in this situation. I hope it hasn't been too obvious. Maybe you're just very observant. I would have thought you would be, with your background.'

I blink slowly. 'You know my background.'

'Yes.'

I pause for a moment, the minor notes of Chloë's voice like a memory of a haunting folk song in my ears. She isn't saying anything else. It's as if she's waiting for me to ask more questions. And I have plenty of those.

'Why?' I say. ' Who are you? What's this war? I don't . . .'

She nods. 'You don't understand.'

'No.'

I'm sitting on the bed, with my legs folded underneath me. Chloë's on the chair. She sighs, stands up and walks over to the door. She opens it and looks out. Then she closes it and walks back over to the chair.

'We can't talk much here,' she says. 'What's on either side of you?'

'The kitchen is on that side,' I point. 'And a cupboard on that side. It's pretty safe to talk in here.' I suddenly think about the wires in the walls. Paranoia, paranoia. Still, I reach up and switch the radio on quite loud. 'If we talk quietly we should be OK,' I say.

I haven't retuned the radio since Ben set it to Zion Radio. I worry for a moment that it never existed, and that all I'll find now is static, but when I switch it on I instantly hear the sound of a guitar feeding back and then the woman's voice. I hear the words *Slitscan* and *Laney. Idoru*, I think.

Chloë laughs gently. 'I hoped you'd be like this,' she says softly. 'But we just didn't know . . .'

'Who is "we"?' I say. 'You're some sort of anti-PopCo thing, I guessed that. But . . . How do you know my background? Why the coded notes?'

'OK.' Chloë looks around and then half-sits on the chair again. 'This has been hard. We badly wanted to recruit you but we didn't know how. Until yesterday, you were a bit of a mystery to us.'

I'm still confused. 'Who's "us"?'

'I'll tell you in a moment. I'm . . . I'm new to this, or at least to doing things in this way. I suspect you could probably teach me more.' She looks at the radio, burbling away. 'It's a kind of paradox, like those puzzles we were doing last week. We decided we wanted to recruit you to help us, but we weren't sure you would actually want to join us. We can't afford to compromise the secrecy of what we are doing so we couldn't ask you outright. But, without asking you outright we could never work out whether you would want to join us.' She laughs again. 'OK, I'm talking like a spy thriller now. It was only when we heard that you were leaving PopCo that I felt bold enough to send such an obvious message. But even now I am nervous about telling you more. I want to say, "This is what we're for! Are you with us?" but I am scared that if I do, you will tell someone else.'

'Who would I tell?' I say.

She raises her eyebrows. 'Georges?'

'Georges?' I'm fiddling with the end of one of my plaits but now I let go. Shit. 'How . . . ?'

'How do we know about you and Georges?' She looks at her hands, a little embarrassed. 'Hmm. Yes. He sent an e-mail to a friend about you. He said, "What do you do if you are falling in love with a creative? Do you have to sack them before you make a move?" Then it said something like, "Find out some stuff for me." Then he gave your name. Bit of a stupid thing to send as an e-mail actually, if you're Georges.' She looks at me. 'A bit of a heartbreaker, aren't you?'

I feel sick. 'Does Ben know?'

'No.'

'Will you tell him?'

'No. But we were – are – concerned at your closeness to the PopCo Board. Trying to recruit you directly seemed like it would be too risky. We had to try to find out if you really were Little Miss Corporate or not.'

'So . . .' Shit. It's falling into place now. 'So you sent Ben to spy on me?'

She laughs. 'No, Alice. We sent Esther. Whatever is between you and Ben is entirely natural.' She laughs again. 'Well, I don't know about natural, exactly – I know Ben – but it's your thing. No one sent Ben to you.'

'But Esther . . . ?' I thought Esther was my friend.

'Esther refused to play along, actually. She said she didn't want to compromise her friendship with you. She never follows instructions. Her latest thing is she refuses to lie . . . I don't know what I am going to do about Esther, actually. Anyway, I believe you had one conversation where she talked about how much she hates the PopCo Board. After that she refused to do any more. But we still didn't know where you were on the whole PopCo thing. I mean, Christ . . . On file you're a model employee.'

I think about this and nod. 'Yes. On file, I probably am.'

Chloë smiles and shakes her head gently. I notice she is still wearing those earrings with brown feathers on them that almost seem part of her hair. I don't think the feathers are real, though. I wonder what they are made of.

'You haven't done anything rebellious at all,' she says.

'Haven't I?' I think back to earlier on today; the feeling of that seam splitting against my fingers. I look at Chloë, sitting on the chair. I wonder what she sees when she looks at me. Is it just that: *model employee*?

'The only good sign was that you didn't seem to tell anyone about the messages you received,' she says.

I smile now. 'They were pretty strange messages.'

Chloë smiles back and pushes her hair behind her ears.

'Sorry,' she says. 'I'm new to this.'

'Why did you send the one that said, "Are you happy"? I couldn't work that out.'

'I wanted to contact you but I was scared to say anything that would compromise the group . . . Once I'd sent the first message, I needed to follow it up to keep the communication going but I didn't know what to say. I decided to send that and see if you told anyone. Do you mind if I smoke?' she asks.

'Go ahead,' I say, reaching for my bag. I pull out tobacco and papers and roll one up myself. 'Chloë?'

She looks up at me. 'Yes?'

'Not only did I not tell anyone about the messages, I carefully burnt them all, and the keys I made for the decodes. I once kept a secret for over twenty years. Why don't you just tell me what's going on? Look at what you've already got on me. You could tell Ben about Georges if you wanted. You could tell everyone about Georges. Hey – I fiddle my expenses. You could tell them that, too.'

'We all fiddle our expenses,' she says, blowing smoke out into the room. 'And you are leaving, so maybe you wouldn't care if they know all that stuff . . .'

'I'm not leaving Ben.'

'No.' She frowns. 'No, I suppose not.'

This feels like being eleven again. I am offering her the equivalent of 'I kissed Georges' in return for whatever she has to tell me. The thing is, I suspect that what she has got to tell me is much bigger than that. If I was her, would I tell me? Definitely not.

'Look,' I say, suddenly. 'If you don't want to tell me, then don't. But since it is what you came here to do, maybe you should just get it over with. I really won't tell anyone, even if I disagree with you. Unless . . . OK, if I am honest, I do have to say that if I think what you're doing is morally wrong, like if what you're doing hurts animals or children, then I probably would tell someone. But I doubt that will be the case.'

She sighs. 'Yeah, we're pretty much the opposite of that. And you have just said exactly the right thing . . .'

The key to the door, I think.

She reaches for the ashtray. 'We're called NoCo,' she says. She sighs again, as if realising that she has entered a one-way function, and starts talking softly as the music on the radio changes to more Bach, with more *Idoru*. 'We're a resistance organisation, which I think you guessed. We are resisting a world in which CEOs like Mac and all the others earn millions a year while the people who make the products for them to sell are on starvation wages. We are resisting a world in which people like us are employed to mislead people into buying things they don't need.'

I smile at Chloë. 'I agree with all that so far,' I say.

'It's particularly interesting being based in a toy company,' she says. 'All the bitter ironies are so much clearer here. You think about childhood, and what it is, and it is all lies and contradictions. Mummy or Daddy sits there in their leather shoes going "Moo cow" while you look at pretty pictures of cows in a field. You don't make the connection with "Moo cow" a couple of years later when you're begging for your Happy Meal. Moo cow is one thing and a beefburger is another. We don't always know it, but the job of people like us is to keep those two ideas separate so we can sell Moo cow books and Happy Meal toys at the same time. We can sell Finbar's Friends to happy suburban kids who are able to think of toys as something Santa makes, not third-world slaves. We can sell them fluffy animals that they curl up with in bed. How odd that a Western child's source of comfort is such a potent symbol of misery and oppression. We can sell animals as long as they are pretend. The animals will be loved as long as they remain *pretend*. We sell the sort of attachment to objects and sentimentalism that means that a kid will run back into a burning house to rescue a toy rabbit, but Dad won't swerve in the car to avoid a real one. That is the real power of brands, when you think about it. One rabbit has a label on its arse, another one doesn't. You can love the one with the label and everyone accepts that. Risk your life for a real animal and people say you're mad.'

She puts her cigarette out in the ashtray and then I do the same thing. Finding my hands suddenly inactive, I fiddle with a tassel from the blanket on the bed without looking at it.

'Ben made me think a lot about animals and what we do to them,' I say. 'It's funny when you think about all the things we consume and why.'

'A lot of the NoCo people are drawn to the animal-rights side of things,' she says. 'It seems to come naturally. I tend to emphasise human rights more, although the two are very much connected. An animal has a right to live in peace just as a human has a right to the same. I always think that humans are doubly betrayed because you can lie to people, and make them hurt or disappointed as well as exploiting them. But then some people argue that people can at least take up arms and struggle against oppression, which animals can't do. Still, I think if I had to pin down what NoCo is all about, it is about stopping the lies and telling the truth instead.'

Chloë leans back in the chair, then draws her legs up and crosses them. I've noticed that she doesn't move around a lot when she is talking; she doesn't gesticulate. She says and does everything slowly and gently. She goes on. 'We all remember the point when we first found out that Santa isn't real, or that meat is dead animal, or that Mummy and Daddy had to have sex to make you, or that when you buy something in a shop for £4.99 it probably cost something like a penny to make.' She smiles at me. 'You know when you're a kid, and you suddenly find out all this stuff . . . You go a little bit mad for a while. Then you grow up and you find out that there's another level of lies that you hadn't spotted. You realise that if somcone invites you to come in for coffee they actually want to have sex with you; that the advertisement that suggests you will be beautiful and thin if you use a certain shampoo is not true; that

'Stupidly Low Prices', when you go into the shop, doesn't mean that at all; that the guy who e-mails you, saying he will give you a share of a few million pounds, is lying; and whenever you see something advertised as 'free' it just isn't. You just think, "God, I've been conned again," and you eventually get used to it.'

I start unravelling the tassel in my fingers, thinking about lies.

'My favourites are those job ads that say No Selling Involved,' I say. 'You go for the interview and find that, no, you're not actually selling the double glazing, you are merely "making an appointment" for a salesperson to call round.'

'I know! If you stop and look around,' Chloë says, 'you see that we have decorated our world with lies. Every billboard, every shop front, every newspaper and magazine. Everyone knows that advertisements are a form of "lie", but they can live with that. At the end of the day it's maybe just a kind of fantasy contract. The advertiser tells you that having a certain car will make you seem sophisticated and sexy, or frivolous and fun, and then you can buy whichever car matches your image, knowing that all your friends will have seen the same adverts as you and understand the 'code' – they will read the car like it was part of your barcode of identity. Many people actually enjoy this part of consumerism and, well, while it's not what I would have in my own personal Utopia, that's fine, up to a point.

'The trouble is that while a lot of these lies are fun – for some people, anyway – this culture of lying means that some truly evil people can get away with horrible things and tell lies about it which people do not question. Sportswear manufacturers tell people that they do not use sweatshops and people think, "Whew, I can carry on buying my favourite trainers with a clear conscience." But it's just not true. They do use them, but because they are subcontracted they don't take any responsibility for them. Everyone seems to have their own fairy-tale version of how milk is produced, I've noticed. I know someone who thinks that we breed cows to produce milk without the cows ever being pregnant. I know someone else who thinks that cows carry on producing milk after the calf has been weaned and that's how we get our milk. They don't know that cows are forced to be pregnant year after year and their calves are taken away and killed, in terrible pain, screaming, so that we can steal milk that's still being produced for them . . .'

'You don't have to say any more,' I say, quickly, feeling sick. 'I gave up milk myself when I worked that out . . . I just can't deal with the details of it all. It's so horrible . . .' I think about toy farm-yard animals again. Is it any wonder people don't think that bad things happen to farm animals, when everyone grew up with these toys?

'That's very similar to the attitude you get when you talk to people on the streets,' Chloë says. 'I do understand it. Of course no one wants to hear about what they do to calves. No one wants to hear the word 'screaming' in relation to their milkshake or their pork chop. I'm terrible for this, actually. I always feel really guilty about upsetting people. I almost don't want to tell them this stuff, you know? Sometimes when people find out you don't drink milk, they say, "But it's natural and lovely and people have drunk milk for ever . . . ", and so you go, "Well, I could tell you about how milk is really produced", and, nine times out of ten, they will hold up their hands and go, "No, thanks". No one wants to know. A lot of people have a vague idea that horrible stuff goes on, but they decide not to find out about it. We all grew up seeing pictures of starving children on the news every night. We turned into the gener-ation that will not look, that changes the channel, that shuts its eyes. You switch on the TV when you're, like, ten years old, and there's a kids' TV presenter showing you pictures of a famine and saying, "So, kids, what are you going to do about it?" Who can deal with that? Then again, a lot of people did help because they saw those pictures . . . I think what I am trying to say is that a lot of people out there just can't cope with the pain and suffering in the world. They understand that they inflict a lot of it – by voting in governments that go to war for the oil, or by buying clothes stitched in appalling conditions, or eating animals that died in pain – but they also know that if they didn't vote, governments would still get in, and if they didn't buy those products, everyone else would. It's almost logical to do nothing.'

I remember when the Ethiopian famine was headline news. I never saw those reports on TV, of course, but I did see my grand-father's newspaper. I remember the popular kids at school being divided on this issue. Half of them started going around with sponsor forms all the time but the rest just constantly made Ethiopian jokes. Can you turn something like that into a joke if it's that far away?

Is that what enabled them to do it? I think about what Chloë has just said. Yes, as an individual it is logical to do nothing, in a way. That's what I've spent most of my life doing. That was my excuse before.

'So you try to persuade them otherwise?' I say. 'By taking to the streets?'

'No,' she says. 'I gave up pounding the streets years ago.'

'But I thought . . . Isn't that what NoCo does, in some form?'

'NoCo? God, no,' she says. 'NoCo has another agenda altogether. We want to bankrupt the fucking corporations. That's what NoCo is all about. The days of talking to middle-class women in the streets are over. Like I said, this is a war.'

I can't help it. I'm thrilled. 'But how?' I feel my eyes sparkle as I look at Chloë.

She tucks her hair behind her ears again. 'Do you agree with our aims so far?' she says, seriously.

'I think so,' I say. 'A lot of what you have said . . . They're things I think anyway. I can see all the ironies, especially working here. Although, I must admit, it's taken this experience – being here with all the seminars and the creepy teenage-girl stuff – to make me realise a lot of it. I'm probably a bit like what you said. I kind of knew all this stuff but I looked away because I didn't think there was anything I could do about it. Look, do you want a coffee?' I am suddenly desperate for some coffee. I need my brain to be able to keep up with this.

'I'll get it,' Chloë says.

'OK, thanks.'

'Sugar?'

'No.'

While she's gone, four words play again and again in my head. *Bankrupt the fucking corporations. Bankrupt the fucking corporations. Bankrupt the fucking corporations.* Bloody hell. She is back pretty quickly, holding two big mugs of coffee. I have a lot of questions but she starts talking again as soon as she sits down.

'NoCo is a global organisation,' she says, in a low voice. 'We have people in almost every country, in many big corporations. We have three basic mottoes: *Do No Harm, Stop Others Doing Harm* and *Do What You Can.* Do No Harm is what we try to achieve in our personal lives but it's also the overall aim of our organisation. In order to achieve this, we have to Stop Others Doing Harm. We want business to conduct its affairs without exploitation, murder and violence. We all try to throw a spanner in the works of those companies that persist in doing harm. We are pacifists, and some, although not a majority of us, are Marxists.'

'I didn't think there were any Marxists left,' I say, sipping my hot black coffee. 'Isn't the general line on Marxism just that it "didn't work"?'

'What, because of the Russians? The Chinese?' She laughs, then sips her coffee, too. 'It's a bit complicated. I suspect there were some real Marxists in there somewhere, a bit like there are some Christians in the Church of England. But I don't know. I'm not a Marxist myself. I think most of us in NoCo just basically believe in equality – real equality. But not the American Dream version, that says that you can do whatever you want to make a profit, as if making a profit should be the priority in everyone's life . . .'

I frown. 'Of course, not everyone can have "make a profit" as their goal in life,' I say. 'If you are selling, rather than buying, labour, you have to operate on a loss. If you don't sell your labour for less than it is worth, then there's no profit margin.' The mathematics of exploitation.

'Now you sound like a Marxist,' Chloë says, with a smile.

'Oh, I was brought up by my grandparents,' I say. 'They were post-war socialists. They believed in equality, and the welfare state, and trade unions. I don't know what they'd make of the world today. It's changed so fast. My grandfather believed that everyone's labour should be worth the same amount. That everyone in the world should have the same hourly rate for work.'

'I like that idea,' Chloë says, enthusiastically. She sips her coffee again; little sips because it's still hot. 'OK, where was I? Oh, yes. *Stop Others Doing Harm.* We believe that it should be globally illegal to hurt or kill people or animals for profit. We don't know how this would be achieved, but it's not up to us. It's really up to the next generation, or the one after that. We just want to stop what's happening now. As for the No Harm policy in our private lives . . .'

'Everyone seems to be vegan,' I say. 'I noticed that.'

'Yes,' Chloë says. 'It's difficult in a situation like this where there are a lot of us together. Various people have spotted all the vegans, and we were worried that it might be, you know, commented upon more strongly. I was particularly worried that if anyone from the PopCo Board spotted us they might suspect that we were NoCo people – a lot of the corporations do know we exist, of course. Mind you, half of the other people here are on Atkins, or some other mad diet, so you can sort of blend in. I think we've got away with it, anyway.'

'Are all NoCo members vegan?' I ask.

'Not all. We ask that when people join they make some lifestyle sacrifices. Meat eaters become vegetarian. Vegetarians are encouraged to become vegans. We try to reduce consumerism in our own lives. We agree to practise Do No Harm but within the realities of the third motto: Do What You Can. No one in NoCo has to become a monk. Loads of us smoke, although NoCo is very much against the tobacco industry, for example.'

I remember what Ben said. *You do what you can do.*

'It's weird, though,' Chloë says. 'Once you start practising Do No Harm, you can end up looking very odd. Most high-street or cutting-edge fashion – especially the kind of stuff people at PopCo wear – is all sweatshop-made. I mean, that's why there's so much choice now, so much more than when we were kids. They can afford to churn out every style because it's costing nothing to make. Those of us in NoCo will be more likely to reject that kind of thing and go to charity shops instead. But if we're not careful it's possible for us to end up as an army of vegans who look like 80s students lurking around in corporations trying to sabotage everything.' She laughs. 'You'd pick one of us out in a crowd, easy. So every month, when I get my communications pack through, it includes lots of hints and tips on, for example, clothes you can buy that are cruelty-free but still cool, or up-to-date lists of vegan items from the menus of all the main restaurants in each city where lots of NoCo people are based. So you don't have to keep asking, if you're out for lunch with a client or something. You don't have to seem weird even though, of course, you are. I've heard that there are a few NoCo chefs who specifically put vegan food on their menus and then tell us about it. I also disseminate information on box schemes and places you can buy ethical vegan products out of normal hours. We all stay in our offices so long that we are virtually forced into supermarkets. We also have lots of tips on how to Do No Harm in the supermarket if you do have to go. And a bit of sabotage, of course.'

'Wow,' I say, my eyes wide. 'Bloody hell.'

'We wondered about you, you know,' Chloë says, shaking her head. 'You carry a flask around with you, and a transistor radio, and you wear very odd – nice, but very odd – clothes. We were thinking that maybe you were already a NoCo member that we didn't know about, and you were doing a really bad job of covering it up. Then we found out you'd been shagging Georges. It was all very confusing.'

I blush. 'I never slept with him,' I say.

'Sorry,' Chloë says. 'Getting carried away.'

'It's OK. So what do NoCo members actually do?' I ask. 'How are you bankrupting these corporations, exactly?'

'It's very simple,' Chloë says. 'We recruit people, tell them the three mottoes and then they do what they can to help the cause. Our main aims at the moment are quite clear. One is to cost corporations money. Another is to sabotage their operations. Another is to get NoCo people into positions of power within the corporations. Another is to get the anti-corporate message out there, right into the minds of young people and teenagers, where it counts. I guess there are probably two distinct areas, or levels, of activity at NoCo. Some members are fairly low-level in their companies. They indulge in minor acts of sabotage. They put viruses on company computers, spill Coke on their keyboards – Coca-Cola is an excellent tool in resistance, we find: very sticky and dangerous when combined with technology – take time off sick on purpose, ruin stock, operate Go Slows . . .'

'Go Slows,' I say, smiling. 'Sounds like a union thing.'

Chloë shrugs. 'Well, they took away most of our unions, so this is what they've got in return. If you work at a fast-food restaurant, you can't form a union but you can join NoCo. On your weekends off you can write graffiti on walls, mess with billboard ads, knock over displays of eggs in the supermarket or shoplift clothes and donate them to charity shops. It all helps.' She finishes her coffee and peers into the bottom of her mug. As if satisfied that it really is all gone, she then puts it down on the desk. 'In a sense, Esther best represents what can be done on this level if you're in a company. I think you already know that her job is to plug PopCo products online. Of course, she goes online and does the opposite.'

Guerrilla marketing becomes guerrilla warfare. Of course.

'So what about the other level?' I say, fascinated.

'Well, that's people like us. We are well paid, sometimes quite senior members of corporations who have, perhaps, always thought we would "fight the system from the inside", but we have become disillusioned at some point, or we haven't known how. We are beyond the stage where we can simply sabotage our workstation and make a difference. There are lots of possible directions for someone at this level. Some people are what we call "invisibles". They are attached to a local coordinator but they never attend meetings or receive any communications from NoCo. Their role is to climb as high as possible in their corporation. They are not encouraged to be vegans or to do anything out of the ordinary. Their brief is simply to keep their heads down, network like hell and get to the top. We already have one NoCo member at the head of a Human Resources division, apparently. HR is the main thing, I guess. If you can get NoCo members into HR, then you can get the people you want into each corporation. If we can crack HR divisions, then we can start marching people into Accounting and IT like an army of ants. Maybe we can even start getting people on Boards of Directors, who knows? The invisibles get where they're going, then sit there and wait for instructions. In fact, one problem we have is working out systems of secret communication with the invisibles. This is one of the reasons we wanted to recruit you, actually. What else? We have quite a lot of people in marketing departments but we always need more.' Chloë laughs now, and pushes her hair out of her face. 'They have the most fun. Do you ever see a marketing campaign and just think, "Blimey, that company's gone mad"? You know, something that just misses the point so totally?'

I smile slowly. 'Yeah, of course.'

'Well, that's what they do. It's not like their bosses are ever going to know that what they are saying is cool just isn't. Sometimes it's hilarious. There's a couple of fast-food corporations at the moment with these marketing campaigns based around how good fast food is for you, and how good it is for the environment. I'm pretty sure that's NoCo people. But you can never know for sure.'

'So you don't necessarily know who else is in NoCo?'

'Oh, no. It's a classic resistance structure. You only know what and who you need to know. Usually, this means that if, like me, you are a local coordinator, you know your members, and then only one person along in the chain. I think of my contact as my next-door neighbour in NoCo. It's not exactly a hierarchy, it's more of a circle. There are founders out there, though, somewhere. And there are plans for a big uprising eventually, but that's a lot of years off. We need to get everyone in place first.'

'How did you get involved?' I ask.

'I was headhunted by PopCo,' Chloë says. 'I was working for Greenpeace as a developer on the kids' area of their website and PopCo got in touch. They wanted someone to go into their new videogames division, someone who could create a game with the theme "saving the environment". They'd done research and found that children were concerned about the environment, so they looked around for someone they could bring in who'd have the right kind of knowledge. So they got me. It didn't take me long to realise that PopCo wasn't as wholesome as its image – not that I ever really thought it was. I mentioned my concerns to someone I used to work with, who had moved on into advertising. She told me about NoCo.' She laughs. 'I still think it's peculiar that PopCo recruited me from Greenpeace. I think there was some sort of odd recruitment policy going on for a while . . .'

'It's all that new management theory,' I say. 'I was designing crosswords when they brought me in. I'd never even thought of working in toys.'

'I think they find that people who actually want to work for them come up with boring ideas,' Chloë says. 'In fact, that's one really interesting thing I've found with NoCo. Pretty much all the members here were originally headhunted, or they were working for a small company that PopCo took over. Companies like PopCo want to sell cool stuff to teenagers who don't take any bullshit. So they bring in people who are, let's say, a bit cooler than people who would go through the normal application process. And, well, now here we are conspiring to change the world.'

We both laugh.

I start rolling another cigarette. 'So on a day-to-day basis, you'd do what sorts of things?' I ask.

'I do what all the NoCo creatives do,' she says. 'I work out ways to hide anti-corporate messages in products.' She laughs. 'I believe it's called propaganda. This is actually one of the biggest areas of

NoCo. As you can imagine, we have a lot of film-makers, musicians, artists, designers, videogames people who have joined. These people try to make anti-corporate products within corporate environments. Sometimes they are unsuccessful. Producers and people who control funding can often spot that kind of thing a mile off. Videogames is a key area, however. When you "hide" messages in products, you often find the best hiding places are simply places where powerful people cannot be bothered to look. A film, sure, you can watch it in an hour and a half. But who's going to play a videogame right through to the end to find out that the hero has become a vegan and the corporate hooligans have been eaten by monsters they created? To get to that message, you'd need to play the game for more than seventy hours, and you'd have to be good at it, too. At the end of *The Sphere*, we basically tell players the NoCo message. We tell them to Do No Harm, Stop Others Doing Harm and to Do What You Can. But you have to fight the last battle first. Books are another good place for hiding things – everyone has always known that. Powerful people don't read many books, especially not if they are at all long and complicated. They just say they have read them. There have been some big NoCo films recently, however, and even some NoCo advertising.'

I'm intrigued. 'What's NoCo advertising? Just really bad ads?'

'Well, no. There's been some bad feeling about NoCo advertising, to be honest. Some of it has backfired badly. One creative team used anti-capitalism as a message and then the brand did really well. Another NoCo team created an ad that was so obviously a spoof. It was for some trainers, and it was all about how great globalisation is. But it was too subtle, and the message didn't get through at all. One great NoCo success in advertising involved a campaign where the creative team used really shocking social-realist images to advertise clothes. Everyone said, "Bloody hell, it's a bit much that this company is trying to profit from images of people dying," and the brand lost market share. It's pretty well accepted now that this was a NoCo campaign. That was really good. It made people think about the issues and despise the product.'

I know the campaign she means. I always remember wondering how that came into existence and what it was designed to achieve. I never wanted to buy any of the products myself, so it worked.

'So, say some kid plays *The Sphere* and thinks that they will try to live according to the messages at the end, they'd be like a member of NoCo but they wouldn't know it?' I say.

Chloë sighs. 'Yeah, sort of. We want to get some "ground-level" members who do know what they're doing, though. There's an idea that individual members of NoCo will be able to "sign up" ordinary people who don't work for corporations – like schoolkids, students, the unemployed – and then act as that person's contact. They wouldn't tell anyone who they had signed up but everyone would still be connected. When everyone is connected, and when there are enough of us, we should be able to do some pretty exciting things. For example, those of us who can afford it already buy shares. It's nice to feel you own a bit of the company you're fucking up. It gives us options, too. One plan is that we will choose a day to sell all the shares in all the companies in which we have collectively invested. When we are much bigger, we will have "buy nothing" days that we plan in secret. We could send the market haywire. We will send it haywire, and then we will kill it. We will only leave the ethical companies intact. And the coolest thing about it is that we will be able to achieve it from within the market itself. Since we are the workers and the consumers, we have an effect on market forces. We will harness that effect and use it in the most efficient way, that's all. Thatcher – if she's still alive – will weep while her free market fucks itself in the arse. And governments won't be able to do much about it either.'

My mind is racing. So this is the basis for NoCo.

'We are the new workers,' Chloë says. 'The new proletariat, if you like. Our workplaces aren't factories any more, though, but air-conditioned offices, studios and call centres. But, just as we no longer work with our hands and bodies, or have to grapple with machinery, this revolution won't be physical. This will start as a revolution of ideas. They teach us branding. Of course, branding is traditionally what happens to animals, slaves, property. Now, of course, the mark is worth more than the object. Corporate money goes into idea people – like us – advertising, marketing, design people. The products are mostly bits of plastic, fabric, dead animal, chemicals, lies. Our job is to make the label on these pieces of nothing mean something to children and teenagers so that they use their money to buy these things so that we can have small flats in London and our bosses can fly first class.' She gives me the biggest smile yet. 'But we are quietly doing another job instead, using the tools they gave us.' She pauses again. 'So, are you with us?'

'Oh yes,' I say. 'I am with you.'

'There's no membership pack, I'm afraid. We have no official documents, no official membership. They can't abolish us like they tried to abolish unions, because we don't exist. And they can't legislate against us because all we are is a group of people not doing their jobs properly. Sure, they can arrest the kid who paints slogans over the front of his local burger bar. But they can't arrest someone for coming up with a terrible marketing campaign.'

She's right. This is a resistance movement based on not doing your job properly. And in this crazy new world of ideas and brands and thoughts, who really knows if you are doing your job properly or not?

'You said something about my skills,' I say. 'About code-breaking and stuff . . . ?'

Chloë nods. 'Yes, that's right. NoCo needs to develop some sort of code or cipher to help with communications. We need people inside to work on development. I mentioned that every month I get a communication pack from my "next-door neighbour" in NoCo. This has all sorts of information that I disseminate among the members I have here. But it also requests skills and ideas which, if we have them in our unit, can be fed back along the chain. When they said they needed someone with expertise in coding, I remembered your KidCracker kit. Then we checked you out. If you agree, I'll feed your details back and you will probably be assigned what we call a "special task". In other words, you'll be given the brief to develop something for eventual distribution throughout NoCo.'

I frown. 'Surely there are people in NoCo who understand basic RSA encryption.' Chloë looks blank. 'You know,' I say. 'E-mail encryption systems based around huge prime numbers . . .'

'But can it work offline?' she asks.

'Offline? No. But . . .'

'As far as I understand it, we need something that we can stick on billboards and in TV commercials. It's not going to be an Internet-based thing at all. We think we have many more "ground-level" members than we know about. When we need to coordinate action, this might be a good way of doing it. Or, at a higher level, it could be a good way to pass information around the globe without worrying about it being intercepted.'

'You want a code that can be stuck up on a billboard anywhere in the world, that NoCo people can understand but the enemy can't?' I say. 'Bloody hell.'

'Yeah, I can't get my head around it. But maybe you can, if you give it some thought.'

I think about how information was communicated to SOE agents during the Second World War. After the *BBC News* bulletin there'd be lots and lots of 'Personal Messages'. Some of them really were personal messages, usually in code, designed to make sense to one listener out there. Some were confirmations: coded replies to agents' requests or communications. Some were just made up to confuse the Germans. You never knew which was which. My grandparents said that listening to these gobbledegook messages was one of the most interesting things about the war. It was a kind of poetry, they said. Of course, when my grandfather was dropped behind enemy lines, the poetry took on a rather more urgent meaning.

What Chloë is asking is difficult, almost impossible, but I know I am going to have a go at cracking it. It excites me. Sitting here now on my corporate bed in this corporate concentration camp (where you come, literally, to concentrate), I feel a warmth inside me that I haven't felt since I was a child. I remember the day my grandfather asked me to help with the Voynich Manuscript. This is like that but more so. To be honest, I feel like I have just fallen into a very exciting film, where life and death don't matter as much as defeating the enemy. Or maybe I am in a videogame with my friends and my sword and my spells. For most of my adult life, I have attempted challenges for fun, as a kind of leisure activity. Even my job felt like some crossword puzzle. And although it was nice filling in the blanks and making my bosses happy, well, this is just so much better than that. Even the mathematics of this adds up. You can get huge, thriving patterns on John Horton Conway's Life game, patterns that keep changing but seem that they will never die. But sometimes, you can give life to one new cell and the whole thing terminates a few moves later.

A code that could be widely published but only understood by NoCo people? It sounds impossible. But there must be a way. Since e-mail encryption became easy to do and impossible to break, there hasn't been such a push towards new forms of cryptography. The ball is in the cryptanalysts' court. Once they work out how to break RSA, then it'll be up to the cryptographers to invent something new. Most people believe that the breakthrough for cryptanalysts will come either with the invention of the quantum computer, or work coming out of research on the Riemann Hypothesis. If someone worked out how to predict primes, the Internet would crumble in a day. There'd be no e-commerce, no secure sites, no credit-card transactions. I know for a fact that big banks and credit-card companies employ people specifically to watch what is going on in the mathematical community. If you were on the verge of this kind of breakthrough in prime-number research, would you turn around one day and find a bullet going through your head? Probably. People make billions of dollars out of the fact that we don't know how to predict primes. I wonder, not for the first time, what my grandmother would have made of this new world, where her primes are like vast corporate diamonds. When she died, no one apart from a few academics used e-mail. No one really imagined that less than ten years later, we'd all be dating and shopping and even living online. What would she have made of the virtual worlds? I doubt she could even have imagined them.

Are there mathematicians in NoCo? I hope so.

'Tell them I'll do it,' I say to Chloë.

She grins. 'Fantastic.'

On the radio, a drum and bass version of the Tarantella is playing. I remember reading that a folk remedy for the bite of the tarantula spider involves getting a passing troupe of musicians to come and play the Tarantella, while the victim of the bite dances the venom out. I feel tired now. I might need more coffee.

'You won't be the only person working on the problem, of course,' she says. 'But if you do come up with something, I will feed your results along the line and we'll see what happens. At the very least, we will want to use whatever you come up with in the local organisation here at PopCo. As you can see by my attempts to contact you, it's not very easy.'

'How many NoCo people are there at PopCo?'

'In PopCo Europe, which I coordinate, oh, about 200.'

'200! Bloody hell. I thought it was just you, Esther, Ben, Hiro and a couple of others.'

'We are getting quite big, now,' Chloë says. 'And you know what? I really think we are going to win. People are coming over to us all the time. I heard about one thing – you don't often hear about things like this, but somehow the information got through. You know all this offshoring that's going on with call centres at the moment?'

I nod. It seems to be like everything else. Any job that isn't connected with ideas, accounting, management, marketing or face-to-face retail is being moved offshore at a startling rate. It's what happens in a global economy. Someone works out that an Indian call centre can be run more cheaply than one in Britain, and *bang*! Before you know it, the English one is closed down and suddenly you are in the odd position of calling a number to book a train and knowing that the person you are speaking to is thousands of miles away. I heard a programme about this on Radio 4. Now I suddenly wonder about retail assistants. If we move into a virtual economy, will their jobs go, too? Imagine if you could order anything you wanted online, and luxury branded items became things you bought for your avatar, not yourself? It doesn't take an economics degree to work out who the online retail assistants would be. They'd be people who have the lowest cost of living in their real-world environment and can therefore work for the lowest price. What would we become then? A nation of creatives, truck drivers and postal workers?

'Offshoring scares me,' I say.

'Well, NoCo got into the Indian call centres pretty quickly. When a group of call-centre workers in Liverpool lost their jobs, they just phoned up and spoke to the Indian workers and became friends. One of the Indian workers was already in NoCo, and organised resistance at the call centre. There was one week where, on this particular call centre, which handled directory-enquiry services, they gave out wrong numbers something like 60 per cent of the time. No one wants to use them, now. It's all connected.' Chloë rubs her eyes. 'Imagine the day when there are more of *us* in corporations than there are of *them*. We could melt it down in a day. I've often thought about how fantastic it would be if, on a particular day, someone gave the signal and we just shut the

world down. Imagine, all over the world, accounts people trans-
ferring millions into housing projects in poverty-stricken towns,
or making huge donations to workers' pension funds and paying
them out immediately, because of a 'mistake'; workers deleting
their company's files, losing passwords, shredding documents,
selling shares, closing down public transport systems. At the
moment, someone calculated that we could cost them something
like 75 billion dollars on one day of calculated action. That potential grows every day. Of course, a lot of people argue that the
collapse should happen slowly and organically, not overnight. If
the big corporations go bankrupt overnight there would be severe
chaos. We don't necessarily want that. We don't want what the
enemy calls "collateral damage". We don't want to affect organic
farms and hospitals, for example.'

For some reason I find myself thinking of the Emperor's New
Clothes. I think about how the weakness of all the big corporations nowadays is that they have to employ people to think, and
thinking is everything. Perhaps once, say in the button factory in
which my father worked, you could get rid of the workers and still
have something of value left: the raw materials, the machines, the
design of the object you were making. But the things that have
value today are the invisible ideas and the marketing plans and the
logos and labels that are created on invisible machinery in our
minds. We own the means of production – our minds – and we
can use our brains to produce whatever we want.

'Why is the group called NoCo?' I ask suddenly. 'How does that
work in, say, non English-speaking countries?'

Chloë smiles. 'Oh, it's not called NoCo everywhere. Every company
has its own name. It's like mirror-branding. PopCo has NoCo.
Another company will have its own version. You could have a
company called, say, Smith and its version of NoCo might be called
Jones. And just as we call the whole global organisation "NoCo",
they will call it "Jones". It's great because it means we can't be
pinned down or traced or understood. We have no brand name,
no logo, no paperwork, no database. Only two things are important: that we remain connected and that we all follow the main
principles. When you join NoCo – or whatever your version is
called – you simply agree to use your labour in a positive rather
than a negative way.'

'That's really clever,' I say.

'No one knows for sure,' Chloë says, 'but most people believe that the concept and the structure were created by two refugees in America – an Indonesian economist who'd spent time working under-cover in a sweatshop, and an Iranian science-fiction writer. But like I say, no one knows for sure.'

'Wow,' I say.

Chloë and I sit in silence for a moment, while a single drumbeat comes out of the radio, pounding, like a fist.

'Chloë?' I say.

'Yes?'

'Do you have to be anywhere for, say, an hour or so?'

She shakes her head. 'No, why?'

I take a deep breath. 'You know that I mentioned a secret I have kept for twenty years?'

'Yes.' She looks intrigued. 'What's that all about?'

I take some more deep breaths and then look at the ceiling and then down at the blanket on the bed. 'Look, I haven't been able to tell anyone about it for various reasons. I mean, I literally haven't told a soul in my life. Not my best friend, not any boyfriends. The only two other people in the world who knew about it are dead. But I really, really need to tell someone.'

She looks flattered. 'You want to tell *me*?'

'Yes,' I say. 'If you want to listen. You are the first person who has ever told me something that is bigger than it and therefore the only person I could logically tell. It's a pretty good story, although it doesn't have an end yet.'

'Cool,' says Chloë. 'Shall I get more coffee?'

'Yeah, I think that would be a good idea.'

She picks up the mugs and turns towards the door.

'What's it about?' she says.

'A necklace,' I say. 'And quite a lot of treasure.'

Chapter Twenty-nine

There are five of us squashed into Esther's car, on the way to Dartmouth. As well as me and Esther, the small car contains Ben, Chloë and Hiro. I have the navigation equipment carefully stashed in my canvas bag, along with all the usual junk I carry around with me. My head feels heavy after staying up half the night talking. But I have never felt so carefree in my life. The sun is shining and we are on the road. I have finally managed to tell my secret. Oh, and I am now part of a global resistance movement as well.

Ben squeezes my leg. 'How are you feeling?' he asks.

'Overwhelmed,' I say back. 'But in a good way.'

'We have to get you on our boat, somehow,' Chloë says. 'We can have a NoCo meeting at sea. We could do with you as well, Esther. And Grace, actually.'

'Boats are the best places for secret meetings,' Hiro says. 'Who could ever overhear you on a boat?'

'I am so glad we can talk properly in front of Alice now,' Esther says.

'Me too,' says Ben, giving me a big smile.

'Is Grace in NoCo too?' I say, a lovely warm feeling, like the opposite of an ache, spreading inside me. They want to have a NoCo meeting today, and they want me to be there. For the first time in my life I feel part of something – almost a gang – and I know I can be myself inside it. I know that if my grandparents were alive they would recognise the person I am now, the person I can be with these people.

'Oh, yes,' says Chloë. 'She's great. It's very impressive the way she's got into the virtual worlds group as well. We really need someone in there. Someone to unsettle things a bit. Have a bit of fun with the "delete" key.' She laughs, the wind blowing through her long hair.

We drive through Totnes again, avoiding the town centre. I look at the soft green hills swelling out of the ground; the wavy graph where the land meets the sky. And it's all so beautiful. But when we stop at some traffic lights I see something with which I am more familiar: tiny weeds and grasses forcing their way between paving slabs and bits of cracked tarmac. A small clump of dandelions. A few daisies. Lots of little patches of grass. I realise suddenly that this is much more beautiful to me. You can tarmac the earth as much as you want but still the grass will struggle through.

'So basically we want everyone from Dan's boat on our boat, apart from Dan,' Hiro is saying. 'That's going to go down well.'

'I bet Dan would jump at the chance to get on the virtual worlds boat,' I say. I remember that they were all in the same sailing team: Kieran, Violet, Frank and James. 'If there was one less boat . . .'

'Chloë'll disable ours, then, won't you?' Ben says.

'No. Then we'll get distributed evenly among the others,' she says. 'Alice will disable Dan's boat and then she, Grace and Esther can come with us. Dan, I'm sure, will naturally drift off to Kieran's team. There, sorted.'

'I can't disable a boat,' I say. 'I've never even been on a boat.' I look around the car with some panic. 'Esther?'

'Oh, I can't be trusted to do something like this,' she says.

'I'll explain what to do,' Chloë says. 'It'll be fine.'

We drive along a long country road lined with trees and hedgerows. Little cottages are snuggled into the sides of hills. I expect in the winter you would see smoke rising from their chimneys but it's a hot day today and it's impossible to tell whether these places are inhabited or not. We drive through a village with a little bridge and then another one with a large, old church. I look at this landscape and I think that this is the kind of place battles used to be fought, where armies would march on foot or ride on horseback. They'd get their food from farms, and safe house networks would spring up. I think I prefer this new war, fought in people's minds, fought against the people who fund other wars and then watch them play out like global baseball games. I imagine trying to hide in this landscape, running through a forest avoiding poachers' traps. And then I think about how well hidden I am in the landscape of my life, a world in which being British and middle class and talking about the state of the world is something that can go entirely unnoticed.

We take a left and then a right-hand turn and then we are on a smaller track, with tall hedgerows on either side of us.

'I'll take you the scenic route,' Esther says. 'Along the sea.'

'Can't we go the quick way?' Ben says. 'If we got there before the others, Chloë could disable any one of the boats.'

'Too late,' says Esther. 'Sorry.'

'Put this on,' Hiro says, passing Esther a black cassette tape.

I look at Hiro, this skinny, geeky-looking Go champion, and I wonder what's on his tape. Esther grumbles a bit about people who get in your car and then expect you to play their tapes, but she slots it in the machine anyway. It turns out to be the Velvet Underground and we all sing along as we hurtle along this odd little road, the wind blowing through our hair like a cosmic fan.

The sea appears in front of us and we turn left, driving along with the cliffs on our right. I feel happy just being part of this. *Change the world.* Maybe I will have something to report to my mother after all.

When we get to Dartmouth everyone else is already there. I am feeling anxious about having to disable a boat but it turns out that we are one boat down anyway, due to some sort of error on the part of Gavin's company. Dan has already defected to Kieran's group, and as we walk past them, I hear him trying to convince Frank that he should be skipper. Violet is standing on the embankment, watching the river, looking pissed off. We walk down some concrete steps to a rickety pontoon and then, wobbling a bit, right to the end, where people are waiting to be taken on a small launch out to the mooring position of their team's boat. The idea is that we will motor down the river to the point where it becomes the sea and then switch off the outboard and practise sailing. Our picnics have already been put on the boats, apparently, along with some other items PopCo think we might need: wine, towels, bottle-openers. All this fuss because of what our minds do for them.

Esther has gone to find Grace, and a few minutes later I watch the two of them walk along the pontoon towards the rest of us, laughing together. I also notice Hiro watching Grace and the way he casually looks away when she gets closer. As we stand there taking it in turns to get into the boat, his hand softly brushes hers. Whatever is between her and Kieran, I realise, is not going to last.

When it is my turn to step into the launch, I copy what Chloë does and slip off my plimsolls and chuck them in the boat before, in bare feet, stepping onto the bow, balancing precariously for a moment, before I am able to take another step onto one of the little seats in the hull. Ben is already in, and offers me his hand. As soon as I sit down I feel excited. I am so close to the water now, I could trail my hand in it. The guy who is ferrying the teams backwards and forwards stands on the pontoon and unties the boat. Then, in one deft movement, still holding the untied rope, he pushes away from the pontoon and steps in to the boat, never looking as though he might fall. He starts the outboard motor and the boat fills with the sweet muggy smell of diesel. He swings her around and we are off, chugging upriver.

'Are you all right?' Ben says to me.

'Yeah, I think so. You?'

'Oh, yes. I love this.'

I think I do too. I look at his feet.

'What happened to the deck shoes?'

'I decided to go *au naturel*.'

'Me too,' I say, smiling as he takes my hand.

'Ben,' I say. 'I want to ask you something later.'

'What?'

'It's going to involve you taking some time off work.'

'I'm intrigued,' he says.

'You will be.'

We smile at each other and watch the land go by on either side of us until suddenly we are approaching a small blue yacht, rather fast.

'Fend off!' Chloë suddenly says.

We don't know what she means but we copy her anyway as she sticks out her legs and places her feet against the side of the yacht to prevent us from colliding with it. No one comments on this, so it must be normal. Then the launch is tied to the yacht and we clamber from one to the other. I stow the navigation equipment while the others bustle around doing what they've been taught while I was ill. Ben is unfurling the main sail; Esther and Hiro are attaching the jib to the forestay and then tying it down, I assume so that they can unfurl it more easily later.

'Do you want to help me navigate?' I say to Grace.

'Yeah, sure,' she says. 'Hey . . . I'm glad you're here.'

I return the smile she gives me. 'Yeah, me too.'

Chloë unties the boat from its mooring and starts the outboard motor. She's stuck her hair up in a loose ponytail and her face is relaxed and suntanned. I've never done this before; I've never been on the water, looking at land, only the other way around. And from the land you just can't imagine what this is like. Everything feels different. On land, things feel hard and certain but out here everything is soft. The smell of diesel mixes with salt and cool air as we travel further towards the mouth of the river.

'Do we need to start navigating yet?' I say to Chloë.

'No,' she says, her foot on the rudder. 'Not for a bit.'

We approach an old castle at the river's mouth and I think for the second time today about forms of warfare. I imagine sitting in the castle, firing arrows from a tiny window, trying to hold off a sea attack: something wet, dark and menacing that you probably couldn't even properly see.

'Check out the river chain,' Esther says, pointing.

'The what?' Hiro says.

She points again to a large bolt stuck into the side of the valley, with what appears to be a large link of a large chain attached to it.

'It's really old,' she says. 'When ships tried to invade Dartmouth, the townspeople would raise the chain. It joined from there,' she points, 'to the other side of the river. They would pull it up from the river bed to catch the keels of the ships as they came in.'

'That's clever,' I say.

We are at the mouth of the river now and the air is fresher; the water choppier underneath us. I shiver and pull my cardigan out of my bag.

'Right, Alice,' says Chloë. 'You'll need to start navigating in a minute. If you get the map out, I'll show you where we're aiming.'

'OK.' I climb into the little cabin and immediately feel sick. I quickly get out the map and try to straighten it out as I come back up to the deck. But now that we are properly in the sea, the small yacht has started to buck and heave with the increasing waves and doing anything at all is difficult. As I try to get my position back, the boat tips upwards with some force and I almost fall.

'Is it supposed to be doing this?' Grace asks Chloë.

'Yeah, don't worry,' she says. 'Careful, Alice.'

I think about Francis Stevenson and for the first time I can imagine how lonely and terrifying it must have been at sea. But it's exhilarating, too. Chloë starts shouting orders at the others and they hoist the sails while she cuts the engine. All I can hear above their voices is the slap, slap, slap of the waves and the vague memory-sound of motors somewhere in the distance.

My insides really don't like this. I feel sick. I make a strangled, gulping noise and clutch at my stomach.

'It's going to be a bit wallowy for a second,' Chloë says to me. 'You could go down below if you want, but it'll make you feel more sick. Don't worry. You'll be OK in a minute once we start moving properly.'

This feels like being in a bottle that someone is plunging in and out of a bowl of water very fast. This boat is tiny and the sea suddenly looks like it's the rest of the world. On a map, it would seem like we were quite close to land. But being out here is very different. I hold on to the handrail as the boat heels over violently.

'Hold on,' Chloë shouts.

'Bloody hell,' Grace says.

I am still trying to open the map.

'Did you think it would be different, out at sea?' Ben says to me.

'Did you?' I am drawing a line on the chart, working out where we are. We still have land in sight, and, just as Dan showed me, I am using the lighthouse and the Day Beacon – a peculiar, grey triangular structure on the headland – as reference points.

'Yeah. I thought it would be calmer.'

My stomach has settled down now. I actually like this, the violence underneath us.

'*Ready to gybe!*' Chloë says. This is Ben's cue to start pulling the sail round via a rope attached to a cleat just behind my back. I lean forwards and when Chloë gives the command Esther lets out the line on the other side of the boat and Ben frantically pulls his rope in, before tying it off on the cleat.

'What did you want to ask me, before?' Ben says, once the activity is all over.

'It may involve more boats,' I say.

'Bloody hell.'

'*Ready to gybe!*'

'I'll tell you more later,' I say, licking salt off my lips and sitting forward again.

Somehow I manage to navigate us to the cove Chloë has chosen on the map. Ben goes with her to lower the anchor. Chloë worked out from the wind direction that it would be sheltered in here, and it really is calm and still. The little yacht bobs around as we all stretch, or sigh, or light cigarettes.

'So, who likes sailing, then?' Chloë says.

A few of us groan.

'I do,' Ben says.

'Yeah, me too,' I say.

Hiro looks a bit green. 'I'm going up front for a bit,' he says. 'Just need to get some air. Get my head together . . .'

We take the picnic out from the galley store. Inside we find crusty baguettes, lemon and coriander hummus, deep-fried potato fritters with chilli jam, roasted vegetables, couscous, plump queen olives marinated in smoked paprika, onion tarts, guacamole, crisps and big, sturdy flasks of coffee. As well as a bottle of chilled white wine, there's a big pack of beer.

'Not too much,' Chloë says as we all fall upon the beer.

Hiro comes back just as we start eating. 'Oh, beer,' he says, taking a bottle. 'Cool.'

'So, Alice,' says Chloë, once we are all settled. 'Any more questions?'

'Just one,' I say. 'How did you find out about my background?'

'That was me,' Hiro says. 'Sorry. Personnel files.'

'I see,' I say.

I bite into some crusty bread and take a swig of beer. The cold liquid hits my throat at the same time that a small breeze blows in off the sea. I turn my head towards the breeze and sip more beer.

'Look, it's a seal!' Esther says suddenly. We all look. Sure enough, there is a seal playing in the water. We all keep completely still as the seal's smooth, brown head emerges from the water and looks around.

'Hello,' I whisper.

'That is the most beautiful thing,' Ben says.

Then the seal is gone, gone deep into the cove and possibly out to sea.

'So, are you still going to leave PopCo?' Esther says to me.

'I don't know,' I say. 'I thought . . . I thought I might write a book.'

I talked about this with Chloë last night. I have always wanted to write books – real books, not just the little guides I do for PopCo. It was something she said that properly put the idea into place.

'You can hide things in books,' she said. 'Everyone knows that.' I am going to have a go at coming up with this impossible-sounding code for NoCo, of course I am. But I'm not sure about staying in the company. The idea of staying at home with my crosswords and the Voynich Manuscript appeals to me too. And, I don't know, perhaps a bit more hands-on sabotage, a bit of toy-wrecking on a Saturday afternoon.

'What sort of book?' Ben asks.

'A novel,' I say. 'All about PopCo. All about what PopCo is, and what it does, and how you can wake up to it and decide to make a difference.'

'Ah,' Grace says. 'A *NoCo* book.'

'I think it's a great idea,' says Chloë.

'I have some other things I want to write about too,' I explain. 'Something I promised my grandfather I'd do before he died . . .'

'But you won't be able to use PopCo's real name. Or NoCo's,' Esther says.

'I'll change them,' I say. 'When I was talking to Chloë last night it hit me that it doesn't matter how many people know that NoCo exists. No one really knows what it's called, or who's a member. I'll make it the kind of book that young or interesting people read and powerful people ignore. I've got some of it in my head, already. I'm going to include all the toys we never made, all the ideas that got scrapped, all the dreams that went wrong. That will be how I'll build up the image of PopCo. After all, no one can sue me for using concepts that never made it into existence. And then of course there's the other stuff. Something about a treasure map, an old puzzle . . . Oh, you'll see when it's done.'

'Cool,' says Hiro.

'So you are leaving?' Chloë says.

'Yeah,' I say. 'But I'm still in NoCo. Like we said.'

'Yeah. Like we said.'

She smiles at me. People drink more beer, and make odd little sandwiches out of the salad, the hummus and the crisps. Chloë starts talking to Esther about her 'outbursts' and Grace sits there with Hiro, smiling softly at him while he opens another beer for her. Seagulls screech overhead, looking for any scraps we throw overboard. In the far distance, an aeroplane marks the sky with a thin white trail.

Ben looks sad. 'So you're still going home on Sunday,' he says to me.

'Yeah, which only gives me five days to work out what to make you for dinner when you come to stay.'

'You want me to come, still?'

'Oh, yes,' I say. 'I do.'

'And what was that thing you were going to ask me?'

'How do you fancy going on a treasure hunt?' I say.

Postscript

The Pacific Bird Sanctuary
1 May 2005

Dear Miss Butler,

Thank you so much for your recent letter. We are very much looking forward to your visit in the week of the 15th. We have made arrangements for you and your companion to stay at the Melody Inn, which is a lovely guest house on the south side of the island, not too far from the sanctuary. On the 17th, we would be honoured for you to attend the opening of the Peter Butler Community School, and the Peter Butler Animal Care Centre. We can also show you the plans for the Francis Stevenson Museum, the initial building work for which, as you already know, will go ahead next spring.

I still cannot quite express to you what the last year has been like not just for me but for all the trustees. To find that your bird sanctuary, or to be more specific, the public picnic area of your bird sanctuary, is the site of treasure worth almost two billion dollars – this is certainly something that doesn't happen every day! As you know, the Peter Butler memorial buildings have been constructed on land that had been earmarked for development by a US toxic-waste-management company. We were thrilled to be able to buy back this land ourselves. As for the rest of the money, well, we can discuss it further when you are here. Obviously, we will now be the richest bird sanctuary in the world, but we have been rather touched by the 'generosity bug'. Can you suggest some other uses for the money? Some worthwhile charities? I never thought we would be able to say this, but we really have too much!

With love and warm wishes – and wishing you a safe trip!

Helèna Rico
Pacific Bird Sanctuary

From *The Cryptogram*
2005, Issue —

Those of you out there working on the Stevenson/Heath Manuscript – stop writing. Put down your pens. This puzzle, almost four hundred years old, has, at last, been solved. The late Cambridge, UK-based cryptanalyst Peter Butler (known to members of the ACA as 'The Cam Buster') came up with an answer back in 1982. Now, almost three years after his death, we talk to his granddaughter, Alice Butler, about just how he solved the puzzle and why he kept it a secret for so long.

'My grandfather started working on the Stevenson/Heath Manuscript just after the Second World War finished,' she says. 'From what I've been told, he worked on it every single day until he had cracked it.' Butler didn't announce his success with this code, however, because he was concerned about the environmental impact of people going to get the treasure. Butler, a keen bird-lover, had discovered that the treasure was buried right in the middle of a bird sanctuary on an island in the Pacific. 'He just didn't want to be rich,' Alice tells us. 'He didn't do it for the treasure. For him it was just the thrill of solving the problem that was important. But then he found he couldn't tell anyone about his success. I remember him being very frustrated about this conundrum!'

Butler did tell two people, however, his wife, the mathematician Elizabeth Butler, and his son in-law, Alice's father William Bailey. He did not tell anyone exactly how he had done it, of course, but he did reveal that he had cracked this notoriously difficult puzzle. But what about the proof? Is there any point in solving a puzzle unless you can tell everyone about it? While he considered this, Butler had a locket made up with a code of his own engraved within it. This code took the form of the following: 2.14488156Ex48. He placed this locket on a chain, gave it to his then nine-year-old granddaughter and told her never to take it off.

'As a child I lived with my grandparents,' Alice says. 'My mother had died some years earlier. I was fascinated with my necklace and tried my hardest to understand it but it took me years to work out what it meant. I remember having one breakthrough when I was about twelve. I was fiddling around with my calculator and I suddenly understood the way the letters and numbers were arranged. I realised that it was shorthand for a longer series of digits, and expanded it accordingly. So then I had a string of digits – but I still didn't know what to do with them. Then teenage life took over and I stopped trying to work it out. It was only after my grandfather died that I properly looked at it again. When I finally realised what to do with all these digits, I saw that my grandfather had taught me how to decode my necklace years before. It was quite clever of him.'

The code that Francis Stevenson used to create his treasure map was based on a numbered system similar to that found in the Beale Papers, in which, as readers will know, each number in the ciphertext stands for a word from a famous document. In the Beale Papers, the first of the three documents was decoded using the American Declaration of Independence. But no one has had any luck cracking the next two texts, (Unless . . . ? No, Alice Butler assures us that Peter Butler didn't also work this out in secret.)

'I knew that my grandfather had worked out which text Francis Stevenson had used to create his code,' she explains. 'He had told me that much. But of course he wouldn't tell me what the text was. He did, however, drop clues sometimes but I didn't pick them up until much later. I remember once he said that he'd had to reconstruct the text, as it didn't exist any more. When I finally cracked the code on my necklace, I knew immediately what the text was. All I had to do then was find my grandfather's reconstruction of it, although that was harder than it sounds. I had all his papers but, of course, so many of these papers – including the ones I wanted – were in code!'

Then Alice had to work out what she would do, now that she also knew the location of the treasure. 'More than anything, my grandfather wanted his achievement to be recognised. However, in his lifetime, he never saw a way that this would be possible. You can't just suddenly tell the world you have a treasure map. You'd have absolute chaos on your doorstep! After a while, he stopped talking about Stevenson/Heath and immersed himself in his new challenge, the Voynich Manuscript. And no, he didn't solve that one either.'

So what to do about the treasure? It turns out that Alice Butler didn't want it either. 'I felt it was wrong for me to have it,' she says. 'So I did something that seemed logical. I simply gave the information I had to the trust of the bird sanctuary on which the treasure was buried. I thought, "Well, it's really your treasure, since you own the land." I also thought they would know how to dig it up without disturbing the birds. I made an arrangement with them that if there did turn out to be treasure down there, they would use some of the money to build a school and a rescue centre for animals. I also suggested that a Francis Stevenson museum would be a nice idea, too. His story is very fascinating, and deserves a much wider audience. I left it up to the trustees to decide what they wanted to call these structures. But I know my grandfather would be very proud to know that they chose to honour his name. And now that the Peter Butler Community School and the Peter Butler Animal Care Centre are both about to open, I can finally tell everyone that he worked out the location of the Stevenson treasure. The treasure is of course now gone, so there is no risk of people pounding on my door in the middle of the night wanting a copy of the map.'

However, Alice is more reluctant to tell us the name of the document which Stevenson used to encode his map.

'I thought I would leave that as an open puzzle,' she says, with a smile. 'Now that everyone knows what was on my necklace, it should be easy for your readers to work out.'

There's another reason, too. Alice Butler has written a novel. 'It's not just about the Stevenson/Heath Manuscript,' she says. 'But the story is there. In the first UK edition of the book I have left the puzzle open, so I don't want to spoil it for any potential readers by revealing it now.' Never fear, though, you don't have to wait for later editions of the book to come out to get the answer if you really want it. The whole story of the solution to the Stevenson/Heath Manuscript will be a key exhibit in the Francis Stevenson Museum, due to open in the fall, and the answer will also be posted on their website.

Across

1) Erase game backwards on mathematician's computer, perhaps? (5)
3) Unity found in loneliness (3)
6) No right to French silver for SOE Operative (5)
7) Group would have more assets without donkey (3)
8) Rumour about conflict, we hear, with bad end (4)
9) There are seven of these (7)
12) Neat? Help sort out this beastly mess (8)
13) Make your own portable instrument out of fragment (3)
14) A short farewell, during cricket game, perhaps? (3)

Down

1) Mage is plucky but confused (4)
2) Cube me (5)
4) Scrambler finds fish in backwards north-east American casualty (7)
5) In mix-up, Premier of Norway swears to reply (6)
7) Maisie very carefully sifts through clue (5)
10) No clue here. Explain missing piece today! You! (5)
11) Wholly. Except? (4)

Frequency of Occurrence of Letters in English

The following table is from Fletcher Pratt, *Secret and Urgent: The Story of Codes and Ciphers,* Blue Ribbon Books, 1939.

Rank	Letter	Frequency of occurrence in 1000 words	Frequency of occurrence in 1000 letters
1	E	591	131.05
2	T	473	104.68
3	A	368	81.51
4	O	360	79.95
5	N	320	70.98
6	R	308	68.32
7	I	286	63.45
8	S	275	61.01
9	H	237	52.59
10	D	171	37.88
11	L	153	33.89
12	F	132	29.24
13	C	124	27.58
14	M	114	25.36
15	U	111	24.59
16	G	90	19.94
17	Y	89	19.82
18	P	89	19.82
19	W	68	15.39
20	B	65	14.40
21	V	41	9.19
22	K	19	4.20
23	X	7	1.66
24	J	6	1.32
25	Q	5	1.21
26	Z	3	.77

Let Them Eat Cake cake

Ingredients

2 oz ground almonds
6 oz self-raising flour
2 tsp baking powder
4 oz light muscovado sugar
150 ml corn oil
200–250 ml soya milk
zest of two unwaxed lemons
juice of 2 lemons
1 tbsp orange flower water
1 tsp natural vanilla extract

Preheat the oven to 190 degrees, or less if it's a fan oven.

Grease a cake tin. A deep six-inch tin is good but any will do.

Sift the flour and the baking powder into a bowl and then add the sugar. Mix in the ground almonds and the lemon zest. Add the oil and the milk. Use slightly less liquid to make the end result more of a cake and less of a pudding. You don't have to be 100per cent precise with the liquids in this cake.

Now add the lemon juice and mix in thoroughly. Add the flower essence and the vanilla extract and mix again. The result should look like a thick batter.

Pour into the cake tin and bake for about forty minutes. The outside should be brown and the inside very soft. Turn out, cool and decorate with fresh mint leaves and strawberries.

2	3	5	7	11	13	17	19	23	29
31	37	41	43	47	53	59	61	67	71
73	79	83	89	97	101	103	107	109	113
127	131	137	139	149	151	157	163	167	173
179	181	191	193	197	199	211	223	227	229
233	239	241	251	257	263	269	271	277	281
283	293	307	311	313	317	331	337	347	349
353	359	367	373	379	383	389	397	401	409
419	421	431	433	439	443	449	457	461	463
467	479	487	491	499	503	509	521	523	541
547	557	563	569	571	577	587	593	599	601
607	613	617	619	631	641	643	647	653	659
661	673	677	683	691	701	709	719	727	733
739	743	751	757	761	769	773	787	797	809
811	821	823	827	829	839	853	857	859	863
877	881	883	887	907	911	919	929	937	941
947	953	967	971	977	983	991	997	1009	1013
1019	1021	1031	1033	1039	1049	1051	1061	1063	1069
1087	1091	1093	1097	1103	1109	1117	1123	1129	1151
1153	1163	1171	1181	1187	1193	1201	1213	1217	1223
1229	1231	1237	1249	1259	1277	1279	1283	1289	1291
1297	1301	1303	1307	1319	1321	1327	1361	1367	1373
1381	1399	1409	1423	1427	1429	1433	1439	1447	1451
1453	1459	1471	1481	1483	1487	1489	1493	1499	1511
1523	1531	1543	1549	1553	1559	1567	1571	1579	1583
1597	1601	1607	1609	1613	1619	1621	1627	1637	1657
1663	1667	1669	1693	1697	1699	1709	1721	1723	1733
1741	1747	1753	1759	1777	1783	1787	1789	1801	1811
1823	1831	1847	1861	1867	1871	1873	1877	1879	1889
1901	1907	1913	1931	1933	1949	1951	1973	1979	1987
1993	1997	1999	2003	2011	2017	2027	2029	2039	2053
2063	2069	2081	2083	2087	2089	2099	2111	2113	2129
2131	2137	2141	2143	2153	2161	2179	2203	2207	2213
2221	2237	2239	2243	2251	2267	2269	2273	2281	2287
2293	2297	2309	2311	2333	2339	2341	2347	2351	2357

2371	2377	2381	2383	2389	2393	2399	2411	2417	2423
2437	2441	2447	2459	2467	2473	2477	2503	2521	2531
2539	2543	2549	2551	2557	2579	2591	2593	2609	2617
2621	2633	2647	2657	2659	2663	2671	2677	2683	2687
2689	2693	2699	2707	2711	2713	2719	2729	2731	2741
2749	2753	2767	2777	2789	2791	2797	2801	2803	2819
2833	2837	2843	2851	2857	2861	2879	2887	2897	2903
2909	2917	2927	2939	2953	2957	2963	2969	2971	2999
3001	3011	3019	3023	3037	3041	3049	3061	3067	3079
3083	3089	3109	3119	3121	3137	3163	3167	3169	3181
3187	3191	3203	3209	3217	3221	3229	3251	3253	3257
3259	3271	3299	3301	3307	3313	3319	3323	3329	3331
3343	3347	3359	3361	3371	3373	3389	3391	3407	3413
3433	3449	3457	3461	3463	3467	3469	3491	3499	3511
3517	3527	3529	3533	3539	3541	3547	3557	3559	3571
3581	3583	3593	3607	3613	3617	3623	3631	3637	3643
3659	3671	3673	3677	3691	3697	3701	3709	3719	3727
3733	3739	3761	3767	3769	3779	3793	3797	3803	3821
3823	3833	3847	3851	3853	3863	3877	3881	3889	3907
3911	3917	3919	3923	3929	3931	3943	3947	3967	3989
4001	4003	4007	4013	4019	4021	4027	4049	4051	4057
4073	4079	4091	4093	4099	4111	4127	4129	4133	4139
4153	4157	4159	4177	4201	4211	4217	4219	4229	4231
4241	4243	4253	4259	4261	4271	4273	4283	4289	4297
4327	4337	4339	4349	4357	4363	4373	4391	4397	4409
4421	4423	4441	4447	4451	4457	4463	4481	4483	4493
4507	4513	4517	4519	4523	4547	4549	4561	4567	4583
4591	4597	4603	4621	4637	4639	4643	4649	4651	4657
4663	4673	4679	4691	4703	4721	4723	4729	4733	4751
4759	4783	4787	4789	4793	4799	4801	4813	4817	4831
4861	4871	4877	4889	4903	4909	4919	4931	4933	4937
4943	4951	4957	4967	4969	4973	4987	4993	4999	5003
5009	5011	5021	5023	5039	5051	5059	5077	5081	5087
5099	5101	5107	5113	5119	5147	5153	5167	5171	5179
5189	5197	5209	5227	5231	5233	5237	5261	5273	5279
5281	5297	5303	5309	5323	5333	5347	5351	5381	5387
5393	5399	5407	5413	5417	5419	5431	5437	5441	5443
5449	5471	5477	5479	5483	5501	5503	5507	5519	5521
5527	5531	5557	5563	5569	5573	5581	5591	5623	5639

5641	5647	5651	5653	5657	5659	5669	5683	5689	5693
5701	5711	5717	5737	5741	5743	5749	5779	5783	5791
5801	5807	5813	5821	5827	5839	5843	5849	5851	5857
5861	5867	5869	5879	5881	5897	5903	5923	5927	5939
5953	5981	5987	6007	6011	6029	6037	6043	6047	6053
6067	6073	6079	6089	6091	6101	6113	6121	6131	6133
6143	6151	6163	6173	6197	6199	6203	6211	6217	6221
6229	6247	6257	6263	6269	6271	6277	6287	6299	6301
6311	6317	6323	6329	6337	6343	6353	6359	6361	6367
6373	6379	6389	6397	6421	6427	6449	6451	6469	6473
6481	6491	6521	6529	6547	6551	6553	6563	6569	6571
6577	6581	6599	6607	6619	6637	6653	6659	6661	6673
6679	6689	6691	6701	6703	6709	6719	6733	6737	6761
6763	6779	6781	6791	6793	6803	6823	6827	6829	6833
6841	6857	6863	6869	6871	6883	6899	6907	6911	6917
6947	6949	6959	6961	6967	6971	6977	6983	6991	6997
7001	7013	7019	7027	7039	7043	7057	7069	7079	7103
7109	7121	7127	7129	7151	7159	7177	7187	7193	7207
7211	7213	7219	7229	7237	7243	7247	7253	7283	7297
7307	7309	7321	7331	7333	7349	7351	7369	7393	7411
7417	7433	7451	7457	7459	7477	7481	7487	7489	7499
7507	7517	7523	7529	7537	7541	7547	7549	7559	7561
7573	7577	7583	7589	7591	7603	7607	7621	7639	7643
7649	7669	7673	7681	7687	7691	7699	7703	7717	7723
7727	7741	7753	7757	7759	7789	7793	7817	7823	7829
7841	7853	7867	7873	7877	7879	7883	7901	7907	7919

Solution

It was a beautiful scarabaeus, *and, at that time, unknown
to naturalists – of course a great prize in a scientific point
of view. There were two round black spots near one
extremity of the back, and a long one near the other. The
scales were exceedingly hard and glossy, with all the
appearance of burnished gold.*

'The Gold Bug' by Edgar Allan Poe

It's late September, and I am washing up in the small kitchen in my house in Gypsy Hill, looking out of the small window at the moon. It's like someone has taken a sheet of blotting paper and covered the whole sky with it, smudging everything, taking the edges away. And this is all I am thinking about: the blotting-paper moon. I'm not thinking about switching on the radio, or playing videogames, or even doing any work. For a while now I have been planning to start writing a book about PopCo, and about my childhood and the Stevenson/Heath manuscript, but I keep putting it off: the NoCo code project has been taking up all my time. But tonight I am thinking of nothing apart from the moon. For the past few years or so I have been frightened of this, of letting my mind roam un-supervised in this house, because it always goes back to the same thing: my grandfather and how much I miss him. It's OK when I am at Ben's house (and I have been there a lot recently) but I am worried about my book. It's going to be made of memories, after all. But tonight, for some reason, it's OK. Tonight I seem able to just look at the moon without anything bad happening.

I finish washing up, dry my hands on a thin cotton tea-towel and fetch a tin of cat food from the larder. Atari weaves through my legs as I open the tin on the small table next to the sink (we never did get a fitted kitchen), still looking out of the window. I think about a note I wrote in my 'ideas' book yesterday, about the moon looking like it had been punched in the sky like a hole. But today's moon has been ripped, not cut, from the sky, and the fabric is frayed around it. So now I have two ideas. I have a blotting-paper moon, and a moon ripped out of a fabric sky. I put Atari's dinner down on the kitchen floor and walk through the hallway and up the stairs. I'll put both ideas down in my tattered red book (already stained with green tea) but I probably won't use either of them. What's the point? And how can I possibly think of writing a book when I don't have a proper ending? I have the PopCo story to tell (I'm pleased with that name for the company: PopCo. I think it's better than the actual name – maybe I'll win another case of champagne if I suggest it to the board) but what's the point of telling the Stevenson/Heath story when it has no end? Nothing about that half of my story seems to have an end. No proof for the Riemann Hypothesis. No solution to the Voynich Manuscript. And the one thing that there is an answer for, well, I know there is an answer, but I don't know it.

The study has always been the warmest room in this house. When we moved here, my grandfather and I took the most care over the decoration of this room: in fact, it's the only one we really changed. The downstairs sitting room was left wearing its house-sale yellow paint, and the hallway still has the woodchip we'd vowed to remove. But we took a lot of care over the study. After all, it was the most used room in the house. My grandfather would sit in there all day, burning coal in the small Victorian fireplace, setting crosswords or working on the Voynich Manuscript. In the evenings I would join him, and we'd work in silence together before I would make our supper: soup and homemade bread (if he made the bread during the day), or scrambled eggs on toast (if the bread was yesterday's).

After supper we would go back into the study and play chess or Go for an hour or so before getting back to work. I'd lost interest in the Voynich Manuscript by then. Or, not exactly lost interest . . . To be honest, it was making me angry. I felt that my grandfather was wasting his life on it; that there probably was no solution. But still he'd sit there with his books and his new copy of the manuscript that he'd obtained from the Beinecke Rare Book and Manuscript Library at Yale University. I had hoped he would go back to the idea that he'd worked on for a time in the mid-nineties, that the book had been forged by Voynich himself. At least that hypothesis was fun. Voynich had claimed to have discovered the manuscript in a Jesuit monastery in 1912, but there was never any record of this. And Voynich was not only a rare-books dealer but also a trained chemist with access to vellum – and experience forging documents for the Polish *Proletariat* movement. But hardly anyone who works on the Voynich Manuscript wants it to be a forgery, and my grandfather moved on from this hypothesis after a year or two. After that, he worked on another theory that has become very popular: that the book had been created by John Dee and Edward Kelley to further their chances of patronage in Europe.

But in those last couple of years before he died, my grandfather had gone back to the task I'd helped with when I was ten: counting words and letters and putting the results into mathematical functions to see what happened. Nothing ever did.

One night, after he had beaten me at Go for the fourth night running, my grandfather sat down in his big brown armchair and, after poking the fire, took out his magnifying glass and set about recounting the letters on one particular page. It happened to be one of the most famous pages in the whole manuscript. I remembered my grandfather telling me about William Newbold, who worked on the text from about 1919 and came up with a crazy mixture of cabalistic Gematria, anagramisation and hocus pocus to eventually decipher a section beginning '*Scripsi Rogerus Bacon* . . .', although, with the method he used, the text could have said anything he wanted (and it has been recorded that both Newbold and Voynich believed the manuscript to be the work of Roger Bacon). James Martin Feely attempted a decipherment based on only one plate from Newbold's book, one showing the same page that my grandfather was now working on. Feely thought he had found a simple substitution cipher, from Latin to 'Voynichese', and part of his translation reads: 'Well humidified, it ramifies; afterward it is broken down smaller; afterwards, at a distance, into the fore bladder it comes.' Not totally convincing, but the page does appear to show 'plumbing', and naked women in strange tanks of green liquid. So now my grandfather was obsessed with this page too. If he could make the total come out as an odd, rather than an even, number of letters, then something interesting might happen. He didn't tell me what this would be. I could see that he had his original calculation on his side-table, along with a small blue exercise book I hadn't seen for years.

'Is that my book?' I said to him, intrigued.

'Mmm hmm,' he said back, still looking through his magnifying glass.

'Can I see?' I asked.

He passed me the book and I opened it. It was just as I remembered it: columns of numbers neatly labelled in my funny ten-year-old's handwriting. I laughed.

'God, I took all this so seriously,' I said, flicking through the book. Towards the end were the results of the most difficult and boring task: the prime factorisation. 'Bloody hell,' I said to my grandfather. 'I'd forgotten I'd done all this as well. It took ages, didn't it?'

He looked up at me and frowned for a second.

'Do you know what the funny thing is?' he said.

'What?'

'You got all of them right. All the calculations you did were correct.'

I smiled. 'Wow.'

He smiled back. 'Hmm.' He returned to his magnifying glass again.

'I always wondered . . .' I said.

'What?'

'Did you give me that task to, you know, take my mind off those two men and my fear of the dark and everything? Because it did, you know, and . . .'

He looked up at me and frowned again. 'No,' he said. 'No. I wanted you to learn about prime factorisation. I wanted to be sure you would always know how to do it.'

I'm standing outside the study now, remembering this, and I'm thinking, *Why this conversation? Why now? Why, when I thought I could fill my head with nothing more complicated than thoughts about the moon, is this suddenly not enough?*

I haven't been in the study much since my grandfather died: it's as if all those conversations we had, and everything we ever did together, are locked up in there. But now I am opening the door and going in. And I am not going to cry. It's hard: there's a sad little pile of coal in the fireplace with two firelighters and some kindling. I remember building that fire the night after my grand father died. Of course, I couldn't light it. I remember sitting in his armchair, looking at his notes and his magnifying glass and everything and wondering why these items hadn't realised that some thing in their world had changed, that they didn't belong to anyone any more. I wished that they could have just tidied themselves away so I didn't have to do it; so I didn't have to be the one to admit that it was all over and I didn't know what came next.

I must have sat there for almost ten minutes before I just got up, went downstairs and plugged in my videogame.

Today I do light the fire. I hold the flame close to one of the white, greasy firelighters until it catches, and then I calmly pick up the magnifying glass and the pencil and the stack of papers from my grandfather's small table and put them away. Then I take all the books from the pile on the floor by his chair and put them on the shelves, slotting each one neatly into place. It's funny how he always left an odd kind of code explaining exactly what he was working on at the time. A magnifying glass, a page of the Voynich Manuscript, my blue book, lists and lists of numbers and mathe matical functions . . . Perhaps you have to know him well to be able to read the code, but it's there. The things around his chair tell a story, quite a simple one: that he was working on the Voynich Manuscript, and nothing else, on the day he died. And this is what I am thinking about now. I'm not thinking *He's dead, he's dead, oh God, he's dead*, any more, like I used to. I'm thinking about how much I loved him, which is different, and for a moment I see him in Heaven, reading some transfinite book. As the fire catches and the red walls glow with reflected flames, I consider moving my desk back up here after all (it's been downstairs ever since he died). I bet he knows the answers now. I bet he knows whether or not the Voynich Manuscript was a forgery. And I bet my grandmother knows everything she would ever want to know about the Riemann Hypothesis.

There's only one thing still bothering me: the living world doesn't know about the Stevenson/Heath manuscript and my grandfather's solution. It's supposed to be part of my book but I never did work out the code on my necklace. And what would be the point of writing a book with no solution? All I ever did work out was that 2.14488156Ex48 is shorthand for a longer number. It was when I was learning about Gödel's Incompleteness Theorem and trying out his number code. Every calculation I did came out with a number so big that it wouldn't fit on my calculator. And when this happened the calculator displayed something similar to my necklace number. 2.14488156Ex48 really means 2144881560000000000000000000 000000000000000000000000000. Ex48 just means you raise the number by 10^{48}. It means the number you want is too big to fit on your calculator, so the calculator rounds it up and gives it to you in this form. I remember the afternoon when I worked this out – it was rainy and grey and a snail kept crawling up and down my bedroom window – and I thought it was a major breakthrough. I even remember what I was doing: I was trying to write 'I love you' to my grandfather, using Gödel's code. I'd written the letters out first as numbers according to their place in the alphabet: I=9, I.=12, O=15, V=22, E=5, Y=25, O=15, U=21, and then I had tried making the code-number. What I needed to calculate was $2^9 \times 3^{12} \times 5^{15} \times 7^{22} \times 11^5 \times 13^{25} \times 17^{15} \times 19^{21}$. This was a list of the first eight primes, with each raised to the power of the corresponding number in my sequence.

I worked out that 2^9 was 512, and 3^{12} was 531,441. But then it started to go wrong. 5^{15} came out as 3.051757812Ex10. I checked my calculator instructions and found out that this actually meant 30517578120. I wrote this down in my notebook and moved on. But 7^{22} was even bigger. It equalled 3.909821049Ex18. But that was when I got suspicious. I realised that this number would end in a zero (in fact, in nine zeroes), implying it was divisible by 2 and 5. But I knew that a number with one prime factor – 7 – could not be divisible by 5 and 2. It was very confusing, so I looked back at my instructions again. And there it was: *This calculator is accurate to 10 digits only.* All those zeroes weren't really zeroes: they were other numbers – but the calculator couldn't display them. And this made me feel uncertain and confused about my necklace code. Why give me an inaccurate number? Maybe it wasn't inaccurate, but I couldn't work it out. Of course I tried to prime factorise it, but it was too big. I could tell just by looking at it that it would be made up of lots of 2s and 5s. Was my grandfather trying to tell me something about 2s and 5s? I couldn't see why he would want to do this. Even if you lop off all the zeroes ($2^{40} \times 5^{40}$) and concentrate on the rest of the number, you end up with another 2^2, 3, 23 and then nothing that I could find. The prime factors obviously became pretty big. It felt wrong. If 2 and 5 related to things – letters or words from another document, perhaps – why would you need so many of them?

There's a large metal trunk on the other side of the study, a larger version of the two small ones I have in my bedroom. I haven't looked in any of the trunks since my grandfather died. The silver one in my bedroom contains everything to do with the Voynich Manuscript, and the other one, a sort of brassy colour, contains all my childhood diaries and bits and pieces. But the one in here contains older papers – all the stuff my grandmother told me I would inherit when my grandfather died. And then a snatch of another conversation comes into my mind. My grandmother: *. . . if you want to, you can work out the code and then make your own choice about what to do about it.* How did they think I would do this? Did I miss the clues? Have I forgotten them?

I open the chest, using the combination my grandfather taught me.

Inside are manuscripts from his Mind Mangle collections, and flat proofs corrected in his large, almost unreadable handwriting. There are bundles of letters and old photos, some going back to the thirties in Cambridge. Then there are the papers that I always vowed I would put aside a weekend to sort out: reams and reams of handwritten notes, mostly unreadable due either to my grandfather's handwriting or, more often, to the fact that they were written in code. I know that part of the answer is here, and part of it is on my necklace. But I don't know how any of it fits together.

I sit back on the floor, cross-legged, with a bundle of papers. I start going through them, but an hour later I haven't found anything that looks like it will help. There are a couple of essays, handwritten in English, on the subjects 'Exploitation in the Workplace' and 'SOE: Remembering'. But most of the papers are lists of numbers, a Beale-type code: a Stevenson-type code. It's unclear how I would go about sorting and arranging them. Shall I take them downstairs and make a cup of tea? Shall I leave this until another time? No. The fire is now going and it's starting to get warm in here. Maybe I will make a cup of tea and bring it up. I will bring my tea upstairs and actually go through these documents properly – however long it takes. That decided, I grab a handful of photographs – something to look at while I wait for the kettle to boil – and go downstairs.

Atari is asleep on top of the Aga, and I don't blame him: it's a cold evening. I put the kettle on and lean against the Aga myself, warming my back, and start flicking through the photographs. There are quite a lot that I haven't seen before. Photos of my father, with his beard and jeans, and, every so often, my mother: sitting in the sun in my grandparents' old city garden, or reading. There's one of my grandfather in his old study, sitting posed at his desk, with a little twinkle in his eyes suggesting that somewhere behind the photo is a serious occasion that he is not taking entirely seriously. I remember the layout of that little study only vaguely, although I do remember that it always smelled of earth and pencil shavings. In the photo my grandfather sits slightly back from his desk with his legs crossed, right loosely dangling over left. The picture is well composed and has been taken side-on, with my grandfather in the right-hand side of the frame and the desk in the left. It's a mess, as his desk always was.

I wonder who was behind the camera. It can't have been my grandmother, as she is in the next photo, sitting on his lap, laughing and – bizarrely, because I never saw my grandmother in anything other than full dress – wearing a yellow bathing costume. Was it my mother? Did she take these? The next photo is of my grandfather reaching to pin or unpin something on the notice board that hung above his desk. I look at the series again. They seem like a text that has fallen out of order: a non linear narrative. But the actual story is clear. My grandfather was busy working in his study, getting a document off his notice board, when someone, perhaps my mother, disturbed him with a camera. 'Come on, Dad, we're all having fun outside,' she'd probably have said. And then she would have made him pose at his desk for his own inside-while-everyone-else-is-out-in-the-sun photo. Then my grandmother would have come in and teased him and joined in, sitting on his lap for another photo.

Except that this isn't what happened, because my mother was already dead. 'Long, hot summer, 1982,' it says on the back of the photos. 1982. The year before I went to live with them. The year before my father disappeared. I didn't see my grandparents much during that year, especially after that big argument that my father had with my grandfather.

The kettle is whistling, so I put down the photos, pick it up and pour water into my mug. Then I add a pinch of green tea from the caddy on the shelf. *Especially after that big argument that my father had with my grandfather.* Of course . . . That argument was about the solution to the Stevenson/Heath puzzle. My father was asking my grandfather to tell him the answer so he could sail off and get the treasure. Shit. When was that? Autumn 1982? Winter? I don't think it was in the summer. What did we do that summer? I certainly didn't see my grandparents. What did I do in the long hot summer of 1982? *Come on, Alice, your last summer with your father.* It's too difficult to remember. I remember one summer when we went to Margate with Nana Bailey, but I don't think it was that one. Except . . . Oh, God. Of course. 1982 was the summer that we went to Wales and stayed in a caravan with a horrible woman called Sandy, and her son Jake. My father wanted us to all become 'a family': him, me, Sandy and Jake. But on the last day of the holiday, a cold, rainy bank holiday Monday, a big man with tattoos came and asked Sandy to 'come home'. She did. And now I remember something else: it was the night we got home from that holiday that my grandfather came over with my necklace. It was still raining. So much for the long hot summer. And of course my father and grandfather argued then as well. 'Why do you keep spying on me?' my father shouted at my grandfather, before leaving the flat wearing his long, black raincoat. It was while he was out – at the phone box telephoning Sandy – that my grandfather gave me the necklace and told me never to take it off.

Back upstairs, I switch on the lamp and settle down in my grandfather's chair with the photographs. The one that most intrigues me is the one where he is sitting at his desk, before my grandmother comes in with her bathing suit. You can see everything on his desk, including the piece of paper he was reaching to take down from his notice board. I recognise the piece of paper anyway: it's in the trunk – I saw it as I was rifling through before – but it's something that my grandfather has always had pinned up around his various desks. It's a copy of Fletcher Pratt's 'Frequency of Occurrence of Letters in English'. There are other interesting things in the photograph as well, items scattered on my grandfather's desk: a World Atlas, a red pamphlet, a collection of Edgar Allan Poe's tales and stories, and a book I remember well, the one about Gödel's Incompleteness Theorem that I read when I was doing all those prime factorisations the first year I lived with my grandparents (and the one that inspired me to try to write 'I love you' in Gödel's code). There are other bits and pieces, mainly sheets and sheets of paper. His fountain pen is there, lid off, resting on the frequency table document.

I sit and look at the photograph for about twenty minutes. It is extraordinary really, and I am sure that no one else would see what I can see in it, but it is clear now that this photograph is a perfect snapshot of my grandfather's desk just after he cracked the Stevenson/Heath puzzle. The red pamphlet is, of course, the one containing the Stevenson/Heath manuscript. My brain feels creaky, but it is still registering the significance of all this. My grandfather gave me my necklace at the end of August 1982, which means he must have arrived at the answer earlier that summer. The World Atlas on his desk implies that, at the moment this photograph was taken, he had reached the stage where he had coordinates to plot. So what do the other things mean? Why would he be taking down the frequency table? What would he have been doing with it?

I go over to the trunk and find the frequency table, the same faded photocopy my grandfather used for all those years. Of course, it is different from the cleaner, newer version of itself captured in the photograph. It now has about five holes in the top, from the drawing pins with which it has been secured to various notice boards over the years. There is a doodle in the top right-hand corner – a few cubes and a triangle – and somewhere in the middle of the right-hand margin is that kind of faded-but-becoming-clearer blue squiggle you get when you try to get ink to flow out of a new biro. In the bottom left-hand corner there is a phone number beginning 01, the old London code. For a moment I consider ringing this number (would it now be *020 7* or *020 8*, I wonder) until I notice another way in which the piece of paper differs from the photograph from 1982. This one has tiny blue dots by several of the letters on the table: E, T, A, R, I, S, L, C.

For a few moments I look from the frequency table in my hand to the photograph. Then I get up and take my grandfather's magnifying glass out of the drawer. I study the photograph again and, now it's magnified, I can see something peculiar in it. In the frequency table in the photograph, just by the lid of my grandfather's pen, it is now possible to pick out the letter E, at the top of the table. It has a blue dot by it. But none of the other letters have blue dots. Could it be that this was what he was doing when he was disturbed by the photographer: marking off this set of letters? But why? It doesn't make any sense to me. It's 1982, and he's just finished cracking the Stevenson/Heath code, which uses numbers, anyway, not letters. He's got his Atlas on his desk. So why would he be needing to use a frequency table at that point? And why mark off letters on it? I know my grandfather well. He hadn't started on something else, not with his desk still cluttered with Stevenson/Heath-related stuff. Whatever he had on his desk – his most precious working space – would have been there for a reason.

And of course there's the other thing: although he had that frequency table pinned up by every desk he ever had, I never saw him use it. He knew those frequencies by heart.

My head hurts. Perhaps there's nothing here for me to see.

I finish my tea, which is now cold. The fire is almost dead. I was right about all the memories in here. It's not just my grandfather I remember, though, but myself as a child – even though I was never a child here. I remember the crazy recipes I used to concoct, thinking I would chance upon something that would make me invisible, or give me amazing superpowers. I would have been about nine or ten, and I would spend whole afternoons in the kitchen, mumbling to myself as I tipped things into a mixing bowl. 'Hmmm,' I'd say to myself. 'The merest pinch of plain flour combined with a small teaspoon of jam. And then all you need is a pint of water, a few grains of baking powder and an eggcupful of hundreds and thousands . . .' At that age I believed that all inventions were accidents. Of course, I'd been brought up on stories of serendipitous scientific discoveries: Alexander Fleming, I knew, had accidentally grown life-saving mould on some unwashed plates; but so many other things had been discovered by accident. Ice lollies were invented by a kid who left a beaker of soft drink outside with a stirring stick in it all night, and Velcro was conceived when George de Mestral got covered in cockleburs while out on a walk. I knew that if I kept fiddling around in the kitchen, doing random things, eventually I would have my own moment of serendipity. But it never came. And, since then, I think I can honestly say that I have never had a 'happy accident'. Every achievement I have made has been through logic and deduction. And although I always take shortcuts, these are shortcuts through a definite system.

This is why I can't believe that what I have found now is significant. I have not used any system here. But that doesn't stop me writing those letters – E, T, A, R, I, S, L, C – down on a piece of paper and seeing what anagrams can be made from them. Of course, I do this methodically, trying to begin words with E, then 'I', than A. And although you can make other things from this jumble of letters, including 'recitals', it is the word ARTICLES that I find first. And then it all starts to fall into place.

And is *this* a happy accident? No. Because my grandfather taught me the following two important lessons: if you see a big number, prime factorise it, and if you see a jumble of letters, start making anagrams. Perhaps seeing the photo was a happy accident. Perhaps that was it.

Of course, it takes me the rest of the weekend to really work it out. 'Articles', of course, is the answer, up to a point. It refers to the Articles of the pirate ship, a document that John Christian would certainly have had in his possession, and the text that Francis Stevenson used to create his number-code. And now that I know this was the text used I feel like it was so obvious all along. All those clues my grandfather gave me . . . He never said it was a book, ever, and he said that the 'text' didn't exist any more and that he'd had to put it together himself, backwards. If only I had sat down and made a list of all books and texts mentioned in the story. Perhaps I would have got it then.

So how does this relate to my necklace? Why did my grandfather make me wear it for all those years? Could I ever have worked back from that ridiculous number and got 'Articles' as a solution? No. But, gradually, over the weekend, I work out what it does mean, and why it was so clever.

I remember when I tried to write 'I love you' in Gödel's code and how frustrated I got with the big numbers I was generating. Of course, 'I love you' does contain various letters that are way down in the alphabet, and that will generate very big numbers, like 13^{25} and 19^{21}. But even a simple word can lead to huge numbers if you try to encode it this way, and I gave up on Gödel's code pretty quickly. The alphabet was just too complicated for it, with 26 letters all needing to be assigned a numerical value. And it didn't help that T, at number 2 in any English frequency table (which meant you were going to see it a lot), was always going to be number 20 in the alphabet.

But my grandfather had always been very fascinated with Gödel's code and its potential use in cryptography, so it's not surprising that he did actually use it this one time, when he simply had an eight-letter word to encipher. But even the word 'Articles' is problematic when you try to put it into Gödel's code. It contains the letters T and S – and S is the eighth letter, which would imply having to calculate 19^{19} right at the end of the process. And this is why my grandfather used Fletcher Pratt's 'Frequency of Occurrence of Letters in English' to assign numbers to letters, rather than position in the alphabet.

A	3
R	6
T	2
I	7
C	13
L	11
E	1
S	8

I wonder what my grandfather thought as he finished formulating his idea for a coded proof that would show that he knew what the missing document was. Did he think that he'd be able to create a sensible number that he could have engraved on a necklace for me? Something I would know to prime factorise, then recognise as a Gödel code and then compare to the frequency table? He can't have done. The number that you get when you run that lot through Gödel's code is 49 digits long. It doesn't even fit on a calculator properly . . .

Sometime on Saturday afternoon I actually do it, though: I get my calculator and I type in the calculation. $2^3 \times 3^6 \times 5^2 \times 7^7 \times 11^{13} \times 13^{11} \times 17^1 \times 19^8$. And when I see the result, I almost pass out. It is exactly what is on my necklace: 2.14488156Ex48, a number that, all my life, I have known better than my phone number. The number is not correct, of course, but it *is* what you get when you type that sum into a calculator. And at that moment I understand. My grandfather, for whatever reason, never intended me to break the necklace code and get the answer. The necklace code was the way you *checked* the answer, not the way you obtained it. My grandfather must have hoped that I would, at some point, come up with the word 'Articles', and that I would know how to run it through my necklace, via Fletcher Pratt, via Gödel, and understand that it was the right answer.

Or maybe not. Maybe he always meant to simply tell me how to do it, but never got around to it. After all, towards the end of his life he was so obsessed with Voynich that nothing else really mattered. No. I think I know what the necklace was actually for: it's obvious. If anyone disputed the fact that my grandfather had come up with the answer – or, say, if someone else said they'd come up with it first – all he'd have to do would be to get the necklace, prove I'd been wearing it since 1982 (and, yes, of course there are pictures of me wearing it then) and then show his challenger that if you put the word 'Articles' through Gödel's code in the way he did, you get exactly what is on my necklace. He knew that the people who would challenge him would not necessarily be mathematicians, and might be from the press, or even the police. And the last thing you would want to use as proof in a case like this would be a number too big to show on a normal pocket calculator. This way was perfect. My grandfather would have imagined it, I know he would. He would have imagined standing there with his calculator, putting the numbers in, and coming up with exactly what was on my necklace.

Late on Sunday night I am still sitting by the trunk, looking through my grandfather's papers. And it's about 1 am, after a takeaway pizza and lots of green tea, that I finally see the actual number. It's at the top of a ten-page document: a list of other, smaller numbers. It says: 214488156000192018589680534412530480932377694600.

And that's it, the 49-digit number. And yes, if you prime factorise it, you get $2^3 \times 3^3 \times 5^2 \times 7^7 \times 11^{13} \times 13^{11} \times 17^1 \times 19^8$. So maybe my grandfather did imagine that one day I would find it, this piece of paper, and that I would know what to do with it.

I smile, deliberately casting my eyes upwards (to Heaven? The ether?), and I wish he was here so I could tell him that I have already done it: I've worked out his code. But I know what he'd say to me next. He'd say, 'Go on then, clever clogs, do the next bit. Work out what the Articles say, and then work out where the treasure is.' I sigh, knowing that this bit is going to take the most time, even if I don't have to construct the Articles from scratch as he had to. No. The Articles are here in this document, with the Gödel number for 'Articles' at the top. What I have to do now is work out which text my grandfather would have used to encode it. And so I look at the photograph again, I consider everything he ever taught me about code-breaking, and then I go to the shelf and take down the book.

Acknowledgements

Thank you to Tom Boncza-Tomaszewski, as usual; Simon Trewin, for facing the world on my behalf; Leo Hollis, for rescuing me back in 2000; Jenna Johnson, for doing such a great and thoughtful job with the American edit; Suzi Feay, for giving me the best job in the world and all the amazing books that go with it; Hari Ashurst-Venn, for the guitar sessions; Emilie Clarke, for letting me treat her bookshop like a library; Lucy Wright, for talking to me about seeds; Allen Clarke, for teaching me about sailing; Jason Kennedy, for the sanctuary; Sam Ashurst, for one particular conversation; Mel McMahon, for all the homeopathic books and advice; Tony Mann, for checking the solution for me, and providing about twenty missing zeros; Francesca Ashurst for reading; and Couze Venn for looking after me.

Thanks also to the American Cryptogram Association for letting me use their name, and that of their publication, *The Cryptogram*. Thanks to Stewart Dean for letting me use his Life game on my website. Thanks also to the Torbay Local History Library and all the Torbay librarians. I couldn't have done this without all the books and the many hours of research.

I couldn't possibly list all the books I have used in this project. Many of them, although useful, don't deserve a mention. They are the marketing books, the trend studies and the guides on selling products to children. These will be recycled. The following list contains the books which I most loved during the PopCo project, and the ones I think readers may also enjoy.

- *The Code Book* by Simon Singh (4th Estate, 2000)
- *The Codebreakers* by David Khan (Weidenfeld & Nicolson, 1967)
- *The Magical Maze* by Ian Stewart (Weidenfeld & Nicolson, 1997)

- *The Music of the Primes* by Marcus du Sautoy (4th Estate, 2003)
- *Gödel, Escher, Bach: An Eternal Golden Braid* by Douglas R. Hofstadter (Penguin Books, 1981)
- *The Man Who Loved Only Numbers: The Story of Paul Erdös and the Search for Mathematical Truth* by Paul Hoffman (4th Estate, 1999)
- *The Colossal Book of Mathematics: Classic Puzzles, Paradoxes And Problems* by Martin Gardner (W. W. Norton, 2001)
- *Six Degrees of Separation: The Science of a Connected Age* by Duncan J. Watts (William Heinemann, 2003)
- *Obedience to Authority* by Stanley Milgram (Tavistock, 1974)
- *Toy Wars: The Epic Struggle Between G.I. Joe, Barbie and the Companies Who Make Them* by G. Wayne Miller (Times Books, 1998)
- *No Logo* by Naomi Klein (Flamingo, 2000)
- *Fences and Windows* by Naomi Klein (Flamingo, 2002)
- *The Algebra of Infinite Justice* by Arundhati Roy (Flamingo, 2002)
- *Animal Liberation* by Peter Singer (Pimlico, 1995)
- *Fast Food Nation* by Eric Schlosser (Penguin, 2002)
- *So Shall We Reap* by Colin Tudge (Allen Lane, 2003)
- *Woman on the Edge of Time* by Marge Piercy (Women's Press, 1979)
- *Between Silk and Cyanide* by Leo Marks (HarperCollins, 1998)
- *Nancy Wake: The Inspiring Story of One of the War's Greatest Heroines* by Peter Fitzsimons (HarperCollins, 2002)

Read on for a taster of Scarlett Thomas's
next novel . . .

Now available in paperback

ONE

YOU NOW HAVE ONE CHOICE.

You . . . I'm hanging out of the window of my office, sneaking a cigarette and trying to read *Margins* in the dull winter light, when there's a noise I haven't heard before. All right, the noise – crash, bang, etc. – I probably have heard before, but it's coming from underneath me, which isn't right. There shouldn't be anything underneath me: I'm on the bottom floor. But the ground shakes, as if something's trying to push up from below, and I think about other people's mothers shaking out their duvets or even God shaking out the fabric of space–time; then I think, Fucking hell, it's an earthquake, and I drop my cigarette and run out of my office at roughly the same time that the alarm starts sounding.

When alarms sound I don't always run immediately. Who

does? Usually an alarm is just an empty sign: a drill; a practice. I'm on my way to the side door out of the building when the shaking stops. Shall I go back to my office? But it's impossible to stay in this building when this alarm goes off. It's too loud; it wails inside your head. As I leave the building I walk past the Health and Safety notice board, which has pictures of injured people on it. The pictures blur as I go past: a man who has back pain is also having a heart attack, and various hologram people are trying to revive him. I was supposed to go to some Health and Safety training last year, but didn't.

As I open the side door I can see people leaving the Russell Building and walking, or running, past our block and up the grey concrete steps in the direction of the Newton Building and the library. I cut around the right-hand side of the building and bound up the concrete steps, two at a time. The sky is grey, with a thin TV-static drizzle that hangs in the air like it's been freeze-framed. Sometimes, on these January afternoons, the sun squats low in the sky like an orange-robed Buddha in a documentary about the meaning of life. Today there is no sun. I come to the edge of the large crowd that has formed, and I stop running. Everyone is looking at the same thing, gasping and making firework-display noises.

It's the Newton Building.

It's falling down.

I think of this toy – have I seen it on someone's desk recently? – which is a little horse mounted on a wooden button. When you press the button from underneath, the horse collapses to its knees. That's what the Newton Building looks like now. It's sinking into the ground, but in a lopsided way; one corner is now gone, now two, now . . . Now it stops. It creaks, and it stops. A window on the third floor flaps open, and a computer monitor falls out and smashes onto what's left of the concrete courtyard below. Four men with hard hats and fluorescent jackets slowly approach the broken-up courtyard; then another man comes, says something to them, and they all move away again.

Two men in grey suits are standing next to me.

'Déjà vu,' one of them says to the other.

I look around for someone I know. There's Mary Robinson, the head of department, talking to Lisa Hobbes. I can't see many other people from the English Department. But I can see Max Truman standing on his own, smoking a roll-up. He'll know what's going on.

'Hello, Ariel,' he mumbles when I walk over and stand next to him.

Max always mumbles; not in a shy way, but rather as if he's telling you what it will cost to take out your worst enemy, or how much you'd have to pay to rig a horse race. Does he like me? I don't think he trusts me. But why would he? I'm comparatively young, relatively new to the department, and I probably seem ambitious, even though I'm not. I also have long red hair and people say I look intimidating (because of the hair? Something else?). People who don't say I look intimidating sometimes say I look 'dodgy' or 'odd'. One of my ex-housemates said he wouldn't like to be stuck on a desert island with me, but didn't say why.

'Hi, Max,' I say. Then: 'Wow.'

'You probably don't know about the tunnel, do you?' he says. I shake my head. 'There's a railway tunnel that runs under here,' he says, pointing downwards with his eyes. He sucks on his roll-up, but nothing seems to happen, so he takes it out of his mouth and uses it to point around the campus. 'It runs under Russell over there, and Newton over there. Goes – or used to go – from the town to the coast. It hasn't been used in a hundred years or so. This is the second time it's collapsed and taken Newton with it. They were supposed to fill it with concrete after last time,' he adds.

I look at where Max just pointed, and start mentally drawing straight lines connecting Newton with Russell, imagining the tunnel underneath the line. Whichever way you do it, the English and American Studies Building is on the line, too.

'Everyone's all right, at least,' he says. 'Maintenance saw a crack in the wall this morning and evacuated them all.'

Lisa shivers. 'I can't believe this is happening,' she says, looking over at the Newton Building. The grey sky has darkened and the rain is now falling more heavily. The Newton Building looks strange with no lights on: it's as if it has been stubbed out.

'I can't either,' I say.

For the next three or four minutes we all stand and stare in silence at the building; then a man with a megaphone comes around and tells us all to go home immediately without going back to our offices. I feel like crying. There's something so sad about broken concrete.

I don't know about everyone else, but it's not that easy for me just to go home. I only have one set of keys to my flat, and that set is in my office, along with my coat, my scarf, my gloves, my hat and my rucksack.

There's a security guard trying to stop people going in through the main entrance, so I go down the steps and in the side way. My name isn't on my office door. Instead, it bears only the name of the official occupier of the room: my supervisor, Professor Saul Burlem. I met Burlem twice before I came here: once at a conference in Greenwich, and once at my interview. He disappeared just over a week after I arrived. I remember coming into the office on a Thursday morning and noticing that it was different. The first thing was that the blinds and the curtains were closed: Burlem always closed his blinds at the end of every day, but neither of us ever touched the horrible thin grey curtains. And the room smelled of cigarette smoke. I was expecting him in at about ten o'clock that morning, but he didn't show up. By the following Monday I asked people where he was and they said they didn't know. At some point someone arranged for his classes to be covered. I don't know if there's departmental gossip about this – no one gossips to me – but everyone seems to assume I'll just carry on my research and it's no big deal for me that he isn't around. Of course, he's the reason I came to the department at all: he's the only person in the world who has done serious research on one of my main subjects, the nineteenth-century writer Thomas E. Lumas. Without Burlem, I'm not really sure why I am here. And I do feel something about him being missing; not loss, exactly, but something.

My car is in the Newton car park. When I get there I am not at all surprised to find several men in hard hats telling people to forget about their cars and walk or take the bus home. I do try to argue – I say I'm happy to take the risk that the Newton Building will not suddenly go into a slow-motion cinematic rewind in order that it can fall down again in a completely different direction – but the men pretty much tell me to piss off and walk home or take the bus like everybody else, so I eventually drift off in the direction of the bus stop. It's only the beginning of January, but some daffodils and snowdrops have made it through the earth and stand wetly in little rows by the path. The bus stop is depressing: there's a line of people looking as cold and fragile as the line of flowers, so I decide I'll just walk.

I think there's a shortcut into town through the woods, but I don't know where it is, so I just follow the route I would have driven until I leave the campus, playing the scene of the building collapsing in my mind over and over again until, realising I'm remembering things that never even happened, I give up thinking about it at all. Then I consider the railway tunnel. I can see why it would be there: after all, the campus is set on top of a steep hill and it would make sense to go under rather than over it. Max said it hadn't been used for a hundred years or so. I wonder what was on this hill a hundred years ago. Not the university, of course, which was built in the 1960s. It's so cold. Perhaps I should have waited for the bus. But no buses pass me as I walk. By the time I get to the main road into town my fingers have frozen inside my gloves and I start examining roads off to the right, looking for a shortcut. The first one is marked with a no through road sign, partially obscured by seagull shit; but the second looks more promising, with red-brick terraced houses curling around to the left, so I take it.

I thought this was just a residential road, but soon the red-brick houses stop and there's a small park with two swings and a slide rusting under a dark canopy of tangled but bare oak-tree branches. Beyond that there is a pub and then a small row of shops. There's a sad-looking charity shop, already shut, and the kind of hairdresser that does blue rinses and sets for half price on a Monday. There's a newsagent and a betting shop and then – aha – a secondhand bookshop. It's still open. I'm freezing. I go in.

It's warm inside the shop and smells slightly of furniture polish. The door has a little bell that keeps jangling for a good three seconds after I close it, and soon a young woman comes out from behind a large set of bookshelves, holding a can of polish and a yellow duster. She smiles briefly and tells me that the shop will be closing in about ten minutes, but I am welcome to look around. Then she sits down and starts tapping something into a keyboard connected to a computer on the front desk.

'Have you got a computerised catalogue of all your books?' I ask her.

She stops typing and looks up. 'Yeah. But I don't know how to use it. I'm only filling in for my friend. Sorry.'

'Oh. OK.'

'What did you want to look up?'

'It doesn't matter.'

'No, tell me. I might remember dusting it.'

'Um . . . OK, then. Well, there's this author called Thomas E. Lumas . . . Have you got any books by him?' I always ask this in secondhand bookshops. They rarely do have anything by him, and I've got most of his books already, but I still ask. I still hope for a better copy of something, or an older one. Something with a different preface or a cleaner dust jacket.

'Er . . .' She screws up her forehead. 'The name sounds sort of familiar.'

'You might have come across something called *The Apple in the Garden*. That's his famous one. But none of the others are in print. He wrote in the mid to late nineteenth century, but never became as famous as he should have been . . .'

'*The Apple in the Garden*. No, the one I saw wasn't that one,' she says. 'Hang on.' She walks around to the large bookcase at the back of the shop. 'L, Lu, Lumas . . . No. Nothing here,' she says. 'Mind you, I don't know what section they'd have put him in. Is it fiction?'

'Some is fiction,' I say. 'But he also wrote a book about thought experiments, some poetry, a treatise on government, several science books and something called *The End of Mr. Y*, which is one of the rarest novels . . .'

'*The End of Mr. Y*. That's it!' she says, excited. 'Hang on.'

She goes up the stairs at the back of the shop before I can tell her that she must be mistaken. It is impossible to imagine that she actually has a copy up there. I would probably give away everything I own to obtain a copy of *The End of Mr. Y*, Lumas's last and most mysterious work. I don't know what she's got it confused with, but it's just absurd to think that she has it. No one has that book. There is one known copy in a German bank vault, but no library has it listed. I have a feeling that Saul Burlem may have seen a copy once, but I'm not sure. *The End of Mr. Y* is supposed to be cursed, and although I obviously don't believe in any of that stuff, some people do think that if you read it you die.

'Yeah, here it is,' says the girl, carrying a small cardboard box down the stairs. 'Is this the one you mean?'

She places the box on the counter.

I look inside. And – suddenly I can't breathe – there it is: a small cream clothbound hardback with brown lettering on the cover and spine, missing a dust jacket but otherwise near perfect. But it can't be. I open the cover and read the title page and the publication details. Oh, shit. This is a copy of *The End of Mr. Y.* What the hell do I do now?

'How much is it?' I ask carefully, my voice as small as a pin.

'Yeah, that's the problem,' she says, turning the box around. 'The owner gets boxes like this from an auction in town, I think, and if they're upstairs it means they haven't been priced yet.' She smiles. 'I probably shouldn't have shown it to you at all. Can you come back tomorrow when she's in?'

'Not really . . .' I start to say.

Ideas beam through my mind like cosmic rays. Shall I tell her I'm not from around here and ask her to ring the owner now? No. The owner clearly doesn't know that the book is here. I don't want to take the risk that she will have heard of it and then refuse to sell it to me – or try to charge thousands of pounds. What can I say to make her give me the book? Seconds pass. The girl seems to be picking up the phone on the desk.

'I'll just give my friend a ring,' she says. 'I'll find out what to do.'

While she waits for the call to connect, I glance into the box. It's unbelievable, but there are other Lumas books there, and a couple of Derrida translations that I don't have, as well as what looks like a first edition of *Eureka!* by Edgar Allan Poe. How did these texts end up in a box together? I can't imagine anyone connecting them, unless it was for a project similar to my PhD. Could someone else be working on the same thing? Unlikely, especially if they have given the books away. But who would give these books away? I feel as though I'm looking at Paley's watch. It's as if someone put this box together just to appeal to me.

'Yeah,' the girl is saying to her friend. 'It's like a small box. Upstairs. Yeah, in that pile in the toilet. Um . . . looks like a mix of old and new. Some of the old ones are a bit musty and stuff. Paperbacks, I think . . .' She looks into the box and pulls out a couple of the Derrida books. I nod at her. 'Yeah, just a real mix. Oh, do you? Cool. Yeah. Fifty quid? Seriously? That's a lot. OK, I'll ask her. Yeah. Sorry. OK. See you later.'

She puts the phone down and smiles at me. 'Well,' she says. 'There's good news and bad news. The good news is that you can have the whole box if you want, but the bad news is that I can't sell individual books from the box, so it's all or nothing really. Sam says she bought the box herself from an auction, and the owner hasn't even seen it yet. But apparently she's already said she hasn't got the space to shelve loads more stuff . . . But the other bad news is that the whole box is going to cost fifty pounds. So . . .'

'I'll take it,' I say.

'Seriously? You'd spend that on a box of books?' She smiles and shrugs. 'Well, OK. I guess that's fifty pounds, then, please.'

My hands shake as I get my purse out of my bag, pull out

three crumpled ten-pound notes and a twenty and hand them over. I don't stop to consider that this is almost the only money I have in the world, and that I am not going to be able to afford to eat for the next three weeks. I don't actually care about anything apart from being able to walk out of this shop with *The End of Mr. Y*, without someone realising or remembering and trying to stop me. My heart is doing something impossible. Will I collapse and die of shock before I've even had a chance to read the first line of the book? Shit, shit, shit.

'Fantastic, thanks. Sorry it was so much,' the girl says to me.

'No problem,' I manage to say back. 'I need a lot of these for my PhD, anyway.'

I place *The End of Mr. Y* in my rucksack, safe, and then I pick up the box and walk out of the shop, clutching it to me as I make my way home in the dark, the cold stinging my eyes, completely unable to make sense of what has just happened.

THE END OF MR. Y

SCARLETT THOMAS

If you knew a book was cursed, would you read it?

When Ariel Manto uncovers a copy of *The End of Mr. Y* in a second-hand bookshop, she can't believe her eyes. She knows enough about its author, the outlandish Victorian scientist Thomas Lumas, to know that copies are exceedingly rare. And, some say, cursed. With *Mr. Y* under her arm, Ariel finds herself thrust into a thrilling adventure of love, sex, death and time-travel.

'A masterpiece . . . A brilliant, engaging story that makes you rethink the nature of existence and the true structure of the world.' Douglas Coupland

'Ingenious and original. A cracking good yarn, fizzing with intelligence.' Philip Pullman

'Has a delightful whiff of decaying books, and a strong pinch of sulphur.' *The Times*

£7.99

ISBN 978 1 84767 070 0

www.meetatthegate.com